Reviews for *To Hear a Nightingale*

'A delightful novel . . . a novel pulsing with vitality and deeply felt emotions, it is filled with unexpected threads. Full of grit and sparkle, Cassie McGann is an entrancing heroine' *Sunday Express*

'A story to make you laugh and cry' *Woman*

'A lovely sprawling saga with a heroine you can't fail to love' *Prima*

'Excellent' *Options*

'Powerful' *Best*

'A delightful book that fairly zings along' *Cleo*

THE BUSINESS

Charlotte Bingham

BANTAM BOOKS
NEW YORK • TORONTO • LONDON • SYDNEY • AUCKLAND

THE BUSINESS
A BANTAM BOOK 0 553 40163 7

Originally published in Great Britain by
Michael Joseph Limited

PRINTING HISTORY
Michael Joseph edition published 1989
Bantam Books edition published 1990
Bantam Canada edition published 1990

This book is set in 10/11 pt. Imprint by
Goodfellow & Egan Cambridge Ltd.

Bantam Books are published by Transworld Publishers Ltd.,
61–63 Uxbridge Road, Ealing, London W5 5SA, in Australia by
Transworld Publishers (Australia) Pty. Ltd., 15–23 Helles Avenue,
Moorebank, NSW 2170, and in New Zealand by Transworld Publishers
(N.Z.) Ltd., Cnr. Moselle and Waipareira Avenues, Henderson,
Auckland.

Made and printed in Canada

UNI   0 9 8 7 6 5 4 3 2 1

For the Duke from Sweetpea

I can remember. I can remember.
The months of November and December,
Although climactically cold and damp,
Meant more to me than Aladdin's lamp.
I see myself, having got a job,
Walking on wings along the Strand,
Uncertain whether to laugh or sob
And tightly clutching my mother's hand.
I never cared who scored the goal
Or which side won the silver cup.
I never learned to bat or bowl
But *I* heard the curtain going up.

Nöel Coward

ACT ONE
BEGINNERS

PROLOGUE

Somewhere in the world there might be a place, perhaps in the middle of the African jungle, or the rain forests of the Amazon, where the atmosphere was more electric, where the apprehension preceding the start of some religious ritual was more intense, where the savage primeval feelings that concern survival were more evident, but nowhere, Meredith knew, could there be a place where there was as much attention focused on so few by so many.

And yet on what? On something that would be over in a few hours, the news flashed around the world, and then as easily forgotten; except in the business. In the business it would always be remembered, because that was where it mattered, where the outcome of this particular annual ritual was always remembered, for ever and ever.

Meredith arranged her blue silk gown carefully around her. She knew she looked wonderful. Her auburn hair dressed by Alexandre, her jewellery loaned from Biagini, her make-up by Austin Ferrel. She had deliberately chosen to wear a cool colour, to stay cool. She was determined that there would be no fluffing or fluttering for her. Her lines had been written long ago, and she knew her moves, and soon she was sure she would know just how it felt to have reached the ultimate goal in the business. And she would hold up the prize and shout to the past, to the person she had once been, to little Mary Zumpone of the thin shoes lined with paper and the paper-thin coat, 'Look, we did it! We did it! You and I, we did it!'

11

Because Mary Zumpone, the person Meredith had once been, she would be just as much the victor as the person the world knew as Meredith Browne.

And somewhere out there too was Max, surrounded by his entourage, as Meredith was surrounded by hers, his banner flying high, his hopes pinned on the ultimate prize. He also would be as much part of her glory as anyone, which is why Meredith had sent him a card.

It was a drawing of a small boy and a girl holding hands. On the girl Meredith had drawn a large pair of false eyelashes, and inside she'd written a message. It read:

'Best wishis', Max. And when they open the envelope please God it will be my name and not yours.

M

1

London, England
1948

Every day started the same, and every day Merry would feel a little sick in case her name wasn't called. Even if her name was called she would feel sick, because she knew having your name called was only the start of the long hard battle to win a part.

She was small for her age, which was good, but she was red-haired, which was bad, because it tied her down, even though she had no freckles, because not all casting directors liked red hair, and not all directors liked red hair either.

Having your name called at Nora Gloucester's School of Stage and Drama was the only thing that really mattered, not just to Merry, but to all the children there, because it meant they would be going up to see a casting director, or even, although rarely, a director.

She was lucky to be at Nora Gloucester's school. Her mother would remind her of her luck daily, as she brushed her hair up into a pert little chignon on the top of Merry's head.

'If it wasn't for Jim you wouldn't be able to go to Nora Gloucester's, you know that, you little brat? You should show him more respect, all he does for you.'

Jim was 'Uncle Jim' to Merry. He worked as an assistant cameraman at Twickenham Studios, and he'd come to live with Merry and her mother the previous year. He paid for Merry to go to Nora Gloucester's and, although he took no interest in her, and seemed to care less if she got a part, or didn't get a part, Merry's mother was always most insistent that Merry should show proper gratitude to Uncle Jim.

13

Merry hated having her hair scraped up into a chignon, because her mother did it so tight that it hurt her head for the rest of the day, but she had to let her, because her mother said the chignon made her look prettier; so Merry put up with the pain and the smell of her mother's cigarettes. She stood quite quiet for her until the whole agonizing business was at an end, and until she at last opened the front door of the flat where they lived and Merry was able to run down the stone stairs and out into the main road.

And every day as she ran to school from the dingy block of flats that she knew as home, she would feel the weight of the 'just-in-case money' that her mother had sewed into the pocket of her blouse. Bang, bang, bang. It knocked against the bones of her chest as she ran along the road, head down against the dust and the dirt of the morning traffic, her hands clenched in the mittens that were sewn on to strings on her coat.

Her mother never bothered to take Merry to school, the way the other girls' mothers took them to school, but Merry didn't mind. She liked running to school on her own, and coming home she would often stop off at Polly Stephens' house to have tea with her and her mother, and Polly's Aunt Tam. And that was a great deal nicer than having tea on her own, because her mother worked afternoon shifts, which meant she was never there to have tea with Merry, even if she'd wanted to be, which she wouldn't.

It was Uncle Jim who had first noticed that Merry was pretty. Too pretty not to be making money from, he'd said to Merry's mother, and sent them both off to Nora Gloucester's for an interview.

The first thing that Nora Gloucester had done was to change Meredith's name.

'Can't go on stage with a "zed" dear, Zumpone is not a theatrical name at all. And Mary is altogether too plain Jane. You want something with more of a ring to it, really you do.'

14

Miss Gloucester had frowned across her desk at Meredith who was having trouble sitting upright on the low stool provided for her.

'No, we'll have to change your name, dear, and straight away.'

So overnight, at Nora Gloucester's suggestion, Mary Zumpone became Meredith Browne. The Meredith bit was after her mother's maiden name, and the Browne bit was Miss Gloucester's idea, because, as she said, it would mean that Meredith would always have to mention it.

'You'll always have to say Browne with an "e", see dear? And the time that takes means that they'll have to look up at you, for however briefly, and that one look can get you a job, see dear?'

Miss Gloucester always said 'see dear?' about everything.

Every day started with a dancing class. All the little girls and all the little boys would line up to stand at the bar and begin their limbering up, and Miss Gloucester would pass down the line, occasionally stopping and taking one of the children's feet, and making them point their toes more stiffly.

'See dear?,' she would say, 'more like that, see dear?'

Every morning, as she ran to school, Merry could feel hunger pangs in her stomach. They always came on at the same point, just as she passed the disused bomb shelter that now had grass and weeds growing out of it, but which old tramps still used to sleep in, and which smelt dreadful, of sick, beer, and other things. Breakfast wasn't something that Merry's mother bothered to give her in the morning, so when she passed the old tea shop on the corner she'd keep on holding her nose, the way she had when she passed the bomb shelter; only this time it was to stop her being able to smell the freshly baked bread, and the buns, and the cakes, and all the other things that the local baker proudly displayed on trays in the window. He used to leave the door open, no matter what the weather, so that no one could pass by his shop without feeling hungry, even if like Polly Stephens they had just had their breakfast.

Polly Stephens was the star of Nora Gloucester's school. She had long blonde hair which her mother twisted into papers at night so that in the morning Polly's hair would fall in perfect corkscrew curls down her back. Polly had had a number of jobs already, even though she was still only seven, and she had been in a winter tour of *Peter Pan*. She had a fur coat unlike any of the other children, and a fur muff to match the coat too. At night Merry would lie alone in the dark and long to become Polly Stephens.

Jobs, jobs, jobs, that's what mattered most; to get a part so you could say you had a job, that you were working.

That cold frosty morning as Merry ran to school she repeated the name of the film director who was coming to school to look over the girls that morning. It was Basil Landun.

'A bloody awful director he is too,' her mother had told her as she brushed and scraped at Merry's long hair. 'Bloody awful.'

But even so she had repeated the titles of all his best known films over and over to Merry, so that even as Merry pulled the door of the flat to behind her, carefully making sure that the string holding the key didn't break, but lay hanging on the other side waiting for her return when she would haul it up and let herself in, even so she already knew the names of all Basil Landun's most successful films off by heart.

Miss Gloucester looked nervous, as she always did when she was bringing a director round the school to look over the pupils. Looking up at Basil Landun Merry felt reassured. He was round-faced, smoked a pipe, and looked every inch a kindly dad. Nothing to worry about there, she thought, but even so he probably didn't like red hair.

'That one, that one, and that one.'

He put a heavy hand on each of the children's slight shoulders as he walked down the line. To her astonishment Merry was one of them.

Her face grew scarlet as she lined up in front of him together with two of the other children.

16

'And what's your name, little girl?' he asked Merry in a nice voice.

'Meredith Browne with an "e",' said Meredith clearly, remembering to pronounce her name with a nice round sound as Miss Gloucester liked.

'Have you ever acted in a film before?' he asked her.

'No,' said Meredith, her heart sinking, 'I have never acted in a film before.'

And she thought longingly of Polly Stephens, and of her rabbit-skin coat and matching muff, and knew that she would never have either herself.

'Good, that's just what I want,' said Basil Landun.

Merry stared at him. What was he saying? Normally no one would give her a part in a film just because she'd never been in one, and now here was this director saying that was a good thing. What could he mean?

Basil Landun looked up at Miss Gloucester, and smiled warmly.

'She's "Karen" to a tee,' he told her. 'It really is quite extraordinary.'

He looked down at Merry.

'Can I see your knees, please?'

Merry looked up uncertainly at Miss Gloucester.

'Just lift your skirt a little, Merry dear, that's all he wants, just to see your knees, dear.'

'Very good.' Basil Landun nodded approvingly as Merry quickly dropped the skirt of her dress again. 'Good, no knock knees.

'I can't believe it.' Basil Landun shook his head disbelievingly again at Miss Gloucester. 'It's quite extraordinary, it really is. To walk in here and find the perfect "Karen", right down to the red hair and the pale skin, it's really quite extraordinary.'

'What about the other two?' Miss Gloucester asked.

'I'll take the one to the right with the fair hair for the part of the little girl who gets run over, otherwise that'll be all, thank you.'

Merry walked back to her place, her face still fiery. She

17

couldn't believe it, she just couldn't believe it. For her to be called up for a part in a film, and for her to get it, and for the director actually to want someone with red hair, it didn't seem possible. Wait till she told her mum, just wait, it was going to be quite something when she saw her face.

'You've got it, you've got it, you've got it.'

Polly Stephens pumped Merry's right hand up and down as the door closed behind Basil Landun and Miss Gloucester. Merry stared at Polly. So it was true, she really had got it, a real film part for the first time.

She ran back to the flats that afternoon, straight back to the flats to wait for her mother's return, even though it meant skipping tea with Polly Stephens and her mum and Polly's Aunt Tam, even so, she ran back as fast she could. She couldn't wait to tell her mother the good news.

But her mother didn't come back that evening, not until it was so late that Merry had put herself to bed with a bowl of porridge that she'd managed to make for herself, so that by morning when Merry woke, and found her mother at home once more, all the excitement had gone from the news. She wished she'd just gone round to tea with Polly Stephens as usual, and not tried to wait up for her mum. But there it was, she still had to tell her, she'd still want to know, just so she could ask Miss Gloucester how much Merry would be getting.

'Imagine you getting a part,' her mother said laughing and coughing when Merry told her the good news. 'I can't believe it. Well, I never. He's not blind, is he, by any chance? Basil Landun's not blind, is he?'

She pushed Merry away from her.

'There, you'll do,' she told her, even though she hadn't put Merry's hair up into the statutory topknot. 'If you've got a part we don't need to bother, do we? Just tie it back with a ribbon. Well, I suppose I'll have to come and see Miss Gloucester about your fee, won't I?'

She started to dress. Merry ran from the room. She hated being in the same room when her Uncle Jim was in bed beside her mother. She didn't know why, but she just hated it.

Nora Gloucester was proud of Merry being cast, but Merry's mother wasn't, she wasn't proud of Merry, and she wasn't proud of the fee Miss Gloucester'd got for her, she thought it was too little, much too little. It would be the last time her daughter'd ever have a fee like that, she told Miss Gloucester, the very last time, which made Merry feel quite sick, because she knew just how lucky she was, it was just that her mother didn't know.

Getting to the location bus in the morning was dark and cold, Merry had to run from the flats, past the bus stops, down to the river, then across the river and over to where she could get a taxi to pick up the coach. Nora Gloucester had got her a better fee for doing without a car to fetch her in the mornings, so Merry's mum had agreed.

'You'll be all right, it's just a bit of a walk and then you're across the river and you'll pick up a cab in no time at all. Coach'll be waiting at Hammersmith to take you on with the others, so you'll be all right. You don't want me to have to get up at five, do you? I never could stand getting up at that hour.'

So Merry woke herself with the help of an old alarm clock under her pillow, and she clawed her way towards her clothes, and dressed quietly so as not to wake her mum and Uncle Jim.

Down on the ground floor there was a shiny plaque in which she could see her reflection to brush her hair. And then she started running because London was very dark in the early, early morning, and as she ran across the bridge the river looked so dark, black dark, it made the five o'clock winter sky seem light. When she paused to catch her breath from running, looking down towards it, she thought she could see bodies floating in it, because once she and Polly had seen a man's body brought back by the river police.

'You get hundreds of suicides every night,' Polly had told her. 'Hundreds, and by the time they haul them in they look like they're a hundred years old, me Aunt Tam told me. The Thames is famous for its suicides, me Aunt Tam told me, really famous. She was once walking along the shore looking for coins and she found a hand sticking out of the mud, but she didn't get no reward for finding it. And there were no rings, so it weren't worth nothing to her. More's the pity, she said. I like murder, do you like murders? I like murders best.'

Merry had agreed, she did like murders best, but now, on her own, she thought she might have changed her mind. Other people's murders in papers they were all right, but when you could hear something coming along behind you, very slowly, and the mist from the river was rising up, and you were running and running, but it was still behind you, it seemed as though it might be your murder Polly's Aunt Tam would be going to read about. Merry ran and ran, but still the taxi followed her – until it stopped, and a man got out, and though she tried to cross the road to get away from him the driver crossed the road too, and caught Merry by the arm, and Merry's large green eyes stared up in terror into the horrified eyes of her captor, and although she pulled and pulled, still he held her.

''Ere, what's a nipper like you out here on your own for? You shouldn't be out in the streets on your own at this hour!'

'I was running to the cab rank, the one on the corner, you know?'

'Your mother should be shot, she should, letting you out wandering about London on your own.'

The cabbie took her by the arm and steered Merry as carefully across the road as if it were as crowded with traffic as the rush hour.

'Hop in,' he commanded her, and opened the back door.

Merry looked at him doubtfully.

'Well, I don't know as I should,' she said slowly.

'Said you were looking for a cab, didn't you? Well, here you are. Go on, hop in. Lucky I'm an insomniac or you'd have been walking all the way.'

Merry hopped into the back of the cab as commanded. It smelt of cigarettes and disinfectant.

'Where to then?'

'Got to get to the location bus to meet my chaperone,' Merry shouted through the window that divided off the driver from the passenger. 'I'm filming, see, so I can't be late.'

'Oh, you are, are you? Well, if that's how it is, I'd better come and pick you up myself every morning. Save you wandering about on your own.'

'My mum's ill or she'd have brought me herself.'

'My eye and Betty Martin,' said the driver. 'Come on, tell me where to, and I'll get you there before the cab turns back into a pumpkin.'

'Shepherd's Bush, that's where,' said Merry, sticking a piece of paper with the directions typed out on it through the window.

The taxi stopped in the car park of the cinema where the location bus was waiting, several people already seated in it.

'I'll pick you up tomorrow morning,' the driver told her, 'what's your address?'

'8a Albert Mansions, just over the river, you know?'

Merry struggled with her small plastic handbag to find the money for the fare, but the driver waved a large paw in her direction and laughed.

'You keep your money, pet, you look as if you could do with a nice cup of tea right now.'

Merry grinned suddenly.

'I can get two bacon butties with this,' she told him.

'You do that. And one on me. See you tomorrow.'

'Thanks, mister.'

The driver raised his eyes to heaven.

'My name's Bob, and that's who'll be calling for you tomorrow, nipper.'

Merry turned away from the kind ugly face under the cap and started to walk towards the waiting coach. First day of shoot: she'd be lucky if she got near enough to a bacon butty even to smell one, whatever the rules governing the use of child actors, that's what her mother had told her. She just hoped she wasn't right.

They ticked off her name as she climbed on the coach. Meredith Browne with an 'e'. The man with the list nodded towards a woman in the corner seat.

'Child chaperone's over there, love,' he told Merry. He pointed to a small woman in a mottled tweed coat sitting at the back of the coach, smoking.

'Hello duck, got here all right, did you?'

She blew out a puff of smoke from her large lipsticked mouth and bared small nicotine-stained teeth at Merry.

'You're the only child on the shoot, you are going to be spoilt, aren't you?'

Merry stared straight ahead of her as the coach started and the low murmurs of the rest of the cast filled the coach as it journeyed towards the studio. There would be no other children on the shoot. She wished suddenly that she hadn't got the part.

'You've been called the first two weeks, and the other two, they're only needed at the end of the shoot. So you're lucky, aren't you?'

Of course she was, Merry thought, and then she held her breath and tried to breathe through her mouth to avoid the smell of cigarettes. They made her feel sick. But she was lucky, she knew that. She took out her lines for that day. They were 'Mum, don't please, don't.'

Not words that she would ever to say to her mother. Her words were always unspoken words, and what she would like to say was buried in the small frayed bathroom towel that she would put over her face as she cried silently to herself at night. Other times she would just sit and stare out of the window on to the vista of blackened chimney pots, holding on to some dream of escape.

Stepping into the harsh, hot lights, the lines that she had to remember buried themselves away from Merry's beseeching memory. Basil Landun's voice was all that she

22

could hear, and all that she could see were the shaking hands of the woman playing her mother. She caught hold of Merry's own, as she was meant to do, but, because they were wet with fear and Merry could see that there was perspiration around her mouth, it was difficult to imagine that she was meant to be angry with Merry, and that Merry was meant to be frightened of her.

Merry looked up at her face, concentrating. She was only too glad that it was the woman who had a long speech to start, that it was her voice which was to be heard first in the strange thick silence that always followed the command, 'Action'.

Merry heard the sound of the camera. She heard someone breathing way back in the darkness behind her. What she couldn't hear were the correct lines. How could a grown-up get so many lines wrong so many times? Didn't she have to bring home the bacon?

'Cut!'

'I'm sorry, Basil, really I do know it.'

Again the shaking, and the sweating followed by the command, 'Quiet studio please'.

'You're a blighter, and you need to be fixed—'

'Cut!'

Now she couldn't even get the start of her speech right. Looking at her made Merry want to laugh and go to the toilet, both at the same time. Make-up had already been called on to the set twice, to repair the sweat on the poor woman's upper lip and on her forehead, but it was still coming through.

All at once it wasn't difficult for Merry to imagine that she was frightened of her, because seeing a grown-up woman so afraid made you afraid. Again and again they did it and each time Merry prepared to say her reply, and each time her cue was wrong.

'I'm sorry, Basil, really I am.'

Basil Landun strolled on to the set. He put his arm round the actress's shoulders.

'Don't worry, love, we all understand. Go off and have a

23

cup of tea, and when you come back I'm sure it'll all be fine. OK?'

The actress raised a pair of hopeless eyes to his kind face and nodded wordlessly.

'I knew it this morning, really I did,' she said finally. 'I knew it on the coach.'

'We'll take a break now,' Basil Landun told the studio. 'And we'll start on singles of Merry when we come back.'

A break? A break meant breakfast, bacon and eggs and tomatoes that Polly and she called 'train smash'.

'Merry, Merry, stop, stop!'

Merry could hear her chaperone panting behind her, but Merry didn't stop running. Real proper breakfast lay in front of her, and she even had enough money for it.

'I don't know, I don't know,' her chaperone grumbled, 'anyone would think you'd never been given breakfast before.'

'Only when I'm working,' Merry told her as the wonderful aromas drifted towards them. 'You work, you eat, that's what my mum says.'

The chaperone put a cigarette in between her lips, and lit it.

'That stupid cow playing your mother's going to be sacked by the end of the morning, mark my words,' she said to Merry as they started to queue.

Merry hardly heard her, she was staring ahead at the food, but then as she finished eating her chaperone's words began to assume a reality. If the stupid cow playing her mother could be sacked, so could Merry. She stared at the words lying on the sheet of paper. She mustn't dry, whatever happened, she mustn't forget her words.

Back on the floor there was a new lighting set-up.

'We're just going to do singles on you, darling, all right?' Basil Landun told Merry.

Merry nodded. Her heart was beating ten times its normal rate, but she'd been back to make-up and she knew her lines. In the thick black silence that followed the word, 'Action', she opened her mouth, and she heard her own voice pleading with her non-existent mother.

'Cut!'

There was a long, long silence, and then Basil Landun appeared and smiled down at her.

'Well, well, well,' he said, and then he turned to the camera again. 'Merry,' he told her, 'meet your new friend.'

Merry gazed past him. She didn't know what he meant exactly, but on the other hand she did know what he meant, he meant she was working.

After that the days welded themselves together. Every morning Bob would call for her, and every morning Merry would sit on the bucket seat near the window that divided the driver from the passenger and shout to Bob through it. Bob liked to hear all about the goings-on at the studio. He took all the movie magazines, knew all about the big stars. Merry would be a star, he predicted. A big star like Shirley Temple, only British.

Merry didn't think about anything like that, she only thought about her lines. Ever since the actress playing her mother had been replaced she'd been convinced that she would be too. And Polly Stephens would be cast in her place, that was the kind of thing that happened in real life.

But Bob knew different.

'You've been discovered, you have,' he told her, 'I heard them all talking about it in the car park. You're Basil Landun's new discovery, that's what they're saying.'

'Hear me my lines,' Merry said, ignoring Bob as usual, and as they sat together in the back seat of the taxi waiting for the coach to arrive Bob heard Merry's lines. And Merry had them off without a pause or a fluff. Every night she'd copy out the next day's lines, because that's what Nora Gloucester had told her to do. Copied lines stayed in your head, she said, and although Merry didn't understand the story of the film, she knew the lines, and that's all that mattered.

The following day there was a break in the filming, the

25

producers were coming down to the studio. Merry didn't exactly know what producers did, but she knew enough to understand that they were even more important than the director, particularly when she saw just how nervous he was before they arrived.

The whole cast was assembled, straight from make-up, and made to line up in order of importance. To Merry's amazement she was placed number three in the line-up.

'Best foot forward, darling,' murmured the actress now playing her mother.

Merry stared straight in front of her. Blooming Ada, it was worse than meeting the King and Queen. She shook the hands outstretched to her, two gentlemen, both smoking cigars, and a beautiful woman in a fur coat. To each of them she bobbed a curtsy as Nora Gloucester had taught, but to the two children who followed she just held out her hand. The little girl was the first to greet her, and then she held out an autograph book to her.

'Can I have your autograph, please?'

Meredith could hardly believe it. She'd never yet had to give anyone an autograph. Solemnly she wrote 'Meredith Browne' in her best writing on the pink page, and then she stopped and added at the bottom 'with best wishis'.

She did the same in the little boy's autograph book, on a green page, and added the same greeting.

He turned the page towards himself, and then burst out laughing.

'Look, look, she's put with best "wishis", she can't spell—'

He ran to his parents' side and held up his autograph book for them to see.

Everyone laughed as he showed his book around, so Merry laughed too. It had to be funny, it must be funny, otherwise they might fire her. As it was they might anyway. Supposing they didn't want children on their film who couldn't spell? They might hate children who couldn't spell, the way she hated that boy in his perfectly cut grey flannel jacket and trousers, and his clean white shirt. She hated his dark hair, and his blue eyes. Most of all she hated the way he laughed, as if he was used to laughing at other people. She'd make sure never to forget him, or his name: Max Kassov.

Merry's cheeks burned so red that she knew they must look really ugly next to her long auburn hair. Perhaps the boy's father noticed her discomfiture, because he came over and put what felt like a very heavy hand on her slight shoulder.

'It doesn't matter she can't spell,' he told the assembled company, 'she can act. I've seen the rushes, and she lights up the screen. She's going to be big, very big.'

Louis Kass looked down at Merry and nodded encouragingly.

'I'm going to put you under a three-picture contract, you know that? You're going to be England's Shirley Temple – better, you're going to be Meredith Browne, and I'll see to it that you know how to spell best wishes, and any other wishes you want to spell. My son can spell, and he can read, but he can't act his way out of a paper bag.'

He walked off, nodding to the rest of the cast who were still meekly lined up.

'Thank you, thank you,' he said to no one in particular, but it was to Meredith he suddenly turned round and waved and winked.

Soon he was gone, and so was the hateful little boy and his very pretty sister and their mother in the wonderful fur coat, and Merry was back on set again, and the lights were hot, and make-up were dabbing at her nose, but all Merry could think about was what the producer had said. A three-picture contract. That would mean she would really bring home the bacon, and that was for sure. That would mean her life would change, if it were true; she'd be able to have a really pretty coat like Polly Stephens.

But she put that thought quickly out of her head as she started to say her lines. She'd think about all that on the coach back, now she must work, just in case none of that came true, none of what that man had said.

* * *

From that day onwards Merry's life did indeed change. Her life changed so quickly and so radically she wished that Louis Kass had never visited the set that day.

She signed a three-picture contract, and Louis Kass who was a powerful agent as well as a producer became her agent, and her mother became her self-appointed manager.

Now Merry longed for the days when she had run out of the flats on her own and jumped into Bob's cab clutching her script. Now she walked out, followed by her mother. And her mother sat in the taxi, and on the coach, and the chaperone was no longer needed because Merry's mother had decided she would look after her, and that was all there was to it.

'You're going to earn more money than Polly Stephens, my girl, and I'm going to see that they treat you right while you're doing it, mark my words,' she'd say over and over to Merry until Merry felt like screaming and kicking her on her precious nylon stockings that she treasured so much.

Because that was her mother. She could never get out of bed while Merry was just going to school and that, oh no, but the moment it was clear she was going to earn not just a little bit, but a big bit of money, she got out of bed before Merry, and she took her through her lines in the taxi, and she even let her buy breakfast, proper breakfast, not like before when she'd scream at her for spending money at the studio.

She'd also taken to calling her 'my little lambkin' which was far worse than when she called her a little bastard. Merry only knew how to hate her mother, and she felt quite comfortable hating her, so to find herself having suddenly to try and like her was so confusing it made her stomach tie itself into knots, and she'd feel sick. And knowing that she was there somewhere, it didn't really matter where, on the set, watching her, put her off her acting too.

'I wonder how we can get you through this scene,

28

Merry darling, it's an immensely difficult scene, even for a grown-up actor.'

Basil Landun frowned down at Merry in his usual kindly avuncular way.

'You see, your mother is dead, and the nurse – where's the nurse, please where's the nurse?'

'Just coming out of make-up.'

'Good, good, ah, there you are, yes, now this nice nurse is going to tell you your mother's dead, and so naturally, as Karen, you're going to be very upset, aren't you?'

Merry nodded. She'd been quite looking forward to this scene because there hadn't been many words to learn.

Basil Landun leaned down and placed a brand-new teddy bear in her arms.

'This is your teddy, hold him tight, he's your favourite toy. You must have a favourite toy, haven't you?'

Merry nodded. She did have one toy. A cat called Binkie. Uncle Jim had won it at a fair, in the shooting gallery, and he'd given it to Merry. At first she hadn't liked the cat even though she had no other toys, because Uncle Jim had given it to her, and that seemed quite enough. But then, lying all alone at night while her mother and Uncle Jim went to the pub, she'd found that Binkie was quite a friend, and she would fall asleep talking to him.

'Right, pretend the teddy is your favourite toy and let's see how you take the news of your mother's death.'

Merry stared up into the grim face of the actress playing the nurse, and tried to look sad. Her mother was dead. No more Mum coming to the studio in the mornings with her. No more Mum smoking in the taxi, and going out at night with Uncle Jim. Well, so what? She tried not to think those two words, but they kept popping back into her head.

'Right, take eight, and action!'

Merry felt hot and uncomfortable. She'd never had so many takes before, not ever. She always got a scene straight off; or had until now, the most takes she'd had was five, and that hadn't been her fault.

29

Again the nurse leaned down to her, and again Merry tried to imagine her mother dead, like Aunt Tam had seen the body washed up by the river, but it was impossible, no tears would come.

By take ten they had to put glycerine on her cheeks, but it was no good, still Merry couldn't cry. It was getting later and later, she could tell from the way everyone was standing, first this way and then that. She'd seen that happen so often, but for other actors, never for her.

'It's no use, she's not going to get it,' she heard Basil Landun muttering to the assistant director and the cameraman. 'We'll just have to go again in the morning.'

'You stupid little bastard.' Her mother barely waited until she was inside the flat door, and then she raised her hand in the air and went to hit Merry on the face. 'Stupid, stupid little bastard, now they'll cancel your contract, wait till you see, you stupid little bastard.'

'Don't hit me, you can't hit me.' Merry ran from her down the narrow corridor and flung herself into the bathroom and locked the door. 'You can't hit me,' she yelled through the locked door as her mother pulled at the handle.

'I'll get you when you come out, see if I don't.'

'No, you won't, you crummy cow,' Merry yelled, 'no, you won't, because it'll show on camera.'

She leaned against the door as she heard her mother walking off. Still three more days on the shoot, she couldn't do anything about that, couldn't hit her until after that time, she had to leave off her for three days anyway. She sank to the floor and put her head between her knees. She was seven years old. She must get the scene. Tomorrow she just had to cry when they said those words 'your mother's dead', not want to laugh with relief, but cry. She'd get a pin and stick it in her hand. She'd pinch herself so hard the tears would come springing into her eyes. Whatever happened she'd get that scene.

Five minutes later she crept out of the bathroom. She could hear her mother laughing with Uncle Jim.

'And the little bastard turns round and says, "You can't hit me, I've got to do my scene tomorrow!" How about that?'

She heard them both laughing. Not long after they went out, slamming the thin front door behind them so that Meredith's key on its string rattled and banged against the door. Merry lay down on her bed with Binkie in her arms. She'd get the scene all right, she'd found a drawing pin on the side in the kitchen. She'd push it into her thumb until it bled, that would help.

'Why don't you bring Binkie with you this morning, little lambkin? He could do the scene with you instead of that teddy they kept putting in your arms. You'd probably get hold of it better, don't you think? With Binkie?'

Merry paused, and frowned, and then she ran to get Binkie.

'See you brought a new friend with you this morning, then?' said Bob as Merry climbed into his taxi after her mother.

'Yes, going to bring me luck,' Merry told him.

'It'd better,' her mother said, lighting up her first fag of the morning, and then she slid the glass window shut so Bob couldn't talk to them. 'Silly old tosser,' she said, staring out of the window at the bleak, black morning.

Sitting beside her on the seat Merry had one arm round Binkie and a hand in her coat pocket which carefully held a drawing pin.

She jumped out of the taxi ahead of her mother as they pulled up beside the coach that took them to the studio.

'Make sure the cat gets good billing,' he said, teasing Merry, 'and don't forget to shine for Bob, eh?'

'Silly old tosser,' said Merry's mother again, but only when they were out of earshot of the taxi, because Bob brought Merry free of charge to the bus every morning.

Nowadays she walked ahead of Merry down the coach with a self-important swagger. She was the mother of Meredith Browne, so people had better watch it.

In the make-up room at the studio Merry watched her face being made up as she had every morning for the past weeks. Gradually Meredith Browne would disappear and 'Karen' would start to appear.

She must cry, 'Karen' must cry, whatever happened.

'You'd better get this scene, you little bastard,' her mother murmured as Merry walked past her on to the set.

Basil Landun looked anxiously down at Merry. They both knew what had to be done, but no one's mouth was drier than Merry's, she was sure.

Merry held up Binkie. 'I've brought Binkie instead.'

'Ah, I see, thought it might help? Good girl. Good. Now you're sitting there, and you're holding – what's his name?'

'Binkie—'

'You're holding Binkie, and you're holding him very tight because you know there's something wrong with your mother, but you don't know that she's dead.'

Merry nodded. She held Binkie up to her face. Bad news always made her want to smile, but that was real life.

Basil Landun twitched her skirt, and stood back.

'Good, yes, now hold him a bit tighter, good.'

The actress playing the nurse leaned down to Merry. She had an ugly wart on her chin, Merry hated the sight of it, but it didn't make her want to cry.

'Good, fine, all right, and action!'

The nurse fed Merry her lines, and Merry stared up into her face, and tried to imagine how it would feel, but she felt only ice inside her, not warm treacly sadness, not the way she might feel if she read a sad book.

'Cut!'

As on the evening before, the takes rolled on, and Merry sat on clutching Binkie, her mouth getting drier and drier and the sadness refusing to come, and the tears too.

'FOR CHRIST'S SAKE MEREDITH, YOUR MOTHER IS DEAD. Dead, dead, dead.'

Merry found her arm clutching Binkie tighter and tighter and she felt her eyes getting larger and larger, but it was fear, not grief, that filled them. Fear that the food would stop

32

coming, that there would be no more money for her mother, money that put her in a good mood with her, that left her free to go round to see Polly Stephens, do what she wanted.

'Cut! Take the bloody cat away. Someone take the cat away. It's no good.'

Suddenly a voice spoke out of the darkness.

'Leave it to me, Basil, I'll get her to cry.'

Merry froze. It was her mother's voice. The voice of hell from the darkness beyond.

'Who's that?'

'I'm her mother, Basil, I know how to make her cry.'

Merry's mother leaned over her, she could smell her familiar smell of nicotine and lavender water.

'Give me Binkie, my lambkin,' she purred.

Merry looked at Basil Landun for rescue, but he had his back to her. Wordlessly Merry watched her mother walking away from her into the darkness beyond the light.

She sat on, and there was a long silence as the technicians rested, watching the director who was leaning back and sighing.

Suddenly Merry's mother was beside her again. She thrust Binkie back into her arms. Merry clutched him to her, as she heard her mother muttering quickly to Basil Landun, and then the board going and the sound of his voice saying, 'Action', and yet again the nurse leaned over her, and Merry held Binkie up to her face; but then suddenly it was in front of her, Binkie's face, and he was blind. Oh God, he was blind, not like the man who sold the matches on the corner who had a black patch over his eyes, not like him at all. Binkie had huge gaping holes instead of his eyes.

Binkie. She clutched him. Where were his eyes? Oh, but where were his eyes? Someone had taken his beautiful blue eyes and pulled them out.

Binkie, her Binkie was blind. Merry started to howl with anguish.

'And cut!'

At last they had their shot.

Having won movie-goers' hearts in Comes the Dawn, *child
star MEREDITH BROWNE is all set to have fans reaching for their handkerchiefs once more. Her new role, a
starring one, is in a Basil Landun directed picture –*
Poverty Line. *This time the frail poppet, who lists as her
hobbies ice skating and reading* Picturegoer, *is cast as a
child who is implicated in a murder by her father's lover.
Mrs Edie Browne, MEREDITH's number one fan, is
worried that the role might prove too taxing for her talented
tiny.*

*'MEREDITH puts everything she has into a role,' she
told us in an interview in her airy apartment overlooking
London's River Thames. 'It worries me that she should be
taking on another heavy role so soon after the last, but
she's a real little trouper, and Basil Landun is a talent I
would really trust.'*

*Meanwhile Mrs Browne has had to call in extra help to
cope with her daughter's fan mail.*

Eff, eff, eff, eff, that's all her mother kept saying. Eff, eff, eff men. In between she was moaning and being sick. Merry left the room and went to the kitchen to fetch a bucket. It was enamel and it had bits chipped off the side, and the kitchen cloth had holes in it, but it was better than nothing.

'He didn't have to kick me in the face, did he?' she asked Merry when she got back with the bucket and cloth.

Merry said nothing, but leaned down to mop up the sick. Going round to her mother's flat nowadays was horrible, but today it was even more horrible than usual.

Not that Merry wasn't glad that Uncle Jim had left the silly bitch at last, but she hated to see her mother looking even more disgusting than usual, her face all swollen.

'He didn't have to kick me,' she said again as Merry left the room to get rid of the dirty water.

Merry banged the bucket down on the bathroom floor and flushed the toilet. One day she'd be rid of coming round to see this mother of hers, but until then she had to visit her, just to give her money, just to try and keep her from coming round to Polly Stephens' place to see Merry there.

Merry had done a clutch of pictures, and had her own fan club run by Polly Stephens' mum before she finally left home to live with Polly and her mother, and Polly's Aunt Tam. It had taken a lot of doing, but finally she had managed it, with the help of her agency, Kass and Vogel.

They'd been lunching her at the studio on her tenth birthday when she'd suggested she went to live with Polly and her mother.

'It'd be much easier for me. See, nowadays she's always getting drunk and having rows with Uncle Jim, and it's giving me bags under my eyes, and I can't learn my lines. If you said it was all right, she'll have to say yes. Please, Uncle Louis?'

Louis Kass removed the large cigar from his mouth and smiled at Merry.

'Merry darling, you're a minx, you're going to break

35

hearts, but what I can say? You're box office and I'm your agent and a producer on this picture, what can I say? No, tell me what you want me to say, and I'll say it.'

'I want you to tell her I'll give her money, same as always, but I want to live with Polly Stephens.'

'Leave it to Uncle Louis,' said Louis Kass benignly. 'Now open your present, I spent hours choosing it, you know that? Hours. I want to see if it suits you.'

Merry grinned up at him. She knew and he knew that the publicity lady at the studio had chosen it, but that's what was fun about Uncle Louis, he played pretend games all the time – but he never pretended they weren't, not like her mother.

That had all been two years ago, and now Merry was twelve. Quite a small twelve, but no longer a child, except in front of the cameras.

'You're better off without him,' she told her mother in a small cold voice, but she didn't sit down and try and comfort her, or put her arm round her, the way she knew a director would tell her to do when she was acting a scene; she stayed standing up, and near the door, because she was still frightened that her mother would beat her, even though Merry was famous and had her own fan club and money and a fur coat, she was still frightened she'd beat her, and that was why she always stood by the door, near her exit, just in case.

Her mother turned on her suddenly. 'You didn't tell him, did you, you little cow? You didn't tell him about Alec Swinley, did you?'

Merry shrugged her shoulders. 'How could I?' she asked. 'How could I? I don't know who Alec Swinley is, do I?'

Her mother lit a cigarette with fingers that shook.

'I don't know who told him, I was never seen out with him, you know that? Never.'

Merry shrugged her shoulders again. 'I've left the money on the mantelpiece,' she said, and went quickly out of the room.

36

As she closed the front door behind her she could hear her mother being sick again. She looked at her watch. It was well after five o'clock, and she still had her lines to learn for the next day's filming, three pages of long speeches. Still, at least her mother'd got to the bathroom this time.

'You didn't tell Uncle Jim about that Alec Swinley taking your mother out, did you?' Polly asked Merry.

'Well, I did and I didn't, but then I didn't have to, not really.'

Merry sighed contentedly and stared out of the window. The two girls were on their way to a film location outside London in a hire car.

'Go on then, how did you do it? What did you say?'

Polly sat back against the leather seats and holding on to the passenger strap watched Merry's face closely.

'What I did,' Merry told her, and she started to laugh at the memory, 'I showed him the box of chocolates that Uncle Louis sent me last week, remember?'

Polly nodded silently. She remembered all right.

'I was round at the flat see, and she was getting ready to go out, and as soon as I offered him one, what with sweet rationing and everything, he looked suspicious. "Where did you get these?" he asked me. "Just a present from Mum's friend Alec," I said, and then I left. I thought he'd be angry, but I never thought he'd leave her, I must say.'

They both laughed.

'Now all she does is get drunk.'

'That's all she ever did, Aunt Tam says,' Polly told her. 'Remember last Christmas she didn't even send my mum a card? Well, Aunt Tam says it's because she was too drunk to hold a pen, that's what she says.'

Merry looked at Polly thoughtfully. 'It's just like that film I did last year, remember? And the mother got beaten up?'

Polly nodded. She remembered.

37

'That's where I got the idea from about the chocolates, from that script.'

'I'm afraid your mother's dead, dear.'

The nurse leaned over to Merry, and Merry was glad that she had brought Binkie with her, because she could hold him up to her face to stop herself smiling.

She was glad too that she had done this scene before. Not just once either, she'd done this kind of scene several times since her first picture, so she was getting quite good at it.

'She died at half past two this afternoon,' the nurse went on, as Merry still clutched her stuffed cat to her face. 'It was very sudden, heart failure. I'm so sorry.'

From underneath her long black eyelashes Merry could see several other nurses watching her. They'd all go home and tell their families that they'd seen Meredith Browne, the child star, being told her mother was dead. It would be quite something for them.

'Too old to be taking that toy around with you.'

Those had been her mother's last words to her.

'Try stopping me,' Merry had replied, knowing that she was on her way back to ham and eggs with Aunt Tam, and there was no way her mother could stop her.

She'd left her mother muttering to herself. She'd got very thin and papery in the last weeks. Merry had felt quite sorry for her, but even so she hadn't wanted to stay with her, and never would, and now she was dead she was glad, because it meant she wouldn't have to go and visit her any more, or pretend that she liked her at all. It meant that she could go straight home from the studio, and not have to stop off and do some more pretending.

'Would you like to come and see her, dear? She looks very nice now.'

The nurse nodded encouragingly.

'No thanks,' said Merry softly, and then she carefully wiped her manufactured tears from her cheeks. 'I think I'll go home now, if you don't mind.'

'Have you got anyone to go to, dear?' asked the nurse as they walked back towards the entrance to the hospital and Bob waiting for Merry in his taxi.

'Yes, thank you. I live with Mrs Stephens and Aunt Tam, they look after me.'

Merry opened her large green eyes wide, and she saw the nurse struggling with genuine emotion as she looked down at her, so she must have done the scene quite well.

'Take care, dear,' said the nurse, and she bent and kissed Merry on the cheek, before turning and going back into the hospital.

'Poor old bag,' said Bob when Merry told him, 'still, there wasn't much left of her, was there? Probably better off where she is, eh?'

Merry didn't care where she was, as long as she wasn't too near her.

Back at Polly's mum's flat Aunt Tam took Merry in her arms as soon as she heard what had happened.

'Oh, you poor darling, you're an orphan now,' she said to Merry. 'A poor little orphan.'

'No, she's not,' said Mrs Stephens comfortably, 'not so long as she's got us.'

'Oh but she is, an orphan,' said Aunt Tam, and once again she suffocated Merry with an embrace.

Polly was in the room too. She was weeping, but only in the approved Nora Gloucester fashion, she wasn't crying properly. Polly wouldn't want to cry properly over Merry's mother any more than Merry would.

'You come to your auntie,' said Mrs Stephens. 'What's Tam talking about? You're going to stay here with us, going to be part of the family, same as what you've always been.'

Both the Stephens ladies smelt of chips when they hugged Merry. But Merry didn't mind, she quite liked it.

'You'll live with us permanently now,' said Mrs Stephens, and her brown button eyes flicked over the crowded tea table to check that all the dishes that should be there were there.

'You've never forgotten our Polly,' her mother went on, 'and now we'll make sure we don't forget you in your bereavement.'

They all sat down at the table, and she pushed a plate of eggs and chips, tomatoes and thick bacon cooked crisp the way she liked it towards Merry. Merry started to cut up her bacon and then pierced the eggs with her knife so that the yolks ran into the chips.

Aunt Tam looked at her approvingly.

'That's it, you eat up. Nothing like food for grief they always say, don't they?'

Merry nodded silently because she couldn't speak, her mouth being just too full of eggs and chips. Soon they were all eating and sipping their tea at the same time.

'It's what she would have wanted,' said Aunt Tam to no one in particular.

Merry agreed. It was just what her mum would have wanted. She never had enjoyed giving Merry her tea, or anything else for that matter.

'You were a bloody great mistake, you were, so don't start eating me out of house and home now you're bloody here,' she would say to Merry if she did give her something to eat.

Well, now Merry was here, and her mother wasn't, and her mother wouldn't have to feed her any more, not ever. She had other people to do that now. Merry looked up from her plate as she finished.

'More, duck?' asked Aunt Tam quickly.

Merry shook her head.

'No, thanks,' she said slowly, 'that was lovely. Now I've got to learn my lines.'

She got down quietly from table, and went to the room she shared with Polly.

There would the funeral to be got through. But that shouldn't be too bad, she could get the wardrobe lady at the studio to lend her some black clothes. And she'd wear her hair down, and carry Binkie, that would look good in the papers.

*　　*　　*

Marion, the lady from the publicity department, stood back and sighed.

'That's really lovely, darling, you look just like you did in *Susie*. My mother saw that film fourteen times.'

Merry looked at herself in the full-length mirror of her dressing room. The costume department had done really well by her, she had a long black coat with a black velvet collar, and a hat edged with velvet that sat on the back of her head making her look a great deal younger than she was. And she wore black patent leather shoes with side buttons. Louis Kass was taking her in the car, a big black limousine. He had insisted.

Just looking at herself made Merry feel quite properly sad. Marion must have felt the same because when Merry turned away from the mirror to pick up her gloves she noticed that her pretty grey eyes were full of tears.

'Oh, but I shouldn't talk of such things.' She hugged Merry carefully to her so as not to disturb her hair. 'You poor, poor darling, now she's gone, now your darling mother's gone, I'll have to be a mother in her place.'

'Would you?'

Merry raised her eyes, large and vulnerable, to Marion's face, it was the look she always made sure to keep for close-ups. Marion hadn't been pretty enough to be an actress, so she'd gone into publicity instead. She would always be useful to Merry, Merry knew that; even if she wasn't working at this studio, she'd be at another, publicity people always were. She'd always be one of Aunt Tam's famous 'contacts'. That was all the business was made up of, Aunt Tam said, 'Contacts'.

'I'd love you to be my mother, Marion.'

Merry held Marion's hands between her own gloved ones.

'I shall need one now that – I'm alone.'

Marion turned quickly away and, picking up Binkie from a chair, she placed him gently in Merry's arms.

'I'm afraid we have to go now. The studio car is waiting to take us to join the funeral cars.'

41

Merry nodded bravely. Marion had even put Binkie into a black coat.

It was strange for everything to be so formal and proper, and everything to be going forward without anyone stopping it. It was really strange. All during the car ride to the church Merry kept looking around and waiting for someone to call, 'Cut!', and for the funeral car to have to turn and go back several times. Merry found herself worrying suddenly about whether she would have any 'lines' in the church, but she was too proud to ask, and then too busy counting how many photographers were following them in the cars behind. A lot of them were agency photographers, but even so the next day every paper carried a picture of the newly orphaned Meredith Browne at her mother's funeral.

Back to work and a new film contract, and then it started to happen. The little itches, the feeling that everything was growing, and that no matter how small she tried to stay inside, her body was growing, with or without her.

Polly's mother had given her gin when she was small to keep her that way, but Merry's mum must have been too busy drinking the stuff herself to spare her any.

Her feet seemed to grow first, and then her hands, and then the studio dresses, made tight and flat not to show anything but a flat shape, they started to look curvy at the top, and she kept having to go for alterations.

'I don't want to grow up,' she told Polly one evening in desperation.

'Has it happened yet?'

Polly tried to look sympathetic, but she was too busy trying to make the ends of her hair curl.

'No, nothing's happened yet,' Merry admitted, 'it's just that I look fatter to me, I mean, no one's said anything at the studio, but I can feel them thinking I'm fatter.'

'Mum says you're bound to grow, can't be a child star for ever, she says.'

The next day Merry stopped eating.

42

She'd show them, she'd starve to death rather than grow up and not be Meredith Browne any more.

But as the months went by and she grew thinner and thinner it didn't stop her body growing, and she hated her body for growing, it made her feel ridiculous.

'It had to happen,' said Polly's mum, 'it had to happen, duck, not everyone can be like Polly here, be a child still at fourteen. Really.'

Nowadays Merry tried to pretend that she couldn't hear what Mrs Stephens had to say. Yesterday at tea, while they ate and Merry watched, she'd told her that no child star in England had ever made it to be a grown-up star.

I'll be the first, Merry thought as she punched her pillows later on that evening, I'll be the first and show everyone.

She let her hands slide down her body. She could feel her hip bones jutting through her skin as sharp as anything, but unfortunately she could also feel her breasts, and they were sticking out as much as her hip bones. There was only one thing she could do. She'd have to carry on starving until her breasts just disappeared again, that's all there was to it.

'What do you think you're doing to yourself, Merry darling?' Louis asked.

Merry had been called into his office. She'd been driven in to see Louis by Bob. Poor Bob, he'd had to stop three times on the way to let Merry get out to be sick.

'Don't let the fans see,' he'd joked.

But Louis wasn't joking now, he was deadly serious, which made Merry feel even sicker.

'I don't know what you mean,' said Merry edgily.

'Oh yes you do, young lady, you know just what I mean, you're starving yourself to death. And you know what?'

'What?'

'It won't work.'

'What won't work?' Merry asked him.

'You know. Trying not to grow up. It won't work,

Merry, really it won't. I've seen it before, in variety, they're always trying to keep themselves small, or build themselves up, and it won't work, not for you.'

'Why not?' asked Merry.

'Because,' said Louis smiling and handing her a match to light his cigar, the way he'd always done, 'because, darling, you haven't got an act, that's why.'

Merry sighed. Louis was right. She hadn't got an act. She was an actress, that was different.

'Look, I don't want a skeleton on my books, you understand? I want you to grow up into a beautiful young girl. Grow up, you understand. Eat something, stop being so scared, I'll look after you, the way I always have.'

Merry looked at Louis. She trusted him, because she knew what he wanted, the same things as she wanted, for her to have a job. He was about the only person she really did trust.

'Stroke the Lions of Judah, darling, you haven't stroked them in an age. They've missed you.'

Merry smiled at him, and then did as she was told. There were four Lions of Judah, as Louis called them, round Louis's desk, one at each corner.

'There, now you feel better, don't you?'

Merry nodded, and tossed her long auburn hair back.

'What's going to happen then?' she asked.

'What's going to happen,' said Louis puffing on his cigar, 'is that you are going to go out and buy a bra, and I'm going to get hold of a script for you where you have your first screen kiss.'

Merry looked at him amazed. She'd been right to trust him. She thought she had.

'Hey, what was I saying you hadn't got an act for? What was I saying? Cut out my tongue,' said Louis, and he laughed as Merry turned several cartwheels right in the middle of his office.

On the way home she made Bob stop off at a department store so she could buy herself a bra.

*   *   *

44

She finished the film she'd been making, and then she sat back and waited for Louis to find her the right script. She was due to make another picture in the autumn, but the way she'd been growing she knew they'd take one look at her and re-cast.

When the call came from Louis to say that was just what they were going to do, Merry was hardly disappointed. After all, Louis had warned that that's how it would be. And anyway, soon she'd get into the growing teenage market. There was one in America already, it had to move over to Britain.

'It's not your fault, Merry duck,' Aunt Tam told her, and almost nightly, 'it's the star system. If it wasn't for you having been a star you would have work. I've always been against it myself.'

Merry nodded, it was a stupid thing to say, but it didn't stop it from being true.

'Come and have tea at my place,' Bob said the following day. 'I'll show you round my place, it'll cheer you up.'

Merry looked at Bob in surprise. In all the years Bob had been driving her around and looking after her the way he had it had never occurred to her that Bob lived anywhere except in his taxi.

'OK,' Merry agreed, 'it's certainly not worth waiting in for the telephone not to ring.'

Bob's flat was nearly underground it was such a basement flat. And it was full of canaries in cages, as if he were using them like miners use them underground.

He'd set out a large tea on a checked cloth, and lit the gas fire, all bars.

'That's something, isn't it? And you can eat as much as you like now you don't have to watch your weight, can't you?'

Merry sat down dutifully. She could eat as much as she liked, but she couldn't either, she had to grow up to be beautiful. Besides, she didn't like Bob saying that that way. It was like he thought she was finished or something.

Hot cups of tea and scones were irresistible though, and

45

Merry knew that Bob would have saved up coupons for the jam which was still rationed, and for the biscuits, so she ate heartily.

'You've done me proud,' said Bob looking at her clean plate. 'I've been worried about you lately, I can tell you now, not eating like you were, determined to starve yourself to death.'

He took her over to the far end of the room.

'Take a butchers at that then,' he said.

Merry looked up and saw the whole of the end wall of his room was covered in carefully cut-out press cuttings. Hundreds of them. Meredith Browne in her first film. Meredith Browne in her greatest hit *Susie*. Meredith Browne waving to the fans, Meredith Browne at her mother's funeral in black clothes. Meredith Browne opening a fête. He had a cutting of everything that had ever appeared about her.

'You'd never guess I was a fan, would you?' he joked to her. 'I got every single one of your cuttings. Which is more than your mum ever had, I'll warrant.'

Merry snorted.

'The only thing she ever kept was my money,' she told him. 'And then only for a minute before she ran down to the pub with it.'

'I've been more of a mother to you than she ever was,' Bob agreed. 'I call this my Meredith Browne corner, and I'll always keep it. You know why? 'Cause I reckon I discovered you that morning you were running along. You know that? I reckon I discovered you all right.'

Merry felt suddenly chilled at his words. He was talking about her in the past tense.

'You'll get work. Louis will get you work, but it'll take time,' Bob told her, seeming to guess her thoughts. 'You know the business backwards now, so you'll get a job soon. They all do. It just takes time. But you want to put all this behind you, you know? Otherwise, it'll make you bitter.'

'You know something, don't you, you silly old tosser?' Merry demanded suddenly. 'You know something I don't. I can tell.' Bob turned away.

'Now, Merry, you know I don't like it when you call me that,' he pleaded, 'you sound like your mother, you know that, that woman had a mouth on her like a camel driver.'

Merry grabbed him by the tie and pulled him back.

'Come on, come on, out with it, I may be a has-been, but I'm not a bloody fool.'

Bob backed away from her, but Merry followed him and for the first time in her life she knew what seeing red really meant.

'Tell me, you tell me or I'll kill you, what do you know that I don't?'

'Nothing.'

'Not nothing, something. Come on, out with it.'

'It's Polly, Polly Stephens, she's got your part, you know the one they'd passed you over on? Well, Polly's got it, see? She went up for it after they passed you over, and last week they rang, and she's got it.'

Merry let go of his tie, and Bob backed away from her.

'Red-haired women, they always do say they flare up like fireworks,' he muttered.

Merry turned away from him and, grabbing her coat, she ran from the basement and its canaries and its pictures of her as a child.

Outside it was raining. Not just spitting little drops, but proper rain, stair rods, the kind that hurt your face and that directors liked, which was why they always used fire engines for those scenes, so the rain really soaked you. She pulled her coat around her and ran on heedlessly, not knowing where she was, and caring less. So that's why Aunt Tam had suddenly moved her things out of Polly's room and put her in the little room at the back that was only used for visiting children. Not because Polly had a cold, but because Merry was moving down the billing, and Polly was moving up. She no longer had the number one dressing room, Polly did.

'Now, now, Merry, what is it now?' Louis asked startled as Merry pushed by his secretary into his room. 'Don't tell me your new bra doesn't fit? You're going to end up on a calendar, you know that?'

Merry looked up at him. Her long hair was soaked, her thin dress was clinging to her new contour in great damp patches.

'Why didn't you tell me?' she asked Louis. 'Why didn't you tell me Polly Stephens had got my part?'

Louis led her to the fire.

'Is that what this is all about?'

'She's got my part, the part I was up for—'

'And which you grew out of? What is this? You knew someone else had got the part, you knew you hadn't got it. What does it matter who's got it if you haven't?'

'It matters to me,' Merry shouted at him,

Louis smiled.

'You always did do those scenes well, Merry darling, you know that? That's why you'll go on.'

Merry stopped suddenly.

'What do you mean?'

'I said that's why you'll go on,' said Louis, smiling, 'but first we have to groom you up, teach you to dance, get you into shows, into the theatre. You've only done films. You've got to do theatre, musicals, revues, go on tours, grow up, change your bra size twice more. You're beautiful already, you know that? Very beautiful, and you're going to get more beautiful.'

Merry stared at him. What was he talking about? Louis took her to the mirror over his mantelpiece.

'Look at that, you're a beautiful young girl. In another few years you'll be a beautiful young woman, and I'm going to look after you, you know that? All the way. Here, take my handkerchief and wipe the rain from your hair.'

Merry did as she was told, and Louis watched her, smiling.

'There, that's better. Now, sit down and I'll get you something to drink, and then you can go home and wait for me to call you, and it won't be long.'

Merry sat and sipped her drink and Louis watched her.

'Your colour's come back,' he told her after a few minutes. 'Now, don't ever not trust me again.'

Merry stood up and walked to the door. She still had to go home and face Polly Stephens and Aunt Tam, and all that smugness they'd been hiding for the last week.

'Polly Stephens won't last, darling, really she won't,' Louis said, showing her to the door. 'Believe me, I know.'

Merry turned at the door.

'Why are you doing this?' she said suddenly. 'Why are you doing this? What's in it for you?'

Louis smiled down at her, and pulled on his cigar, and then blew a perfect celebratory smoke ring.

'What do you think, Merry darling?'

'I think you might want something from me,' Merry said.

'Quite right,' said Louis, and he nodded his approval, 'I do want something out of you.'

'Yes? What?'

'Ten per cent,' said Louis.

2

Sloane Street, London
1949

The Rolls-Royce stood below in the street. Reaching up to the window sill and balancing on his tiptoes Max could just see the top of Mayber's hat, but he really had to stretch to see it. Mayber was his father's chauffeur. Max liked Mayber. It was just as well since he saw him more than he saw his own father.

'Why can't I go to school like other boys?' Max had asked his father once or twice, more out of curiosity than desire.

'Because you've got no Mummy now, and Daddy knows best,' his father would say, and then his eyes would fill with tears as they drifted over to the portrait of his mother over the fireplace, and Max would turn away defeated by the sight of his father's ever-present grief.

'But Trixie goes to school.'

'Trixie doesn't go to school,' said Nanny indignantly. 'Trixie shares a governess with three other little girls. That's not school, Master Max, that's private that is.'

Max gazed at Nanny's whiskered face remembering how lovely his mother's had been. She had had large violet blue eyes, and black lashes that his daddy had always said of proudly, 'They're double top and bottom.'

How pretty she had looked when she'd come into the room, her long shiny nyloned legs pitched a little forward, on shoes that often showed one little red toenail at the front. Not like Nanny's lisle stockings that wrinkled and had mends in them, and her lace-up shoes that were so tightly done up that sometimes when she tied them before they went out Max felt sure that the laces must break she tugged at them so hard.

50

'Time for our walk now, Master Max, and then back to tea and Muffin the Mule on television.'

Max hated Muffin the Mule, but Trixie and Nanny loved it. Max was always longing for him to fall off Annette Mills's piano, and for Peregrine the Penguin to snap off one of her fingers, but nothing exciting like that ever happened. In fact nothing at all exciting seemed to happen now that his mother had died, just people coming to see them, and his tutor arriving in the mornings, and then going for a walk.

Max ran ahead dizzily. Too fast, on purpose so that Nanny would become anxious, and then he jumped down the steps to the pavement outside, two feet at a time, using his arms for impulsion.

'Careful, Master Max,' said Mayber, 'we don't want nothing happening to *you*.'

He always said it like that. Mayber always said, 'We don't want nothing happening to *you*', as if to remind Max daily that now his mother was dead it was his moral responsibility to stay alive.

'Oh, yes, we must be careful of ourselves now, mustn't we?'

Mayber opened the car door. Max paused, his foot in its highly polished shoe on the running board.

'Can I see the engine, Mayber?' he asked.

'Not now, Master Max, Nanny'll want to get on with the walk. But when we get back I don't mind opening the bonnet for you.'

The walk. Driving round the park sitting beside Nanny with your feet together in front of you didn't seem like a walk to Max.

But every day it was the same. Mayber driving, Nanny and Max in the back, then Mayber stopping when Nanny tapped on the window. Then Max stepping out of the car and Nanny following, calling anxiously from the moment the fresh air hit their faces. Sometimes their destination was the boat house in Hyde Park, sometimes it was Peter Pan; wherever it was it was always too far for Nanny.

'Onl̰ as far as the Daisy Walk,' Nanny would gasp on her bad days when her bronchitis was playing her up.

But even if Max raced ahead of her and left her way behind, even if he got to Peter Pan first, he knew it would never make any difference, that someone would always be behind him, tailing him, making sure where he was, making sure that he wasn't running too fast, or picking up a stick that was dirty, or getting his shoes muddy.

Once he'd run away from Nanny. Out into the street, and down to the bottom where he'd run up and down, and down and up, and played hopscotch on the squares the way he'd seen other children play. But then Nanny had cried so when he'd gone back, and the French maid had had to give her one of her special pills to calm her, and Mayber had been so cross, bringing him back to the flat, holding Max tightly by his arm, so he'd never done it again.

Instead he'd let life go back to being as it had been. Lessons with his tutor who was old and dry and ate his lunchtime sandwiches very noisily, then the walk, then tea and bed. Always the same, except for Saturday which was always the same too, except it was Saturday.

On Saturday his father and his uncle took Trixie and Max out to lunch.

Uncle Baz's arrival was always signalled by heavy breathing, even though their large, airy flat was only on the first floor, and even though he could have taken the lift, he didn't, and he would arrive breathing heavily and holding a large box of glacé fruit for Max and Trixie.

'Thank you very much,' Trixie would say, curtsying as her dancing mistress had taught her, and Uncle Baz would smile, and pointing to his cheek he would say, 'Kiss me there, Trixie, I don't mind.'

And Trixie – who to Max looked like an angel – would kiss Uncle Baz, and Max would shake his head and pretend to be surprised by the box of glacé fruit. After this they would both follow their father and uncle down to the waiting Rolls with a sense of relief, of duty done, as if they had remembered to clean their teeth both before and after breakfast.

'Uncle Baz' was not a real uncle. He was their father's business partner, they were Kass and Vogel, theatrical agents.

'Soon we'll be as famous as the Grades,' Uncle Baz would laugh and tell the waiters in the restaurant every Saturday, and Max noticed how much the waiters bowed and how they ran for the menus, and it made him feel good to be so rich you could make other people run around that way.

'Your father and I never had anything when we arrived in this country,' Uncle Baz would tell Max and Trixie, as he and their father tucked their napkins into their collars and spread the starched material over their waistcoats and started to eat, 'nothing at all, and yet—'

Here he would pause and the children would look up, again trying to seem surprised.

'And yet we had everything, because we had our mothers who loved us and we had talent, and that's all you need, isn't it, Louis?'

Max's father, who was older, but looked younger than Uncle Baz because he was thinner, would nod and smile at this speech, and then he would wave his fork at his children and say, 'Eat, eat.'

The food was of all kinds, but whatever happened they had to eat it, because of their father and Baz having 'arrived in this country with nothing', and because of the war, of course. That was another reason they had to eat; because no one in the war had been able to eat, Trixie and Max had to make up for it.

'I remember the first time I saw an orange. Remember the first time you saw an orange, Louis? Remember?'

Max's father would nod, bending over his food, but not looking up, keeping his eyes down on his plate.

'What a thing that was, an orange.'

Max hated oranges. He hated the smell of them in the cinema, and he particularly hated them because they

53

hadn't made themselves known to his Uncle Baz earlier on in his life, thereby making it impossible for Uncle Baz to be so surprised by them.

This Saturday though, it was different. Uncle Baz brought the glacé fruits as usual, of course, but he didn't talk about oranges, he ate, and Max's father waved his fork and said, 'Eat, eat', as usual, but there was nothing about the oranges, and neither man seemed to be willing to talk much, they seemed more in dread of something.

Trixie had said something about an aunt neither of them had ever met coming to see them, but Max had ignored her. He loved Trixie, even more than Nanny loved Trixie, if that were possible, but he didn't listen to her any more than his father had ever listened to his mother. His father just smiled and waved his cigar and carried on out of the door to the office. Always back to the office. From early morning to late at night his father had been at his office, but his mother hadn't seemed to mind, filling the house with girlfriends, and twice a week the masseuse would arrive, and once a week the chiropodist, and when they weren't arriving his mother would be going out of the door to have her hair done, so she can never have noticed much that their father was never there, not the way that Max had noticed.

'She was so beautiful.'

Uncle Baz stood beneath the portrait of her as he always did every Saturday after lunch, and he wiped his eyes and turned away, as he always did, but then the doorbell rang and the maid announced a visitor.

'Ah, there you are.'

Max never forgot the image of his mother's elder sister. He couldn't imagine that she and his ethereal mother could have been related. Could have even shared the same house. This woman was tall, and though not big boned, she might as well have been, for her voice was deep and commanding as if she was used to shouting across a field in a high wind. He saw his father and Uncle Baz stand their ground before it, clutching their cigars, and drawing on them even as they shook her hand.

54

'So you're Max.'

The words were ominous. Max looked up at her and tried his most winning smile, the one that always got Nanny to leave his light on later than it should be.

'What a pampered poodle you are, to be sure. What are you doing dressing him up as a girl this way, Louis? I mean, to look at him, to look at him you'd think, well, I swear I'd have taken him for his sister. We can't have this.'

Max had never been referred to as 'this' before. Now he was he didn't think he liked it, but he went on with his best charming grin even so.

'I thought, I suspected this was what I would find,' said his aunt grimly. 'Leave two men to bring up a couple of children on their own and before you know where you are they're eating caviar to the sound of trumpets.'

Louis turned and looked uneasily at Baz who shrugged his shoulders.

'Susan, please—'

'Look at the colour of these children.'

She turned from Max and Trixie to the two men.

'Pallid, pale, pallid, wispy little poodles. They look as if they spend their whole lives in restaurants and night-clubs.'

'Susan, would we take children to night-clubs, please? I mean.'

Louis turned to Baz who shrugged again, and once again the air became thick with anxious cigar smoke.

'That's it, Louis, I've made up my mind. I'm taking them both up to Scotland with me, and then the boy can be sent on to his grandfather's prep school. It's my duty, my poor dear sister had the brains of a flea, leaving you two to bring them up indeed.'

'Take the boy, don't take Trixie.'

Max stared up at his father, he'd never seen him daunted this way before. Why, now he was even pleading. The great Louis Kass pleading for his own children with this tall woman in her severe suit and three strings of pearls.

'Very well, the boy's more important. Where's Nanny?'

Max looked confidently from his father to his uncle and back again. He was still smiling, until he saw the tears in his father's eyes.

'I can't stop her, Max, it's what your mother would have wanted. She would have wanted you to be a gentleman, and you'll never learn to be a gentleman staying here. Baz and I, we haven't got the time. The office. You know how it is.'

'But I want to stay here with you. I'm fine here with you.'

'That's as may be,' said Susan grimly to no one in particular, 'but you're coming up to Scotland with me – ah, Nanny? Pack up Master Max's things, would you? Just two or three Aertex shirts, some jumpers, a thick coat if he's got one, and some strong outdoor shoes and wellington boots. In fact you can take him off with you now, change him, pack him, and bring him back.'

Max walked back to his father and put his hand in his. 'I don't want to go to Scotland,' he told him firmly.

'Do you think I want you to go? But it's what your mother would have wanted, and the schools, that's what she would have wanted. Here – it's not right for you, not if you're going to grow up as you should, grow up nice.'

'Please.'

Max pulled on his father's hand, and the scream that had been preparing itself in his throat flew from him. His Aunt Susan looked unimpressed.

'You see what I mean?' she said to Louis and Baz triumphantly. 'Spoilt brat.'

And then she picked Max up bodily and threw him to the door. 'Won't have that, go on, get out, won't have that at all.'

Max tried to run back to his father and Uncle Baz, his screams becoming so hysterical with terror that long stretches of sound separated each breath that he took.

'Take him away, for God's sake, Louis, take him away,' Baz begged. 'My heart, you know, it's not good for my murmur, please, have him taken away.'

56

'I don't want to leave you,' Max screamed, 'don't let her take me, don't want to, don't want to.'

'Be a good boy,' Louis kept begging him, 'just be a good boy, and, you know, just be good.'

Susan now had him by the scruff of his neck again.

'He's going to learn to be a good boy, and the first thing we've got to do is get that hysteria knocked out of him. That's the trouble with bringing up boys in incubators, Louis, it makes them hysterical. See where your efforts have got you?'

The door closed behind Max's screams and Susan turned to the two men with a slight colour in her cheeks, a triumphant look in her eye.

'Point proven I think, don't you?'

'He's never *been* away from home before, Susan,' Louis protested. 'Only to the Isle of Wight for his holidays.'

'He's too old for a nanny anyway. If you had any sense at all you'd send the girl away too, but never mind that now.'

'Where are you going, Susan, please, where are you going?'

'Where do you think, Louis? To straighten out that boy of yours, my poor sister's only boy, and make a gentleman of him.'

'Yes, yes, you're right. We haven't the time, we haven't the time, have we, Baz?'

'No, no time, not with the office,' Baz shook his head miserably, 'not with the office, so many shows. The tours, there's a great deal on at the moment.'

'Of course there is,' said Susan briskly. 'Don't worry, I'll soon lick him into shape.'

The darkness of his bedroom in Scotland was made worse by the blackout blinds left over from the war. To Max, in his new-found hell, the blackness was bad, but better than the day when the blinds would be forcibly pulled up and the light would flood the large room with its heavy old-fashioned furniture, and he would hear his aunt calling him from his bed in the same way that she whistled up her dogs to go walking.

Every day, she dressed, he undressed in only his swimming trunks, she would run him down to the edge of the grounds and watch grimly as he 'did his lengths' in the icy lake before going back upstairs to change and face another day of walking up the mountains, or into the village. Walk, walk, walk. Sometimes when he returned home the backs of his heels would be rubbed raw, sometimes in the mornings he could hardly do his shoes up so sore and swollen had his feet become.

'Better colour, much better colour, you're beginning to look less bleached,' she would comment occasionally.

How he hated her! In the blackness of his room at night Max would conjure up images of her dead, hanging from a rope, or lying bleeding only half dead, like the birds she shot and made him run ahead and pick up with the dogs.

In between the silences of their lunches together she would tell him about his mother. Not the mother that he had loved, who had smelt of flowers, and worn pretty clothes and furs. Not the mother that he had walked so proudly beside on the days they went to his father's charity matinées or to visit the actors on a film set. Not the beautiful girl in the picture that his father and uncle cried before every Saturday.

The mother his aunt talked about was 'a fool'. A girl who had thrown herself away on a 'cheap showman'.

'She could have married anyone,' Susan would say, staring out across the lawns. 'Anyone at all, and yet she fell for your father, of all people. Hold your fork properly. No, don't do that, no gentleman drinks while he still has something in his mouth. Ah, good, custard. Now, don't forget to eat with a fork, only people in insurance eat custard with a spoon.'

Max could do nothing for himself when he'd arrived in that bleak Victorian-Gothic house that called itself a castle. He had never even tied his own shoelaces; and now when he tied them, if he tied them wrong, she would hit

58

him with a paperknife that had her late husband's crest stamped on it. An eagle with wings outspread. There were plenty of eagles around them in the mountains, she told Max. They'd been known to carry off babies.

Occasionally he had a letter from Nanny. She hoped he was keeping well. Trixie missed him and sent her love. He must be a good boy.

It was too frightening to run away. Outside was nothing but the estate, miles and miles of it. Miles before you even reached the gates that led up to the little road, and then miles more of little roads until you reached the station that brought the train up to London.

London. In the blackness he would think of it. Mayber and the car, his cap shining in the afternoon sunlight as he waited for 'Master Max' to come down. Max would cry remembering how he had run away from Mayber that day, he shouldn't have done it, he shouldn't have run away from Mayber, he should have been good that day, and then maybe his father wouldn't have sent him to live with his Aunt Susan.

'You can scream your head off here,' she would tell him with satisfaction, 'no one to hear you, not for miles, and Mrs Braddock, she's as deaf as a housekeeper should be, as deaf as I want her to be, that's if she wants her pension.'

Max knew he would never forget what was happening to him, and he knew it was wrong, but he didn't know when it would ever stop. And he didn't know why his father hated him so that he had sent him away like this.

Still, inside, right down inside, in the black dark of his heart, he knew it wouldn't go on for ever, because like the dying birds who struggled and struggled until finally their wings were still, like them he knew finally it had to stop, like his screaming had had to stop.

'Well, now we've made a bit of a man of you, and a bit of a gentleman too, we can take you to London, and buy your school uniform.'

He walked up the steps to the flat. Nanny and Mayber, his father, Uncle Baz, Trixie, specially Trixie, he was going to hug them all, and never ever again would he leave them, and he'd never be naughty again either. Not ever.

'Are you all right? Are you all right?' Trixie kept asking him anxiously. 'You seem different. You seem much older.'

Max looked at her. She was right. He was older. He was nine.

'Where's Father? Where's Uncle Baz?'

'They're at the office, Master Max.' Nanny stroked the top of his head. 'They'll be back tonight for dinner. Not long now. Uniform fit all right, I hear.'

She sighed and looked at him.

'Trixie's right, you are older, I never thought to see you walking upstairs one at a time, the way you just did. Still, I suppose it's – how shall we say, it's just as well your Aunt Susan took you off like that. Made a man of you before you go to school. You always did want to go to school, didn't you, Master Max?'

Max looked round the flat. The French maid was laying the tea on the dining-table. A proper tea with two or three sorts of sandwiches, and a muffin dish, and cakes. The fire was hissing and spitting, and Trixie's little bright face was hanging on to every word of what a horrible time he had had. Suddenly school didn't seem so inviting.

'I don't think I want to go to school after all,' he told his father when he came to say good-night.

His father laughed.

'Of course you do. You used to nag me to go to school with other boys. You've got to go to school to make up for me and Uncle Baz not going to school. You've got to go to school to get on.'

'But I could stay here, the way it was.'

'No, you're better off away. It's done you the world of good, I can see that. Made a bit of a man of you. I don't like your Aunt Susan, even though she is your darling mother's sister, but she's done a good job on you. I have to say that. She's done a good job. Max Kassov, you're going to be a

60

great man, mark my words. You're going to inherit an empire.'

Max didn't want to inherit an empire. He just didn't want to go to school. Not any more, not now he was back. He turned his face to his pillow. Now he didn't just hate his aunt, he hated his father too.

Excerpt from Rodney Young's show business page, *Sunday Express*, 6 May 1951

Great impresarios are the stuff of show business legends, and Louis Kass, genial backstage éminence grise, is all set to prove that he is no exception. We met in his chic offices in London's West End, and he lost no time in bringing me up to date with his plans.

'My partner and I have just acquired a substantial share in Dillington Theatres Ltd,' he said, offering me an expensive Havana cigar, 'and now we're all set to move into the film business. People need to be cheered in these post-war times, and that's what we're dedicated to doing, bringing much needed entertainment to the British public. Who needs drear after a war?'

Pulling with difficulty on the hand-rolled cigar he had generously offered me, I could only marvel at the energy of this formidable man whose day starts at dawn.

'I only sleep when the lights of the West End go out,' he boasted.

His only regret is that his son Maxwell is not able to see his latest show.

'He's enjoying himself so much at school, I'm lucky if he even gets time to write to me,' he said laughing.

The cold of it, the bitter, bitter cold. Max stood on his narrow iron bed in his pyjamas and stared out of the window above it. Down below there was no sign of Mayber's cap, only the stiffly laid out flower beds of the housemaster's garden. He hated his housemaster's garden. He hated his housemaster, and he hated all the other boys at the school. He hadn't known how to make friends with them, and now he'd been at the school for over two years, he didn't care if they never spoke to him. He didn't care if they kept him in 'Coventry', as they called not talking to you at the school. He didn't care.

Night was the time that he liked best, the only time. To wait until all the other boys were asleep, and then to fall asleep yourself dreaming of the day when you would no longer wake up at school. His only wish was to sleep away all the days and nights until the end would come to the grey-black days spent in the grey uniform trotting from one grey building to another.

'And Max Kassov will be collected at Victoria Station by his nanny.'

The laughter that had greeted that announcement at the start of his first half-term had finished Max's career at the school. And Mr Townsend, that tall beadle-like figure in his headmaster's gown, how he had smiled and smiled at the laughter, at Max's flushed cheeks, at the tears that sprang so shamingly into his eyes as the laughter grew and swelled, as the other teachers joined in.

'Max Kassov will be collected at Victoria Station by his nanny.'

'Why, Master Max, what have they been doing to you?'

Nanny stared at Max's torso as he undressed for his bath.

'Nothing, nothing, I just fell in the playground off the ropes by the swings. That's all, I just fell over.'

Nanny turned away, momentarily accepting.

'I hope Matron keeps an eye on you,' she said vaguely. 'And I hope she puts some aquaflavin on that cut of yours.'

She sighed, and folded one of the large monogrammed bath towels and put it carefully on the heated towel rail. Now Max had been away at school she seemed less interested in him. He was more a boy on loan now. Not like Trixie who was always there.

Max climbed into the warm water. His eyes travelled over his own body. He could put a name to every bruise. That one there, that was Holmes, and that one there, that was Cahn, a small ginger-haired boy. But the lump behind his ear, that wasn't Cahn. Max put up his hand and felt it; that was Cardew. And then there was Walker, and Trepte – their speciality was beating 'squits' on the soles of their feet.

'Please, please, don't send me back.'

Louis sighed, and then drew on his cigar and patted the top of his son's head. It was good to see him again.

'You'll get used to it. We all get used to it. You're having a privileged schooling. You should be grateful. Baz and I, we only went to the school of life. We only had our mothers.'

His eyes travelled towards the portrait of Max's mother.

'Besides, you know, it's what *your* mother would have wanted.'

Max stared up at the portrait. Was that true? Was that what his own mother would have wanted for him? To be beaten up by other boys, to be made to perform after lights were out?

'Go on, perform, Kassov,' they would taunt him. 'Go on, everyone else has. Go on, pull yourself off.'

Max whispered in his head to his dead mother, 'If this is what you wanted for me, I hate you. I hate you.'

He turned towards his father, despairing.

'Now, Maxie, don't cry, it's necessary, we all have to suffer a little – make a man of you. Baz, and I, Baz and I in the East End, you know what that was like? My mother worked in a sweat shop, a real sweat shop, not like nowadays where they have plastic fans and people pay you double to work all night, no, this was real. The damp ran down the walls, and she had bad eyesight, that's why she went blind in the end, bending over that machine, day, night, night, day, that was all she did, making Italian sheets, you know, like they say it's made by nuns? Well, it isn't, it's made by people like your poor grandmother, day, night, night, day, and going blind all the time.'

He shook his head, and then he waved his cigar at the portrait of his wife.

'She never knew anything like that, your mother, all she ever knew was the best, and I saw that she got it too, right to the end. I never let her know she was dying, not ever, gave her everything the way it always was.'

Louis looked up at the painting and, as he did every evening, he willed the slender young girl standing beside the marble plinth with her hand to her cheek to step down out of the painting and to touch his cheeks the way she always had just before she went out or came back.

'Class, that's what she had with a capital "C", and that's what you've got to have, Maxie – class, that's why you've got to go away to proper British schools.'

'They make fun of me.'

'Everyone makes fun of everyone. And don't cry, it's bad for Trixie to see you crying when you come home, really, think of your sister.'

Think of his sister! Max couldn't think of anything except the pain of parting.

'Don't send Nanny to the station, please, at least don't send Nanny to the station!'

'Maxie please, you're meant to be a young man, please, don't be childish, you're going to be twelve in a few months' time. At twelve, Baz and I were out mixing concrete for an Irishman by the name of O'Riordan; now, he *could* make you cry. He used to hit us with the back of his shovel every time we stopped mixing. You knew what mixing was you'd know what crying was. Of course Nanny goes to the station. She'd be upset *not* to go to the station, she'd worry.'

'Just Mayber, please, just send Mayber, and to the side entrance.'

His father looked at him, and then slowly raised his drink to his lips, and drank deeply before he spoke again.

'Nannies, chauffeurs, Rolls-Royce to take you everywhere, and all you want to do is go in the side entrance? All right' – he pointed his cigar at him – 'all right, just Mayber, and the side entrance, but you've got to take Nanny and Trixie in the car with you, I don't want *them* upset.'

Max nodded and wiped his eyes on the grey flannel of his sleeve. No more Nanny, at least that was something.

But it wasn't. No more Nanny on the platform still didn't stop him being 'that boy'. The one Mr Townsend had said would be collected by his nanny. All that happened was that you learned to live with it. Somehow.

And as Max grew up, he made sure he was good at everything. Swimming, football, maths – particularly maths. He was up there with them all. He played clarinet in the school orchestra; sang in the choir; athletics he excelled at, running faster than most (although not as fast as some); until finally the hell of his first school was over, and he could walk down the platform towards the waiting car and know that with any luck he would never see any of them again. Not Mr Townsend, not Trepte, not Cardew, none of them, they could all go to hell, the one that he had constructed for them every day and every night of that four years.

'See? It wasn't so bad was it?'

They were in his father's favourite restaurant. Friday night and Uncle Baz had his napkin spread out over his now increased girth. Max dropped his eyes, he didn't want to see that, that napkin spread out over his Uncle Baz's waistcoat. He knew it was wrong. People might laugh. He clutched his own stiff white napkin under the table.

Louis beamed round the restaurant. It was wonderful to be out on a Friday night dining at Le Caprice, all the stars passing by their table, and his son beside him, his big son, a gentleman every inch of him.

'And you passed into Harrow just like that.' He waved

66

his hand in the air in a parting of the waters gesture. 'Just like that.'

Max put his hands under his knees and swung his legs. He wished he hadn't heard his father boasting about how much he'd paid towards the school building fund 'to help get Maxie in'.

'You'll be in all the teams there, mark my words, you'll carve a name for yourself. I know you will. You'll have your name written up in gold on all the school records. There'll be no stopping you now. I know that, Maxie, no stopping you at all. You'll be bigger than us. Remember, just remember that your school, the school you're going to – that's Winston Churchill's school, remember that, Maxie.'

Max stared at the menu, and a wonderful warm feeling came over him. He was going to eat proper food again, no more grey meats with stale cabbage, no more potatoes with all the black eyes still in them, no more slimy fat that you had to swallow, that made you feel sick, and then sometimes you even were sick. No more smells of the 'bogs', and boys' urine, not for the moment, a whole two months before there was any more of that.

A beautiful woman passed by their table. She smiled at Louis and Baz.

'Hello, Louis,' she said in a husky voice, 'remember me?'

It was always the same no matter who it was, if anyone greeted Louis Kass and Baz Vogel, it was always, 'Hello, Louis', and then, 'Hello, Baz', a fraction later.

'Gloria, you're looking wonderful.' Louis beamed. 'Really wonderful.'

'Of course I am, Louis, I'm rich.'

Her laugh was in her eyes, which were large and green and slanting, and her long red nails ran through her short curly auburn hair.

'I'm rich, Louis, and I'm loving it.'

'So am I, Gloria, so am I.'

'But you always have been rich, Louis.'

'Not always, Gloria, not always, but long enough so that I don't feel cold when I look back.'

The sounds of the restaurant filling up, the smart faces from the gossip columns, the warmth, the food, that was what it was all about.

Max watched her walking off. His father and Uncle Baz did too. Through the floating panels of her dress Max could see that she had long slender legs, beautiful legs set on slim ankles, and she swayed her backside gently as she proceeded on her way.

'She was a cloakroom ticket girl in the Trocadero when we spotted her,' Louis told him proudly. 'She used to say to me, "Until you put me in your shows, Louis, I didn't even know what an aitch was unless it was 'anging off an 'anger"!'

'Mr Kass?'

Louis and Baz raised their eyes to the head waiter. Their table was always assured, in the window, never a problem. He handed each of the men the heavy menus.

'And this is?'

'My son, Max Kassov. He can afford the extra two letters, I was so poor at his age I had to pawn them.'

Max took his own menu, but his eyes still followed the woman. He watched her secretly as she swung her way across the restaurant, pausing briefly at other tables. Her tiny waist emphasized the roundness of her breasts. Around her neck was a necklace that sparkled. Max longed to be sitting next to her, not between his uncle and his father in their reading glasses. They were both arguing over the hors d'oeuvres in the same way that they must discuss deals at the office. In just a few years, only just a few now, Max thought, he would make sure he wouldn't be sitting between them any more, he would be beside a woman like that, and he would smell her perfume, not cigar smoke, and he would feel the silkiness of her dress, and she would let him touch her breasts with his hands, and that would be very nice.

His father was telling the waiters that Max was about to

go to Harrow. The head waiter, yes, but the *waiters*. Even the one pouring the water, even he had to know that Max was going to the same school as Winston Churchill.

'Probably going to sit at the same desk as him, the one he carved his initials on. Sir Max Kassov, that's what you're going to be, aren't you, Max?'

Max looked up from the menu.

'I'll have the pâté, please, and then the steak mâitre d'hôtel.'

'See?' Louis beamed round at everyone, and even Baz smiled.

'He even speaks French like Winston Churchill.'

Max remembered his first day at Harrow most of all because of the people. They all looked so shabby, so completely different from the people to which he had been used.

There were no slender waists and beautiful clothes in evidence, just the browns and greys of the men's suits, beautifully cut but old, not like Louis and Baz whose suits were always so new. And the mothers, they didn't look like his mother in the portrait, they looked more like his Aunt Susan, three strands of pearls and tweed suits and shoes that were comfortable. And not all of them even wore nylons, some of them wore thick woolly-looking stockings on their legs, and they walked ahead of the men and the chauffeurs and the boys, as if they knew they ran England, which they did.

'It was the women of England who won the war,' his Aunt Susan had instructed him. 'Our women picked the fruit, and grew the food, and ran the schools and organized ourselves; it was the English women in the country who defeated Hitler. We out-knitted, out-dug, and outwitted him, that was what we did, and we didn't give in. It wasn't just the men, you know, it was us behind the men bringing up our domestic cavalry charge, we did as much as anyone.'

More school, more of the same, except now he could see

69

and smell the West End, it was no longer so far away. Sometimes, when the fog lifted, he imagined he could see his father's theatre, and even hear the orchestra starting to play, and the clatter of the showgirls passing the stage door, and their heels ringing out on the stone steps as they went up to their dressing-rooms. For since he was thirteen his father and Baz had sometimes allowed him to hang around outside the theatre, or inside the theatre, and even taken him backstage.

'The boy might as well start to learn the business in his holidays,' Louis told Baz. 'After all it's his heritage, it's him I'm doing it all for.'

'And Trixie,' said Baz.

'And Trixie, of course, and Trixie. But it's Maxie who's got to have the brains, hasn't he? He's the one who will be doing the deals, not Trixie. Trixie's going to marry a prince, we don't want her near the business, the business is for Maxie.'

Louis smiled, and Baz nodded and turned away. He had no children, never wanted any. Didn't like women, not to live with; they were all right for the things he wanted them to do, but not to live with.

Baz was how Max had found out that there were such things as brothels. Of course Max knew about prostitutes because no boy growing up in London could avoid seeing them as they stood in clusters smoking and walking outside the cinemas and theatres. They actually frightened Max, with their strange lurid clothes, and the way they smoked their cigarettes over the top of men's shoulders as people passed them in the dark, and the way the men all looked so intently at them; but Max didn't, he hurried on. They were no more for him than the maids at the flat with their odour of onions.

Baz had far too grand a taste to go near a prostitute. Where he went to see girls was very chic, a nice address, and the door was opened by a maid.

'Very expensive,' he would grumble when he climbed back into the car and sat beside Mayber. Max wasn't meant to know what it was exactly that Baz had been doing that was costing his father's partner so much money, but he did. And he longed to be able to afford the same thing himself.

By the time he was fifteen Max was allowed to stand by Wally, the stage doorkeeper and watch all the beautiful girls arriving backstage for his father's shows. Wally called it clocking in.

'And you're having a clock too, in'tyer, Master Max?' he would say every night that Max arrived, and then he would laugh and fold his racing paper and mark out his bets for the following day. 'You'll strain your eyes you will, be wearing glasses by the time you're sixteen if you carry on clocking those birds the way you are.'

Max grinned. Sometimes he brought friends with him and they 'went round after the show'; that was good, that meant they had to do you favours back at school, that they ran around as if you were a prefect because you could take them to look at beautiful girls, because they didn't have beautiful girls to look at on their estates at home, just fields and trees, and they'd grown out of those, most of them, and into staring at pictures of girls in magazines and cutting out pictures to put on the walls.

'Will you really take me round to see them, Kassov?'

Howard. God, his family were so old they kept having to learn about them in history, even he crawled to Max now. Girls, girls and more girls, and they were all part of the Kass Empire, all part of what Max had on tap and they didn't.

Max looked at Howard and then he grinned slowly, and he opened his eyes wide.

'Yes, I'll take you, Howard, if you take *me* home!'

Howard shifted uncomfortably as Max's grin grew wider. Home was a castle and a moat and even footmen. Home was everything that Harrow stood for, but it didn't have girls, not lots and lots of girls.

'It's difficult, you know how it is, Max, my mama – she's

such a stickler, you know. You can come to the flat, she's hardly ever there, the flat's fun too because it's near Harrods and my brother keeps a motorbike and he's going to try riding it through the banking hall next holidays.'

'OK.' Max shrugged his shoulders. 'OK, Howard, I'll let you come to the show, and backstage, but first you take me to the flat.'

Again, everything at Howard's flat was so old and so worn, not at all like Louis's flat. Max looked round, his hands in his pockets. He had no fear of Howard. Howard wanted to see showgirls too much.

'My father's been right through the first row of the chorus,' Max told him proudly on their way to the show in the chauffeured Rolls. He didn't know if he had, of course, but he hoped he had, for both of them, for him and Howard, and for Uncle Baz; for all of them. Anyway, he couldn't stand the idea of his *not* taking an interest in all those beautiful creatures who passed by Wally's window every night.

Howard loved every moment at the show. He might have a castle and a moat but seeing so many beautiful girls at such close quarters sent him white with excitement.

'You're so lucky,' he said thoughtfully in the car going back to their respective flats. 'So lucky. I wish my father did something exciting. Land, that's all that interests him, land.'

He said 'land' in a way that made it sound very, very flat, and very, very dull, and very, very boring. Max looked across at Howard.

'I am lucky,' he agreed, 'but you could be lucky too, Howard, you could go into the business too.'

Howard's eyes lit up. 'Do you think?'

Max shrugged his shoulders, and nodded.

'For a percentage of course,' he said laughingly.

'He shouldn't have taken you there, it's wrong, it's really wrong. You shouldn't have taken him, Baz.'

'Why? Why? The girls are clean, guaranteed; it's

72

expensive, he's eighteen. By eighteen you and I hadn't just hired all the girls on our books, we'd had them too.'

'I know, I know,' said Louis, but he still shook his head. 'I know, Baz, but you know Max, it's meant to be different for Max, everything's meant to be different for him.'

'He enjoyed himself,' said Baz defensively. 'You know they're very skilled, those girls. Every one of them is French, every one Louis, and they're chic. I mean you know what they did for me. You know what Ginette did for me? Remember the problem I had, after Mama died? Remember that?'

'Sure I remember, how could I forget? The whole business knew about your problem, Baz, but Max hasn't got a problem, he's young, he should be going around with nice girls, not being taken to see French girls.'

'He *loved* it' – Baz was shouting now and waving his fingers under Louis's nose – 'he loved it, he hugged me when he came out. He danced down the street, didn't you Max? I mean Louis, really, it was the boy's *birthday*.'

'Well then, buy him some shares, but don't take him to brothels.'

'It's not a brothel, Louis, you know it's a cut above that. The French do these things very well. This is an exact replica of that one in Paris. I mean, he should be so lucky to lose his virginity with a top-class girl like that.'

'You spoil him,' Louis grumbled reluctantly. Then to Max, 'He spoils you, if he'd had children of his own now that would be different. But now he has to make it up to you because he doesn't have children.'

There was a small pause, and then he looked up at Max who at eighteen was taller than his father and Uncle Baz put together.

'Well, go on, tell me, how was it?'

Max's eyes danced with mischief, dreadful wide-eyed sparkling mischief. 'FANTASTIC.'

His father laughed, and turned to his partner.

'How about this boy?'

He shook his head and then said again, 'How about this boy?'

For Max, following Uncle Baz up the steps of that discreet but chic London address, and actually having the door opened to him, and not just being left waiting in the Rolls, it had been the realization of a dream.

The maid was so pretty he would have been quite happy with her! Instead he followed Uncle Baz's example and just gave her his coat. And then it was into the drawing room, or the *salon* as the maid called it, where he found himself shaking hands with a beautiful older woman, her dark hair swept up into a chignon, around her neck three strands of fine pearls, in the middle a large turquoise and diamond clasp which lay to the front, on her wrist a matching bracelet. Her eyes were dark and sparkling and she greeted Uncle Baz with a charming kiss.

'Baz. And you've brought a young friend, huh?'

Her voice was French accented but light and modulated, and Max, who was over six feet in height now, appreciated that she was tiny and delicately made so that even though she was older he could gaze down on her, and it made him feel more confident.

'Champagne?'

'It's the boy's eighteenth birthday,' said Baz, sitting down heavily. 'Eighteen yet.'

'Eighteen today! Well now, that calls for vintage champagne.'

She smiled at Max delightedly, pronouncing champagne 'shamp-pannyere', which made it sound even more exciting, foreign and exciting.

'I have heard so much about you, Max.'

She sat down beside Max on the deep red velvet-covered button-backed sofa.

'It is always Max this, Max that – you have two fathers I think, huh?'

Max felt his eyes swimming with excitement, her perfume was wonderful.

74

Soon they were drinking the vintage champagne brought in by the maid, and Max was dizzy, heady, and hopelessly in love. Not just with the maid, but with her, with Annie.

And then, and then, and then, and then, and then, and then – God, it was wonderful, and *she* was so wonderful, and he knew just how he wanted to spend the rest of his life, with firm-breasted girls who made him feel so good, who were as beautiful as 'Lucille' was. He would never ever forget her. Her little white teeth and her pink tongue and her long slender body, and how she let him sleep afterwards.

And when he woke the car and Uncle Baz were still waiting, as if they knew what a great time he was having and didn't mind because it was his birthday.

He ran down the steps and wrenched open the door of the Rolls-Royce.

'Thanks, Uncle Baz, my God, THANKS!'

Uncle Baz looked up from the *Financial Times* and shrugged. 'The French do these things very well,' he said.

In those days Paris was fashionable, Paris was it. Movies were being shot in Paris, everyone went to Paris. People who couldn't speak French and couldn't understand it either boasted of going to the theatre in Paris. It was chic to see everything there. To know how to pronounce the names of Jean-Louis Barrault and Edwige Feuillère, and to quote from the plays of Jean Anouilh.

So it took little for Max to persuade his father to send him to Paris to stay with an incurably fashionable family in the sixteenth *arrondissement*.

To be young, to be handsome, to be Max and to be in Paris at the right time, it was everything that Max knew life must always be thereafter. He loved every hour of every day, all he lacked was love. Still, at least he could watch girls, all Paris watched girls, and all the girls walked Paris to be watched. And they weren't on the game, they were just beautiful and chic, and he wanted them all.

Sometimes a car would pass near where he would sit out on his favourite sidewalk, and he would watch a beautiful woman climbing out. So chic, so special, something so different about French women after the fussiness of English girls; not pretty like the English girls, more than pretty, insouciant.

He began to long for one of them to stop and look towards him and, seeing him appreciating her, call him over. It became an obsessive fantasy, the way he had for so long as a boy fantasized over following Baz up the steps of that London address. And if one fantasy came true, why not another? He developed a belief, the only belief, and that was that he had only to believe for it to happen. It was not long until it did.

'You are English, no?'

Max shook his head.

'Not exactly.'

He grinned and widened his eyes, which he had an idea made him look more attractive.

'No, no, I'm a little bit of everything. English, Scottish—' He stopped; he wasn't going to go on, he'd found it better to dissemble the 'Englishness' when in Paris. Too many boulevards named after Napoleon, too many reminders of, if not Agincourt, at least the old enmities; so, nowadays, he was only a little English, and mostly Scots – well, the French loved that. To be Scottish was as good as being French – well, not quite as good as being French, but good enough to get you a free drink in the Quartier Latin on a Saturday night, good enough to be asked for Sunday lunch now and then.

So here he was now only a little English, and getting more Scots by the minute as this beautiful blonde woman (for she was definitely a woman and not a girl) looked at him with speculative eyes and slowly raised a glass to her lips.

Max had already kissed her hand, something he had practised a great deal in private. Just kissing a married woman's hand was intoxicating enough, particularly when their scent was subtle and expensive, particularly when their nails were polished and manicured, lovely red talons that you could imagine resting lightly on your arm, that you longed to rest lightly on your arm.

'You are here to study, no?'

He loved the way the French so often posed a question at the end of their sentences, it seemed so generous, so polite to be apparently ever ready for contradiction. The only way he would ever like her to say 'no' was ending with a question mark, never with a full stop.

Her skin was very, very pale. Max immediately decided that he liked pale skin on a woman, although a tanned body was wonderful in a girl, and currently very fashionable in Paris.

Yes, of course he was there to study French, wasn't everyone? But he was failing dreadfully, he told her gaily, except studying French was after all to study the French too, for they *were* their language, precise, colourful, sentimental, joyous, changeable, were they not?

He watched her face carefully as he hesitatingly spelt out the adjectives that he had mastered, and saw that he was winning; more importantly he saw that she wanted him to win.

'Oh, Jacques.' She turned to Monsieur their host, Max's genial landlord, if someone so grand could be described as such. 'May I not have *ce petit monsieur* beside me?'

She looked at the *placement* reproachfully as if Monsieur had promised her, and for many months, that he would seat her beside Max. Their host nodded to his wife who shrugged genially. Max's conquest was a woman with many aristocratic connections, even the Queen of Spain was a close relative.

And so Max found himself in the sublime company of a beautiful woman on a beautiful day, seated at a white damask cloth while the sun flooded in through the old shutters of the apartment and falling hopelessly and passionately in love, which was of course to be highly recommended to anyone who was over eighteen and living in Paris in the 1950s.

She took him away with her and no one seemed to notice. How sophisticated! Kissing her in the back of her chauffeured car, feeling her roundness and her softness through the silk of her dress and the little bumps where her suspenders held her stockings in place, Max knew now and for the rest of his life that you only had to believe something and it would come true. It was as simple as that.

'You have *got* to come home!'

Louis was screaming down the telephone at Max who was leaning his naked back against the silk wallpaper of Marie-Gabriella's boudoir – and God it really was a boudoir. He had been smoking a Gauloise feeling quite 'superb', as in the French, when his father rang from London.

'Please, Pa—'

'I'm not your Pa, I'm your FATHER!' Louis shouted. 'Remember that, and you're not yet twenty-one!'

'I know, Pa – Father – but you know how it is. I'm not costing you anything. And I'm learning more French each day—'

'You should be here learning the business. French – where does French get you when you're putting a show together? How many deals are you going to make in *French*?'

'Look, I'll be home soon.'

'Soon? What's soon? May I ask? What is *soon*? We had soon last month, soon last week. Soon you'll be without anything to come home to, and that *will* be soon.'

Max exhaled his Gauloise. It tasted so good after love, after coffee, after a walk down the Bois. Quite wonderful.

'It's your Uncle Baz's fault,' Louis carried on, his scream descending to a shout as his secretary must have come into his office. And then in a hoarse voice he hissed into the telephone, 'I told him, I told him taking you to Frenchwomen that day, on your birthday, would be the end, but he wouldn't listen, and *now* look at you.'

Max looked at the end of his Gauloise, it glowed red. He sighed slowly. No, not exactly a sigh, more of an exhalation of breath, even though he had long ago blown the smoke from the cigarette into three perfect rings. Marie-Gabriella had bought him many things, but he often thought she had bought him nothing better than the trousers he was wearing at that moment. They were so beautifully cut, they made him feel taller, slimmer, and even sexier than she made him feel already, than he had discovered that he was. For since that lunch, since that day, he had never ceased to make love to her, and he had been impressive. He must have been because they never left her apartment, because she took no calls, 'not even from the *docteur*', she had murmured to her maid.

Sometimes she had protested that he 'tire-red' her, but then, since he only treated this as a challenge, she soon stopped protesting, and Max continued to make love to her so that in the end, although she was older than he, perhaps even by ten years, he could see that she had become his slave, and that he could do as he wanted, when he wished, and that she would give him anything in return for not leaving her. It was perfect. And of course they were in love.

But how could he explain this kind of love to his father who liked only showgirls with no class or real style? How could he explain heavily monogrammed sheets and scents for the bath that clung to your skin, and a woman who had such a perfect body and such beautiful clothes, so many rooms of such beautiful clothes that she would command Max to wander from one *armoire* to another and choose her something to wear, while she lay in bed and sipped 'shamp-pannyere'.

Max sighed again, but this time it was a true sigh, it was a 'you'll never understand' sigh. It was a 'there's more than the Channel between you and me' sigh.

'Max.'

His father's voice dropped.

'Maxie—'

Max could hear the tears in Louis's voice, and imagined them in his eyes. He had seen him use this technique before, usually before he fired someone.

'Maxie, Baz and I – well, we're not getting any younger. Your mother dying like that, so suddenly, bringing you up on my own. It hasn't been easy. Imagine, try and imagine. Everything I have is invested in you, everything I've done is for you – now get out of that woman's bed and come to London, or I leave everything to Trixie. Now did you—'

Max put the telephone back on its receiver before his father could finish. It always made it sound as if they had been cut off and that worried his father. Power, that's all he had. Max had everything else. Most of all he had Marie-Gabriella.

He moved in front of the long mirror that was opposite the bed. He had other things too. Look, the body, tall, but not too tall, slim, but not skinny. No, he could do without his father, what was power against what he had?

Marie-Gabriella came back into the room, her hair about her shoulders, one beautiful long leg poised gracefully in front of another. She smiled at Max, and he moved towards her. Oh, those breasts! Oh, those legs! And when she stood on tiptoe like that he knew just what she wanted. To hell with his father.

She had taken to going to the cinema on her own. Not in the Champs Elysées where the films shown were always subtitled in English, but to small *quartier* cinemas where the films were intellectual, all in French and no subtitles.

After a while Max let her go on her own. It pleased him to resume wandering around Paris on his own, and besides sometimes, just sometimes, it was good to be away from the apartment, from her scent which was heavy now the warmer weather was with them, from the endless wardrobes of clothes, from her maid who spoke French with such a thick southern accent that Max couldn't follow what she was saying.

Not only that but he had made friends with other

English-speaking students, American journalists who hung out in the bar of the Georges Cinq, sophisticated English boys who were waiting to go 'up' to Oxford, and who were envious of Max and his sophisticated affair with an older woman in the sixteenth *arrondissement*.

Altogether, when he looked back, when he was older, a few weeks later, it was hardly surprising to find that Marie-Gabriella's visits to the cinema were visits of another kind, and that inevitably he would return one day, a little earlier than usual, a little fed-up with the hot Parisian streets outside, and find another man in her bed, another outline of a body beneath the sheets.

'I'll kill you, I'll kill you,' he screamed at her, and at him, an older man, a man of her own age, a man with dark hairy armpits that sprouted obscenely over the top of the embroidered sheets, and who lit a cigarette, one of her cigarettes from her small gold case, and looked at Max having hysterics with a mixture of amusement and boredom.

'I'll kill you, I'll kill you.'

She shrugged her shoulders, and Max couldn't help admiring her courage as she turned her back on him.

'You are very young and very stupid,' she said in French.

The tears on Max's cheeks were cold now, and he was in her dressing room, and he still wished to kill her, but they had sent for the doctor and the doctor had given him something, and now he just hated her. He had given up everything for her: his father, Uncle Baz, Trixie, everyone.

Except he hadn't. He had forgotten one person, another person that he hated, that hated him, or so he thought.

'Come on, Max, carry my bag and stop standing about like a wet week in Whitstable.'

Max picked up what could only be described as his Aunt Susan's 'portmanteau', so old and so dilapidated was it, and followed her dismally into the hotel. They were in the

South of France. Very fashionable, but thankfully it was off-season, for he would have committed suicide rather than be seen with Aunt Susan on the *Promenade des Anglais*.

The hotel with anyone else, even with Howard, would have been quite fun, but with Aunt Susan it became just another place to keep your voice down, to lower a newspaper and stare if someone rattled their hotel key too loudly, or over-tipped the hall porter, or said something in *French*.

Because of course, unlike Max, Aunt Susan hated the 'Frogs'. On what particular principle or basis Max never quite dared to question her directly, but hate them she did, if only in a general kind of English way that was, it seemed to Max, more to do with the fact that they weren't the same as her, and what's more didn't seem to mind.

'You're my heir, you know,' she said one night over her gin and tonic without ice or lemon.

Max looked at her blankly. She had caught the sun sitting out at the back of the hotel and it had made a red 'V' underneath her rather yellowing pearls, and her earlobes were heavy with larger even more yellow pearls, and not even the smell of mimosa could overpower the slight tang of mothballs from her thickly woven woollen stole.

'Uncle Harold, as you know, has been dead many years.'

Max didn't know how long Uncle Harold had been dead for the simple reason he had completely forgotten that his Aunt Susan had even been married. He couldn't imagine her ever doing the kind of things he had been doing in Marie-Gabriella's boudoir in the sixteenth *arrondissement*. He couldn't imagine her even kissing a man, not properly, just a little kiss on the side of his face, the way she let Max kiss her as they parted at night.

'You may kiss me,' she said every night.

Max bent over and then sat down in his chair again. The night sounds of other guests' voices, the taste of the brandy that she always ordered for them both every night, kissing his aunt's soft powdery cheek, it was all so strange, a dream from which he would wake up and find himself once more in Marie-Gabriella's arms, and her waiting for him, her eyes sleepily aware of his, waiting for him to come alive for her.

'Yes, your Uncle Harold has been dead these many years.'

The kiss seemed to have satisfied Aunt Susan that Max was properly grateful, and consequently, it seemed, she was prepared to confide in her nephew.

'Being childless now, having lost our son in the war, naturally we always thought you would be our heir, and now of course you are nearly grown up so we might as well be frank. How much money do you need?'

Max stared at her. It had all seemed so simple, in Marie-Gabriella's boudoir, life had been love, food, wine, and he had thought it would go on for ever and ever, that it must go on for ever and ever. That he was her prisoner, and she his, although for different reasons, and that they would never need anything else except each other. But tonight was reality, it was business, the kind of business his father talked about, his father who would have nothing more to do with him, his father who had even cut off his small allowance.

He heard himself saying, 'I could set myself up in an agency. Howard, he's a friend of mine, he wants to come into the business, he always did, and *his* father's prepared to back him, to help him.'

Aunt Susan sipped her brandy, and for a minute Max wondered whether his aunt, who after all had spent all her life either as a hostess to shooting parties, or battling with the elements in her large historic garden, would even know what 'an agency' was?

She nodded, seeming to savour the brandy, the night air, the softness of the evening weather.

'Jolly good, jolly good,' she said slowly. And then she turned to Max. 'And just think how cross it'll make your father and your uncle, Max dear, as cross as two crossed sticks. Now, how much do you want?'

Max's eyes widened. Cross? *Cross*. What an incredibly Trixie-type word to use for how his father and Uncle Baz would feel. Cross? They would rage, they would scream, they would beg God to tell them it wasn't true, they would cry to each other, to their friends they would sigh and shrug, to their enemies they would pretend it was *they* who were backing Max.

'I don't know how much I'll need,' said Max slowly, 'I'll have to price West End rents, we'll have to have a West End office, a secretary, it's not a question of a huge outlay. But what about you? You'll want a cut, won't you?'

Aunt Susan picked at her stole, and rearranged it slightly around her shoulders.

'I'll take a "cut" as you call it after five years, by that time it'll be worth it, up until then it'll be cheese parings.'

Having kissed Aunt Susan once more, and with a great deal more respect than he had ever felt before, Max left her and went for a walk by himself.

He hadn't known, not until that moment in the garden, he hadn't known just how much he *knew* about the business, not until then. Hadn't really thought, but now he did think he knew a great deal. All those days kicking around 'the office' waiting for his father or Uncle Baz, listening to the deals, no, half listening to the deals, leafing through *Spotlight* to see the pictures of all the pretty actresses before he went back to his prep school – it was second nature to him now, when he thought about it, once he'd stopped thinking about Marie-Gabriella and how he would like to murder her, once he stopped that, well it was suddenly very clear to him, he knew quite a lot. What's more, he knew the language. 'Availability check.' 'Say yes to everything, you can always back out later.' 'Say yes to everything, and nine times out of ten you find you're left with no deals anyway.'

Poaching, he knew about poaching. Not Aunt Susan's sort of poaching, not the man with the beard and the cudgel and a sack full of rabbits, no, he knew about poaching other people's clients. Especially in the provinces. Especially girls – they were the most vulnerable. First-night presents, dinner at the local Grand, sending the Rolls for them, it always worked.

He knew about 'stalking', again not Aunt Susan's stalking, not like deer stalking, but again a little like deer stalking too. Going after a talent when you knew it was in the mood for a change. Not giving it any idea that you *were* after it. Just always being around, being nice, being charming, not mentioning any unhappiness they might have with an agent, with their present agent, just being sympathetic and friendly, and then letting them do the suggesting.

'You know, Louis, I was thinking, I don't suppose – but your list must be so full.'

'Never too full for a beautiful girl, never. It's always been our principle, Baz and I, we can always find time for a beautiful girl.'

He remembered glimpsing his father saying those very words. His father standing and smiling, the girl in question, a well-known character actress of plain looks sitting and smiling up at Louis, trying to believe him, wanting to believe him.

And how Max grumbled afterwards to his father.

'But she's *not* pretty, she's not at all pretty.'

'Of *course* she's pretty,' Louis had corrected him. 'She's famous, she's talented, she's class, and we need her on our books – so of *course* she's pretty.'

Max had kicked his black school shoes up in front of him, and then let them drop with a thud against the leather of the Rolls-Royce. It was silly telling someone they were pretty when they weren't, because they had only to go home and look in the mirror to discover that they weren't anyway, and then they wouldn't join the agency because they'd know that Louis was a liar.

Except it wasn't true. And he remembered going to the actress in question's first night, and backstage, and he remembered the audience applauding and applauding, and his father escorting her proudly to the Rolls, and Max and Trixie being sent home in a taxi to Nanny. And his father winking at him as he closed the cab door.

'See what I mean Maxie – she's pretty, and wait till you see the notices. You won't believe them. They'll be as good as if I'd written them myself. You'll see.'

And they had been. Decorated everywhere with the words 'elegant' and 'beautiful', and 'divine'.

'Now that's what a good actress is, Maxie, not a bit of tat in a pretty skirt. Someone who can *act* beautiful is what you want, not someone who *is* beautiful. You want a beautiful girl, you can pick 'em up anywhere, anywhere at all. You'll see. What an agency needs is class. How come you think Baz and I got so rich, so we own the theatres and the performers? By going for the best. It's always cheapest in the end, remember that. Like this Rolls-Royce, expensive? Never, cheap, because it'll always be a great car. Go for class. Remember that, go for class. Like I did with your mother.'

As always the mention of Max's mother filled his eyes with tears, real tears.

'If only she could hear me.'

'Maybe she can.'

Remembering him that day, Max felt bad. The way he'd felt bad when he'd been sent to Aunt Susan's that time and he'd cried himself to sleep thinking of how he'd upset Mayber by running away.

But then, as he turned towards the hotel again, he shrugged off his feelings. His father had cut him off. He'd cut *him* off, not Max. Max had just stayed where he was, not costing him anything either. It wasn't as if he'd had to give him any money, for God's sake.

He slipped quietly into his own suite and lay down on the large comfortable bed with the sea view. It was a superb hotel and it was high time that he started appreciating it, and the food and the wine, and the good weather, and even Aunt Susan – no, especially Aunt Susan, after all she was prepared to back him. He'd have his own office, his own secretary. In the morning he'd ring Howard in England and see how much he was good for, and after that he'd spend the rest of the time exploring the South of

France. On the beach, tomorrow morning, he wouldn't just stare at the beautiful girls from behind his dark glasses while Aunt Susan shook yesterday's copy of *The Times* and checked her shares, he would *look* at them, the way someone who might sign them up would look at them, and that would make staring at them a great deal more fun, and looking at them a great deal more interesting.

'Girls, women, it takes some time to get your eye in,' Uncle Baz once said as they drove away from the chic private address with the very pretty French maid. 'It's like painting, Maxie, you've got to look and look, and look some more, and in a little while you start to see what there is, and then you start to appreciate, and then you can criticize. It pays to work at all these things, really. I'll take you to an art gallery tomorrow and we can start to look at the female nude, and when you can stare at one without giggling then we'll know you're beginning to get your eye in.'

To give Max his due he had never been prone to giggling when it came to staring at the female form. He had stared up at pictures in company with Uncle Baz and only longed to step into them, to lie beside those wonderful rounded forms. The female body never ceased to cause him wonder. It was much bigger than a man's even when the woman in question was small, like Marie-Gabriella. Even when it was slim and perfect like Marie-Gabriella's, there seemed to be more of it, and that made it more wonderful to him, the fact that there was so much more of it. No wonder painters in the past had made women look large, had painted them large, because they were, to a man, to a boy, they were large; wonderfully large.

'I think it's time for lunch,' said Aunt Susan.

Max sat back down on the sand beside her. He had been swimming, and the water had been cold and clear and blue and perfect, and the unexpected warmth of the off-season weather was just a bonus because the coldness of the water had made him feel even more alive than ever, even more than when he awoke that morning and realized that he was going to be able to be himself, nothing to do with his father, nothing to do with Baz. From now on he would be himself, Max Kassov. No, MAX KASSOV. And even Marie-Gabriella, she would be nothing. Just a French girl, no one special.

3

North of England
1959

Jay's hand slipped over the polished wood of the carved mahogany bannisters. Probably because the hotel was the Grand, and built in the 1880s when staircases in England were really grand, the bannister was not only ornately carved, it was highly polished, irresistibly highly polished, so highly polished that her hand slid up and down, and down and up quite effortlessly over its silken surface.

Down in the lobby, far down below, below the vast chandelier, stood William Kennedy, the publicity man for the publishing house, her chaperon on the book tour, an acquaintance of two days. Besides him, there was no one in the front hall – obviously there was a lull in the early-evening activities of the Grand.

Jay swung one nineteen-year-old leg over the side of the bannister and, with the kind of blissful expression that she normally reserved for a new book, a bag of Sharp's toffees and a nice rainy afternoon, she allowed herself to whizz, not slide, for the polish was really good, down the bannisters and into the lobby.

William drew on his cigarette, and then turned slowly towards the grand staircase, for from the expressions on the faces of the newly arrived visitors and the hall porter, who were emerging in unison from the swing doors, there was obviously something quite interesting happening on the staircase. When he saw what it was he ran forward and helped Jay dismount from the bannisters.

'Do you want to get us thrown out?' he hissed, helping her down.

Jay looked up at him from under her too long brown fringe, and then tossed back her braid of hair.

'Don't be stuffy,' she hissed back.

'I am not being "stuffy",' said William, leading her over-firmly to one of the leather chairs in the residents' lounge. 'You can't behave like that, not here.'

'Oh pooh,' said Jay, flinging herself down into the armchair. 'I never could resist sliding down a highly polished bannister, not even when I got whacked for it.'

'Well, you'll have to resist them now, you're an author now, you're famous.'

'I know, so you keep saying.'

Jay stared out of the window at the trees which had no leaves on them, at the greyness of the afternoon, and then back again at William. He might be very nice, but he was a grown-up, and although she was not officially a 'grown-up', she was still required to behave like one, which, to her mind, was sort of cheating. Tonight she had to make a speech, and tomorrow she had to make another speech, and after that it would be nothing but speeches and hand-shaking, and if the truth be known, and she couldn't tell it to anyone, not even her best friend Tilly, if the truth be known, she would rather not be a grown-up, not for a long while yet, she would rather put it off.

Apart from everything else she didn't look like a grown-up. Her mother had put her in a tartan dress, and her long braided hair ended in a black ribboned bow, and her skirt wasn't short enough, and her shoes weren't the right kind, so she wasn't even a success as a 'young' person. If you picked up a newspaper anywhere you could see what 'young' people were looking like, they didn't still have a braid, and skirts that went halfway down their legs. She sighed.

'I think I'd like a Scotch,' she said suddenly.

William matched her sigh.

'No Scotch, not until after the speech,' he said firmly. 'Anyway, what would you want a Scotch for now, Jay? Come on. Be a good kid, have a lemonade.'

'I don't know.' Jay wrinkled her nose. 'I just thought I'd try and have something sophisticated, you know, just a little more Scott Fitzgerald rather than teeny bopper author.'

'Scott Fitzgerald ended up a pretty unsophisticated lush, drinking thirty cans of beer a day, and that was before lunch.'

William stared over the top of his horn-rimmed glasses at Jay.

'Oh, but every writer should die young,' said Jay, her large grey eyes shining suddenly, 'otherwise no one remembers you. I intend to die of boredom by the time I'm twenty.'

'Who brought you up on these clichés?'

'I did.'

William lit another cigarette and beckoned to one of the hotel staff.

'Could we have a lemonade, and a double Scotch, please?'

Jay watched the waiter walk away. He had that perennially flat-footed walk that all waiters acquired. Fallen arches. Her uncle had been a waiter. He'd suffered from fallen arches.

'I bet you wish you were taking J. B. Priestley on a tour rather than me,' she said suddenly.

'Yes, I do,' said William, 'I wish I was taking Jack Priestley *and* Tennessee Williams – at least they wouldn't slide down bannisters.'

'I always heard Americans were very direct,' said Jay, looking at the pattern on her tartan dress. 'No, not direct so much as slightly rude.'

'Yes, well, in that case, you heard right.'

'Obviously,' Jay agreed miserably, and wished she'd worked harder at school at those subjects that would have got her a glorious entrance to a university. All her friends were at university. All clever, except her. And you had to be very clever to get into university in 1959, much, much cleverer than the boys.

So that was the reason why she had had to write a book, that was why she had worked so hard and for so long, every night, every weekend, in between her job as a secretary for Burnes, Burnes, Burnes and Burnes Ltd; because life had stopped happening to her, and had gone on happening to her friends.

She had got through her secretarial course all right, she had done that, and she had managed to find herself a job. Her mother had been pleased with the money she'd brought home. And even Jay had been quite pleased at first, for at seventeen to be employed as an office junior in the legal department of a big firm seemed quite nice really. But life in the English provinces, once you grew up and looked around, was definitely not full of the excitements that Jay had read about in books. Far from it, it was still and wet and dark, very dark sometimes, and it made her feel as if she were already just a tiny cog, a little stick person, and that nothing would ever be any different.

That was the second reason why she'd had to write her book: to give herself some feeling that she was still alive, that something was happening to her, and not just to her friends, who had all to a girl turned out to be outstandingly brilliant and were having a really good time being young with people their own age who understood exactly why it was necessary to die young – although only after you had written a great poem, or a scintillatingly great novel.

But William Kennedy, he wasn't like that. He was nearly twenty-eight, really quite old, and cross most of the time. Sort of sharp and cross in spurts, so that sometimes you thought he didn't mind you, and then other times you thought, well – he did mind you, and quite a lot.

'You'd better go and change.'

Jay nodded grimly. Her dress for the Literary Dinner was going to do absolutely nothing to lighten her mood. She didn't know why she'd bought it. She never knew why she bought any of her clothes, really. But this dress was a real dud. It was pale blue with little bits round the collar and hem, sort of organdie frills, and her mother had bought her a pale blue head band to go with it, and then covered it with matching pale blue velvet.

It wasn't her mother's fault, she couldn't blame her dress on her, poor thing. No, it was just that Jay herself had no taste.

Just for a minute, when she put the dress on and before she turned and looked at herself in the mirror, Jay had nurtured a little hope that it might not be too bad, but then she had turned and seen herself, and the dress was just as she had feared. It was truly horrible. It made her look not nineteen but a kind of over-developed thirteen.

She had washed her hair in the bath and dried it quickly in front of the electric fire, and now, brushing it out and putting on her mother's lovingly made, pale blue bandeau, she turned quickly away from the mirror; she looked like a macabre sort of Alice in *Through the Looking Glass*. An authoress should dress in black velvet with pearls as big as ostrich eggs. Or a sort of intellectual serge green, or even just serge, anything but pale blue with a velvet bandeau.

She sat down on the edge of the large mahogany hotel bed and took out her speech. She had memorized it, but even so it was worth going over it again.

'My lords, ladies, and gentlemen—'

The sound of her own voice, tremulous and reedy, echoed round the large Victorian hotel room. Oh dear, why, oh why had she thought it would be fun to write a book, and why had she let her mother send it off to her friend who had a friend who knew an agent, and why had she let herself go to London? She should have just said 'no' to everything, and then she would still have been working in Burnes, and Burnes, and Burnes, and Burnes, having a nice little job, going home to her mum at night, eating a quick supper, and then up to her room and the long hours of sitting and staring at her small, grey, portable typewriter, trying to make something happen, trying to make a good story, something that someone, somewhere, would want to read. It had all, as they say, seemed so simple then, but now it was different, not at all like she had thought it would be when she was little and she had dreamed of being a famous author. This was just hard and cold and full of people like William Kennedy who didn't like you, and just wheeled you around like the puddings on the trolleys in the dining-room downstairs.

'My lords, ladies and gentlemen—' she began again, and again she stopped as the nerves started to claw at the base of her stomach. Time to go to the bathroom, time to 'grip the porcelain', as her cousin Jimbo called it.

The applause was tumultuous. Even William Kennedy looked pleased – no, more than pleased, he actually looked delighted. Smiling and applauding and his eyes were crinkling with pleasure from behind his glasses. Jay sat down in the large carved chair and smiled feebly in front of her. The speech, arriving, going up to the top table, seeing the microphones laid out either side of her chair, it had all been a nightmare, and now it was over, she just had that cold sweaty feeling that you had when you woke up from a delirium. What on earth had she said to make them all so pleased, and then led them to applaud that loud afterwards?

William nodded appreciatively down at her as he led her to the book display where she was to sign copies of her nineteen-year-old autobiography. So many smiling faces, so many nice people.

Jay wanted to ask William if she was really all right but she sensed somehow that it would be wrong, that this tall owl-eyed American would just put her down, so she said nothing, and just followed him over to the table where there was already a long queue of people waiting for her, 'Jay Burrell', to sign their copies. Suddenly her name looked different, suddenly she was someone else, not Tilly's friend, not her mother's daughter, not her dead father's only child, not her cousin Jimbo's cousin, she was 'Jay Burrell', a writer – not *the* writer of course, but 'a writer' was good enough for her, quite good enough for

her, and judging from the way the display table was empty-
ing of copies it was even going to be good enough for
William too.

'Now may I have that Scotch?'

William signalled with one finger for the waiter, and then
pushed his glasses up his nose with the other.

'You'll be sliding up the bannisters after a Scotch, but—'
he shrugged, and then said to the waiter, 'Two Scotch, one
single, one double, please.'

Jay watched him uncross his long legs and then re-cross
them. He wore nice clothes. Not stiff and 'British' the way
everyone else she knew did. She liked his soft-collared
shirts, and the more relaxed jackets that he wore during the
day; she even liked him in his dinner jacket. And all this
because the dinner was over and the speech was behind her.

'Were you nervous for me?'

'Never you mind.'

'I'm sorry.' Jay bit one of her nails and William hit it
lightly.

'Biting your nails isn't something famous authors do.'

'No, well, no. But you see, well, what you don't see is that
I – well, I only have you to ask. I mean I don't have anyone
else, so if you don't tell me, who else should I ask?'

'I suppose that's a point,' William agreed, and then after a
long pause he said, 'you were good, but you know, you can
get away with murder at your age, looking as you do.'

'What – you mean silly?'

'Yes – silly. No, of course I don't mean "silly", no, of
course not. Did I say that? Did I say "silly"? Is that a word
that I would use?'

'Yup.'

Jay went back to biting her nail.

'I said, and I mean it, I said looking like you do. Young.'

The waiter put down the drinks and William paid him.
Jay frowned. She'd had quite enough of William's patroniz-
ing ways, and his 'there, there dear' tones. Yesterday –
yesterday she'd had to put up with a whole conversation
carried on over her head where a television producer and

several others debated whether or not she was just a flash in the pan. Well, she didn't mind, but talking over the top of her head that way, referring to her as 'she' even though she was very much present, it was rude.

'You know, it may not have come to your notice but I am NOT a stick of furniture, William Kennedy.'

'Now, did I say you were?'

'You know yesterday was the absolute pits with all those television people—'

'So you said.'

He picked up his drink and lit a cigarette.

'You were quite vociferous about it all the way to that nightclub where you had to pose with the boa constrictor.'

'Yes, I was, and I wish—'

'What do you wish?'

'Nothing.'

'Don't say "nothing" that way, it's childish.'

Jay took a large gulp of her Scotch and stared fiercely ahead of her at the carpet.

'My cousin Jimbo always refers to this kind of carpet as "sperm" carpet. He always says it looks just as if—'

'And that's quite enough of that!' William leaned forward. 'There are – older people present.'

Jay looked round. She saw a great many older people having their brandies and sodas before going to bed with a nice copy of Agatha Christie.

'I thought I'd have a grown-up conversation with you, that's all.'

'That's too grown-up,' said William, clearing his throat, 'haven't you something in between?'

'*Tout l'un, tout l'autre,*' Jay muttered.

'There's no need to turn to French, we're not that desperate.'

'Who's not?' said Jay.

'What is the matter?'

William leaned forward and removed his glasses. He had beautiful eyes, large and grey with long black lashes.

'Oh God, that's not fair,' Jay protested, 'that's really not fair. Give me your eyelashes – you don't need them.'

William shrugged.

'It's a medical fact they grow better under glass. Now what's the matter? I'm only here to help you – what's the matter?'

'I don't know.'

Jay looked at him helplessly. How could she explain to this tall American who wore soft-collared shirts and had been to Harvard, and was just about to give up everything to become a real live screenwriter full-time, how could she explain to him how she felt about what was happening to her? He would just yawn, or look bored. Or shrug his shoulders and say, 'You stand up in the market-place you gotta learn to have cabbages thrown at you.' Things like that, things that everyone said, one way or another. No one but she knew how uncomfortable she felt, how cut off from everything, how much of an orphan.

To her mother it had all been a fairy tale, and one that she had been celebrating ever since. Toasting her photograph of her daughter every night. Cutting out each little press cutting with all the pride of someone who had reared a precious orchid and had just won a medal for it at the local flower show. She couldn't talk to her mum about the bad bits, or rather about it seeming now to be nothing but bad bits. The only child of a widow had a duty to tell her only the things that she wanted her to hear, and Jay knew every bit of every single thing that her mum would *want* to hear. Just how loud the applause had been after the speech. How many people had bought the books? What had she had to sign in all of them? There would be no detail that would be boring or 'silly' to Jay's mum, Mrs Burrell, in her small, over-clean house at 57 Warrington Avenue, Danby, Yorkshire, England.

In her head Jay ran through the things that she couldn't tell her mum about. Friends not talking to you, and if you rang them up the feeling that they were thinking, you're different from us now, you've been in all the papers.

Feeling you should give all the money you'd made away because it didn't seem fair for you to be so lucky when everyone else wasn't. Things like that, things that were boring and just 'clichés' to someone like William, and would be disappointing, even wounding to her mother.

'You're on your way, you're on your way, my lamb,' she'd said to Jay the moment she'd had The Letter from the famous London publisher. 'You're going to be famous, just like I always wanted you to be. And you're going to go down to London, and you're going to know other famous writers, and that will be only what someone as talented as you deserves.'

It had been wonderful, that moment, those worn eyes of her mother's shining with delight; really believing, as Jay had, that a door was opening and that the world was really going to turn out to be as beautiful as you believed, as they had both believed, that somewhere down south away from the narrow streets of Danby a new life was waiting to be lived, and a transformed Jay would be there, in the thick of it, mixing with all the famous people, with all the people who, up until then, had just been print on the outside of books in the library to Mrs Burrell and her daughter Jay.

'To have the power with words, that's what I envy, even though I know envy is wrong, Jay, that's what I've always wanted, the power with words, and as soon as I saw you had it, the way I do believe your poor father would have had it had he lived, why I knew where my duty lay – to you and your talent. And now you're going to go places and you're going to prove to them all, to everyone, just what a talented daughter I've got. And no getting married and having children, mind? Because we all know where that leads to, don't we?'

This last was always said with a brisk nod to the houses opposite which, in Jay's mum's opinion, were peopled with women whose whole existences had been brought to degradation and ruin by their devotion to hearth and home.

Sometimes it had occurred to Jay that even without her

98

father having been taken to his maker at an early age as a result of a misdiagnosis from the local doctor, even if he hadn't been in the habit of attending the Greek doctor who didn't understand a word of English, let alone the symptoms of his patients, even so he would have had to have departed this life some way or another because the poor man could never have shared their house with Jay, her mother, and 'Jay's talent'.

Only good books were read. Nothing of a 'childish' nature was allowed by Mrs Burrell. No comics of any kind, no Enid Blyton such as other children enjoyed, no strip cartoons on Saturday morning. A new word was learned every day and spelled out just before she went to sleep. The Bible was allowed because it was written in good language, but belief in God was for the other folk who needed it, the folk that allowed their children to read comics. Jay was going to be different from every other child in the street, right down to her beliefs. That had been her mum's way.

And that had been only the beginning. That was all before Miss Tilson came into their lives. Miss Tilson was a pretty woman, rounded and blonde with grey eyes – not blue the way you would think from looking at her thick chignon of blonde hair, for it was a chignon not a bun, not a neat little screw of hair, but a large sweep of hair piled up into a generous mound and fastened with pins that would stray erroneously down to her shoulder if she had one of her 'quivers', as the children all thought of them.

Because like it or lump it Miss Tilson didn't just teach Jay and the other pupils at St Hilda's Secondary School English, she lived and breathed it. And on occasions she quivered and shook with it, her voice rose and fell with it, the power of the English language could never be forgotten by anyone who had been through Miss Tilson's hands. She knew what she wanted from her pupils, she wanted every single one of them to view the world through other eyes than their own. She wanted them to walk the Yorkshire moors with Emily Brontë and her dog, to dance

99

every Hampshire dance with Jane Austen, and to ride every inch of a pilgrimage to Canterbury with the Wife of Bath. Miss Tilson burned. And from the moment she clapped eyes on Jay's first essay she not only burned with the zeal of her mission, she adopted a cause too.

Jay was going to be a famous writer, she told Mrs Burrell, and Mrs Burrell, having agreed with Miss Tilson wholeheartedly, redoubled her efforts on Jay's behalf. She had to, for Miss Tilson was only a supply teacher at St Hilda's Secondary School, waiting to go to America where, she assured Mrs Burrell, she would continue to burn on behalf of the English language, but from where she could not do more than write and advise Mrs Burrell on a monthly basis.

Monthly. How much Jay would dread those letters — closely written in small neat writing. Miss Tilson made comments on Jay's latest essays. She advised Mrs Burrell as to which books Jay should be reading, by which authors, about which authors, and which plays. She strongly condemned any form of entertainment outside the theatre. Not even the cinema was encouraged, being, as she wrote to Mrs Burrell, 'tasteless and without due regard to the beauty of the English language, devised as it was to entertain people who couldn't read by other people who couldn't read, and performed by many who were similar.'

So, as neighbourhood houses started to sprout television aerials and as Jay started to hear about programmes that she was missing, and as she felt more and more isolated from her school friends, the list of books that she had read at a precociously young age grew, and grew, until the Danby library seemed hard put to find anything new, until they were down to lending her books by French and Russian authors, which were normally never asked for by anybody but visiting American university professors who had taken leases on houses in the neighbourhood with a view to spending their sabbaticals walking the Yorkshire moors.

'It sounds the perfect childhood to me,' said William, poker-faced.

It was half past one in the morning and he had had four Scotches, or 'Scotch' as he called it for some reason, and Jay had had two, and they were sitting in Jay's hotel suite, and she was feeling strange and over-excited, and he had his glasses on the top of his head, and she'd made him laugh quite a bit, which was also strange and very exciting because from the way he'd been before she could have sworn he really thought she was – well, nothing really. Just a duty, a last duty before he left to write for the silver screen.

'It *was* the perfect childhood,' Jay agreed, 'but, well, it was lonely too.'

'Aaah—'

'No, really. It's pretty difficult to find anyone in the average playground who wants to discuss Virginia Woolf and her influence on the stream of consciousness in the novel.'

'Yes, I guess that could be a problem. Although I would have been quite happy to oblige.'

Jay grinned at William.

'That's very nice of you,' she said, but then she found when she looked across at him, for some reason, she found that she dropped her eyes, just like a dog.

'I'd better get to bed and learn that new speech, hadn't I?' she said suddenly.

William nodded, drank his Scotch down, and stood up to go.

'Sleep well,' he said, and walked towards the door.

When he reached it, and Jay opened it, William kissed her briefly on the cheek, so that when she closed it after him it seemed as if that door, and then those walls next door, and that long length of carpet, well, it seemed to Jay that they were all just paper thin and at the same time as thick as anything ever built, that was how close she'd felt to him when they had been talking, and how far she felt from him once he'd stood up to leave.

'Mr Mayor, my lords, ladies and gentlemen—'

Tomorrow's speech. William liked her to learn them, as near as possible. It was important, he said. 'William.' Jay fell asleep thinking she'd never much liked the name, but now, it seemed different, quite nice even.

Jay put her finger to her lips and motioned to the maid to stand behind her. Day five of the tour, and this morning for the first time she had no speech to dread, no butterflies in the stomach, no feelings of terror that kept breakfast on the plate and coffee cold and undrunk.

The maid stood behind her. She was a small freckled local girl with a mass of red hair. 'Marauding Danes,' William muttered every time he saw red hair in one of the local towns or villages. Red hair came from the Danish invasions: sea ports, border towns, they were all game to the fierce warriors of ancient times, he said.

'It's just like going everywhere with my mother or Miss Tilson,' Jay had complained.

Now she was going ahead of the maid to wake him.

'I'll tickle you if you don't wake up,' she said, standing over his long pyjamaed frame.

William groaned.

'It's no good, we rang and rang' – Jay turned to the maid – 'didn't we? And now it's nearly nine-thirty and breakfast is off at ten, so I've had it brought up to you.'

'This girl's a sadist.'

William reached for his dressing gown and turned to the maid who was busy laying the breakfast table in the window. 'A sadist, and in one so young.'

The maid smiled shyly.

'She's written a lovely book. Mother read it out to me, bits of it, from the Sunday paper, very nice it was too. We all enjoyed it, even Grandad who doesn't usually like that kind of thing.'

'Thank you very much,' said Jay, and then as the door closed she stuck a small pink tongue out at William.

'See – some people *like* the book.'

This was now fast becoming a 'book tour' joke, ever since William had admitted to Jay that he had made up his mind to resign from his job at the publishing house the moment they had accepted *As Soon As I Can*, so downhill had he considered that the world of literature had gone by publishing Jay Burrell's book.

'Not that again, not now, please, not this early.'

'You wait, William Kennedy, you wait,' said Jay, 'you wait until you go freelance and your back's against the wall, you'll soon wish you were back in Mayfair having nice little lunches and wheeling authors round.'

She watched William loping slowly over to the window where his breakfast was carefully laid. He looked at it and then pulled his glasses further down his nose, and really looked at it.

'There's a plastic fireman in my cereal,' he said and held it up.

'I know,' said Jay, sitting down opposite him and helping herself to his coffee. 'We thought you might like it, the maid and I, we thought you might be collecting them.'

'As a matter of fact I am,' William replied straight-faced. 'In a few months' time I hope to have the whole crew.'

Jay sipped her coffee.

'When you go freelance you'll need more than a fireman,' she said, unable to keep the triumph out of her voice.

'Will you stop threatening me with writing that way—'

Jay leaned over the table and the laughter was uncontrollable.

'You mustn't laugh at old men of almost twenty-eight who are being brave for the first time in their lives.'

Twenty-eight. Jay looked out of the window. She was nineteen, William was old. Not as old as she had thought yesterday, but old. He must know things, things that you couldn't even talk to your mother about, things that people talked about to you, but that you didn't dare talk about to them. Well, not dare so much . . . well, yes – dare.

'Have you had a lot of sexual relations?' she asked William suddenly.

'"I keep in touch with all my relations, we're a very united family, he said quipping lightly over the breakfast table."'

'Ha, ha. No, but you must have, you know because of going to university and all that.'

'Look, you leave my sexual relations alone and get on with learning your speech for tomorrow. Or read me out something tedious from the newspaper.'

'Oh, all right.'

Jay sighed, and then slowly picked up the newspaper and sighed again.

'Now what?'

'Nothing.'

'Not "nothing" again, I can stand anything but "nothing".'

'Well.'

William put his coffee cup down.

'Well is not a way to start a sentence, and shouldn't ever be used in dialogue.'

'OK. *So*. So I want you to tell me about sex.'

William picked up his coffee cup and sipped at it, and then he replaced it and pushed his glasses up his nose.

'What do you want to know?'

'Everything really.'

'Not *everything*.'

'Yes, everything, because, well – I mean so then I'll be able to write about it. At the moment I can't, because I don't know anything *about* it.'

'Please, not a talk on sex at breakfast, please?' William looked at her pleadingly. 'And not when I'm in my dressing gown and unshaven.'

'Oh, all right.'

Jay sighed and looked out of the window again. It was always the same, if you ever asked anyone they always said 'not now'.

'You must have been given a book by your mother, even you? Or heard things in that famous playground?'

Jay continued to stare out of the window.

'I did get a book out of the library, but it all seemed so, well – so medical really.'

William put his hand over hers. Jay looked down at it. It was nicely shaped even if it was dark and hairy.

'We'll take a walk after breakfast, and I'll tell you anything you want to know.'

Jay looked up at him mischievously.

'*Everything?*'

William sighed.

'Well, maybe not everything, some things I may well save for after tea.'

Their walk was around the seaside town. Still in its winter grey, there were few others around. Just old people walking slowly, and slow people looking old, and besides them just William and Jay. The waves washed the shingle and Jay picked a stone from it 'to keep'.

Now she was alone with William, just walking along, and not to and from somewhere with some other purpose, she felt really alone. She hated to think of the tour ending. The days until it did would rush along, she knew, because being with William was being with someone to whom she could say anything, anything at all, and that was very strange, because she'd been out with a great many boys of her own age and she just hadn't been able to talk to them.

'You can hold hands with someone, and just love them like that, can't you?' She looked up at William anxiously at one point. 'I mean that's what Rupert Brooke did, didn't he?'

William sighed, and looked down at his own hand, which was holding Jay's, and then at her worried face, and then he frowned and looked out to sea, and then he said, 'How about if we had tea at that café along the way?'

Jay nodded. 'Great.' She started to half walk, half run beside him, which made William slow down and call her 'titch'.

'I'm not that small, and anyway I've got long legs,' Jay protested.

'Long legs compared to whom – Charlie Chaplin?'

'That's hitting below the belt.'

Jay slid along the banquette in the café and sat opposite William.

'I have long legs even though I'm not as tall as I would like to be.'

'Don't worry, I don't like tall girls that much.'

Jay blushed.

'I wasn't worried—' she protested.

'Some tall girls, of course. My last girlfriend was very tall.'

There was a short pause and then Jay said in a small cold voice, 'Oh, did you go out with her a lot?'

'No, we stayed in most of the time . . .'

William turned to the waitress. 'Two teas please, and some buttered toast, and—'

'Scones with strawberry jam, and some biscuits.'

William lowered his glasses.

'Are you sure you can eat that much, Jay?'

Jay nodded briskly while tightening the ribbon on her long plait of brown hair.

'Absolutely sure, in fact I think you'd better add a cup cake or two as well. It's the sea air you know, it makes you very eaty.'

'There's no such word as "eaty".'

'No I know, that's why I said it, I knew you'd be stuffy.'

'Will you stop calling me stuffy!'

Jay grinned.

'I can't. I never knew Americans *could* be stuffy!'

'So, what do you want to know about the facts of life?'

'Oh, you know, how, when and where, and if – well, if it's nice, and – you know, if it's worth trying?'

William looked at her and then shook his head slowly.

'Jay. Sex is not something you "try". It's not a new hairdo, it's not a face cream, it's something that happens to you, for God's sake.'

'Yes, but supposing it happened to you and you didn't like it?'

'Then you stop.'

'You mean like in *Alice* – you go on until you stop? You see – you see I keep trying to imagine it, and – and – I can't.'

'What do you try and imagine?'

'Oh, you know, being in bed with someone and kissing them without your clothes on and then, you know – having a cigarette.'

'You don't smoke.'

'Oh, but I would if I was having sex with someone.'

'Why?'

'Because people always do.'

Their conversation went into a state of suspension as the waitress reappeared with a loaded tea tray, and Jay's eyes wandered lovingly over the scones, and the jam, and the buttered toast, and the biscuits, and she seized her napkin eagerly.

'This is nice, this is fun,' she said and, having helped William to some toast, she put a scone on her plate and started to heap it with strawberry jam.

'You'll get fat,' said William.

'No, I won't, I'm not a fat person. My waist has never been more than twenty-one. Never.'

'I'm not interested in your measurements,' said William, 'I'm interested in these extraordinary ideas you have about kissing people with your clothes off and then having a cigarette.'

'They're not so extraordinary—'

'Put some more scone in your mouth, I can't hear what you're saying.'

'I said you'd have them if you were me. You see' – she leaned forward – 'you can read about things, and you can hear things, but the things themselves are – probably quite different.'

'You're only nineteen – give "things" a chance,' said William. 'Really, you've got time on your side.'

'Oh, I know,' said Jay hastily, 'of course I'll give everything a chance, it's just that, well it's just that you're

107

the first person I've ever really felt like talking to, you know, about it. But I quite see that I shall probably end up like Queen Elizabeth I and Florence Nightingale, and women like that. Dedicated but untouched. I mean, even when I was at school everyone had had – well, you know, they, well, they all went out with boys, and held hands and kissed them, so I didn't. Because they did, I suppose. "Always trying to be different, Jay Burrell," our headmistress used to say. So I thought I, well, I would be.'

William picked up her hand and turning it over, he kissed the palm.

'You shouldn't do that,' said Jay, her cheeks burning from the tea and the scones and the conversation, 'that's the sort of thing that starts "things" off. At least it always seems to in books.'

'Just remember books are written by people like you – people who eat scones and toast, and other people's cup cakes.'

'Oh, I am sorry, I thought that one was mine.'

'It is,' said William. 'It's all yours. And let me tell you something, you're the first—'

'Yes?'

Jay brushed the crumbs from the cup cake from her mouth with a little dusting movement.

'You're the first girl I've – ever given a cup cake to.'

'To *whom* you've ever given a cup cake,' Jay said, straightfaced.

William just looked at her, and then he smiled.

'I'll always have my stone,' said Jay, and she nodded at something in the distance down the platform. It was snowing now, and the book tour was ended; the 'teeny bopper author', as William frequently referred to her, was making her departure, back to Danby, back to Mum, time to start another book, another life. Time to try and prove that she wasn't just a 'one-book' person.

'Sure, we'll always have Manchester,' William joked.

Jay smiled ruefully up at William.

'We didn't think we'd like each other, did we?'

'No—oo,' William agreed, and then he touched her cheek briefly. 'But we do. We had fun. It was good.'

'Yes,' Jay agreed. 'It was, wasn't it?'

'And you're the first author I've ever looked after who slid down bannisters.'

'And the last,' Jay reminded him. 'Now you're going to discover what the *real* world is like – the one room, the typewriter, being on your own all day long. You'll be running back to your cosy office in one year flat.'

'Wanta bet?'

'Yes, I'll bet you my stone you don't last.'

'Done.'

They shook hands, and William pulled her towards him and kissed her gently on the lips. Jay was amazed. It was the first time he'd kissed her, but she was more amazed at the effect.

'Wow!'

She looked up at William and started to laugh.

'You shouldn't have done that.'

He turned.

'Quick, the train.'

Jay snatched up her suitcase and started to run towards it. William wrenched open a carriage door, she jumped in and he threw her suitcase after her.

'I'll see you in a year, OK?'

Jay waved a gloved hand, and called to him, 'I shall probably be dead by then.'

'Don't say that—'

'What else is there to do – after all this?'

William was running beside the train.

'Don't be an idiot, you've got a talent, use it.'

Oh God, oh God, how often Jay heard those words of William's in her head in the next few months. She even wrote them down and put the words over her small, grey portable typewriter, but it was no good. Every time she sat down to write, every night (for she slept right through the

109

day) William's words – meant to be encouraging, of course – William's words came back to her, and not a word, not a single sentence would arrive. Her brain remained frozen into an ice block. Frozen into a little hard grey thing that would not release a single coherent thought.

And of course all the words from the publicity tour, and all the words in the now yellowing press cuttings, they all came up and hit her gently round the head, the way her mother's wet washing hit her when she walked into the kitchen on a Monday morning. Warm but dampening. 'You can never tell at this age, it's so often just a one-trick pony.' 'Anyone has one book in them.' 'Everyone has one book in them.'

She took to walking the streets in the early morning when her useless meant-to-be-hard-at-work night was finished. She stared into the faces of everyone that passed her by. Did they all really have 'a book in them'? Could the whole world write a book as everyone suggested? Would that woman scrubbing the doorstep, would she be able to tell a story and keep everyone enthralled? And if this was so, what future was there for Jay Burrell? Not a lot, it seemed, for if the whole world could write, then writing seemed somehow pointless, an exercise no more interesting or individual than brushing your teeth.

Months went by, and Jay slid into a kind of self-induced lethargy. Getting up when everyone else was going to bed, going to bed as her mother and the rest of the world got up. Pulling down the black-out blind left over from the war twenty years before. Pulling the curtains tight shut so that not a crack of light could filter into her small room, and then as darkness came getting up and making herself breakfast.

'It'll come, love, it'll come,' was all her mother said, in the same kind of voice that she would use when Jay was a child and no one was talking to her in the playground because she 'talked funny'. 'Let things be, they'll soon come round.'

Sometimes Jay lay awake in the afternoons when her

mother was out, and hated her. Why had she wanted Jay to be different? Why had she wanted her to talk posh? Why had she sent her to elocution lessons so that she 'talked different' from the rest of the class?

But hatred for a woman as good as her mum was pretty futile. It was as useless as hating nature. Her mother was a mother, and Jay was her sole egg; her reason for living was Jay; she often said so, and her eye would travel to the precious book of cuttings, and she would stare into the fire her arms crossed over her stomach and would see visions of Jay receiving the Nobel Prize, and Jay would creep away upstairs to her little room and once again try to write, and fail.

*In these times of fast-made reputations, and fast lost too,
JAY BURRELL, the teenybopper authorette once tipped to
be England's answer to France's bestselling Françoise
Sagan, seems to have vanished from the literary scene.*

A call to Blanchards, the publishers of her bestseller As
Soon As I Can, *left this columnist marvelling at the speed
at which literary reputations are made and lost. No one
there seemed to know anything about her at all.*

'*I think she's in France, but I'm not sure,*' *said a
representative for the publishing house who had been
responsible for such literary lions as William Grieves and
Desmond Bassett (one of whom is rumoured to have left the
esteemed publishing house in protest over the publication of*
As Soon As I Can*).*

'*We prefer to leave very young talent such as JAY
BURRELL's to develop unaided,*' *went on Blanchards'
representative,* '*if you try to influence it in any way you
might well crush its development.*'

Quite so.

*Our next call was to JAY BURRELL's literary represen-
tative, the equally esteemed D.B. Wyatt & Son. They had
some difficulty recalling whom JAY BURRELL might be.
Or even whether they did in fact represent her. We assured
them that this was indeed the case, but it took several calls
before they were able to confirm this.*

'*We think she's in Italy, or it may be that she's taken a
sabbatical and gone back to Yorkshire. We do know that
she's working hard on a novel, but we have no authority to
say exactly what its content might be.*'

*If MISS BURRELL would care to contact this column
we will be quite happy to pass on any information she might
care to give us – to those parties least concerned, namely
her agent and publishers.*

Jay stared at the cheap give-away calendar above her desk. There it was, carefully ringed, the date when she should have been meeting William.

'Somewhere in London', he'd said, but although he must still have her address, and although he had used to telephone her, not a word came from him, and the only time Mr Bell's invention rang was when her mother's friend Alice telephoned to tell her that she wouldn't be attending church on Sunday.

Jay watched the date tick by, and she thought of William and his new life, and she saw that she was not only fading in the eyes of others but in her own too. Once or twice she rang the publishers, and once she called on them; but the receptionist no longer pretended to know who she was, there were other authors on the walls now, and a new man in the publicity department, and anyway soon they were moving offices.

So Jay had caught the train home to Danby and gone back to her room with a feeling that she was as dusty as the book that she had written. Her poor book: it had seemed to promise so much, but now its jacket had a faded look to it, the air of a once too fashionable dress, and for the same reason it now looked a little foolish.

'I don't see why you should have to change your name.' Jay's mum looked puzzled and hurt. Jay Burrell was a good name. 'A writer's name,' she'd always said. 'I can see that on book jackets,' she would tell Jay. 'Up there with all those others.'

'I have to, Mum, otherwise, you know, everyone knows who you are, and they won't want to employ you.'

'Do you have to go to London?'

Jay nodded.

'Yup. I'm sorry to say, but London is where it's at, and I'll get better pay.'

'You be careful with your little nest egg, Jay, don't get done by those Southern sharks down there. I hear London is full of sharks.' Her face softened. 'Mind, it was good of you to pay off my mortgage for me.'

Jay looked at her mother. She was small, grey-eyed, vivacious, with a rounded little figure, just like Mrs Tiggywinkle. She had small sturdy legs, and her brown hair was lightly streaked with grey now, but it wasn't all grey, just enough to make Jay feel that it was she, Jay, who had put it there. No, it wasn't easy to leave her mother, knowing she'd be on her own; just Alice ringing up, and the little house to polish.

'Life's like a nettle, Jay,' her mother said suddenly, 'you've got to grasp it when you pluck it, no good being a coward or it'll sting you. Now be off with you to London, just don't sign anything without Jimbo's father throwing his eyes over it. And don't trust anyone with your purse. And keep your wits about you. Things'll soon come right for you, you'll see. The words, they'll come back to you, I know they will, it's just you that's blocking them, but you don't know it. Maybe London will do the trick, unlock something.'

Jay's nest egg was just that. A nest egg, and she had to get a job to keep it that way, to keep it intact so that she could buy herself a flat; no, not a flat, she hated flats, coming from a house they seemed like rabbit hutches. No, what she wanted was a studio, a large airy studio with a garden running off it, and a staircase which would lead to a place to sleep.

She found one. It was in a fashionable street, but not too fashionable, off the King's Road, but not so near to it that the noise of the traffic penetrated its walls. At the same time she found a job, under the name 'Nicola Jameson'. It was a theatrical agency. Max Kassov Associates. Max Kassov was young and energetic, and at least it was something to do with entertainment, and he was funny. He had sparkling eyes and a wicked grin, and when Jay said her shorthand was nil he hired her on the spot. She was the first honest girl he'd interviewed, he said, so the shorthand could go whistle.

To the agency came so many of the famous. The properly famous, faces that Jay knew from magazines, and from theatre, and cinema a little. They would sit restlessly for a few seconds waiting to go into the inner office, and Jay would offer them drinks, or tea or coffee, which sometimes they readily accepted and sometimes they declined as if they were superstitious that she might spike them.

Everyone who was famous looked smaller than those who were there because they were hoping to become famous. Sometimes it seemed to Jay that once they had become so-called 'famous overnight', and had a hit under their belts, they would almost immediately seem to shrink, and look smaller than they did when they strode about the stage or the screen as someone else.

At the end of the day 'the boss' would ask Jay into his office, and she would take him his first drink, and it was always something nice and strong with plenty of ice. 'A Marthreeni, not Martwoni' was the office joke when it had been a particularly hard day, and then Jay – or 'Nicky' as she was known – would be regaled with jokes and anecdotes about what had gone on. But she never knew more than he wanted her to, she saw that he was careful to shut the door when he was on the telephone sometimes, and she respected him for that, as much as she loved him for his funny wry jokes, and the habit he had of rolling his eyes, or shrugging his shoulders, or putting his feet suddenly above his head so that he could think better.

Of course Jay loved her boss, Max Kassov. But only in the way that girls who work for a man often love them, with a sort of mixture of schoolgirl crush and wanting him to like what she did – the way she would, she imagined, if she had a father.

'Oh what a day, what a dead fish of a day, throw it out and bring me a Marfourni, not even a Marthreeni will do today, Nicky.'

Jay looked at the vodka bottle and tipped more than usual over the pile of ice in the Waterford glass. Everything in the office was nice, and pleasing to the eye, everything chosen with care. She liked that.

'You must be tired—' She handed over the drink, and the blue eyes smiled wickedly.

'Yes, but I won – I won!'

It was always a case of 'winning' or 'losing'.

'I got him five times what they offered in the first place.'

'Hey, that's terrific.' Jay smiled, holding the small silver drinks tray in front of her. 'That's really terrific.'

There was a small silence, and then the telephone rang once more.

'Shall I take it?'

'No, I'll do it, you go off, you'll be late.'

Jay went, and he called out 'enjoy' after her as she went, and then, 'I like the micro skirt, Nicky, or should I call you Nickers?'

Then she heard him say to the telephone, 'OK, come round, no, now is fine, really, come round.'

'I'll leave the keys on my desk,' Jay whispered back through the door, and waved.

Jay looked at her watch. There was just time to change in the loo and make herself look glamorous before she was due at the Aldwych theatre.

'Oh, I like that, that's great!"

Max whistled from his still open office door as Jay reappeared transformed.

'Who are you going with? Who's the lucky fellow?'

'Oh, no one, just going on my own.'

'But I gave you two tickets.'

'I know, I know,' Jay agreed, 'but the person I was going with had to cancel.'

'I'd come with you myself, but –' Max shrugged his shoulders – 'but I've seen the show, twice.'

Jay waved at him, and then pulled a little face.

'Don't worry, I'll soon pick up someone in the bar in the interval,' she joked.

'Looking like that you should pick up several in the interval and quite a few will follow you home too.' Max was glancing down the weekly takes on a show he'd invested in. He could read three columns of figures and come up with the correct total in five seconds flat.

There was the sound of a light quick footstep on the stairs. Max went on reading the next sheet of figures.

'Just let him in, Nickers, would you?'

Jay went out to the outer office and as she did so, while she could still hear the sound of that quick light step, she had a feeling of unreality, and yet she didn't know why, and then as she picked up her small evening bag and glanced up to the door, she knew why; and there was no way that reality in the form of William coming towards her could be denied.

He stood there in one of those mackintoshes that every attractive man always owns. It had been raining and the collar was up, and he had his hands in the pockets.

'Max Kassov, please?'

He hadn't quite seen her. Not really, not the way someone sees someone and can afterwards say exactly what they were wearing and what colour hair they had, so for a few seconds, as he turned away from a photograph of one of Max's more famous clients, Jay too was able to turn quickly, so that he didn't see her full face but just caught sight of the back of her head and her now blonde-streaked hair.

'In here, William,' Max called out. 'Nicky, bring in another Martini please, but not too strong: Mr Kennedy is a writer, and he needs to stay sober. You can act drunk and you can play drunk, but no one ever made it writing drunk.'

'Not true, Max, not true,' said William, turning from the line-up of stars' pictures on the wall. 'Some of the greatest things ever written have been written in a blind stupor.'

He walked past Jay who now had her back to him and had started to mix a fresh Martini.

'Yes,' Jay heard Max say, 'maybe, but not comedy. George Kauffman never wrote on drink, Moss Hart never wrote on drink.'

'No, not comedy,' William agreed, 'not comedy. Why do you want me to get into comedy, Max?'

Jay could almost hear the eloquence of Max's shrug.

117

'There's more money in it, William. And besides, you're funny. It's good to be funny.'

'Not on paper, Max, not on paper. It's a short way to insanity. Do you want me to go mad and for my hair to fall out?'

'Writers, you all feel so sorry for yourself, and you never even have to go to an office in the morning.'

'No, we just stay locked in cell fifteen.'

Jay peered through the crack in the door. She knew William; he'd look round Max's office now. He always did that, prowled about looking at everything – he was like a cat. The moment his back was turned she put the Martini down on Max's desk and then fled. Not even Max seemed to notice, for he was still staring at some figures on a sheet of paper. The atmosphere was very relaxed, they obviously knew each other well.

'Night, Nickers,' Max called as he heard her go out, but Jay didn't reply. She daren't.

The play at the Aldwych theatre was good – no, not good, it was excellent, and Max's client was very good. A small but showy part. Jay went round backstage afterwards and took him for a drink, on Max's instructions. All Kassov clients were nursed and looked after, most especially while their careers were in their growing stage.

'You've always got to give bloody actors the impression you've been in a lot,' Max had instructed Jay when she had first joined the agency. 'Make them feel you're keeping an eye on them. Your job won't stop at six o'clock in the evening.'

Jay didn't mind, not even a little bit. Going to the theatre every night was her idea of bliss, and although she was nearly always on her own, she never let Max know that, for she sensed that he preferred to think that she had hordes of admirers. Max liked success in all areas, he didn't like anything that wasn't what he called 'up'. He never went 'down' himself, and he never expected anyone else to.

Even Jay knew how to massage an actor's ego, make him feel good, even if he hadn't been. How to listen to his stories of what had gone wrong on stage that night, and how much better it had been the previous night, or the previous week. Of how badly or well the director had been treating them, of how little or often he had come in to see the show.

The stories were always the same, and yet always different. Some were funnier than others, but more often than not they grumbled, and that surprised Jay, knowing how long their list of 'available' actors could be in a bad week.

'No actor is a happy person,' Max intoned pretty regularly. 'I've never known a bloody actor who was a happy person. You want to be miserable – be an actor. They're miserable in work and they're miserable out of work. They never like the play, and if they do then they hate the bloody author, and if they don't hate the bloody author, they hate the bloody director. And if both of them are all right, then it'll be someone in the bloody cast, and if not someone in the bloody cast, then it'll be the dresser, and if not the dresser, then the cleaning woman, or the woman at the box office, or the bloody stage doorkeeper, that's actors. The most miserable bloody bunch of people you'll ever meet.'

Jay thought Max was going too far, in fact she was quite convinced that he was. Actors seemed a warm-hearted bunch to her, with a fine sense of the ridiculous, telling stories against themselves, informal and friendly. She thought of them affectionately, even if they were a little inclined to grumble.

She allowed Max's client to kiss her on the cheek, and then she hailed a taxi. It had been a nice long day, and when she got home to her beloved studio she would write to her mum all about it, and all about what a fine time she was having, even though her mother would never believe her because her mother was still convinced that Jay would soon return home and take up her pen once more and write

119

another book that would be another success. She simply couldn't accept defeat for Jay. Didn't realize that Jay had, quite thankfully, left 'Jay Burrell' behind and was enjoying being 'Nicola known as Nicky' more than she had ever enjoyed being the teenage writer of *As Soon As I Can*.

'It's off the King's Road,' she told the driver, and he turned into 'her' road, the road where she had bought her beautiful studio with its long white walls and its northern light and its stripped wood floors. Where her bed was up above where she lived, up a little flight of stairs in a minstrels' gallery, so that when she awoke in the morning the first thing she did was to look down at the studio room.

The big white room was gradually being furnished with large eccentric furniture, furniture that when she described it to Max would make him laugh and say to her, 'You've bought another prop from the sound of it. You're nothing but a prop collector, Nicky.'

But laugh as Max might, large eccentric furniture was very cheap to buy, and in Jay's mind it was perfect for a big room with white walls.

Jay always looked forward to going back to the studio; putting her key into the outer lock, and treading quietly across the inner hall, past the odd-smelling smoke that was always wafting from under a neighbouring studio door, and then opening her own door, putting on the lights, and seeing the now increasingly familiar sight of her own things.

The taxi started to draw up as Jay leaned forward and told the driver, 'By the lamppost, just by that lamp.'

She jumped out of the cab and paid, plus a too-generous tip that would make Max grumble in the morning when he saw her expenses, and ask her what made her think taxi drivers were in need of benefit? And was she trying to break him? Which he never meant at all, but loved to say, and which Jay guessed was something that he had heard people say when he was growing up.

She put her key in the outer lock and felt the familiar mixture of comfort and relief as the door swung open, and then she heard a voice behind her say, 'You shouldn't have left the stone on your desk, I'd have known it anywhere.'

She turned and saw William. He was standing behind, just two steps below her, those funny steps that London houses sometimes have, where the top one is tiled and the rest aren't.

'William,' she said, and tried to sound surprised, and failed, because part of her had known all evening that she would see him again. 'I—'

'You knew damn well I'd be here,' said William angrily. 'Imagine being in that office, seeing me there, and not saying anything, just going away. If I hadn't seen that stone on your desk, that stone you picked up on the beach – what would you have done? Just let it go?'

Jay shrugged, and looked down at him, still occupying the top step, blocking him following her into the hall.

'I suppose so, yes.'

'Oh, you "suppose so", do you?'

Jay hadn't ever seen William angry before. She'd seen him off-hand, casual, wary, all sorts of things, but not angry, he was usually so un-angry.

'Do you know how long I've been looking for you?'

'Oh, come on, William Kennedy, pull the other one, it's got Big Ben on it.'

Now she was angry. In fact she was furious.

'You knew where I lived, you knew my name. You have no right to be angry. None at all. You knew the date.'

It was very bewildering, but suddenly she was even angrier than he was, not even able to think she was so furious.

'I had my address book stolen in Florence, OK?'

'No, it's not OK. You still knew where I lived, Jay Burrell, Danby, England, there aren't that many Jay Burrells in Danby, England, so don't try to pretend there are.'

There was a long silence, and then William leaned back against the railings, and half closed his eyes.

'Danby. *Danby*. Dear God, I've been writing to you in *Denby*, no wonder all the mail's been returned.'

'Oh, very quick,' said Jay. 'Like that trick you taught me about not knowing someone's name.'

'What trick?' asked William momentarily wrong-footed.

'You know, where you say "I've forgotten your name" and then the person says it, and then you say very quickly, "No, I know your *Christian* name, it's just your *surname* I've forgotten."'

'I never taught you that—'

'Yes, yes, you did, when you were standing on the station and you met that author whose name you'd forgotten.'

'Your memory—'

William shook his head, and then he joined Jay on the top step and, looking down at her, he managed to look as hurt as it was possible to look.

'Why did you? Why did you do that? Why didn't you let me know it was you there? If I hadn't seen the stone, I would have gone off, we might never have seen each other again.'

'I thought – well, I thought that's what you wanted,' said Jay, 'of course that's what I thought.'

She wished most heartily that William was a million miles away, and not standing so near her on the doorstep with the door open, and her studio just across the hall.

'Can I come in?'

'I'd rather you didn't, not tonight, not really.'

William looked back down at the street, and then up at the sky.

'It's beginning to snow, I won't stay long.'

'Oh, all right,' said Jay, without any kind of grace, 'but you can't stay very long, I have to get up in the morning, you know. And I've had a long day.'

'Don't be such an old woman,' said William, following her across the hall to her own door. 'You sound like my grandmother back in Connecticut.'

'I *feel* like your grandmother,' said Jay. 'You don't seem to understand. What you can't understand is, well – is that I've changed.'

She put her key in the door.

'I'm not the girl, as they say in the song, that I used to be. I've even changed my name.'

'You're exactly the same,' said William, following her into the room and sighing loudly, 'exactly. Going blonde and streaky and changing your name to Nicky – Christ, what a terrible name, what made you think you looked like a *Nicola*, Jay?'

Jay switched on the studio lights from the door. She was very proud of the lighting. Someone Max knew had helped her, and he had lit shows, so that all the best bits were now softly lit and all the other bits had 'downlighters' and other very modern contrivances, so it all looked even more marvellous than it was, to her mind, already.

'I don't know,' she said in answer to William's question, 'I thought it sounded nice and posh, you know?'

'This is good,' said William, looking round the large room and suddenly forgetting to be angry.

'I did it all myself,' said Jay, and then she thought for a moment and realized that that wasn't quite true, so she added hastily, 'well, not all, I didn't do the lighting, I had help with that. It's very modern, the lighting. My mother hates it, but I love it.'

William turned round and looked at her.

'You've got good taste, kid, everything's just right.'

Jay turned away from him looking at her.

'Would you like a coffee?' she asked.

'And?'

'And – a whisky?'

'You've done this very well – really well.'

William took off his mackintosh and hung it up, meticulous as ever, and now he was prowling and staring, and staring and prowling, and again Jay was reminded of a cat before she turned towards the galley kitchen and started to put out glasses for William to pour whisky.

It was strange to see William, someone so much from her past, the person who had escorted Jay Burrell on her literary promotion tour, standing in her studio. And even

123

stranger to hear him saying, 'You've done this very well, kid', just as he would look up at her all that time ago on the tour and murmur, 'Well done, kid', when she'd got through a speech all right, and hadn't what he called, 'Gone through laughs', or fluffed or anything. And they were going to drink whisky, the drink she'd first drunk with him, the drink that had made him like her that first night when she'd disgraced herself by sliding down the bannisters.

'What are you thinking about?'

'I'm thinking about – whether or not I've put enough ice in your drink,' said Jay.

'No, you're not,' said William, staring up at the first and only picture that she had bought. An oil painting of a field of corn that she had bought in a fit of excitement from an art gallery in Kensington Church Street. 'What on earth made you buy this?' asked William, giving Jay a puzzled look.

'Four glasses of white wine, if you really want to know.'

'At least you're truthful,' said William, quite seriously. 'It's terrible, plain terrible.'

'Oh really, and how much do you know about painting?'

'Studied it in Florence before going to Harvard,' retorted William. 'I spent a year in Europe majoring in aestheticism, if it's of any interest.'

'You Americans, you come to Europe to stare at our heritage, and then go away thinking you know all about it.'

'The survival of Florence owes just a little to the US of A, madam.'

Jay smiled suddenly, because she'd lost.

'Here's mud in your hatch, and polish on your duster,' she said.

William sighed.

'I just wish you'd changed a little,' he said, 'just one tiny, little, bit.'

'I've dyed my hair blonde, lost half a stone in weight, grown older, changed my name to Nicola, and you dare to tell me I haven't changed?' Jay demanded. 'You're crazy, William Kennedy.'

She turned up the central heating, because the snow was really falling down outside now. Even so the studio was warm, or maybe it felt warm because they'd both become mesmerized by the sight of it falling in cold silent blossoms outside the windows.

'Turn out the lights,' said William suddenly. 'It will look better in the dark. No, wait, first I'll put on some music. Where's your hi-fi?'

Jay pointed to her new hi-fi set which was becomingly housed in an old washstand in the corner of the studio. William walked over to it and opened the lid.

'Girls,' he said with resignation, 'I wish you'd get advice when you buy hi-fi. I never yet went into a girl's apartment and found a decent hi-fi. These your records? At least they show a little more judgement.'

'Do they? Do they really?'

Jay hurried over to where he was standing, her eyes blazing with anger. She tried to snatch the record William was holding away from him.

'Why don't you stop criticizing everything here? This is my place, not yours.'

William leaned forward and kissed her gently on the lips.

'Shut up,' he said, then turned to the offensive hi-fi again, and carefully placed the LP of Johnny Mathis's 'Warm' on it. It was one of Jay's favourite records, but it was very romantic. And somehow not conducive to conversation. She didn't want William there, in her studio, not with that record playing in the background, not with so much to say. Because William always did have a way of making her talk, making her say things, things she wouldn't dream of saying to anyone else.

She went to the window because he was still at the hi-fi. The cool of the glass would give her the necessary overall cool. She could look at the silent white snow and try and remember what it was like not to have William around. It had been fine, quite fine. So why wouldn't he go away

125

again, then everything could be fine once more. Without him.

She felt his hands on her. He'd followed her to the window, and now slipped his arms through hers, holding her to him, but still holding on to his whisky glass, in the way that you would if you knew someone very well.

'It's so blue,' he said into her hair, 'snow is always so blue. When I was a boy we used to have skating parties—'

'Oh, I know, you used to skate down the rivers and stop off at friends' houses, and all the girls would be dressed in red velvet—' Jay interrupted sighing.

'So hard and sarcastic for one so young. To get back to the scenes of my early childhood, we used to have skating parties, and they put flares on the side of the ice. I think we should have flares in this garden, don't you?'

'It would be nice,' Jay conceded.

'I'll order you a costume in red velvet, and then we'll skate together, arms around each other, locked together in effortless movement.'

'Not if you're skating the way I skate,' Jay murmured.

William let go of her suddenly, and equally suddenly Jay felt a sense of disappointment. She watched as he put his glass of whisky down, and then took hers and put hers down. It was all so strange, but she knew that it wasn't very surprising, not really, not if she was going to be honest. When she'd seen him standing there in Max's office she knew he'd come back into her life and that everything was going to change again, but not because she'd made it change, but because he'd make it change.

'Did you really look for me in Denby?' she asked.

William frowned down at her for a second, before taking her in his arms and starting to dance with her.

'Of course I looked for you in Denby,' he said, his cheek against hers, 'of course. I looked for you so long and hard I knew the Denby directory off by heart.'

'But why didn't you just ask the publishers, why didn't you just ask at Blanchards?'

'I did, and they gave me Denby, the girl there gave me Denby, twice. I'll put that track on again.'

Jay stood watching as William returned to the hi-fi and reset the record so that the luscious tones of Johnny Mathis resumed the title song of the record. William had changed physically almost as much as she had. Now he was a writer he was wearing softer clothes: a cashmere sweater, and trousers that were cut to show his long legs, and a pair of fashionable suede boots that would never have been allowed at Blanchards.

He came back to her side and took her in his arms again.

'Where do you live now?' she asked. 'That is if you are living in London?'

'Not really, I'm living in Hampstead, and I never think of that as London.'

'It's a long way away,' Jay agreed.

'You bet. Too far to go back to in this weather.'

William stood back from her for a second, and removed his glasses very solemnly and seriously, and then he put his hand under Jay's chin, and for the first time he kissed her long and lingeringly; and things happened to Jay that had never happened to her before, and she realized why she hadn't been able to find out about love from books.

Oh, but it was wonderful. To kiss and be kissed with the snow falling outside and the warmth inside.

'I've missed you so much, all this time, you don't know how much I've missed you. Wondering what's happened to you, wondering what was going to become of you, no one knowing. I thought you might be married—'

'Oh really, William, you know I don't like marriage, I could never get married, not ever.'

They had only stopped kissing to resume again, and then the kissing seemed to have a snowballing effect to go with the weather outside, because they were both taking off each other's clothes, and still kissing and stripping going up to the minstrels' gallery, until they fell together on Jay's bed, and then William hesitated.

'Are you sure? Are you sure you want this?'

'Oh, William,' Jay whispered impatiently, 'why wouldn't I?'

He was so tender with her, and so clever. Jay was amazed, and when it was all over and he lay across the pillows looking at her she could see that he too was amazed, and then she knew that although this was the first time a man had made love to her, and although it must have been the umpteenth time that William had made love to a girl, even so it was different for him too – even though it wasn't his first time.

'Your breasts are stunning, they're quite, quite perfect.'

He kissed one and then the other.

'Quite stunning,' he said again. And then he looked at her and asked her quietly, 'Are you sure you're all right?'

Jay nodded.

'Is there anything you'd like?'

He took her in his arms again.

'Is there anything you'd like?' he demanded.

Jay nodded sleepily.

'Mmm, a nice cup of tea.'

William started to laugh.

'Oh God, you're so *British*. You make love like that, and then all you want is a cup of tea!'

He pulled on one of her dressing-gowns and, as she lay against her pillows and laughed at him putting on her dressing-gown and at herself for wanting tea, he went back down to the galley kitchen and made her a cup of tea, which seemed to take hours.

'Just like after an operation,' Jay said as she sipped the sweet tea, and William sipped another Scotch.

'That's the first time my love-making has ever been compared to an appendectomy,' William sighed with mock resignation, but seeing her sitting up in bed with her hair tousled and the light from one of the downlighters making shadows across her young body and strange patterns on the pillow, seemed to arouse him again, and he quickly finished his Scotch and removing her cup from her hand he started to make love to her again, and to Jay's amazement their love-making was even better the second and the third, and the fourth time.

'I have to get some sleep, William,' she begged. 'Please, I have to go to work in the morning.'

'Don't worry – I'll ring Max,' said William, pulling her to him again. 'I'll tell him you're with me, and he'll let it go.'

'But I don't want to let it go,' Jay protested, 'I love my job.'

'Have a headache just this once,' William pleaded, but Jay shook her head, and pulling on his shirt she pattered downstairs.

'No more tea, please,' William groaned from upstairs.

'No, a nice strong black coffee,' said Jay as she switched on the percolator.

Then she curled up in the large what she called 'King Lear' chair she had bought a few weeks before from the Portobello Road, and as the snow fell softly she let the happiness of being made love to for the first time suffuse her. Happiness of a different kind was not new to her, but her present feelings were so strong and so physical, because she and William, well, they were so unlikely.

She hardly heard him padding down from the minstrels' gallery, so when he stood over her and she looked up at him it was a shock, one of those suddenly-seeing-someone-for-the-first-time sort of moments. He looked so tall and dark and dominant. He pulled her to her feet and started to kiss her, and his face was so rough she could feel it marking her skin, and then he started to pull her upstairs again, but Jay shook herself free.

'Oh no—' she began, but William had other ideas, and although she struggled and wriggled, and protested, half laughing and half serious, it was no use, he just held her wrists more firmly, until finally she found herself being pushed towards the studio couch.

'Oh no,' she said again.

'Oh yes,' said William, 'oh yes.'

* * *

'This is awful.'

Jay stood in front of the studio mirror and looked at her early morning face, and groaned. Her mascara and eyeliner had run together. She looked like a panda.

'Don't go,' William pleaded from high above in the minstrels' gallery, 'really, I'll ring Max.'

'You'll do no such thing,' said Jay, and she smeared some eye cleanser over her eyes, and then quickly wiped it off with a Kleenex. 'I didn't realize that—'

'What? What didn't you realize?'

William stared down at her from the gallery. Jay turned.

'I didn't realize how over-sexed you were,' she said crossly.

'I'm not over-sexed,' William protested, 'Jesus, I've been in love with you for what seems, what has to be – years. Please, don't go to work. How can you go to work? Think of what you might be doing here with me. Just think.'

'If I think about that,' said Jay to herself in the mirror, 'if I think about that I won't be able to type a word, as it is I'm late, and Max hates "late". Late is for other offices, for Max you're there at eight, or forget it.'

The last thing she heard as she closed the studio door was William calling to her, 'You'll regret it, you'll see, you'll regret not giving up your career for me.'

The day seemed twice as long after that, and twice as short too. It seemed twice as long because Jay felt that somehow, since last night, she was different, that everything about her had changed, and that Max was busy noticing; and that every time he looked down at her while he was dictating or she looked up at him when she took a call in his office or put his coffee in front of him, or performed any of the other day-to-day tasks that she did for him, she felt herself about to redden. But then again it seemed twice as short because every time she thought of William something inside her raced, and dear heavens if there was hardly time to turn around and she was back outside the office again, and Max was offering her a lift in his cab and dropping her off at the end of the road.

'Thanks, Max,' said Jay, giving a little wave before she shut the door.

Max grinned at her from out of the cab window.

'That's OK, Nicky. Give my love to William.'

For the first time that day Jay's face did colour, in fact a positive tidal wave of red flooded into her cheeks.

Max pulled on his cigar.

'Just don't keep him from his writing, or there'll be two of you out of work.'

Jay nodded, and smiled just a little awkwardly. Damn Max, he would notice. But even he didn't know that William was her first lover. Max would probably give his disappointed shrug if he did know, the one he gave if the figures for a show he'd invested in were down, not the one he gave which meant, 'How *about* that?' Jay guessed that Max liked to think that she had had one or two lovers before coming to London. Certainly she had always been careful to let him suppose that she had a very full social life, so now, she hoped, he'd just think that William was one in a short line, just as she was for William one in a long line.

It seemed that he had gone. She stood in the studio doorway and looked at her beloved white room and saw that it was quite empty of any signs that it had been occupied by lovers until early that morning. There was not one dirty tea cup, not one stray cushion, and no ashtray was unemptied. William had gone back to Hampstead from whence he had come; probably, knowing William, he had walked back through the snow thinking about Connecticut.

It was better that way, Jay decided immediately, as she slowly removed one cold hand from her glove, and then another. Love was better that way, and life too: that it should be brief and wild and impossibly joyous was absolutely right, she wouldn't have it any other way, and she was very glad that her first lover obviously felt the same.

'Hi—'

He leaned over the side of the minstrels' gallery and

131

smiled down at her. Now that he was there, looking relaxed and happy and dressed in his cashmere sweater and shirt from the night before, because she had absolutely determined that he wouldn't be, Jay felt unaccountably angry. It wasn't right that he should still be in her life when she had made up her mind that he was back in Hampstead and their one-night affair had been brief, wild and impossibly joyous, but over.

'William.'

She looked up at him. William. Still tall and dark and in her studio. Still there in her life, not a part of a wonderful night that was over.

'I thought you must have gone home.'

'That disappointing, is it?' asked William lightly.

'No, not disappointing, and not the opposite either, I just imagined that you would have gone, that's all.' Jay shrugged her shoulders.

He sat on the bottom of the gallery stairs and slowly pulled on his boots as Jay quickly put the shopping bags into the galley kitchen.

'You are.' William stood up. 'You're really disappointed, you wanted me to have gone out of your life. What's the matter?'

'Nothing, nothing's the matter,' said Jay, 'don't be silly, nothing's the matter.'

William walked towards her, and Jay stayed still, because not to stay still would mean that there *was* something the matter. He frowned down at her, and then put a hand on her shoulder.

'Tell me,' he commanded, 'what is the matter? This morning when we parted you were besotted with me.'

'I wasn't,' said Jay, frowning, 'I'd just gone to bed with you, that's all.'

'Oh, really? And that's all, is it? I don't believe it. We make love as few people have ever made love in the whole history of the world, and you call it "going to bed, that's all". What's the matter with you? Are you auditioning for hard-hearted Hannah, or what?'

'Look, William, last night was last night, and tonight, well it's different.'

'For whom may I ask?'

'For me for a start. You, me, it's ridiculous, you're very clever and talented and I respect you a lot of course—'

'Please, no speeches, just tell me *what happened*?'

Jay turned from staring out at the snow.

'Max knows.'

'I'm sorry?'

'I said, Max knows.'

William started to laugh and then, seeing the hurt in Jay's eyes, he stopped.

'Is that it? And you're feeling suddenly self-conscious? Of course Max knows, I told him.'

'You *what*?'

'I told him I was in love with you.'

'How *could* you?'

'Because he's a friend, and my agent – Max has a short list of writers on his books, remember? I'll be working here, he has to know where to call me.'

Inexplicably Jay became suddenly and instantly angry, and little red dots appeared in front of her eyes. How could he? William Kennedy standing there in *her* studio, how could he tell Max that he was going to live with her? How could he tell Max he was in love with her? He'd probably even told him her real name. She slapped him, right across the face and it was wonderfully satisfying.

'That hurt.'

'It was meant to. How *could* you tell Max? And what else did you tell him?'

'I told him you were fantastic,' said William, teasing her, 'and that we'd made love six – no, you're not going to slap me again, the first time hurt quite enough.'

He caught her hand, and Jay wished that instead of slapping his face she'd taken a kitchen knife to him. How could he? She'd never be able to look Max in the face again, not ever, ever. She stormed and raged at him. She wished that she'd never met him, she wished that all the

133

worst things would happen to him, not once but a million times. She hated him.

When she ran out of words William took off his glasses, very slowly and very carefully, just as he had the night before, and put them on the table, and then took her by the hand, and led her up the stairs to the gallery and there was a long silence broken only by the sound of Jay sobbing as William undressed her slowly and deftly, and then laid her under the top cover where she lay until he joined her.

It was all strangely dark, the cover, his body, the studio, and her eyes hurt from the tears, but this new thing, this making love was so wonderful, so out of this world, and William was so passionate, so amazingly passionate, that Jay forgot that she hated him, and why she hated him, and even that he had hurt her, that he was hurting her, pulling her hair back and telling her that she was a bitch and that he hated her too, and that he would leave her, just as soon as he had finished making love.

'*Petite mort*, that is what the French call it,' said William matter-of-factly some time later, as he poured them both a drink. 'It doesn't happen to everyone, you know.'

'Really?'

Jay started to unpack the shopping in front of him, and then remembering, she stopped.

'Are you going to make us both *quelque chose* very special, because I could eat the room.'

'Yes, yes, of course, of course I am.'

William frowned.

'*Now* what's the matter?'

'Nothing really, I was just remembering that I've got something in the little top freezer, something more suitable.'

Jay crossed and went to the freezer, but William crossed behind her and went to the shopping.

'Just what I wanted,' he said with satisfaction. 'Forget the freezer, there's everything here for two hungry lovers,

134

and champagne for breakfast. My, my, my, anyone would think you'd had an affair before—'

'I have, didn't you know? A raging affair with the man across the hallway.'

William turned and for a split second she could see that he had forgotten, and then he remembered, and smiled; and then again he seemed to remember something else.

'There's two of everything here, there's *two* of everything. You knew all along I'd be here when you got back tonight.'

'No, I didn't—'

'All that nonsense about not wanting me here.' He pulled her towards him, and Jay started to laugh. 'You're nothing but a minx. For that I shall stay here for the rest of the year, and make love to you twelve times every morning, and twelve times every night.'

'Ow.'

Jay tried to wriggle out of his arms.

'Do you hear that? That is your punishment for lying to me, slapping my face, and forcing me to make love to you.'

'You're hurting me.'

'Really? Am I really? Well, isn't that just too bad, Jay Burrell?'

Jay nodded.

'Yes, it is.'

'So what are you going to do about it?'

'Nothing, nothing at all,' she said happily as the telephone rang. They both stared at each other.

'If that's Max?'

'No, it's not Max,' said William, suddenly letting go of her wrists and leaving Jay to rub the marks he'd left, 'it's a call I booked to America.'

Jay went on rubbing her wrists, as William walked to the telephone. Even on the book tour all that time ago they'd always joked about his 'other life' in America. But then, well, then things had been different.

'I'll go and take a shower,' she said.

William nodded.

'Don't sing too loud in the shower,' he warned her, 'my mother's hard enough of hearing as it is!'

His mother. Jay shut the bathroom door, and then leaned against it the way people always did in movies. She was terribly glad William was American and that his parents lived so far away.

Then she tore her clothes off and stepped into the shower and sang 'Onward Christian Soldiers' right off key. She was living in sin, as people still called it, for better or for worse, but somehow with William around it didn't seem to matter.

ACT TWO
SWINGERS

4

'Meredith? Meredith?'

The voice sounded uncertain, as if the person who owned it couldn't quite believe that Merry was in fact Meredith Browne. Merry turned slowly to see who it was calling to her as she had strolled past them down the Burlington Arcade and on to lunch with a prospective agent.

The face belonging to the voice peered at her.

'It is, it's Meredith Browne, don't you remember me? Polly Stephens? We grew up together, remember? Albert Mansions, you used to live at Albert Mansions? I lived down the road with my mum and my Aunt Tam, remember?'

Merry pretended to frown uncertainly, and then she dug Polly in the ribs.

'Course I remember you – you silly little cow! How could I forget you?'

They hugged each other, and as they did Merry smiled smugly over the top of Polly Stephens' cheap tweed coat. She hadn't lasted long as a teenage star, had she? After pinching Merry's chance to become a teenage star she'd been given every opportunity, but 'it', Polly's so-called stardom, had lasted about two blooming minutes. So much for talent, dear. So much for doing your best friend down too. So much for life, because, standing back from her now, Polly was having ample opportunity to discover just how well Merry had been doing. She had on a full-length banded red fox fur coat and special hand-knitted Women's Home Industry white stockings, which were all the rage and very expensive, and a pair of shoes that shouted MONEY. And gloves. And a wristwatch like a man's that was pure solid Swiss gold. MONEY. Lots of it, that was what her clobber shouted.

Poverty was what Polly shouted. Flat shoes, lank over-blonded hair, no gloves to cut out the cold of that snowy London winter, nothing on her that said anything except poverty. Not real poverty of course, not the kind that made you think of cooking your dole card, not the kind that made you think twice before you got on a bus, but thin-clothed poverty, having to watch how much you put in the gas meter, that kind of poverty, that was what Polly stunk of, poor little cow.

'What's doing then?'

Merry stood back, automatically folded her arms across her body, and grinned at Polly.

'What's my little Polly been up to then?' she asked in deliberately 'stage' cockney.

Polly had no such indulgence. No sending up cockney for her, because she still was one, same as when she was still living on the wrong side of Battersea Bridge, and not frequenting fashionable nightspots and newly opened boutiques, and restaurants with Italian names; she was still trying to speak 'proper', as they used to call it at Nora Gloucester's school, proper English with careful vowels, and 'tees' that were as crossed as Merry's arms.

'The truth is – I'm not up to anything myself, Merry, how about you? Well, I don't have to ask, you look marvellous,' she said nodding sadly at Merry's fur coat.

Merry smiled. Polly was right. She did look marvellous. That morning when she had got out of bed everything had been just right: her hair, long and shining with just the right auburn lights in it to go with her coat, her dress to go under the coat (specially imported from Italy) had clung to her in just the right places. Standing in front of the mirror she knew that Max Kassov would have to fall for her, of course he would – she'd fall for herself, if she was taking her to lunch.

140

He'd come round after the show the night before, brought her some flowers, told her that she was wonderful but that the show wasn't, and that she must call him in the morning. Of course she'd remembered who he was. The spoilt little boy on the set that day, the boy who had made everyone laugh at her. But now she was back where she should be, with her name only second on the billing in a hit musical, her wardrobe full of expensive clothes, out every night if she really wanted. She didn't care any more, not a jot, if Max Kassov was that rude little brat that day. Those days, those far-off days of poverty, the days on the other side of the river, they seemed as far off in time as Polly and her mum and Aunt Tam, and those early days of making movies.

'Look, I can't stop now,' Merry continued, 'I'm going to lunch with an agent, Max Kassov, you know? Give me your number, and I'll give you a call.'

'I'm not on the phone, Merry,' Polly replied, 'I can't afford the phone, you know?'

Merry looked at Polly. Not on the telephone, that took them both back a bit, back to the smell of over-cooked kippers and tea at four. Back to worn floors that had dirty patches in the corners and the sounds of someone being sick by the dustbins as you hurried home from school. Not being on the phone: that brought it all back again, and made her want to hurry on, hurry on to work and warmth and a nice restaurant, a fashionable restaurant where people would stop by her table and talk, and then pass on again – leaving you hoping they'd say, 'That was Meredith Browne', as they met who they were lunching with, which would make their lunch more interesting, because 'Meredith Browne' was a name again, once more 'up there', up in the lights, in the warmth, no longer hurrying off to try and see some two-bit producer in her lunch hour. Hoping, always hoping. And even when they did see you it was always the same.

'Show us your legs, love. Legs and tit – that's all that they're interested in.'

That's all they were interested in, sleazy buggers.

'Look—' Merry rubbed the side of her nose with a gloved fist suddenly. 'Look, call me at the theatre, Poll, call me tonight, and we'll have lunch, OK?'

Polly nodded. She was still staring at Merry's coat, and they both remembered the days when it was Polly that was always hurrying to Nora Gloucester's School of Stage and Drama in *her* fur coat, and Merry was in the thin tweed. No, not thin, papery, it was that thin, her so-called winter coat. She hugged her new fur coat to her, she couldn't help it, and then leaned forward and kissed Polly briefly either side of her head, taking care not to smudge her lipstick.

'C'mon, take this.'

She had started to hurry on, smiling, but she ran back, she couldn't help herself.

'Take this, get yourself something hot, you look frozen stiff.'

She pushed a fiver into Polly's hands, and Polly took it.

'Thanks, Merry, I'll pay you back.'

'Yeah?'

Merry laughed and ran on. Pay her back indeed, when had Polly Stephens ever paid her back? Except by pinching a job from her. She laughed when she thought about it, and then as she got round the corner, at the bottom of the Arcade, she stopped running and slowed down to a halt, and laughed again, the cold air hitting the back of her throat so it hurt a little. Pay her back, that was rich!

She peered at herself in the window of a shop, and powdered her nose quickly to stop any ugly shine. Her two pairs of false eyelashes made her orbs look huge. She started to walk on slowly, savouring every minute.

Inside the building Max Kassov's agency was up a short flight of stairs. Merry paused and sprayed a little perfume either side of her head, and a little on each wrist. 'Joy', very suitable for her mood.

The secretary was a pretty girl. She smiled as soon as she saw Merry, and Merry could see from her smile that she knew who Merry was, that Max Kassov had warned her that she was coming, and that she had been told to look out for her, and that he wanted to know as soon as she did arrive. Very nice to realize that.

She took Meredith's coat and hung it up with some reverence, they both knew that not everyone had a fur coat like that. The secretary didn't. Merry could see inside the cupboard: there were two other coats there, one was a man's, probably cashmere and wool, and the other was a girl's, very definitely just wool, and obviously belonging to the slender girl with the blonde-streaked hair caught up in a velvet bow on the back of her head.

'I'll tell Mr Kassov you're here. I expect he'd like you to go straight in.'

Merry nodded and crossed her legs. And what fabulous legs they were nowadays, she thought, stretching them out in front of her. Long and slender. All those years ago how ugly had she been, and how skinny; seeing Polly had reminded her of that. But now, now that she was older, it was so much better. It was fashionable to be skinny, shapely but skinny, and the long skinny legs had grown into long shapely legs, legs that suited her five foot seven inches, and her twenty-two inch waist, and her thirty-four inch hips, not to mention her all-important thirty-eight inch 'tits'. Because they were tits. They weren't 'bosoms', or even 'breasts'. Merry's bustline was not designed to heave and sob, it was designed to tempt the eye, and a lot else as well.

She hadn't had much time to take in what Max Kassov looked like the night before. Sure she remembered he'd looked rich, but then an awful lot of the men that came backstage to see her looked that. She also remembered his blue eyes wandering over her appreciatively, and his voice, which had been attractive, and his hair that was thick and wavy; but what she hadn't remembered was his smile, just a little arrogant, just a little 'cocking a snook' at the world as the cockneys called it, just as full of spoilt mischief as that day on the set all those years before.

But thank God he didn't remember her. Why should

he? Mary, had she even been called 'Mary Zumpone' in those days? She couldn't remember, and at that moment as she shook Max Kassov's hand, to be truthful Merry didn't wish to. Why should she make herself miserable thinking of the distant days before she was beautiful and on the billing? She was here now, in a young and handsome agent's office, on her way again, that's all that mattered, and that's all she cared about.

It was electricity between them as soon as they shook hands, and Merry knew at once that he wanted her like crazy; she wanted to laugh because it was so obvious, and he knew that she knew and he could do nothing about it.

'You don't want a drink here, do you? We'll go straight out, shall we?'

Merry nodded, and then waited patiently as the slender girl who was the secretary re-entered with the beloved fur coat, and held it for her as she slipped her arms into it.

'Take any messages, Nicky, and tell them I'm out at a meeting, would you?'

They swept past her and, as they did so, it suddenly seemed to Merry that that must be a code between them, that last remark that he'd made. 'I'm out at a meeting' must mean that he had every intention of enjoying his lunch. Well, so be it, let him enjoy his lunch, and she would too.

It was great, to walk into a restaurant ahead of Max Kassov, knowing that he wanted to represent her, and knowing that he was crazy for her too. Merry swayed a little, and her green eyes swept the restaurant recognizing some faces, not recognizing others. It was all such a game, but it was a game that you had to play right, and this time she was going to play it right, just right, so right that she would get to the top, right to the top, and not just as an actress either. She was going to be as big as any one of them, starting here, today, at lunch.

They sat at a corner table with a good view of the room, so that they could talk and watch at the same time. It was nice they both wanted to do the same thing, it made them

144

feel at ease with each other straight away. The sofa they sat on was plush and velvet and matched the dress she was wearing to perfection.

'You're very clever to wear red,' Max said. 'Red is great with auburn hair.'

Max's eyes raised themselves appreciatively to Merry's thick shining hair, and then lowered themselves to her glossy lips and her matching nail varnish.

'You should wear pink too,' he added, 'a quite shocking pink.'

Merry allowed her lips to part and show her little white pearly teeth, and she saw Max noticing them, which he was meant to, and she saw how much he wanted to kiss her too. She often wore shocking pink, but she wasn't going to tell Mr Kassov that, any more than she would tell him about her bad times, all those times when the telephone had never rung.

'Really? Do you think I should?'

'Sure, a lovely hot pink would be wonderful on you. Shall we have a glass of champagne to start with?'

Merry nodded. Champagne was a great start, but she mustn't drink too much of it, because it would make her lose her head. It would make her too easy.

And then a terrible thing happened, and it was the most terrible thing that had ever happened to Merry, something that was to have lasting consequences on her life. Max made her laugh. She could never remember what it was that he said, or how he said it, but suddenly for the first time in her life at the ripe old age of twenty Merry laughed at something a young man had said, not something that a girlfriend backstage said, but a real live man, and she didn't laugh to make him feel better, or to make him feel good, she laughed because he was funny, and what he said was funny, and how he said it was funny, and she saw that Max Kassov desired her even more because of it, that he liked a girl to laugh with him, and that maybe not every girl he took out did.

'To eat a superb lunch, and then to make love in the afternoon,' he said suddenly, 'that is perfection.'

They were sitting with their coffee, and he had made his remark so casually, so dreamily, his eyes roaming around the restaurant, and then coming back to her face, that for a split second Meredith couldn't believe that he had said what he had, and she looked at him a little fascinated, but not surprised. His face wasn't as handsome as she had remembered it when he came round after the show, but the expression in his eyes was so lively, and his confidence so tangible, that the overall impression was of a handsome man. She hadn't met anyone like him before, and she wondered if Max had met anyone like her before, and she suspected that he had, that he had known many beautiful girls.

'The afternoon is the best time for most things,' Merry agreed.

'As a matter of fact I thought I'd sign you up this afternoon.'

'Where do you want to "sign me up"?' Merry said laughing, unable to help it.

'The office,' Max replied poker-faced. 'Where else?'

'I already have representation,' Merry heard herself saying, probably because as soon as he said office she had felt a little dagger of disappointment, and found herself wondering why he hadn't suggested his flat, or his house, or even the Ritz. So many other men in her life, men she had only half liked, they had been ready and willing straight away, but not this Max Kassov. He was proving different, and she didn't want him to be different, any more than she had wanted him to make her laugh, and be different that way too.

'Have you signed with him? Who is he?'

Max had quickly taken advantage of that momentary pause, and his voice had changed and lost its dreamy quality, and Merry could see him working out a deal, working out how to get rid of this other man.

'No, I never signed with him,' Merry replied. 'I don't know why, but I'm still with him, and I like him, and well – I owe him everything. He's a nice fella.'

146

'I'll buy him out. What's his name? You can get rid of him.'

Merry sighed, and then she laughed, because really it was very funny, particularly now that she saw how much she meant to Max Kassov, that he wanted to sign her up that urgently, and, of course, wittingly, or unwittingly – she didn't really care which – he had played straight into her hands. That was good, because she'd never before felt that little dagger of disappointment over a man – and that was ridiculous, men were in and out of your life, this day, or any day, and you took good care of yourself with them. But you didn't get involved, you didn't feel miserable if they called you or they didn't call you, unless they had a job waiting for you. That was different, quite different.

'Get rid of him,' said Max again as he leaned over the table. His blue eyes had lost their arrogance and their mischief, and he now no longer cared whether she was wearing red or sky blue, she could see that, he only cared that she was with someone else, with another agent, and he wanted her with him.

Now it did come back to Merry, with wonderful clarity, that little boy's voice, that mocking little voice saying, 'Look, look she's put with best wishis', and as she moved back against the plush sofa and smiled at Max she savoured her little moment, she couldn't help it. And at the same time she couldn't help laughing, because it was funny, but not in the way that Max had been funny earlier, in another way, in that way that made your life seem very black and white, and seem to have a grand purpose, a conductor, a magician even, only at this moment she was the magician, and boy, oh boy, was it fun to put your own hand into the hat and pluck out that fat little bunny yourself.

'I can't get rid of him, not just like that,' she replied finally. 'He's been too kind, he's been a father to me really. Besides, I've been with him since I was a child. Before him, well, before him I was always having to run from job to job, after him I only had to walk.'

147

Max's impatience was all too evident. His head swayed slightly to the side, and he sighed.

'Come on, if he hasn't signed you up, what's the problem? What's his name? Do I know him?'

'Yeah, you know him. Louis Kass? Ring a bell?'

Max shrugged, and then he said coolly, 'In that case it's even easier.'

'You wouldn't rob your own father, would you, Mr Kassov?'

'Sure. And he'd rob me,' Max replied, grinning suddenly. 'He poached someone only last month, and he was actually signed with me, but you can't sue your own father. Particularly when you haven't spoken to him for years.'

He'd stopped smiling and was laughing, and Merry could see it was very good acting, his acting, and then she knew why he was so successful, the other people, the agents and so on, they had to be good at acting too; and they were, they really were, better than what was happening on most West End stages every night of the year.

'So,' he continued, 'that's all right then. You can call him when you get back to the office, tell him you're with me, tell him you're with Max, and he'll understand, he won't hold it against you. Not really. He'll pretend to, but I know, believe me, he won't, not really.'

Merry took out her red lipstick and her gold powder compact with her initials on it in the corner, and she flicked open the compact, and slowly, very slowly, she traced her mouth with the lipstick, and Max watched her. Her lips were quite full, very attractive she'd been told, not least by Max's father.

She snapped the powder compact shut with a satisfying sharp sound, and then she smiled, allowing those small pearly teeth to gleam entrancingly at Max.

'I can't do that, you know? I owe him too much.'

'Oh, come on. He's an old man now, he's got everything he wants, and he's not that interested in the agency any

148

more anyway. He's more interested in playing the impresario. I should know, I'm having a hard enough time trying to find shows for my clients that he hasn't put on.'

'Well, I'll think about it. OK?'

'Think about it? Thinking about it is not going to change anything, what will thinking about it do? No, come back to the office, call him, and sign with me.'

Merry nodded slowly. It sounded like a nice idea, and if it hadn't been for that little dagger of disappointment, she might, just might have done exactly that, but now, now it was all changed, everything had changed since he'd made her laugh, and she knew there was only one way to play it, and that was her way.

'So, that's settled then?'

Max got up quickly. Merry followed him. The maître d'hôtel signalled for their coats (and his *was* cashmere) and they strolled out of the restaurant into the snow again.

He took her arm as they walked along, guiding her through the slush on the pavement, and watching carefully when they crossed the road, but she could tell, from the way that he was holding her and the way that he was walking slightly ahead of her, that he was holding her and guiding her not as a girl that he was crazy about, but as an actress that he couldn't wait to sign up. He wanted not her, but her signature.

In the office he sent Nicky for some coffee, and then handed her the telephone.

'Call him.'

It was time for Merry to do some acting. She took the telephone, and started to dial, and then she quickly replaced it.

'No, no, I can't really. Louis – he's been everything to me: father, agent, everything.'

She looked across the desk at Max.

'And he always said he never laid a client,' Max joked.

'And he hasn't,' said Merry factually. 'Not this one anyway. He's been a friend, a dear friend, the only one I've ever had in the business, as a matter of fact.'

'A friend in the business? Now there's a thought,' said Max, and then added, 'Think about it. There's a great deal waiting for you here, and I'm younger, in case you hadn't noticed.'

Merry got up to go. Always be the first to get up to go, Louis had taught her that. 'I think I'll let it go,' she said, and she went.

During the intervals of the play, Merry let a more lowly member of the cast, an ex-member of the chorus called Moppet (who had changed her name from Doreen for obvious reasons) come and sit in her dressing-room for a cup of tea and a gossip. The subject for the evening's conversation was, as usual, men, and in particular Max Kassov.

'When in doubt, do nothin',' Moppet advised, during a close examination of her nail varnish. 'Least that's what my nan always said. It's for the best, she said. When in doubt, don't do nothin' at all.'

'When in doubt don't do anything at all,' Merry corrected her, while wondering all the same whether it was such good advice after all.

Because that's exactly what she was doing about Max Kassov. Sweet nothing at all. And she wasn't doing anything about Louis either. She didn't ring Louis and try and talk it over with him, and she didn't ring Max. She just did the show and went out afterwards to eat and sometimes to dance with men who quite openly admired her, but that's all they were allowed to do. Just admire her, because that's all Meredith allowed her escorts to do when she was working. They could pay for her, they could drop her back home, sometimes they might even get a kiss. But always they were left standing on the doorstep with the promise of a telephone call in the morning which they never got, but so what? It was fun. That's all it was. Fun.

But Max not ringing wasn't fun.

Because much as Merry hated to admit it, she was dying for him to weaken and telephone her. She wanted to hear

150

him beg once more, she needed to hear how much she was wanted. And yet because he didn't weaken, she admired him all the more.

'You seen that bloke then?' Moppet asked her one evening as she helped Merry brush out her hair. 'You seen that bloke in Row E?'

'I never have the chance to look as far as Row A let alone Row E, stupid,' Merry replied, studying her reflection carefully in the mirror. 'Besides, I'm so much in character now, I never even notice the audience.'

'He's in every Friday,' Moppet continued, unabashed. 'Same seat, same bloke. Every Friday, regular as clockwork.'

'So what? I know somebody who's seen the show eighteen times.'

'You'd think they had better things to do. It's bad enough being in the bleedin' thing, without having to see it eighteen times.'

'He doesn't come to see the show, Moppet,' Merry sighed. 'He comes to see me.'

'I don't think this bloke does,' Moppet replied. 'Every time you comes on, he puts his 'ead down and 'alf covers 'is face.'

Merry stopped admiring her own image in the mirror for a moment and stared at that of Moppet's. Why should anyone hide his face when she came on? Unless they didn't want to be seen. And why wouldn't they want to be seen? They wouldn't want to be seen if they were—

Meredith's reverie was broken by the voice on her dressing-room tannoy calling the five, and she rose immediately as if programmed to finish her change and put the final retouch to her make-up.

Moppet yawned and rose too, although she had no reason to hurry – her next appearance wasn't until well into the second act. But since she was understudying Merry, she felt it her bounden duty to shadow her, in case Merry tripped and broke an ankle in the wings and Moppet would find herself suddenly called to go on.

151

Merry knew and understood this, because she'd been there. She'd done the same on countless occasions when she was covering one of the stars. But she'd never got the chance to go on. And much as she liked Moppet, Meredith was quite determined come hell or high water she'd never give her the chance to go on for Merry either.

Merry hurried down the stone steps which led down to the stage in response to the call on the tannoy for beginners, making sure nonetheless to keep a good hold on the polished brass rail just in case she slipped, or in case anyone behind gave her an accidental push – that anyone in this instance being Moppet – and before taking her position onstage, she took a quick peek at the audience through the spyhole in the prompt corner. After all, it was Friday night, and she was now very curious as to who the mystery regular might be. Row E was full up, except for the aisle seat which was empty. Merry scanned the row of faces, but recognized none of them.

Then, just as the lights started to fade in the auditorium, Merry saw him, a figure waiting at the top of the aisle until it was dark enough to take his seat unnoticed. But even in the dimming light Merry could recognize who it was, the moment he started to walk towards his seat, by the way he nervously ran a hand over one side of his hair, a gesture that itself was a trademark of Max Kassov.

Merry grinned to herself, and felt even more special than she normally did when she was waiting to go on. So he'd been there every week, had he? And for how many weeks? All the time she'd been hoping he would ring her, he'd been sitting out there, admiring her, loving her, applauding her. And now as she went onstage and took up her position, she realized how grateful she was that she hadn't known he was out front. Because she might have tried too hard, and by doing so she could have broken the spell. If she had known Max was out there sitting in the dark watching, she could all too easily have lost it. You inevitably did when friends or relations told you in advance of their visit to the show. As soon as you knew they were out front, the magic went.

And if she'd known Max was out there. . . . Merry gave a little shudder as she waited for the curtain to rise, unable to bear the thought of what might have happened. She remembered what had happened one night when she had learned one of the most influential casting agents was in the audience. The effect of the news was catastrophic. Merry lost all her co-ordination and, like in those half-sleeps where your pillow turns to stone, her limbs had all started to feel twice their weight and size, and her voice had risen ever higher and higher. By the time they had started Act Two, the casting agent's seat was quite visibly empty.

But tonight she felt as if she had wings. Because Max had been once, and had obviously been so entranced he had returned again and again. So Merry had nothing to fear, and as a consequence she gave far and away her best performance of the run. It was as though she had the entire audience on a string. If she wished them to laugh, they roared, and if she wanted them to be silent, it was like the grave. At the end, someone even threw a rose on to the stage. A red rose. Max?

She could hardly contain herself during the curtain calls, and finally, before the curtain fell for the sixth and final time, Merry sneaked a direct look at Row E. But the aisle seat was empty. Max Kassov was gone.

He must have rushed round backstage, Merry thought, as she hurried back up to her dressing-room. He'd be there outside her dressing-room, surely, with a huge bunch of flowers and a bottle of champagne. And Merry would know she hadn't a hope. She would be lost before he followed her into her dressing-room with that strange mixture of arrogance and mischief. And his blue eyes would dance and sparkle, and they would laugh, and finally he would tell her how wonderful she was.

'Butterflies,' she heard Aunt Tam saying in her head as she clattered up the long flight of steps from the stage. 'That's what you lot are. Nothin' but a lot of flippin' butterflies.'

153

And Aunt Tam was right. Of course she was. Of course actresses were like butterflies, with their pitifully short lives before their looks went, their lips puckered and their cheeks sank. And there was nothing to look forward to except books of yellowing press cuttings, or running a boarding house, or digs, or a pub with photographs of stars they had only met since they went to work behind the bar. Merry had seen a lot of those sort of hostelries in her part of London when she was a child. Not that she ever was a child as such. But when she should have been a child, she'd seen them. Tired old tarts with puckered butterfly mouths, their arms thickened by gin and their eyes watery with the same. And even then Merry had made up her mind not to end up like them. Butterflies they may all be, but Merry was going to keep flying till she dropped out of the sky.

She rounded the corner to her dressing-room, but there was no one waiting outside in the echoing corridor. No Max Kassov with a bouquet and champagne. He wasn't inside the room either, and there wasn't even a note, nor a message with the stage doorman. For a moment Merry felt like kicking the one armchair in the room really hard, before deciding otherwise and starting to disrobe. One or two visitors, all from the business, popped their vaguely known heads round her door to breathe how marvellous she had been, but no one knocked and asked if they could come in because they were Max Kassov.

The night air was sharp and cold and caught in her throat as Merry hurried out of the stage door. She tightened her silk scarf round her neck as she asked Harry the doorman to find her a taxi.

'That won't be necessary,' said a voice from the darkened alley behind her. 'I have my car.'

Merry didn't even turn. She'd show him how cool she was. And how unsurprised. She stood where she was and made the final adjustments to her scarf before tucking it back inside her coat.

'Hello, Max,' she said, still without looking. 'Good house.'

154

'Good house,' Max agreed, coming to her side and taking her arm. 'Lousy play. Great performance.'

He steered her to where his Rolls was waiting, and opened the door for her.

'Where are we going?' Merry asked.

'That,' Max replied, his hand still on her elbow, 'all depends on you.'

They sat in the stationary car in silence for a while, as Max carefully prepared a cigar before lighting it.

'Was that the first time you've seen the play, Max?' Merry asked him, in all fake innocence.

'No,' Max answered, 'but I hope to God it's the last.'

Then he turned and smiled at her, and Merry was disarmed. One of Max's number one smiles, and Merry found she was fighting for her life. She didn't know what it contained, or why it had that effect on her. All she knew was that for the first time she found herself caring for a man. No one, but absolutely no one had ever got through her defences before.

Even so, Merry tried to maintain her composure.

'Didn't you like the play, then?' she enquired, after a small pause.

'I have an aversion to comedies set in Swiss chalets,' Max said, laughing. 'I'm always afraid that before being bored to death I'll get killed by an avalanche.'

Merry laughed, despite herself, and despite the fact that it wasn't all that much of a joke, for Max had good delivery. Very snappy.

'Actually,' he said, leaning back, his teeth clenched around his cigar, a cheeky look in his blue eyes, 'my worst fear was that you'd get killed in an avalanche of crap. That's a terrible play you're being brilliant in.'

He removed the cigar and smiled. There it was again – that smile. Max had smiled and Merry could feel her head swimming.

'Now,' he said, brushing the cigar ash off his knee, 'will you please tell me whether you are going to sign up or not. The ink's getting dry in the pen.'

'Why do you need to know right now?'

'Because I need to tell my driver where to take us to eat. If it's no, we'll do a trattoria. If it's yes, it's the Savoy.'

Merry looked at him, and then shook out her luxuriant hair.

'Tell him to go to the Savoy,' she replied, before looking out into the night, and up at the other stars which were high above them in the sky.

Besides the fact that she knew she was in danger of falling in love, Merry also knew that it was no bad thing, to let it happen. How could it be? Max and his impudent charm had caught her unawares, because he made her laugh. She knew that's where he scored where others had failed. Aunt Tam had always said that. If a man made you laugh, you might as well strip off there and then. Even so, she must be careful. An affair that went wrong could do you more harm than good. And survival was everything, and Max could be her lifeline. At the end of the famous day it didn't really matter a damn how talented you were. What mattered was who you knew. And how well you knew them.

Meredith sipped her champagne cocktail and looked Max in the eyes as she'd learned to do. Not directly, but first in one eye, and then in the other, which was much more flattering for the subject of your attentions, and much less demanding. A look straight in the eye was a challenge. A searching look from one to the other showed interest. Deep interest. Constant interest. Max smiled at her in return, probably only subconsciously aware of the effect of the trick. But the smile was warm and genuine, and the look – even though he was still mid-anecdote – the look he gave her was open to only one interpretation.

'It's true,' he told her, now trying to catch her searching eyes. 'Uncle Baz was responsible for getting Jack taken off the show and the two of them didn't speak again – not a word – they never spoke again for ten years. Until one day Burnett Meyer, you know, the producer? Well, he had this idea for a charity auction, and he asked Jack to be the auctioneer. It was brilliant. I mean the whole thing, Uncle Baz was sitting in the front row, and Jack never looked at him all evening. Right until he was auctioning off the very last item. Some pissy little silver plate gravy boat. And he says – you're going to love this – he says "Who'll start me at £5000 for this quite priceless antique?" Big laugh. You can imagine. "Come on!" says Jack. "This is for a very good cause! It's worth every penny of £5000!" And there's more laughter. And it's then that Jack chooses apparently to let bygones be bygones, so he smiles and nods at Uncle Baz. And Uncle Baz smiles and nods back to Jack. And Jack knocks down the gravy boat to him for £5000.'

Max grinned like a child with delight at the story, and then the grin turned to a big broad smile when he saw how much he had made Merry laugh. And Merry saw how delighted he was with her delight, and chose that moment to stop searching Max's face, and fix his eyes with hers. And they both fell silent as they exchanged the look a man and a woman exchange which says although they know they're not yet in bed, they just as well might be.

Meredith couldn't remember much else that was said over dinner that evening. Later on she couldn't even recall what she ate, or rather what she ordered and then left. Max didn't eat either. They just drank some more champagne, and then found themselves in bed in Merry's flat. She couldn't even remember whether or not she dreaded Max might not be as good a lover as she hoped he might be, because it all happened so quickly, so seamlessly. One minute she was shutting the flat door behind them, and the next she was in Max's arms – not standing there by the door but lying in his arms in bed, and he was making love to her, strongly yet tenderly, his arms through hers and his hands up on her shoulders, his mouth everywhere. On her mouth, on her neck, on her breasts. And when he was inside her it was as if he'd always been inside her, filling her with his strength, and pulling her to him, and seemingly into him. And then when she lay back gasping, numb, the most alive she had ever been, and yet suddenly and momentarily dead, Merry was aware of him smiling. Even though she couldn't quite see him full face, she knew he was smiling.

'Are you smiling for the reason I think you're smiling?' she finally whispered to him.

'Who said I was smiling?' Max replied.

'I can feel you are.'

'Yes, I'm smiling. And so would any man be after such love-making.'

'That's not why you're smiling, Max Kassov. You're smiling because you know you've got me.'

'Got you?' Max laughed, and turned, slipping an arm under her and pulling her to him. 'I got you the day you first walked in my office.'

Merry bit Max on the shoulder, hard. But Max just grinned the more.

'Talk about *hutzpah*,' she sighed, as she rested her head on his chest.

'If you're going to talk about it, Meredith Browne, it's *huztspa*,' Max corrected, giving the word its correct guttural sound. '*Huztspa*. And to say it properly, you might need to change your faith.'

'What is it exactly, Max? I mean I know roughly what it is. But what is it actually?'

'It's not what it is, it's what you need. It's the something you need to survive in this bloody business. It's the daring. The cheek. The neck. Without it, you're strictly back row of the chorus. Now turn round and kiss me. I want to make doubly sure I'm doing the right thing in signing you on.'

Max slept, but Merry didn't. She sat propped up on her pillows, staring at the full moon that hung in the sky. She didn't want to go to sleep. She didn't want to succumb to unconsciousness, and lose this wonderful feeling that glowed through her body. Because for the first time in her life she was quite genuinely happy. Up until now her life had been cheap. Like all those awful films she had made. And the terrible plays she had been in. The moon had only been a paper one, hanging over a cardboard sea. But now it was a real moon, and what she was feeling in her heart and head was just as real as the clear limpid light that shone into her bedroom and on the body of her lover sleeping beside her.

Merry turned and very gently kissed Max on the shoulder. He didn't stir, so she kissed him again, and kept her mouth pressed against his warm flesh. She would always love Max for that night, Meredith decided. Even if he got up in a couple of hours' time, dressed in silence, and walked out of the door and she never saw him again, she would be eternally grateful to him for showing her how it felt to be happy. He'd kicked the door down. And she'd stepped through it with him. Into a light which she had never known could be so warm.

In fact it was Meredith who got up first and silently dressed while Max slumbered on. He woke when Merry was pulling on her shoes, just before preparing to write him a note.

'I have an interview out at Elstree,' she explained, 'and you know how long it takes to get out there.'

'You've left something behind,' Max said, picking the something off the pillow.

He held it up to her, and Merry saw it was one of her false eyelashes. Then Max reached over for his jacket and put the eyelash in his wallet.

'A little memento,' he said. 'Now, what's this part you're up for?'

'Nothing,' Merry replied. 'It's that epic they're finishing making out there. What's it called? Yes – *The Nile*.'

'*The Nile*,' Max scoffed. '*The Crock*.'

'They want to see me for one of Cleopatra's hand-maidens.'

Max sat bolt upright in bed and stared at her.

'You're out of your bloody head.'

'It's work.'

'It's work – it's shit. Now come over here and get back into bed.'

Merry hesitated. The film might be a crock, but the director was big-time transatlantic, and Meredith knew just to get seen by him for a part was almost better than actually getting a part with lesser directors.

'And that's even greater shit,' Max retorted with a grin as she explained. 'So come over here at once and take your clothes off.'

Still Merry hesitated.

'I at least ought to ring and give some sort of excuse.'

'You ring and give some sort of excuse and you're like every other bloody actor. You turn up and stand in line for some pissy little walk-on and you might as well kiss it all good night.'

'Max – Rosie Roberts was just *seen* by Herman Stein for *Bad Day Tomorrow* and look what happened to her.'

'Everyone knows what happened to Rosie Roberts. Rosie Roberts got laid by Herman Stein, got a three-scener in *Cheer Leader* and is now advertising shampoo on television. Now do as you're told and come and take your clothes off. If you're going to have to take your clothes off today, Meredith Browne, I'd much rather it was for me.'

It was the grin that did it. The little boy cheeky smile. And the confidence behind it. Meredith sat down on the edge of the bed and took her shoes off. That was as far as she got. Max removed the rest of her clothes. And as he pulled her back into bed, Meredith knew in her heart of hearts that by not going out to Elstree she wasn't kissing anything goodbye. She was in fact doing the very opposite.

The day Max signed Merry up, he stopped taking her out. She found out the first day she was officially on the agency books when she rang him to make plans for the evening.

'No,' Max said. 'Not tonight. Tonight you go home to bed, and early. And tomorrow I'll call you and tell you what you're doing.'

'What we're doing, I hope,' Merry replied as tartly as she could.

'What you're doing, sweetheart,' Max countered, grinning (Merry dared swear) as he said it. 'I know where I'm going.'

At first Meredith couldn't believe it, that anyone could be that transparent. Despite the promises she'd made herself the night before, that she would just be forever grateful to Max, whatever he did, and however he might subsequently treat her, now she felt like kicking him in the head.

'Max—' she started to protest, but Max cut her short.

'Not now, Meredith. I've got a lot on my desk today. A light supper, an early night, and I'll call you tomorrow.'

Meredith stared helplessly at the now silent telephone she was left holding. That wasn't the way she'd planned it. Tonight she'd planned on Max picking her up from the theatre, and then dinner at Le Caprice, so that the business could see who was walking in on Max Kassov's arm. She'd even planned her outfit, down to the last detail, as she'd lain there awake after Max had left her sleeping. And now she'd been ordered straight home for a light supper and an early night. Alone.

Even so, despite Merry's overwhelming desire to disregard Max's strictures and go out on the town with one of her many escorts, after the curtain had come down that evening, Merry found herself dutifully heading home in a taxi by herself, to a late-night dinner of chicken breast and salad. She also found herself in bed for the first time in months the right side of midnight.

At five to twelve her telephone rang. It was Max.

'I just rang to say good-night, sweetheart,' he said.

'Yes?' Merry replied. 'And supposing I hadn't been in?'

'If you hadn't been in, young lady,' answered Max, 'you'd have been looking for a new agent in the morning. I'll pick you up at quarter to nine.'

And that was that. No pleasantries, no sweet nothings, just bald facts. Max hadn't even said what he was picking her up for the next morning.

'Voice lessons,' he told her, as he ordered the taxi to head for Marble Arch. 'Your voice needs to come down half a register.'

'I've got a very nice voice,' Merry protested. 'The man in the *Western Evening Argus* said it was sweet and clear. Like a bell, in fact.'

'Sweet and clear and like a bell and half a register too high. You're going to Jeannie Costelow. She's the best voice coach in the business. Remember Lewis Felton? You won't remember Lewis Felton, at least you won't remember the old Lewis Felton. Great looks, great physique, and a voice like Tweetie Pie. I sent him to Jeannie and the next season he was playing Othello. You can't play Othello with a voice like Tweetie Pie.'

'Who said I want to play Othello, Max?'

'All you'll play with your sweet clear little soprano, sweetheart, are *ingénues*. And wide-eyed soubrettes. We're going to give you a nice throaty voice, low and sexy, like Bacall. Then you'll sound interesting. Sweet isn't interesting. Clear is for the weather. And bells are for ringing. You want to sound as if you drink whisky and smoke forty a day.'

'You mean you want me to.'

'You were the one who wanted to come to me.'

'I didn't know you were going to play Svengali.'

'I'm not. That sort of thing doesn't interest me. In business terms, you're an investment. That's what interests me. And the way you are now, I'd lose my money.'

Max was looking at her, grinning, as if the smile would take the heart out of what he was saying.

'I thought you bought what you saw,' Merry said.

'I never buy what I see,' Max replied. 'I buy what I *can* see. What I see is a picture like every other picture in the casting directory. What I can see is a great big star.'

Meredith conceded, warmed by his smile and fired by his flattery. She smiled back at him and then slipped her arm through his, leaning on his shoulder.

162

'We're going to have to change not only the way you say things,' Max continued, 'but also the things you actually say.'

'I don't see why,' Merry argued. 'The way I talk's very fashionable.'

'Fashion,' Max sighed. 'Fashion only exists to become unfashionable. What survives is what's classic. Kelly was classic. Dietrich was classic, Garbo was classic. You've got the looks. You've got the talent. You've got the *huztspa*.'

He turned and grinned at her, then covered her hand with his.

'Now all you need, sweetheart, is the class.'

After privately damning him, Merry knew Max was right. She had everything going for her except the thing that makes you stand out. That indefinable quality that makes you a star and your rival an also-ran. For a while she argued with Max that star quality was something you couldn't create. But Max told her that was sheer nonsense, and quoted her example after example of star actresses who had been nothing and nobody until they had been 'taken over'.

'So now I'm a commodity,' Merry complained over dinner at her flat.

'From a business point of view, certainly,' Max agreed, pouring himself some wine.

'And from the other point of view?' she enquired.

'You mean there's another point of view?' Max replied, poker-faced.

'If you need reminding, Max, you could always stay the night.'

'I'm all for being reminded, sweetheart. But I'm afraid I won't be able to spend the night.'

'You're not married, are you, for Christ's sake?' Merry asked him, as the thought occurred to her for the first time.

'You see? See what happens to your voice when you become excited?' Max laughed, completely ignoring her question. 'On the breath! Breathe! Remember what Jeannie said!'

'God Almighty, Max! The curtain came down an hour ago!' Meredith protested.

'All the world's a stage, sweetheart!' Max replied. 'And you never ever know – not at any time, at any moment – just who's watching. And just who may be listening.'

It was the same if not worse when Max took her shopping. Meredith, like all girls about to be taken out on a spree by their lovers, had been looking forward to it intensely. She had her hair done specially the day before, and for the day itself she chose to wear her expensive new suede dress and knee boots.

She was ready and waiting for Max half an hour before he was due. He arrived dead on time, as usual, except this time he was carrying several shopping bags.

For a moment Meredith thought she'd been pre-empted. Max soon put her right.

'OK,' he said, after briefly kissing her on the cheek. 'Now go and put these on.'

He handed her the shopping bags.

'I'm already dressed, Max,' Merry replied. 'Or perhaps you hadn't noticed?'

'You're not going out in that, Merry. No way. No more cheap clothes.'

'This dress cost me over a hundred pounds, Max!'

'I'm not interested if it cost you three times that. It's wrong. It's the wrong image. You look like every two-bit dolly bird. And what *have* you done to your hair?'

'I had it done, Max!' Merry practically shouted. 'I had it done specially to go shopping with you!'

'Well, you shouldn't have done, sweetheart,' Max replied quite calmly. 'You should have waited for me. That haircut is piss.'

'This hairstyle, Max Kassov—' Merry started

'I know,' Max interrupted. 'Everyone's got it. But we don't want you to be everyone, do we? Now go and put those clothes on I've bought you.'

'You haven't actually bought me clothes to go shopping in?' Merry asked disbelievingly.

'Where I'm taking you,' Max told her, 'the assistant will be dressed better than you.'

He held the bags out to her. Merry took them from him and disappeared obediently into her bedroom to change her clothes. Or rather, she thought more appropriately as she closed the door behind her, to change her costume.

Only recently Meredith had seen a film where the heroine sat with her lover on gilt chairs in a thickly carpeted salon while mannequins modelled, especially for her, the very latest in couture clothes. Meredith had always considered such a notion romantic in the extreme, and watching the film she had tried very hard to imagine what such a moment could be like. And now she could actually find out, because here she was, seated with Max in one of the most fashionable salons in Bond Street, while the models walked up and down the catwalk showing off the latest designer creations *especially for her*. How had Max arranged it?

On the other side of her sat the *vendeuse*, who described every dress in detail. If Meredith wished to see any particular garment in even more detail, she would summon the model over, and the girl would turn and stand and stand and turn, right there in front of Meredith while the three of them pondered whether or not it would be quite right for *madame*.

Max made the final choice, and Meredith was deeply grateful, because she herself had found it quite impossible to make any sort of definite selection. Meredith was then shepherded to an enormous changing-room, which was fully mirrored and lit with soft and subtle lighting, the complete opposite to the communal scrums which were so fashionable in the new boutiques, where you were lucky to leave in the clothes you were wearing when you came in. The *vendeuse* even helped Meredith undress, down to the new silk underwear and stockings Max had bought her that morning.

165

She was then put into the dress by the *vendeuse* and her young assistant, who was, as Max had predicted, much better dressed than Meredith would have been had she not taken Max's counsel. The fitting took some time as there were so many interior fastenings.

'The *toile* for this was fantastic,' the *vendeuse* told her. 'I went over myself to Paris to view it. It's not something you can hear about, you see. One simply has to view it oneself. Ah – and if I may say so, *madame*, there is absolutely no doubt at all that this was made for you.'

Merry looked at herself in the mirrors. The woman was right. The dress, so utterly complicated to fit, and yet which looked so utterly simple on, could have been made especially for her. It didn't fit Meredith so much as embrace and caress her. The superb cut enhanced the shape of her own superb body, so much so that every movement she made in the dress, be it a turn, or a step, gave her a greater awareness of her sexuality. It was as if she was wearing a corset made of the finest silks and wools, a corset which shaped her gently but firmly into something and somebody no man could resist.

Max regarded her in silence as she stood compliantly before him. Then he shook his head slightly, as if in disbelief, before ordering her to walk away from and then back to him.

Meredith walked the length of the room in silence. By the door she stood for a moment with her back to him, so that Max could appreciate the way the dress accentuated her quite perfect hips and backside, before falling away into a skirt of deceptively simple pleats which as she turned back swung easily around her elegant long legs.

'Perfect,' said Max, without emotion. 'Thank you, Marie.'

'Thank you, Mr Kassov,' the *vendeuse* replied, before making a small and quite superfluous adjustment to Meredith's new dress. 'It is always a great pleasure, albeit a rare one, to fit a young woman so perfectly proportioned. Sometimes I find myself saying a dress is made for a client, and trying to make myself believe it. Today, I am glad to say I had no such problem.'

'Good,' Max nodded. 'Now that white two-piece suit, with the dark blue braid. I think we'll see that next, please.'

The *vendeuse* nodded and signalled to her assistant to take the suit to the changing room. Meredith took the opportunity to buttonhole Max.

'You own a bank or something?' she hissed at him. 'You know how much a dress like this costs?'

Max stared at her, almost as if he was momentarily displeased with her, although Meredith was only anxious to try and save him money.

'Do you like the dress?' he asked her.

'Like it? I love it!' Merry replied, still *sotto voce*.

'Do you like the suit?'

'The suit's incredible!'

'So shut up and stop being so cheap.'

Meredith was about to take offence, when Max suddenly grinned at her.

'And in answer to your first question,' he added, 'no, no, I do not own a bank. But by the time I've finished with you, you're going to look as if you do.'

He bought her three outfits from the salon. The dress, the suit, and an evening gown, a long sheath of unadorned black silk. Other designers might have been tempted to add something around the bodice, lest the cut of their gowns might prove monotonous. But the artist who designed this particular dress knew that any extra embellishment would only detract from his masterpiece, particularly when worn by someone as stunningly beautiful as Meredith.

'It's cut on the bias, you see,' Max told her, cigar in mouth as he ran an appreciative hand down her side and on to the top of her hip. 'Something like this – it just wouldn't work, you see. Not unless it's cut on the bias.'

He took as much interest in her shoes. They must have visited the best six shoe shops in and around Bond Street in the search for the finest shoes. Most Max rejected before Merry even had a chance to try them on. He just held one of the pair in his hand and studied it, as if it was an ornament. And then when he found a pair of which he approved, he would set them down on the floor in front of him and walk round them, puffing at his cigar, and grunting now and then under his breath.

Finally Meredith would be ordered to try them on, while Max sat slouched in a chair, a deep frown furrowing his brow. And there would be more grunts from under his breath, and deep sighs, and long silences, before he made his mind up finally whether to buy or reject them.

'You've got a shoe thing,' Meredith said to him en route from one shop to another.

'Of course I have,' Max agreed. 'I love women's shoes. It says everything about the woman wearing them. And the man she's sleeping with. But I only think about shoes when I'm buying them. Or admiring them. I don't think about them at any other time.'

He turned round and looked at her evenly.

'What do you think about then, Max?' Meredith asked him in her new smoky voice.

'I think about how incredible it is,' he replied. 'Particularly with you.'

Then he walked on ahead of her, staring into the windows of the shops, Meredith followed him after only a moment. But in that moment, Meredith's heart stopped a thousand times. So far in their relationship, although Max had loved her passionately by making love to her passionately, he had said nothing of how he felt. On the other hand Meredith had. Not by telling Max she loved him, but by showing him in ways for which she despised herself. By the over-eagerness in her greetings, and in the drama of their farewells. Max would have to be a fool not to know she loved him.

But Meredith, although she had felt the power of his love every time he took her to bed, knew nothing really of Max's inner feelings. But that moment he stopped on the street and looked at her, the moment he told her how incredible she was, she knew she had him. Not as a possession, but as a true lover. He was as much enthralled as she was. And so when as now she ran to catch him up in the street, there was an even greater spring in her step.

He spent the rest of the day buying her handbags which he preferred to call purses, like the Americans, and gloves, and all the other fashion accessories about which men don't usually bother. But then Max wasn't like other men, he was, in his own words, 'making her over', and he intended to do so from top to toe.

In the taxi back to Meredith's flat, they sat in silence for most of the journey, Max deep in thought, and Meredith deep in wonder at the pile of parcels with which she was surrounded.

At one point Max caught sight of her reflection in the window and turned to stare at her. She took his hand and kissed each finger.

'Thank you, Max,' she said. 'I mean it.'

Max turned her to him, and put one hand on the back of her neck up under her hair as he looked at her.

'You're my slave now,' he whispered. 'I shall buy you a gold chain for your ankle, and one for your waist. Which you will wear all the time. And you will do everything I ask.'

'I'll do anything you ask, Max.

'Good,' said Max. 'We'll start this afternoon.'

Then he let go of her, and went back to staring out of the taxi window. But this time Meredith couldn't see whether or not he was smiling.

Moppet came in for her tea and gossip in the interval, and Meredith gave her an abridged version of the day's events. Moppet sat listening like a child and was so enrapt she let her tea go cold.

'Christ, Merry!' she said. 'What's your trick?'

'Nothing special, Mopp,' Merry told her. 'Anyway, when it comes to tricks, next to Max I'm a beginner. He's incredible.'

169

'I know lots of tricks,' Moppet said rather glumly, dipping a biscuit in her stone-cold tea. 'But they don't seem to get me nowhere.'

'It's not like that with Max and me,' explained Merry. 'It's something other, you know. For instance the other afternoon something happened, and you know what, Moppet? I went out like a light. Really. Max says the French have a word for it.'

'Yeah,' said Moppet. 'Well, the French would, wouldn't they? You'd think they'd bloody invented it.'

'It was unbelievable, really, Mopp,' Meredith continued, undeterred by Moppet's comment, as she was by the sight of Moppet laboriously attempting to retrieve her biscuit from her tea with one nail-chewed finger. 'Max learned to make love really well in France, he says they really have got a corner in it. He's so considerate, you know?'

Moppet looked up at her, having finally scooped out the remaining bit of her biscuit, and dried her fingers on the underside of her skirt.

'Reckon 'e'll ask you to marry 'im?' she asked Meredith, with more anxiety in her voice than interest. ''Cos I mean if you're going round fainting, reckon 'e'll be obliged, won't 'e?'

Moppet frowned at herself in the mirror, and then turned to look at Meredith. It would be too much for her, if Meredith married Max Kassov. Moppet might well top herself. Bad enough that she had to cover for Meredith, but if she married the mighty Max Kassov, well, that would be it.

'I don't think I'd marry him, Mopp,' Meredith answered carefully. 'Max's kind don't marry. They dominate. And it's all right dominating outside of being married. But once you're married, that's it. Nothing else happens to you.'

'Why not?' Moppet asked.

'I don't know, but it just doesn't. Think about it. You just become the same as that mirror over there. A reflection, that's all.'

The idea of Max and her being married hadn't actually entered her head. But now the subject had been brought up

170

Merry considered it briefly, and then dismissed it. A Pisces and a Scorpio? It would be murder. With neither of them ever giving in? It was great in bed, and great out of it, as long as it was an affair. Because half the fun of an affair, it seemed, was doing battle. Enjoying what Max called a duel in the middle of life's great battle. But if they ever were to get married the duelling, with its thrusts and its parries and its scores, that would all stop. And change into fighting.

At least that was the line of reasoning Meredith chose to follow. Because the more time they spent together the more obvious it became that Max most certainly wasn't thinking along those lines.

Meredith once mentioned something about being uncertain as to how she could ever repay him.

'By becoming a star,' Max replied, without even looking up from the script he was reading. 'How do you think?'

'It could be ages before that happens, Max. If at all.'

'No ifs, Merry. When, maybe. But no if about it.'

'But supposing it does take an age, Max?'

'Who cares? I'm not in the loan business. The risk I've taken, I took on my own behalf. And in the meantime, you mean you're not enjoying yourself?'

'I was thinking of you, Max.'

Max stopped reading and looked up.

'I'm fine.'

Then he returned to his reading.

Perhaps that's all he did need to make him content, Merry thought as she lay beside him in bed that night. Perhaps that's all he wanted for her and from her, to become a star. For the magic to happen to her, and then that would be that. Everything else would take care of itself. Because to Max, brought up from birth in the business, stardom took care of everything. Once you were a star, there was nothing more that could happen to you. Once you were a star, you had the secret of the world. Once you were a star, you were fixed. You were a mark. Once you were a star there was no going back.

Maybe that was the most you could ever want for anyone.

*It's not often nowadays that I meet an actress with more to
say for herself than the famous symbol of the Gainsborough
lady so beloved of British pictures. But MEREDITH
BROWNE is an exception. For not only is she beautiful,
but she has something to say too.*

*'Dotty, I knew nothing,' she told me, 'you know how it is
when you grow up in the business?'*

*'I do indeed, my dear,' I agreed, remembering just what
a big star this luscious titian-haired five foot sevener was
as a child.*

*'After a childhood spent in movies I was determined to
get myself an education. And I did. I worked really hard,
paying for private lessons, visiting art galleries and
museums. There's nothing I don't know nowadays about
eighteenth-century art history, I can tell you. I've missed
out on some real opportunities because of it, but I don't
regret it one bit. I honestly think I've become a far, far
deeper actress now, benefit of being away from the business
and being able to view it from afar. I even know who
painted the Gainsborough Lady,' she added laughingly.*

*In my opinion this delightful young actress has only one
way to go, and that's up. And with young agent-about-
town, Max Kassov, controlling her ascent my bet is there is
one British star that the Yanks won't be able to match.*

One day, weeks later, just after Meredith had returned from Jeannie Costelow's, Max rang her to say he'd found the play. At first Meredith wasn't sure she knew what he meant.

'You mean one you've lost?' she asked.

'One I've lost!' Max laughed. 'A play I've found for you!'

'Is that where you've been?' Meredith asked him, because she hadn't seen or heard from him in three days. 'Touring the provinces?'

'The provinces?' Max roared. 'I've been to Broadway!'

That was Max. He hadn't even told her he was going to America. But the reason he hadn't told was that if he'd had to come back empty-handed, he wouldn't have had to tell her that either. He blew her a kiss down the phone and said he was sending a copy round for her to read at once. It was basically a two-hander, and, he assured her, like the famous dress he'd bought her recently, it might have been tailor-made for her.

It could well have been tailor-made for anybody, was the conclusion Meredith reached after her first long and laborious read-through of the play. Because she could make neither head nor tail of it. Whenever she had done a play before, Louis had read it for her, told her what it was about, and what her part was like. Meredith had never had to draw her own conclusions on some known or unknown author's piece of work. Sometimes even as the play was running she would have been hard pressed to write a comprehensive synopsis of the plot. She was always word-perfect in her own scenes. But what the other actors were doing and saying while she was offstage was of no interest to Meredith whatsoever.

Max put it down to all those early films, where as a child star she had just had to learn her scene, parrot it, and then go home to learn the next day's scene.

'But that won't do now, sweetheart,' he told her when she asked him for guidance. 'If you're going to be a leading lady, you're going to have to understand what you're doing.'

'But I can't, Max!' Merry argued. 'I can't follow the story!'

Max took the playscript from her and flicked through it. Meredith had carefully ringed all her speeches, and underlined the cue lines of the preceding ones. Max grinned and then tossed the script back at her.

'Of course you'll never follow the story if you just read your own speeches, you idiot!' he laughed. 'You got to read the whole thing! Stage directions and all!'

'Stage directions?' Meredith frowned. 'Those are for the director, surely?'

'No, they are not just for the director, you klutz!' Max replied. 'They're for the bloody actors as well! Writers work just as hard on their stage directions, you know, as they do on their dialogue! And yet the bloody actor comes along and refuses to read them! And it's not only bloody actors, Merry, I can tell you! I've even known some directors who deliberately ignore them! With the grandiose excuse that reading them will impair their own vision of the play! As if they'd written it! Now, sit down and read it, sweetheart, from first to last word, like it was a book. Even a child of ten could understand that play!'

Meredith had long ago stopped being stung when it came to people telling her how to do her job. Long ago, when she had realized she couldn't be a child star for ever, she had swallowed some of her pride and resolved to shut up and listen when her elders and so-called betters in the business started holding forth, because she reckoned that however much nonsense they talked, somewhere along the line there would here and there be some good and useful home truths. And now, much as she'd like to kick Max up the backside for the way he was laughing at her, and shaking his head as if she was the village idiot, she knew she had to learn how to read a play properly and efficiently. She knew it was going to be an essential part of her armoury, so that when she could afford the luxury of turning a play down, and when some pompous ass of a director wanted to know why exactly, she could tell him.

So, instead of kicking Max up the backside, she kissed him and thanked him for his help. Then she took herself off to bed and proceeded to read the script from cover to cover. Shortly before dawn the next morning, after she had read the play slowly and thoroughly and at least four times, she woke Max up and thanked him properly.

'What are you doing?' Max gasped as they finished making love and rolled slowly apart to lie on their backs and stare at the ceiling. 'Are you trying to make me old before my time?'

'That was for the play, Max,' Merry told him. 'It's terrific.'

'You'll bet it is,' Max replied. 'It's terrific, and you'll be terrific in it. All we need to get you now is a great leading man.'

This seemed to take a lot longer than it should have taken, at least to Meredith it did. In her naïvety, she had thought that anyone Max decided to offer the play to would leap at the chance to star in a new two-handed comedy with, as Max now described her, the hottest whisper in the business. But the first half-dozen leading men on the list all refused, some of them reluctant to star with an unknown, however hot the whisper, the others because they were wary of sharing the bill with Max Kassov's lay. Naturally Max relayed none of this to Meredith. Whenever she asked how the casting was getting along, he would simply reply 'bloody actors', and turn the conversation to the latest scurrilous piece of backstage gossip. And if Meredith persisted with her enquiry, Max would tell her not to worry and concentrate on learning her part.

'Remember what Coward said,' he told her. 'He insisted every actor should be word-perfect before they even sat down for the first read-through. So learn it. Forget all that

175

method shit. Learn the words the author wrote, and the rest will follow. Why shouldn't it? You're beautiful. And talented. And have got the greatest arse I've ever seen on anyone.'

Nevertheless, despite Max's deliberately lighthearted approach, Meredith worried. She'd been around too long already to know what the wrong chemistry could do to a play. And there were one or two suggestions for her co-star floating around which made her seriously worried.

Moppet was the one who took especial delight in telling her the latest on the wire. 'Dickie Nesbitt's been offered it, Merry,' she told her one night in the interval. 'And he's out front.'

That was enough for Meredith. The rest of that evening's performance was a nightmare. She'd heard such terrible things about Nesbitt that when she went back · onstage for the second act she was almost inclined to give the worst performance she possibly could in order to deter him. But unfortunately the audience that night was a particularly good one, and Meredith was too much of a pro to squander a good audience. Also she had just found out, at the eleventh hour and no thanks to Moppet, that James Francis, the director of her new play, had decided to look in that night on Act Two, and pay his respects to his new leading lady.

So Meredith had to be good, and she was good. At one point she managed to glance down at the front row where Jimmy Francis was sitting and she could see his big white face wreathed in happy smiles. She also noticed to her surprise, but not to her displeasure, Dickie Nesbitt making a rather unanonymous exit halfway through the act.

Max brought Jimmy Francis backstage afterwards, and he embraced Meredith to him as if he had known her all his life, instead of barely two weeks. 'Darling,' he sighed, holding her against his over-large stomach, 'no, darling, you were *marvellous*. I'm no great fan of the author, in fact I think the play's shit, but no – you were simply *marvellous*.'

'I don't think Dickie Nesbitt would agree with you,' Meredith said, disentangling herself and wondering how she was going to cope with three weeks of rehearsals with a man who had such terrible halitosis. 'I saw him leaving rather noisily halfway through the act.'

'No, no, darling,' Jimmy said, mopping his ferociously sweating brow. 'No, I talked to him in the interval, darling, and he thought you were *marvellous*. No, no, he said he was leaving early because he's filming tomorrow at sparrows'.'

'Why are you so worried abut Dickie Nesbitt?' Max asked over dinner afterwards. 'Who's Dickie Nesbitt?'

'Just someone who you offered the play to, Max,' Merry replied. 'As if you didn't bloody know.'

'I never heard of Dickie Nesbitt,' Max said and signalled the waiter over.

'It's just as well, Max,' Meredith said. 'When they did *Lovers* together, he made all Chrissie Gale's hair fall out.'

'No no, that's not what I heard, darling,' Jimmy said, dropping sauce all down the front of his old Marks and Spencer's jumper. 'No, I heard poor Chrissie's hair all fell out because she'd lost her bottle.'

'Because of playing opposite Dickie Nesbitt,' Meredith insisted.

'No, no, darling,' Jimmy persisted. 'Poor Dickie got a hiatus hernia because of playing opposite Chrissie. Whom rumour has it they had nightly to push onstage.'

'Don't pay any attention, Meredith,' Max said, taking her hand under the table. 'Because you needn't. Because I have got your leading man.'

'You have?' Meredith asked.

'No, you haven't?' Jimmy Francis echoed.

'Who is it, Max?'

Max grinned, at Meredith, and at the timing of the waiter who had produced the champagne at the perfect moment.

'Craig Matheson,' he announced.

'Craig Matheson?' said Meredith.

'Good God,' said Jimmy Francis.

'Craig "Hello-In-There" Matheson,' laughed Max. 'And if you're asking me if that's good. I'll tell you it's terrific. Because not only is Craig Matheson the flavour of the month, thanks to his big hit TV series, *Hello In There*, but even better—'

The waiter uncorked the champagne.

'Even better,' Max continued, 'I've just signed the bastard up!'

It had all seemed so good, Meredith reflected some weeks later. It had all seemed so auspicious. The new hit comedy from Broadway, starring the most popular light comedian on television at the time, teamed with the girl tipped as the most likely to succeed; both with their names above the title, not one above and one below the other, but side by side, equally billed. Certainly there had been a dispute as to who got the number one dressing-room, and Meredith could see Craig Matheson's point of view that he was entitled to it because he had starred in the West End on two previous occasions, both times with his name above the title. But Max assured him, publicly, that he knew Craig Matheson to be a gentleman, and Craig Matheson withdrew his demand. Nonetheless, he made it part of his contract that when they came into town the number two dressing-room should be refurbished up to the same standard as the number one dressing-room, and that the two doors should be numberless.

'He can't be serious,' Meredith quizzed Max the evening he told her the news.

'Abble-dabble,' Max replied enigmatically.

'What do you mean, Max, abble-dabble?'

'Bloody actors' abble-dabble, that's what I mean, Meredith Browne. They've always got to kvetch about something.'

'Even so, I don't see the point in giving me the number one dressing-room, Max, if there's no number on the door.'

'Don't start, Meredith. Because it doesn't matter. It's just a bit of sparring. Bloody actors' abble-dabble. Just learn your lines and get on with it. And don't worry about the number. Everyone will know it's the number one dressing-room, because I'll have a bloody great star painted on it.'

The following night, Max took them all out to dinner. Meredith had never met Craig Matheson, although she had seen him once or twice on television on the few occasions when she wasn't working. She had never caught his latest show because she'd been in the West End.

So she knew what he looked like: fair, curly-haired, with an almost angelically baby face, and a quick-fire delivery. She knew nothing of his reputation, other than that he was a perfectionist. When she shook hands with him in the restaurant he smiled at her, when they sat down at table he joked with her, joined forces with her in a series of teases against both Max and Jimmy, and regaled them way past midnight with hilarious stories of his television series. And when they left he helped Meredith into her fur coat and after kissing her on both cheeks, told her how much he was looking forward to them working together.

Max didn't have to ask her what she thought of him when they got back to her flat. Meredith told him in bed and without words.

'You're the most wonderful man in the world, Max Kassov,' she told him much, much later. 'You're a fantastic lover, a brilliant agent and an inspired producer.'

'That's what I call good bill matter,' Max murmured in reply. 'With credits like that, I'd sign me up.'

Rehearsals started the following Monday, in a no-longer-used morgue off the North Circular Road. Meredith was well accustomed to working in odd places, but there was something particularly depressing about rehearsing a comedy in a place where they used to lay out dead bodies. Max just laughed when Merry remonstrated with him, and said he hoped it wasn't prophetic. It didn't seem to worry

179

anyone else. There was still one of the actual old marble slabs in the room where they were rehearsing, and the stage staff had utilized this to lay out the coffee and biscuits.

'I don't think that's very appropriate,' Meredith remarked, with a shudder.

'Why not?' Craig Matheson asked, lighting a small cheroot.

'I just don't,' Merry replied. 'It gives me the creeps.'

'Really?' Craig said, nodding thoughtfully. 'It doesn't bother me at all. But then my father was a mortician.'

Jimmy Francis actually found it funny, and made a lot of camp jokes about corpsing and stiffs. Meredith joined in the laughter although she felt uncomfortable, as she thought Jimmy was obviously doing his bit towards lessening the tensions which always precede rehearsals.

'No – right! Shall we read then everyone, please?' Jimmy called, clapping his fat hands together once. 'Let's have a little read, shall we? And find out exactly how deep a hole we're in.'

Meredith laughed at this as well, thinking it to be another of Jimmy's jokes and, settling herself at one end of the table, she opened up the brand-new folder with her name embossed in gold letters on the cover which she had bought especially for the occasion. As she did so, she became aware that Craig had already taken Jimmy aside to point out and discuss certain passages of the play. At one moment during their confab, Jimmy looked up from his script with a worried look on his face and caught Meredith's eye. He at once changed the look of unabashed concern into an unconvincing smile.

'No, good!' Jimmy called, as he sat down at the head of the table. 'Good, everybody! Jolly good! But just before we start charging through, I might as well give you these few cuts, and one or two changes that have been made, to save you the bother of reading them.'

Jimmy then proceeded to itemize the few cuts and changes. It took him over an hour. And the part most affected by the cuts and changes it seemed to Meredith was hers.

She asked Jimmy who had authorized these cuts.

'We all have, love,' he answered blandly, wiping some coffee from his chin with a grey handkerchief. 'Why?'

'Because it just seems to me that I'm the person who's suffering most by them, Jimmy, that's why,' Meredith said. 'And I don't understand what you mean by "we all have". Nobody told me.'

'No – oh dear,' Jimmy replied with a very good worried frown. 'Well, the thing is, love, we only made them last night. And although it might seem a little brutal now, love, actually when you come to play it, you'll see your part has actually been enhanced by the changes. Refined really. Yes, better, your part has really been refined. Right, Craig?'

Jimmy looked to Matheson for reassurance, but Craig simply smiled back at him and lit another cheroot.

They then read through the play. But the last-minute changes meant that Meredith was no longer word-perfect. In fact she floundered dreadfully, trying to make sense of speeches she had committed to memory, but which had now either been totally expunged, or cut from ten lines to two. Last night when she had read the play out loud with Max for the last time, she had her part off perfectly. Now she could make no sense of it at all.

Craig Matheson didn't help much either. He made no attempt whatsoever either to characterize or inflect his part. No trace of the famous quick-fire delivery. He simply read it all out in a rather flat monotone, which at times was practically inaudible. The only time he betrayed any interest in the piece at all was when Meredith fluffed a line, or misinterpreted a speech, when he would pause before reading his next lines and look at her in puzzled surprise.

'You're a big girl now,' Max said when she related the events of the day to him later. 'You can look after yourself.'

'I may be a big girl now, Max,' Merry replied. 'And of course I can look after myself. But this is this big girl's biggest chance. And she doesn't want it screwed up by her co-star and director.'

'You worry too much,' said Max, picking up his copy of *Variety*. 'Actors.'

Jimmy Francis also told her she was worrying too much.

'No, stop it, love,' he directed her at the end of the first week. 'No, stop looking so *worried*. This is a romantic comedy, Merry, set in laughter land. Not some boring bloody BBC2 drama set in a cancer ward!'

But Meredith was finding it practically impossible not to worry. Whatever she tried was met with that look of bewilderment that Craig Matheson was famous for. She would try a new way of saying a line, and Craig would stop and frown at her. And then turn and address Jimmy Francis.

'Sorry to stop, Jimmy,' he'd call. 'But I don't quite understand what she's trying to do here!'

She. From being Meredith, Merry, Meredith sweetheart and Merry dear, she had now just become 'she', and was hardly if ever addressed directly by her co-star any more. He talked to her through Jimmy. Through fat, baggy, bad-breathed Jimmy Francis, who would listen to Matheson's litany of woes while staring at Meredith as if she was a waxwork. Then he would trundle across to where Meredith was standing friendless, and slip his arm round her waist as if they were old lovers.

'No, Craig's got a point here, Merry love,' he would explain. 'It really is so much better if you go offstage entirely during his telephone call, because, no – it adds more *tension*, love. And the audience, knowing you've just quarrelled, will be wondering when you're coming back, if at all, do you see? And then it will also leave Craig clear to do that wonderful juggling thing he does with the telephone and all that business with the flex, which, no – he would hardly do in front of you, would he? No, not if you'd just been arguing. You see, don't you, love?'

Meredith didn't, and Max wasn't interested when she asked him for his advice.

'Max – you're my agent for Christ's sake!' Meredith argued.

'I'm Craig Matheson's agent too, sweetheart,' Max replied. 'I've got him on the telephone six times a day kvetching about you!'

'About me!' Meredith yelled. 'I haven't done anything!'

'That's just what he says, Merry darling,' Max grinned. 'When's this famous new star of yours going to do something, he asks me? When's she going to produce the goods?'

'He won't let me, Max! Every time I try something, he stops rehearsals and goes into conference with that fat old pansy you hired as a director!'

'I didn't hire him, Merry. He came as a package with Craig.'

So that was it. Meredith sank into a chair and stared at the ceiling. What chance had she got now? Craig had brought along his tame director. By the time they opened in Oxford he'd have her playing the whole thing in a mask with her back to the audience.

'How come, Max?' she finally asked. 'How did anyone get that one by you of all people?'

'I wanted Craig Matheson, sweetheart,' Max replied, rolling an unlit cigar between his fingers to test its freshness. 'Craig Matheson is bums on seats. You're not. Not yet. I want people to see you. I don't want you playing to empty houses. So if Matheson wants to bring along some worn-out old director, so be it. The advances for the tour are already fantastic.'

Meredith got up from her chair and went and knelt beside Max, taking one of his hands and looking beseechingly up at him. 'He's killing me, Max,' she said. 'There's nothing left of what I wanted to do.'

'He's making you, Merry,' Max replied. 'By the time Craig Matheson's finished with you you'll be ready to kill. And that's exactly how you've got to be. If you really want to be a star. You've got to be a killer.'

183

That was Max's last word on the matter. From now on any further discussion of what was happening in rehearsals was a forbidden subject. Meredith once or twice tried to broach the matter over dinner, or in bed after they had made love, only to be met either by Max's best number one steely stare, or by him turning his back on her and falling fast asleep.

As for Meredith, she couldn't sleep for the worry. She couldn't eat either, so much so that by the time they reached Oxford preparatory to opening, she had lost more than half a stone in weight, and looked the colour of a newly laundered sheet.

Craig took Jimmy aside after the technical dress rehearsal and, while Meredith sat on a sofa onstage waiting for any notes, earwigged the director within Meredith's earshot about how dreadful she was looking. Ten minutes later she found Jimmy settling his cumbersome frame down beside her.

'We think you should see a doctor, Merry love,' he said, breathing last night's garlic all over her.

'I don't need to see a doctor, Jimmy,' Merry replied, trying to avoid the director's rancid breath, 'I'm just a little tired, that's all.'

'No – of course you are, love,' Jimmy murmured, putting his moist hand over one of hers. 'We all are. But dear Craig—'

'*Dear* Craig?' Merry expostulated.

'No, darling, dear Craig is worried about you,' Jimmy continued before Meredith could really let fly. 'I know. He's a funny old thing. But you see he only really cares, no, once we're in rehearsal this is, you see his only *real* care is getting it right. And quite rightly he doesn't want to take any chances with your health. No, we could be in for a long run with this one, you know. And Craig quite rightly says if your health can't take it—'

'There is nothing wrong with my health, Jimmy!' Meredith said sharply, removing her hand from his clammy grasp. 'I'm just over-tired and haven't been eating!'

'Bovril,' said a voice suddenly from behind her. Craig Matheson's voice. 'I beg your pardon?' Meredith asked, as icily as she could.

'Bovril, sweetheart,' Craig replied. 'A cup of Bovril three or four times a day, and a little less of the night life.'

'For your information,' Meredith said, 'I'm in bed every night by half past ten. With a mug of hot chocolate.'

'Really?' Craig enquired. 'It must have been somebody else Max has been seen with.'

Meredith rang Max from her hotel at the earliest opportunity. But there was no one at home. She banged the phone down and then went and poured herself a brandy. Normally Meredith never drank, but due to the ever-increasing strain of the last few days prior to opening, and her increasing lack of sleep, she had taken to the habit of downing a couple of large brandies in an effort to get off to sleep.

And tonight she needed a drink more than ever before. Max had only been round to her flat twice that week, and on neither occasion had he spent the night. In fact, both times he had just looked in, before dashing off to go backstage somewhere. And then where? What had he done after that? Where had he been?

She finally ran him to earth at half past two in the morning.

'Max?'

'What the hell are you doing ringing at this hour?'

'What the hell are you doing staying out to this hour?'

'I was with a client.'

'Who?'

'Does it matter?'

'Yes, Max. It does. Who were you with?'

'You won't want to hear, Meredith sweetheart.'

'Try me.'

'You've got quite enough on your mind. You open tomorrow.'

'I know when I open, Max. Are you going to be there? Or will you be going out?'

185

'Of course I'm going to be there, sweetheart. You know I'm going to be there.'

'So where were you tonight, Max?'

'I was out with a client, Merry. Now take a pill and go to sleep. Jimmy tells me you look like a ghost.'

'Craig tells me you've been seen on the town.'

'You want an agent who stays indoors watching TV?'

'Max, he told me you've been night-clubbing.'

'Jesus. Bloody actors. Of course I've been night-clubbing. I went to Danny's three times this week because I'm trying to woo Reg Rogers. You trying to tell me my business?'

'Is that where you were tonight?'

'No – no, I was at The White Elephant tonight. Now will you please put your light out and—'

'Who were you with, Max? I want you to tell me.'

'No, you don't.'

'I want you to tell me, Max.'

'I was with Craig Matheson.'

Meredith felt her blood change. Craig had driven down to London after the dress rehearsal? What for?

'What did he want, Max?'

'That you certainly don't want to know.'

'Yes I do, Max. If you don't tell me, I'll only imagine worse.'

'Then imagine. Because I'm not telling. What I am telling you is that Craig Matheson is a son of a bitch.'

And with that the line went dead. Meredith rang through to Jimmy Francis's room. The phone was answered at once, but not by Jimmy. By a boy's voice. Meredith heard Jimmy in the background remonstrating with the boy for picking up the phone, and then he came on the line himself.

'Who is this at this hour anyway?' he demanded.

'It's Meredith.'

'No – are you ill or something?'

'No, I'm not ill, Jimmy. Just—'

'You do know what time it is, Merry dear?'

186

'I'm not ill, Jimmy. I'm just curious as to why Craig found it necessary to drive all the way down to London—'

'Who told you that?'

'To drive all the way down to London to bend Max's ear.'

There was a silence, followed by a click of the tongue, followed by a sigh.

'What Craig chooses to do, Merry dear, is entirely his own business.'

'I thought you were included in Craig's business. I was told you both came as a package.'

'Meredith love. If you've just rung up to bitch me at this unearthly hour – I am busy, love. You know. Really.'

'What was Craig doing with Max Kassov, Jimmy?'

'You wouldn't want to know, even if I told you.'

Another silence.

'He's trying to get you re-cast, Meredith darling.'

He put the phone down before Meredith could ask him why. And after a moment Meredith was glad he had done so, because otherwise she might have found herself begging for further information, information which she was sure Jimmy Francis would be only too delighted to give her. Instead she went into the bathroom and washed her face in cold water, and then stared at her image in the mirror.

Why should Craig Matheson want her out, and why at this late stage? Yes, it was obvious he had decided to do everything in his power to make her life impossible since they'd started rehearsing, but if she was *that* bad surely it would have been apparent early on, and surely any move to replace her would have been made then? But if she was going to be replaced Max would have told her. Of that at least she was sure. As sure as she was that whatever happened Max wouldn't replace her. Max had bought the play for her. Max had cast her in it first. Max had got the play financed before he had even thought of casting Craig Matheson. And, most importantly, Max was in love with her.

So this just had to be part of Craig Matheson's warfare. This was his final attempt to destroy Merry's confidence so he could achieve what he had set out to do from day one, namely make a two-handed play a virtual one-hander. Well, he wasn't going to, Meredith told her white and tired reflection in the mirror. He might succeed with somebody a little newer to the game. But not with Meredith Browne. Meredith Browne had been born in the proverbial hamper.

Max was due to arrive an hour before curtain up. He had already sent a simply enormous bouquet of flowers to Meredith which arrived at lunchtime, as Meredith was busy preparing her dressing-room for the opening night. Craig was at the stage door when they arrived, and Meredith, who had ignored him all morning, made quite sure Craig knew who the flowers were from by reading the label out loud right under his nose. Craig had then followed her back down the corridor and into her dressing-room uninvited.

Meredith asked him what he wanted. And Craig told her that he wanted to give her some more notes, concerning various points he'd been considering since the final dress run.

'Not now, Craig,' Meredith said, reopening her dressing room door.

'When then?' Craig asked, blowing smoke from his cheroot just past her face.

'Never,' Meredith replied. 'Stick them up your arse.'

And then she laughed and shut the door in his face. But before the door closed right over, Meredith had time to see the look of blank astonishment on his face. He hadn't really known what he'd taken on, but now he was going to know, although Meredith wished she'd been a bit quicker off the mark. She'd been slow because she'd been too much in awe of what was happening to her. Name above the title in a brand-new comedy earmarked for the West End. She'd taken it all too much to heart, as Aunt Tam

188

would have remarked. Instead of realizing it was only another round in the constant prize fight that was the business.

No, there was no way Craig Matheson was going to get the better of her, Meredith had told herself the night before, because she'd been at it far too long. She'd been hard at it, since those dark black dawns when she'd rubbed her eyes awake as a child and staggered out half-blind with weariness into Bob's taxi, to go off to yet another full day in the studios, before returning in the evening to find her mother sick, or drunk, or both. While Craig Matheson had been growing up, the little boy favourite dandling on his mother's knee, Merry had been sitting at the kitchen table learning her lines for the next day, and getting her knuckles rapped for every mistake. As a child she had learned not to let anything or anybody throw her, not actors, not directors, not anyone. So why should she let Mrs Matheson's spoilt little bully boy throw her? There was nothing really he could do that hadn't in some form or other been done to her already.

Besides, he was so much more vulnerable than her. Meredith had worked it all out during the night. Craig Matheson needed the audience to love him. He needed that continuation of love, which he had first tasted on his mother's knee, and which had been supplied to him by his mother all through his childhood, so that by the time it was decided he should be an actor, he was addicted. The audience had become his now dead mother, and Craig Matheson would not be able to live for a minute without its adulation.

But not Meredith. She wasn't vulnerable like Craig because she didn't need the audience's love. Because no one had loved her as a child. And she had thus grown up free from the need to be loved and the dependence that love brings. It even applied to Max, whom she did love. But without whom, should he walk out of her life the very next day, Meredith knew she could survive perfectly well.

Because she had survived perfectly well before she had loved him.

And that was why Craig Matheson wasn't going to beat her, and why Meredith was going to win. In fact when the chips were down, Matheson didn't stand a chance. And Meredith reckoned that he knew it. Which was why he was fighting so dirty. Because he was frightened. Frightened for his professional life. The reason Craig had tried to depose her was because he had recognized the fact that Meredith was a star in the making.

Max had known it, too. Of course he'd known she was going to be a star, because he'd kept so patiently telling her. But Meredith now believed he also must have known that the contest taking place in the rehearsal room and about to go on tour was a one-sided affair, heavily weighted in Meredith's favour.

That's why he'd kept so cool, and teased her, and told her not to worry. He could see what Meredith then couldn't see. That she wasn't sugar and spice and all things nice. But the stuff that stars are made of.

And once she had come to those conclusions, Meredith got back into bed and slept for the first time since they'd started rehearsing for six hours without waking.

And now Max was sitting in her dressing room, smoking a cigar and signing letters on the top of his briefcase as if it was the end of yet another day in the office, instead of the biggest night of Meredith's career.

'Don't you ever get nervous?' Meredith asked him.

'What makes you think I'm not nervous?' Max replied.

'Because you're sitting smoking a cigar and signing letters as if you're back in the office.'

'You think I'd be doing this if I wasn't nervous?' Max looked up at her and grinned. 'It's like owning a really good racehorse,' he said. 'It's not a question of whether you'll win or not. It's a question of how much by.'

But Craig Matheson didn't go down without a fight. From the moment Meredith got her first laugh, exactly where she should have got her first laugh, and then, instead of sitting down as she had been directed to do, had moved just slightly upstage of him, Matheson must have known he was in trouble. But he didn't panic, because as Aunt Tam would have said, it takes one to know one. So he simply moved into line with Meredith and played back to her new position. And duly got his first laugh. But it wasn't as big as he had hoped. And this was entirely due to Meredith coming in on the laugh, and topping it by cutting her next two lines to get to her second laugh early.

And now instead of Meredith having to watch and follow what Matheson was up to, as had been the case all through rehearsals, Matheson was forced to watch and follow Meredith, in an effort to anticipate any other little changes she might try and make. Because Meredith had got in first. Meredith had named the game. And Meredith was dealing it. Craig was thrown and Meredith could see it quite plainly. And halfway through the act, the light of panic was clearly visible in his eyes.

So Meredith eased off, and played the rest of the scene as rehearsed. The laughs were coming easily now, and, as a team, they were working in near perfect harmony. But Meredith never took her inner eye off her opponent, which was how she thought of Craig. Not as her fellow actor, but as her adversary. Her visible eyes sparkled and shone, but her inner eye was steely and unwavering. Craig, on the other hand, thought the danger was past and started to grow in confidence, stretching the pauses between his double takes and slow burns to almost unbearable length in the attempt to wring more love and laughter from the audience than Meredith was getting.

And Meredith let him get away with it. He wasn't doing anything directly damaging to her; so as long as he behaved, she let him carry on. Up until the end of Act One, and even after the interval and well into Act Two. Until Craig, unable to stop himself, committed the unforgivable offence of poaching one of Meredith's best lines.

191

He took it quite simply. As Meredith opened her mouth to speak, Craig held up his hand and interrupted.

'I know what you're going to say, darling,' he said. And then said her next line.

Which brought the house down, and actually got a round.

Meredith smiled at Craig and felt the cold stab of genuine hatred. But revenge is a dish to be eaten cold, so she waited. She waited until Craig's set piece, the piece she'd been sent offstage for by Jimmy Francis, the telephone call from Meredith's character mother. The piece of business which Craig thought he'd been rehearsing in secret, but which Meredith had watched him do through a keyhole in the rehearsal-room door.

She waited onstage long after the moment she should have exited, and watched Craig's puzzled look in her direction as he mopped his brow as rehearsed and waited for the telephone to ring. Which it duly did.

And when it did, Meredith, who was standing nearer the desk than him, picked it up and answered it.

'That will be for me,' Craig ad-libbed quickly, moving to the desk and preparing to take the telephone from Meredith. Who simply put the telephone in her other hand and turned her back on him.

'Hello?' she said into the phone. 'Oh hello, darling!'

And then she turned back to Craig and smiled.

'It isn't for you, sweetheart,' she told him. 'It's for me. It's my mother.'

And she then proceeded to do the entire phone call changing the dialogue to suit her character, but incorporating all Craig's carefully and secretly rehearsed business, including the climax with the flex where it appears to get a life of its own and nearly ends up strangling the person on the phone.

It was brilliant. An inspired piece of comic invention. And it stopped the show.

And while the show was stopped and the audience

192

were still quite helpless with laughter, Meredith looked over at Craig Matheson, who had been left onstage with nothing to do while Meredith had daylight-robbed him, and winked.

Then she picked up the reins again and drove for home.

'You even won the curtain calls,' Max told her afterwards when the last of the visitors had left her dressing-room. 'You should be in opera, not light comedy.'

'Did you like the way I made it look as if he was pushing me forwards?' Meredith enquired.

'I thought for a moment he *was* pushing you forwards,' Max grinned.

'The only place Craig would have wanted to push me at that moment was under a bus, Max. I made it *look* as though he wanted me to take a single bow.'

'And I threw the rose.'

'I know, Max. I saw you. And thank you.'

Meredith kissed him.

'I've only got one note,' Max said, 'while we're on the subject of kissing. Craig shouldn't kiss you like that at the end of Act One.'

'Like what?' Meredith enquired in all innocence.

'Like he's got his tongue halfway down your throat,' Max replied. 'I don't know what he thought he was doing. It looks disgusting. He lost his audience completely at that point.'

'That wasn't his tongue, Max,' Merry grinned. 'That was mine. Look – I'll show you.'

And she took Max in front of the mirror and made him kiss her again, with his eyes open. As he kissed her, Meredith rolled her own tongue round the inside of her cheek so that it looked as if Max was French-kissing her.

Max held her away from him and stared at her in a mixture of astonishment and admiration.

'Where the hell did you learn to do that?' he asked her.

193

'Yeah,' Meredith replied in her best street cockney, with a grin. 'And wouldn't you like to know, I'll bet!'

The play was an immediate success with audiences and critics alike. By the time they reached Brighton, their third and final date before coming in, the word of mouth was so strong that as far as the box office went, it was returns only for the whole run three days before they opened.

As far as Craig and Merry's relationship went, they had reached and settled upon an uneasy truce. There was no doubt in anyone's mind whose star was in the ascendancy, but even so, the impression Merry got was that Craig had not quite yet conceded victory. Which was perfectly understandable. From her own experience of touring and coming in, even Merry knew that the leap from provincial audiences to West End ones was quantum. So Craig was playing let's wait and finally see. Craig Matheson's audience was all ready and waiting in Shaftesbury Avenue. Meredith Browne still had to make sure of hers.

But now at least they talked. And did the play as written and rehearsed. And Craig was kind enough also to offer Meredith one or two tips, which Meredith politely but firmly ignored. She was quite well aware that once she started taking advice again from Craig, she would immediately lose the ascendancy. So even if the advice was good, which it was on one or two occasions, Meredith didn't act on it, and that way kept her position one rung up from Craig on the ladder.

Oddly enough the play wasn't the unqualified success it had been in Oxford and Bath. Brighton could often be a notorious watershed for touring comedies, and on this occasion thoroughly lived up to its reputation. It was also a dangerous date as far as the profession itself went, since it was near enough to London for the business to visit in force. Which they did. And they came not to praise, but to bury. Craig Matheson's dressing-room was crowded with visitors every night after the performance, while Meredith had barely a caller.

But she would leave her dressing-room door ajar so she could catch some of the comments of Craig's camp followers as they left. They had plenty to say, and what they said they said loudly and without discretion, as if they were somewhat more than anxious for Craig's co-star to overhear their opinions.

And the verdict was, by and large, not good. The comedy hadn't 'transferred'. It was too typically brittle and Broadway. Waspish and witty, without being genuinely funny. Craig was far too busy doing his usual nothing, while the *girl*. Well. Whereas in Act One she was running away with it, by Act Two she was quite out of control. No wonder Craig was so intent on doing so little, it must be like acting with a bleeding windmill, my dear.

By the end of the first week, Meredith's dressing room was kept firmly closed. Her dresser luckily was an old hand, and had marked Meredith's card about the Brighton Expressers, as she called them.

'I remember doing Brighton with Jean Stevens' first starrer,' she told Meredith one night. 'It wasn't much of a play, but then they didn't have to be in those days. Remember? Vehicles, they used to call them. Good star vehicles. And this one was handmade for Jean Stevens. Who was being wonderful in it. Quite wonderful. Until we got here. To the Theatre Royal. And then the Expressers arrived, night after night. Like carrion crows they were, because the word was out that a new star was about to be born, and they wanted – like they always want, I'm telling you – they wanted to abort the birth.'

'But why?' Meredith had asked her. 'Why should they want to?'

'Because the business doesn't like stars, my love,' was the reply. 'They love you when you're in the ranks. When you're comrades in arms, all dreaming of your names up in lights. But the moment one of you gets to do it, gets their name above the title, and a star on your dressing-room door, then the only thing they're going to love about you after that is your obituary.'

So the Brighton run, unsettling though it was initially for Meredith, was finally the best thing that had happened to her on the tour. Because the unconcealed bitchery of her fellow professionals, instead of decreasing her self-confidence, had only increased it. Now she was quite certain Max was right. And that she was going to be a star. And that it would only be a matter of time.

Nonetheless, she took heed of the one prevailing note of criticism. Because, as Aunt Tam would forever remind all and sundry, there was never no smoke without some fire. By the end of Act Two, Meredith was running too free. Out of control was probably a little over the top, but she was certainly over- rather than under-playing. It was fine when the audience had become convulsive, as they had in Oxford and Bath. But if you weren't quite carrying them to that point of dementia, then the comedy became strained, and Meredith knew that in the last ten minutes she was pushing too hard, and she was losing the audience. While Craig was cleverly pulling back from the brink, and subsequently keeping them. The applause was still warm and generous enough at the end, although not ecstatic, but it was Craig who was getting all the backstage visiting. Not Meredith.

Max visited Brighton twice. On the second night, and the second last night. On the final visit, he sat in Meredith's dressing-room while she undressed, smoking a cigar and attending to some papers.

'I'm losing them, Max,' Merry told him.

'I know,' Max replied, without looking up.

'So help me, Max.'

'I'm not a director, sweetheart.'

'Neither is Jimmy Francis. I really need your help, Max.'

'No, you don't, sweetheart. You know what to do. You just want to hear it confirmed.'

'Fine. So confirm it.'

Max put his pen down and looked up at her, with a boyish grin.

'What do I like when we make love?' he asked her. 'No – better, what *don't* I like?'

Merry stopped wiping her make-up off and looked at his reflection in her dressing mirror.

'What don't you like? I don't know, I don't know what you don't like.'

'Yes, you do, sweetheart. Think about it.'

Merry thought about it.

'You don't like it when I make the running.'

'You got it.'

'That's what I thought.'

'Like I said, you only needed it confirmed.'

'I'm seducing the audience—'

'No, you're not. That's exactly what you're not doing. What you're doing is telling the audience they're going to get laid. Just go back to seducing them. Enticing them, but all the time you're on your back with your neck bared. Let them make love to you. They got all dressed up specially to come and spend the evening with you. The last thing they want is you taking your own clothes off and saying: Right! How do you want it! The audience wants to make love to you, sweetheart. They don't want you coming on and making love to them!'

Meredith stopped looking at Max's reflection, and turned round to face him directly.

'For those words of wisdom, Max Kassov,' she said, 'I would like to do quite unspeakable things to you. But of course I shan't. Instead I shall get dressed and let you take me back to the hotel, and allow you to do quite unspeakable things to me.'

Max grinned at her, and blew a kiss at her from the end of one elegant long finger.

'That's my girl,' he said.

Craig was totally unprepared. What he had expected to happen on opening night in London, and what he had catered for happening, simply didn't. He had thought Meredith would go a couple of notches up. He had thought Meredith would build on the size of the performance she had been giving on the tour. He had believed that, owing to her theatrical virginity, inasmuch as she had never carried a play fifty-fifty before, when confronted with the London audience, Meredith would go not just over the top but out into orbit. While he, the real star, the man with the track record, Craig Matheson, would do even less than the famous nothing, and thus assure himself of victory. Of the victory that really mattered.

Instead he lost hands down. From Meredith's first entrance, she had the audience in the palm of her hand. She even got a round when she came on, an unheard of accolade for a semi-unknown. That was almost enough to throw Craig, until he reckoned that the applause must have been started by a Max Kassov claque, and spontaneously taken up by the rest of the house.

But what happened consequently failed to confirm that theory. Meredith could do no wrong, with anybody. Craig could almost sense the audience's impatience with him during his speeches and comic business, as if they could hardly bear Meredith to be silent, or offstage. When she came back after the famous telephone call, which Craig played impeccably, the applause that rang out was for Meredith's return and not for Craig's *tour de force*. And yet it wasn't really until well into the second act that Craig could define the difference in Meredith's performance, so busy had he been concentrating on his own.

Meredith was doing nothing.

At least she was, she was acting quite superbly. But she had reduced what had been a slightly larger-than-life comedy performance, full of wide eyes, breathless gasps, and uncertainly bitten lower lip, to a perfect miniature, making herself utterly vulnerable, and utterly lovable.

And making Craig panic. For the very first time in his career, Craig Matheson lost control and, feeling the play slipping away from him, it was he who went over the top. Meredith was even sacrificing laughs in order to keep her characterization within its new bounds. But although some of the laughs she was getting were smaller, there was little doubt that they were also warmer. And they built, so that the smaller laughs she had been getting later in the play, when previously she had been going for broke, now got larger. And they were becoming laughs of recognition as the audience recognized themselves in Meredith, and identified much more personally with her seemingly insoluble dilemmas.

And Craig could do nothing. At least he could do 'nothing' no longer, and so before he realized that the laughs hadn't in fact stopped coming, but were just coming differently, he pressed the panic button and blew his own performance up in his face.

By the time the curtain fell, the battle had long since been over and the day won and lost.

'Jesus!' Craig hissed as the audience disappeared from view and the applause broke out. 'Jesus Christ Almighty!'

'I know,' Meredith whispered, smiling sweetly and coolly at his sweat-lined face. 'Wasn't it *wonderful*?'

And then the curtain rose for the first call, and the cheers started to ring out, and Meredith took Craig's sodden hand in her ice-cool one, and stepped forward into the starlight.

The notices were all for Merry. Max sent his driver off from the party to Fleet Street for the first editions, and every paper carried an unqualified rave. Meredith's performance was considered by the critics variously to have been the most warm-hearted, modest, unassuming, underplayed, understated, charming, deft, impeccable, unselfish, sincere, totally accurate, unquestionably convincing, achingly funny study in bewilderment, innocence, wonder, perplexity, naïve confusion, unpretentious marvel, artless candour and affectionate naïvety that the West End had corporately seen in a decade. She lit up the sky. She warmed the heart. She made you laugh till you cried, while making your spirits soar. She was wonderful, astonishing, astounding, marvellous, brilliant, incredible, divine, exquisite, sensational and phenomenal. A new star had last night been added to the constellation.

Craig Matheson was considered to have given her first-class support, although one or two critics opined that his performance was, for him, surprisingly wild and undisciplined.

The play was even better than it had been on Broadway, thanks entirely to Meredith Browne.

Max gave her his best told-you-so look and also a watch with tiny diamonds round it.

Meredith gave him a small gold locket. Inside it was a false eyelash, Meredith's. The one Max had kept that night as a memento, and which Meredith had stolen from his wallet in order to have it fashioned into a permanent reminder.

On the inside of the locket opposite the glass-covered lash, she had ordered an inscription. It read:

Best wishis. Merry to Max.

Max kissed the locket, kissed Meredith, and said what a pity they'd misprinted it. And Meredith smiled to herself when she saw he hadn't remembered.

Then Max turned his attention to selecting the best of the notices for putting up outside the theatre.

Just before they left the party, Craig Matheson came over and sat down beside Meredith. They hadn't spoken since the final curtain call. Now he took one of her hands in his and nodded into the distance in front of them.

'What we need now, love,' he said, 'is someone to write something especially for us.'

*CRAIG MATHESON, young West End star of hit
Broadway comedy* One Every Minute, *was looking upset –
it seemed he had lost his dresser.*

*'Bunny's been with me on all my tours, Barry love, I
can't remember my own name without him.'*

I could have told him, it was outside the theatre in lights.

*Relief all round when Bunny was discovered in the
next-door dressing-room gossiping with co-star MERE-
DITH BROWNE.*

*At last we could settle back for the interview. CRAIG,
evergreen star of TV's* Hello In There, *lit a cheroot.*

*'It's been a helluva year, love,' he told me, 'you know,
the tour, and the series, and then waking up to find that
MEREDITH had stolen the show from right under my
nose.' He laughed wryly. 'But I love her for it. It's what the
business is all about, and we so love working together
we've commissioned a comedy from the writer of* Hello In
There. *It promises to be great. He knows just how to write
for me.'*

Tentatively entitled Needless to Say Darling! *it will go
on tour next year, same cast. Must be a hit. But Craig's
going to take care not to let MEREDITH BROWNE steal
all the limelight next time.*

*'I know she's a girl, but she can't expect to have it all her
own way every time,' he joked as I left, and the now
famous Bunny passed me bearing a bowl with what he
called 'Sir's footbath'.*

5

Max grinned at William. He didn't like most writers. Most writers were a pain in the arse. Some of them were even bigger pains in the arse than bloody actors. But William was OK. William didn't take himself too seriously. Yes, he took his writing seriously. He'd have been no good as a writer if he didn't. But William still saw the funny side. William Kennedy was *hombre*.

Max selected a fresh cigar from his humidor and carefully bit off the end, while William sat the other side of his desk, swilling the ice in his glass, and staring at the remains of his drink.

'Have another drink for God's sake,' Max offered.

'I don't want one, thanks,' William replied. 'I don't usually drink at this time.'

'Jesus, William,' Max sighed. 'Every bloody writer does rewrites.'

'I'm not "every" writer, Max.'

Max knew that perfectly well. Max knew William wasn't just good, he was actually one of the best writers in town, and certainly was not a writer who did rewrites, rewrites, that was, of other people's work. But as William's agent he also knew that all William was being offered at the moment was the other sort of work William despised: screenplays for the fashionable 'instamovies' that were currently being set up and churned out in Swinging London.

'A dog can bark his head off, Willy boy,' Max said. 'But sooner or later he has to eat. Let's start again. Craig

202

wanted someone to write something especially for him, OK? So we got him someone.'

'The wrong someone,' William replied.

'Which is why I'm asking you, Willy boy.'

William swilled the ice round in his glass again before replying.

'Who do you mean by "we", Max?' he asked. 'You mean you and Meredith? Or you, Meredith and Craig?'

'This guy had been banging on at me for yonks,' Max admitted. 'Telling me how much he'd always wanted to write a stage play. And seeing he'd written Craig's last television series—'

'Co-written, I guess you mean,' William interrupted. 'Nobody gets a script past that bastard without him scribbling all over it.'

Max drew on his cigar and smiled, but more to himself than at William. Craig Matheson's reputation amongst writers was not good. Not so long ago one had even taken a swing at Craig in the television studios when he discovered during the taping of the programme the length and breadth of the actor's unsolicited alterations.

'Anyway,' Max continued, checking his cigar was properly alight. 'Like they say, it seemed like a good idea at the time. And the first act was excellent.'

'You know what they say, Max,' William replied. 'Anyone can write a first act.'

'This poor old sod has written two first acts. I tell you, watching this play – in the interval it's like changing buses. Only to find yourself back on board the one you've just got off.'

'What about the script I've just sent you?' William asked.

'It's terrific,' Max replied. 'Terrific.'

Behind his horn-rimmed glasses, William's face lit up, almost childlike.

'No kidding?'

'Straight up.'

'So, what are you offering me a rewrite for then?'

'Because, old chum, I can't do a thing with it. Nobody wants this sort of thing at the moment, Willy boy. It's too good for this town. Don't laugh! I'm serious!'

Max took the cigar out of his mouth and pointed it at William to emphasize his seriousness.

'They don't want witty, sophisticated comedy on the box! They want vulgarity! Tits! Double meanings! Jokes about ugly women! You're too good, that's your trouble, sweetheart! The English like their jokes to be about lavatories! Or failing that, people failing to get to lavatories! Sure – things will change. They always do. And when the country falls on hard times again, yes, they'll want love and romance and wit by the yard. But while they're never having it so good, in their heads they want to slum it!'

William sighed, and drained the rest of his now watery whisky. Max was right and he knew it. Everything William had tried to set up and sell recently had been met with a lukewarm response. Everyone agreed he was a good writer. Everyone wanted the chance of working with him. But nobody wanted to work on the sort of thing William wanted to write. Things had got so bad he was even considering going back to America. At least in America they showed reruns of the Burns and Allen show. The goddam English hated wit. Even the merest sniff of it sent them running from the theatres crying American smart-arse.

Nonetheless, William held out. Max tried everything. From charm to bullyboy tactics. But William remained unmoved.

'It's a one-way ticket, Max,' he said, rising. 'And once they find out I'm play-doctoring—'

Max tapped the ash of his cigar and nodded.

'You're right,' he said, suddenly agreeing. 'I don't know what I can have been thinking of. Ring me later in the week, and I'll try and have news of your script.'

William nodded and went. Max waited until he was out of the room, then pressed his intercom.

204

'Sweetheart?' he said to his secretary. 'Get me Jay Burrell on the phone. And now.'

Jay wasn't in when William got back to the studio. William threw his newspaper in a chair and went to put the kettle on. He hated it when he came home and Jay was out. It was as if he was only half alive when she wasn't there. Anyway, dammit, she was supposed to be writing. So where was she?

She'd left a message though. On the blackboard by the kitchen telephone she chalked the one word 'Wow!'

Wow what? William wondered? Wow good? or wow bad?

'Wow fantastic!' Jay told him, when she returned and after William had hugged her and kissed the breath out of her.

'I'll bet you say that to all the writers you sleep with,' William teased.

'You should know,' Jay retorted, producing a bottle of champagne.

'I know this scene!' William said suddenly. 'This is when we discover you're having a baby and don't know whether to laugh or cry.'

'Guess who rang when you were out?' Jay asked him. 'Max.'

'What did he want? I was just with him.'

Jay smiled and put her arms round William.

'The most wonderful thing you could imagine, William,' she said. 'He wants me to rewrite this play.'

Even after a good night's sleep, induced by a particularly inspired session of love-making, William still couldn't work out how it had happened. At every turn he had said no. First he had said no to Jay working on the play for what he thought were ethical reasons. Then he had said no because he really didn't think it was the sort of thing Jay should be doing either. Then he had said no because even if it had been an all-right thing for her to do, he wasn't going to have her talent mauled about by the likes of Craig

Matheson. And then he had said no because from the sound of it the job wasn't exactly suited to Jay's talents anyway, and she'd be going down the market to do it, not up. And if she really wanted to write plays and scripts, it would be far better for her to start in her own right, and not as some poor unfortunate other writer's play-doctor.

And then he had said no because he was jealous of her being asked to do it, even though he himself didn't want the job. And then Jay had said, after a fairly heated discussion, that he had one or two points, but not them all, but even so how about this for an idea? Why didn't they work on it together? Whereupon William started to get stuck into the Scotch and said that was possibly the worst idea he had ever heard. And Jay asked him why? And William got further stuck into the Scotch because he couldn't think of a reasonable answer, and while he fell silent, Jay became more and more persuasive, reminding William about all the great boy and girl scriptwriting teams which had preceded them, and what fun it would be to form a new one, as a kind of homage to those who'd gone before them. Besides which, they both enjoyed exactly the same sort of comedy, and admired the same sort of actors, and loved exactly the same films and plays and everything, so what had they got to lose?

To which William replied their separate identities.

Which was when Jay produced all the household bills she'd carefully been hiding.

Even so, the next morning, William still couldn't remember the exact point at which he had surrendered.

'I must have been drunk,' he told Jay over breakfast.

'We were both a bit drunk,' Jay replied. 'So that doesn't change anything. Now I'm going out to the shops. Is there anything you want?'

'What are you going out to the shops for?' William asked.

'To buy some pencils,' Jay said, sighing happily. 'To buy some pencils, and erasers, and notepads, and notebooks, and everything else we'll need.'

'Don't forget some brain food for the muse!' William called out after her as she left.

They read the play for the umpteenth time on the train up to see it performed in Manchester.

'Actually it's not all *that* bad,' Jay said with a frown during one of the train's many siding stops. 'Some of it's quite funny.'

'Educate me,' William replied.

'That joke about her cooking's quite funny.'

'It's a "like" joke. Never write "like" jokes. Similes are the impoverished writer's jokes.'

'The run about her hair. That made me laugh.'

'It's not organic.'

'What do you mean by organic, William? You mean her hair's not organic?'

'I mean the comedy doesn't grow out of the action. The run about her hair's dragged in, it doesn't belong. Which is why I'll bet anything you like it's not getting a laugh.'

'You must have liked the scene where she gets dressed, surely? Or rather the scene where she doesn't get dressed?'

'I've seen it one and a half million times, in some form or another. The scene would be funny if it were *he* who couldn't decide what to wear.'

'You're very strict, William.'

'You betcha.'

'I think you're also very right.'

'Even more you betcha.'

'Still,' Jay smiled a little bleakly. 'It's not *all* that bad.'

'It's a crock of the proverbial,' William answered.

Unfortunately, nothing finally could dull Jay's enthusiasm. She was as excited as hell not only about rewriting a play, but about working in the live theatre, with real live actors. And not just actors, but stars.

'The stars are in the heavens, Jay,' William would sigh at her. 'The only stars you'll see are the ones in your eyes.'

'You're as bad as Max,' Jay would retort. 'When I was

working for Max, that's exactly how he would go on. Bloody actors, he'd say. It was always bloody actors this and bloody actors that.'

At which William would simply sigh and give her his best just-you-wait-and-see look.

The trouble was Jay could hardly wait. Despite William's stories on the journey up about actors measuring each other's billing outside the theatre with tape measures, and putting little sharpened pins in the top of each other's make-up sticks, and gluing down each other's props onstage, Jay couldn't wait to get backstage and meet the cast.

The first person she met was one of the supporting players, Jon Partridge, a tall, razor-thin man with a crinkle of sandy hair. He had bright sparkling blue eyes, and an immaculate way of dressing.

'I say,' he said when he was introduced to her by Jimmy Francis who was once again directing. 'I think I'm rather going to look forward to being doctored by you!' Then he squeezed her arm and gave what Jay later came to describe as his clubman's laugh, before wandering off to his dressing-room with one arm round the understudy.

Craig was the next to be presented. He was both courteous and funny, and left William silent for once.

'You're just cantankerous, William,' Jay said as they followed the director down the passage towards the number one dressing-room. 'He couldn't have been sweeter.'

'No, Craig's frightfully misunderstood,' said Jimmy. 'No, all he really cares about, you see, is getting it right. To me, you see, that's a true pro.'

Then he knocked on Meredith's door.

Jay was quite staggered by how beautiful Meredith was offstage, let alone on. She wasn't exactly dressed to kill when they met either, since she was in her rehearsal clothes, with her long auburn hair tied up on top of her head in an old scarf. But she had the most perfect

208

complexion Jay thought she had ever seen on anyone and a bone structure that defied description.

And of course her figure was already the stuff of legends.

'We've been dying for you to arrive,' she said in her now famous husky voice, extending a perfectly manicured hand rather regally to be shaken by William. 'We really are in the shit, darling.'

'It's going to be marvellous,' Jay enthused, as William and she walked back in the rain to their hotel.

'What is, Mary Poppins?' William asked.

'This is, William! Working on this play!' Jay replied. 'I can't believe it's all actually happening! It's like a dream!'

'You said it,' William agreed. 'So why don't you pinch us both? And with a bit of luck we might wake up.'

But nothing shook Jay's enthusiasm. William was cynical, but then William was thirty.

'What's so marvellous,' Jay continued over what William described as the worst dinner he'd had since his schooldays, 'is to be able to help someone like Meredith.'

'It's still not too late for you to become a brain surgeon, Jay,' William replied.

'We're going to make this play into a smash hit,' Jay said, quite ignoring him.

'Stop trying to paint everything white, Jay. Not everyone can live in goddam perfectly painted white houses.'

'I don't see why not,' Jay argued, returning to an old bone of contention. 'It's only because people can't be bothered.'

William sighed.

'And do stop sighing, William,' Jay scolded. 'This could be the most wonderful opportunity.'

'What for?' William asked. 'Having a major nervous breakdown? Or ageing prematurely?'

'You wait,' Jay said. 'Just wait till you see what we can do.'

The tune changed slightly after they'd been to the theatre and seen the show.

'You were right about the bit with the hair,' Jay said over drinks in the interval. 'It's embarrassing.'

'Because it isn't organic.'

'I went red all over.'

'What about the new bits? That new scene with the best friend?'

'I didn't understand that business with the cards.'

'He was doing a conjuring trick.'

'Why?'

'God knows.'

'And what happened to the best friend's character in the scene before the interval, William? When he tries to blackmail Craig? It was just silly.'

'That was meant to be funny.'

'I didn't hear anyone laughing.'

'Is there anyone else here?'

William looked round the almost deserted stalls bar.

'Anyone that's still alive, that is,' he added.

During the second act, the man in the row behind them, the only man, stretched out over two seats, fell asleep and snored until the end. Meanwhile a couple of old ladies in the row in front talked at the tops of their voices about how much better television was than this rubbish, before tipping up their seats and leaving as noisily as possible.

In one of the stage-side boxes, Jimmy Francis sat looking like a beached whale, but braying like a donkey at all the supposed jokes. His misplaced loyalty was rewarded by a series of filthy looks from both Craig and Meredith.

Long after the curtain had fallen, William and Jay were to be found still sitting in their seats.

'We're going to have to face the music sometime,' William told her.

'I don't know what to say,' Jay muttered. 'And I don't know what I'm going to say either.'

'Tell them they were lovely,' William said, getting up and yawning. 'And that you don't know how they did it.

That's all any actor wants to hear. Whatever you do, don't mention the play.'

'But that's the whole purpose of us being here!' Jay protested. 'To work on the stupid thing!'

'They are actors, Jay Burrell,' William replied. 'These people are actors. Not human beings.'

They looked in on Craig Matheson first.

'Not much of a house,' he said, in between brushing his teeth over the sink. 'There's been sod all publicity, you know.'

'You were very funny, Craig,' William said, accepting a paper cup half-full of warm white wine. 'I don't know how you did it.'

'We've been up here a week, you know,' Craig grumbled. 'And no one's asked me to open anything.'

'That's disgraceful,' William replied.

'How do they think they're going to get people into the theatre? That's what I want to know, sunshine. If no one knows I'm here, they're not going to come and fucking well see me, are they?'

'Good point.'

William nodded and looked into his drink. Craig turned his attention to Jay, looking at her as if he'd only just realized she was there.

'Well?' he said.

Jay frowned as deeply as she could, to indicate concern.

'Absolutely,' she agreed. 'If nobody knows that you're here—'

'Too right,' Craig interrupted. 'They're not going to fucking come and see me, are they?'

William and Jay walked in solemn silence down the ill-lit corridor to the number one dressing room. William cleared his throat and knocked on the door.

'Who is it?' said the now famous husky voice.

'William and Jay!' William answered.

'Who?' the husky voice enquired.

'William Kennedy and Jay Burrell. The writers!'

'Lovely! Come on in, darlings!'

211

William opened the door and stepped aside to let Jay in. Jay took a step inside the door then stopped dead. William crashed into the back of her.

Meredith was standing facing them, stark naked. And washing herself down with a sponge. Her magnificent body glistened with the sheen of soap as she worked the sponge round her perfect firm breasts.

'Sorry,' said Jay, trying to back herself out but running into the still stationary William.

'Do shut the door, William,' Meredith said with a total lack of concern. 'Unless you want me to die of pneumonia.'

William closed the door behind him and stood staring at a wall. Jay, with her back now turned on Meredith, stood staring at William.

'I asked for a shower, you know,' Meredith informed them. 'I don't know how I'm expected to run around out there like a demon, and then come back here and dry myself off like a race horse.'

'Too many similes,' Jay muttered at William.

'You'd think the least they could have done was install a bloody shower,' Meredith concluded.

'Not much of a house,' William essayed, after a moment's thought.

'And whose fault is that, do you think?' Meredith asked.

'No publicity, I'll bet,' said William.

'Oh, there's publicity all right,' disagreed Meredith. 'But it's all for Craig. You'd think I'd never been born.'

'It's understandable though,' William argued, 'because isn't he from round these parts?'

'Like hell,' replied Meredith, from the sound of things now towelling herself off. 'Craig Matheson was born in Chepstow. He just talks like that because it's bloody well fashionable. We've been up here a week, you know, and nobody's asked me to open anything.'

Jay bit her lip and tried as resolutely as she could not to look at William's poker face because it almost made her worse.

'And of course nobody'll come and see you, will they?' Jay managed finally to say. 'I mean not if they don't know you're here.'

'Darling – you don't know just how right you are,' Meredith replied, now from the sound of it pulling on her panties. 'That's precisely what I was saying to Craig in the interval.'

William and Jay sat in silence in their hotel room. It was well past midnight. William was surrounded with a lot of thin strips of paper he had carefully torn from an old magazine, and Jay was confronted by a dressing table arrayed with a row of twelve perfectly sharpened pencils.

Finally, round about a quarter to one, William put both his hands behind his head and spoke.

'Well,' he announced. 'I wouldn't know where to start.'

Jay nodded in glum agreement, but said nothing. Because she had nothing to say. Instead she took the last pencil from the end of the row on the left and promoted it to being first pencil on the end of the row on the right.

'We could start at the beginning,' Jay said, pulling her long braid of hair over her shoulder preparatory to chewing the end of it. 'We could start at the beginning, then go on until we come to the end, and then stop.'

William nodded.

'That's not as funny as you think, Jay,' he sighed. 'Because I'm afraid that's exactly what we're going to have to do.'

'That bad eh, partner?'

'That bad, partner. And then some.'

Jay started in on the end of her hair, and then demoted the second pencil from the end of the row on the right down to being the second pencil from the end of the row on the left.

William tore some more strips of paper from his magazine.

After another five minutes of strip-tearing and hair-chewing there was a sudden and, although surprising, welcome knock on their door.

213

'Are you awake?' said the now famous husky voice.

'Yes!' Jay called with a what-do-you-make-of-this look at William. 'Just about!'

The door half opened and Meredith's head appeared.

'Can I come in?'

'Of course.'

Jay got up and pulled a chair round for their visitor. William nodded a welcome.

'Hi,' he said, offering her a strip from his magazine. 'Like a piece of paper?'

Meredith smiled and, tossing her mane of hair back carefully, sat down opposite them both.

'Look, I won't keep you,' she said, 'because I really should be in bed. But I thought I'd better mention what some people think is wrong with Act Two.'

Jay leaned forward. At last a clue. A message from the front line.

'That would be interesting,' William agreed. 'What is it that some people think is wrong with Act Two?'

Meredith bit her lip while carefully considering whether or not to go through with it. Then she put both hands behind her ears and stroked out her long mane of hair.

'The hat,' she announced.

'The hat,' William repeated.

'The hat,' Meredith confirmed.

'The hat you wear in Act Two?' Jay asked just to make quite sure.

'Of course,' Meredith replied. 'Craig says it's killing the comedy.'

William thought about it, while tearing another strip of paper out.

'And that's what some people think's wrong with Act Two?' he said.

'Ridiculous, isn't it?' Meredith laughed.

'I find it somewhat absurd,' agreed William.

'I like that hat,' Jay said stoically. 'I think it's a great hat.'

'Thank you,' Meredith said, rewarding Jay with a dazzling smile. 'You're sweet.'

214

'No, really,' Jay continued. 'I love the hat.'

'You really are sweet,' Meredith assured her. 'But I'm afraid Craig is convinced it's killing his laughs.'

William nodded, and so did Jay, uncertain now whether or not they were expected to continue the discussion. William had obviously concluded there was no need, because he had returned to tearing more strips out of the magazine.

'I just thought I should tell you,' said Meredith, coming to Jay's rescue. 'Because I thought it might be of some help.'

'You're right,' Jay replied. 'Because it is.'

The phone suddenly rang beside William.

'Yes,' William said, answering it.

'This is Craig,' a voice said in his ear. 'I hope I haven't got you at a bad time.'

'You've got me at a bad time,' William replied. 'Because it's not a good time. If it was a good time, I'd be full of ideas and working. And if you'd called me then, and I'd been flowing, then that would have been a bad time.'

Jay smiled vacantly at Meredith, hoping she couldn't hear as well as Jay could precisely who was on the phone.

'I really should be in bed,' Craig said, 'but I think I know what's wrong with Act Two. And I think it might help if you knew.'

'I know,' William said. 'I know what's wrong with Act Two.'

'The hat,' Craig hissed. 'It's that bloody hat.'

'No, it isn't,' William replied.

'I tell you it is, sunshine. Nobody's looking at anything else! Nobody's looking at what I'm doing!'

'Nobody's looking at what you're doing, because you're not doing anything very interesting.'

Meredith smiled and gave one nod of triumph to Jay.

'And the reason you're not doing anything interesting is because your character hasn't been given anything interesting to do. Neither has Meredith's. Which is why she's found it necessary to come on in that hat.'

Meredith's smile turned to a frown of concern.

She looked to Jay but now it was a look for reassurance.

'William's right,' Jay found herself saying. 'It's not your fault. But William's right.'

'So what do *you* think's wrong with Act Two, sunshine?' Craig asked defiantly.

'Act One, basically,' William answered.

'Yes?' said Craig, a little less belligerently. 'And what do you think's wrong with Act One then?'

'Oh, that's easy,' William yawned. 'What's wrong with Act One is Act Two.'

By the time they had got to rehearsals the next morning, it had been decided to go for a total rewrite. Or rather it had been decided between William and Jay to go for a total rewrite. Jimmy Francis wasn't so sure.

'Yes, but I'm sure that's not what the trouble is, loves,' he told them, stuffing some of the digestive biscuit which had lodged on his chin back into his mouth. 'No, I mean fair enough. If it was as simple as that, fair enough. A total rewrite – fine. But you see I don't think it's as simple as that, much as I'd like to.'

'What could be more simple than an entire rewrite, Jimmy?' William enquired. 'If we rewrite the entire play, leaving nothing of the old one, how the hell could anything be simpler?'

'Ah yes, but that's easily said, old love. But we also have to consider what Craig wants. And what Meredith wants. And what the Management want.'

'They don't want a dead body, Jimmy. Which is what you've all got. You've got a goddam stiff on your hands.'

'No – no, but will *rewriting* it be the answer? These things are all very well in theory, love. But there's many a slip, as I'm sure you well know. There's many a slip between the silly old cup and lip.'

William moved back to Jay's side as the director waddled away to try and flirt with the young male assistant stage manager, who from the appalled look in his eyes certainly wasn't having any.

216

'What was he saying?' Jay asked William in utter bewilderment.

'I haven't a notion,' William sighed. 'The man's a walking disaster.'

'You'd think he'd be pleased you'd offered him an entire rewrite.'

'Jimmy Francis bears the impression of the last man who sat on him,' William replied. 'And I'd say from the flatness of his face that last person was none other than Craig Matheson.'

By now Craig had come into the theatre and, hopping up on the stage, had buttonholed Jimmy to give him an earful. There was as yet no sign of Meredith.

'Let's go home, William,' Jay said suddenly. 'You're right. This isn't the sort of thing you should be doing.'

'We should be doing,' William corrected her. 'We're a team now, remember?'

'You shouldn't have listened to me, William. I have some of the worst ideas in the world.'

'We can't go home, Jay. Believe me, there's nothing I'd like more in the world than to tell this lot to go hang, and hightail it back to the studio. But that'll only upset Max. And that's not something I can afford to do right now. Upset Max Kassov. So I guess we're going to have to at least give it our best shot.'

William draped his long legs over the seat in front of him in the stalls, and carefully unwrapped a peppermint, which he handed to Jay.

'How come plays as bad as this actually get put on, William?' she asked, popping the sweet in her mouth.

'Because actors don't like good plays, Jay, that's why. Put an actor in a good play and there's not a lot more he can do to it. Not only that, put an actor in a good play and he might get found out. He might be seen not to be up to it. But put an actor in a mediocre play, particularly a mediocre comedy, and he can embellish it. He can bring his bagload of tricks to it, and everyone will say how brilliant he is, and won't think about the play at all. And

217

should the play be *so* bad that he can't finally do anything to it, he can just walk away from the wreckage with a shrug and say just that. "I tried, old love, but there was absolutely nothing I could do with it." Who'd be a writer? Particularly a living writer? The only person damn fool enough to be a writer is a writer.'

At that moment Meredith arrived amidst a whiff of pungent scent and, setting down a large leather duffel bag on the seat next to Jay's, looked up at the stage.

'What are those two bastards up to?' she asked. 'No good I'll bet.'

'They're trying to find out how to rewrite the play without actually rewriting it,' William told her. 'It's a bit like waiting for Moses to come back down the mountain with the tablets.'

Jimmy Francis came downstage and clapped his pudgy hands for silence.

'No, if you could all come up here, loves!' he called. 'It's time to go to work!'

They all sat down round a rather rickety trestle table, the cast with cannibalized versions of the playscript in front of them, the stage staff with their clipboards.

'Jimmy tells me you think the whole thing needs rewriting,' Craig said, opening the meeting up and staring in a deliberately provocative way at William.

'It would be a start,' William replied laconically.

'But that would mean a lot of changes, sunshine. That would mean throwing away a lot of good stuff.'

'Perhaps you'd like to be more specific, Craig. I can't say from what we saw last night I remember any "good stuff".'

'A lot of what I'm doing, sunshine. You want all that to go?' As if they were suggesting throwing out the crown jewels.

'What you're doing, Craig, is "business". What we're talking about is *text*.'

'What I'm doing is working, sunshine. All you have to do is rewrite the bits that aren't working.' With a slow burn directed pointedly at Meredith.

218

'With respect, Craig,' William said, 'my partner and I were asked up here as writers. To rewrite where necessary. You're employed as the actors. To do, if agreed, what we rewrite.'

Craig smiled round at Jimmy, a smile of complicity, the smile of an old shared joke. Jimmy returned the smile, pursing his over-red lips.

'Yes, we may just be the actors,' Craig replied with a sigh. 'But you see we're the people who have to get up here and do it, old love. You don't.'

'That's beside the point,' said William.

'That *is* the point,' said Craig.

'No, I think we should listen to what they have to say, Craig,' Jimmy interpolated. 'Because, no, there isn't any doubt that there's *something* wrong with the play.'

'We know what's wrong with the play, Jimmy,' Craig argued. 'We've already talked about it.'

William nodded at Jay and stood up.

'Where are you going, old love?' Jimmy asked in some surprise.

'Back to London, "old love",' William replied. 'You obviously don't need us any more. Now you've found out what's wrong with the play. Just take the hat off Miss Browne here—'

'Over my dead body you will!' Meredith exclaimed.

'Or don't take the hat off Miss Browne, as the case may be,' William continued. 'But since you think the hat is the sole cause of any problems, it shouldn't take too long for a crowd of grown-up people to discover what to do with it. I know what I'd do with it. But then I'm only a writer.'

There was a silence, broken only by a giggle from one of the stage staff, a half-strangled laugh which the unfortunate girl did her best to turn into a cough.

Craig lit a fresh cheroot, and blew the smoke slowly out the side of his mouth.

'So what do you suggest, sunshine?'

'I suggest my partner and I go back to our hotel room and start soaking the towels,' William replied.

Craig looked round to Jimmy. Jimmy smiled weakly and shrugged.

'No,' he said. 'I don't suppose there's any real harm in them having a go, love.'

Jay walked half a step behind William on their way back to the hotel, in deference to his seniority. It also enabled her to sneak a look in the shop windows.

'It's basically another two-hander, right?' William announced as they crossed a road. 'He needs her, she needs him. But it takes near disaster with their two best friends for them to come to their senses, that old run.'

'You said it,' Jay agreed, taking his hand. 'I get a sense of *déjà vu* at every line.'

'The main problem is, partner, besides the fact that it's a crock, the main problem is that it's a male-female play written by a male who doesn't know how to write females.'

'Which is why in Act Two Meredith is hiding under a hat.'

'It's a wonder she doesn't come on in a tank,' said William. 'I've never seen such a badly constructed role.'

By evening they had the first ten pages. By midnight the first twenty. They got badly stuck round about a quarter to three in the morning, so Jay had a bath and washed her hair, and William tore up a fresh magazine. By dawn they had an entirely new first scene.

They read it through over breakfast. It was good. In fact even though they said so themselves it was more than good. It was bloody good.

William bathed and shaved while Jay rang Jimmy with the news. From his reaction, or rather from his lack of one, it seemed he wasn't at all surprised they had written a whole new first scene in less than a day.

'He was probably expecting the whole first act,' William said as they hurried to the theatre. 'If not the entire rewrite.'

'No—' said Jimmy as he flicked through the new pages, 'I suppose what one really should do is read it.'

220

'It might help,' William agreed.

'But you've only done two copies, old love. It's not going to be that easy.'

'We only have a portable typewriter, "old love",' William informed him. 'You're lucky to get two copies.'

'Oh dear,' the director moaned, sucking his lower lip. 'This means we'll have to get it photostatted.'

William looked at Jay quite blankly, and Jay opened her eyes very widely back at him.

'In the land of the blind,' William sighed.

'Couldn't you have typed out another four or five, love?' the director enquired. 'This means we're going to have to look over.'

In the event, to read it the actors looked over each others' shoulders, and the director just sat and looked on.

And even though it was being sight-read, it was immediately apparent that William and Jay had worked wonders with the rewritten scene. Meredith's part now had definition, and a proper female point of view, and Craig's part had been honed right down so that his character was infinitely more real, besides being much quicker-witted.

Except Craig didn't think so. The more he read, the more he mumbled and fumbled, and sighed and paused. And every time he paused he looked up at Jimmy with a you-tell-me look.

When they finished, there was an embarrassed silence, broken finally by Craig Matheson.

'Yes,' he said stubbing out his cheroot. 'Well, that wasn't exactly brilliant, was it?'

'Nooo,' said Jimmy Francis, drawing the negative out for as long as he could.

'No, it wasn't,' William agreed very pleasantly. 'In fact it was terrible. So why don't we start again from the top and this time try and read it properly?'

'I'm not talking about how we read it, sunshine,' Matheson said.

'I am,' William replied.

'I'm talking about how *it* read,' the leading actor continued. 'And it read dreadfully.'

'"It" can't read by itself, Craig. "It" can only be read. Which it was. By you. Very badly. Which is why I suggest—'

'Isn't it up to Jimmy to suggest whether or not we read it again, love?'

Craig was leaning across the table to William now, his face set in determination and the veins standing out in his neck.

'I thought it was terrific,' Meredith suddenly interrupted, 'It's a hundred and fifty times better.'

'You mean your part is a hundred and fifty times better, Merry,' Craig replied. 'Mine's disappeared up its own fundamental.'

'Perhaps in the first act we should put Craig in a hat,' Jay suggested to William.

They were sitting either end of a now lukewarm bath at two o'clock the following morning, having been ordered to return to their hotel room and reinstate certain stipulated sections of the cuts in Craig's part.

'This is getting more and more absurd by the minute, Jay.'

William rubbed some soap between his index finger and thumb and blew a large bubble which floated across the bath before landing on one of Jay's firm young breasts, where it lay for a moment before silently bursting.

'This is like painting by numbers.'

It had been a terrible day, followed by an even worse evening. Both William and Jay knew the rewrites were a vast improvement on the original, yet here they were, faced with the quite impossible task of trying to dovetail into their new draft certain lines and speeches for Craig which no longer fitted in with what they were trying to write.

'It's worse than painting by numbers, William,' Jay said. 'It's like doing one jigsaw from two boxes.'

'Hmmm,' said William getting out of the bath. 'Too many "likes".'

Jay slept for two hours and only woke up when she suddenly heard the typewriter clacking away furiously. She pulled her dressing gown round her and went and looked over William's shoulder. He was working in a white heat, and actually laughing out loud, something he certainly hadn't done since they embarked on this miserable enterprise.

'I don't much like the sound of that laugh, William Kennedy,' she said.

'It's brilliant, Jay!' William replied. 'I've got the stupid bastard!'

'How?'

'By putting back most of what Matheson wants, but not in the same order, nor with the same intention! His character is taking a rise out of himself, see?'

William pointed out certain passages with his pencil.

'But Craig won't realize that! He'll take what he's saying at face value! But because of what we've now given to Meredith – it'll bring the house down!'

Jay carefully read through the second rewrite of the first scene and when she'd finished, she marvelled at William's skill. On the page it looked almost bland, although certainly Craig appeared to be the one in control of the scene. But as William had just said, because of the changes they'd made to Meredith's role, the meaning below the lines was entirely different, and made the scene funny because it was ironic.

Craig was grudgingly acceptant, and willing to give it a try, while remaining innocent of the time bomb ticking below the surface.

William and Jay were privately delighted, and waited for Meredith's reaction, which they considered to be a foregone conclusion.

It wasn't. Meredith hated it.

'Why?' said Jay, as they sat at the back of the stalls during the coffee break. 'We haven't changed a thing of yours.'

'Yes, you have, darling,' Merry replied. 'You've put that bastard back in the driving seat.'

'It only looks like that, Meredith.'

'It reads like that, my darling.'

'It won't play like that, Meredith.'

'How do you know, poppet? You don't have to get up there and bloody do it.'

Just before they started rehearsing the new scene, Jay found William at the back of the dress circle tearing a theatre programme into little strips.

'You can please some of the people, eh William?' she asked, settling down beside him with a sigh.

'It would help if we had a director,' William told her.

'We have,' Jay answered gloomily, 'judging from what's happening down there.'

On the stage below them, Jimmy Francis was seated submissively by the proscenium arch, watching while Craig Matheson conducted the rehearsal. After watching half an hour of indescribable chaos, William got up, took Jay by the hand and marched them out of the theatre and across the road into the pub, where he ordered them both large whiskies.

'I thought this was really going to be exciting, you know, William,' Jay said a little sadly, as they settled at a table in the corner. 'I thought it was going to be just like on the movies.'

'Fairy tales don't come true,' William replied and downed his whisky in one.

He then pulled his notepad out of his old battered briefcase and uncapped his pen.

'Act One, scene two,' he said.

they'd done four pages by the time the cast and stage staff broke for lunch. Unfortunately they all chose to come and eat in the pub.

But there'd been a sea change. Craig was actually smiling and buying everyone drinks, Jimmy was groping and fondling any of the young men in the entourage who were foolish enough to come within arms' length, and

224

Meredith actually had her arm through Craig's as they stood at the bar.

The next thing William and Jay knew, a bottle was being plonked down in front of them on their table.

'Champagne,' said Craig Matheson. 'Champagne for the scribes.'

'Isn't that a mite premature, Craig?' enquired William.

He sat back in his chair and, taking off his glasses to clean them, stared levelly up at the leading actor.

'Not a bit of it, sunshine. Keep you going. Anyway — you deserve it. You both deserve it. The new scene's great. Mind if we join you?'

Suddenly Jay forgot all her disappointment. This was exactly how she'd imagined it would be. Champagne, laughter, *bonhomie*. Everyone mucking in, helping to make a silk purse out of a sow's ear. There were bound to be difficulties, Jay knew that. But she'd always believed the difficulties would be ironed out, and by opening night there really would be no business like it.

Which was when she felt the hand up her skirt.

Jimmy, Meredith and Craig had all sat down at William and Jay's table for lunch. Meredith had sat herself next to William, and Craig had sat down next to Jay. But he really hadn't taken that much notice of her. There'd been some initial small talk, and some flattery about how clever she and William had been to incorporate the cut sections from the original draft, but after that he'd turned his attentions to Jimmy, and started talking to him in some detail about the staging of the new scene.

And now suddenly he had his hand up Jay's skirt. No, suddenly wasn't quite right, Jay decided. Because she had felt a hand on her knee once or twice during the course of the lunch, and at first had thought it was William fooling around. But William was just that bit too far away to put a hand on her knee without having to half disappear under the table to do so.

Which was when she realized it was Craig.

She didn't do anything at first, trying to kid herself that

225

it was probably quite innocent, and anyway she was among actors, and actors apparently were notorious for doing this sort of thing without thinking and without really meaning anything by it. Craig probably didn't even fully realize himself that he was doing it, Jay reasoned. Most likely it was a sort of conditioned reflex.

And then the hand, which was now resting not on her knee but under her skirt and on her thigh, began to work its way up higher and higher.

Jay froze, and sat quite still. And the hand, obviously taking her lack of reaction as encouragement, now positively raced up towards the edge of her panties. By the time Jay had picked up her fork and dropped it below table level, Craig had even managed to get a finger under the edge of her panties and was trying to work his hand underneath her backside.

And had just about succeeded when Jay stabbed him in the offending hand as hard as she could with the fork.

He was some actor, Jay thought, seeing him hardly flinch. He just kept his back half-turned on her, while he continued to talk to Jimmy Francis, and simply removed his hand without anyone being any the wiser.

Jay, red in the face but feeling positively purple, got up and, excusing herself to no one in particular, fled to the ladies' loo.

It was a pretty miserable room, in keeping with the general tattiness of the pub, but at that moment it was a haven. Jay leaned on the handbasin and stared at herself in the mirror, the writer in her at the same time wondering why it was that at times of upset people did such clichéd things. Then she washed her face in cold water several times, as if she was the sinner and not the sinned against, before carefully repairing what little make-up she wore, and deciding finally that it had been just a minor aberration. Craig was an actor, it was as simple as that. And she was one of the writers. And he probably thought in his naïvety that she'd enjoy being groped. And that if she enjoyed it, she'd go away and write something for him.

Something he wanted her to write for him. That's what happened in the business. William had told her plenty of cautionary stories, so she should have been forearmed. Craig was an actor, and actors were a race apart. And that was all there was to it.

And with that Jay put her lipstick in her bag and marched back out to face whatever music it was the band was now playing.

By the end of the week, William and Jay had completed an entirely new draft of the play. They had sat every night well into the small hours, drinking black coffee and eating Mars Bars, sometimes literally with wet towels wrapped around their aching heads, until at last the play had fallen into a new and, as they both considered, better shape.

William for his part was delighted with Jay's input. Working alone, he had often found it difficult to deal with his female characters' motivations, but now with Jay at his side he experienced no such difficulties. It was interesting working with a woman, and a lot more fun, once he got used to a woman's more lateral approach to problems. And her habit of making lists in the middle of a hiatus. And disappearing off in pursuit of some wild goose while he was struggling to think up an exit line for the leading lady. And trying out a new hairstyle on him at the start of the evening session, and then sulking for the rest of the night because she thought he hadn't liked it. And making him look at the new moon through her petticoat just as he was on the brink of discovering how to get the hero's best friend back out from under the bed. And cheering them both up when he felt like cutting his throat by making them both up as tarts and standing in front of the mirror till the tears of helpless laughter ruined everyone's make-up. And then taking him to bed and making such tender love to him that the problems of trying to balance the dialogue evenly between his two leading players no longer seemed of the slightest importance.

227

Yes, William decided, working with a girl certainly had its advantages.

Even so, William knew they were fighting a losing battle. He didn't say anything to Jay, because as their new scenes finally went into full rehearsal, she was brimming over with enthusiasm and confidence. She knew their rewrite was good. She had known from the moment they had got the first scene right. And then each subsequent scene. The play had come alive. The characters now existed for real.

First thing every morning after they had bathed, they would read through the previous night's work, and do a final polish on it before trotting off dutifully to rehearsals to hand in their homework. And as they walked down the rain-soaked streets, they were quiet in their confidence, as they had heard for themselves how well their new scenes had read. They never laughed out loud at anything they wrote. Instead they stared at the typewriter and frowned at each new line.

'Do you think that's funny, William?' Jay would enquire nervously.

'Yes, that's funny,' William would reply, nodding his head and looking even more worried than usual. 'Yes, I think that really is funny.'

And then they would hand it in, endure the agonies of a mumbled sight-read by the principals, and the list of criticisms and suggested improvements which Craig Matheson invariably offered, before disappearing back to their hotel room to work on the next scene.

'How much are we being paid for this, William?' Jay had once asked him, during a particularly long and unfruitful hiatus.

'Not nearly enough,' William had replied. 'A flat fee and no percentage of the box office. If I'd known what it was going to entail, I'd have asked for twenty times as much. And we'd still have been underpaid.'

Jay thought all their troubles were over when they handed in their new version of the last scene, because for three days there had not been one single complaint from the cast, nor one expression of doubt from the director.

They had met as usual every evening in the hotel bar for a drink in the break between rehearsals and before the performance, and it had seemed from the warmth and friendliness of the gathering that William and Jay's picture was most certainly up there on the company piano. Craig was relaxed and affable, Meredith was positively affectionate and grateful, and even Jimmy Francis grudgingly considered the writers had performed something of a small miracle.

On the Saturday night when they met for drinks, William asked when they were going to put the new version before the public for the first time.

'No, the week after next, I think, old love,' Jimmy told him. 'We'll rehearse the entire new version next week, and then open the magic box in Sheffield.'

'Good,' William replied. 'We shall be looking forward to that.'

Jimmy Francis smiled at him and nodded.

'Oh good,' he said. 'You'll both be coming back up for it then.'

'Coming up?' William enquired. 'Why should we be coming up? We'll be staying up.'

Jay saw the glance that Jimmy and Craig exchanged over the tops of their drinks, and for a moment her blood ran cold, although she didn't know quite why.

'No, there's no need for you to stay up, love,' Jimmy smiled, patting one of William's hands. 'You've done quite splendidly as it is.'

'I suppose because we're the writers,' William replied.

Craig shook his head,

'You're not the writers, sweetheart,' he announced, smiling. 'You two are the re-writers.'

And so it was they were banned from rehearsals. William was furious, and Jay was astounded, but on the Monday when they made their one and only attempt to sit in on rehearsals, Craig downed tools and refused to work.

Jay was sent by William to lobby Meredith that afternoon, but Meredith, although she was greatly saddened, as she said, by this unfortunate turn of events, had no option but to comply with the company's request, otherwise they would never get the play on at all.

'Believe me,' she told Jay over tea. 'It really is going to be fine. You've both done such marvellous work, there's no way anyone's going to spoil it. We're all *so* grateful. I'm particularly grateful. Really. In fact I think you're both so marvellous, once we're open and running in town, I'm going to ask Max to get you both to write something just especially for me.'

Jay was greatly mollified by this promise, and reported back to William.

'Abble-dabble, as Max would say,' William said. 'Bloody actors' abble-dabble.'

And with that he pulled their suitcases out from under the bed.

'So that's it then,' Jay asked. 'End of story.'

'Not quite,' William replied.

'But we're going back to town.'

'Yes, sure. We're going back to town. But the reason we're going back to town is to see Max.'

Max listened attentively, and because he did so, William knew he wasn't interested. When Max was really interested, he walked about the room, and interrupted, and took his jacket off, and loosened his tie. All he was doing now was sitting at his desk smoking a cigar and nodding in punctuation.

'Jesus Christ,' he said when William and Jay had finished. 'What did I tell you? Bloody actors.'

'So pick up the phone and tell them it won't do.'

'No, I have a better idea, Willy boy,' Max said, relighting his cigar. 'Leave it for now and we'll all go up to Sheffield together.'

* * *

Sheffield was a triumph. The audience roared with laughter from the moment Craig appeared in his Union Jack boxer shorts until the final curtain where Meredith, in scarlet camiknickers and a large black picture hat, collapsed on the bed and it broke in two. The cast took eight curtain calls, and a red-faced man in an open-neck nylon shirt rushed onstage and tried to kiss the leading lady.

When the house lights went up, Max was beaming from ear to ear.

'Great!' he said turning to William. 'Magic! Everything you say about it is true!'

William was sitting with his head in his hands. Which is how he went on sitting.

Max turned to Jay.

'You too, sweetheart!' he said. 'What a team! Kauffman and Hart – eat your heart out!'

Jay managed to smile back at Max, but only because she could never resist the childishness of his enthusiasm.

'Come on!' Max exhorted them. 'Let's go and get pissed!'

Still William didn't move. Jay neither.

'What is it with you two?' Max enquired, sitting down on the back of the seat in front of them. 'Look at the audience! They're still pissing themselves!'

'The matter is, Max,' William answered slowly, looking up at him, 'is that this is a travesty. A vulgar travesty, which won't last five minutes in London.'

'Believe me. You've done a terrific job.'

'Max, what you saw tonight – that was nothing to do with us!'

It was now Jay's turn, having found her tongue at last.

'There's barely half-a-dozen complete speeches left of our rewrite!' she continued. 'Craig's readapted the whole thing just so he can go on doing what he's always been doing!'

'Viz. *Hello In There*,' William added morosely. 'He's not interested in getting the play right, Max. He just wants a vehicle to show off all his old tricks from television.'

231

'You heard the audience, William,' Max sighed, turning the palms of his hands upwards to emphasize the point.

'I heard the audience, Max. But all they laughed at was what Craig and to some extent Meredith were doing. They weren't laughing at the play. The play, old friend, *elle n'existe pas*. With respect, this is Sheffield. And tonight was an outing to see a television star in the flesh. By the time you get to London, if you get to London, you're still going to need a play.'

They all three adjourned for a drink in the stalls bar before going backstage, where William told Max his only salvation was to do the play as rewritten.

'Not here,' William urged. 'But for when you're nearer London. In Cambridge. And Windsor. And get them to play it as it is on the page. Stop Craig mugging, and cut Meredith's performance not in half but in quarter, and believe me, you'll be in business.'

William and Jay passed on the celebratory dinner, and ate *à deux* back at their hotel. Jay was still optimistic, betting William anything he liked that Max could persuade the stars to give the play a chance. But William remained unconvinced.

'But you heard him in the bar, William!' Jay argued. 'He said he was going straight round backstage to have it out with Craig!'

'Sorry, partner,' William replied. 'Max nodded. And when Max Kassov nods, it means no.'

Max joined them at their table for breakfast the next morning, looking more than a little red-eyed.

'You missed a good evening,' he told them. 'Craig did his Amateur Talent Contest.'

'What about the play?' William asked.

'He did the Seven Dwarfs auditioning as well,' Max continued. 'Have you ever seen him doing the Seven Dwarfs auditioning? Get him to do you the Seven Dwarfs auditioning. It's a knock-out.'

'Did you ask him about the play, Max?'

'He thinks you two are geniuses, William. He said

you're two of the most talented writers he's ever come up against.'

'Why does he have to come up against writers, Max?' William asked. 'Why can't he just work with them?'

'Meredith thinks you're the answer to a prayer, too. In fact she has plans for you three to work together once the play is up and running.'

'You ask him, Jay,' William suggested. 'Maybe he'll listen to a pretty girl.'

'What about the play, Max?' Jay enquired.

'We're practically booked through to Windsor now, do you know that, kids? Never ceases to amaze me, the power of the box.'

Max poured himself another cup of coffee and turned William's newspaper round to read the headlines.

'What did I tell you, partner?'

William wiped his mouth on his table napkin, and pushed his chair back.

'We might as well go pack our bags.'

'Max,' she said. 'You're not really going to let this happen?'

Max looked at her, and shook his head.

'Don't be fooled,' William said. 'That shake means yes.'

'Jay, sweetheart,' Max said, taking her hand. 'This is business. I have such advances on Craig Matheson's name alone you wouldn't believe. The feedback I'm getting from the theatres we're booked into is incredible. They're just showing the third season of *Hello In There*, and I understand it's topping the ratings. They're interested in Meredith, too. She made a big impression in that last play, and people are already talking about her. What do you want me to do? Put my foot down and say you do the play these two writers have sat up night after night rewriting? You do it or else? You know what happens if you say something like that to someone like Craig? They tell you to piss off. Or if you're fool enough to insist on it, they piss off. And then where are you? I have to re-cast at the last minute with someone else, somebody who's not Craig Matheson. And all the theatres we're booked into, suddenly they're saying I'm not so sure. Or the money gets frightened. And the word gets out the show's in trouble. At the moment, everybody's happy. The stars are getting their laughs, the advances are getting better by the minute, and the audience are pissing themselves. Why should I make waves now? Everybody's happy.'

'Except us,' said Jay.

'It's not your play, Jay sweetheart! Stop eating, yes! When it's your play! But this was just a job. And you did it fine. We'd never be in this shape if it wasn't for you!'

Jay looked to William, but William wasn't saying anything. He was just tearing the newspaper into very thin strips.

'But there's nothing of what we've done left, Max!' Jay added as a confused afterthought.

'You breathed life into it,' Max replied, rescuing the sports page before William could shred it. 'And you gave the stars back their confidence.'

William taught Jay how to play gin rummy on the train back to London.

'It's an essential for every writing partnership,' he told her. 'You're not a team till you can play gin rummy.'

'You mean we're still a team?' Jay enquired.

'You betcha,' said William, laying down a winning hand. 'Why in hell shouldn't we be?'

It was the best bit of news Jay had heard in days. Despite what had been thrown at them, despite being taken off the show and sent back to London, they were still in harness.

'You do know I love you, William Kennedy, don't you?' Jay asked as William redealt.

'You betcha,' William replied. 'I wouldn't be any sort of writer if I didn't.'

There was nothing for them back in London. William went in to see Max at the beginning of the following week, but all he came home with was the news that the play had broken

234

the box-office records in Coventry, Leeds and Birmingham.

'Any interest in the show we've proposed for Meredith?' Jay asked.

'Oh yes,' William replied. 'Apparently that's a foregone conclusion. Once the play is up and running.'

'Great,' said Jay. 'So let's just keep our sights on that.'

William looked at her over his glasses, but didn't say anything. Sometimes it wasn't such a bad thing to be born yesterday.

By the time the play reached London, William and Jay were broke. The pittance they had been paid for their rewrite had long since gone to pay off the outstanding household bills, and the only work William had been offered was an adaptation of an extremely salacious paperback, which he had turned down.

They stayed well away from the opening night, and took a long time to get around to reading the notices, even though Jay had rushed out and bought every morning paper. William finally took a couple up to the bathroom and locked himself in.

Jay sat with the others in front of her on the dining table. She opened the first one and turned to the arts page.

'Christ!' she heard William shout from the bathroom. 'Christ, I just don't bloody well believe it!'

Jay read through the notice in her paper. It was a rave.

'Jesus Christ!' William shouted again. 'Jesus Christ, they've all gone bloody mad!'

Jay read the notice in her second paper. It was another rave.

William appeared wet, dripping and totally naked by her side.

'What do yours say?' he demanded.

'Mine say it's the best and most original and wittiest comedy to hit the West End since *Private Lives* stroke *Pygmalion* stroke *Boeing-Boeing* stroke—'

'Mine all say the same!' William shouted. 'What's the

matter with everybody? Have they all taken leave of their goddam senses!'

They went to see the play the following week, in the aftermath of a spate of wonderful notices, from the weeklies as well as the Sundays. Outside the theatre the front of house was plastered with bills which extolled the comedy as the wittiest, lightest, and most brilliantly sustained piece of writing it had ever been the critics' unalloyed joy to witness.

Inside the theatre the cast were now playing William and Jay's rewritten version of the play, word for word, minus all extraneous comic business.

It was deft, subtle, light as a soufflé, and all their own work.

They left as the audience started cheering and walked in silence all the way back to the studio where, once they'd let themselves in, William poured them both a very stiff drink.

Then he threw a copy of the evening paper, folded open at a particular point, to land in Jay's lap.

'One final nail in the coffin, partner,' he said, smiling a weary little smile at her.

Jay frowned and looked at the news item.

It simply read: 'Meredith Browne, star of the new hit comedy *Where Were You Just When It Mattered?* to star in own TV series.'

The series was to be written by the original author of the play.

6

On tour or on location 'it' didn't count, so the saying in the business went. Max had been brought up with it, but he didn't believe it, he always thought 'it' counted.

Coming off tour this time Meredith was changed. She seemed more in control of their relationship, and he less, almost as if something had happened to make her think she had the upper hand. Max started delaying going to the office. He would find himself ringing and making excuses about why he couldn't go in, and then he would turn his attentions to Meredith, to his private passion.

'You'll wear me out,' Meredith protested once or twice. 'I've been back a fortnight, you know.'

Max lay back against her pillows and smiled. She had made love to him, he had made love to her, they had made love together; she should be worn out.

'You're a great lay,' he told her affectionately.

'I'm a great actress,' Meredith corrected him.

'Some things you can't fake, not ever.'

'No,' Meredith agreed, 'maybe not.'

She walked towards the bathroom, and as she went she kicked various small items of underwear from her path. She was such a slut, Max thought, watching her. She was like so many girls he'd known, didn't matter what he bought them, it ended up on the floor. He picked up a pink and grey silk item from the bedside table. It might as well have been some cheap chain-store item the way she treated it; not silk, not the best.

'You're the best,' he called to her, but she couldn't hear because she had started to run the shower. He could see the outline of her breasts through the shower curtain, and her hands seemed to be touching herself, sponging and soaping, just for his benefit.

'If I didn't have to be at a meeting at midday. . . .' he said out loud. 'Stop doing that, it's turning me on again. And again.'

She was singing now, so she heard even less. Max swung his legs to the carpet, and walked across to the chest of drawers.

He'd been in to see the matinée of the show the day before, and it had been very good. Full house, terrific ovation at the end, particularly for a matinée. Even Max had enjoyed it, despite the fact that he knew the damn play in his sleep by now; even so, he had enjoyed it. Until he noticed Craig looking at Meredith in a different way. In a way that, it seemed to Max, meant that he too was hypnotized by her.

Meredith laughed, in that new confident way of hers, when Max mentioned it at supper afterwards. She paused by the door of the kitchen and looked at him.

'Craig's terrified of me, Max, wouldn't you be, if you were him? He knows he's got to get up so early to get the early worm, doesn't he?'

Max relaxed. So that was it, the new confidence, the added swagger to her walk, it was just the actress who had won the latest round against her co-star. That's all it was. No sudden bout of passion in some touring hotel. No hate turning to love the moment the play started to come right for both of them.

Not that he would have minded, he told himself, as he too headed for the bathroom. He wouldn't have cared a damn. He stopped as the telephone started to ring, and tracked back to Meredith's bedside to pick up her white telephone with its expensive brass fittings.

'Meredith, please.'

The voice was all too familiar, and it was speaking before Max had spoken, so that he had time to think quickly, and to make up his mind that he wouldn't answer, that he would remain silent, and replace the receiver before Craig had time to go on.

He wouldn't ring again, because Max would make sure of it. He leaned forward and pulled the telephone point from the wall before walking slowly back to the chest of drawers and picking up his cigar case. Shit. So he had been right after all. The whore had had Craig on tour.

Max chose a cigar and lit it.

Meredith emerged from the bathroom, a towel wrapped around her head, but her beautiful body still quite naked. She started to laugh when she saw Max.

'That's one of the funniest sights around,' she said, doubled up with laughter. 'Oh God, that looks funny. That looks really funny.'

Max laughed too, but his eyes were narrowed, from the cigar smoke, and from the effort not to show her what he was feeling. She was just like Marie-Gabriella. Just another version of the same old song. Why couldn't he keep girls interested in him? He bought them everything, did everything for them, and they just, as the French said, pissed on his shoes.

'I'll have to take pictures of you naked with that cigar,' Meredith gasped, slowly recovering from her fit of giggles.

Max walked past her to the shower. Craig. So she'd had Craig, had she? Why? Over a year ago she'd bested him on the famous first night, what did she want *him* for? Max turned on the shower and let cold water, freezing cold water, splash over him. Something to cool him, please, something, or he'd murder her.

By the time he stepped out of the shower, and in that short length of time, his passion for Meredith had fled. He had learned from that first love. Love came, love went, Max stayed. What was she anyway? A two-bit actress whom his father had picked up, put on his books and turned into a comedy actress. She was an *actress*, for Chrissake. An actress whom Max had turned into a star. What did he want, a nun? Sure she was beautiful, and

239

she was a great lay, but she was no reason to commit murder. Not now, not now he'd had the cold shower.

She turned from her dressing table, slowly brushing her hair, and looked at him as he collected up his keys and his money clip.

'Will you send the car for me tonight?'

Meredith turned back to the mirror again, seemingly hardly able to bear leaving it.

'Will you?' she asked again, as Max considered it.

'Sure,' said Max, 'I'll send the car, but I won't be in it.'

Meredith widened her eyes.

'Why not?'

'Boys-only night, meeting of the Rat Pack. British branch.'

Max kissed his hand to Meredith.

'Take care,' he said, but Meredith ran to him, and put her arms around him, and kissed him properly, on the mouth. Max didn't like the taste of her lipstick, not for a moment, but he still smiled.

Every two or three months Baz called Max and they lunched.

First he rang a few weeks before and asked Max to lunch, always somewhere very new and very fashionable, because Baz worried about these things, especially now that he was getting older. The routine therefore was always the same while the restaurant changed, but not, alas for Max, the conversation. It was always the same, and it always started the same, just like when he was a little boy and Baz came round to the flat to go out for lunch on Saturdays, then the conversation had always been the same, and now it was always the same.

'Why don't you call your father?'

Baz took off his half-moon spectacles and stared at Max, and his eyes were very sad, so sad they even made Max feel sad, and at the moment nothing made Max feel sad, just full of a sort of inner anger, against women, against actresses, and against Meredith. But it would go.

'Why doesn't my father call *me*?' Max demanded.

'Because he's your father, Maxie, fathers don't call sons when the sons set out to ruin them. Sons call fathers and ask forgiveness. That's how things are.'

'Do you want the pâté?' asked Max, ignoring him.

'No, I want you to answer me,' said Baz, and he opened his eyes and tried to look pathetic. But the pathetic look didn't come off because just at that moment a very young girl sauntered past their table, and she was wearing only the briefest of leather mini-skirts, and the longest of soft leather boots that came up and over her knees. Both Baz and Max smiled appreciatively at her, and she walked on, knowing that they were still watching her and enjoying it as much as they were enjoying watching her.

Baz nodded towards the girl.

'When we were young,' he told Max, 'when we were young the erotic zone was a girl's ankle. A glimpse of stocking around the ankle – that was enough to make a boy run home and dream for the rest of the week. I used to lie awake trying to imagine what the rest of a woman looked like, what shape she would be. Now there's a new erogenous zone, the gap between the hem of the mini-skirt and the top of the boot. It's quite something, a new era, a new zone, and the rest is covered. She was wearing suspenders though, wasn't she? I think that's sauce. But enough of that. Why don't you call your father? Call Louis and ask his forgiveness?'

'For what?' asked Max exploding. 'For never asking him for anything? For owning everything I've got? Why should I ask his forgiveness?'

'Poaching, that's for a start, you poached Meredith.'

'Meredith? OK, I poached Meredith, but tell him he can have her back, and then he can call me,' said Max, shaking the menu as if he had his father by the shoulders.

'Don't get so angry, why get so angry?' Baz pleaded.

Max put the menu down.

'Every time we lunch it's always the same, we've got to

241

learn to leave it alone, Baz, really. It's no fun. I hate things that are no fun, and right now that's not.'

'Louis will change his will, Max, he'll change his will in favour of Trixie.'

'Let him, who cares? Now, what are you eating?'

'I don't feel like eating when you're angry, you're never angry. Best-tempered child I ever came across, that's not exaggerating,' said Baz, sighing.

It was Max's turn to sigh. Baz always knew how to get to him. He had only to look doleful or to sigh and it would bring back memories of Baz and his father on birthdays, or at Christmas, when they would arrive laden with parcels, their faces glowing like children, making up for the time they hadn't had anything, the time they put the note up the chimney asking Father Christmas for an orange each, and all they got was soot. Any minute now Baz would mention the oranges. But he didn't, not until the dessert.

'Caramelized oranges, we'll have caramelized oranges,' he told the waiter, and then looked across at Max, challenging him to change the order.

That was one whole unvaried routine that he and Baz went through. The next was Baz following him back to the office. Here he would stand around while Max sent Mona in ahead of him to 'tidy up'. Tidying up was Max's code to Mona to put away any papers that he might have left out on his desk, and empty the wastepaper basket, so that finally the office Baz walked into would be pristine, and tidy, and all the drawers would be locked, because Max knew Baz and his father as well as he knew himself, and there was no way he would leave anything out when they were around.

'You don't even trust me to be left with the wastepaper basket,' he complained as he passed Mona on her way out with the refuse.

'I don't trust myself, why should I trust you?' Max would answer, and then, yet another routine having been observed, they would settle back in the leather armchairs that graced Max's offices, and it would be very nice, just the two of them, and Baz would wax lyrical about how much it meant to him, if not to Max's father, to see Max doing so well on his own, making his own way.

This afternoon though, Baz didn't settle down in the leather chair that Max offered him, because his eye was arrested by something, not Mona's flowing skirt and regulation secretarial footwear, but by some new pictures that Max had bought. Pictures of Dutch interiors.

'Who bought those for you?' he demanded, peering at them through his bi-focal spectacles.

'I bought those for me, that's who,' said Max, bracing himself for Baz to hate them.

'If you're the who who bought them, then you've bought wrong,' said Baz triumphantly. 'And whoever sold them to you, don't do business with him any more.'

'Howard sold them to me,' Max told him. 'Howard, my partner in the agency, he sold them to me.'

'And you bought them? Without advice? I thought you had more sense. Buying pictures from your partner, what's happened to you? Too much has happened to you. You've been conned, he flattered you and you let it get to you.'

'Those aren't fakes,' said Max indignantly. 'They belonged to Howard's father.'

'Then he sold you fakes,' Baz said even more triumphantly, as if he was paying Max back for not leaving any papers out. 'I hate art, never go near it myself, but I know a fake picture the way I know a fake gem. Fakes are terrible things. One thing you can't fake is talent though. You know that, I know that. It's what your father and I built our reputation on, what we built the business on — our ability to spot talent, to weed out the fakes. That's how I know that painting's a fake, because it's got no real talent, not really, not when you look at it, not when you know.'

Max went up to the picture and stared at it. It was true, now when he looked at it, Baz was right, it was a fake, they were both fakes, both pictures.

As soon as Baz went, he took the damn things down from the office walls and had Mona parcel them up. He was going to stay with Howard for a short weekend. The first time that Howard had dared to ask Max Kassov up to Norfolk. It'd been the subject of a great deal of Max-type teasing. Even so, Howard seemed a bit nervous about it all, as if he was afraid Max would suddenly be sick in the middle of the fish course, or steal the Charles I cup from the Great Hall.

'Take any messages, say I'm at a meeting,' Max told Mona briskly, and then buttoning up his overcoat once more he walked down into the street carrying the pictures.

He thought about the pictures a great deal as he walked along. If Howard had sold him fakes then he'd deal Howard one back, because that was all he needed, a partner who sold him fakes. As it was he knew Howard was only asking him up for the weekend because his father had seen Merry's play three times and was wild about her.

One day he'd have a country house as big as Howard's father's house, and he'd live in it with a beautiful girl, but she wouldn't be Meredith, even though he knew he still had to take Meredith to Norfolk; even so, she would never be part of that side of his life again. His passion for her had frozen over, so that even that morning he'd turned away from the photograph of her on his desk. She could be just another actress. Just another beautiful girl he represented. But he'd revenge himself on her, even so, he had to, because no one double-crossed Max Kassov, not ever. He frowned with pleasurable spite at the thought. The day had turned freezing, and he should be in the office enjoying himself, dealing on the telephone, doing things he liked, not brushing the sleet from his hair and stamping his feet to bring some feeling back into them as he turned into the auction house.

And then he suddenly saw her.

He hadn't wanted to see her, he hadn't come to see her, but there she was in front of him, and she was beautiful, and because, seconds before, his heart had been in turmoil, and only yesterday his passion for Meredith had been in the

244

centre of his life, he could see just how beautiful she was. He was in that softened state that is necessary to fall in love at first sight; he had already gone a round or two with love.

He felt his eyes opening wide, as if by doing so he would take in her beauty better, and he could no longer remember why he was standing there, and he was aware only of her beautiful face, and her gentle gaze, and her skin that looked so soft that it seemed to him that to touch it must be like touching the peaches that Howard sometimes brought back with him from the country on Mondays.

'Can I help you?'

The voice was everything. Now in one sentence Max realized that no one, no voice teacher on earth, could give a person a true voice, not one that swam and danced on the air, its carelessly lilting notes speaking of hundreds of years of dining off mahogany tables, and eating with real silver forks, and going to bed in crumpled linen. This girl had never posted her Christmas letter up a chimney and received only soot in reply.

'What's your name?' Max demanded.

The girl standing behind the counter looked startled. It was obvious that she was not used to people demanding her name from her so abruptly. Men arriving in off the streets with brown parcels full of paintings to value, or *objets d'art* to be passed on for advice, that she would be used to – not wanting to know *her* identity, only the identity of their pictures.

'What's your name?' Max asked again, because that's what he was used to. In show business your name was the first thing you gave, it was the thing you made into an object, a stock or a share that people bought to put above the title.

'Seraphina Lucy.'

'Yes, but Seraphina Lucy what?' asked Max almost impatiently.

'Seraphina May Lucy. Lucy is my surname,' she said, blushing.

Dear God, she actually blushed! Max's eyes swam in

245

front of this phenomenon. The last time he saw a girl blushing – he couldn't remember the last time a girl blushed. Merry never blushed. She reddened. He didn't suppose Merry would ever have known what it was like to blush. Not ever.

'Dutch interiors. Fakes?' Max asked, and he rapidly undid the brown paper Mona had done up just as rapidly not many minutes before.

'I'm not an expert,' she said softly, 'I'd have to show them to our expert.'

But nevertheless she turned the paintings round towards her, and as she did so the charms on her gold bracelet sang out her childhood interest in horses. As her eyes ran over the two small paintings, Max's eyes ran over her. Pink cashmere twinset, beautifully tailored skirt, real pearls in the ears, pearls that reflected the pink of her twinset. She was anything but fake. And how beautiful she was.

'Can you leave them with us?'

She looked up at Max, and she was still blushing, as if she knew that Max was looking right through her, right through the white, lace-trimmed, virginal petticoat that he knew Seraphina Lucy would be wearing under her cashmere twinset. Everything underneath would be bright white, Max knew that. It would be wonderfully white.

'I, er – what was that you said?'

'I said, I wonder if you could be so kind as to leave these with us?' she said slowly.

I wonder if you could be so kind as to leave these with us? Max's eyes half closed in delight. What a way to ask someone to leave something. The sentence took the listener on a verbal detour round the park and past the earliest of the spring flowers, before depositing him back at his own front door.

'Yes, of course.'

For a second they both stood looking down at the paintings which were still facing Seraphina, and then she raised her eyes to Max's and smiled.

246

'Can I have your name?'

'Max Kassov,' said Max, and he watched her carefully and correctly writing it down on a receipt. 'The Shropshire Kassovs,' Max couldn't help adding as she finished writing it in a large rounded hand.

She tore off the receipt and handed it to him and smiled.

'I have an aunt who lives in Shropshire,' she said.

'I had an aunt who lived in Scotland once, but she died.'

'Aunts are very precious.'

'Aunts maybe, but not those paintings,' said Max grinning.

'You never know,' she said suddenly anxious, almost maternal. 'You never know.'

Max put the receipt into his crocodile-skin wallet.

'I shall come back after the weekend,' he told her.

She smiled, and then Max moved away to allow another man to present his brown paper parcel to Seraphina Lucy, and leave Max to walk back into the cold air outside feeling jealous not just of him, but even of the brown paper that she would by now be touching.

'You're a credit to me,' said Max, only half-jokingly as Meredith emerged from the stage door and followed him to the waiting car.

It was ten o'clock at night, and they had a long drive ahead of them to Howard's old family house in Norfolk where they were expected to arrive for a very late supper, prior to a Sunday and Monday of civilized leisure.

'I'm a credit to me,' Meredith retorted as she stalked round to the passenger door. Max shrugged his shoulders, and let himself into the car without opening her door for her. She could take care of herself, so let her.

As he headed the car towards North London, and the roads that would take them to Norfolk and the tail end of a shooting party, Max found himself trying to find something to talk about to Meredith. It was absurd. Only three days before and he wouldn't have given it a thought; but now, suddenly, after leaving his pictures to be assessed by

247

a slip of a girl in a cashmere twinset, he was struggling to think of something to say to Meredith. When passion flew out of the window, so did talk.

He settled on talking about the business. Meredith hardly ever talked about anything else anyway. She was always happiest talking shop, gossiping salaciously about who was doing what to whom, and for what reason.

But Max was too distracted by the thought of Seraphina, and as Meredith rattled on, his thoughts wandered to how she would be spending the weekend, and he fantasized about what he would be doing if he were spending it with her, and how she would look, and how beautiful she'd be.

'So – you don't think that's funny?' Meredith suddenly demanded, interrupting his reverie.

'I thought it was funny,' Max stated.

'Sure, that's why you didn't laugh,' said Meredith, and she crossed and recrossed her legs restlessly in front of her.

'I do, I think it's hilarious, it's just that I was wondering if we had the right road.'

Max peered through the windscreen and up at a small country signpost.

'By the looks of it they haven't repainted that since the war. And even then it was only put there to confuse the Germans,' he joked, having decided to take a right instead of a left.

'It's spooky in the countryside,' said Meredith, and drew her fur coat tightly round her. 'I wish we hadn't come, I don't know why but I don't think country weekends are my thing. I've never even played in a country house play.'

'You'll be all right, Howard Senior thinks you're incredible, he's seen the play three times.'

Max drove on slowly in the dark wishing to himself that he hadn't come, and more especially that he hadn't brought Meredith. It was true, she had never even played in a country house play.

'Look, when we get there, if there are a lot of courses,

248

just remember you start from outside and work your way in.'

'What do you mean? I thought we were just expected for a late supper after the show.'

'That's tonight,' said Max impatiently, 'I'm talking about tomorrow. Lunch, dinner, whatever, there may be more courses than you're used to, so just remember you always start from the outside and work your way in, and if there are meat—'

'What do you mean?' asked Meredith again, a note of hysteria entering into her carefully trained voice, 'what do you mean there'll be more courses than I'm used to? I'm only used to a sandwich in the interval.'

'Calm down,' Max ordered her, 'and just give your performance.'

'Which one? Disarmingly shy and sexy? A simple girl made good? Which one?'

She plucked at her bag and put on some more lipstick.

'Disarmingly sexy will do,' said Max, wishing even more heartily that he'd left Meredith in London.

The house was lit up on every side, and since it was set back from the road and approached by a long drive, its lights could be seen from afar.

'Buckingham Palace,' said Meredith, and she looked at Max accusingly. 'A small shooting party for a few close friends, my eye. They've asked the world and his wife by the looks of it.'

She shivered once more, and her teeth started chattering just the way they always did when they called the 'five' backstage.

'Good luck, and break a leg,' said Max as they drew up in front of the great double doors, but Meredith quite obviously didn't think his send-up of backstage behaviour on a first night was funny, because she didn't smile, just powdered her nose before alighting from the car.

The butler flung open the doors as they approached. And then he stood surveying them from the top step so that they felt themselves to be under close scrutiny. Max knew this was disconcerting Merry by the way she flung the scarf of her coat back around her neck in one defiant gesture.

'Welcome to Hardway Hall,' said the butler.

Just for a second as Max listened to his overdone greeting he wished that Meredith would make some outrageous reply, if only to see whether it would disconcert him.

But Meredith didn't utter a sound, she just stalked by him employing her swaying, self-taught, graceful walk to such good effect that even the butler couldn't help glancing at her appreciatively. She certainly looked a picture. Max had seen to that, and she'd even remembered not to drown herself in perfume, something about which Max had been trying to get through to her for months.

'The family are in the library,' the butler informed Max, 'a little supper will be served to you in there, if that would suit Miss Browne and yourself.'

'Oh, that would suit admirably,' Max assured him, 'and here are the keys to our suitcases.'

He handed the keys to the butler, and a man appeared from nowhere to unload the car.

'You're much posher than you let on, Max Kassov,' said Meredith out of the corner of her mouth, and then she flung off her fur coat, and prepared herself for her number one entrance, her svelte outline encased in a dazzling after-theatre dress, her auburn hair beautifully arranged into the nape of her neck and held in place by a diamond-scattered snood.

She paused as she stood framed in the library doors, long enough for everyone to look up and see her making her entrance, and long enough for Max's eyes to grow accustomed to the soft light that the oil lamps threw over the assembled company.

One glance told him that Meredith had got it wrong, and he had got it wrong for her. No one there was in the least costumed. Or rather they were dressed, whereas Meredith was costumed, as in a play, and as in the kind of play that Max would tell her to turn down. Straight away Max found this very funny. He didn't mean to, but in the back of his mind he thought that it was a kind of perfect snub to Howard after all this time. And he could see that Howard was going to have a hard time with the rest of the house party because of Meredith's over-the-top dressing, although his father – because he was a fan, and had fallen madly in love with her from the stalls – was quite happy to look down her *décolletage* and admire her publicly in front of his guests.

Only her stage training saved Meredith during the next sticky half-hour. And God, how sticky the English could be when they wanted! Their conversation condescendingly leaking in little droplets from half-closed mouths, their eyes narrowed at Meredith in disapproval. Meredith would be too used to getting the feel of an audience not to be aware of it, and Max knew just how much it must have got to her when the butler presented her with a supper tray immaculately laid and beautifully arranged with food.

'No supper, thank you,' she said grandly, 'I'm far too full. We ate in the car coming up.'

Max swallowed a smile, and noticed their host doing the same. Not the lines that Noël Coward would have written for her. And what's more Max knew she must be starving with hunger, because he was. Only the terror of using the wrong knife or fork had made her dismiss her supper.

No such problem for him. He ate, and he was happy for anyone who wished to watch him.

'Please, Max, please, can't we go home?'

Meredith was walking up and down the vast area between Max's magnificent bed and the end wall of his room.

'I'm cold and I'm tired and I'm hungry, and I want to go home. I've never done a play with a shooting weekend, I'm not that kind of actress.'

'Stop getting yourself so worked up,' Max begged her, 'it's only two days. Old man Howard thinks you're the best.'

'He's a dirty old man,' Merry fumed, 'I've met his type before, always sniffing round dressing rooms when they can

251

get the opportunity. He should go to a proper tart and get it out of his system.'

'He does,' said Max, lighting a cigar and grinning. 'He goes to the same place as Baz.'

But Meredith wasn't in the mood for gossiping, she was in too much of a state.

'You should have had something to eat,' Max went on, 'you know what a state you get in if you don't eat. And after a performance and a long drive. You're crazy. If the staff hadn't gone I'd ring down for something for you.'

'It's all right for you, you were brought up posh,' said Meredith, now close to tears. 'I come from Albert Mansions, remember? Flat 8a Albert Mansions, and the nearest I ever came to having a nanny was when I played in *Peter Pan*, and dogs aren't snobs the way your nanny was.'

'You'll be all right,' said Max, pulling on his cigar, 'really. Just relax.'

'Take the line again, you lack conviction, director,' said Meredith, and she turned and walked off towards the door.

'Get some sleep, get some sleep,' returned Max, and he yawned and picked up a book from beside his bed. Actors' abble-dabble, that's all that Meredith was going in for, just kvetching in a different form.

Breakfast downstairs in the dining room was held in silence. No one spoke, they collected papers from the sideboard and they ate quickly, and that's all that could be heard as Meredith stalked into the room slightly ahead of Max who had had to all but put his knee in her back to get her into the dining room.

Laid out on electric heaters was every kind of English breakfast food, and in enough quantities to keep even country appetites satisfied.

Max helped himself to porridge and cream, and then perfectly cooked bacon and eggs and sausage and tomato, but Meredith just toyed with one small piece of toast and lemon tea.

'Stop being afraid of dropping your props,' Max said in a

low whisper as she sat staring ahead of her in petrified silence.

He tried to smile at her once or twice, but she lowered her eyes and picked at the lace tablecloth instead.

'I just want to go home,' she moaned after breakfast as Max got ready for the rabbit shoot.

'See you at lunch,' he said, kissing the air around her head, and going quickly. He wished to God she would go home, but it was too damn far. He was enjoying himself.

'Go downstairs and join the ladies, that's always more fun,' he advised. 'You can't stay in your room until lunchtime.'

But as he left her, and she went back to her bedroom, Max knew that that's precisely what Meredith would do, go back to her bedroom and sit brushing her hair in front of the mirror, or doing her nails; or she'd ring a girlfriend and moan. He knew all that because that was precisely what she would do if she were backstage.

At the shooting lunch the men sat down at trestle tables and were served by the staff and joined by the ladies. Meredith arrived in the company of old Mrs Howard who seemed more unbending now that morning was come, but no one could do anything about the coat and skirt that Meredith had been allowed to pack, a bright purple affair. It made Max want to laugh when he saw how new and wrong Meredith looked beside the other ladies, and how nice and faded their coats and skirts looked, and how they all tried not to look at Meredith but in trying not to look appeared to be staring quite hard.

Meredith was too cute not to notice what a guy she looked, and Max could only guess what she was feeling, until after lunch when she put out her hand and took his cigar from him, and drew on it as if it was pot, and then in the half-silence that surrounded this piece of action, she blew a series of large, round cigar rings.

'Very good, my dear,' said old Mrs Howard, 'I used to do things like that, before the war, particularly when I was back from hunting.'

It was a nice moment, and one from a nice play, but Meredith had had two gins and tonic.

She turned an unsmiling face on old Mrs Howard.

'I bet you bloody didn't,' she said, and then she turned to the butler and said, 'I know how you feel, really, I do, I know how you lot feel.'

Max grinned, but it was a smacked-into-the-wall version of his usual delighted grin.

'That's in the play, isn't it?' he said to Meredith, and covered the moment, before going on to tell a funny story against himself.

As he finished he saw Meredith staring at him, and he could feel the power of her resentment, and her anger at what he knew she thought was her social humiliation; then a look came into her eyes that Max had learned to recognize, and it meant trouble.

She was being upstaged, and she didn't like it.

From then on she gave the performance of her life, and even Max had to admire it. She was superb. She seemed to forget her previous sulks, and set about charming the whole house party as to the manner born. She was funny, and she was graceful, and having been a flop she turned herself round and became a huge success.

She was perfect, but Max knew that the real thing was not what Meredith was doing, but what Seraphina would be doing if she were here.

They left after breakfast on Monday, and the other guests waited until they had gone, as if they were royalty, because by then Meredith had practically convinced even Max that she was.

She climbed regally into the car, and sat quite quietly beside Max until they had passed through the large gates. The moment they hit the open road once more she sat back and put her stockinged feet up on the dashboard.

'Well,' she said, 'if that's what it's like to be a lady, you can keep it.'

Back in London the day when Max was due to pick up his pictures seemed as if it would never come. He took to walking past the premises of the auction house where

Seraphina worked in the vain hope that she might suddenly emerge from its doors and see him, and see how much he loved her already, how she was never out of his thoughts.

He longed for her to have imperfections, just so that they might cool his feelings, so that when he finally walked into her place of work he was relieved, overjoyed even, to see that when she smiled she had a front tooth that crossed slightly over her other front tooth. It wasn't noticeable, but was imperfect, unlike Meredith's perfect little white teeth, and Max loved Seraphina Lucy even more for that.

He ached to ask her out, to tell her that he was already passionately in love with her, that he worshipped every part of her, that he wanted to kiss the little mole by her gold watch strap, that he'd thought of nothing but her, that he had had to pretend to Meredith – and only the night before – that he was too drunk to make love to her, because it had seemed to him that to do so would be to be unfaithful to Seraphina.

'I'm glad to tell you that our expert has said that the pictures are genuine,' she said smilingly to Max. 'Isn't that wonderful? I am so glad.'

She held the pictures up for Max momentarily as if she wanted him to see them again in a new light, and then she rewrapped them in their brown paper.

Max stared at her for a few seconds as she frowned at her task of redoing the parcel for him, carefully knotting the string.

'Could you put your finger there, please?' she asked leaning over it.

Max put his finger on the place where she was tying the knot. It was laughable how his hand shook, and how when he raised his eyes and saw her pushing her blonde hair behind her ears, how he had to hold on to himself not to lean forward and try to do it for her.

She handed him the parcel. He looked at her, his eyes devoid of their usual impudent mischief.

'Seraphina is such a beautiful name,' he said to her, apropos of nothing, and everything.

She didn't blush, but her face most definitely became edged with pink, as a daisy is, it was noticeable against the navy blue of her dress, and the white collar, and the charms on her bracelet sang a little as she pushed her hair back yet again.

'It's always been an embarrassment to me, actually,' she told him, 'but now I quite like it. At least not many other people are called Seraphina.'

'No,' Max agreed, and he picked up the parcel.

How to ask her out? What to say? Imagine being able to make the kind of deal that would make even Baz blush, and yet not have the courage to ask a girl out. Maybe it was because suddenly, in front of her, he knew he was a little older, and she was a little younger, and he knew he risked being turned down, and Max wasn't used to being rebuffed. Maybe that was it? Not that it mattered, because he was already at the door and, although the place was still empty, even so he hadn't had the courage to say, 'What are you doing this evening?' Or 'Will you come out to dinner?' Bald words that were necessary if he was ever to get so near to Seraphina that he would be able to hear her heart beat.

'Mr Kassov?'

He turned and looked at her almost wretchedly, imagining that he must have left his cheque book, or that the parcel needed more string.

'Yes?'

'Would you like an invitation to a Private View tonight? It might not be of interest, but a friend of mine does rather good paintings – horses and so on – not at all modern or anything, but she is being taken up by quite a few people, and she does do some quite fine things. Well, at least, I think so.'

Max was by the door, it was half open, and the cold air was already making his face feel chill.

'I hope you don't mind my asking, but there are still a few invitations I should have placed – you know how it is. I suppose it's working in here with all these poor dead artists' work, I feel I ought to be nice to living ones. But that doesn't mean to say that you'd necessarily feel the same. I mean I'd quite understand if you're busy.'

'What time?'

She held out an invitation. Cork Street. Six-thirty.

The place was already crowded when he arrived just a little before seven, but she saw him immediately and waved her catalogue at him and smiled as if he was an old friend.

'Mr Kassov? Mr Kassov?'

'Max—'

'Max.'

As soon as she said his name they both knew. Max. Seraphina. Their names had become entwined, and she looked up at Max wonderingly as if she, too, suddenly couldn't believe it, that what was happening to them didn't happen to people, not people like her anyway, not people who had been properly brought up.

'Would you like to meet the artist – Susan, this is Max Kassov, he's a . . .' she paused and looked up at Max briefly, 'he's a friend of mine.'

They walked round the room looking first at their catalogues and then at the paintings, and Max stood behind her, and occasionally her hair swung in his face, or her arm touched his arm, and then very soon they were walking along the road and both turning every now and then to see if they could find a taxi, and he was opening the door of one for her, and she was climbing in, and he didn't have to look at her legs to know that they would be slim, and fine and, although not unbelievable like Merry's, coltish and charming, and that she would wear slightly 'older' shoes of the kind that would be bought because the wearer knew that they would 'take them through the day'.

Sitting back beside her in the taxi, Max wanted to lean forward and kiss her, but instead he held on to the strap and talked and looked out of the window, and she did the same because the driver was speeding along to the restaurant, and if they didn't hold on tight they would both be thrown

257

together, and although it was already too late it was too soon too.

Dinner passed as all dinners do when the moment that two people are really waiting for has yet to come. She ate delicately, and drank little; in fact he could see from the way she drank that she would have been 'quite happy with bitter lemon'.

'Shall I drop you home?'

'Are you sure?'

'Can I see you again?'

'Would you like to come in for a drink?'

It was her parents' London flat. They had another, in Rome. A country house in Sussex. A shooting lodge in Scotland. Max's heart sank. He was two Scotches in and he hadn't a hope.

'Seraphina—'

He leaned against the frame of the door.

'Seraphina? Seraphina. Seraphina. I'll start again. Seraphina, would you come out with me again?'

'I'd love to,' she said quite seriously, and then he noticed that she was quite pale, and he leaned forward and took her in his arms, and she went quite willingly into them, standing with her face against his before they started to kiss, and to kiss some more, again and again, until, stunned by her passionate response, he followed her back into the sitting room and, taking off his coat, led her by the hand to the sofa and started to make love to her.

'I can't.' Max straightened up suddenly.

Seraphina lay back against the chintz cushions and stared up at him.

'What's the matter?'

'I can't. I can't make love to you. Not here. Not now.' He stood up and walked away from her. 'I love you, you see. I'm in love with you. I fell in love with you the first moment I saw you. I didn't think that kind of thing happened.'

She went to him.

'I love *you*,' she said, reaching up and putting her arms round him. 'I love you terribly.'

'Maybe you'll improve with practice,' Max joked, but he took one of her hands and kissed the palm. 'I must go home. I'll call you tomorrow.'

'Very well.'

She was so passive now. Max turned away from her, his desire for her so painful that he found himself suddenly wishing that they had never met, half hoping that by morning it would all be over. She would have flown to Rome. He would go back to Merry. Nothing would have changed. It would just have been a passing fancy, or a fancy pass.

The next day he was hardly in the office before he rang her.

'I'm sorry about last night, I got carried away.'

'You didn't mean those things then? You didn't mean what you said?'

'I meant every word, no, what I mean was I'm sorry – I'm sorry if I got carried away.'

There was a long silence, and then she said faintly, 'It doesn't matter.'

'Oh, but it does,' said Max quickly. 'Because I want to marry you.'

She made a strange little sound, and put down the telephone, and Max went round to see her straight away.

'Please?'

'No, I can't.'

'*Please?*'

'All right. One o'clock then.'

He'd upset her, he could see that. He went back to his own office feeling suicidal. He was sure that she looked as if she had been crying.

Lunch was what Seraphina called 'utterly wretched'. They knew nothing about each other. Where would their relationship begin or end? He confessed that he had been in love with someone else. It was all over the moment he met her. He promised. Seraphina stared from him to the view out of the window. People walking along, people hurrying by, none of them in love, all of them going somewhere.

'Let's go back to my flat,' Max suggested after they'd walked halfway round the Park in the bitter weather.

Seraphina said nothing, knowing. He drove them. Back there, Max knew, it would be different. It would be his flat, and he would feel less guilty. He would be able to undress her slowly and tenderly. He would be able to lay her on his bed and kiss her, every part of her, and she would love him.

'I love you, I love you.'

Her cry soared across the bed, and as he took her Max felt almost guilty. She was so beautiful, blonde, and white, and so beautiful, and utterly unlike anything he'd ever known. Such gentle eyes, and such demure manners, and yet she responded to his love-making with such passion that when he lay back and stared at her it seemed to him that it was someone else who had been in bed with him.

He kissed her smooth forehead as she lay sleeping, her head against his shoulder. Now for marriage.

Looking back, years later, when he was living in America where he liked to take his memories of England out and look through them without pain remembering only those things that he had loved, those things that were to him England, his corner viewed from a foreign field, Max marvelled at Seraphina's courage. She had gone to him, and he had taken her, and she had loved him, and it seemed to him that she had looked neither to the right, nor to the left, but only followed where he had chosen to go. She'd given up everything she'd known for him, and, it seemed, without a backward glance.

'We must be married straight away.'

He had taken her to Brighton for the day. Catching the old-fashioned train, the Brighton Belle, with its lace mats and courteous rail attendants. Walking along the sea front, lunching at English's famous fish restaurant. It seemed the right place to discuss marriage. He had a picture of her that day, her arms crossed, the wind blowing her hair away from her face.

260

'Yes, I'll marry you, Max, but let's do it quickly.'

She clung to him, and he wondered at the sudden passionate way that she had said those words.

And then he knew what it was that she meant. That marriage to him would mean the end to everything else. That her mother and stepfather, her sister, all of them, they couldn't be told. Perhaps she couldn't even tell herself what she was doing? Perhaps she wouldn't need to if it all happened too quickly.

'I'll arrange everything,' said Max briskly, and he felt suddenly impatient that their day out in Brighton was delaying his return to London, and their arrangements.

Back at the office Max knew that he had to get Meredith out of his life, and quickly, but short of murdering her it seemed an insuperable task.

They had never lived together, because that had always been one of Max's rules, never to let a girl move in with him. Visit each other, make love, but no rows of high-heeled shoes in his cupboard, and mascara brushes left by his tooth glass.

As yet, besides the famous night when he had had to pretend to be too drunk to make love to her, luck had been on his side, because following their visit to Hardway Hall she had contracted a virus, which had kept her barely able to go onstage let alone question Max's lack of passion.

When he went round to see her at her flat he was at pains to make her laugh, and to be his usual cheerful self, but she could never hold his eyes, and he had to pretend that he was afraid of catching her virus to cover for the fact that he couldn't face kissing her, not after Seraphina.

'Max?'

Max stopped by the door and turned round. He was all too aware of the sudden anxiety in Meredith's voice, and yet all he could think about was that it was now only four weeks until he and Seraphina were due to be married.

'Max, are you all right?'

'Fine, fine, why?'

261

Max turned towards her, and smiled. He would have felt like Judas, if he hadn't thought that she and Craig had knocked each other off.

'Nothing,' said Meredith, 'nothing, it's just that you don't seem to be yourself. These last few days you've seemed so distant.'

'I'm a hypochondriac, I'm terrified of disease!'

'Stale news,' said Meredith flippantly. 'No, there's something else. Is it the show? We're still getting full houses, aren't we? The returns aren't down, are they?'

Max could have sworn that she knew, and he started to sweat. He wasn't afraid of Meredith, but he was afraid of women in anger. Particularly red-haired women.

'All right, I'll come clean.'

Max went up to her bedside. The poor girl looked quite pale, but still beautiful. Meredith was still very, very beautiful indeed.

'I'm worried about you, it's not like you to be ill, you know.'

Meredith threw him an old-fashioned look.

'Pull the other one, Max, please, it's got Big Ben on it,' she laughed, and as she did so the telephone beside her bed rang, and she picked up the receiver. Hearing who it was she looked up at Max and pulled a little face.

'Can I ring you back in just a minute?' she asked the caller. 'I won't be a minute.'

She replaced the receiver again.

'You won't believe who that was,' she told Max, 'he's driving me mad. And God knows why, I can only think that the more you crush men the better they like it.'

'Who's he?' asked Max and, quite obviously for old times' sake, he felt jealous. 'Who?'

'If I said Craig Matheson, what would you say?'

'You must be joking?'

'Quite. But I'm not. Trouble is the more I tell the silly bastard to run along the more he pesters me. It's unbelievable, he's – well, he seems to have some kind of schoolboy crush. Has that ever happened to you, Max?'

Meredith was a good actress, but not that good. Max watched her long-nailed fingers stroking his hand, and try as he could he knew that he felt as guilty as he'd ever felt.

'He's just trying it on,' he told her, 'ignore him.'

'I can't be as rude as I would like,' Meredith said truthfully, 'because of the show. It's all but a two-hander and I can't, I really can't face battling with him every night, not again, and not feeling like I do, like an old granny.'

'Marry him and make your partnership permanent,' Max suggested, and he laughed to take the sting out of the suggestion.

Meredith looked up at him affectionately.

'Now there's a notion,' she said, and she too laughed.

'No, marriage is not for me, Max, not ever. Love, but not marriage, that's one thing that Jay and I have in common, our dedicated aversion to wedded deadlock.'

The relief that Max felt was the much-needed Martini at the end of a dead fish of a day. It was the shower after exercise. It was a deluge of gratitude to God that in marrying Seraphina he was robbing Meredith of nothing. Because he had loved her. He knew that now he was leaving Merry, he had loved her, and a great deal, but it would have taken him nowhere; he knew that now, because she wouldn't have married him.

'I can tell you why I've seemed a bit strange,' he said, 'it's because I've been planning a film for you, and I wanted to keep it as a surprise, but now that you're ill I'll tell you anyway, and then you've got something to look forward to, OK?'

Meredith flung her arms around his neck, and Max could do nothing to avoid her kiss.

'Oh, Max, how wonderful you are. I owe you everything.'

'You certainly do,' said Max, retreating to the door once more as the telephone rang again.

He waved to Meredith as she once more picked up the receiver.

263

'See you,' he called.

As he closed the door he heard Meredith saying, 'Oh hello, Craig darling, hello.'

But this time Max felt no feelings of jealousy, just panic. He must now find her a film, and like yesterday.

Baz had bought the rights to a book, many years before, just another property, but in the middle of the night Max remembered it. It was a terrible book, but terrible books made good movies, and it had a wonderful central role in it, the part of a fallen woman. Perfect for Meredith. He rang Baz at six in the morning, both their times.

'What do you want to buy that from me for?' Baz demanded.

'I need a property for Merry, Baz, she's feeling low, she's ill, and you know actresses, they must be wanted day and night and night and day. Merry goes one better though – she needs to know she's in work Sundays too.'

Max could hear Baz yawning.

'Call me in the morning, Maxie, really.'

'This is the morning, now come on, how much?'

'Take it, have it, I don't want it,' said Baz wearily, in the tone of voice he would use to a young boy borrowing his car. 'Just let me get back to sleep, OK?'

'Thanks, Baz. Really.'

Max surprised even himself. The book, the money, he had them all in a week, now all he needed was a writer.

'Not in a fortnight, Max, we can't do it in a fortnight,' said William, pushing his glasses back on to his nose.

Everywhere was winter, except in Max's office. William had his coat off but he still felt as if he had it on. He looked round at a rubber plant with sudden dislike.

'I hate rubber plants—' he murmured apropos of nothing.

'I love your play by the way—' Max interrupted.

'A fortnight's impossible. Did you, did you really? I was wondering when you were going to mention it.'

'It's really terrific. Seriously, I know I can get a management for it. And stars. No problem.'

'We thought you didn't like it, Jay said you didn't like it,' William told him.

'Like it? I *love* it. I've read it three times now. Ask Mona. *She* loves it. It's funny. It's tender. It's terrific. No problem.'

William sighed with relief.

'Do you know, Jay and I were really beginning to think that you didn't like it, but Jay did say you'd been snowed under, that Merry was ill, and you were worried.'

'Sure, sure, Jay was right, she knows me, she knows I never read anything in a hurry. I like to do a property justice.'

'What – what did you think of the "reveal"? I mean, did it fool you?'

'*Fool* me? I couldn't believe it, really. I – well, ask Mona, I went through to her and I said, "I can't believe what they've pulled off here." Really.'

William smiled at Max delightedly.

'I can't tell you what this means to me, really. What it will mean to Jay. She believes in it so much. So very much.'

Max put his arm round William.

'Now leave the play to me. What about the film? Everyone wants to write a movie. You must want to write a movie. Jay must want to write a movie—'

Max stopped suddenly. Even to his own ears he could hear how like Baz he was beginning to sound.

William sighed.

'Oh, all right, Max, for you. But no, I don't want to write a movie, and nor does Jay. It's not a writer's medium, it's a *director*'s medium.'

'So, become a director?'

'I don't want to become a director, Max, I want to write. Directing bores me. I directed at Harvard. I hate the mechanics of it. I hate having to flatter actors and tell them they look great in their wigs. Really.'

265

'All right. So leave the play to me. I'll take care of the play, will you do the film?'

'Yes, yes, of course. A fortnight though.'

William pushed his glasses further up the bridge of his nose again.

'It's all there in the book,' Max tried to reassure him. 'Really, you'll see. The story's all there. And now's a good moment, people are making pictures everywhere.'

'I know,' said William glumly, 'I've seen some of them.'

He took the book from Max, and then got up to go. At the door he turned suddenly and cautioned Max, 'We'd want it to be good. You must understand that.'

'Of course. Of course, you can make it as good as you want.'

'Oh – good!'

'And I'll pay you,' said Max happily. 'I'll pay you well.'

'A film in a fortnight? You sure you know what you're doing? I mean, can you afford two funerals, Max?'

But Max was already pressing the intercom for his secretary.

Max always moved fast, that was his way. His enthusiasms, his ability to feel bored, to feel as he put it 'the seat of his pants' after only a few seconds at a show or at a meeting, to dismiss anything that didn't grab him by the throat, they were something to which Meredith was quite used, and why she found him enthralling. But now even Merry was amazed at how he was getting everything together, hiring everything in sight even before the script was on his desk.

If Max had had the time he too would have marvelled at himself, but time was an indulgence if he was to get Merry off his hands before his wedding.

Of course she had to know what was happening, and all the time, which slowed Max down, and made him want to spit with impatience.

The worst day was when she rang him because she'd read the book, or at least Jay had read the book, and Jay had told her it was rubbish.

266

'Of course it's rubbish, darling, it's terrible rubbish, dreadful awful stinking piss, but it'll make a great movie, the worst books make the best movies, you know that.'

Meredith didn't know that, but she agreed that she did nonetheless.

'Look' – Max pulled on his cigar slowly and talked slower into the telephone – 'look, you've got a movie being written for you by your favourite writers, you've got the best costume and art design around, you've got a cracking new young director, you'll have London, Paris and New York at your feet, so what else do you want?'

'Oh God, Max, I know, I didn't mean to sound ungrateful, really.'

'I worship you, and soon the whole world will join me, what else do you want – really, tell me.'

Meredith laughed her husky, throaty, well-developed Jeannie Costelow laugh.

'God, I love you. You're incredible. I owe everything to you. Everything.'

'You're a star, Merry darling, a great big star. Remember that's what matters. Always. It's the only thing that matters—'

'You're beginning to sound like Louis – you're sounding like your father,' said Merry laughing.

Max replaced the telephone. He had to keep up the brainwashing. Stardom, I, me, my face for the world to see, that's all that mattered to Merry really. And she must be encouraged to think that way even more. She must be made to see that she was the only person who mattered to her, and then what happened to Max, what happened to him, wouldn't matter to her.

Seraphina was different. She was so wonderfully different that whenever he wasn't with her, and he thought of her, Max could only marvel at her rarity. She didn't say 'I' or 'me', she said 'one'; and that only occasionally. She always seemed so anxious to talk of Max and what he wanted. She never interrupted him. She never leaned across him to talk to someone else. She never raised her voice. And she was so soft, and her eyes were so kind, and she looked at Max as if she couldn't believe that he existed.

Max's eyes swivelled from 'Act One' of William and Jay's play to his diary, and he flicked through it quickly. The movie should be in full swing by the time he and Seraphina were ready to slip away to Scotland after the registry office wedding. By the time anyone found out, they would be locked up in the castle he had hired for the honeymoon. And that would be that. After that all they had to be was happy.

'Easy,' he said to himself. 'Easy.'

He went to the window and looked down at the traffic moving slowly in the street below his office window. Happiness. That wasn't something he'd ever contemplated before. Success yes, but happiness?

Seraphina wore a pink suit with a matching pillbox hat and brought three rapturous girlfriends to the registry office with her. Their eyes shone as they looked at Max and then at Seraphina.

'It's all so romantic,' they murmured, and sighed after the brief ceremony was over and everyone was busy kissing everyone else.

Seraphina was as pale as the little bouquet of flowers that she carried. She didn't seem able to look Max in the eyes until they were in his car, and held up at the traffic lights outside the hotel where Max had arranged a wedding lunch, and then she flung her arms around his neck, and hugged him tight.

'I'm free, I'm free,' she said.

For a second Max looked at her in astonishment. He hadn't until that moment been aware that she was, or had been anything else, but now he saw by the radiance in her face just how much parental duty had meant to her, and that in marrying him she had freed herself from being a daughter and a stepdaughter and a sister, and he could see just how much it meant to her to be his, to be free to be herself, to be the wife of Max Kassov.

268

Until that moment he had never been quite sure that he meant as much to her as she did to him. And he hadn't minded. It hadn't seemed to matter, because so much did he love her, so much did she seem to be the only person ever created whom he could love as he loved her, that he was convinced even if she didn't feel the same, then after a little she would, because his love would double and redouble. He would love her even more for not loving him quite as much.

But now he could see he didn't have to. They loved each other equally.

'Just remember you're only free to do as I wish,' he said teasingly, but Seraphina didn't seem to hear him, she just gazed ahead of her, into the future.

The Scottish castle which Max had rented for the fortnight's honeymoon was small and cosy, and had central heating, and wasn't what Seraphina was expecting; no ghosts or draughts or winds whistling round the turrets, just rain and beautiful views and a housekeeper and a cleaning woman to look after their needs. Even so they were truly alone.

Seraphina loved to walk, and Max who had always hated walking learned to pretend that he didn't. They wandered the woods and hills around the castle talking about everything, but most of all about their future home. A house in the country. Max was obsessed by the idea, and he knew just where he wanted it: in Norfolk, where Howard's family came from, a house near theirs, so he could forget to ask Howard to his house, the way Howard had always failed to ask him. He didn't tell Seraphina that, he just said that he wanted to buy her a beautiful old house.

Nor did he tell her that he wanted her to live there all week, because he wanted to keep Seraphina to himself. He didn't want her to become any part of his business, or indeed to have anything to do with the business itself.

'The business is for bastards, not nice girls,' was how he

put it, and she seemed to accept this, as she seemed to accept everything.

'I'd like to live in the country,' she agreed, 'quite honestly I only really like animals and children.'

When Seraphina said things like that Max's spirits soared. She was the perfect girl, she would be the perfect woman.

'Do you mind?' she added, 'I'm afraid I'm a little dull like that.'

Max hesitated as if he was afraid of her dullness. It was a game, only a little game, but it made him feel even more in control of her.

'I don't know anything about show business,' she added apologetically.

'And you don't need to,' Max told her. 'Forget the business, it needn't concern you.'

And then he undressed her and made love to her in front of the fire with even more passion than usual.

One night they made lists of what they liked. Seraphina's list was so 'Seraphina' that it made Max take her in his arms and caress her as if she was about to be torn from his life.

Seraphina's list read:

> White aertex shirts
> Sweet peas in large bunches
> Pink satin slippers
> A large straw hat with a velvet ribbon
> Old silver photograph frames
> Any orangery anywhere
> Button hooks

Max's list read:

> The Taj Mahal
> Betty Grable's legs
> Rubinstein
> Spinach *en branche* as made by Franco
> A yacht on a sunny day
> Cashmere
> A clean handkerchief

Seraphina found two bicycles at the back of the empty coach house. She presented them to Max all newly washed and polished. Max folded his arms and looked from her eager expression to the bicycles and back again.

'You're not catching me riding a girl's bicycle,' he announced.

'There isn't a boy's bicycle,' Seraphina told him apologetically, and then she pushed hers across the cobbled courtyard into the rough drive that lay in front of the little castle.

'I want to bicycle to the village to buy a Mars Bar,' she called back to him, her voice floating serenely back to where Max was still standing.

Max watched her disappear through the arch of the courtyard, and then he groaned and pushing his bicycle ahead of him he sat astride the old jalopy and started to peddle after his young bride. Seraphina was like his sister Trixie. She could get him to do anything.

The village shop was the only shop. There was nothing else for miles. Knitting patterns for babies' bootees jostled with packets of cigarettes, some of which Max knew had long since ceased being made. Large skeins of thick wool were draped from iron rods, themselves hung with chains and bearing the weight of mackintoshes and woollen jumpers. Everywhere winter was in permanent expectation, or rain.

Max picked up a small child's penknife and just as Seraphina was carefully handing over her money for the Mars Bar, he added the little penknife. The old woman behind the counter was pleased by the sale. Max felt the coarseness of the skin on her hand as she took his two shillings and sixpence. It scraped against the softness of his own, and he thought of his father, and how his grandmother would whiten doorsteps for a halfpenny a time in the East End. Her hands would have felt like this old biddy's hands.

Outside the shop Seraphina took the wrapper carefully off the Mars Bar, and then took Max's penknife, and cut the chocolate and toffee into six little slices, like a cake.

Max looked at her and grinned delightedly. They'd both been to boarding school and both cut their chocolates up with penknives. They had that in common. The same way they had both learned to ride bicycles by falling off them. The same way they'd been taught to try and enjoy cold showers. He had a lot for which to thank Aunt Susan.

He jumped aboard his bicycle and this time he sped ahead of Seraphina, arriving back at the coach house long before her.

'Well done,' she said as she finally drew up, and Max's heart contracted at her generosity.

If that had been his sister Trixie he had been racing against, she would have complained that Max hadn't waited for her, and then sulked for the rest of the afternoon. But not Seraphina. Seraphina delighted in the fact that Max had won the race, and was full of praise for the way Max had handled his bicycle.

'I wobble too much,' she told him. 'As soon as I try and go fast, I wobble about all over the place.'

'That's because you're pushing down too hard,' Max replied. 'First one side, then the other. You want to lean forward and try to pedal evenly.'

Seraphina just smiled back at him angelically, and then kissed him on the cheek.

'I'll beat you at Scrabble instead,' she said.

Mrs McKenzie had laid tea in the kitchen, which was in the basement of the castle. There was a good fire burning in the grate, and as they came in Mrs McKenzie was busy piling home-made drop scones on a plate. After they had feasted on the perfect strawberry-jam-covered scones, and the rich home-made Dundee cake, they turned their chairs round to the fire, and sat warming themselves and staring silently and dreamily into the flames.

Then they excused themselves and, thanking Mrs McKenzie for the quite splendid tea, they retired upstairs to their bedroom where, warmed by another roaring log fire, they made love in the four-poster bed.

Or rather Max made love to Seraphina, who as soon as

272

Max started to undress her seemed to be about to faint. She was completely suppliant, and utterly submissive, and this excited Max all the more. For Max had been used to women who showed him things. Or women who, once he had made the initial advance, responded quite vigorously and creatively to his love-making.

But not Seraphina. Seraphina closed her eyes when he kissed her, and never opened them again until Max had brought them both to a palpitating climax. She would moan softly as he entered her, and again as he started to love her. And she would sometimes let her head fall back from his embrace and open her mouth as if she could hardly breathe and was dying. And her arms might hold him round his waist, or his neck, and she might raise herself back to him, to kiss him slowly and voluptuously, her tongue rolling slowly around his own, or her small white teeth biting softly into his lips. But she never made a move, not a conscious one, not one of which Max was aware. Yet their union was perfect, sublime in fact: a form of love-making quite different to anything Max had experienced before, on a higher plane it seemed, on a threshold nearer the heavens, somewhere far nearer the vicinity of the gods.

And as he made love to her, and when he finished making love to her, Max felt superhuman. As if he had been elevated above mere mortality and become an eternal.

'Seraphina,' he whispered as she lay naked in his arms, 'I love you. I love you more than I've ever loved anyone before. Before you, there was nothing. Not anything at all. Because now I know what love really means.'

And at that very same moment, so did someone else find out what love really meant. A girl all alone in her bedroom, far away in another country, in England. And as Meredith Browne discovered the nature and meaning of love, she reached for a phial of sleeping tablets and a bottle of brandy she had positioned by her bedside and, wiping away her tears, mixed herself a lethal cocktail.

7

'If they'd been barbiturates,' the doctor told Jay, 'you wouldn't be visiting her now. Well, you might be, but those flowers you're carrying would be a wreath. The fact the pills were of the tranquillizer family no doubt saved her.'

The doctor stopped outside Meredith's private room.

'That,' he continued, 'and your opportune arrival.'

'It was pure chance,' Jay said. 'When my partner – when the person I was with saw how drunk she was getting in the restaurant, he said "Meredith's found out". And so when I rang her—'

'I'm not handing out medals,' the doctor smiled, reaching for the door handle. 'I'm just saying If. Not more than five minutes now.'

And he swung the door open for Jay.

Meredith could have been Ophelia. Except instead of floating in flowers she was surrounded by them. But the sleep she was in, as Jay tiptoed to her bedside, might have been the sleep of death, so still was she lying, and so pale was her skin. Jay sat and stared at her, at the beautiful complexion now stretched a little tautly over those quite perfect bones, and at Meredith's hair, lying in beautifully arranged patterns on the pillow, and her long elegant white hands resting above the bedding. It was as if she had been prepared, and arranged by make-up and wardrobe especially for Jay's visit.

I am a camera, Jay thought, as she continued to stare down at the sleeping beauty. But then as far as actresses go, she concluded, I suppose we all are.

After a while, Meredith opened her eyes and stared up at the ceiling. Then she frowned, and looked slowly round at Jay.

Jay kicked herself inwardly, in an attempt to stop herself from feeling that the whole thing was a scene in a movie.

Meredith stretching a lily-white hand out slowly to grasp one of her own, and smiling weakly at Jay didn't help to dispel the illusion.

'Darling,' she whispered huskily. 'You are sweet.'

Having to face a would-be suicide for the first time, Jay found herself at a loss for words. In the taxi on the way to hospital she tried to imagine how she would handle the scene as a writer, but every opener she dreamed up, every approach she envisaged just emerged as a long string of clichés. So in the end she found herself settling for a concerned and sympathetic silence.

'How long have you been here?' Meredith asked.

'I've just arrived,' Jay answered.

'You're a darling,' Meredith whispered. 'And you're very, very sweet.'

Then with another brave but rapidly weakening smile, Meredith turned her head away and once again closed her eyes.

But she hadn't let go of Jay's hand, so Jay sat there for as long as Meredith slept, still holding it. While she sat, Jay cast her mind back to the events of the night before last, when William and she had been taken to La Terrazza by a visiting American film producer who had spent the evening pretending that he was about to commission William and Jay to write a modern-day version of *When Our Hearts Were Young and Gay*, but had in reality only asked them along so that he could justify his expenses. Jay knew that William had realized the scam from the word go, when the producer had asked them what they'd like to drink and William said champagne.

Meredith came into the restaurant halfway through Jay's Vongole Romana, which were quite delicious. She was with her leading man from the film she was making,

Lawrence Brere, who possessed a beautiful voice but the looks of a car salesman, and who was famous for undoing his trousers at dinner parties and showing the assembled company what had got him to the top. He was already very drunk, and when Meredith stopped to introduce him to William and Jay he practically fell on to their table. William saved him from that humiliation, and propped him up while Meredith exchanged pleasantries with them, before taking Brere off to join the rest of their party who were busy gathering around a large centre table, where they finally all sat shrieking with hysterical laughter at each other's scurrilous anecdotes.

Until Jay noticed a passing stranger stop by Meredith's table and, having introduced himself, pull up a chair and show Meredith something in the evening paper. Then as Meredith read the item the stranger took a notebook from his pocket and started asking Meredith questions. A row then broke out, but Jay couldn't hear or see why. But what she could see was one of Meredith's party trying to get rid of the stranger whom Jay assumed to be a reporter, and him refusing to go. Lawrence Brere then threw a glass of wine in the man's face, and within moments a waiter, one of the patrons, and one of Meredith's friends took the intruder by the seat of his pants and expelled him. And the incident, the sort of incident that happens in crowded fashionable restaurants all around the world, was soon forgotten by the other diners, and the good humour of the evening was quickly restored.

Jay would have put it out of her mind as well, had she not known one of the protagonists so intimately. William too was distracted by it, but had no chance to discuss it at the time with Jay. But Jay kept a weather eye on Meredith, and noted how much she was suddenly starting to drink, and how very drunk she was getting when it was time for William and Jay to leave.

When they were back at the studio and William was pouring them a nightcap, Jay suddenly thought of the evening paper. It didn't take her long to find the relevant item. The whirlwind courtship and marriage of Max Kassov and Seraphina Lucy was the lead story in 'Londoner's Diary'.

'You don't reckon Meredith *knew*?' William asked after poring over the article.

'Judging from her reaction,' Jay answered, 'no.'

'Meredith and Max were like Nichols and May,' William said. 'Jeezus. They were fixtures and fittings.'

'You seem to forget, William Kennedy,' said Jay. 'There's no business like show business.'

And that had been that, until Jay had suddenly sat bolt upright in bed at three o'clock in the morning.

'I have to ring Meredith!' she announced, reaching for the telephone. 'I've just had this terrible dream!'

'Sure it can't wait till morning?' William groaned. 'A dream is a dream is a dream.'

'This one was of Meredith's funeral!' Jay replied, waiting in vain for an answer from the number she was ringing. 'It was awful! They were burying her in a pauper's grave!'

William yawned and pulled the pillow over his head.

'She won't thank you for waking her at this hour,' he said.

'She will, William!' Jay answered, jumping out of bed and starting to get dressed. 'That is if we're not too bloody late!'

It wasn't the first time in her life Jay had experienced precognition, but it was certainly the most vital. When she had been a little girl she had often known things were going to happen in advance, but it had always been put down to the phenomenon known as *déjà vu*. Or, more specifically by her mother, to glands.

But William had always been intrigued by this side of Jay, and that she might have believed some sort of extrasensory perception. As a partnership, although still a young one, they had already started to thought-transfer, and test each other out on what they were thinking at particular moments when they were apart – with quite rivetingly accurate results. Which was why William went along with Jay in the middle of the night to Meredith's flat and persuaded the night porter to open Meredith's door.

And which was why Jay was now sitting holding the hand of a live Meredith Browne, instead of attending the funeral of a dead one.

On her third visit, Jay found Meredith sitting up in bed painting her nails. Jay put down the magazines and books she had brought Meredith and pulled a chair up beside the bed. Meredith barely looked up at her.

Jay spent the first quarter of an hour or so of her visit talking business small talk, concentrating mainly on the bad time she and William were having at present working on a story outline for a film for the producer Michael Spiller.

'He has the foulest mouth I've ever heard on anyone,' Jay laughed. 'He even has cushions with obscenities embroidered on them.'

Meredith paid little attention to her anecdotes, but just continued painting her fingernails. Every now and then she would hold a hand away from her to examine it, and then she would flick a glance at Jay before continuing the manicure. Finally she put away the varnish, brush, files and emery boards in a special leather case and, straightening out her bedsheet, turned to Jay with a formal smile.

'Well then,' she said.

'Yes?' Jay enquired.

'I gather I have you to thank for me still being here,' Meredith announced.

Jay had been anticipating this, but still hadn't been able to come up with a suitable reply.

'I know. Weird, wasn't it?' she found herself saying. 'I just knew.'

'Thanks.'

Meredith looked Jay right in the eyes, challenging her. Jay frowned and bit her lip.

'Do you want to talk about it?' Jay asked, hardly able to believe what she was hearing herself say.

'What's there to talk about?' Meredith replied. 'I tried to kill myself. I wanted to kill myself. Then along comes the Good Samaritan.'

Jay knew what the next line was. The next beat was no man was worth it, surely. But Jay left it unsaid, preferring instead to sit this one out. Or better, and perhaps more in keeping with the scene they were playing out, take it on the chin.

'I've been sitting here wondering why it is that suicide's so bad,' Meredith continued. 'It's not as if I'm here by my own request. My mother got pissed at a wrap party, drank the best part of a bottle of gin, or so I was later told, and that's how this little darkie got born. Courtesy of the distiller and the carelessness of a film technician. So what if I decide to call it a day? Life isn't a bowl of cherries. It's a crock.'

Jay stared at the floor and wished she could stop wanting to rewrite everything Meredith was saying. But it was an itch of which she couldn't rid herself. Meredith was in deadly earnest, she knew that. But because she was expressing herself so badly it was all sounding like a first draft. The draft you threw away.

'I think people should commit suicide,' Jay suddenly said in an inspired moment. 'Just to make other people jealous.'

Meredith looked at Jay, and then suddenly laughed quite genuinely.

'Jay, you're great!' she said. 'If somebody had to find me, thank God it was you!'

Meredith then insisted that they open a bottle of champagne one of her many well-wishers had sent her. Jay could see no harm in it. Particularly after the first two glasses.

'What did the papers have to say?' Meredith asked her.

'Quite a lot,' Jay replied. 'The consensus of opinion was nervous collapse.'

'Did they say what it was caused by?'

'Pressure of work. Filming by day, theatre by night, meteoric rise to stardom, and all the usual etceteras.'

'Any connection with that bastard Kassov?'

'Not directly. Plenty of innuendo, but then how would they sell papers without innuendo? William and I have often thought of starting a paper called *The Innuendo*. You couldn't go wrong.'

'What exactly was the innuendo?'

'I'm not quite sure if innuendo can actually be exact,' Jay replied, refilling their glasses.

'The gist,' said Meredith.

'Meteor crashes on set. Meredith Browne, the girl nursed to stardom by West End Whizzo, collapses filming. Real Life Drama as Star is rushed to hospital from location.'

'Sounds as if the publicity department were right on the ball, as usual.'

'At least they got your name right. Don't you remember last year on *Sabotage!*? When poor David Burns collapsed and died, and they gave it out as Terence Bond?'

'Oh Christ, yes!' Meredith laughed. 'And Terry Bond apparently picked up the newspaper on location the next morning and said, "I knew I was miscast, but I didn't think I was that bad"!'

The door of Meredith's room was opened, and Sister, alerted by the noise, looked in.

'Is everything all right in here, Miss Browne?' she asked. 'I thought I heard screams.'

'Everything's fine thank you, nurse,' Meredith replied. 'Except I think we may need another bottle.'

'This is a hospital, Miss Browne,' said the nurse, coming to try and confiscate the remains of the champagne. 'Not a hotel.'

'It's very like some of the hotels I've stayed at on tour,' Meredith told her, keeping the bottle out of reach. 'And you're a dead ringer for some of my bloody landladies.'

Jay took the bottle from Meredith and put it on the

floor, reassuring the Sister that she wouldn't give the patient another drop.

'You theatricals,' the nurse sighed as she returned to the door. 'You're all the same. You think the world owes you a living.'

'She believes it was a put-up job,' Meredith confided to Jay when the nurse had gone.

'Never,' said Jay. 'She's Craig Matheson's mother.'

They were both now fairly drunk, otherwise they would never have found such a remark that funny. But Meredith found it hilarious and collapsed with laughter until the tears ran down her face. And then suddenly Jay noticed that the tears weren't of laughter any more, but had turned to tears of genuine anguish.

'The bastard!' Meredith sobbed. 'The rotten bastard. Why couldn't he have told me?'

'I thought you said she said she didn't want to get married?' William asked Jay when she returned home.

'I think that was only because she knew Max wouldn't ask her,' Jay replied.

'How so?'

'Because Meredith's an actress.'

'Oh, come on!' William laughed. 'These are the 1960s! Not Victorian England!'

'Seriously, William,' Jay argued. 'I agree with Meredith. I don't think Max would ever have asked her to marry him. Actresses are for affairs. Not for marrying.'

'Even to impresarios?'

'I'd say particularly to impresarios. There's no novelty. They've been backstage too often.'

'So what do impresarios want, Jay? Or more specifically – what does Max Kassov want?'

'That's easy, William. Max Kassov wants to lay a bit of Old England.'

They took Meredith abroad with them when they went on a short holiday to Positano. It was Jay's idea, and although

William had baulked at it in principle, in practice, when he saw the state Meredith was in, he could only condone the notion.

Meredith was wrecked. She was as pale as death, and had lost nearly two stone in weight. William had been quite convinced the suicide attempt had been the traditional cry for help, but now he had seen her, he knew this had not been the case. Meredith Browne had genuinely intended to end her life.

'I never realized she was that serious about Max,' William confessed to Jay as they were packing.

'I don't think Meredith did either,' Jay answered. 'I think that was the whole trouble.'

'It wasn't just nose out of joint.'

'If it had just been nose-out-of-joint trouble, she'd have gone round and kicked Max in the neck.'

'But people don't usually go and try and kill themselves the moment they hear the bad news, Jay. They usually sit and brood awhile. And then cut their wrists.'

'Who's people, William? What's usual? People don't usually have a long-running smash-hit affair with someone and then suddenly up and marry somebody completely different. Max Kassov did.'

The Mediterranean sun and air did Meredith immediate good, as did the food. Immediate physical good that is, because although William and Jay could see the weight going back on her skeletal frame, and the colour returning to her cheeks, they could have no idea what was going on in her head. Particularly since Meredith spent most of the time sleeping under her beach umbrella during the day and hardly saying a word to them at meals.

Then one night as they sat up in the hills eating the best home-baked pizza William and Jay had ever experienced, Meredith dropped the bombshell.

'I think I've had acting,' she said.

Jay looked at William, uncertain whether or not to pursue the topic. Meredith made her mind up for her.

'I'm serious, you two,' she continued. 'I'm really thinking of giving it up.'

'Why?' Jay asked. 'At this moment in time when at last you've made it? When everyone wants you?'

'Nothing like going out at the top,' William said, in an attempt to take the steam out of it.

'It's not that, William,' Meredith said with a shake of her head. 'There just doesn't seem to be a point any more. And when acting loses its point, it's just ridiculous.'

Meredith had given it a lot of thought. She had thought about it all the time they were in Italy. Lying under her beach umbrella, often feigning sleep so that no one would talk to her, she had thought about how impossible it was going to be to go on acting now that she no longer had Max. Because the one thing that Max's treacherous marriage had finally taught Meredith was that no matter how you tried to kid yourself you were doing it for everyone out there, you weren't. At the bottom line, you were doing it for one person. It might be your mother, or your father, or your lover. But whoever it was, what drove you on to succeed in the business as an actor was the need to please that person who loved you. Or more importantly whom you wanted to love you. And if that person died, or disappeared from your life for one reason or another, your motivation went, and the process of acting became pointless. You did it for someone. There had to be someone special out there in the dark.

At least this was the way Meredith figured it, after days spent lying in silence on the beach, and nights spent lying alone in her bed. She hadn't known this when Max was alive and with her, not consciously, but now that he was dead and gone from her, she knew it only too well. She'd done it for her mother, but she might as well never have bothered.

Her mother would have pushed her under a bus if the director had thought it would improve the shot.

She'd never heard her mother's applause. Her mother had never hugged Meredith to her and told her well done. Her mother had never said that's my girl.

But Max had, Max had done all of those things. Max had clapped her to the echo, and cheered her with the crowd. Max had sent her first-night flowers and waited for her in the wings. It was Max who had told her she could do it. It was Max who had believed in her. It was Max who had made her a star. And what more love could anyone want than that?

Max had been the face in the darkness. It had been Max out there to whom she'd been playing.

And now he was gone, and without a word. He'd thrown her a scrap, a movie to do, like a burglar might throw a dog a bone to distract it. And then when she wasn't looking, he'd sneaked out of the stage door and into the arms of someone else.

And now there was no one out there. They could put up the House Full sign every night for the rest of her life, but it wouldn't make any difference. The aisle seat in Row E would always be empty.

By the time Meredith met Louis for lunch, she was already formulating a plan. She wasn't entirely sure of how to execute it, but she knew in outline what she had to do. And she also knew that Louis was the man who could set it all in motion.

So when Louis asked her if she'd meet him for lunch, she wasn't the least surprised. She had already thought that one out. As soon as the news had broken about Max's whirlwind marriage, Meredith knew Louis would start wondering about her future representation, and that after observing a 'decent' interval, as if someone had died, he would be on the telephone asking her out to lunch at Le Caprice.

'I'd rather go to the Connaught, Louis,' she'd said. 'If you don't mind.'

'The Connaught isn't the business,' Louis grumbled.

'That's why I'd rather we went there,' Meredith replied.

'You don't want to be seen with me, is that it, Meredith?'

'On the contrary, Louis. I'll be delighted to be seen with you. As always. But not yet. Least of all, not yet at Le Caprice.'

'The Connaught is for visiting American stars,' Louis grumbled on. 'Visiting American stars and greedy English publishers.'

'Nonetheless, Louis darling,' Meredith concluded, 'I'll see you there at a quarter to one.'

Meredith was starting as she meant to go on. From now on if anyone was going to make the running, that person was going to be her. In future any jumping that was going to be done was going to be through her set of hoops.

'This is just a phase, Meredith,' Louis told her over his Châteaubriand. 'You'll act again, believe me.'

'Why?' Meredith asked. 'If I go on acting, I wouldn't be able to eat a lunch like this.'

'Figures,' Louis shrugged. 'Women and their figures.'

But all the same Meredith noticed he couldn't help casting an appreciative eye over the great shape she'd managed to get herself back in. Thirty-eight, twenty-two, thirty-four. Louis wouldn't want her any different. More importantly, even though her life was about to change direction, Meredith didn't want herself any different. So OK – she wasn't going to go on being an actress. But nonetheless, that thirty-eight, twenty-two, thirty-four hourglass was still going to need to earn its living.

'Listen,' said Louis, carefully wiping his mouth on a corner of his napkin. 'You give up acting, and Max wins.'

'No, Louis,' Meredith corrected him. 'I don't give up acting and Max wins. I stay an actress, I remain a butterfly. And butterflies, however beautiful, don't live long enough.'

Louis opened his mouth to say something and then thought better of it. Meredith smiled, and chose this moment to put her hand on his.

'I know what you were going to say, Louis darling,' she

said. 'And quite right, too. Yes, what's somebody doing talking about butterflies and their short lives when only a few weeks ago she tried to top herself?'

'Nothing was further from my thoughts, Meredith my dear,' Louis replied.

'I wouldn't blame you,' Meredith continued. 'Bloody actors, as Max would say. Always overdoing everything.'

She smiled as she said his name. Max. The first time she'd said it out loud since he'd gone. And she smiled as she said it as convincingly as she could. But so deep had the wound gone that the smile nearly turned to a cry of pain.

'You'll get over him, my dear,' Louis said, now taking the initiative and putting his hand on her bare arm. 'And even though he's my son, let me tell you, you'll meet someone better. To behave in such a way – Max doesn't deserve you.'

'No, I think Max and I were well enough matched, Louis,' Meredith said softly, in her huskiest tone. 'The person Max doesn't deserve is you.'

Meredith had now recovered her composure and was looking up from under her beautiful long eyelashes and smiling gratefully at the face across the table. Louis was smiling back, unable to take his eyes off her, and patting her arm comfortingly. Meredith then let her eyes meet Louis's directly, and held them in a challenging stare. And when she saw the look deep in the old man's eyes, she knew then he was hers.

So at first she demurred when Louis invited her back to his office for coffee, saying she wasn't sure, making the old man feel younger by pretending in the nicest way that by coming back to the office with him Meredith was putting herself at some risk. This amused Louis, as well as flattering him, and when she finally agreed to come back just as long as he behaved himself, Louis felt twenty years younger.

They sat on either side of Louis's vast mahogany leather-topped desk, with the famous four bronze Lions of Judah stationed at each corner. Meredith stroked the lion nearest her, and then looked across at Louis, who was sipping his brandy and watching her.

'You used to stroke those, remember?' Louis asked her. 'Whenever you weren't working, I'd tell you to stroke them. I'd tell you they were magic, and you'd look at me with that wonderful laugh in your eyes, and say, 'Balls'. 'Balls', you'd say. And what would happen?'

'The phone would ring,' Meredith recalled.

'The phone would ring, Meredith. Not next week. Not in a couple of days. But a few minutes later – the phone would ring.'

'It was a fix, Louis Kass. It was a put-up job between you and Baz.'

'Never!' Louis laughed. 'How could we do such a thing! It was magic!'

Meredith knew that it wasn't, but even so, because she wanted her plan to succeed, she found herself nonetheless stroking the lion as if it was indeed a talisman.

'That's a pretty ring,' Louis observed, lighting a large cigar. 'Present from an admirer?'

'From an ex-admirer,' Meredith replied, turning the ring Max had given her once round her finger.

'The stone's too small,' Louis said, having leaned over the desk and taken Meredith's slender hand in his. 'What was it? End-of-run present?'

'No,' Meredith answered. 'It was a first-night present actually.'

'First-night present!' Louis exclaimed. 'Yes – that's Maxie! That's like the way the Chinese pay their doctors only when they're well! Yes, that's Maxie all over. A first-night present it would be.'

Louis shook his head and blew his cigar smoke in a swirl above his balding head. Meredith by now had risen and worked her way round to his side of the desk, by way of stroking each lion.

'I've always loved this office,' she said, standing by him and staring out of the window at the traffic below her. 'Remember when you used to let me sit on your knee?'

287

'I remember when you used to sit on my knee,' Louis recalled.

'I remember once when some bastard choreographer—'

'Ed Giles.'

'When that bastard Ed Giles had made us all dance until our feet bled. And I cried and sat on your knee. And you stroked my hair and said that whenever I was in trouble, or upset, I could come and sit on your knee.'

'You want to come and sit on my knee now?' Louis laughed. 'Imagine.'

Meredith turned and stood behind him, then putting one hand on each of his shoulders bent down low and half whispered in his ear.

'No. That's not what I want right now, Louis darling,' she said.

She felt him breathe in deeply of her scent and incline his head back just enough to touch her half-bared breasts.

'So what exactly do you want, Meredith my dear?' he asked.

'I want to come and work for you, Louis darling,' she whispered.

And even though she was behind him and couldn't see his face, Meredith knew for once Louis Kass was having a lot of difficulty keeping his big cigar in his mouth.

She also knew there would be strenuous opposition from Baz.

'Old man's toozle,' he groaned when Louis told him. 'It's always been just the two of us, and now you're bringing old man's toozle into the office.'

'She's not toozle, Baz,' Louis argued. 'And I'm not old.'

'She's toozle, and you're old,' Baz insisted. 'And she'll kill you. She'll kill us both. What are you thinking?'

'I'm thinking, Baz, how good she'll be for the business. Star crosses the floor. It has to be good business. Look how she looks. She looks sensational. The Americans will be queueing up outside her door. It has to be good for business.'

'Business is already good, Louis. Or perhaps you haven't had time to notice?'

'Business can never be too good, Baz. Meredith will be a gilt-edged asset.'

'You're going to make her a partner? Or better still, a sleeping partner?'

'That's cheap, Baz, and thoroughly undeserved. I'd rather you kept vulgar thoughts like that in your head.'

'I know what we'll do,' Baz decided. 'I'll treat you to the new girl at Annie's. Now she really is sensational. You remember what I told you about poor Robert? Well, his troubles are all over. And all thanks to this new girl. She gave him this ring, yes? She gave Robert this ring see, which every time he wants to do it, he—'

'I'm not interested what this floozie does for Robert, Baz!' Louis shouted, beginning to lose patience. 'This is nothing to do with that sort of thing! All I'm doing is thinking of the business!'

'Thinking of the business indeed,' Baz sighed. 'What you're thinking about is what you've always been thinking about. What you're thinking about is dick.'

'I'm thinking of the business, Baz!'

'Toozle, Louis. Old man's toozle.'

Meredith waited while the two men fought it out. Louis would take her out to lunch and bring her up to date, and while he still promised her everything, Meredith was patient, and never pushed him an inch.

Instead, after a couple of weeks when the two men were still locked in an impasse, she went and saw Baz.

The next day she had her very own office. And she was on her way. It had been very simple, she thought as she stood in the empty room, trying to decide how to furnish it. It had been a very simple tactic she'd employed, but a very effective one. One she'd learned from watching Max. You simply took your opponent's side.

She had sided with Baz against herself.

Baz had been quite right. It had always been just the two of them, so what could Louis be thinking wanting to bring in a klutz like her?

No, no, Baz had demurred. Meredith a klutz? Meredith would be an asset.

No, no, Meredith insisted. She was – what was that wonderful word Baz used to describe her? Toozle. That was it. Meredith was toozle, and Louis was infatuated

Who could blame him? Baz had sighed, and then sighed even more when Meredith put one of those cool and elegantly manicured hands on his. Who couldn't help but be infatuated with Meredith? No, no, it was perfectly understandable.

Take him to Annie's, Meredith had insisted. If it was something Louis needed to get out of his system, Baz was right. Buy him a piece of young at Annie's.

Perish the thought, Baz had replied. As if he could suggest such a thing. As if that was the way Louis was thinking. All right, so Louis's head maybe was a little turned. But that's not how he saw Meredith. That's not how either of them saw Meredith. Meredith would be an asset to the business. Not just an asset, positively a gilt-edged one.

Meredith was unsure. What could she possibly bring to them that they hadn't got already?

Sex, Baz said. Her sex. They were getting old, and who wanted to woo a couple of old men? But Meredith Browne? With her looks and her twenty-two-inch waist? And her personality? Meredith, Baz was telling her, America will be queueing at your door.

And it was Baz who had finally shown her into her office. This was to be Meredith's room, he had decided. Not the one Louis had suggested. But this one. With the better view. Overlooking Claridge's. Meredith was going to be far happier in here than in the room Louis had suggested.

It was a great tactic, and the pleasure of it working so well was made infinitely more pleasurable because Meredith had taken it from Max. Side with someone unexpectedly, he had always counselled. When they think you're going to

290

leap one way, go jump the other. And preferably down on their side of the fence.

And of course Meredith could be even more convincing than most, because she was such a good and convincing actress. When Meredith told people that of course they were quite right, those people would almost feel ashamed of their rectitude.

By the next day, Meredith had her own desk. A very expensive desk, a genuine antique. She had financed the purchase by selling the ring Max had given her. And, with the money she had left over, she had also bought a small but excellent oil painting to hang on the wall behind her. And a large comfortable leather chair, which tipped back and swung all the way round.

Meredith sat in it and, swinging herself round to look at the traffic below her in Mayfair, thought how funny it was that Max, albeit indirectly, was actually helping to pay to set her up in business against him.

Because that was the whole point of the exercise. It wasn't based on a desire to escape from the ephemera of acting. Nor was it simply in pursuit of power. Meredith's motive was one of revenge. The day Max married Seraphina Lucy, he was a dead man.

Meredith swung her chair away from the window and back to face her desk. She spread her hands across its leathered top and, staring into the time that now stretched invitingly ahead of her, started to formulate her plans.

And the first of these was to poach some of Max Kassov's best clients.

Meredith already knew one of the secrets of Louis and Baz's joint success in the business. They were always and always had been early birds. Other people might start trading at half past nine, but Louis and Baz were in their office planning and scheming at six o'clock in the morning.

'Two things you need to succeed in this business, Meredith,' Louis told her. 'Enthusiasm and a loud alarm clock. The English – they're so slow. They talk about the early birds catching the worms, but by the time most of them are in their gardens, all that's left are the slugs.'

Meredith, who as an actress had never been an early riser, preferring to start her day at noon, nonetheless was outside the offices of Kass and Vogel Ltd on her first day at work at five to six, ready and waiting for Louis and Baz when their chauffeured cars drew up.

Neither of the men referred to it, and Meredith was flattered. But before they locked up the offices that night at seven, they presented her with her own and freshly cut set of keys.

Then she spent the best part of a day ploughing through the volumes of *Spotlight*, the business's casting directory, annotating a list of all Max's clients, male, and female, which she then redrew up into a list of priorities, before studying it patiently to see which clients it would hurt Max most to lose.

It was a very prestigious list. One of the best lists of clients in London. It was even more prestigious than Kass and Vogel's own. And there were several names on it which it would hurt any agency badly to lose.

But Meredith only needed one. One scalp, one major defection, and some of the other stars would begin to worry. Why had so-and-so left? Had Max done a bad deal for him? Were others thinking of leaving? Was there another agency on the upgrade? Had the fashion changed? Was it time to look around, time to find some new enthusiasm, time to refresh a static career? Just one scalp and the cat would be among the pigeons.

One big one. And it didn't take long for Meredith to home in on him. Tom Kenny. Probably the best and most wanted actor in England at the moment. Certainly the most exciting, Meredith thought, as she drew a big circle of ink round his picture in *Spotlight*. Big, tough and genuine working-class, the real stuff, the flag-bearer of the latest fashion. And Hollywood was already beckoning.

And what was even better, he had just opened in Jack Crawford's new play at the Royal Court, a play in which

Meredith's old sparring partner Polly Stephens had finally landed a good character part.

So Meredith at once set about securing her first client. Polly Stephens.

She knew Polly was represented by possibly the worst and laziest agent in town, so it shouldn't prove too difficult to woo her away. But what was of vital importance was the manner of the courtship. Because Polly Stephens was just the sprat to catch the mackerel.

Meredith attended the opening night with Louis, whom she took backstage to meet Polly. As they fought their way through the first-night crowd round to the dressing rooms, Louis grumbled and wondered aloud why he should be taken to meet some two-bit supporting actress.

'It's not as if she's much good, Meredith,' he complained. 'She has a voice like a screech owl.'

'Polly's going to be vital to us, Louis darling,' Meredith assured him. 'Just be patient.'

Then she slipped her arm through Louis's and guided him to the number one dressing-room.

The door was open, and Kenny was holding court to a throng of admirers within. But there was little chance of him missing seeing Meredith. Nobody had missed seeing Meredith that night, she had made doubly sure of that by the way she was dressed, in a cream silk and wool hand-crocheted mini-dress, worn beneath a knee-length open fur coat.

Meredith paused by the star's dressing-room door, once she was certain she was fully reflected in his dressing mirror. Kenny stopped talking for a moment and looked round at the vision in the corridor. As he stopped talking, the rest of his entourage stopped talking as well, and looked in the direction in which he was now looking. At Meredith. And at who was attached to her arm. Louis Kass.

Meredith waited just long enough to make sure of her impression, before she turned to Louis and smiled up at him.

'No, not in here, Louis darling,' she said. 'You said you wanted to see Polly Stephens.'

Then she hustled him away up the stairs to a dressing room of far less importance.

Polly was overwhelmed by their visit, but Meredith made no promises. And she kept on making no promises throughout the week, whenever she brought someone new to see Polly in the play, which she did five times in six days.

Kenny soon got used to Meredith's sensational back-stage appearances, but he never got bored with them. By the Saturday of the first week he was totally intrigued by the stream of important casting agents and directors, most of them handled by Kass and Vogel incidentally, which Meredith brought round to introduce to Polly Stephens.

Max, on the other hand, couldn't make the opening. He was in America, setting up a movie deal. Meredith was well aware of this, and was making his enforced absence work in her favour. Because she knew that although Max had a perfectly valid reason to miss the first two weeks of the play's run, by the time she had saturated somebody as relatively unimportant as Polly Stephens with her all-important backstage visits, a star as luminous as Tom Kenny was going to begin to wonder, however unfairly, about his own personal representation.

'Hello,' he finally said after the show had come down on the first Saturday night. And when Meredith was hurrying her way through the backstage crowd with the director, Ted Scofield.

'Hi, Tom,' said Scofield, happy to be hailed by the hottest name in town.

'I was addressing the lady on your arm,' Kenny said, grinning round his cigar at Meredith.

'Hello,' said Meredith lightly, and then continued on her way to see Polly.

Kenny was waiting for her by the stage door when Meredith finally emerged.

'Dinner?' he asked as Meredith smiled politely and tried to pass him.

'That's very kind of you,' she replied, 'but I'm already going out.'

And with that she guided Polly to her waiting limousine, Louis's borrowed limousine, and swept her off into the night.

She finally agreed to dine with him at the end of the following week. They met and had lunch at The White Tower. All the heads turned when they came in, and all the staff danced attendance. They made a sensational duo, Kenny loose and in no shirt, just jeans and a crew-necked black jumper, and Meredith all buttoned up in the very latest Chanel suit.

'What do you want?' Meredith enquired, as she glanced at the menu.

'I'm buying,' said Kenny, lighting up a cigar.

'I know,' Meredith replied. 'But I'm still curious as to what you want.'

'What I really want, darling,' the actor replied, scratching his chest under his sweater, 'is *you*. Preferably in a hammock on a hot afternoon.'

'A lot of people want me, Tom,' Meredith answered, still studying the menu. 'I'm afraid you're going to have to stand in line.'

Kenny laughed so loudly, everybody looked round. He waved his cigar at them.

'Mind your own bloody business!' he said. 'And eat your lunch!'

The scolded diners all found this highly amusing and returned to their food in a state of some excitement.

'Wankers,' Kenny stated, putting his hand on Meredith's knee.

Meredith replaced the hand where it belonged. On the actor's own knee.

'What's the matter?' he asked her. 'Don't you like me?'

'I don't know anything about you,' Meredith told him. 'And I think I'll have the scampi.'

'You like my acting.'

'I quite like your acting.'

'What the hell do you mean – quite?'

'I mean I quite like your acting.'

'What's wrong with my acting?'

'There's nothing wrong with it, Mr Kenny—'

'Tom, for Chrissake.'

'There's nothing wrong with your acting at all. Except the esteem in which you hold it.'

Meredith didn't even look up, but just continued to peruse the menu. Even so, she held her breath, waiting for the explosion. She quite expected him to walk out. She half hoped he would. It would make good copy in the gossip columns, and hot talk in the business.

But the explosion didn't come. Instead out of the corner of her eye she saw the actor nodding, and grinning.

'You're absolutely bloody right, of course,' he agreed. 'Me mam says exactly the same bloody thing.'

'There you are then,' said Meredith, closing the menu, and handing it to the now hovering waiter with a smile. 'And I think I definitely will have the scampi.'

From then on the actor was eating out of her hand. Meredith had got away with it, as she thought she would, or rather as she thought she should, since she was a member of the club. She was an actress, had been an actress, she had got up there and she had done it. Nobody other than a fellow actor could have told Tom the-talk-of-the-town Kenny that he was getting too self-conscious and got away with it. A man would have had his nose split, and a woman would have been publicly foul-mouthed. But Meredith could get away with it because she was kosher. She had been up and running since she was a child. Meredith Browne was the business.

If she'd been so inclined, Meredith could have had him on her books before they'd finished eating. It wasn't just that he wanted to take her to bed. It was because he was in awe of her dedication. All Meredith did was talk business, right the way through lunch. No small talk, and no flattery. Just what was being done, what was about to be done, who was going to do it, who should do, who might do, who wanted to do it, and what was Tom Kenny going to do with the rest of his life?

'I'd have thought that was pretty obvious, love,' he said with a grin and another scratch of his chest. 'Show 'em.'

'You've got it all mapped out then?' Meredith enquired.

The actor looked at her blankly.

'Mapped out?'

'You know, all your next moves.'

'How do you mean?'

Meredith allowed a little silence to fall before she answered, the way you would with a child who seems unable to understand your questions.

'You've got your career planned,' she reiterated.

'That's the bloody agent's job,' Kenny replied.

'Well – yes,' Meredith said, with just enough doubt in her voice to worry him, before switching the subject.

But Kenny wouldn't leave it alone, and kept returning to the subject.

'But when you were with Kassov,' he finally asked, 'didn't you just leave it all to him?'

'Max is very good,' she replied, on a tangent. 'Max is brilliant at just letting things happen. But as a matter of fact, with hindsight, I'd have liked a little more planning. And a little less . . . a little less *que sera*.'

Meredith smiled enigmatically, and saw she had totally baffled her companion.

'You don't reckon that Max is that on the ball then?' he asked.

'I think Max Kassov is brilliant,' Meredith replied. 'And of course now that he's turning his energies more to film production. . . .'

She let that one hang in the air.

Kenny soon picked it up.

'Yeah,' he nodded. 'A lot of people reckon he's not going to have as much time as he did for his clients.'

'Oh, I don't know about that, Tom,' Meredith said

297

without conviction. 'So many agents nowadays are diversifying.'

'Are you? Are Kass and Vogel?'

'We're about as diversified as we'd ever wish to be,' Meredith replied. 'And as for me—'

'Yeah? As for you what?'

'As for me, Tom' – choosing this moment to eyeball him for the first and only time – 'as for me, nothing comes between me and my clients.'

They stood outside the restaurant for a moment in silence. Then Kenny started looking for a cab. Meredith told him not to bother, as she had her car.

'Great,' Kenny said as the limousine rolled up. 'Your place or mine?'

'You're very welcome to come back to the office,' she told him, as he climbed inside next to her.

'That's where your place is?' he asked.

'That's right,' she replied.

He came back to the office but he didn't come up. Instead he chewed on the remains of his cigar, and pawed the pavement with the toe of one of his gym shoes.

'Max is away a lot of the time now, you know,' he said.

'Is he?' Meredith asked extra innocently. 'Yes, yes, I suppose he is.'

'He hasn't been to the play yet.'

Meredith smiled sympathetically and said she really must get back to her desk.

'What's your interest in Polly Stephens?' Kenny asked her, following her to the door.

'Polly and I go back a long time,' Meredith explained. 'I'd like to see Polly succeed. Yes, all right, so she'll never make star status. But this business isn't built just on stars. There wouldn't be any stars – there wouldn't be any business – without the Polly Stephens of this world.'

Then Meredith, seeing that he was going to try and kiss her, theatre-style, put out her hand to be shaken, and took her leave.

When she got up to her office, and looked down to the street below, Kenny was still there, leaning against a lamppost, staring at the main doors. He stayed there for about another four or five minutes, before ambling away down the road, deep in some thought.

For the next few days, Meredith was out to his calls. She was either in meetings, or at casting sessions, even when she was sitting at her desk with nothing to do. She went twice more to see the play, each time with someone important. Louis saw to that, no problem.

Not that there was ever any shortage of people wanting to be seen with Meredith. Agents didn't look like Meredith Browne. People who looked like Meredith Browne became actresses. So – Louis argued – who wouldn't want to be seen with her?

Tom Kenny most certainly did. She relented again, although privately she didn't find doing so all that tough, and on the Saturday night allowed him to take her to Quaglino's.

After they had wined, dined and danced, he set about once again trying to seduce her. But Meredith just smiled and shook her head.

'For Christ's sake, what's the matter?' he shouted at her over the band. 'Don't you find me attractive?'

'Of course I find you attractive, Tom,' Meredith replied, leaning slightly back from him as if in contradiction. 'I'm just not that sort of girl.'

'What sort of girl?' the actor demanded.

'Not that sort,' Meredith laughed, and then wandered back to their table. 'I don't want to cheapen our relationship.'

Don't handle the fruit, Louis had said. We're like greengrocers. We can look, but we can't touch.

'Suppose I sign with you,' Kenny demanded, grabbing Meredith by the arm before she could sit back down. 'Supposing I leave Kassov and sign up with you?'

'Suppose you did?' Meredith echoed, retrieving her arm

299

and sitting. 'You think that would get me into your bed? And what would you think of me then? You wouldn't think much of me, Tom. You'd lose any respect that you might have for me if you thought I was the sort of agent who could only get clients by going to bed with them.'

Kenny sat down beside her and wiped his hand across his mouth.

'Jesus,' he said.

'We'd both lose our respect, Tom,' she said, taking his hand. 'And I wouldn't want that to happen. I have far too much respect for you. As an actor. And more importantly, as a person.'

'Really?' Kenny said, with more than a hint of derision. 'And what about you and Max Kassov?'

'Exactly,' Meredith sighed, making her point.

'Do you know? I've never wanted anyone, love,' the actor growled, 'half as much as I bloody want you.'

Me too, sweetheart, Meredith thought, but to fulfil quite a different want. So instead of replying, she just smiled in return.

'So what do I have to do then? To get inside your knickers?' Kenny enquired, as if he was asking the way home.

'Learn to underplay maybe,' Meredith replied, and then rose, deciding that right now it was time to go home.

For a while, Meredith thought she'd lost him, that maybe she'd overplayed her hand. He didn't ring, and Meredith didn't see him, because she had long since run out of visitors to take backstage to Polly.

And now Max was back in town. He'd arrived back from Hollywood, having cemented a deal, and the papers were full of it. It was Max Kassov this and Max Kassov that, and Max Kassov everything. There were even rumours that Max Kassov was going to America permanently. Thanks to the newspaper saturation, Meredith couldn't escape Max Kassov.

And, as it happened, nothing could have worked more in her favour.

Because it finally brought Tom Kenny across.

He arrived unannounced in Kass and Vogel Ltd one morning, and walked straight into Meredith's office.

'Good morning, Tom,' said Meredith, concealing her utter surprise. 'And what brings you here this fine morning?'

'Because I'm fed up with reading about my bloody agent, love, that's what!' Kenny announced. 'Anyone'd think he was the bloody starker!'

And that was that. Max had finally done it to himself. Max the showman, Max the thwarted actor, Max the exhibitionist had inadvertently upstaged his biggest star. And by doing so, he had pushed him over the road and into the arms of his new and most deadly rival.

Not that Meredith hadn't quite brilliantly paved the way. But she might never finally have secured Kenny had not Max himself come to her aid, by standing in his biggest star's limelight.

'I told you she'd be an asset, Baz!' Louis crowed that evening as the three of them drank champagne at the Ritz. 'Didn't I tell you she'd be good for business!'

Meredith further proved her worth, and soon, when Max Kassov Ltd suffered three further defections, and all of them regrettable. Guy Benyon, Robert Roberts and Shelley Bird, three of Max's biggest earners, and all of them worried by the new direction their agency was rumoured to be taking, signed with Kass and Vogel and were assigned by Louis to Meredith Browne.

There was no word on Max. The more Louis, Baz and Meredith listened, the less they seemed to hear.

'Maybe he's gone out of business,' Louis grinned early one morning as they all scanned the papers.

'I don't think so,' Baz contradicted, tapping an item in a paper. 'It says here he's just bought a theatre.'

'And,' said Meredith tapping another item in another paper, 'that he's just signed up Clint Fraser.'

'Even so,' Louis said, carefully removing the band of the day's first cigar, 'I knew a man who was bleeding to death inside for four years before it ever showed. That'll teach him to be trendy and not sign his stars!'

As for Tom Kenny, he made several more attempts to pull Meredith, but the sallies became increasingly more half-hearted. Not because he knew Meredith wasn't going to come across, but because he realized Meredith was right and it would damage their relationship.

And he was very happy with their relationship. Meredith was everything she had promised she would be. Diligent, single-minded, and devoted. Her advice was first class and her sense of planning impeccable – with the result that for the first time in his short but meteoric career, Tom Kenny actually knew for certain exactly where he was going.

'The way my bloody career's shaping up, darlin',' he said to her over one of their infrequent lunches, 'you won't need to represent all these other bastards. You could just represent me, and you'd be rich for the rest of your life.'

'It's a lovely prospect, Tom,' Meredith replied, 'because there's no one of whom I'm fonder.'

'I get top billing then,' Kenny grinned.

'You're up there above the title in a box and lights,' Meredith laughed. 'But I'm never going to put my eggs in one basket ever again. There's a younger and prettier Meredith Browne setting out somewhere on the bottom rung of the ladder already.'

'There'll never be another Meredith Browne, kid,' Kenny replied, putting his strong arm round her waist and pulling her to him across the restaurant banquette. 'Just don't ever bloody forget that.'

She hadn't quite told the truth to Tom Kenny over lunch, but then what agent ever does? Any agent who believes in telling the complete and utter truth to his clients, Meredith considered, would be selling matches on Waterloo Bridge in no time.

She'd told Kenny that there was no one of whom she was fonder, and there was. And it wasn't one of her clients. It was Louis.

302

And it was inevitable. She saw more of Louis than she did of anyone else, she was closer to him, they shared one and the same life. Every day except Sunday they met at six, and even when they finished in the evening, they would usually go on to see the opening of a new show, or the première of a new film, and then on however briefly to the party or the reception afterwards. Then Louis would drop her home at her new flat, and she would snatch a few hours' precious sleep before being up at five the next morning, ready to see Louis again at six.

His energy, for an older man, was incredible, and his company left his younger rivals in the shade. And although he was over sixty, he kept himself hard and fit by watching his diet and walking ten miles every Sunday, whatever the weather.

And he made Meredith laugh. Just as Max had done, except perhaps more so. Because Louis was the originator of so many of Max's stories, and the original star of so many others. Sometimes they would manage to find an evening free from business involvements, but instead of going home to a quiet evening *touts seuls*, they would go out together and quietly dine *à deux*. And Louis would have Meredith helpless with stories of his beginnings in Variety, and the tricks and treacheries of a trade even more precarious than legitimate theatre.

'One comic I remember,' he told her one night over their dinner, 'George Bright – the Safety Valve of the Nation. That was his bill matter. George Bright, at one point of his career, he could never get over that, wherever he played, his act died the death. And he knew it was a good act. And then George saw this other comic, Len Buxton, who was a nothing, he saw Buxton in the wings one night when he was onstage, writing down all George's act. So George did a bit of detective work and found out that Buxton was playing the same circuit George was playing – only the week before George was. And he was doing George's act. For true. So, one day – and this is the sort of trouble they went to, Meredith my dear – one day

303

George hears Buxton's opening somewhere way up north in some club or other. So he drives up to the club and makes a special appearance, an hour or so before Buxton's due to go on. And he does his act. And it's a wow. Then he gets into his car and drives three hundred miles all the way back to London. What I like is he didn't even wait. He didn't have to. He knew Buxton would come on and die the death and worse, because he'd be doing George's act which they'd all just seen.'

Meredith and Louis sat there with tears of laughter rolling down their faces, Meredith laughing at the joy of the story, and Louis at the joy of recounting it.

Then they fell silent for a moment, as comfortable in each other's silence as they were in each other's conversation.

After a long while, they both suddenly started to talk together, but Louis was the one who insisted on being heard.

'There are lots of things I want to say to you, Meredith dear,' he said. 'But I haven't a notion how to say them. Instead, I've bought you something.'

And taking a small box out of his pocket he pushed it across the linen tablecloth in front of Meredith.

Meredith opened the box, and saw within it an emerald and diamond ring exactly like the ring Louis's son had given her, and which she had sold to buy her desk, except this ring was twice the size of Max's, and must have cost twenty times as much.

'This is the most beautiful ring I have ever seen, Louis darling,' she said. 'But why?'

'Look, my dear,' Louis said, lighting his cigar. 'Everyone thinks you're my toozle, as that vulgarian Baz puts it.'

Meredith smiled.

'Everyone thinks you and I are lovers,' Louis continued, 'and I don't like that.'

'I don't mind,' Meredith told him. 'I'm flattered.'

'It's not that I mind about, Meredith dear. What I mind about is that it's improper. And I'm not. And neither are

304

you. We're proper. At least I am. And I'm quite sure so are you. It's different when you're the same age. Nowadays. It's different. Times have changed. But I'm an old man, and I'm proper. And I don't want to think I'm advantaging you. After all, I've looked after you all your life.'

Meredith took one of Louis's hands between both of hers.

'I wouldn't mind if you were "advantaging" me, Louis,' she said. 'Nobody means more to me than you do.'

'So that's why I want you to marry me,' Louis said. 'I want you and I to be proper.'

'If I was going to marry anyone,' Meredith told him that night, after they had become lovers, 'I promise it would be you, Louis. But I'm not going to marry anyone.'

For a moment Louis couldn't care less. For Louis was somewhere in heaven. He was somewhere in heaven, and Meredith was an angel, and angels didn't get married. So who cared?

'It's difficult to explain, Louis,' his perfect-breasted angel was saying, as she lay propped up on one elbow. 'Whatever I'll say is only going to hurt you.'

Louis smiled. His angel's long titian-coloured hair was falling gently on his face, as she leaned over him. Nothing she could say could hurt him.

'If I got married, if we got married, it would only spoil everything. Being married's not going to make any difference to us. It won't make anything better between us.'

How could anything be better between them, Louis wondered? He had never experienced love-making like it. If marriage wasn't going to make things better, so what? Who needed it? This girl was amazing. Her body was amazing enough, that was for sure. But what she could do with it was even more amazing.

'The point is, Louis darling,' the angel was now saying, 'the point is I'm married already. I'm married to our business. And I don't want and I don't need to become a wife. I can be everything a wife is to you, and more. Marrying you isn't going to do anything more for either of us.'

'It would be more proper,' Louis groaned, as Meredith started to make love to him over again. 'That's all I was thinking. I don't like to be thought improper.'

'Why not?' Meredith whispered, slipping down between the sheets. 'It's much more fun.'

And so it was that Meredith side-stepped that one. And it was one that she had failed to see coming. She thought to herself how extraordinary it was, that however carefully you planned it all out, invariably there was always one little wrinkle you hadn't considered.

And Louis wanting to marry her was this particular one. Louis falling for her she had worked out. Herself getting fond of Louis she'd also prefigured, but had concluded that their relationship would be that of good friends, good and very close friends, but nothing more.

She'd never thought Louis might want to marry her.

She'd put Louis Kass down as the sort of older man who would be far happier to have a mistress rather than a wife. Or just something on his arm, rather than something round his neck. So when he proposed to her it had come as something of a shock. Yet to turn him down could hurt him, and by hurting Louis she would be hurting herself. Her refusal, unless carefully thought-out and phrased, could bring down her oh-so-carefully-built-house-of-cards. Louis was vulnerable. He was of an age when rejection hurt more than ever. And a hurt and angry Louis was not somebody Meredith fancied facing across the battlefield of the business.

Which was why she took him into her bed, and made love to him in the best ways she knew, before teasing him gently out of any notion of marriage. She knew once she had him in her bed she would bedazzle him. She would stun him with her skill and variety until he was bewitched, and she would silence him and leave him quite breathless with her athleticism and sexual prowess. And then once he was bewitched he would put all thoughts of anything except their next union out of his mind. He would be besotted. He would be obsessed. He would be mad for it.

After they finished making love the second time that night (and it had been many years since Louis had made love twice in one night, so that now he felt like Adonis), Louis lay on his back with Meredith held in his arms, and told her wonderingly that she must have had a lot of lovers.

'Some,' she replied, in her best husky voice, 'but none as good as you.'

Louis never bothered to raise the subject of marriage ever again. Not till the day he died.

*Larger than life is a cliché much used to describe many of
the occupants of Tinsel Town. But how else can you
describe Kathy Summers, the star of over twenty-five
films, which include most notably* Death Kiss, Two Weeks
in Another Time, The Girl Most Likely, Bohemians,
Paris Sings, *and of course most recently,* Now Cry the
Heart, *for which, as the schizophrenic mother, she won the
Oscar as Best Supporting Player? The phrase was custom-
made for Kathy Summers, who flew into London last week
to start filming* Intimacy, *to be directed by John Savage.
Miss Summers has made herself internationally famous for
her on-screen portrayals of giant-sized characters – (who
can ever forget her nymphomaniac landlady in* The House
On East Street?) *and also for her extrovert behaviour
off-screen.*

'That's all behind me now,' *she told me when I called on
her in her riverside suite at the Savoy yesterday.* 'Since my
divorce from Victor, I really have reconstructed my entire
existence. Hell,' *she continued, sipping a straight tomato
juice, and refusing the offer of a cigarette,* 'hell, life's not a
dress rehearsal, you know? At my age it's high time to find
out where you're really at.'

*Did this mean, I wondered, a total reform of her
lifestyle? An end to her famous 'open-ended' parties?
Abstinence in place of indulgence?*

'Too right,' *she assured me.* 'What I care about now is
my work. Getting it right, and giving my best to the
wonderful guys and dolls I work with. I've put my centre
back in the middle. And believe me, from now on that's
where it stays. You know, this is a very wonderful business
that we're in.'

8

Jay had never seen so much lasagne. There was lasagne everywhere, in long white dishes on the floor, on the tables, on the furniture. Mostly it was uneaten, a plate taken and filled by someone on set, and then carelessly abandoned somewhere about the house. Some of it had been trodden into the carpets, or dropped on the upholstered furniture, but no one had made any effort to remove the mess, or wipe away the stains. It might have been forgivable if it had been a children's party which had got a little out of hand. But this wasn't. This havoc had been caused by a lot of grown-up people being paid an awful lot of money for doing very little.

Because this was the main location of *Intimacy*, which was being shot largely in and around Holland Park, London, and on which William and Jay had been brought in to do some 'additional dialogue'. At least that's how the deal had started out. But the more they worked on it with the director, the more it became apparent they were being expected to do a total rewrite, but for only the original 'additional dialogue' fee.

'OK,' William had agreed. 'So we're being conned. But it's a good credit. It's a major movie, the director's big potatoes, and they've promised us a single credit up front. So I reckon here we bite on the bullet, keep our heads down, and make this one work for us.'

Jay had little trouble in concurring. They'd had an up and down couple of years, with nothing of any substance coming their way, while all their friends seemed to be getting film after film. William said it was because they were too choosy, meaning that Jay had become too choosy. And William was right. They might still want to write a *Sunset Boulevard* and maybe one day they would, but in the meantime they were going to have to make do with additional dialogue credits on movies such as *Intimacy*. Jay knew all too well that beggars never can be life's choosers.

She finished her own plate of lasagne, and put it as neatly as she could back on a table, then watched in disgust as one of the crew stubbed his Gauloise out in the half-eaten portion he'd just left. She wondered what on earth her mother would make of it? When her mother shopped for meat she shopped for the exact amount. If it was eight ounces, then up went her arm when the scales tipped the half-pound, and she wouldn't take an ounce more or an ounce less. Everything at home had been carefully budgeted, no unnecessary waste had been allowed. It was awful to think what her mother would make of such profligacy.

Jay walked out of the drawing-room, and into the hall in search of William. On the staircase she saw a well-dressed woman in floods of tears remonstrating with one of the crew, who was standing nodding and rapidly chewing gum. The woman was pointing to the desecration of the house and Jay suddenly realized that she had to be the owner. But before Jay could hear exactly what the now quite demented woman was saying, another assistant started clearing the hall of unwanted people in preparation for setting up the next shot, at which the gum-chewer took hold of the woman by the arm and, still nodding disinterestedly, steered her back up the stairs and out of everyone's way.

The house was in a terrible state, of that there was no doubt. Jay looked around her. Everywhere there were lights and wires and booms and trolleys, and all the heavy paraphernalia that comes with a film crew. Someone had made a half-hearted attempt to cover the best of the furniture which wasn't in shot with dustsheets, but they had long since ceased to do an effective job, and now the tables and sideboards, the commodes and even the grand piano were covered with dirty plates, glasses, empty bottles, and makeshift ashtrays. Someone had even managed to get some food on their shoes, and had trodden it in all the way up the expensive stair-carpet.

Jay finally found William in the kitchen. He was sitting at the table on the same side as Kathy Summers, who was dressed in a large flowing kaftan, which was doing its best to conceal the volume of the figure underneath. Kathy Summers had her arm round William's shoulders, while speaking earnestly and quietly into his left ear. Jay came and sat down opposite them.

William saw her and pulled a private face. Kathy Summers paid no attention to her whatsoever, but continued to talk non-stop to William, every now and then blowing smoke in his face from a cigarette she was holding in her free hand. At one point the cigarette started to burn too low, so the actress just chucked it over her shoulders and clicked her fingers for someone to hand her a fresh one.

Which a young man standing just behind her did, having carefully lit it for the star first. He then trod on the discarded cigarette and extinguished it.

'Should I be in on this?' Jay enquired at one point, when Kathy Summers stopped to draw on her cigarette.

'As a matter of fact I think you should,' William replied, trying to ease himself free from the bear hug round his shoulders.

The star then looked at Jay for the first time, through a haze of smoke.

'And *who* is this?' she asked of William.

'You remember, Kathy,' William sighed. 'This is my partner Jay. The girl I write with.'

'Go screw,' Kathy Summers told her. 'When I need you I'll whistle.'

She didn't bother to look at Jay as she ordered her off. Instead she reached for the glass in front of her, which looked very much as if it contained whisky, and, draining it, held it up in the air for a refill.

Jay looked at William for guidance. William grimaced, but nodded his head all the same in the direction of the door. Jay got up and left.

'There was nothing I could do,' William explained as they drove home. 'I'm sorry, honey.'

'It's OK, William,' Jay sighed. 'I've got quite used to it. The men don't speak to me because they're afraid, and the women don't either because they're women.'

'Just as long as we keep speaking to each other,' William said. 'That's all that matters.'

'You saw what they've done to that poor woman's house,' Jay asked, changing the subject.

'That's film crews,' William replied. 'She's getting well paid. And they make good when they wrap.'

'You can't make good damaged antiques!' Jay protested, surprised at William's apparent disinterest.

'They'll replace them if necessary,' William told her. 'That's why writers are paid so badly. Our money goes on repairing the damage inflicted by the crews.'

Jay laughed.

'I'm not joking,' William said. 'Two things never to let into your life. A woman, and a film crew.'

Kathy Summers didn't just want rewrites. She wanted rewrites on the rewrites on the rewrite of the rewrite. The original writer had long since packed his bag and returned to the comparative sanity of Los Angeles, content that he had his first-day-of-shoot money, and worldwise and weary enough not to care what happened to his baby after that.

Which was really where William and Jay came in.

'Everyone else must have turned it down,' Jay had said when they were originally offered the additional dialogue job. 'We must be the end of the line.'

'Not according to Max we're not,' William had assured her. 'Max says John Savage asked for us particularly.'

'Once Max had told him how cheap we come.'

'We do not come cheap, Jay Burrell.'

'William, additional dialogue money is pin money. Even I know that. What we need is an original screenplay, that actually gets to first day of shoot. That's when the writer makes his money.'

William knew Jay was right. This job was in essence just marking time for them. Whatever screen credit it got them, it was still an incidental job, a stopper, an in-between.

And then Kathy Summers put her foot down. During about the tenth retake of a scene upon which William and Jay had not been required to work, the star didn't wait for the cut. She pre-empted the director by storming off the set.

'This is shit!' she announced to the producers in her trailer. 'OK! So for a lot of the time we have to do shit! But this shit ain't even beautifully cooked!'

Her trailer door was then closed so that the all and sundry that was collecting with gathering interest around it were going to be denied the fine details of the ensuing battle.

Two hours later, William was summoned to the inner sanctum. Not Jay and William. Just William.

Kathy Summers was lying on her bed with a face pack on, a cigarette stuck in the middle where her mouth had to be. The director, John Savage, was sitting in one corner, drinking vodka straight from the bottle, while the two producers, whom Jay had christened Bill and Ben, sat shinily suited at the table.

'Ah,' one of them cried as William entered, 'Walter.'

'William,' William corrected him.

'Honey,' said the star. 'Tell these horses-arses what you think of their script.'

'Not a lot,' said William.

'We had a script, Kathy,' the director chipped in, 'until you started pissing all over it.'

'Go screw yourself,' the star said, throwing her cigarette on the floor. 'Because sure as hell nobody else is gonna.'

'The trouble with the script as it stands—' William began.

'The trouble with the script is it sucks,' the star interrupted. 'Which is why you're gonna rewrite it, honey.'

'We'd better have dinner,' one of the producers said, smiling meaninglessly at William.

'Forget it,' announced the star. 'If he has dinner with anybody, he has dinner with me. D'you hear?'

Then she turned her head in William's direction and one white-caked eyelid flicked open. From within, a bloodshot red orb eyeballed him.

'OK, honey?'

'If you say so, Miss Summers,' William replied, before turning back to the producers. 'But if you're serious about a total rewrite, you'll have to speak to my agent.'

'I don't think that'll be necessary,' replied Bill, or it could have been Ben. 'I think your contract covers your obligations well enough.'

'You'll bet your sweet arse it don't!' yelled the star, sitting up and grabbing a fresh cigarette from her ever-attendant young man. 'You pay this poor bastard what he's entitled! Or you know what you can do with this goddam lousy picture!'

The star presented a formidable picture, as she rammed the cigarette back in her mouth and sat staring red-eyed and face-packed at the two mohair-suited executives. Then she grabbed a whisky bottle from the table and poured herself about four inches of neat spirit, which she proceeded to down in two.

'OK!' she then yelled. 'So do we go to work or don't we for Chrissakes?'

Not only did they go to work, but Max managed to negotiate a whole new deal for them, which would pay them the same as if they were writing an original first draft. There was no first-day-of-shoot money, naturally, but as a sop they were to be given a collaboration credit, rather than just an additional dialogue one.

Jay was ecstatic, and even William felt optimistic.

'The great thing is, Jay,' he said, 'Kathy actually likes all our ideas for the script. Which is why she insisted that we did it. She may be foul-mouthed, and she may go right over the top, but underneath she really isn't all bad.'

'We're going to make this a really good film,' Jay said, tidying up the desk in preparation. 'I mean this really could be our break, William. How long have we got to do it did you say?'

William explained the logistics. Obviously since the film was already shooting, they couldn't just shut down and wait for the complete and finished version. They were to be given four days to get as much written as they could, while the second unit went off and shot all the mute footage which had already been agreed, and then, once they had started shooting again, they were to be allowed a minimum of two weeks to finish, handing in as they went, and a maximum of three and a half.

It was back to the cold towels and the black coffee routine they had first perfected on the road with *Where Were You Just When It Mattered?*

At least it was for the first forty-eight hours. And then the phone started ringing.

'How's it goin', honey?'

Jay could hear the star's voice from the other side of the room. William looked at Jay and held the receiver a foot from his head, while he told the star how well they were progressing.

'Great!' the star announced. 'I've been givin' it some thought too, honey! So come on over – we can have a session!'

William tried to make his excuses, but the star wasn't having any. She also made it perfectly clear that she wasn't expecting Jay to come along.

'You'll have to go,' Jay told him. 'We can't afford to put her back up.'

'I'll be as quick as I can,' William said as he prepared

315

to leave. 'Apparently the director and the producer are going to be there, so you don't have to get out the chastity belt.'

Jay grinned and kissed William goodbye. Then she closed the door and leaned against it with her fingers crossed.

Kathy Summers wasn't staying in a hotel. Most hotels she'd stayed in when she'd been in London previously were reluctant to have her back, even though she had now 'reformed', so in order to allow her to live in the luxury to which she was all too well accustomed, the film company had been required to rent a house for her in Mayfair.

A maid opened the door to William and took his coat, before indicating where he was to go. Upstairs.

William went, thinking he was to be shown to a first-floor drawing-room. But the maid continued on up the stairs, and William followed with a little less certainty.

He was shown into the star's bedroom.

Where Kathy Summers lay in wait for him, a monstrous figure draped in green nylon, lying on top of a huge round canopied bed, her hair held up in place by a scarf and plenty of thick and visibly sticky hairspray.

'Hi, hon!' she called as she stubbed her cigarette out in a plant by her bed. 'Come on in!'

William heard the door shutting quietly behind him as he hesitated before wading across the thick white carpet to the star's bedside.

In vain he looked for a chair to sit down upon.

'Here.'

Kathy Summers patted an area on the side of the circular bed.

'Park it there, hon,' she commanded.

William had no alternative. He could hardly stand there all evening, briefcase in hand, and work. So he sat. The bed was incredibly soft and took him by surprise, so that before he could check himself he toppled half-over.

'Whoops!' said the star. 'Isn't it a little early for that?'

Then, grabbing his cheek with a baby's pinch, she shook his jowl before releasing him.

'Jesus,' she laughed. 'Is that all you writers ever think about? Maybe it's from sitting on your butt all day.'

William readjusted his position on the bed until he was sitting a little more comfortably and a little more safely. Opening his case he got out his notebook and started to run through the ideas Jay and he had been working on, and talk the star through the first pages they'd written. As long as he kept talking, William thought, he was safe. So he talked.

And to her seeming credit, Kathy Summers listened. She smoked incessantly, and drank absolutely regularly all the time William was talking, but she appeared to be attending. And when William came to a halt, an hour or so later, she smiled at him and gave his cheek another ferocious baby's pinch.

'Great!' she exclaimed. 'I love it! I love you! You're such a clever little writer-person!'

'I'd be interested in hearing your ideas now,' William said, leaving her a copy of the new pages on her bedside table.

'My ideas on what, hon?' the star asked him, dropping her voice register to husky.

'You said you had lots of ideas,' William replied. 'That you'd been giving it a lot of thought.'

'Sure as hell I have, hon,' she whispered. 'I've done nothing else but think about it.'

'And?' said William, frowning at her like an earnest student.

The star stared at him, and then smiled in what she must have thought a seductive and secretive way.

'I guess I'm old-fashioned, hon,' she said. 'I like to hear ideas coming from a man.'

The silence that followed seemed interminable to William. He found himself frowning ever more deeply, so that he reminded himself of Stan Laurel. His perplexity was so acute that he was only just short of scratching the top of his head.

317

Then the telephone rang. It was so loud in the middle of all that silence it could have been the bell on a fire engine.

'The telephone,' he said, quite unnecessarily.

'Forget it,' the star announced, but she picked it up.

One thing William was eternally grateful to actors everywhere for was their total inability to ignore a ringing telephone. Kathy Summers was no exception.

A couple of minutes later, and William might just as well not have been there, so deeply had the star become involved in her call. It was John Savage, the film's director, and if God ever found Himself put on hold when deciding to call an author upstairs, William reckoned, He could bet His last dollar the person He was giving best to was a director.

William took this golden opportunity to slip away. He picked up his case and snow-shoed it through the thick white carpet to the door. The star glanced up for a moment, as William waved a small goodbye, and mimed that he would call her on the phone.

As he closed the door, for a moment he could have sworn the star was no longer sure even who he was.

William managed to avoid any further summonses to the bedroom for a week by coding their telephone calls. They told Max, the director, the producers and their closest friends if they wanted them urgently to ring twice, hang up and then ring again. Otherwise they didn't and wouldn't answer the phone.

It worked beautifully and so did they, managing the first fifty pages in less than seven days. Savage thought the new draft excellent, and took it to the star who also thought it excellent, and for that reason so did the producers, Bill and Ben.

Savage called them after the first thirty pages had been reviewed and said Kathy Summers was so excited she wanted to tell William personally, but William managed to persuade Savage to act as a foil.

And then at about half past three one morning, when William and Jay were both fast asleep, the phone rang. And it didn't ring twice. It rang and rang. William, awakening from a pill-assisted sleep, forgot all about the code and picked up the receiver.

'Get over here,' said the voice. 'At once!'

William groped for the alarm clock and held it close to his face.

'Come on, Kathy,' he said. 'It's half past three in the morning.'

'You come on over here, you son of a bitch,' came the reply, 'or I'll have your ass.'

The phone clicked dead. William sat up and stared into the darkness. Jay stirred beside him, then with a sigh, fell into an even deeper sleep. Nothing, but nothing awoke Jay Burrell.

William left her a note by her bedside, just in case he wasn't back by the time she awoke. He hoped he would be, he prayed he would be, but knowing the business, anything might happen. Then he let himself out into the start of a fine summer morning, and headed himself for Mayfair.

'Hi, hon,' the star said, rolling over off her back and turning to lie on her stomach to stare at him, chin propped archly on heavily bejewelled hands. 'Long time no see.'

'We've been working, Kathy,' William replied. 'You know that.'

'Too right,' the star replied. 'And I love it. I love it to death. You're a clever little son of a bitch, I mean it. And I'm going to take you all the way back to Hollywood with me, do you know that?'

It wasn't until she smiled then that William realized how drunk she was. He knew she was one of those regular and heavy drinkers whose behaviour never seemed to change that much except when the scales finally tipped, but from the lack of co-ordination in her smile and the way she totally mistimed it, William reckoned she had now entered that one-bottle-too-many zone.

'Is something the matter, Kathy?' he enquired, his mind racing ahead as he tried to plan his escape.

'Nothing's at all the matter, hon,' she said, rolling on to her back again and putting her arms up to the ceiling. 'Nothing that a good rolly-in-the-hay won't put right.'

'I hear you're very happy with the rewrite,' William said, doing his best to ignore the solicitation, and staring down at his feet rather than the monstrous upside-down woman on the bed in front of him.

'What's the matter with you, for Chrissake?' the star asked, tilting her upside-down head back at him until it dangled off the bed edge. 'Are you a fruit or something?'

'It's not that,' William replied hesitantly. 'No, that's not really the point, as a matter of fact.'

'So what is it?' the star demanded. 'Can't you get it up or what?'

'That's not what it is either, I'm afraid,' William answered.

The star rolled back round on to her front again, and as she did so her huge milk-white breasts tipped out of the top of her bright pink nylon nightie. She gave the matter no thought, choosing instead to try and focus her weeping eyes on the man somewhere in front of her.

'Listen, dick,' she hissed vaguely in William's direction. 'Half the men in the world out there' – she gave a wave roughly in the direction of the world – 'half the men out there – would – you know that? They would, to have me.'

'I know that, Kathy,' William sighed. 'I just don't want to spoil anything.'

For a moment, a silence reigned. William thought he might have bought his ticket out of there. The star was staring up at him, with her hands clasped together under her rapidly doubling chin, and smiling. And then suddenly she grabbed him by a leg and pulled him down on top of her.

'OK!' she yelled. 'If you can't make love to me, I guess I'll have to make love to you!'

She was strong. The strongest woman William had ever encountered. And she was fighting drunk. Before he knew what was happening, she had his sweater and shirt ripped off him and was tearing at the fastening on his pants. Short of punching her on the chin, and hopefully knocking her out, William hadn't a chance. As it was, the way she was wrestling him, he'd be hard put to aim a decent blow, let alone land one.

And then what would the papers make of it? he wondered. Even as they were rolling about the bed, the writer in him could see the subsequent news story. 'Film Writer Attacks Star. In the early hours of the morning, William Kennedy, a little-known film writer, entered the apartment of his leading lady and, having knocked her out, proceeded to rape her.'

He was going to have to give in. As she lay panting on top of him and tearing at his zip fastener, William realized the only way out of it was to give in. To close his eyes and think of the contract. Even if he could reason with her, he was still going to have to. Like every other grown man, William knew all too well quite how hellish a woman scorned could be. So even though everything in him was crying no! no! he was going to have to concede and cry yes! yes!

And then suddenly it all went very quiet. Far too quiet. At first William thought she must be dead, so still was she lying on top of him, and so heavy was the weight. He couldn't move to get a better look, because she was flattening him, her legs either side of his, her arms outstretched, and she had him pinned to the over-soft bed as if she was a plane that had belly-flopped on top of him. And so deep and luxuriant was the mattress, so heavy the body on top of him, William thought he was going to be quite unable ever to free himself.

Then the body shifted slightly, and gave a deep snore, and as it altered its position William was able to extricate half of himself from under it. And then slowly and surely the rest of himself. He was very careful, just in case he

321

might wake her, but the more he eased himself out from under her, the more he realized how fast her sleep was.

For she was now snoring quite regularly, and very deeply, with a beatific smile spread over her wildly smudged face. In the struggle her multi-layered nylon nightie had rucked itself both up and down until it was just a band of pink around her waist, exposing a large and white dimpled backside. William took the counterpane from the floor and draped it over her, more for aesthetic reasons than out of gallantry, before pulling his torn sweater back over his head and letting himself quietly out of the house.

'Oh dear, poor William, poor William,' Jay gasped, holding her sides as he tried to relate just how terrible his experience had been. And then, suddenly seeing the funny side, he too started to laugh.

'Of all the people for her to try and gang bang,' Jay cried, now falling on the sofa and actually having to hold her sides. 'Oh, dear, so typical of an actress to make a pass at you. I could have told her.'

She stopped laughing for a second as William started to look serious again.

'Oh dear, your mouth's gone all small. Don't go back to looking serious, please. Oh, what a party piece! Just wait till Meredith hears this! She'll kill herself!'

'Please, Jay—'

'All right, all right, I'm sorry, I'll make us a brilliant brunch to make up for the hysteria.'

The telephone rang.

'Oh no,' said William retreating from it. 'I'm not taking that, thank you. That'll be Big Fat Nellie coming to and wondering where lover boy has gone.'

They both glanced up briefly at the list kept above their desk. It said 'KATHY SUMMERS CALLED' in block capitals and then underneath it there were times. 'Nine-fifteen, nine-thirty, ten, ten-fifteen, ten-thirty.'

'What a dreadful woman,' Jay muttered, wiping her eyes. 'No one would believe you if you told them.'

She picked up the telephone with great caution as if she was afraid it was going to sting her, and paused before answering.

'Yes?' she asked briefly.

It wasn't Big Fat Nellie, as William referred to Kathy Summers, it was Meredith. She was crying. It was Louis. He was dead.

'Do you know what Dorothy Parker once said?' asked Jay over-brightly of William an hour later, as they walked into the expensive apartment block situated just off Sloane Street, where Louis had lived for nearly all his career, and with Meredith for the past two years.

'Dorothy Parker said an awful lot,' said William, 'most of which she overheard in the interval at the theatre.'

'She said no one ever lived happily ever after.'

'She was famous for her optimism,' said William, getting out of the lift white in the face, because he enjoyed lifts not at all, and Jay had had to cover his face with her hands all the way, all of one floor up.

'We could have walked,' William protested to Jay, but she seemed not to hear, and rang the doorbell.

William frowned down at her. Jay was looking very young, far too young, as she had a habit of doing when there was a crisis. He reached forward and pushed her hair out of her eyes a little.

'You'll get a squint,' he said crossly. And then a second later, 'I don't know why we came.'

'Friends. You want your friends at times like these,' said Jay, and her large grey eyes reproached William, as they had a habit of doing when he said what he thought.

A maid opened the door, Spanish, dressed in a black dress and a little white apron, just like the movies. She'd been crying. Maids always did cry when people died, even William knew that. His grandmother in Connecticut had always told William that maids loved to cry. That they thrived on it. It gave them something to do, she'd said.

The hallway was large. Jay looked round it anxiously as

if she expected to see a body already laid out, and then she looked up at William, because she could hear voices coming from the main room. Raised voices. Angry voices.

'We shouldn't have come,' she whispered.

'Tell me something new,' William growled.

William could feel Jay shrinking back against him as the maid re-emerged from the main room, the door opening and shutting behind her, the raised voices from within flinging themselves in and out of the hall as she did so.

'Miss Meredith's coming,' she told them.

Meredith walked towards them calmly enough, but when she put out her hands they were trembling.

She had changed into a little black dress. Somehow it looked familiar. William found himself wondering if it was the same dress that she'd worn in Act Two for the funeral scene of *Where Were You Just When It Mattered?* The scene had been remorselessly unfunny, even after Jay and he had tried to breathe some magic on it.

He felt Meredith's nails digging into his arm and tried not to flinch. They were long red nails. Real woman's nails, not like Jay's which were usually chewed from high anxiety when they got stuck on a scene. But then Meredith was a woman, probably always had been, even when she was a child. Jay was still a girl, probably might stay that way too.

'Baz is very upset—'

Meredith raised her beautiful green eyes to William's.

'He says I killed Louis.'

'Has he called a Press conference to announce it yet?' asked William.

Meredith didn't smile, and neither did William or Jay.

'He can't think you killed him,' Jay whispered, 'that's ridiculous, really.'

'Well, I know,' Meredith was still looking at William, so now Jay did too; they both seemed to expect him to think of something.

'He wasn't found covered with stab wounds from the kitchen knife, and you weren't found with a smoking gun,

324

were you? It was his ticker that gave out,' Jay went on fiercely, and she put her hand on Meredith's arm to comfort her, but Meredith didn't seem to notice, she was still looking at William.

'What do you want me to do?' William asked her, and suddenly found that he too was whispering.

'Could you go in and speak to him? Max was, is, your friend. Louis – Baz – he's so angry with me.'

'Death makes people angry,' said William to no one at all, but he went into the room ahead of them, leaving Meredith and Jay in the hall.

The grief on Baz's face was dreadful to see. Sitting sprawled across a Knole sofa at one end of the room, he had tears everywhere. Ordinarily, because he came from Connecticut, and so did his grandmother, William did not like the sight of a man crying, it made him want to shake the man in question. But at that moment he saw on Baz's face forty years of friendship shredded. He saw him as a little boy, probably standing with Louis in the playground of some down-at-heel East End school, the two of them planning what the future could hold, where they were to go, how it all was going to be, once they got out of the prison camp of poverty. And they had made it happen. Every dream that they had ever had had come true, and they had enjoyed their life together, probably been closer than any married people would ever be, had better memories – but suddenly it was gone, finished, for ever. He had a right to cry. William went over to him, and put his hand on the old man's shoulder.

'There, there,' he said, 'you cry, you cry, it's best.'

'There's only one Louis, only one. Maxie, he's not Louis, how could he be? Maxie never built anything on his own, not with his own sweat, he got given, that's different. Louis and I, we never got given, we made, we built. It was us that did it, and it was better because of it, but it was only better because we had each other, because we could look across the table at each other Friday nights and we could say, "Remember when we were cold? Remember when we had nothing to eat?" That's what being good together is, it's starting out with nothing and ending up with something.'

William was sitting beside Baz now, and he was listening, which Jay said he was adept at, but which William sometimes wished that he wasn't.

'You're a writer,' Baz said, raising his head, 'you're a writer, you understand these things. Louis always said writers are different. He always said they shouldn't be in show business. It wasn't their place to be in show business, but he never did find a way of putting on a play without one.'

'I expect he tried—'

'Oh, he tried, we all tried, but even variety needs writers.'

'Sure, it's a problem—'

'Come and see him,' Baz begged, 'come and see him, come and see Louis, he's never looked more beautiful.'

The bedroom was large and ornate, ornately masculine. William could imagine Louis being presented with the designs of it, and rejecting them. Not King Louis enough he would have said, until the designer got it right. Just the right amount of gold, just the right amount of heavy furnishings. Sixteenth-century bed, brought from some castle, a replica from Cotehele in Cornwall perhaps? The drapes were very expensive, embroidered with swirls and fantastical in just the right way. It was a set, a good set too, a proper set for a king, and Louis was lying in the middle of it, as Baz said, never looking more beautiful than he did now.

'I had them come and lay him out straight away, so he can lie in state the way he should,' said Baz, and he looked down at Louis with love and took his hand. 'My old friend must have the best, always.'

William's arm went round the old man's shoulders again.

'He looks great,' he told him.

'Yes, he does, doesn't he?' Baz agreed. 'He really does.'

As they stood looking down at Louis, William thought of all kinds of things. He had to. He hadn't even known Louis very well, and yet here he was, for no good reason he could think of, staring down at him, alone with his grief-stricken partner.

'We've telephoned Max, he must come, even though they never spoke since he went to France. Not once. I used to say to him "Louis, he's your son. He's your own son." But he wouldn't speak to him, not when he went into business against him. Not a word passed between them, not even at Christmas. I think it was because Maxie proved he didn't need him, not like Trixie. Trixie's in the States, she's flying back. Louis needed people to need him. It made him feel better, what he didn't need is out there, that's something none of us need. Why did he go and do it? It was his rule. Never, never go with an actress. Love her, represent her, worship her onstage, but don't mix the pleasures of business with sex. You're the green-grocer, we were the greengrocers, we used to tell each other that, and greengrocers mustn't touch the *fruit*.'

As he helped Baz Vogel out of Louis Kass's bedroom, William knew he needed not just a Scotch but a double Scotch, no ice, no Perrier, no soda, no nothing.

Meredith and Jay were sitting in the drawing-room when William eventually, very eventually, got Baz back to it.

'Do you want to see him?' Baz asked Jay with a kind of desperation. 'Go and see him, he looks beautiful.'

William loved Jay, but never more than at that moment. He knew how much she hated reality, how she would turn her head away if she saw someone spit in the street, or if 'there was something on the news'. How she would skip pages in a book if they even touched on subjects that she found appalling, or were what she called a bit 'real'. But now she got up and followed the maid out of the door as calmly as if she had been invited to view a new painting.

'You don't need to see him. You've seen quite enough of him already,' said Baz to Meredith.

327

He turned away from Meredith, and William wanted to take the stone out of his hand because he'd looked at her with such despite, and even William didn't believe she was that much of a fallen woman. What had she done that Louis hadn't done too? She'd used Louis, sure she'd used him, but then Louis used people, Baz used people, they were all the users of this world.

'Could I have a Scotch, do you think?' William asked Meredith suddenly, because the silence that had followed Baz's remark had also been followed by renewed tears from the speaker.

Meredith rang the bell, and the maid was summoned. William could see that the maid was shocked at his wanting a Scotch, but he didn't care. That morning, when he'd got a taxi back from the dreadful Summers woman's rented house, he'd been filled with a sense of relief that he didn't live with an actress, that he had Jay to go back to, that his life was in some way rounding itself into a pattern. He saw the morning stretching ahead of them in a gentle kind of way. They would work on a new idea. They would have coffee. Of course he knew Jay would laugh at his discomfiting experience, and that in the end he would too, but they would then spend the morning harmonizing together. Nothing more of a dramatic nature need be expected. No clothes tearing, no sobbing or groaning, just a day, like any other.

But then the telephone had rung, and it had been Meredith, and suddenly he was involved with her always complicated life again, and being forced to play defendant to a fallen woman, so he was damned if he wasn't going to have a Scotch to help him through, and to hell with the maid's reproachful looks. Now *he* was getting angry, and he hadn't even *known* Louis Kass, not properly. If only Max would come.

But Max wouldn't come. William remembered now. Max was great at not arriving, at not returning calls, not the ones he didn't want, not the unpleasant ones. And how could he arrive here when his father's mistress, his old girlfriend was in charge? Even if he had wanted to see his father dead, which Max would never want, but even if he had, he wouldn't come. It wouldn't be in Max's interests.

'Call him, call him again,' Baz was screaming at Meredith now, and Meredith, white in the face, was reaching once more for the telephone.

She had called him a dozen times, and it had been hard for her, William could see that, speaking to Max's wife, speaking to the girl that was the girl that Meredith had once been. Nevertheless, obediently, almost submissive in her guilt, Meredith telephoned once more.

'Seraphina?'

William could see how difficult it was for her even to pronounce Max's wife's name, let alone speak to her, but Baz was standing beside her, and he might as well have been holding a gun to her head.

'May I speak to Mrs Kassov please?'

Once again Seraphina was called to the telephone and once again Meredith stood and begged her, for Baz, for his father, for Max to come to the telephone.

No one in the room could have guessed from Meredith's face what it was that Seraphina was saying this time, but they could all see that it was certainly not something that Baz would have wanted to hear.

Meredith replaced the receiver without saying 'goodbye', and so quietly she might have already been in the chapel of rest.

'She doesn't know where he is—'

'She's lying,' Baz screamed.

Meredith looked at him. Her eyes seemed enormous, and her face quite tiny as she faced the sight of Baz's terrifying bitterness.

'No, Baz, she's not lying,' she told him, and suddenly her self-possession seemed to return to her, and she looked like a star again, very much Meredith Browne, and she walked across to Baz, and put a hand on his arm.

'She's not the kind of girl that would know how to lie about something like that.'

329

Baz raised his head and shook off her hand from his arm.

'Toozle,' he said contemptuously.

All that William had known was that Louis had died of a heart attack. And that's all that anyone had known, or would know. Louis's death made front-page news second from the bottom on the right, and then page threes and page fives, full half-pages inside.

Meredith knew those clippings off by heart; she sat with them day after day in her office as she tried to get used to the silence.

Was death always this silent? She couldn't get used to not hearing Louis talking on the telephone. The rumble of his laugh, the weight of his step as he got out from behind his desk and opened her doors and summoned her at seven at night with 'Come on, enough is enough, let's go and play at living.'

And then in her head she'd replay the moment that she'd found Louis, how cold he had felt to her hand, and yet he had seemed to be just sitting sleeping. And he wasn't an actor pretending to be dead, he really was dead, and she didn't have to play the scene, she had to really do it. Perhaps that, more than anything, had panicked her. What was she meant to do? Ring a doctor. Ring someone she knew. She'd rung Jay. She sounded so alive, about to have a coffee, so was William, they were on a new idea, she'd told Meredith, before Meredith had told her that Louis was dead, that life was no longer in him, that the 'Louis' bit of Louis had gone, and would never be coming back.

It was strange, but the first person Jay had insisted she telephoned was Max, and when Meredith had refused, Jay had offered to do it for her. They had a strange kind of bond, Max and Jay, not exactly friendship, certainly not male and female, because Jay wasn't Max's type, but still something more than business. Perhaps it was just the kind of intimacy that comes from working in close proximity. You know how someone breathes, and eats, and drinks their coffee. What they feel about rain, or how much they hate the postcards friends send from abroad. You know all the little things. Maybe Jay even knew Max better than Meredith did, than even his father had? She'd probably spent more hours at a time with him.

Max.

Meredith looked up at the clock. Six o'clock tonight he would be coming round to the flat to meet her. She got up from her desk, and went to her mirror. She was looking terrible. Pale, and thin, far too thin, and her hair was lacklustre. No one's death, not her mother's, not anyone's, had affected her this way. Certainly no death had ever come between her and her looks before, but there was nothing to be done. She smoothed down her skirt, and as she did so she could feel her hip bones jutting out.

She could still feel them when Max walked some three hours later into the drawing-room of his father's flat, the flat where he had grown up. Underneath her hands were those hip bones, and those bones, jutting out that way, they reminded her that she was once a skinny little kid, so skinny that Louis had had to tell wardrobe not to put her legs in black stockings.

Max had black lines under his eyes, but they weren't the really bad ones that mean that you have a weak heart, they were nicely shaded ones that told the world only that he was working long hours.

Meredith had been brave up until that moment when she saw Max. She hadn't cried, or wanted to keep someone else up late telling them about how bad she felt. She'd gone to see Louis's doctor, he'd prescribed some pills, she'd gone to the office, done a full day, and then returned to the flat, eaten supper alone, taken her lone pill, and gone to sleep until one-thirty or two when grief, and the space around her in the bed, had woken her.

But now, for the first time since Louis had died, her routine had been broken, and it had to be Max who was the one to break it. Max who had broken her. Max whom she had loved, but who hadn't loved her.

Just before he'd died Louis had taken her to the opera.

331

Opera had opened Meredith's eyes to the grandeur that could be emotion. Before seeing opera she had only witnessed the smallness of people's emotions. People cutting each other up in small ways. Not giving someone a part because they hadn't gone to bed with them. Giving them a part because they had. Ruining each other's scenes by 'corpsing', as actors call giggling onstage. Or coughing in the middle of someone else's big speech. All those things she knew about, and it was water off a duck's back, she could cope with all those things, things she'd grown up with; but now with opera she'd seen and heard something different, something written in a different language, a language which, up until then, was not one that she'd really understood, but to which she had listened, nevertheless, enthralled and astonished. Now, seeing Max, she felt all of those large emotions that she'd seen and heard opera stars sing about: love, despair, hatred. Because she knew, without any doubt, that Max was the cause of all her present hell.

It didn't help that his voice was so like Louis's voice, or that he had Louis's way of opening his eyes suddenly, the way Max was opening them now, very suddenly.

'I didn't know you were going to be here, I thought it would be only Maria.'

He turned to the door as if Maria was still in the room, although she hadn't even let him in.

'Maria, the maid, she told me you were coming.'

Meredith's voice was perfect, accentless, spanning the Atlantic but not landing mid-pond. It ought to be, she had worked long enough on it for him, for Max.

She walked across the room to the drinks table, and her walk was perfect, from the hips, her movements as she lifted the whisky decanter a perfection of grace; they should be, Max had sent her to the best movement coach in town.

'No, thank you. I won't have anything. I just came for the painting, really, that's all.'

'I think you should,' said Meredith and, as always when

332

she looked at Max, she had to hold on to herself not to hear that little boy laughing and saying, 'Best wishis'. 'There are things we must talk about.'

'Really? Trixie been trouble, has she? She thought she was getting the flat, did she?'

'No. At least, I don't know.'

Max's habit of being direct disconcerted her, because Louis had never been direct that way. Louis had made speeches. Even Baz made speeches, but Max, she now remembered, even though it wasn't so long ago, Max just made little disconcerting statements. She'd forgotten that. Just as she had forgotten how he was taller than his father, and that he wore a signet ring on his little finger, and that he was very elegant, and quite slim.

Meredith's hand was still poised over the heavy cut-glass whisky glasses that Louis had always liked to drink his evening Scotch and soda from, but Max, she remembered suddenly, didn't like that. Max only liked clear glass for his evening Scotch, and no soda.

'Oh, very well, just a small one.'

Max shrugged, and then he went to stand underneath the portrait of his mother, and look up at it.

It was a beautiful painting. The most beautiful painting in the place, because the girl in it was so beautiful, because she had such a beautiful face and she was so ethereal. Meredith had stood often enough gazing up at her, the way Max was now gazing up at her. Her dress was magical, a ball dress of tiered lace, blue to match her eyes, and sashed tightly to show off her tiny waist. The sitter seemed to be asking the onlooker, 'Is there anything more important in life than to be as beautiful as I am?'

'She was so beautiful,' said Max softly, and Meredith waited to put a glass in his hand, the way she had used to wait until Louis had finished looking at the same painting, and saying the same thing. 'So beautiful,' he said again, and then he took the glass from Meredith, but didn't turn to look at her, just went on gazing up at his mother, the angel.

It's always something small that changes the emotions suddenly. Milk that's not quite right in a cup of tea. A bad-tempered reply, just one too many that scuttles across the dinner table, one date too many that gets broken, one hour too many to be kept waiting, and then, suddenly, the mistral, sirocco, and madness breaks through the dam. For Meredith it was that moment of *not turning*. The way Max put out his hand and took the glass, and didn't even turn, didn't even bother to look at the prop that she was handing to him, but went on gazing up at his mother, that pure angel above his head. Louis would have taken the drink, and he would have said 'thank you' one way or the other, but most of all he would have turned and looked at her. She would have been someone to Louis. She was no one to Max, and yet Louis had made her into something when she really was nothing. All Max, spoilt Max had done was gild her a little.

'You're never going to be the man your father was, are you, Max?'

Meredith smiled as Max turned to look at her surprised. It took living with someone to know just how to hurt them.

'I hope not,' he said slowly. 'I wouldn't want to be like Louis.'

The 'cut off' in the voice, the way he used his father's name instead of calling him 'Dad' or 'Daddy' or 'Father' or whatever, it was all so cool, and it fanned Meredith's anger. She had so many, many reasons to hate Max.

'You couldn't be like him, Max, never in a million years, you're too spoilt and selfish. Too egotistical.'

Max's eyes widened and he grinned suddenly.

'Louis didn't have an *ego*?' he asked incredulously.

'Yes, he had an ego, Max, but he used it to help other people, and he had a kind heart. You have an ego you just splash people with, daub them, ruin them, and you haven't a kind heart.'

'Listen, I just came for the painting.'

Max turned back to his mother, the beautiful woman

that Meredith had heard him speak of so many times, when he was a little drunk, when he was in love with Meredith, when they were enjoying themselves, always his beautiful mother. The dresses she'd worn, the way she'd laughed. He'd wanted Meredith to develop a laugh like his mother's laugh – she'd even tried, God help her. She'd worn blue for his mother. She'd given up smoking, because his mother never smoked. Not even occasionally.

'I don't need this.'

'You can take the painting, and its history, Max.'

He knew then, because of the way she looked at him, they both knew that he had to know what she knew, and that what she knew wasn't good.

'What history? What history? Have you suddenly become an authority on a painting of my mother? Ring for the maid, and get her to bring the ladders.'

Meredith had never seen Max panic before, but she was seeing it now, and she was enjoying it. She was enjoying it for herself, for those days and weeks of despair that Max had caused her. She was enjoying it for Louis. For the years he'd spent pretending that he didn't mind that his only son didn't speak to him, stole his clients, married without telling him. She was enjoying it for them both.

'Your mother, Max, was a whore.'

Meredith said the line in a surprisingly clipped way. She even surprised herself. She sounded suddenly so English, so precise, so 'country house'.

Max laughed.

'You're mad with grief,' he said, and the fear went out of his eyes. 'You've gone mad. I don't blame you. I really think you loved my father. Baz, well, Baz, he's mad with grief too, but he doesn't believe you loved him. I actually think you did, because like it or not, Meredith, try as hard as you may, you're a nice girl. You see I don't think you ever loved *me*, you thought you loved me, but what you loved in me was my father.'

He paused and shrugged his shoulders.

'It's simple psychology, you loved the man who brought

you up, the only man who never tried to sleep with you, the father you never had. You loved Louis, not me. I loved you, not the way I love Seraphina, but I loved you nonetheless. But that's another story.'

'That's the most I've ever heard you say,' said Meredith after a short pause, but she wasn't going to let him off the hook. She was poised, the dagger was in her hand, this was her aria, she was the star tonight, not Max. 'Even so I think you should know about your mother. It's important to know about your parents, if you're talking psychology, Max. Your mother was a nymphomaniac. She slept with all London. She couldn't help herself. She even loved Baz, and Baz never got over her, which is why he goes to Annie's. He could never look at another woman after your mother.' Meredith looked up at the portrait. 'And you couldn't really blame him, could you?'

'Do you really hate me that much?' asked Max. 'Do you really hate me that much that you have to try and lie like this?'

'Oh yes, I've hated you, Max, I've hated you with all my heart, and all my soul for what you did to me when you went off and got married. But even so, to tell the truth I never hated you quite enough. Not to tell you about your mother. Now I hate you enough, because of what you did to Louis. Because he went on hoping, right to the end, that you would call him, or write to him, because he used to cry in front of your picture. The one of you when you were a little boy going off to stay with your Aunt Susan. He went on hoping, right to the end, that somehow you'd come back and be a son to him. But you preferred being a son to a dead woman, someone who never existed, someone who, because she was rich and spoilt and well bred, treated your father like dirt, because he'd been poor and never had anything, and came from an immigrant family. That's how much I hate you, not for me, for him, for Louis.'

Now they both knew she was telling the truth and, if she'd still loved Max, Meredith's heart might have been touched by the way he turned to the picture of his mother, pleading to her with his eyes to come down from the picture and tell him it wasn't true, that she'd been as pure as she looked beautiful. Yet as beautiful as she was when they both looked up at her now, they knew what Meredith had said was true. For now, when viewed again, the lips that had seemed to curve in a delighted smile, now curved in secret delight.

'She loved Baz?'

'She loved everyone, Max, all London.'

She could see him now realizing how true it must be. Quickly, and how quickly, Max's mind would run around all the evidence. He would be remembering secret smiles from people, people who'd known both his parents. He'd be remembering how people would talk so fondly of his mother: men, other men, not just Baz and Louis. How his Aunt Susan would have kept silent on the subject of her sister, how – it would seem to him now – how little she had talked of her younger sister. How she had insisted on bringing him up in her way, taking him away from his father, making him into 'one of them', rather than Louis's son.

And then he would be worrying that he wasn't really Louis's son, that he was perhaps Baz's son? He would be thinking about that on the drive home, as he headed towards Seraphina and the life that they had together in remote Norfolk, in the house that she never left to come to London.

'You know you should never have said that, don't you? You know you should have gone to your grave rather than tell me secrets you learned from your trade?'

Meredith didn't have a drink, she didn't have a glass with anything in it as Max did, because if she did she would surely have been unable to resist throwing it in Max's face. But as it was she watched him in silence as he rang for the maid, and rang for the ladders, and carefully took down the portrait. And then waited for the porter to come from downstairs to help him carry it out to the street below, where a van was waiting to take it to Norfolk, and Seraphina.

In spite of herself, in spite of the courage that it had taken to stand up to Max, to tell him what would hurt him most, for her sake, for her revenge, and for Louis, Meredith's heart was cold with terror. She knew the business, and Louis knew the business, and Louis had always said, 'When the word's out, and it doesn't take much, you can't get people to send you an old apple skin, let alone any business, remember that. I've put the word out, the words been put out on *me*, and I know what it's like, but it just takes that – the word, the one word – TROUBLE.'

Meredith was trouble. She knew it as Max walked past her to the door. What fresh hell would he make for her now? She lay down on the sofa. Let him, she suddenly cared less.

The office was strangely silent. Just at first Meredith thought it was because Louis wasn't at the centre of it any more, or as if the whole place had been put in permanent mourning. And then Meredith saw her secretary's face and she turned away from Meredith as if she hadn't seen her, and walked rapidly towards the ladies' cloakroom. Meredith frowned at her retreating back and then, turning towards her own office, and having to transverse Louis's to get to it, she suddenly saw the packing cases. Not many of them, not so many, just enough to take Meredith's effects.

She bumped into Baz as he emerged from her room. He was looking grim and determined, and she could see past him into the room where his secretary was carefully removing ornaments from Meredith's desk and wrapping them in newspaper.

How Meredith longed for William and Jay at that moment! They could write her some fresh lines, something original; as it was she could think of nothing to say, but gave a little cry when she saw the secretary picking up a small china ornament of an eagle that Louis had given her when she'd poached Tom Kenny from Max.

338

'Don't touch that,' she cried out, 'don't touch it. What-ever happens. It's not yours. Put it down, put it down.'

The girl put it down, and in doing so, so suddenly had Meredith cried out, she knocked it over breaking off its head.

'Look at that,' Meredith sobbed, 'look at that! You bitch, you've broken the most precious thing I own, you bitch.'

She looked up at the girl's white face and she aimed a slap at her which caught the girl full in the face.

'Bitch, bitch, bitch,' she sobbed, but Baz pulled her away from her before she could slap her again. 'You leave my things alone. Leave them alone I tell you.'

Suddenly her voice was no longer husky, but sharp and hysterical, yet she didn't care. She picked up the little bird and let it lie in her hand just as if it was a real bird that she had found dead in the road instead of an ornament.

'Go and get yourself a drink,' Baz said to the girl, and he nodded his head towards the door, and as she passed him with her white face and the slap mark reddening on her cheek he slipped a five-pound note into her hand. 'Get yourself an early lunch too,' he added, 'and I'll see you afterwards.'

The girl half walked and half ran out of the room, leaving Meredith to sink into the antique chair she had spent many months saving up to buy, and about which Louis had used to tease her saying that she was saving up to pay for a fake, that all antiques were fakes unless they had come with papers to prove otherwise.

'Fakes for fakes,' was what Meredith had replied grin-ning, but what she felt now wasn't fake. Black despair, that wasn't fake.

To make matters worse Baz was smoking one of Louis's cigars. Meredith knew just from the smell that it was one of Louis's cigars, and it was macabre, that Louis should be dead and Baz should be smoking something that was pure Louis, and which was nothing to do with Baz and never had been. It was as bad as seeing him in one of Louis's old suits.

'You've got to go, Merry, you know that. I thought of

keeping you, because you've worked hard, and you've brought clients to the agency, good ones too, I'll give you that. But now, I can't. Especially not now. You'll have to go, and as soon as possible. Really. I can't have you around me, not now.'

All those bloody 'nows', Meredith thought dully. Did you ever in your life hear so many bloody 'nows'?

'Now' meant that Max had rung Baz, and they did good business together, especially *now* that Max was branching out into film production, trying to set himself up. Baz was very sensitive towards Max. He loved him, despite how Max did or didn't treat Baz, Baz still loved Max. And he had been so passionate about Max's mother.

Meredith looked up at Baz, still smoking Louis's cigar. Not the way Louis would have smoked it. Not really pulling on it hard and confidently, but making short little pulls and then little stabbing movements with his hand, quite the opposite to Louis who used to leave it to rest in one surprisingly long-fingered hand and use his other hand to gesture.

Of course! Baz had loved Max's famous, now infamous, mother, that's why Meredith had to go. In taking revenge on Max she had not only stabbed herself in the back, she had mortally wounded Baz.

She could see by the cold look in Baz's eyes that he would be quite happy if he never set eyes on Meredith again. And, as Louis would say, that would be too soon. No one but no one could sully the name of Mrs Diana Elizabeth Kass and be allowed to get away with it. It didn't matter that what Meredith had said was true, not a hangman's curse did it matter, no. All that mattered was that she had dared to talk of the beloved in a derogatory way, to Max of all people, who was her son.

Meredith narrowed her eyes against the too-rapid cigar smoke that was weaving a noose around her neck.

'I've got a share in the business,' she said, 'Louis said he'd changed his will.'

'He didn't have time, thank God,' said Baz with some

relish. 'Not enough time, you stupid toozle. That was one thing you overlooked.'

'I heard him booking the appointment with the lawyer. I heard him myself.'

'You're right, you did, but unfortunately he had to cancel, to go to a meeting, and he never did remember to book another. Such a pity,' said Baz, and he smiled.

'I don't believe you,' said Meredith, standing up as the truth of her situation exploded in her head. It meant starting again, all over again. Jesus, starting again. Trying to find new actors to put on her books, trying to find new stars. This meant she'd lose Kenny, he was signed with Kass and Vogel, all of them, she'd lose all of them.

'I don't believe you,' she told Baz, 'this is just one of your scams, you and that smart lawyer of yours, the one you pay twenty guineas an hour to, it's just something you've cooked up.'

'Even if it was, Merry darling, what could you do?'

'I could screw you.'

'No. I'm one man you're not having, Merry. Louis yes, he could kill himself over you. Max – well, he's only young, but me, never, never, never. And try taking me to court, I should love it to pieces. Really. It wouldn't only ruin you, it would double ruin you. I'm a millionaire, you don't find millionaires in prison, do you? No, you find poor people, people who believe some smartarse lawyer when they say they can win against the big guns, and they lose, and they find themselves up to their ears in debt, and up to their necks in crime to pay for the debt, because that's the system, Merry darling, and you know it. Sue me and you might as well take another of your famous overdoses, only this time it would be better for all of us if you made it to the other side. You understand what I'm saying, don't you? You know where I'm at, as you kids say nowadays. So why don't you help me pack up your stuff, and then you get out of here? It's the right thing to do. Really.'

Meredith left a long, long pause, and just stared at Baz.

She knew he was right. If she took a case against him, for no matter what good reason, she wouldn't have a hope of winning more than a few bob off Baz. Unfair it might be, but Baz was right, it was life, her life. She'd had the luck, and now it had run out, like money at the bank. Suddenly she could smell sick, like when her mother was sick and she'd had to clear it up, and she could smell garbage, like when she'd had to run past it in the back alleys on the way to a job. And she could smell cigar smoke, like when the men would say to her when she was small, 'Lift up your skirt'.

She ran past Baz to the ladies' cloakroom. As she rushed in, her secretary was slowly emerging, her make-up freshly applied, and she smiled in triumph at Meredith. She'd never dared spend so long in there when she worked for Meredith. Never. But now, her smile said, Meredith was gone, blown, and she could do what she liked.

I'll be back, Meredith thought, gazing dully round the expensive wallpaper after she'd finished vomiting. I'll be back, and then no one will get rid of me, no one. I'll be at the top of the tree, and it won't shake, and I won't look down, just up to where I'm going next.

She freshened up her make-up, redid her hair and making sure that she put on her best walk, she stalked back to her office and picked up her briefcase.

Baz was still there, guarding the tea chests. She smiled at him.

'It's all right, Baz, I'll go quietly. But I'll beat you at your own game, you wait. I'll take every sodding star off you until you cry for mercy.'

Baz shook his head.

'You'll never be as big as me, Merry darling, never. You're too venal; to succeed you've got to stay clean, and you'll always succumb to someone, you can't help it. It's the way you're made.'

'Clean! You've spent half your life at Annie's!'

'By clean I don't mean not having sex, you silly toozle, I mean the actors. You'll never be able to stay away from

342

them, because you're one yourself. Clean! Get yourself some brains, or you'll starve.'

Meredith stared at him, and then she said, 'You know years ago, when I was making *Nobody's Child*, one of the extras told me a ghost story. It was about this posh woman who wouldn't give an old tramp a meal until he'd swept up leaves for her. So he takes the broom, and he says he'll sweep her leaves even though he's dying, but when he does die he'll come back and make her life hell, haunting her, see?'

Baz nodded.

'You can still remember your cockney accent then?' he said, surprised.

'And that's what I'm going to do to you, Baz,' Meredith told him, resuming her husky tones. 'I'm going to haunt you, Baz darling, I'm going to make your life hell, you wait, because you may have money, but you're old and I'm not.'

'You're wearing too much lipstick,' Baz called after her.

Meredith paused by the front entrance to the offices and, picking up a white silk cushion, she pressed her lips to it, leaving a beautiful red bow imprinted on its expensive surface.

'I'm not now,' she called back to him, and sashayed out into the morning.

9

some boxes only partly full, and that was meant to be sad somehow or even funny.

Meredith got up from the desk, stalked over to the window. Why am I standing up? What's the need of that? Oh, well, no sense of stage. I was about this most of my life. You need ... Oh, no ... here's a real nail-biter, this one say fifteen bucks. Too late the ground, and I've gotta keep. He wanted to punch he'd had this box around the hall, and then the polishing for . . .

Meredith was allowed to leave with a token list of clients.
Actors and actresses Baz found dispensable – and when
Meredith sat at her desk examining their recent credits she
well understood why. Seven out of the eight names would
be lucky to see £20,000 between them even in a good year.
And ten per cent of twenty grand wasn't going to keep
Meredith Browne Ltd in business very long.

The eighth name was the only one that might keep
Meredith up and running, at least for a while. Polly
Stephens, when she discovered Meredith was leaving, had
refused to stay on at Kass and Vogel, even though she was
still signed with the agency for another year, and Baz for
some inexplicable reason had stood aside and released her
from her obligations. It might have been the fact that Baz
didn't like Polly personally, or it might have been in a rare
moment of chivalry, since Polly was the first client Meredith had brought to Kass and Vogel when she joined.
Whatever the reason, it was a definite advantage having
Polly, because Polly was working: nightly in a minor role
in a big West End musical and daily in a new television
situation comedy. Between the two jobs Polly was earning
around £180 a week, which meant that Meredith's commission on that would just about pay the rent.

Which was just as well, as none of the other clients
Meredith had been donated were working at all. Meredith
despaired of them. They were the sort of people you could
never imagine becoming actors and actresses, and of
course perversely they were the very last people who
would ever think of giving the business up. Meredith

could only imagine that Louis and Baz had been forced to take them on as part of an overall deal, or that perhaps they were all at some time lovers or hard-up relatives of some of the stars Kass and Vogel had once signed.

But they all had to be rung every so often, and each call cost. Because if Meredith didn't ring them, they'd ring her in a fury and occupy her precious telephone all day. She could of course drop them all, slowly but surely, but firstly Meredith didn't quite have the heart and secondly, while Polly was her only present earner, there was always the chance that one of the has-beens might just pick up the odd and possibly lucrative job.

For a short while after Meredith had been moved out of Kass and Vogel her phone rang constantly. It was the business commiserating on her change of luck, or wanting to hear all the dirt about the drama. After that there was silence. Nobody wanted to know. It was as if she was being punished for once again having been so precocious. The word was out against her.

And of course while she was representing no one of any true worth, there was little reason for anyone to return her calls. Even the so-called great friends she had made of certain casting directors and producers while she was top gun at Kass and Vogel now ignored her approaches.

Meredith knew she would probably be the same in their position, but that didn't stop her growing increasingly bitter. As she sat in her overcoat and gloves in her unheated office, she remembered how different the tune had been when she was calling about Tom Kenny, or Louise Rosse, or Jack Blond. But now she was down to the unheard-ofs, the un-remembereds, or the long-since-forgottens, everyone was out to lunch.

She was being shunned, and through absolutely no fault of her own. She was being shunned because Louis Kass was dead, and the business, even those who had hated Louis and were happy to see him gone, the business had chosen to blame her, because every apparent tragedy had to have a villain.

But most of all she was being shunned for her success. The business was shunning Meredith Browne because she'd been seen as an opportunist, as a climber, and as a ruthless go-getter. Meredith considered this, the real reason behind her shunning, as the height of irony, since those who were choosing to ostracize her were either all of those things themselves, or at the very least aspired to being them. Why Meredith stuck in their throats was because she had broken out of the rat pack and done it. She had seen her name both above the title and on the brass plaque. 'Meredith Browne In,' the West End lights had read, and the engraved lettering had spelt out 'Kass and Vogel Ltd, incorporating Meredith Browne.'

And that was what was at the root of it all. Resentment. Jealousy of her success. And there is little in life so disenchanting as the success of others. Meredith knew that and understood it, because she had seen others rise when she was falling. But what distinguished Meredith from many of her rivals was her ability to get up off the floor and carry on with the fight. While others called it a day, and unable to stand the heat fled the kitchen, setbacks only made Meredith Browne more resolute. Which was why she was now determined to make her humiliating expulsion from Kass and Vogel Ltd into one of the most significant and important moments of her life.

Such was her single-mindedness that within three months of setting up on her own she had all her small list of clients working. Granted, with the exception of Polly Stephens, none of them were being asked to do much more than a spit and a cough, which initially most of them resented – until Meredith spelt out the ultimatum. Either they wanted to work, or they didn't. And if they didn't want to work, they could leave. They stayed. And Meredith got them all working.

She did so by simply wearing down the opposition. Having been in power, Meredith knew that the weakest line of approach was by letter. Every day at Kass and Vogel her mail was full of letters from actors extolling the virtues of their acting, and by the time she was through reading them all, Meredith was word-blind. So she eschewed the plea-by-mail, and instead went to face the opposition in person, all too aware of the humiliations which could possibly lie in store.

And which indeed they did. Those she had been appointed to see kept her waiting endlessly, often all the morning or the afternoon. Sometimes after waiting in certain outer offices, without a cup of coffee or a smile from the receptionist, they wouldn't see her at all, but instead would convey, via their secretaries, that unfortunately something important had come up and their meeting with Meredith would have to be postponed indefinitely. Meredith would bite on the bullet and accept all the specious excuses with good grace, before returning home to write down the names of those self-same producers and casting directors in a little black notebook she had bought specially for the purpose.

The names were all filed under the heading 'Don't Forget'.

Some would go further in their attempts to wound and dismay. They would invite Meredith into their offices immediately, and talk warmly of the old times, as if they were quarter of a century ago, and not just a few months dead and gone. They would then promise her work for her clients, and recommendations for her list, besides giving her privileged information about what new shows, films, and plays were on the stocklist. If Meredith hadn't long since been completely dry behind the ears, she might well have believed them, and gone away encouraged, to tell her struggling clients of the promises that had been made, and perhaps even borrowed money on the strength of the pledges.

But Meredith had been born in the hamper, and learned her walking and talking backstage, so she believed nothing until she saw it, and even then she looked for the wires. Whatever they promised her most faithfully, Meredith discounted, even when at one point a management went so far as to suggest and then start setting up a number one tour of a revival of a twenties comedy starring Maxine Gane, one of Meredith's more notable has-beens. Meredith made all the right noises, and pulled all the right faces, and then went back to her office and kicked all the furniture, because the management that was suggesting the tour was run by Louis's first cousin. Most wisely of all she said nothing to the wretched Maxine Gane, whose disposition was not up to standing the strong possibility of a major disappointment.

Nonetheless the ageing actress got to hear of the proposed revival on the bush telegraph. She arrived one morning in Meredith's office unannounced, with her hair freshly styled and the face below caked thick with make-up.

'Darling,' she breathed over Meredith, 'I just bumped into dear Robbie Pinkerton coming out of the Garrick, and he told me All.'

Meredith put the kettle on for some coffee and said nothing.

'You're a sweetie,' the actress continued, 'not saying anything. Not telling me until it was Definite.'

'You should know better than that, Maxine,' Meredith replied. 'Nothing's definite in this business not only until you've done it, but until you read that you've done it.'

'But Robbie said it was as near as dammit,' Maxine continued, carefully checking her lipsticked mouth in her compact. 'And that they'd talked to you. And that they'd even talked money, Robbie said. And my daughter too.'

The actress then closed her compact and smiled up at Meredith. But all Meredith could see was the pleading in her eyes, and the dying rays of hope.

'You're on the list, Maxine darling,' she confessed, sitting at her desk with her coffee. 'You're on their shortlist.'

'But Robbie said—'

'Maxine,' Meredith levelled with her. 'All we can say with any certainty at this moment in time is that you *are* on the list. If and when it gets any firmer than that, don't worry – you'll be the first to know.'

'You're a poppet,' the actress replied. 'And you know how much I love you. But I really can't believe they've put me on a List.'

'Darling, in the times we're living in,' Meredith told her, 'with the lunatics running the asylum, they're even asking Olivier in to read.'

But, thanks to the grapevine and despite Meredith's regular administration of cold water doses, Maxine Gane became more and more convinced the part was hers, pestered Meredith daily, and finally forced her into phoning the management up in her presence to see what the state of play was.

Meredith was put straight through to Louis's cousin.

'Meredith,' said the voice the other end of the line, 'I've been meaning to call you.'

She knew the signals too well. And this one meant the day was lost.

'I was just wondering,' Meredith enquired, hardly bothering to ask, 'if you'd got any further with the final casting?'

There was a small silence on the phone. A studied silence. A well-planned pause.

'Ah,' the voice finally replied. 'That means you haven't heard?'

No, she hadn't. No, Meredith hadn't heard, and she knew the reason why she hadn't heard. Because they had wanted to force her into ringing them up to find out. She could have held out against them by herself. She could have saved herself this unwanted and unasked-for dose of humiliation, by keeping *schtum*, as Louis would have said, and as Louis would have advised, thus depriving them of their shot of *schadenfreude*. But taking pity on the ageing and anxious face across her desk, she had weakened and as a consequence was now getting it fair and square between the eyes.

Louis, besides advising her not to handle the fruit, also

counselled Meredith when she had joined Kass and Vogel never to feel sorry for her clients.

'They chose this business, Meredith,' he would tell her. 'They chose it for themselves. It was nothing to do with you. If you're a diver, you're going to get wet. If you're a soldier, you're going to get shot at. If you're an actor, you're going to get slapped.'

Now, as a consequence of neglecting good advice, Meredith had to listen to Louis's first cousin positively gloating down the telephone at her.

'I thought you must have heard,' the voice was saying, 'because of course it's all round the business. That we persuaded Sonia Benton from retiring *especially* to play the role. Which is marvellous. Because of course darling Sonia has for so long been the jewel in the West End's crown. And after such a career now to go out in this. And for us.'

There followed another short silence during which Meredith could see the owner of the voice nodding his head reverentially.

'Of course this also means we come in, guaranteed,' the voice continued. 'Straight into The Haymarket, and you can imagine the business we'll do. So all in all we very much feel it was the right decision. Don't you?'

Meredith kept her thoughts to herself, and instead just thanked Louis's cousin for his help, and hoped that they had a long and profitable run.

'Thank you, Meredith dear,' the voice replied. 'And don't forget now. If there's ever anything I can do to help, you just call me.'

Maxine was busy checking her make-up in the mirror of her compact when Meredith put the phone down. Meredith knew full well it was because the actress didn't want to look at her, because she was too well trained in reading other people's expressions.

'There'll be something else,' Meredith finally found herself saying. 'Something else will come along soon.'

The ageing actress looked at her and smiled.

'Yes. Rather like the hippopotamus,' she replied, clipping her compact shut.

Meredith looked at her quizzically.

'Oh, I saw this wonderful cartoon once, darling,' the actress told her. 'There were these two birds sitting in the forest, you see. And in the background just trundling out of sight was a hippopotamus, with his back absolutely jampacked with birds. You know, the sort that sit on the poor creatures' backs? And one of the birds sitting watching the hippo leaving was turning to his chum and saying: "Don't worry. There'll be another one along in a minute." Just like the theatre, darling. Now let's go out and get absolutely tiddled.'

Meredith, although privately wishing to put the matter to bed and get on with her day, agreed out of sympathy.

It turned out to be one of the smartest moves she'd ever made.

Meredith couldn't take her eyes off him all the time she was there. She thought he must notice, but he appeared not to, instead he just continued to go about his business while two of the most penetrating and beautiful eyes in town bored into him. Meredith tried not to keep staring so hard, but every time he moved she found herself watching him, as a starstruck schoolgirl might.

Fortunately Maxine was past noticing what Meredith was doing, now she was well into her fourth large gin and busy reminiscing about her once-famous Ophelia. Meredith kept half an ear open for any gaps in the monologue, where she might be expected to interject something, while never really taking her eyes off the young man in the T-shirt and jeans.

He wasn't classically handsome, and neither was he musclebound, which pleased Meredith as these were two male attributes she considered greatly over-valued. Instead he was quite perfectly proportioned, tall, with long legs and slim hips. Everything visible about him seemed the right size: his hands, his feet, his nose, his ears, they were all either elegant or shapely, and from what she had seen so far, his lightly tanned skin was smooth and unblemished. But it was his face from which Meredith couldn't finally take her eyes. It wasn't a square-jawed, short-haired, blue-eyed face. It was if anything the very opposite, slightly rounded and good-humoured, but well-boned, with a firm jaw and a determined mouth. His hair was thick and dark, and loosely curling, just long enough to keep his overall appearance sufficiently soft and appealing, but not too long to make him look untidy or unkempt.

But it was the eyes that had it.

Meredith knew well enough that if the camera was going to love you, then it had to read you through your eyes. You could be the best cut, the strongest made, the most masculine, but if the eyes didn't have it, the camera told on you.

This man's eyes definitely had it. They turned down very slightly at the corners, giving him a rather droll look. And they were bright, clear and very deep blue.

In fact Meredith had never seen such startlingly blue eyes. She herself had eyes of a wonderful hue, but they couldn't begin to match the depth of this man's eyes. They were what initially drew you to look at him, and they were what finally kept you riveted. And because they were blue, so very deep blue, the camera was going to love them.

The moment Meredith had walked into the bar and seen him, she knew she had discovered a star. She knew it from the *frisson* she got when she saw him. She knew it from the way she saw other women watching him move easily round the room. She knew it from the openly resentful looks he was getting from the other men. The only thing she didn't know was why, looking like he did, he was working serving drinks in a bar.

When he opened his mouth she did.

'Orl right then, gurls?' he asked when he finally made it to where Meredith and Maxine were sitting. 'You done wiv these, then?'

He smiled and, picking up their dirty glasses, wandered back to the bar.

352

Of course, Meredith thought wryly. If he'd had a voice like Olivier, or Redgrave, or Gielgud, he'd have been out of the pack years ago. But with that voice, no way.

It wasn't that he was cockney. Cockney was fine. In fact cockney was flavour of the decade. An actor born Maurice Micklewhite who'd been playing nonentities for years in second features had suddenly been discovered and was busy making it as a 'deliberately unconcealed cockney' named Michael Caine. They'd even managed not so long ago to miscast Caine totally as an upper class British army officer in the film *Zulu*, but such was his charisma that he'd escaped relatively unscathed. So cockney was orl right. Cockney was in.

What wasn't orl right with unconcealed cockney, unless you knew how to deliver it right, was what it did to your features once you started talking. A lot of ordinary people who had particularly attractive faces in repose lost all semblance of beauty once they opened their mouths, and this man was no exception. Caine's cockney was an object lesson. His face held together when he talked. But this man's did not. As soon as he opened his mouth to speak his jaw slackened and went sideways, utterly distorting his previously perfectly shaped mouth. And with it, all his sex appeal vanished.

His sex appeal via the camera that is, Meredith concluded, watching the eyes watching the man. He was fine when he was moving, and fine when he was listening, but hopeless when he was talking, if you thought of him as seen through the camera lens. Up there on the big silver screen, which was well known for highlighting the slightest fault in your make-up, that slack and wandering jaw would be an unmitigated disaster.

But Meredith wasn't in the least discouraged. Temporarily dismayed perhaps. But not deterred. After all, Max had turned her round, so what was to stop her doing the same for this guy? Nothing. Just as long as that's what he wanted. Or, more importantly, just as long as Meredith could convince him that was what he wanted.

When Maxine disappeared slightly unsteadily to the ladies, Meredith took the opportunity to approach the man. She waited till he was busy polishing some clean glasses, and then she sat herself down at the bar in front of him. The man looked up at her, and Meredith, who had prepared exactly what she was going to say, suddenly found herself speechless.

She just stared at him, wordlessly. The man smiled and went on polishing the glasses. Someone came up and ordered some drinks which the man poured and took the money for. And Meredith still couldn't unjam her mind. Finally she took a card from her purse and pushed it across the bar at him.

The man stared at it, looked at her, then read the card.

'Yeah?' he said pleasantly enough. 'You're a featrical agent, yeah? Nice.'

'I want you to come and see me,' Meredith stammered.

The man looked at her with a deep frown.

'Yeah?'

'Yes. This afternoon. When you close. I'm only round the corner.'

'Why?'

'Come and see me in my office and I'll explain. Any time before half past five.'

And then she got up, collected Maxine who was looking rather blearily round the bar for her, and left.

He turned up in her office forty-five minutes later, and stood in front of Meredith's desk, flicking her visiting card against his hand.

'Right then,' he said. 'So 'ere I am.'

He was even better-looking out of that smoke-filled bar. Standing there in front of her, smiling shyly at her and occasionally running a nervous hand through his hair, he could have been the young Hank Fonda, Jimmy Stewart and Cary Grant rolled into one. Meredith drew a deep and private breath, in an attempt to calm her inner self, for she had never been this excited before in her life.

Then she sat him down with a cup of coffee and started

questioning him. He was called Ted Ernstone, he was twenty-five, and since leaving school at fifteen he'd done this and that, work which included spells on the docks, as a lorry driver, and now as a barman. He was unmarried, and still lived at home in Bethnal Green.

He was drifting at the moment, because he hadn't found anything yet that he really wanted to do. He was giving it until next year, and if he couldn't settle down then, he was going to join the Navy.

'Have you ever thought about acting?' Meredith asked him.

'Nah,' he answered, after a tell-tale pause. 'Not reelly.'

'Why not?' Meredith persisted.

"Cos I 'aven't, I suppose,' he said. 'That's why. I wouldn't know where to start.'

'I'm where you start,' Meredith told him quite simply.

She told him he had the looks and the physique to make it. There was absolutely no doubt in her mind. She knew the business inside out, because she'd been in it since she was a child, and he had to believe her when she told him he'd got the famous what-it-takes.

'I know what you're going to look like on camera,' she told him. 'You're going to look sensational. The camera will love you, and that's all that matters. You have a perfect facial bone structure. And as for your eyes.'

Meredith looked into those deep blue orbs. He held her look quite steadily, until Meredith was the one who was almost forced to break the gaze.

'You're goin' to think this a bit cheeky,' he said suddenly, as Meredith was refilling their mugs of coffee, 'but if you're so good at this lark. At spottin' future stars like. Then what you doin' in a pissy little office like this then?'

He looked round at her as she handed him his mug, widening those big blue eyes. His manner had become much more relaxed and confident now, with an air of slight insolence about it, which only excited Meredith all the more.

'I'll tell you what I'm doing in a pissy little place like

355

this, shall I?' Meredith asked him, as she sat herself back down behind her desk. 'Getting cold, and hungry, and angry. Which can only be all in your favour. Because in this business you don't get anywhere unless you're hungry.'

They then talked this and that for a while, for Meredith didn't want to pressurize him in case she frightened him off. The notion of becoming a famous star was obviously something Ted Ernstone had never given any serious consideration, and now the subject had been broached, and the initial shock had worn off, Meredith could see suspicion writ large across his open face.

'I'm not sure,' he said suddenly, putting his coffee mug down on the desk and standing up. 'I mean I'm really not sure about this at all.'

'What aren't you sure about?' Meredith enquired. 'Do you think I might be running some sort of white-slave traffic?'

"Ow do I know what you're at, Miss?' he asked, frowning and looking very vulnerable. 'You could be anybody. You could be – I dunno. Anything.'

'I could just be after your body,' Meredith said straight faced.

'Well, I dunno, do I?' Ted mumbled, looking down at his feet and reddening. 'It takes all sorts.'

'What do you want out of life, Ted?' she asked him. 'Do you just want to go on drifting, into the Navy perhaps, and then out again? And then back to working behind another bar, or driving someone else's lorry. Is that how you see the rest of your life going? I really can't believe that it is.'

Ted shrugged and then turned to look out of the window.

'I'd like to move me mum out of where she is,' he said finally, 'and buy 'er a 'ouse, like.'

'And so you shall,' Meredith replied.

Ted turned back and looked suspiciously at her.

'Oh, yeah?' he said.

'Yes,' Meredith assured him. 'If that's what you want. I will promise you that in five years' time you will be able to buy your mother a house. Who knows? You might be able to buy her one before that. But I promise you that if you haven't, your mother will still get her house. Because in five years from today, if you still can't afford to buy your mum a house, I'll buy it for her.'

The young man stared at her hard, and speechlessly.

'I mean it, Ted,' Meredith said. 'That's how much I believe in you.'

That night when she lay in her bed, Meredith concluded that she must have lost her reason. She knew nothing about the young man she had signed up that afternoon beyond the fact that she was taken by him in a big way. But not sexually. Or rather not just sexually. Of course he had excited her, but it was something other than the normal excitement she felt when meeting a very attractive man. Meredith guessed that perhaps this was how inventors might feel when they suddenly discovered something quite revolutionary. Or how an astronomer might feel when he discovered a brand-new star.

But besides her gut feelings, she knew nothing else. She didn't know whether or not he had any acting talent whatsoever, and as for her confident assertions that the camera would love him, she had absolutely no technical knowledge at all as to what the lens loved and what it hated.

It was just a hunch. Just a feeling inside her. Just a wild shot in an all-enveloping darkness.

But then what was life if you didn't play your hunches? If the favourites always romped home there'd be no bookmakers. It was the rank outsiders who more often than not trotted up, and so why shouldn't Ted Ernstone be one of them? The business was full of totally untalented dimwits who had leapt to stardom just because of their bodies, or their square jawline, or their beautiful blue eyes. To tell the truth, Meredith thought as she fell into an uneasy sleep, perhaps having talent in this business was sometimes a positive disadvantage.

Meredith sold more or less everything she had to back her latest investment, including the small oil painting she had bought for her first office, and finally even the beautiful ring Louis had given her. That was the only thing which gave her any second thoughts about selling. But still she sold it, because she knew that if she was unable to part with it, then her determination would be suspect.

Besides that, she needed the money. In order to pull this one off, she was going to have to kill Ted Ernstone and launch David Terry, as she had rechristened her embryonic star, in his place. And that meant a whole new wardrobe, and a whole new way of life. David Terry couldn't be seen working behind bars while he was waiting for a break. David Terry had to be seen in all the right places, as if he already existed, and was not just a product of Meredith's imagination. And that meant expensive meals at expensive restaurants, and a night life in expensive clubs.

It also meant a long and comprehensive series of voice lessons. David, as both of them now had to think of and call the former Ted, had initially resented this, more even than the changing of his registered name. In fact he found it very difficult to comprehend why it was necessary to change anything about him at all.

He was proud of what he was, he told Meredith. And he didn't see what and why it needed changing. Nowadays it didn't matter any more if you didn't talk posh. Look at all the actors who were making it talking cockney, or Liverpool, or Geordie. And they'd all kept the names they were born with – Albert, Tom, Jim, Alfred and Bert. So why did he have to go all posh and change his monicker then?

Because, Meredith kept repeating to him patiently, because she wanted him to become the sort of star who would be accepted internationally. Yes, agreed, there was a boom of sorts in British films at the moment, and all the actors were going round scratching their chests and dropping their aitches. But Meredith was talking long term. And that ultimately meant America. And America finally just wasn't interested in actors with ugly names and impenetrable English regional accents.

So what about Michael Caine? her pupil would keep insisting. Michael Caine had not gone all lardy-bloody-dah.

Meredith was getting tired of this one, but tried her best not to show her edginess. She finally convinced him that Caine was an exception, and that if he, David Terry, wanted to hang on to his East End accent and all that went along with it, then the most he could hope for was to become known as the poor man's Michael Caine.

This got home. This threat to the actor's growing vanity. Already he couldn't stop looking at himself in every mirror or shop window that they passed, now that he had been carefully redressed and restyled by Meredith. In his Duggie Millings suits, or his John Michael casuals, and with his newly Vidal Sassooned hair, he looked, as he called it, dead sharp. He looked neat.

But the voice still gave him away. Dressed in the height of fashion, he looked what he should until he opened his mouth. Then you'd have bet your last penny that what David Terry was involved in wasn't strictly legal.

'Leave him to me,' Jeannie Costelow sighed, when Meredith revisited her old voice teacher.

'You just have to do for him what you did for me,' Meredith told her.

'By the time I've finished with him, darling,' Jeannie replied, 'he'll think he was born to it.'

He did, too. When he finished his tuition, his whole personality had apparently altered. Jeannie had taught him a faultless standard English accent, which he had embellished by adopting a wonderfully languid form of delivery. Where it came from, neither Meredith nor Jeannie could imagine. But coupled with the doe-like blue eyes, and the slightly cherubic face, the effect was devastating.

'Get him out of here,' Jeannie had whispered to Meredith with some urgency after his final lesson. 'Get him out of here and quickly! Before I tear his trousers off and make a total fool of myself!'

Meredith was delighted. After all, that was the effect she was after. When this man finally made it on to the big silver screen, Meredith wanted every woman in the audience to be feeling just like her friend Jeannie was feeling.

'Are you sure you mean it, darling?' she whispered back to Jeannie. 'It might be the only chance you get.'

'Just get him out of here!' Jeannie groaned. 'Before I let him have all the lessons free!'

The next day, after Meredith had rehearsed him in all the social niceties, they went out for their first meal together in public. Meredith chose to go to Le Caprice, where she had gone so often both with Max and with his father.

The moment they walked in, heads turned. Meredith had been careful to dress herself down slightly, rather than upstage her client. Because of course this time she wanted the eyes to be on him. She had kept all her good clothes, because she knew it was going to be a long time before she could buy herself anything approaching the standard of the gifts Max had bestowed on her, and from them she had chosen to wear a dark two-piece suit with a white silk shirt, an outfit more suitable to the rising executive than the ex-West End star. She had dressed David in a hand-tailored blue mohair suit, which had small cuffs and covered buttons, and a very pale blue voile shirt from Cecil Gee, chosen especially to show off those startling blue eyes.

And the moment they walked in was the moment Meredith knew she was in business. It wasn't the immediate turning of the heads that told her. After all, most people when they're dining look up out of curiosity when anyone attractive enters the restaurant. That's half the fun of dining out. Nor was it the length of the stares they got. Some of those could have been for her, do-you-see-who-I-see? stares. No, what confirmed Meredith in her belief that her protégé was going to be a star was the effect it had on *him*. As soon as they walked into the room, he turned it on. He could have been going onstage, such was the electricity he generated. Once he saw the people looking up and around at him, Meredith saw the lights go on. And he dazzled. Quite positively.

He wasn't just dazzling the clientele either. From the way he was shown to his table you'd think he'd just stepped off the plane from Hollywood.

'Well done,' she whispered to him as they sat down. 'Now, talk to me, and look at me, and remember what I said. Don't look round, and don't look at anyone else. This sort of place and these sort of people must appear to be second nature to you.'

David did as he was told, and most convincingly. And when it came to ordering the food and wine he was word-perfect. So he should have been, since Meredith had taken him through exactly what they were going to eat and drink the night before, basing the projected meal precisely on the lunches she had eaten there before, down to and including Louis's favourite burgundy. The staff were most impressed.

So were the clientele. So was everyone everywhere they went. By the time Meredith took him gaming to The White Elephant one or two of the business's minor notables were coming up to them and volunteering to guess who the actor was.

'Don't tell me,' they'd say. 'You must be David Terry.'

And then Meredith would whisk him away before the conversation became too probing, making a polite excuse about having to introduce him to somebody else before spiriting him away into the night. It was a gamble but a premeditated one. Because from her own experience Meredith knew that what the business didn't know about you they would make up, rather than be found wanting.

361

It didn't matter that the actor's picture wasn't to be found anywhere in the casting directories. That only added to the mystery. Besides, not everyone advertised themselves. Not everyone needed to. And Meredith was determined that David Terry should be one of those who need not.

Meredith rehearsed him in everything. In the evenings when they didn't go out, she sent him to the theatre or the cinema by himself. And then he'd come back to her flat and they'd talk about what he'd seen, and what he thought about the performances. It didn't take long for him to evaluate the actors, and it took even less time for him to start bitching them.

'That bloke in the play tonight—' he'd start.

'Not bloke,' she'd correct. 'That man, that boy, the person, the actor, that idiot, that stupid bastard even, but not that bloke.'

'He was piss.'

'He was awful.'

'He was piss awful.'

'He was hopeless, darling.'

'He was diabolical, doll.'

And then Meredith would start to hoot with laughter, while David would stare at her with that wonderful look of childish bewilderment. She would apologize, and try to control herself, but there was something so intrinsically funny about all this cockney coming out posh that she found it nearly impossible.

'I'm sorry, darling,' she'd apologize. 'It's just your vocabulary.'

'So what am I meant to say?' he'd ask, genuinely trying to help and to please.

'I'm trying to teach you, David.'

'And I'm doing my best.'

'Of course you are. I'm asking the impossible of you.'

'No, you're not.'

'Of course I am. And I'm sorry.'

'No, you're not!' he'd suddenly shout. 'You said so yourself for Christ's sake! Nothing is impossible!'

362

Which was exactly the reaction Meredith was after. Once he stopped being angry, he'd lose his determination. She wanted to rile him, to make him think the task was beyond his range. To extend him, probe him, irritate him. To do anything to him which would make him even more resolved to crack it.

'Actually I think I'm wrong about your vocabulary,' she said to him one night, quite out of the blue. 'I think that could be part of your appeal. This idiosyncratic way of talking. Nobody else talks like you do. Like Noël Coward being played by a lorry driver.'

'You winding me up, doll?' he asked her, in a puzzled rather than a hostile way.

'No, David,' Meredith replied. 'As a matter of fact I'm not. I think, as long as we don't overdo it, the odd bit of cockney colour showing through here and there adds something rather original.'

And so they worked at refining David's act, until they had more or less perfected his way and manner of talking. But sometimes it backfired and the actor would sound like the famous scene in *Some Like It Hot* where Tony Curtis tries to imitate Cary Grant, and Meredith would start to laugh while trying not to, until David corpsed as well and they both started to roll around the sofa in helpless laughter.

It was during one of these sessions, where they both found themselves hopeless with laughter, that the actor kissed her.

Meredith was livid, and slapped him hard across the face.

'Friggin' Ada,' David said, in cockney-posh which under normal circumstances would have rendered Meredith quite helpless once again. But on this occasion she was still very angry, although her fury was really mostly directed against herself.

Even so, she continued to warn him off.

'Don't ever try that again,' she said. 'Not ever.'

'I don't understand,' he replied, innocently puzzled once again. 'Don't you fancy me?'

'It doesn't matter a twopenny damn whether I fancy you

or whether I don't,' Meredith told him. 'The point is you mustn't, and I mustn't – right? Otherwise we'll just screw the whole thing up.'

'I don't see why,' he said, rubbing the sting from his cheek.

'You wouldn't,' Meredith replied. 'Why should you? But I do. Believe me, David, because I know. Once we become lovers, it's over. We'll lose our objectivity. We won't be able to see the wood for the trees any longer.'

He looked up at her from where he was sitting on her sofa, frowning, hurt. But Meredith felt heartless. Whatever she did, she mustn't get involved. She mustn't handle the goods.

In the beginning, that was the closest they came to disaster. After that, David never made another attempt at intimacy, and their relationship became exactly what it had been before he had taken her in his arms and kissed her. Deep in her heart Meredith wished that it didn't have to be, because, when he had kissed her, for a moment the world had stood still. And for another dangerous moment, as she opened her eyes and looked at him, she had been willing to throw it all away for love. For him to lift her up and carry her into her bedroom and make love to her. And then just in time she had seen reason, and slapped him round the face instead.

10

Max had hung the portrait in the hall. He had thought about hanging it elsewhere, in fact he had considered not hanging it at all, after Meredith's disclosures. But Seraphina had talked the sense back into him.

'You don't have to sit in judgement on her, Max,' she had said when he had told her what sort of person his mother had really been. 'You don't have the right to, either.'

'She was my mother!' Max had snapped back at her, raising his voice at her for the first time ever. 'You don't know what this does to someone!'

'Max,' Seraphina had reasoned, 'Max, if you loved her, you loved her for what she was. Whether you knew it or not. You don't have to hate her now, because she's the same person. She's the same person in the eyes of the person who matters.'

Max had still been angry, even though he listened, and even though he knew what Seraphina was saying was right. And his anger was now directed not at his dead mother, but at Seraphina. He was angry because she was saying the right thing. And because she had got there before he had. And because she was so pure and unspoilt she could make the proper judgement and make him feel lesser because of it. And he was angry that she hadn't felt at all jealous at him seeing Meredith and at him speaking to her. Seraphina seemed above all pettiness, and quite unable to do or think the wrong thing. And at this moment in his life it infuriated Max.

He was still angry with her that night when they made

love, and he hurt her, wilfully, almost spitefully. But still she seemed to possess an understanding beyond anyone else Max had ever known, and although she cried after they had finished making love, she said nothing to him. She didn't remonstrate, and she didn't ask why. She just cried.

Max got out of bed and walked round the room, his anger now gone from him. He stood by the bedroom window and looked out at the moonlit gardens below.

'I'm sorry,' he finally said. 'I really don't know what came over me.'

'There's nothing to be sorry about, Max,' Seraphina answered. 'I'm the one who should be sorry.'

'Why?' Max asked, turning round and frowning at the beautiful creature who was now propped up in their bed. 'What did you ever do that you had to be sorry for?'

'I told you something that you knew already,' Seraphina replied. 'And that's why you got so angry.'

Max sat down on the bed and took one of Seraphina's beautiful white hands in his. He looked at it, at every inch of it, stroking every elegant finger before raising the hand to his mouth and kissing it.

'I don't deserve you, Seraphina,' he said. 'Never in my life did I do anything to deserve you.'

Then he made love to her again, only this time very gently, and very slowly.

Which was how the portrait came to hang in the hall, in pride of place, so that it would be the first thing of note that the visitor would see. Max looked at it every day he was home. Whenever he arrived down from London, he would stand for a moment, looking up at the beautiful woman who had been his mother, and first thing in the morning when he came downstairs, and last thing at night before he retired. And because of Seraphina he could look at it without pain.

But one thing he could not do, despite Seraphina's ministrations, was leave her every Monday morning without pain. She would kiss him, and walk with him to the car, sometimes in the winter months when it was freezing and still pitch dark, then she would kiss him again and tell him twenty times how she would be fine until Friday without him, because she had Mrs Joliffe and all her country interests, and anyway the way it was now she so looked forward to seeing Max on Fridays, it made their relationship even more special, if that was possible.

It was what Max wanted to hear and as always with Seraphina he was content to hear what he wanted to hear while he was with her; but when he left her, when he returned to London, the need to make her prove over and over how much she loved him returned, and he would brood about whether she did indeed love him as much as he idolized her. And he would want to know, not once or twice a week, but once or twice a day, and then again at the weekends, just how she felt.

'You don't love me as I love you,' Max would tell her on the telephone in the evenings. 'You don't care what I'm doing here in London. I could be doing anything, with anyone – do you know that?'

'I think about you all the time,' was all Seraphina would reply. 'I think of nothing but you.'

Max knew this was true. It had to be. When he went home there were always flowers everywhere, and bowls of pot pourri, and in the bedroom his hand-embroidered slippers by his bedside and new books set out on his bedside table, along with a fresh supply of biscuits in a tin. Everywhere he looked he could see that indeed Seraphina did do nothing but think of him. But still he upbraided her, and although daily she reaffirmed her love for him, still he didn't believe her.

'I want to be inside you all the time,' he told her once on the telephone, desperate with desire for her, most of all because she was so remote from him. 'And I want you to carry me around with you everywhere you go.'

Seraphina would sometimes sigh at these things he said.

'Has no one ever loved you before?' she demanded once.

'Oh, yes,' Max replied, suddenly mischievous. 'I've always been loved, that's not the point.'

'What is the point?' Seraphina wondered.

'This point is,' said Max slowly, 'the point is this is the first time I've loved someone else.'

But Seraphina never asked Max if he loved her. To Max she would say that if she loved him too much he would tire of her. And, Max thought, damn, she was probably right. A passionately demonstrative Seraphina would be anathema.

He never brought visitors to his Camelot. No friends came to the hall bearing with them gifts and laughter, to demand Seraphina's attention. Max was the king, and Seraphina his court. His neighbours shot, or hunted, or just partied, Arthur had only his Guinevere. But she seemed content. In summer they would sit out in the gardens, Max reading while Seraphina did her tapestry, sitting just far enough away from him on the lawn so that the sound of her needlework didn't disturb him. And in winter they would sit by a roaring fire, while the rains dashed against the windows, and the winds howled around the chimneys.

Seraphina never complained, or sought after company. On long winter evenings when other girls her age might have been bored, she would just smile at the question, and ask Max how she could be?

'It's all right for me,' Max would argue. 'I have a busy week, and then I have you to come home to. You're here the whole time.'

And Seraphina would just smile back at him, and stroke her little dog's head.

'I don't mind, Max,' she would tell him. 'Really. I'm quite happy.'

But Monday morning always came, although Seraphina did her best to make their weekly parting as painless as possible. On the fine light mornings of spring and summer, she would follow his car down the drive, running first and then slowing to a walk as Max accelerated away. She looked so beautiful, her blond hair flowing out behind her, as she waved after him and blew him kisses. Max would smile and wave back, hardly able to believe what he saw was his, the old house, the gardens, the fine trees, and Seraphina. Beautiful Seraphina, so English, so perfect, and all his.

'You spoil that girl,' Baz told him one Tuesday when he caught Max despatching his weekly present to Seraphina. Max always sent her a present on Tuesday. Usually something small, but sometimes something wildly extravagant. This particular week he was sending her a floor-length velvet coat, lined with fur, which he had spotted in the window of a very fashionable couturier boutique on his way to a meeting. Even though he was late Max stopped and ordered it to be sent round to the office at once, from where he was despatching it all the way to wintry Norfolk. Seraphina had laughed about the winter mornings up there, of how the water froze in the taps and Mr Bennett had to come from the village to unfreeze her and Mrs Joliffe. Now Seraphina could get up in the morning and wear what most women wore only when going to a ball.

'Your father Louis used to say never spoil a woman,' Baz went on. 'Keep the lead short he'd say, and keep them fascinated. They think they've got you, you've lost them.'

'What shit, he did nothing *except* spoil my mother—'

'Don't swear. What's with you rich kids swearing all the time? When we were poor it was the first thing we gave *up*, swearing, it was a sign of poverty to use words like that.'

Max ignored this and went on preparing his parcel.

'Besides, everyone spoilt your mother, the whole world spoilt your mother. This wife of yours, maybe you're ruining her, burying her in the country like that. She's a beautiful girl, beautiful women don't like the country.'

'Seraphina loves it in the country,' Max sighed past his cigar. 'She's a country girl. She was brought up in the country.'

'Girls brought up in the country hate the country, that's a fact, they've seen too much of it. Trees dripping. Mud. It's not feminine.'

369

Nowadays Baz was never out of Max's office. He was always stopping by on some pretext, or on no pretext. Either way it was always a punishment.

'Baz? Why don't you go see Annie, huh?'

'I don't want to see Annie, or her girls.'

'I'll treat you—'

'A fine thing. No, I don't like the girls any more, she doesn't have those nice girls she used to, with long hair and red lips, they're all in uniforms now, schoolgirls, long white socks, they look like nurses, stewardesses, that sort of thing. It's just not tasteful. And she doesn't have French girls. Now they have to be American. Annie's taken to having American girls, with those over-white square teeth, and bodies like athletes. If I want an athlete, I'll go to a stadium. I don't like these American girls. They remind me of air hostesses. I like French girls, with those nice round, dark bodies that smell a little of garlic. And what I don't want to do when I go see girls is to talk about the business. That's all they want to talk about. The business. How to break into the business.'

'You're so right,' Max grinned. 'But it's funny also. Because whores, they all want to be actresses. And most actresses – they're whores.'

'That could be your father talking,' Baz said. 'You know that? You even looked like him when you said it.'

The remark went over his head and into oblivion. Max knew the tactic, and nowadays was forearmed. Baz liked to drag the memory of Max's father in wherever and whenever possible, to keep alive the unspoken notion that Louis's death was all Max's fault. It was Max's fault because he had chosen not to speak to his father. And because of that, and their estrangement, Louis had been driven into Meredith's arms, and his passion for too young a woman had killed him. And so that was Max's fault. Max had given his father the fatal heart attack.

But by keeping it alive, Baz had killed it off. He'd talked it out of Max's system, and Max now felt no more guilt about his father's death. People died. That happened. His father had died. That had happened too.

He felt Baz glaring at him in the silence but he ignored it, finishing off the parcel and then turning to see what was on his desk.

'So what's new?' Baz finally asked, having been forced on to a new subject. 'Anything good? I can't remember when I last saw something good.'

'It depends what you're looking for,' Max replied.

'I mean on television,' Baz grumbled. 'I'm an old man. I like to sit at home nights now and watch some television. But what is there on? Nothing. What I'd like to see is a good comedy. Why don't we make a Dick Van Dyke Show? Please tell me why we don't. But we don't. I'd like to see a good comedy like Dick Van Dyke.'

'So why not watch it?' Max asked him. 'It's on every week.'

'I mean a home-grown one,' Baz replied. 'If I wanted to be an American, I'd go live in America.'

Max nodded, half-hearing, as his secretary Mona came in with the second post. In response to his query as to what it contained, Mona told him that among other things it contained the promised script from Kennedy and Burrell.

'So what are those two writing for you?' Baz enquired without real interest.

'They have this idea for a television series,' Max replied, consigning the newly-arrived script to his bottom drawer, as was his habit with all new manuscripts. 'Now, are you quite sure you don't want a freebie at Annie's?'

The script sat in the drawer unread for a month. After the first week, William or sometimes Jay would ring the office for Max's reaction, and Mona would tell them it was on his desk. To which William or sometimes Jay would enquire as to whether or not Max had read it, and Mona would tell them it was on the top of the pile. After four weeks of this William finally lost patience, and told Mona they were coming round to the office in person.

Mona at once went and told Max, who was having a private manicure in his office. Max sighed and fished the script out of the bottom drawer and started to give it a cursory read while the pretty little blonde manicurist finished his right hand.

After the first two pages, he dismissed the manicurist and, having selected and lit a fresh cigar, settled back in his chair to give what was turning out to be a first-class property his full attention.

Mona kept William and Jay waiting in the outer office for nearly an hour when they arrived, to give Max a chance to give the script a second reading. Jay found an old copy of *The Stage* in the wastepaper basket, and gave it to William for him to tear into little strips. While he did so, she sat down and made a list of things they might one day do to the studio.

Max appeared at the doorway in shirtsleeves, beaming.

'My favourite writers,' he said.

'I'll bet you say that to all the derelicts,' William replied as they wandered into Max's office.

'I mean it, William ma boy,' Max assured him. 'You two, to put it in the popular jargon, are something other.'

Max poured them all drinks, then sat at his desk and grinned at them. William smiled deliberately back at him, and Jay stuck her tongue in her cheek and widened her eyes. They knew the rules of the game well enough by now not to open up by asking Max for his opinion. So instead they enquired after Seraphina, and Max enquired after them. And they told Max they were fine, and enquired after him. And he told them he was fine. And then William and Jay got up as one and wished him goodbye.

Max laughed but inwardly cursed them for winning that round. He was inordinately fond of both William and Jay, but he hated the fact that they were writers, because he hated writers. Writers were so smart. They were always that one step ahead of you, and they all sat there with that particular blank look on their faces, as if they were constantly puzzled or uncertain, while all the time they'd

372

already figured out the moves that were going to outsmart you. With actors you knew what they were thinking. They were so transparent. With writers, you never knew what the bastards were thinking.

'OK!' Max called as they reached the door. 'Your round on points! But I win on a technical knockout!'

William and Jay stopped and turned.

'Don't tell me you've read it?' William asked.

'It's wonderful,' Max replied. 'It's the best thing I've read in years!'

'You don't mean it?' Jay enquired hesitantly.

'You bet I mean it!' Max beamed. 'You know what you have here? You have an English Dick Van Dyke Show!'

William and Jay left the office with a spring in their step. Before they went, Jay had reached up and kissed Max, William had offered Max one of Max's own cigars, and Max, in a moment of benevolence, had almost forgiven them both for being writers.

'This show will make your reputations,' he told them. 'I'll see that it does.'

Even so, William had to have the last word.

'As a matter of purely academic interest, Max,' he said, hand on doorknob. 'It was intended as an *hommage* to Burns and Allen. Rather than a look-alike Dick Van Dyke. But there you go. We're only the goddam writers.'

You'll bet your sweet life you are, Max thought, closing the door and chewing on his cigar. Who needed writers? What were they? Old ladies in jeans.

Then he picked up his telephone and asked Mona to get him Barry Philips, his second cousin and Controller of Programmes at City Television.

By the time he left London for Norfolk the script was safely with his cousin, having been delivered to him and recommended in person by Max the previous evening over a long and expensive dinner. Max wasn't normally interested in television, but with this particular property,

Max smelt a hit, and Max could never resist the chance of a score, whatever the environment. Besides, people were now beginning to earn good money from television as the overseas markets were starting to open up, and a runner was a runner, whatever stable it might come from.

'I like the sound of it,' Barry had told him at dinner. 'Sounds like our sort of show. Nice and glossy.'

'Could be right for Craig Matheson?' Max had suggested, but carefully, anxious not to tread on any toes.

'Not for us, I'm afraid, Max,' Barry had told him. 'With respect, I know he's a client, but he's difficult. We had to pull the plugs on the second series of his last show because of what he wanted. And what he didn't want. I'd rather someone else took the strain.'

'Craig's a monster,' Max had agreed, grinning. 'He's his own worst enemy. If only he'd just stick to what he's good at. Acting. And let everyone else get on with their jobs.'

'I'd like to find somebody new, Max,' Barry had concluded. 'I'm getting tired of the same old faces cropping up. Matheson, Nesbit, Singleton. Maybe it's time to find somebody new.'

Max had nodded sympathetically, but hadn't committed himself. It was a perfect vehicle for Craig Matheson, and the thought of getting commission from both the writers and the star was very attractive to Max. Nonetheless, Max was prepared to play along and wait, since he knew that finding a new and untried talent as good as the proven and bankable assets of Craig Matheson was about as likely as making a hit musical out of the telephone directory. So all in all, as he headed out of London, Max felt well pleased with the business they had done over the previous night's dinner, even though it had meant delaying his departure for Norfolk from Friday afternoon to Saturday morning.

Seraphina was waiting for him, by the front door, as she always did. And as always Max shook his head and asked her how she knew he was going to be there.

'Because I do,' she replied, and kissed him.

Max then returned her kiss and teased her, saying that once she knew he'd left London, what she did was stand and wait by the door for three hours in order to impress him.

'Ask Mrs Joliffe,' Seraphina replied. 'I was in the kitchen cooking until two minutes ago.'

Max grinned and, putting his arm round her slender waist, walked her into the house. Nonetheless, he asked the attendant Mrs Joliffe if what Seraphina had just told him was indeed the case.

'Oh yes, Mr Kassov,' Mrs Joliffe answered. 'It's always the same. Before we even see or hear your car in the drive, Mrs Kassov always calls to say you're arriving.'

Seraphina smiled at Max's blank expression and took him by the hand into the drawing-room, where a tray of hot coffee and croissants sat ready on a table by the fire. Then, after he had eaten, she took him upstairs and ran him a refreshing bath. While the water was running, Seraphina sat Max down on the bed and slowly undressed him, until he was quite naked.

Max then made a move to start undressing her, but Seraphina motioned for him not to, and disappeared to turn off the bath. When she returned she was still fully dressed, which was how she stayed while she made love to him.

'You like this, don't you?' Max whispered as he moved her under him, and lifted her skirt.

'You know I do,' Seraphina whispered back. 'It's like something you'd dream.'

'Do you dream much, Seraphina?' he asked, putting a hand up under her cashmere sweater and discovering she wasn't wearing a bra.

'When you're away, I do very little else, Max.'

Her small beautiful nipples were already erect before Max even touched them, and long before he put his mouth round first one and then the other. Seraphina sighed and started to bite the end of her own fingers in ecstasy. Then Max lifted her skirt and eased one hand into the warm cleft of her legs. Seraphina moaned, and

375

squeezed his hand tight between her thighs, as if she didn't want the hand to venture any further. Max obeyed the signal, and just let his hand rest, before suddenly pushing her legs apart and starting to explore her with his fingers.

Seraphina moaned again, softly and then louder, as Max began to arouse her. She implored and beseeched him not to, while all the time doing nothing to prevent him from continuing. And Max continued until her moans had turned to groans and until he had brought her to the very edge, which was when he raised himself up and thrust himself inside her. Seraphina gave a gasp of sheer delight, as her eyes suddenly opened wide.

'My God, Max!' she cried. 'Max – you're incredible!'

And he was. Max knew it, all the time he was making love to her. He was incredible, because that is precisely how Seraphina made him feel.

'Poor Meredith,' Seraphina suddenly said in the silence that followed their love-making.

'Why poor Meredith?' Max asked in amazement.

'No wonder she did what she did to you,' Seraphina said sadly. 'No wonder she tried to hurt you.'

'You mean about my mother?'

'Yes. Of course. She loved you, Max. And any woman who loves you is scarred for life.'

Max turned on his side and grinned at Seraphina, who was lying on her back staring at the ceiling.

'I'm that good, huh?' he said.

'Too good,' Seraphina replied, almost sadly. 'Women will do anything for you.'

Much as he hated leaving Seraphina every Monday, Max still thrilled to his work. As soon as he walked through his office door, the adrenalin started flowing. Max loved his business, he loved doing business, and he was good at doing business. And it meant a lot to him that he was good at doing it, because like his father Max knew that's all there was. One go at it, then it was over. There were no other rewards, there was no eternal prize-giving. One go, and one go only. There were no second chances.

Mona was waiting for him with a list of calls.

'Barry Philips from City Television called,' she said, indicating the top name on the list. 'Twice. He wants you to call him straight away.'

Max raised his eyebrows as he skim read the other calls. There was nothing else that couldn't wait, so he ordered Mona to put the call through at once.

'I knew you'd have to read it over the weekend,' Max said to his second cousin. 'I told you it was that good.'

'We'd like to do thirteen, Max,' Barry replied. 'Seven and six—'

'That makes thirteen.'

'With an option on another thirteen. But give it to the writers in pieces. You and I, we'll agree thirteen with another thirteen, but give it to them in bits.'

'You are talking to their agent, Barry.'

'I know who I'm talking to, Max. This isn't about money. We'll talk the money in a minute. This is about not letting them know how good they are. That's for both our benefits.'

'Now you've gone too fast for me, Barry. I'm meant not to tell my clients how good they are?'

'That's right, Max. That's if you want them to go on producing stuff as good as this. If they know how good they are, they might start worrying. And that could affect their writing. And I don't know about you, but these writers are good and I want to squeeze them.'

'I won't tell them how good they are.'

'Then let's deal.'

'For the first seven I want fifteen hundred a show, Barry.'

'I'm paying seven-fifty.'

'Fifteen hundred.'

'To me, they're an unknown quantity.'

'You've just told me how good they are, Barry. You have to pay for how good.'

'Sometimes I don't think you hear, Max. We don't want them to know how good, remember? So they come in on the agreed minimum.'

'Sometimes I think you don't remember who you're talking to, Barry. Think back a moment. This is their agent in your ear.'

'OK, Max. So what's ten per cent of seven-fifty?'

'It's seventy-five, Barry. It has been for as long as I've been an agent.'

'And what's seventy-five pounds to you, Max? You're a rich boy. You don't need seventy-five pounds.'

'Seventy-five times, say, twenty-six – say times thirty-nine, if you go to three series – that's nearly three thousand. If I dropped that in the street I'd go back for it.'

'If we go to three series, you'll get your three grand. Don't worry. So let's talk from seven-fifty, right?'

'We're talking from seven-fifty.'

Max got William and Jay £750 for the first seven scripts, £900 for the next six, £1250 for any further seven, and £1500 for any further six. The price for any third series wasn't negotiated, although an option on the writers' services was proposed.

Jay was thrilled, but William pulled a face.

'You any idea what goes into writing one of these?' he asked Max.

'I'm the guy who looks at the garden, William,' Max replied. 'Not the one who plants it.'

'The money's piss, Max.'

'It could be a good long piss, think about it.'

'What they're offering for thirteen scripts, Max, you know as well as I do we can make from one movie.'

'First you have to get the movie, pal. And let's face it. Recently the phone's not exactly been jumping off the hook. Besides, this is your baby. This is something you brought to me.'

'Yes, that's right, William!' Jay interjected, jumping up from her chair. 'You're forgetting this is something we

378

want to do! This isn't just any old job! This is something we believe in!'

William gave her a private glare, trying to get Jay to cool it and shut up. William didn't want Max to know how keen they were to do it. Sure, he was their agent, but as William knew all too well, there were deals within deals, and they were usually known as cross-deals.

Max on the other hand was listening to Jay attentively, nodding and smiling in agreement.

'If it's something you want to do that badly, Jay—' Max was saying.

'That's not the point, Max,' William interrupted. 'Because you want to do something doesn't mean you have to pay for doing it.'

'William pal, this is a Writers' Guild figure,' Max sighed. 'This is an agreed payment for a twenty-five-minute script.'

'For a twenty-five-minute script from a first-timer,' William corrected.

'For a twenty-five-minute script for a first-timer in television, William,' Max replied. 'But still. If you don't want to do it—'

'Of course we want to do it!' Jay cried. 'What do you think we asked you to sell it for?'

'Sure we want to do it, buddy,' William agreed. 'Just get us a better deal, that's all we're asking.'

'They won't budge, William.'

'You won't know till you've asked, Max.'

Max 'asked' and came back to them. William put the phone down on the proposal, and Max let them cook. He knew the money was awful, but he could justify it, since Kennedy and Burrell in television terms were a totally untried commodity. And theoretically, whatever they all privately thought of the script, it was a risk. William and Jay might be a one-trick pony. They mightn't be able to come up with another twelve scripts as good as the first. Or even if they did, the show might be miscast. Or misdirected. Or it just might not 'take'. In which case the company would only do seven shows and cut their losses. The television people were right. This was a risk contract. So Max could justify the lousy money.

And any doubts he might have had about doing so had been quickly dispelled by the second deal his cousin had proposed, namely for a series of thirteen fifty-minute spectaculars for one of Max's biggest variety clients, the singer-comedienne Toni French.

The differential between £750 and £1500 very soon became quite beside the point.

Max was therefore in high spirits as he headed his car back home. Certainly, William had kvetched as he knew William would, but Jay was obviously so over-excited she'd probably have done the job for nothing. The deal with Toni French, however, was big potatoes, and the commission from that series alone would buy the time Max needed to develop some of his projected movies. So all in all it had been a good week.

Which is why he'd decided for once to leave London early on Friday, and not at his usual last minute. He'd rung Seraphina to tell her, but the phone had rung in an obviously empty house. Max guessed Seraphina and Mrs Joliffe must have both gone out to shop for the weekend, and gave the matter no more thought. He just wished he could get home before Seraphina returned and for a change surprise her.

The roads for a Friday were surprisingly uncrowded, and Max, in his new S-class Mercedes, made Newmarket in his fastest time ever. From Newmarket he picked up the A11 to Thetford and did the eleven miles between the two points in just over eight minutes. His clear run continued until Wymondham, where he left the trunk road to drive the ten miles or so cross-country to East Dereham, before branching off on the north side of the town on to the B1147, the last lap of his journey.

East Dereham was just getting back to business after lunch, which would account, so Max thought, for the slow-moving traffic on the far side of town. However, when he got to the junction of the two roads which carried the outgoing traffic north and north-east, and took the right fork, Max saw the slow-moving line of traffic stretching ahead of him and realized there must be some other reason for the delay, since all this traffic was being held up going out of the town.

And then when he saw the flashing blue lights ahead of him, and the stream of cars being diverted on to the other side of the road, Max realized there must have been an accident.

It took him a good five minutes before he was alongside the wreckage. There were two vehicles involved, a builder's lorry, and a private car. Besides having spilled most of its load, the lorry was relatively undamaged, but the car was not only a wreck, it was a burn-out. Max didn't want to look, he wasn't a gawper, in fact he was only too anxious to comply with the hurry-on-through signals the police were giving him.

But something caught his eye and made his heart stop.

The car was still recognizably a Mini. Even though it was burned right out, Max could tell from the back of the car which was still more or less intact, that it had been a Mini. And Seraphina drove a Mini.

Or rather had driven a Mini, Max suddenly remembered with a flood of gratitude. Seraphina had driven a Mini before they were married. Nowadays she drove an MGB, which Max had given her as a wedding gift. And which Seraphina adored. And which she rarely if ever drove above thirty.

Max accelerated away from the scene of devastation and drove for home, now only five miles away across country, with a feeling of immense relief. Of course he felt for the occupants of the totally wrecked car, whoever they might have been. But Seraphina wasn't one of them. Seraphina drove what she called her 'Bee'.

And there it was in the garage. Max could see the car in the open double garage as he drove up to the house, and now his relief was final. Because even though Seraphina had long ago sold her Mini, Max still had to have the fact she now drove a sports car and that the sports car had not turned into a Mini proved to him, he had to see it with his very own eyes.

He even went and touched the bright red roadster, running his hand over the deeply polished bodywork, as if to prove to himself it wasn't a mirage. Then he noticed Seraphina had left the keys in the ignition, and with a sigh he pocketed them. She was forever losing her car keys, and little wonder, Max thought to himself.

Inside the house everything was just as he had imagined it would be. It was just as it always was: the freshly cut flowers carefully arranged, and the fires already lit in the hall and the drawing room. Even though he was early, everything was prepared. It was as if the house was kept in a permanent state of readiness for his arrival.

The only thing missing was Seraphina standing by the front door.

Upstairs too, everything was in place and immaculate. On the bed the old Chinese dressing gown, which had once belonged to Seraphina's grandfather and which Seraphina had given him when they were married, was laid out in readiness, and by the side of his bed his hand-embroidered slippers awaited him. The silver biscuit tins were full, as were the water carafes on the tables beside the bed, their bed, a carved oak four-poster, with seventeenth-century drapes held back with silk ropes, a faded and worn silk throwover, and a pile of huge pillows in hand-embroidered lace slips. Max picked a chocolate from the dish on his side of the bed, and bit into a violet cream. He grinned. Seraphina liked violet creams as much as he did.

But where was Seraphina? And come to think of it, where was her little dog Daisy? The house was oddly quiet, and still. Daisy always barked when he came home, half out of joy and half out of anxiety, as if she wasn't quite sure of Max, as if she never knew whether he was going to stay or go. So where was she now? Max looked out of the bedroom window down on to the gardens, half expecting to see the sight he so often saw and loved, Seraphina wandering in a dream up from the wild garden, her arms full of fresh flowers and her little dog running in joyful circles round her heels.

There was no Seraphina, and there was no Daisy. Just a garden in bloom, its plants swaying in a gentle breeze.

Max went out on to the landing and called. Then he went downstairs and called. Then he went through to the kitchen, and then through into the laundry rooms, and finally out into the garden itself and called. But there was never any answer. There was no sign of life.

He heard the car as he was running back inside. From where he was, he couldn't see it through any window, and by the time he had got to one, the car had been parked out of sight below. He thought for a moment it might be Mrs Joliffe returning from a shopping trip, until he remembered that Mrs Joliffe always drove up the back drive and straight round into the yard. He knew it wasn't Seraphina, because Seraphina's car was still in the garage. Unless she'd been out for a drive with someone else. Which Max briefly considered would be an unlikely thing for Seraphina to do on the day she was expecting Max home.

It wasn't Seraphina, and it wasn't Mrs Joliffe. It was the police. Two of them were standing there when Max opened the door, both in uniform.

'Mr Kassov?' the senior officer enquired politely, before introducing himself, and requesting permission to come into the house.

Max stepped aside and allowed the men in. They came past him, and stood in the hall, looking up and around them for a moment before removing their hats.

'If perhaps we might go in there, sir?' the senior officer requested, indicating the drawing-room.

Again Max concurred without query, leading the two men into the room, where again they took one curious look round before turning to face him.

383

'Mr Kassov,' the senior officer said. 'I'm very much afraid there's been an accident.'

'Do you mean just outside Dereham?' Max asked. 'I saw a bad accident just outside the town on my way down today.'

'Yes, sir,' the officer replied. 'That's the one.'

In the silence that followed Max wondered why. So what? What's that accident to me? And then with a stab of horror he remembered Mrs Joliffe. Mrs Joliffe drove a Mini.

'Jesus Christ,' he said. 'Not Mrs Joliffe?'

'Mrs Joliffe being your housekeeper, I take it, sir?' enquired the officer.

'Yes,' Max replied. 'She has a Mini. A green one. The car in the accident—'

'Yes, sir,' the junior officer suddenly volunteered. 'One of the vehicles in the accident was a Mini.'

'Mrs Joliffe's?'

'I'm afraid so, sir.'

'Is she badly hurt?'

'I'm afraid she's dead, sir.'

'Jesus Christ,' Max whispered. 'Mrs Joliffe?'

He sat down on the sofa and stared into the fire while he tried to make sense of what the policeman had said. Mrs Joliffe dead. Mrs Joliffe killed in a car crash. Mrs Joliffe gone. What would Seraphina say? What would Seraphina do without Mrs Joliffe? How could Mrs Joliffe possibly be dead?

Max looked up as if expecting to see the answer on the policeman's face. But the policeman was staring up at the portrait of Seraphina which hung above the fireplace. The other policeman was staring at the floor.

'Have you tried to make contact with her family?' Max asked. 'There's no Mr Joliffe, I'm afraid. Mrs Joliffe is a – was a widow. And I'm not altogether sure who her next of kin was. My wife knows. Of course we can ask—'

'I'm afraid your wife was in the car as well, sir,' the senior policeman said.

384

'She can't have been,' Max replied. 'Her car's in the garage.'

'No, sir,' the policeman corrected him. 'Your wife was a passenger in Mrs Joliffe's car.'

'That's not possible!' Max exclaimed angrily, getting to his feet. 'My wife has her own car! What would she be doing in Mrs Joliffe's!'

'I'm afraid I can't answer that, sir,' the policeman said. 'All we know is—'

'To hell with all you know!' Max shouted. 'My wife couldn't possibly have been in Mrs Joliffe's car! My wife has her own perfectly good car! If my wife wanted to go anywhere, she'd go in her own bloody car!'

Max stood staring at them, feeling his eyes bulging in their sockets, and his heart beating somewhere up in his throat. These men were imbeciles. These men didn't know their job. These men were hick policemen, who didn't know what they were talking about.

And he was right, wasn't he just! Because now the senior one of the two was nodding his head at him, so he must be agreeing with him! Of course Seraphina wouldn't have gone in the Mini! Why should she? Seraphina had her lovely little red Bee which she loved and which she loved driving everywhere! This was all some crazy mix-up, that's what all this was!

'There were two people in the car, sir,' the senior officer was saying. 'There were two people and I'm afraid—'

'But the car was burned!' Max interrupted. 'I saw it myself! There was nothing left of it! You mean you could tell who was in that car – in a car which had burned like that! Are you trying to say the people in that car were recognizable!'

Max had hold of the policeman by his arms. Their faces were inches apart. Then he felt the other policeman take a firm hold of him, and Max let go, allowing himself to be seated in a chair.

'I understand how terrible this must be for you, sir,'

the senior officer continued. 'But we do have positive identification. The occupants were both seen getting into the car in Dereham by several eye-witnesses, as they were indeed seen leaving the town.'

'No!' Max heard himself yelling.

'Both your wife, sir,' the policeman told him, now it seemed from one million miles away, 'both your wife, Mrs Joliffe and from what we're told, your wife's little pet dog.'

'No! No, no, no!' Max shouted.

'They stopped at Lee's garage on the way out of town to get petrol, and Mr Lee himself drove off behind them, and in fact witnessed the accident.'

'No!' Max yelled, banging his clenched fists on his knees, trying to block out this faraway voice. 'It just isn't possible, do you hear me?'

'I appreciate how difficult this must be for you, sir,' the voice continued. 'But Mr Lee saw the whole terrible thing. The lorry was overtaking, it was well over the double white line—'

'No!'

'I'm afraid they never had a chance, sir.'

Max looked up at the policeman and into his face. He saw only kindness and concern.

'No,' he said to him, but now barely audible. 'No. No. No.'

'I'm really very sorry, sir,' the policeman apologized, 'to have to tell you this.'

'You're quite sure it was my wife?' Max asked without hope.

'Both bodies were badly burned, sir,' the officer told him, dropping his voice, 'as well as the little dog. But besides the eye-witness accounts, we do at least have this, sir.'

The policeman was holding something out to him. Something that glinted in the sunshine which was so inappropriately flooding the room. Max saw his own hand reaching out to take it, and then after a moment he saw quite clearly what he was holding.

It was Seraphina's signet ring.

When the doctor had left, Max lay on his bed and, while he waited for the sedative to take effect, wondered what had happened to the world. What sort of world was it, then, where things happened like this? As they had happened that day? To someone as pure and as innocent as Seraphina. Yes, things happened all the time, bad things, evil things, terrible things. Christ, he knew the world was a huge and frightening place. But why did these things happen to the good? To the children, and to the innocent, to the pure and to people like Seraphina? Why not to him? Why could it not have been him, driving too fast up from London in his big expensive car? Why couldn't it have been him, who had done people down and made people sweat on the line, and cross-dealt behind their backs? Why not him? Why her? Why his Seraphina? Why that beautiful angel who didn't know the meaning of the word bad? Who had never hurt a soul. Who had never done a wrong.

And why had she gone out today? Why had she suddenly decided to go into town with Mrs Joliffe after all? He knew now why she hadn't taken her own car, because he had gone for himself to see. And he had tried to start her beloved red Bee, only to find there was no petrol in it. And he had nearly smiled as he found himself half saying 'typical Seraphina'. And then the smile had frozen as he remembered what had happened, and that there would no longer be any Seraphina, and no longer anything typical for her to do.

But if she had wanted something from town, why hadn't she just asked Mrs Joliffe to bring it back? Max knew the only other person with whom she liked driving was him, so what prompted that outing? Perhaps she had gone to buy Max something. The thought froze him up. Yes, perhaps it was his fault. It must be. She had gone to buy him something special, as she so often did when he was expected home. A bottle of his favourite Pomerol. A new tie. A book. A joke present even. Something to surprise him. Yes, that's what she'd done. It was entirely his fault. Of course it was. It was all his own fault. Seraphina had died because of him.

He tried to get up from the bed, but the drugs had made his body heavy and he was half dead himself. His legs wouldn't move and his head swam sickeningly. So he lay back on the huge pillows, the pillows whose very slips Seraphina had so lovingly covered with her own embroidery. He lay back and searched for tears. But there were no tears left. Just an ache. A terrible sick pain which flooded through him as the realization of her death sank deeper into him.

Seraphina was dead.

She was dead, lying somewhere dead, lying in a morgue, lying waiting for his final identification, lying burned, lying dead, lying with no more life or laughter left, no hand to hold, no slender waist to put his arm around. The angel was gone, she was dead, she was no longer there, for him, for anybody. And he was left spinning in space, with time now rushing past him, speeding by on the wind that was rattling his darkened windows, alone and in the night and without her.

She was as dead as those she had remarked upon in the village graveyard, through which they had so often strolled, confident yet that their own calling was still distant. Max would walk ahead eager to return to Sunday lunch, the fire, to life, but Seraphina would stop to gaze at the gravestones in her intense and idiosyncratic way. There was her face now before him, staring at the stone of some young girl who had died too young. Max could see her, quite clearly, standing in the sunlight, her hair falling softly around her beautiful face as she sighed and frowned at the epitaph.

'She was so young,' she said. 'Poor darling. Max, look how young she was.'

And what were you, my Seraphina? Max wondered. What were you but so young like those you mourned in the village graveyard? And now others will mourn you and stand by your grave and say 'so young'. Look, stranger. See how young this woman was!

And then she would smile at Max as she slipped her arm through his and they walked out under the wicket gate and back towards their Sunday lunch. She would smile and say there was a good side too, because the young died before they became old and cross, or bitter, before they had suffered too much. They would have had no time to become bitter, she told Max, no time to have lost their love for life.

So it was for her, now dead. She would have had no time for grieving, no time for suffering, no time for slow decay. She died loved and in love, and in perfect health. She died at midday, before the sun had cooled.

Max slept, quite dreamlessly. But when he woke he found he was still alive, and cursed his fate.

They laid her to rest in the old churchyard, the very place they had so often walked. And all the village came. The business came as well, and in force, overfilling the church so that the service had to be relayed outside. The business hadn't known Seraphina, but it dared not miss her funeral. Max had wanted family and friends only, but no one would hear of it. The business had to pay its last respects to Max Kassov's wife.

Even so, those from the business who came wasted no time, and in the church before the service had started they were surreptitiously looking around to see who had made it and who hadn't. And by the time they were gathering round the grave everyone knew that anyone who was anyone had made the long journey up to Norfolk, even if it had meant they might risk losing a deal; the people who were anyone in the business had all made the effort to attend the funeral of a young woman none of them had known, because she was the wife of Max Kassov.

Max had borne the invasion, the visitors' mumbled platitudes, the embraces of those who counted themselves as his friends, the half-smiles and sympathetic nods of those who wanted in, the two hands of those who hated him clasping his one hand while they searched for any sign of his anguish, and the clicking of the distant telephoto lenses as the hidden Press snapped the departing celebrities.

Max endured it all because he could endure it all – because he had shut himself off from it all. He had walled himself up inside, and taken refuge in his inner self. They smiled, they sympathized, they embraced. But Max felt nothing. His feelings had stopped that day when she died. By the time they had lowered her into the ground his heart was stone.

He stayed up in Norfolk for weeks afterwards, unwilling and unable to go anywhere, except daily to the graveyard.

People called him after a little gap left for mourning, but by then he had employed a girl to answer his calls and his mail.

One day, when he got back from the graveyard, Max found Baz waiting for him in the drawing room. Over drinks they talked, and after observing the conversational niceties, Baz asked Max when was he returning to London.

'Does it matter?' Max asked. 'Suppose I don't go back? Does it really matter?'

'Who am I to say what matters?' Baz countered. 'I just think you'll go crazy if you stay up here.'

'I'll more likely go crazy if I go back to London,' Max replied.

'Tosh,' said Baz, accepting a cigar. 'It's bad what you feel. Of course it's bad. But it's not the holocaust.'

Max paused in the lighting of his own cigar and stared at Baz, and Baz could see in Max's eyes that this was the holocaust, Max's holocaust.

After Baz had left to return to London, Max put the Schubert Impromptus on his gramophone and sat back down by the fire to listen. It was the first music he had played since Seraphina had died.

She had loved those pieces, and so often they had sat in

the very spot Max was sitting now to listen to them. Seraphina had sat at his feet, her head resting on Max's knee, while Max had stroked her hair. But she was no longer there now. She was just an imagining.

And now the happiness was over, finished like the record which had just stopped playing. Max got up and walked to the open French windows and looked out into the gathering dusk. Baz had been right, he had to get back. But not for Baz's given reasons. Not because it would be better for him, or because he would go mad if he stayed in Norfolk.

But because the interval was over, and the house lights were dimming again. He had to go back because he had to get back on, to take his appointed place and continue with the drama.

Because what else was there?

Things had been moving while Max had been away. There had been some very positive reactions to one of Max's projected films from one of the American majors, whose representative, while mindful of Max's personal tragedy, was still most anxious for Max to touch base asap. Mona told Max she'd kept them informed and happy during Max's prolonged absence.

And William and Jay had written three more scripts and, according to the messages from Barry Philips, they were as good if not better than that quite remarkable first episode. Max was well pleased and decided it was time to make a move concerning Craig Matheson.

'I don't think so, Max,' Barry said in answer to Max's call. 'We're still very keen on new. And while we haven't exactly come up with anybody yet, we're still looking. In fact I'm seeing someone today who I'm told is a number one candidate for this year's Man Most Likely. You've probably heard of him. David Terry?'

Max hadn't but lied.

'The papers have been full of him recently,' Barry continued. 'But then I don't suppose you've been following them that closely.'

391

Max admitted that he hadn't. Not that closely. Barry was privately relieved since what the papers had mostly been full of were pictures of Meredith Browne being squired around town by a new heart-throb. So he just made some more of the right noises and promised to let Max know how they were going before ringing off.

Max then fixed to have lunch with the American major's rep, who happened to be free that very day.

They met at The White Elephant, where Max found that although he still had no appetite for food, his appetite for business was undiminished. By the time he walked back out into Curzon Street Max had a firm invitation to fly out to the Coast and take his project to the next level, a direct meeting with the studio heads of Allied Independents.

Seraphina had always packed for him, which was why on his final departure from Norfolk Max had left so many vital things behind him. He could have asked Anna, the girl he had appointed as his PA at The Hall, to forward down to London what he needed, but excused himself from asking her on the pretext that some of the papers he needed were personal, and that he was never quite sure which clothes he would want to take with him to California until he had seen for himself.

The real reason for his return to Norfolk was that finally he could not bear to stay away.

As he left London, he knew it was a fool's errand, because Seraphina was dead. Yet a part of him still believed a mistake had been made, and that as he turned off the final lane and into the long drive, at the end of it by the open front door his beloved girl would be there, in her white aertex shirt, her bare feet and her flowing patterned skirt. And Daisy would rush out from the house behind the car, half barking, half yelping with excitement, and Max would take Seraphina in his arms and they would awake from the nightmare.

He reached the village, now only his village, no longer

theirs, and slowed his car down as he passed the church. It was raining heavily, and Max had to wind down the window to get a sight of the graveyard. Through the rain he could see the gravedigger at work, digging the ground up near where Seraphina lay. A deep chill ran through Max, and he felt his legs weaken at the thought of who lay so near him in the cold, dank ground. Then he pressed the button for his window to close and drove off quickly to The Hall, unable and unwilling to get out and visit her grave.

The house, usually so warm and welcoming, looked cold and forbidding. As Max approached there was only one light on at a first-floor window, which glimmered faintly through the increasingly heavy rain. He rang the bell as a warning, before opening the door with his key and walking into the entrance hall, where he called up to Anna that it was he who had entered.

Then he put on the hall lights, and stood for a moment looking at the portrait of his mother. The small picture light illuminated the painting as it always did, yet there was something different. It no longer looked the same. Max moved closer and stared up at the portrait even harder, but couldn't make out what the difference was. Yet there was a difference, something most definitely had changed. And then he suddenly realized what it was that had changed. It wasn't the portrait, it was him.

The beautiful woman looking down at him was the same as the day she had been painted. But the person looking up at her was no longer who he used to be. Until now it had been a boy staring up at his mother. Now it was a man, and the man was looking at a painting, which was nothing but an impression made by an artist.

Was that what love and death did to you? Max wondered, as he heard footfalls on the stair behind him. Is that what all this had meant? Or had been meant to mean? Because he had found love with Seraphina, and she had tragically died, had this altered his previous complexion? Had the love he felt for his dead wife finally cancelled out the love he thought he had felt for his mother, and the ensuing guilt he must always have been feeling since she herself had died so young? Max knew the answer lay somewhere here, as surely as he knew that the feelings he had staring up at his mother were no longer those that he used to feel for her.

A voice from behind him interrupted his contemplation. Anna was welcoming him home and sighing dutifully about the terrible weather. Max agreed, walking ahead of her into the drawing room, which to his dismay he found dark and shuttered, with its furniture shrouded in dustsheets. At once he threw open the shutters and turned on the table lamps, before admonishing the girl for not having lit a fire. At his scolding, Anna became frightened and nervous, telling him she had thought his visit was only to collect his clothes and papers.

'My wife may be dead, Anna,' Max told her. 'But the house isn't. Seraphina would hate it if we buried the house with her. So light the fires, and put on some lamps, and fill the flower bowls. Or else we might as well all go and form a queue in the graveyard.'

For the first hour or so of his return, Max sat on the sofa in silence. They had removed the dustsheets and lit a huge fire, which roared and crackled as Max sat staring into its flames. In the fire he saw her again, on her bicycle in Scotland, cycling towards him, her fair hair flowing out behind, her face glowing with health and happiness, and she sparkled with delight at his victory in their race.

He saw her lying in his arms, her eyes closed, lying tight against him, as if he was her father and her mother, and she was his child.

He saw her face attentive, looking up at him while he foretold the happiness that lay in store for them, and recalled how they had simply just looked at each other and then had loved.

He saw her running up the lawn in her bare feet, breathless with excitement and bursting to tell him that their swallows were back in the spring.

And then he found her diary.

He had finally gone upstairs, reluctant to leave the warmth of the fire and the memories which played around its, flames, but he knew he had to start collecting up those things he had come for. So he took himself up first to his dressing room, where he selected the clothes he would need, and then to his study where he collected his papers.

When he finished he went into the bedroom and stood by the bed. He touched her pillows and straightened the pile of books on her bedside table. It was an odd selection, which included books on the Romantic poets, *Katherine* by Anya Seton, a much-thumbed copy of *The Secret Garden*, a life of Van Gogh, and at the bottom of the pile, an anonymous-looking hardback copy of *Lolita*.

Sitting on the bed, Max picked up the Nabokov novel and opened the flyleaf. There was an inscription. It simply said, 'S. To the memory of a late spring. My love forever. A.' There was no date.

So what? So Seraphina had had other boyfriends. A girl as beautiful as Seraphina, there would have to be something wrong with her not to have had other boyfriends, Max reasoned. So why then was he feeling so jealous? And what did 'A' mean by 'a late spring'? Seraphina was a virgin when he had first made love to her, so what was this about a late spring? And why *Lolita*? It seemed such an unlikely book for Seraphina to read. *The Secret Garden*, the Romantic poets, sure. But *Lolita* – Max shook his head and wondered.

He also wondered what the book was which was still lying in the bed. Since Seraphina had been killed, Max had always slept in his dressing room, unable to face the four-poster, which had probably not been remade since the day of the tragedy. And someone had left a book under the bedclothes, near the bottom of the bed. Either Mrs Joliffe by accident, or Seraphina herself.

It was a diary. A fairly thick blue leather diary, a five-year diary, and it was locked.

Max looked at it curiously. He had never for a moment thought of Seraphina keeping a diary, and she had never mentioned the fact that she kept one to him. But then lots of people kept diaries, Max reasoned. And half the fun of a diary he imagined must lie in its secret keeping.

But a locked diary somehow seemed to be a thing of suspicion. A locked diary suggested the keeping of secrets you most certainly didn't want discovered. A locked diary was something Max just couldn't imagine his Seraphina keeping. Seraphina and he had kept no secrets from each other.

He made a cursory attempt to find the key for it, but it was nowhere in the dressing-table drawers, or in Seraphina's precious jewel box. So Max instead took a hairbrush and inserting the long handle under the diary's feeble lock prised it open easily. Then with slightly trembling hands he sank into an armchair and, opening the leather-bound volume, flicked through the pages.

Most of them were filled with Seraphina's large sloping writing, which she had seemingly reduced in size for the diary, or perhaps in the belief that if she wrote smaller it would be more secretive. Max wondered what on earth she could have found to write about at such length, leading the quiet country life that she had.

Dear D, (one of the first entries read)

Spent the morning in bed wondering what M was doing in London. The weekend was as fabulous as ever, and I often wonder how I am possibly going to last until Friday evening. I have only been here for two months, but already the time between Mondays and Fridays hangs so still. It seems so interminable. I really wonder how I am going to bear it without M. Daisy has just chewed one of my slippers. She must have been working away at it all the time I've been writing, or probably when I slept this afternoon, and I never heard! I haven't the heart to smack her, she's so sweet, so I let her keep the slipper. I'll buy another pair in town. M will never notice! Mrs Joliffe brought back one of my new evening dresses which Mrs B was altering. It's still far too long, and it'll have to go back yet again. M telephoned and was terribly grumpy about one of his 'bloody actors', but I soon cheered him up. Roll on Friday.

Max sighed, but also smiled. It was sheer Seraphina. Only Seraphina could have bought a lock-up diary and filled it with such innocent trivia. Even so, Max still felt it was an intrusion of her privacy, and was about to set the journal aside when he noticed on several pages Seraphina had marked certain paragraphs with several small stars. So, his curiosity having overcome him, he returned to the diary and flicked through the rest of it. Sure enough, the further he got into the entries, the more paragraphs there were with stars, sometimes as few as one or two, sometimes a row of six.

Turning to a page well into the diary, a page decorated with a row of five stars, he smoothed the book open and started to read, determined now to find what the stars actually symbolised, although not unnaturally he had already formulated a theory that the stars were a mark of appreciation for his love-making.

He was so nearly right. The stars were an award for merit for love-making, but not just for his.

The stars marked Seraphina's appreciation of the skill of other men as well.

Mrs J's day off, and she went to London. Which meant I could spend all day with T, (***) and then the entire night with G (****). It's probably not fair on T to prefer G marginally, but last night! I have never been so captivated (literally!), or felt such total subjugation! T is brilliant, and sensitive, and warm, and funny. And very sexy too, I might add. But G! If it wasn't for his habit of collapsing afterwards as if he was dead (which, mind you, considering what he can do, he has every right to be!) G might well get *******. By

397

the time I've finished with him, maybe he'll make the magic number.

Max put the book down, and wiped the sweat from his hands slowly down the front of his trousers. He could feel the silence that was now in his head, and in his very being, a terrible stillness born out of these words of betrayal.

He read more. He had to, just in case that entry had been a red herring, or a trip wire to catch the uninvited reader. Perhaps the rest of the diary was full of the innocence he had found on the first pages, marked up with the trivial history of Seraphina's early days at The Hall. But as he turned the pages, he knew this could not be so, because every now and then there would be more starred paragraphs, and more initials, and more rows of dots followed by exclamation marks.

For 3 July of that year, only a matter of weeks before her fatal accident, Seraphina had recorded the following entry:

Dear D, my sexy friend, keeper of my secrets, knower of me. I drove all the way to Cambridge to see PB without anything on underneath! No *sous dessous*! Nothing! Just my breasts firm and pushing against the silk of my dress, and my bum naked against the leather car seat. (Or that 'wonderful arse' as PB calls it!) It was a strange and incredible feeling walking round the city without a stitch on under my dress. Knowing that a sudden gust of wind could have lifted my skirt and exposed me for everyone to see. It made me feel very secret, and the more secret I became, the more demure. Almost ashamed by the end, so that by the time I had got to the hotel I was ready to do whatever I might be asked. Which I think was just what PB wanted, judging from the events of the afternoon. . . . What an imagination! The things we do! The things he makes me do. . . . But then I found that today I also had one or two surprises! (*******)

Every week had a similar entry, sometimes two, on occasions even three, which reported in some detail

Seraphina's clandestine rendezvous, and her ensuing and inevitable couplings. Max read on and on, glutting himself on his wife's self-confessed philanderings, until he was gorged and could take no more. Then he closed the diary and placed the book down very carefully on the bed beside him, before sitting in silence for well over an hour while he tried to sort out both his head and his heart.

But whichever way he looked at it, he could only come to one conclusion. Seraphina had been just like his mother, and that was that. His angel was a fallen angel. His angel was a whore.

Later he left the bedroom and went downstairs to the drawing-room, where he piled the fire up with logs until it started to flame. While he waited for it to catch fully, he sat and drank whisky, with Seraphina's diary lying closed on the sofa beside him. On a table opposite him was his favourite picture of Seraphina, one Max had taken himself of her sitting in an apple tree, in spring, their first spring in Norfolk, the picture of perfect innocence.

He sat quite still, one hand on the diary, looking into the eyes in the photograph, the eyes of his dead love. Then, once the fire was roaring, he threw the diary into the flames, and in a fit of silent anguish hurled the photograph, still behind its glass, and still within its frame, into the fire after the book.

He didn't watch them burn. Instead he poured himself another large malt whisky and went in search of Anna.

Anna was in the kitchen, sitting reading at the scrubbed pine table. Max told her he was hungry, and she said there was plenty of food in and that she'd make him something. Max sat at the table with his whisky and told her to fix them both something.

He sat and watched her while she prepared their dinner, and talked to him about herself. She was a shy girl, the only daughter of a land-wealthy family, who had fled London and a traumatically broken engagement for the country in order to try and reassemble herself and her life.

Which was why she didn't mind the solitude of looking after The Hall and dealing with Max's affairs in the country. Basically, it was just what she needed.

She was a handsome girl, good-looking rather than pretty, tall and athletic, the sort of girl you would expect to be a very expert swimmer. She had dark green eyes, a peach-like complexion, and raven-black hair, most of which at present was tied up behind her head. Max had never really noticed her in detail before. He had needed a Girl Friday after the tragedy and a local friend had suggested Anna, a recommendation which had been fully borne out by Anna's ability to deal quietly and tactfully with the aftermath of such a dreadful accident.

She was also a more than competent cook, Max noted, as he ate the dinner she laid before him. They had the remains of some watercress soup Anna had made for her own lunch, and some cold home-made game pie and salad. Max opened a bottle of Château Haut Brion which they drank with it.

'Did you ever meet my wife?' Max enquired halfway through the meal.

'Several times,' Anna replied. 'At parties.'

'But we never went to parties,' Max told her, 'at least not up here. Not anywhere really.'

'These were lunch parties,' Anna explained. 'Girls' lunches. Your wife even gave one here.'

Max made no reference to the fact that this was news to him, but privately wondered how much more there was he didn't know about Seraphina?

'She had an awful lot of girlfriends,' Anna continued. 'She was terribly popular. Everyone thought—'

The girl stopped for a moment, eyeing Max, and wondering whether or not she might have already gone too far.

'Go on,' Max told her, pouring them both some more wine.

'It's just that everyone thought she was about the sweetest and nicest person they'd ever met,' she finished.

'I know,' said Max. 'That's what I thought as well.'

He got up and, taking another open bottle of claret with him, wandered off to the drawing room, having invited Anna to come along and join him. He was drunk, really quite drunk, but Max knew it didn't show. Max knew it never showed when he was drunk.

He sat on the floor by the fire, and patted the ground for Anna to sit beside him. She smiled and sat on the floor as well, but opposite him, her back against the sofa.

'What are you going to do?' Max asked her, giving her some wine.

'When? I don't understand, Mr Kassov.'

'Max, for Christ's sake.'

'What do you mean – what am I going to do?'

'With your life. What do you think I mean? With your hair?' Max grinned at her.

'I don't know. I suppose I'll go back to London eventually.'

'And?'

'I don't know. Get a job I suppose.'

'Don't you have any ambitions?'

'Such as?'

'Such as seeing your name in lights! Becoming famous! Having half London in love with you!'

The girl laughed shyly, astonished.

'Good Lord!' she said. 'I'm the very last person in the world who could become an actress!'

'Garbage,' Max replied. 'You're a fantastically pretty girl.'

Anna looked at him, her green eyes opening wide in amazement before her brow started to furrow in anxiety.

'I don't understand,' she said, turning away to look into the dying fire.

'You don't understand,' Max repeated. 'You don't understand when I ask you what you want. And now you don't understand when I tell you how beautiful you are.'

He clicked his tongue with a sigh, and threw the last log on to the fire. Then he sat back and drained his glass of wine.

'Take your hair down,' he said suddenly.

The girl looked round from the fire now, and stared at him instead. Max knew she wouldn't dare say that she didn't understand, because he had forestalled that by mocking her. But all the same her face said it. Her face said why? Her face quite clearly asked him why, but the look in her eyes was not one of fear, but rather one of interest.

'Please,' Max asked her again, but softly, 'take your hair down.'

The fire crackled as the wood caught, throwing a sudden red glow on the girl's face as she reached up and undid the knot of dark hair. Then, with one shake of her head, the long tresses fell silently down, almost to her waist. Max stared at her, and said nothing. Anna stared back, and with both her hands smoothed her fallen hair back behind her ears.

'Now tell me what you want,' Max whispered.

'I think it might be easier,' Anna replied, 'if you told me what you wanted.'

'Very well,' Max nodded. 'I want you to undo the top buttons of your sweater.'

She was wearing a pink cashmere cardigan that Max suddenly realized could have belonged to Seraphina, and which she had buttoned right up to her neck. At her throat she wore a single strand of good pearls, which at the moment she was fingering, not nervously, but in anticipation. It seemed she was waiting for Max to repeat his command, but he said nothing more, he just looked straight into the girl's eyes.

Anna let go of her pearls, and slowly undid the top two buttons at her neck. Max watched, enthralled. He had seen girls strip, he'd seen the best girl strippers, but he had never experienced the sense of uncontrolled excitement he was feeling now.

'More than two,' he ordered after a minute. 'Open them down to your breasts, and then fold the sweater back.'

For a moment he caught his breath as he thought she

wasn't going to obey. Because there was a look in her eyes, a sudden flash, which initially Max thought spelt danger. Then, as he saw her continue to undress herself, he realized the flash was from the shock of her own desire.

Now five buttons were open, revealing her perfect neck, and more of that peach-like skin. Max wanted to kiss it, and lick it, and bite it, but not yet, he told himself. They had plenty of time. He wasn't going anywhere. They had all night.

'Undo them all,' he told her.

'No,' she said, shaking her head slowly so that long dark hair fell across her neck and face. 'No.'

'Yes,' said Max. 'Do what I say.'

And she did. Just as Max had known she would. Because he was listening to what his fallen angel had told him. She had said that women would do anything for him, and she should know. She if anyone should know.

The girl was seated before him on the floor, lit by the flickering firelight, her sweater open to the last button, exposing her wonderful firm breasts, which seemed to be trying to burst free from the tight white lace of her bra.

'Take off the sweater now,' Max ordered, 'and then your bra.'

Anna looked at him with a sudden frown as if he had hit her, or sworn at her. But she made no reply. She just opened her mouth slightly and licked her lips with a little bit of pink tongue, before slipping out of her pink cashmere. But she didn't take off her bra. Instead, she folded her arms across her breasts and stared at Max.

Max stared back. The look seemed to be endless. Then Max simply nodded to her, and the girl lowered her head, putting her hands up behind her back and releasing the catch on her bra. She sat up slowly and took first one strap off one shoulder, then the other strap off the other, before dropping the white lace undergarment on the floor in front of her. Her breasts were round and firm, larger than Seraphina's had been, with bigger nipples. Max wanted to lean across and touch them, to hold them, to pinch each

403

nipple gently first, then harder, until the girl would bite her lip and frown, but not want him to stop.

Instead he sat back, and merely rubbed his cheek with the tips of his fingers, before nodding again.

'And now your skirt,' he said, 'and your stockings. And your panties.'

God knows what she was feeling, Max thought as he tried to hold his wine glass steady, but he could feel himself gasping inside as the girl stood up and unbuttoned her skirt, which she allowed to fall slowly to her feet. Underneath she wore black stockings, white lacy panties, and a black suspender belt, which she removed having undone her stockings. Then she sat for a moment on the sofa and rolled her stockings off, before finally sliding them down her long shapely legs.

The fire was almost out, but it was casting enough light for Max to see the outline of the girl now standing over him.

'What now?' she asked him, in a voice barely even whispering.

'Now,' Max said as he got to his feet, 'now you will walk upstairs in front of me with your hands behind you.'

'Why?' she enquired.

'Because this is what you want,' Max told her.

They walked out into the hall, the girl completely naked and Max still fully dressed. This is for you, Seraphina, he thought to himself as they crossed the hall, this one is for you. Me dressed, and the girl naked. And it's also for you, Mother, Max vowed, as he turned to the portrait of his mother, lit only by its little picture light. This is in honour of your activities as well. This is for both of you.

Anna, her hands held behind her, was waiting for him at the top of the stairs, uncertain as to where she should go. Max walked past her without a word and opened the door of the main bedroom. He saw the girl frown as he knew she would, but he simply nodded to her to go in.

She stood there, hesitantly, looking at the four-poster bed, and then she turned to Max.

'Why here?' she asked.

'Why not?' said Max, closing the door.

He told her to get on the bed and lie there and not move, which she did, while Max went into his dressing-room. He took his time undressing, pouring himself a brandy while he was doing so and drinking it slowly. He knew the girl wouldn't move. He knew she would just lie there and wait for him, her heart beating faster and harder in her chest as she lay imagining what they might do together. He knew from the moment he had decided to seduce her that this was how and where they would end up, because his fallen angel had marked his card. Women would do anything for him.

And Seraphina had been right. Out there, lying on their marriage bed, was a girl to whom he had barely spoken, a girl about whom he knew practically nothing. Yet he had asked her to humiliate herself, to take all her clothes off in front of him, to walk naked like a bought slave up to his bedroom, and to lie there on the bed waiting for him, which she had done. She had done all of these things, without any objection.

Selecting his old Chinese silk dressing gown, he pulled it on and walked slowly into the bedroom.

Anna was there on the bed, lying face downwards, her hair spread around her, her hands still behind her. Max sat beside her and, easing her hands apart, ran the nail of one index finger slowly down the length of her back. She said nothing, but Max could fee her skin contract at the touch and the deep breath that she took fill her lungs. Then he rolled her slowly over towards him, to Seraphina's side of the bed, until she lay on her back where Seraphina had so often lain, her arms at her side. Max gripped each of her wrists and, pressing his weight down on them, leaned over her and kissed her, hard and long. He held her down by her wrists while she writhed and moaned softly, then still holding her down he kissed her firm breasts and the soft curve of her belly.

Even when he let her go, she didn't move, but lay as if

trapped, as if held by some invisible force. He took off his
robe, but she just lay and watched, and only her eyes
seemed to move and follow him round as he walked to the
other side of the bed, his side, the side where he had lain
so often next to Seraphina, either before he had made love
to her, or just after. Then he got on to the bed and moved
over to Anna, who still didn't move. Max ran his hand
between her legs, into her, then out of her again and up
the line of her firm and flat stomach and across each of her
nipples and breasts, and up the arch of her neck and in
between her open lips. She bit on his fingers hard and then
ran her tongue over them and between them, before Max
started searching her again, until she abandoned her
defences and arching her back gave a great cry, and then a
deep gasp as Max entered her, so deeply and so strongly
that he seemed to be everywhere inside of her. And then
turning her round to him he half rose above her, and
started to make long and passionate love to her, on the
very spot he had made long and passionate love so often to
Seraphina, in the very place where he knew that he was
incredible, because that was what he had been told.

While away down in London, a girl he had once and
suddenly abandoned was about to take the next step in her
long and patient campaign to topple Max Kassov from his
throne.

11

She had got him a part. Or rather David Terry had got himself a part, which was one of the things Meredith had been training him up to do. From her own experience she knew there was only so much an agent, however good, could do for a client, and that once an interview or an audition had been arranged, from there on in the client was on his own. Of course there were other pressures which could be brought to bear to improve the client's chances, and sometimes even finally to land the client the role. But Meredith preferred not to sully herself. One of the things she had decided when she took on representation was that that sort of negotiating was going to be left to her clients.

David Terry she knew would find things easy on the way up. As long as he was up for parts which were in the province of casting directors, with his sensational looks and his carefully groomed laid-back manner, they were all going to want to take him to bed – the women and the men. Most of the powerful casting agents were women, she told her pupil, usually middle-aged women, and more often than not faintly unappealing middle-aged women. He wouldn't be required to go to bed with them, but it was absolutely vital if his career was going to take off that he should always give the impression to these ageing or plain women that the actor could barely think of anything else besides getting them between the sheets.

As far as the male casting directors went, since the majority of them were homosexual, the ploy here was not to come on too butch. The casting directors might suspect that he was straight, but that wasn't going to stop them fancying him. In fact the more dedicated among them would hope to convert him, and, in order for them to believe this wholesale, the actor must give the impression that this was indeed possible. The same would apply, Meredith instructed her pupil, when he got to the stage of bypassing the casting directors and being summoned directly before the directors. Here the tactics became even more complicated, because firstly there were very few women directors, and secondly there were far more heterosexuals among their male numbers than among the ranks of the casting directors. And heterosexuals resented wildly attractive men, particularly since most heterosexual directors were themselves the very opposite of wildly attractive. So the secret with them was to pretend to be homosexual, so as not to threaten the director's precariously balanced psyche.

David Terry listened to all this intensely; read, marked, learned and very visibly digested.

'It's a bit like being on the game, old love,' he drawled, draping his long legs over the edge of Meredith's sofa.

'Too right!' Meredith laughed. 'You're a tart, and I'm your pimp!'

But then, once more in earnest, she put the actor through yet another rehearsal for his interview the following day. He was up for a small but very showy part in a hugely popular television series called *The Marriage Game*. The role for which he was being seen was that of an enormously attractive, very laid-back bachelor who had just moved in next door to the Newly-Weds, and who gave the young husband his first attack of green-eye and the young wife her first regret at being married. The show was the highest rated comedy show in the country and, should David Terry land the role, even though it was only a three-scener, it could well be the springboard he needed.

When the script had arrived, the actor had read it through carefully two or three times and then pronounced that the part could have been written for him.

'It was,' Meredith told him.

The series was by the author of *Where Were You Just When It Mattered?*, Meredith's second starring vehicle, and the play so extensively rewritten by William and Jay. When Meredith heard he was writing a new series of *The Marriage Game*, she called him and suggested they have lunch. They met in a small Italian restaurant round the corner from the author's home, since Meredith didn't want to be seen lobbying him in any of the business's usual haunts. She plied him with plenty of liquor and, once he was well and truly alight, leaned over the table and asked him for a favour. He told her, or more accurately informed her décolletage, that there was nothing he wouldn't do for her, and Meredith put her hand on his and told him he was a love.

'It need only be a small part,' she told him. 'But a showy one. One that'll make people sit up and say – Christ! Who the hell is that?'

'There's a part in ep. nine,' the writer remembered, accepting his second large brandy. 'But the bloke's small and French.'

'Make him tall and English, darling,' Meredith smiled. 'And very sexy. And tell them it's for David Terry.'

'I don't see why not,' the writer agreed. 'Anyway, as you know, I'd do anything for you, Merry love.'

'Would you, darling?' Meredith asked him, putting a cool hand on his inflamed cheek. 'I don't see why.'

'Yes, you do, old thing,' replied the writer, his smile giving way to a look of resignation. 'You know something they don't know. You know who wrote my hit play.'

Terry landed the part without difficulty, and before rehearsals started Meredith hired Marshall Baird, an up-and-coming comedy director, to coach her client privately.

'I take it you don't want this round the business,' Baird asked her after the final session.

409

'You bet your life I don't,' Meredith agreed. 'But what I'm paying you now is just about all I've got.'

'I don't want money,' Baird replied.

'And I don't come over,' Meredith told him.

'Great,' Baird smiled. 'So what's stopping me?'

'The fact that when Terry makes it,' Meredith told him, 'which he will—'

'Oh, he'll make it all right,' Baird agreed.

'Well, when he does,' Meredith concluded, 'what's stopping you from telling is that you'll be there. I promise.'

Baird gave a nod of appreciation, and then kissed her.

'In that case, darling,' he said, 'we'll just make this *au revoir*.'

Everyone who was anyone in the business got a please-watch memo from Meredith the week before Terry's episode of *The Marriage Game* was transmitted. Everyone, that is, except Max Kassov. Something purely instinctive warned Meredith against volunteering the information to Max that she was handling the young actor. If he found out, she decided it could be through the normal channels. The last thing Meredith wanted was Max being given a free go at blocking any of her moves.

Meredith knew that 'please-watches' were usually hardly worth the memos they were printed on. But sometimes, by one of the chances upon which the business runs, somebody up there did watch, and the person you wanted watched was watched. Which was the case with David Terry. The show went out on a Monday night, and most people in the business stayed home on Monday nights. The show went out against a current affairs programme, so that if you were in two minds as to what to watch at that particular hour, there was no contest. At least that's the conclusion thirteen and a half million viewers reached every week at eight o'clock in the evening.

There were plenty of availability checks on David Terry the following morning. Meredith told all enquirers the actor was fully booked.

The actor himself rang in just after midday.

'My mum loved it,' he told Meredith.

'Is your mum making any films, David?' Meredith replied.

'Yeah, OK,' the actor drawled, 'so what did Hollywood think?'

'We've had one or two enquiries,' Meredith told him. 'But none were transatlantic.'

'Who cares?' he said, perking up at once. 'So who wants me?'

'Nobody important,' Meredith answered.

'I don't care,' he replied. 'I want to keep working.'

'You are working, darling,' Meredith said just prior to hanging up the phone. 'At least according to me you are.'

It was Polly who incidentally made the breakthrough move.

'Guess who come round to see me last night then?' she asked Meredith one morning when she called into the office. 'Those writer friends of yours. William and Jean.'

'William and Jay,' Meredith corrected her.

'They really liked me,' Polly told her. 'Said there might be a part for me in their new series.'

'Remind me,' Meredith said calmly, since this was the first she'd heard. 'I can't remember what they're calling it.'

'*Life With Charlie*, in't it?' Polly replied. 'Least that's what I think they said. They said I wouldn't exactly be right for the lead—'

'No,' Meredith agreed. 'I can't quite see you as the girl.'

'Hardly,' Polly grinned. 'I mean she's meant to be small and dark and posh, and I'm tall and blonde and common.'

'The man's not going to be easy,' Meredith ventured. 'Charlie himself, that is.'

'No,' Polly agreed. 'William and Jean—'

'Jay, darling.'

'They was having a right old bitch. Apparently everyone's pushing Craig bloody Matheson at them.'

411

'From what I hear about the part. . . .' Meredith started, before pretending to become distracted by her copy of *Variety*.

'Yeah, Craig Matheson would be totally wrong,' Polly volunteered. 'William said Charlie's got to be dead sexy, but rather sort of dopey. You know, kind of half there. Dead handsome but head in the bleeding clouds. Craig Matheson comes across too knowing. Least that's what William and Jean said.'

'And now I've even forgotten who's directing it,' Meredith said, looking up.

'That idiot David Pepys,' Polly replied.

William and Jay were working when Meredith arrived at their studio. It was somehow exactly how Meredith had always imagined it, and she was so pleased not to be disappointed by what she actually found. They were sitting either end of a long white table supported by two chrome trestles. They sat in front of two large jumbo notebooks, with a mug of pencils each, and that was all. The image was one of precision, and neatness, with strong surgical overtones.

They were even dressed similarly, in blue velour sweaters, jeans, and sneakers. Jay's velour top was designed like a track-suit top, with a seam of red edging the zipper, while William's was a plain dark crew neck.

Meredith drew up a chair and sat in the middle of the table between the two of them, accepting the coffee that was offered to her.

'Are you always as neat and tidy as this, you two?' she enquired.

'Only when we're expecting visitors,' Jay grinned. 'The way we work normally is with me up there in the gallery still in bed, and William sitting over there tearing the newspaper into strips.'

'You laid all this on for me?' Meredith asked.

'We have a photographer coming,' William confessed.

'So we thought we'd rehearse. This is how people like to imagine writers do it.'

'I can't imagine how writers do it period,' Meredith sighed. 'I think you're quite wonderful.'

They talked around the show, and then about the show, and during the course of their intercourse Meredith unearthed the writers' very real anxiety that Craig Matheson was going to be forced upon them.

'We know the guy at the top, the controller of programmes Barry Philips, is anti-Matheson,' William told her, 'which is a big plus.'

'But the producer—' Jay was about to add, when Meredith interrupted her.

'Remind me,' she said.

'Peregrine ffrench,' Jay replied with a little sigh. 'He did *Hello In There*.'

'And according to Peregrine ffff-ffrench,' William grinned, 'there simply is nobody else worth even considering.'

'You two must have some say in the matter,' Meredith said, knowing perfectly well that they didn't. 'After all you wrote it.'

'After all we only wrote it,' Jay corrected her. 'And if Craig Matheson does it, we won't even have written it!'

'Anyway,' William added in despair, 'Jesus, you know nobody listens to the goddam writers, Meredith!'

Meredith asked them who in an ideal world they'd like to see in the leading roles, and Jay produced a list of actors, all of whom had a number of stars by their names, denoting preference. The list was totally predictable. Meredith could have drawn it up in her sleep.

'You want someone new,' she said. 'Barry Philips is right. You want somebody like Scott MacDonald.'

William and Jay frowned at her, then looked at each other. They hadn't heard of him.

'Or Bill Bird.'

Another blank look. They hadn't heard of him either. They wouldn't have done. Meredith had just pinched both names off book spines behind William's head.

'Or better still,' she suggested, 'David Terry.'

'Yes, now him we have heard of,' Jay replied, quite plainly lying.

'Have we?' William enquired, reaching for their copy of *Spotlight*.

'Forget *Spotlight*,' Meredith said, opening her briefcase. 'Here.'

She pushed her latest photograph of Terry across the table to Jay.

'Oh yes,' said Jay. 'Wow.'

'Not bad,' William said, turning the photograph round. 'Not bad at all. But looking like that, there's no chance of him being able to act.'

'You can soon find out,' Meredith told him. 'He's sitting in my car outside.'

At Meredith's behest, William and Jay read the entire first episode out loud to Meredith and her protégé, who was now also seated at the table, having quite obviously won over Jay the moment he walked through the door. Meredith knew William would be harder, but by the time the actor had laughed quite genuinely and helplessly a dozen times in the first five pages, William was weakening, and fast.

'Listen,' Terry drawled at the end of the reading, 'you two should play it. You're hilarious.'

'Don't you just love that delivery, William?' Jay asked her partner.

'It's like Noël Coward played by a trucker,' William replied.

Meredith laughed delightedly, but said nothing. She just hoped Terry had remembered her instructions. To take his tone from William. Not to mimic the writer, but to take the tone from him, and simply amplify it. Let the writers hear their own sound being played back to them.

'You're the Stradivarius,' she had told him. 'They will play you the tune on their fiddles, but when you play it back to them, you'll take the very same tune and turn it into a blasted concerto!'

Meredith read the script with him, playing the part of

the wife. William and Jay read the subsidiary roles, but kept missing their cues since they both seemed unable to take their eyes off the unknown actor.

Who was word-perfect. One of the things they had taught Ted Ernstone well at his primary school was how to read, to himself and out loud. And while it was the fashion among so many actors, once they were known, to mumble and mutter their way through a reading, Meredith insisted on capitalizing on the young man's natural ability with words, because she knew from her own experience that would always get him in good and strong with writers. And some writers, whatever their show of public despair, were sometimes extremely influential in private.

'That was good,' William said, in his typically under-stated way when they had finished the read. 'Thank you.'

'Good?' Jay chorused. 'That was bloody marvellous, William! That was Charlie!'

William nodded curtly and enquired what else the actor had done. Meredith looked wide-eyed at him and asked William if that meant he had missed him on *The Marriage Game*.

While William went into flashback, Jay, the possessor of perfect recall, chimed in.

'Of course we saw him!' she cried. 'He played the sexy new neighbour! This is the actor we meant to write down!'

William looked at him again and afresh.

'Yes,' he said. 'That's right. You were excellent.'

They went out to lunch on Meredith, who by now was beginning to get quite heavily into debt because of her belief in her discovery, but who after that reading no longer had any doubts about recovering her investment.

'All we have to do now,' William said, carefully slicing his stuffed chicken breast, 'is get him ppppppast Ppppp-peregrine.'

'And David,' Jay added.

'David's a time-server,' Meredith stated. 'He'll jump where Peregrine jumps. It's only Peregrine we have to get him past.'

'Any ideas?' William enquired.

'Yes,' Meredith replied. 'We buy him.'

'We do?' William continued. 'With what exactly?'

'With him,' she said, and pointed at her protégé.

People see what they want to see, and believe what they want to believe. If the theatre had taught Meredith one maxim, it had been that. But she had also learned you could play certain tricks which could subtly alter the nuance so that although people still saw what they wanted and believed what they wished, what they were actually choosing to see and believe was not always entirely due to their own persuasion. As an actress she had learned the power of the sub-text, and now as a businesswoman she was well versed in the art of the subliminal. So much so that by the time she had finished preparing David Terry for his interview, Peregrine ffrench would see in him what Meredith wanted him to see, and believe of him what Meredith wished him to believe.

Her hidden persuaders were small but potent. A small leather purse which attached to Terry's belt, an African bone necklace at his throat, just enough daytime make-up to be noticeable, and a uniform of very tight faded jeans and bright white T-shirt, designed to show off every mouth-watering muscle and curve of the young actor's body. And the most hidden and undoubtedly what would prove to be the most persuasive of her persuaders: a middle-aged actor called Noel Blond.

Blond was one of Meredith's has-beens, although he could no longer be called that with any degree of accuracy, so successfully had Meredith rebuilt his career. He was a charming and erudite homosexual, who had taken a vow of celibacy ever since his long-time lover had died suddenly of a heart attack. Subsequently he had developed a heavy drink problem, and while Meredith had been at Kass and Vogel she had taken especial care of him and helped him through his critical drying-out

416

period, critical because his doctors had told him if he didn't come off the drink, he'd be dead in six months.

So he owed Meredith, not that she ever made him aware there was a debt, simply because that was not how Meredith worked. But now that she needed him, she was aware that because of their joint history he would be only too willing to help her in her subterfuge.

Which was why he at once agreed to the suggestion that he should become David Terry's lover.

'I even think he should move in with you,' Meredith proposed.

'Are you sure?' Blond asked her back with a twinkle in his eye. 'You know how wicked people like me are.'

'The worst thing that can happen to David coming to stay with you,' Meredith smiled back, 'is that he'll get given too many hot-water bottles.'

'I still might not let you have him back,' Blond warned. 'I have been *tout seul* for a rather long time.'

'Listen, you bad fairy,' Meredith replied. 'You do as you're told, or I'll have you back in rep before you can say Mary.'

The actor smiled with delight at the mock-scold and, clasping his hands together in front of him, awaited his further orders.

They were quite straightforward, simply for the two men to be seen at a few of the right restaurants, and at several of the right parties. It really shouldn't need more than a week, Meredith guessed, for it to be all round the business. That Noel Blond and David Terry were an item.

They made a very handsome couple, Meredith thought as she observed them from a safe distance at the first night of *Lazarus*. They were catching plenty of eyes too, as Blond moved easily round the party, introducing the young man to all the right wrong people. Seeing who was attending the party, and how many notables Terry was being introduced to, Meredith thought that this one party alone would be enough to give truth to the carefully constructed rumour.

And best of all, there in a far corner talking idly to some friends, was the overweight figure of the red-bearded Peregrine ffrench.

David Terry was called back to see the director and producer for the second time in a week. This time William and Jay were also present, and when the actor was introduced to them, none of them turned a hair. Peregrine had already talked the writers through his shortlist of final choices, and had indicated that should they still not be met on the question of Craig Matheson there was now, thank God, a very possible and extremely exciting alternative.

He didn't nominate who this might be, but you would have to have been blind, deaf and comatose not to guess when David Terry was called in. Peregrine ffrench lit up like Oxford Street at Christmas, and started prancing foolishly round the room, pouting and giggling at everything Terry said.

Then they read the actor in the part for William and Jay's benefit, with the director, a rather lethargic and sarcastic man, taking the part of Terry's wife. Throughout the entire three scenes that the two men read, Peregrine hooted with constant and hysterical laughter, while clapping his two pudgy hands together in front of himself at chest height.

The audition consequently was absolutely appalling, and William had to drape his arm casually round Jay's shoulder so that he could keep pinching her arm in order to stop her from laughing out loud.

In the meantime, Meredith sat patiently at her office desk awaiting the outcome. Terry called her from the studios just before lunch.

'I think I'm in!' he gasped. 'He wants me to have lunch with him!'

'You're not going,' Meredith replied.

'What!' Terry hissed back at her. 'You taken leave of your friggin' senses?'

'Frigg*ing*, darling,' Meredith corrected him. 'Not

418

friggin'. And no, I haven't. Which is why you're not going to go out to lunch.'

'One good reason, doll,' the actor asked her, with more than a hint of exasperation.

'Because you're going out to lunch with Noel, darling,' Meredith said. 'He's waiting for you outside the building in his car, and what you're going to do is give the impression that it's a terrible bore, and of course you'd have loved to have lunch with Peregrine, but. Then pull a face, and leave the rest in the air. And when you get down to the street, Noel is going to make a terrific fuss of you, and you're going to be really pissed off with him, and get into the car and slam the door. And Peregrine ffrench will have watched every move from his office.'

Terry rang Meredith again late afternoon. 'He wants me to go out to dinner,' he said.

'When?'

'Tonight.'

'You're busy tonight, darling. But you could make tomorrow.'

'OK.'

Meredith rang Terry the next day just before she left the office. 'Cancel him,' she ordered.

'Oh, now come on, doll!' Terry protested.

'Do you want this part or don't you?' Meredith enquired.

'Of course I want the part, sweetheart,' the actor sighed. 'I'd do anything to get it, you know that.'

'Then cancel Peregrine. But make sure he knows it's not your fault. It's Noel's.'

The next time Meredith heard from her protégé was shortly after midnight.

'He's just rung again,' he told her, 'and he was well pissed.'

'It gets better all the time,' Meredith replied.

'Lunch tomorrow,' Terry continued. 'At Leith's.'

'Why not?' said Meredith. 'But remember what I told you.'

David Terry did. According to him he played the scene Meredith and he had rehearsed between them to perfection. Peregrine had indicated the part was his for the asking, so Terry had told him he was asking. Peregrine had smiled and said only if he said pretty please. The actor had frowned, and said what sort of pretty please? To which the producer had sighed and told him not to play the young innocent with him, while wrapping two podgy legs round one of Terry's out of sight under the table. There had then been the vexed question of what to do about Noel, but Peregrine had been quite firm in his attitude on that one. He didn't give a toss for Noel, and anyway as everyone knew Noel was two-timing Terry with a young Irish actor who'd been in the play Noel had just finished doing at the Beeb.

Terry told Meredith that he'd nearly 'gone' there, and had to feign a fit of the sneezes behind his napkin, until he could look at Peregrine straight faced again. By the time he did, the producer had turned a very high colour and was gripping the actor's leg ever more tightly beneath the tablecloth.

'At least come back with me tonight!' he had pleaded. 'You'll be crazy if you don't! I really can make you into a household name!'

But still Terry had demurred, and said much as he was attracted to Peregrine, Noel had been so kind to him he couldn't possibly deceive him. Not for anything.

Not even for the starring role?

Well . . . . Terry had conceded. Yes, it was the chance of a lifetime.

Good. So here he was being offered it. The role was his. Yes? If?

If nothing. The role was his. All he had to do was leave Noel.

Listening to him across her desk Meredith could hardly believe how well their pre-constructed scenario had not only come to life but had actually played.

'What did you tell him?' she asked.

'I said I'd think about it,' Terry replied.

'Jesus,' Meredith breathed, 'you're cool. Now I'm certain you're going to crack it. When are you going to tell him?'

Terry told her Peregrine wanted a decision by the time they had dinner that evening. Otherwise he would offer the part to Craig Matheson.

'No,' said Meredith. 'We can't have that. Dinner's dangerous. You tell him over dinner you're leaving Noel and he's going to want to try and get you to bed tonight. You're going to have to fend him off until daybreak.'

She pushed her phone across to him.

'Dinner's out,' she told him.

'I'll need a bloody good reason,' Terry replied.

'Noel's been taken to hospital,' Meredith announced.

'Anything serious?' Terry asked, ringing through for an outside line.

'A rather small overdose,' Meredith grinned.

The actor told the producer over lunch the next day. The producer could hardly contain himself and tried to get Terry to go back to his flat that afternoon. But Terry had his excuses prepared, and left the producer, as Meredith had told him, like you should always leave your audience. Gasping for more.

Meredith promptly got Terry a job 'abroad', and he lay low in her flat for ten days while she accepted the offer London Television made for David Terry's services, and then negotiated, agreed and drew up the contract. Terry signed it on the day of his 'return' from location, and the following week the television company threw a press reception to announce their new comedy series, and the casting of David Terry in the lead.

It got a massive press coverage. It wasn't every day the industry turned up somebody quite as sensational-looking as David Terry.

Peregrine called him in for a meeting with the writers a few days later. After William and Jay had left he poured

421

the two of them drinks and, taking the actor's shoulders in his podgy hands, pushed him gently down on to his black leather sofa.

'Well?' he asked him. 'Pleased?'

'Thrilled, Peregrine,' Terry replied. 'Over the moon.'

'And?' the producer prodded, with what he obviously considered a sexy little *moue*.

'And what?' Terry frowned.

'What about Noel?'

'Oh, I've left Noel, Peregrine. I mean, a deal is a deal, right? And you said I'd get the part if I left Noel, and so that's exactly what I've done.'

'Super,' the producer purred. 'What a lovely boy. So I take it you're free at last, and perhaps even for dinner tonight?'

'I would have loved it, Peregrine,' Terry smiled.

'What do you mean – you'd have loved it?'

The fat man wheeled round and stared at the actor from behind his thick glasses. With his beard and glasses his face was too crowded, but not so crowded Terry couldn't still see his expression.

'Because I can't do tonight, I'm afraid,' Terry replied.

'I'd be interested to hear the reason,' Peregrine hissed, his smile now quite gone.

'I've met somebody else, Peregrine,' Terry told him.

There was a deathly, deadly silence. Peregrine went sheet-white and pursed his lips together so tightly he looked like a pig.

'You said if you got this part, darling,' he seethed, 'that you would. . . .'

The actor let the unfinished sentence die on the air. 'Yes?' he finally enquired.

'You know very well, sweetheart,' Peregrine replied.

'I promised I would leave Noel,' Terry agreed. 'Which is what I have done. Even though he tried to kill himself, I kept my promise and left him.'

'Yes?' Peregrine enquired, jutting his now re-reddening face towards the actor. 'And?'

'I didn't promise I wouldn't meet somebody else, Peregrine,' Terry answered, shrugging lightly, and then looked up at his producer with a smile. 'Did I?'

'That's show business,' Meredith said, raising her glass of champagne in a toast.

'That's what you should have said to Pppperegrine,' Jay laughed and told her star.

William was busy tearing his paper table napkin into strips.

'We are sure we're completely home and dry, I take it?' he finally asked. 'You know that old one about cup and lip.'

Meredith took a contract out of her case and laid it on the restaurant table.

'You know what Sam Goldwyn said about contracts,' William warned.

'Stop being such an old woman, William!' Jay told him. 'You're such a Jeroboam!'

'Jeremiah,' William corrected her. 'I guess it's a trait I've inherited. This constant ability to poop at parties.'

'There's nothing he can do, William,' Meredith assured him, turning the signed contract round for him to read. 'Barry Philips is delighted with "his" new discovery, we have a contract, the Press has bannered the news everywhere, so what's one fat frustrated old producer going to do? Say he doesn't want to use his Programme Controller's brightest and newest young star because he won't come over? I don't think so somehow, darling, do you?'

'Hmmm,' said William almost convinced. 'But he could still make life somewhat unpleasant for poor David here.'

'Don't you worry, old cock,' the actor said in his idiosyncratic accent, leaning forward and putting a strong hand on the writer's forearm. 'I mean it. I may only be an actor, but don't you worry, son. I know how to look after myself.'

The first episode of *Life With Charlie* attracted twelve and a half million viewers, and rave reviews. There was only one dissenter, a failed producer who now wrote a TV guide for one of the Sunday heavies, and who for some reason best known to himself ran a personal war of attrition against the show, a programme which was otherwise sweeping all before it.

'Jesus Christ! What's got into this guy?' William would moan every weekend, ignoring the spectacularly good notices in all the other papers. 'Has he got a corner in misanthropy or what?'

'You're like that old misery-boots in the story,' Jay would tease. 'You know, about the pea in the mattress. There's the whole of this enormous bed to sleep in, but every night, you have to find the pea.'

And this one man's snipings didn't affect the rest of the country, as Jay kept pointing out. By programme four, the figures had increased to fourteen million, making it the top-rated comedy show; by the sixth programme, *Life With Charlie* made it to the top of the pile, knocking *The Rose and Crown*, ITV's phenomenally successful soap opera, off its perch, and staying top of the ratings until the end of the show's first run.

David Terry quickly became a household name. Meredith knew it normally took two or three runs for an unknown actor to make it nationally. But not David Terry. Such was the strength of the show in which he starred, and such was his immediate charisma, before the show had even come to the end of its first series he was no longer, as had been predicted, the Man Most Likely. David Terry was The Man.

Meredith sat back when it all started happening with a sense of tremendous relief. But she only did so to draw breath. Meredith Browne was not one to count her chickens, even after they'd been hatched.

As for the show's originators, William Kennedy and Jay Burrell, they were walking on air. For not only was the show an astounding success, it was, give or take only the most minor of changes, the show they had initially both envisaged and written, something about which very few other writers they knew could boast.

And they had a contract for a minimum of another two series, the first of which they were already beginning work upon. They were happy, successful, and secure.

As indeed they would have been, had they succeeded so triumphantly in any other business than the one in which they were.

Excerpt from the *Daily Mail*, 2 February 1970

If you've ever asked yourself how these hilarious scripts came into being, listen to this . . . Life With Charlie *is for real*
by LAURA LOWE

If ever you're in the supermarket and an attractive young woman suddenly walks off with your trolley, pays for it and takes your shopping home, don't worry. She's not potty, she's most probably Jay Burrell, one half of television's newest and probably funniest script-writing teams.

'That's actually what Jay did only last week,' the other half of the partnership, handsome and debonair American novelist and playwright William Kennedy told me. 'She brought home six packs of disposable diapers and a dozen cans of cat food. We don't have either a baby or a cat. Or a baby who thinks it's a cat, or vice versa.'

Sounds familiar? I can tell you, after spending a morning with William, 37, and Jay, 29, in their lovely studio flat off the King's Road, what I heard and saw might have come straight out of an episode of Life With Charlie, *commercial television's runaway comedy hit, which stars David Terry and Beth Benson.*

'It's all true,' laughed Jay, a small vivacious brunette, 'William is Charlie. Right down to the newspaper tearing, and putting on his pyjamas back to front.'

'Pajamas,' corrected her handsome six-foot partner. 'But at least I don't leave notes out for the milkman which read, "No milk for a fortnight until further notice please".'

So how much of it was true, I asked? How much of their own lives went into the creation of the crazy, zany and wonderfully affectionate comedy that is keeping the nation glued to its sets every Tuesday?

'Remember the episode where Charlie has the frightful argument with a crazy driver in a country lane?' Jay asked. 'And the man later turns out to be their host for that weekend? All true.'

'The odd thing,' William confessed, while, I have to say

426

it, tearing an old letter into very small strips, 'is that the things which really are based on fact, while people find them funny, it seems they don't believe they're true.'

'Yet everything we invent,' Jay finished for him, 'people take as gospel.'

'Which only goes to show,' her partner added, 'that while you can fool all of the people all of the time, you can't fool some of the people some of it.'

Life With Charlie is the couple's first joint hit, although both worked as successful independent writers before teaming up, most notably Jay who at the age of nineteen wrote a biography entitled As Soon As I Can, which became a No 1 Bestseller. William, on the other hand, cut his teeth in his home country of America, script-writing for such notable TV successes as Fort Louis, The Buddy Green Show, and Pooky's Island.

'People ask us all the time what it's like to collaborate—' Jay told me.

'And she never dares tell them,' William interrupted laconically, 'in case they shave off all her hair.'

'And I always give them the same answer,' Jay continued, ignoring her partner's intrusion. 'Because it's so much more fun. If you get over-tired, of course you get ratty just like any other couple. But the fact that we work together doesn't make it any worse.'

'I would reckon it's harder to work with somebody with whom you're not living,' William added. 'Besides that, Jay and I are tuned in to the same station. We even share the same piece of soap. Everyone thinks Jay writes all the women's stuff, and I write the men. But as a matter of fact it's the other way round.'

'Which is why William's wearing that rather nice skirt,' cracked Jay.

But what brought them together in the first place, I wondered? What inspired them to form what is quite obviously an inspired partnership? I asked them both what they thought was each other's vital ingredient.

'William's dialogue,' said Jay. 'It's incredible. He has this fantastic sense of rhythm.'

And Jay? William pondered awhile, before coming up with his partner's best asset. 'Jay's legs, I guess,' he told me. Or was that Charlie speaking?

'But you were his top writer, William!' Jay had persisted. 'And he fired you the day the article came out!'

'There's more to it than that, honey,' William had reasoned. 'David Terry's just on the way up. He wouldn't want to dump on his own doorstep.'

It had happened so suddenly, and for seemingly no good reason. The show's first run was over, and William and Jay were already halfway through writing the scripts for the second series. Everyone was wildly enthusiastic; they had a new director, who mercifully had taken over from David Pepys after show six, and the runaway success of the show had even assuaged the grievance Peregrine ffrench had been quite venomously nursing against David Terry.

So when the blow came, it came out of left field.

Surprisingly enough, it was Barry Philips who telephoned.

'William?' he said. 'Trouble.'

'What sort, Barry?' William enquired. 'Nothing too heavy, please God. We're just off on vacation.'

'Cancel it,' Barry ordered. 'At least till we're out of the shit.'

Jay came out of the bathroom, hearing the phone, and frowned at William. William closed his eyes and shook his head at her. Jay knew what that look meant and sat down on the arm of a chair, trying to make some sense out of William's answers.

'I don't see what we can do,' he was saying. 'I'd have thought that was your department.'

And then: 'Jesus, Barry, we're the goddam writers, buddy! We're not the ones who go round putting out the fires!'

There was trouble, Jay realized, but with whom? The new director maybe?

'Get Stuart to do it. Stuart can be pretty goddam persuasive.'

It wasn't the director, because the director was Stuart. Peregrine?

'Jesus, Barry! This is down to you lot! It's your lot who should have blocked any holes! Isn't that what you pay those bastards upstairs for?'

The bastards upstairs. Contracts! That was it, Jay concluded. There was some cock-up with someone's contract. Somebody was kicking up a storm over their fee. That was bound to happen, seeing the success of the show. But why was Barry ringing them?

'Because he wants us to do the talking,' William told her, after he'd put down the telephone. 'Apparently everyone else, including the very Gods even on the umpteenth floor! They've all had a shot. And we're the very last chance. Because, it seems, he trusts us.'

Jay was still all ends up and, pulling her bathrobe tightly round her, frowned up at William.

'Who?' she asked. 'Who are we talking about?'

'David-would-you-credit-it-Terry,' he replied.

The actor arrived for dinner. He brought Meredith with him. William and Jay had rushed around in the few hours' notice they'd been given, putting together the best dinner they could. Terry loved seafood, so Jay and William had run to Harrods, where Jay bought Dublin Bay prawns and some superb fresh lobsters, and William bought a Corton Charlemagne white burgundy, some vintage Bollinger, and a bottle of Old Landed Pale Hine cognac.

'What the bloody hell are we supposed to do?' Jay hissed at him for the twentieth time as she prepared a thermidor sauce. 'Get him footless, and then force him to sign?'

'I can't believe the idiocy!' William declared. 'They have options on everyone else! They probably even have options on the old dears who sweep the studio floor! So how in hell did they let David through the net!'

'And more importantly,' Jay grimaced. 'Why the hell won't the idiot bloody well re-sign?'

'It has to be a question of money,' William sighed. 'This just has to be a stand-off.'

* * *

'It's not a question of money, darling,' Meredith told them over their champagne. 'And nobody's holding a gun to anybody's head.'

'Then what is it, Meredith?' William asked, as David Terry prowled silently round the studio, examining Jay's art collection.

'You'll really have to talk to David, my darling,' Meredith replied. 'Perhaps he'll listen to you. He won't listen to me. But he respects you. He really respects both you and Jay.'

Jay looked at William, as much as to tell him he should be the one to broach the subject. William pulled a face, poured himself another glass of champagne, and went after the actor, who was still staring at Jay's paintings.

He caught him just by The Apple Orchard, which Jay had bought from a small gallery in the King's Road.

'So,' William opened, standing side by side with Terry and looking at the painting.

'I don't want to talk about it, mate,' the actor replied, chewing his bottom lip. 'Not at the moment.'

'I thought that was the object of this evening,' William said.

'I just don't want to talk about it now,' Terry persisted. 'It's too painful.'

The actor then turned to William and, giving him his best brave smile, put his arm around his shoulder and led him back to the waiting group. Where Meredith and Jay stood smiling in anticipation.

'Know what?' the actor said. 'I love you all. Straight up. I really love you.'

'The way he's carrying on,' Jay hissed at William as they prepared to carry the lobsters through from the kitchen, 'you'd think he'd just had a terminal prognosis instead of a dust-up over his contract.'

'I don't think you're so far off the mark there, sweetheart,' William replied. 'Except I don't think it's him who's had the terminal prognosis.'

Dinner was a disaster. The food wasn't: in fact the Dublin prawns and the lobster thermidor were exquisite,

431

to those who bothered trying them. David Terry hardly lifted his fork to his mouth throughout the entire meal. Already more than a little drunk when he arrived, by the time the lobster was served, he was well gone. Jay did her best to keep the mood light, as indeed did Meredith, but William, once he saw how badly their star guest was behaving, relapsed into near total silence.

In fact, when their guest of honour lit a cigarette as everyone else was just starting on the lobster and then stubbed the end of his smoke out in the middle of his untouched food, Jay thought William was going to take a swing at Terry.

'I'm sorry, David,' she said, leaning suddenly across the table to remove his unwanted plate, and thus block any blow William might have been thinking of aiming, 'I should have asked you if you didn't like seafood.'

'I love seafood,' the actor replied, failing to see the exit his hostess had so tactfully provided. 'I love prawns, I love lobster, and Christ, I love you.'

Terry grabbed Jay by the arm and, pulling her towards him, kissed her full on the mouth. In her surprise, Jay tipped the plate of food she was holding and spilt it all down her new crushed velvet skirt.

William was on his feet in a second, but just as quickly Meredith had a restraining arm on his.

'David,' she said sharply. 'You're a clumsy bastard.'

The actor tried to focus on what he had done, and when he saw the food all down Jay's skirt, he grabbed a napkin and started to try and repair the damage.

'Jesus, I'm sorry, darlin',' he drawled. 'Jesus, I really am sorry. But don't worry, I'll buy you a new one. I'll buy you two new ones. Three new ones. Christ, I'm sorry.'

William sat back down, but pushed his food aside, unable to continue the pretence any longer.

'OK, David,' he said. 'That's enough. You hear me?'

'Oh, I hear you, William my old darlin',' the actor replied, turning to William and grinning fatuously. 'I hear you, mate, and Christ – I love you.'

Whereupon he tipped his chair towards William and, putting one strong arm around William, rested his head face down on his shoulder.

William looked round helplessly to Meredith.

'Do something,' he said.

'What?' Meredith asked. 'I'm sorry, but he just can't handle this. He just finds this all too much.'

'What precisely?' William demanded. 'Exactly what does this ox-head find "too much"?'

Meredith looked at William. She gave him her best sad-tragic look, and put a hand on his.

'Not to be able to go on doing your's and Jay's wonderful show,' she replied.

After the actor had stopped being sick in the downstairs loo, Jay and Meredith had laid him out like a corpse on the sofa. William, stating that he wanted nothing further to do with it, disappeared into the night to walk his fury off, while Jay and Meredith sat down and tried to thrash the problem out.

They were still at it when William made his reappearance.

'Don't tell me the garbage men still haven't called?' he asked icily, as he surveyed the unconscious mummer.

Jay kissed him and, pouring him a whisky, sat him down next to Meredith.

'Apparently David's worried about becoming typecast,' she told him.

'Is he hell!' William retorted. 'He's just had a better offer!'

'There's nothing else on the table,' Meredith insisted. 'Really, William. David just has this thing about being Charlie for the rest of his life.'

'Garbage!' William yelled. 'Complete and utter and one hundred per cent garbage!'

Jay had never seen him angry like this. Come to think of it, Jay realized she'd never actually seen William really angry, period.

'This is just like a goddam divorce!' he continued. 'Except this one's a quickie! Usually guys wait a decent period of time before they ditch the booster rocket! You know, the poor bastard who's put up with him and supported him and encouraged him until he became rich and famous! But not this son of a bitch! No, no! No, this rocket gets one taste of the honeypot, and that's it! The marriage is over! For everyone else, the future is cancelled!'

'I really thought if anyone could talk him round, you two could,' Meredith sighed.

'What in hell are you talking about, Meredith!' William yelled, turning on her directly. 'Whose mess is this anyway? You're his goddam agent! You're the one who agreed his contract! So why no option! They slapped one on everyone else! We have one! Stuart has one! Beth has one! But not this bastard here! So how come you managed to get him contracted with no option for another series, you hear me?'

Jay took William's hand and held it. Normally there might have been tears behind her eyes when she saw how upset William was, but she wasn't going to let her emotions show. Instead she managed to get him to sit down again, and perched herself beside him on the arm of his chair.

'You're quite right to be this pissed off, darling,' Meredith sighed. 'I mean here we have the hit comedy show of the last ten years, and now the leading man doesn't want to go on playing.'

'I want to know how you ducked the option, Meredith,' William demanded.

'It was part of the deal, William love,' Meredith replied. 'Because David was unknown I had to accept a ridiculously low initial fee, and they tried to swing a whole series of options on us. But I argued that if they got him cheap first time round, and if the show was a success, and if David was a success, then next time round he wasn't going to come so cheap.'

'That doesn't explain the lack of an option,' William argued. 'They could have set the subsequent fees to one side, made them TBDs—'

Jay frowned at him, lost.

'To be discusseds, honey,' William explained. 'There's no way the making of an option has to be tied to the next series' fees.'

'Absolutely,' Meredith agreed. 'My very argument. But David wouldn't hear of it.'

'My heart lies bleeding,' William replied. 'David Terry wouldn't hear of it. Who, if you'll pardon me for asking, who was David Terry then?'

'He was the actor, William, whom everyone, including you two, wanted the most, remember?' Meredith reminded him crisply. 'He was the actor who was going to make your show, he was the most exciting talent you had all seen in years. And because he was frightened—'

'Ah,' said William, reaching for his drink.

'Because he was frightened of what might happen,' Meredith continued, 'because he had heard from his mates in the business how quickly you could get lumbered by your television image, and because he is a young actor with everything before him, he didn't want to sign away the next three or four years of his life on a show which could well turn out to be his very own Frankenstein's monster!'

'He didn't, or you didn't?' Jay suddenly asked, as cool as could be.

Meredith hesitated and looked round at Jay. Jay looked right back at her, challenging her right in the eyes.

'I'm only his agent, Jay darling,' she answered. 'Whatever I may or may not have thought about the deal, finally I can only carry out the instructions of my client.'

'Is that right?' Jay replied.

'You know that's how it is,' Meredith said.

But even so, Meredith was the first to drop her eyes. She opened her purse and took out her cigarettes, making the action the excuse for her inability to hold the look.

Then, having lit up, she blew the smoke slowly out above her head and turned back to William.

'I still think we've a chance, William darling,' she said, 'if you'll speak to him.'

'I don't beg, Meredith,' William replied. 'I threw away my begging bowl after I was sacked off the Buddy Green Show. I grovelled when that happened, you see. I went back cap in hand and pleaded for my job back. They were very sympathetic. Very understanding. And promised they'd use me on a freelance basis. Which they did – once, over two years. But by throwing myself on their mercy, I owed them. And they made me pay. Rather Buddy did. That drunken bastard son of a bitch was never out of my head. He called me night and day, reading me other guys' junk material and asking me what I thought. He'd even come round to my apartment late at night after he'd done the show, crocked, practically incoherent, and he'd sit there drinking my liquor and telling me what a great show he'd just done. And all I could do was listen. Which is why I don't beg any more, Meredith. If I wear holes in the knees of my pants pleading with this bastard here to stay with the show, then I'll end up owing him. And believe me, that's not where I want to be. Once, I'm telling you and I mean it, once is more than enough.'

Jay felt like applauding. She knew they'd lost the moment David Terry had walked in through the door ahead of Meredith earlier that night and gone straight to check his now nationally famous good looks in her enormous mirror over the fireplace. It was then she had seen, off-screen, away from the studio, and on her home ground, the monster they had all created, and she knew that they had lost. But she still felt like applauding, because even though the day might be lost, the battle was not. William had made it all too clear that nothing in the world could persuade him to make the slightest effort to drag David Terry back on.

Meredith rose and, having carefully brushed something imaginary off her skirt, turned to William for one last go.

'So,' she asked him, 'what do you want to do about it then, darling?'

'I'll tell you what I want to do about "it",' William answered, starting to pull the slowly awakening actor up from the sofa. 'I want you to tell "it" to get the hell out of here. Personally – although I'm sure I speak for my partner as well here—'

'You bet your bottom you do,' Jay replied, in answer to William's look.

'OK,' William continued, turning back to Meredith. 'So personally, and this goes for both of us, we don't want to see this son of a bitch ever again, OK? Let alone work for the bastard.'

'I'm really sorry,' Meredith said as she kissed them good night.

'Of course,' said Jay.

'You bet,' said William.

David Terry by now was propped up against the doorway, halfway back to consciousness.

'Listen, you lot!' he commanded, suddenly putting both arms up above his head. 'Listen! I just want to tell you something! I love you all!'

Meredith caught him just in time before he collapsed again, and steered him out into the night.

After their guests had left, William lay on the sofa where he was to remain face down and silent until dawn broke. Jay, who now knew her partner's ways, cleared and washed up, and took herself quietly off up the stairs to their galleried bed.

There was silence for a long while also in the taxi which was carrying Meredith and her client homewards, through a now almost deserted Chelsea. Finally, David Terry, who had spent most of the journey looking out of the window, turned to Meredith and smiled.

'Well?' he said to her. 'So how was I, doll?'

'Marvellous,' she told him. 'Fabulous. As usual.'

Following the public disclosure that David Terry had

437

refused to do another series of *Life With Charlie*, there was a small earthquake internally at City Television with very few casualties. However, somebody who did get hurt was Barry Philips, the Controller of Programmes, who came into work one morning to find himself given an hour to clear his desk. He had intended to re-cast the leading role, having argued that one series was not enough to make a leading man irreplaceable in the public's mind, and had already made approaches to several leading light comedy actors about the likelihood of one of them taking over from David Terry. He had offered it to Craig Matheson but had met with a stony refusal, which Philips had well expected. He was, however, a man who always believed in asking, maintaining that the worst answer he could get would only be no.

The next half-dozen pretenders to Craig Matheson's throne were then approached, but it soon became clear that leading actors considered it beneath them to step into the shoes of a previous unknown, and so to a man they all, as they thought, excusably declined.

But Philips was still not without hope as he made his way up to his office that Tuesday morning, since he had a back-up list of aspirants, several of whom, given the strength of the material in the show, could quite possibly become David Terrys themselves. However, owing to a totally unpredicted palace revolution, one hour later the former programme controller was to find himself out of a job.

William and Jay read about it in the newspaper. No one thought of telling them, even though they were contracted to do another twenty-six shows plus for the company. William called Max, but was told Max was tied up. Ever since failing to get Matheson cast as the lead, it had appeared to William and Jay that Max had been constantly tied up.

'Maybe he enjoys it,' Jay had joked.

But William hadn't found it funny. In fact ever since David Terry's walk-out, William seemed to have suffered from a complete sense of humour failure.

438

'What in hell's going on?' William wondered out loud when they had returned to staring at the newspaper report. 'And what's it going to do to us?'

They didn't have to play guessing games for very long. The following day they were invited into City Television to meet Martyn Brett, the new controller of programmes.

'Interesting,' he said, sitting at his desk with his hands clasped under his nose as if in prayer. 'Now what are we going to do with you?'

'For us, I hope you mean,' William replied. 'We hope you're going to find us a new leading man.'

Brett smiled at them without affection, rapidly tapping the fingers of his still praying hands together.

'I don't respond to take-overs,' he informed them. 'I interpret them as a mark of company failure.'

'No leading man, no show,' William offered with a shrug.

'I'm aware of that,' Brett replied, picking up a perfectly sharpened pencil and using it to flick through the ratings sheets lying in front of him.

'So what's the game plan?' William enquired.

'I'd like to see something new please,' the Programme Controller said, without looking up.

Jay, visibly paling, was about to open up with both barrels. William could see that, and to forestall her he put his hand on her knee and shook his head at her. Jay frowned back at him, perplexed, but William just shook his head again.

'Yes?' Brett asked them, still awaiting a response to his statement.

'Pardon me?' said William.

'I just said I'd like to see something new,' Brett repeated. 'And by that I meant from you.'

'We still have thirteen more "Charlies" to write,' Jay reminded him, 'with the possibility of another thirteen.'

'You still have twenty-six more shows to write for us, Miss Burrell,' Brett corrected. 'Twenty-six untitled shows.'

'What's wrong with *Life With Charlie*?' Jay persisted.

'Too much,' the Controller replied.

'Slow down, for Chrissake!' William snapped on their way home.

'Normally you like the way I drive,' Jay replied defensively.

'And today I don't!' William snapped. 'So slow down!'

On the strength of their success, Jay had treated herself to a second-hand red Alfa Romeo GTV, in which she and William loved to roar round about and in and out of London. The underpass into Knightsbridge was perfectly clear, but even so Jay could see that William was knuckling it, so she dutifully slowed down.

When they got back to the studio, William disappeared round the corner only to return a short time later with a couple of tissue-wrapped bottles.

'What's this?' Jay asked, unwrapping one and seeing a fresh bottle of vodka. 'William, we've masses of vodka!'

'Had,' William replied, taking the bottle back from her. 'I killed it last night.'

Jay watched as he poured them both sizeable shots, to which he added about the same again in tonic. Jay took the tonic bottle and filled her glass up to the rim. William took his drink off and sat himself down at their work table.

'Are we going to work?' Jay asked.

'Are we hell!' William answered. 'Speaking for myself, I'm about to get fried. The son of a bitch.'

William downed his first drink in about two and a half seconds and got up for a refill. Jay watched him sympathetically, but was still frightened. Normally William was a man of the most complete discipline, never drinking during the day, and only within the strictest self-imposed guidelines in the evening. Now he was sitting down at their work table with the bottle in front of him as if intending to take on Scott Fitzgerald.

'At least we're still in work,' Jay ventured after a while, and then immediately wished that she hadn't.

'There is no such thing for a writer, Jay Burrell,' William yelled, banging the table with his fist, 'as just being in work! You and I – we write what we want to write! We've always agreed that! And if we can't, we don't! That's what being "in work" is! Doing it for some other bastard!'

Jay apologized, and sat back in silence, preferring not to take William on in this mood. For his part, as the drink got to him, William started to loosen up, and to talk persuasively and passionately about what City Television was trying to make them do. The new controller had killed the goose that had laid a golden egg, not because of a fear that they, the writers, and the actor who finally would replace David Terry might not succeed quite so phenomenally second time round, but simply because he, a newly appointed West Hampstead broom, was determined to sweep his desk completely clear.

'This isn't my show,' he had told them. 'And it isn't my sort of show. If we have to have Light Entertainment, then I think it should be issue-related. What you have written in your series is emotional propaganda.'

'And so say over fifteen million viewers,' Jay had argued.

'My dear girl,' Brett had replied. 'When television began, people used to rush home to watch the test transmissions. There is a time, and a place. And if you find it, you'll find the viewers. What would you choose to watch at eight o'clock in the evening with a current affairs programme as your only rival?'

'You're saying people watched *Life With Charlie* just because it was there?' William asked incredulously.

'I'm saying its figures were over-inflated,' Brett had replied. 'While an autopsy will always find an audience, prize fights sell out.'

'I didn't understand what he meant by that remark,' Jay was later to inform William over his third large vodka.

'Smartass,' William muttered. 'Trendy, long-haired smartass. What he meant was while some people might stare at a corpse, *en masse* they like their people moving. What does he know, anyway? About goddam entertainment? You know where they got that creep? BBC Current Affairs! No wonder he doesn't like comedy!'

Jay suddenly laughed, causing William to stare at her in surprise.

'Christ!' she said. 'You don't think that current affairs programme *Charlie* was going out against was one of his! — shades of *The Marriage Game*? I don't believe this.'

William started to laugh, and then stopped. It was far too possible to be funny.

Max was no help. William went into the agency to find out just how tied up he was, and bumped into him coming out of the john.

'With one bound he was free,' William said, closing the lift gates behind him.

'William,' Max said, grabbing him by the elbow. 'I've been trying to reach you. Come in. I've only got a minute.'

Max steered him into the agency and called to Mona to hold all his calls for five minutes, and then ushered William through into his office. He commiserated with William, he sighed, and he duly cursed in all the right places, but William noticed he was now a shadow of his former self. All the time William was talking, Max stared blankly at an elastic band he kept winding and unwinding round his index finger.

He had nothing to offer William. William asked him what the position was *vis-à-vis* his and Jay's contract with City Television, and Max just shrugged, telling him that it was up to them. William pointed out that it wasn't, that the company were ordering them to come up with something entirely different to *Life With Charlie* which had been junked, and Max swore that they were all idiots who didn't know their arses from their elbows, but the fire had gone from his rhetoric.

William finally slowed it right down, and waited until Max felt the change of pace. Max eventually did, and stopped twitching at the elastic band on his finger to look across his desk for the first real time at William since he'd brought him into the office.

'What is it, Max?' William asked. 'Something's bothering you.'

Max stared at him, and William could see from the expression in his eyes that he was dying to tell him something. Instead Max got up and chose a cigar from his humidor.

'It's this country, Willy boy,' he said eventually, once he'd bitten the end of his cigar. 'It's a piss hole.'

'It hasn't done badly by you, buddy,' William replied.

'You get from something what you put into it,' Max told him. 'All you get back is what you put in. Now I'm not even getting it back.'

'Maybe you need a vacation,' William suggested.

'Maybe I need better than that,' Max said. 'Maybe I need to get the hell out.'

'Where to?' William enquired.

'Where do you think, chum?' Max replied. 'America.'

Max finally left for America three months later. Jay and William knew he was going, but not when. Again, they read about it in the newspaper.

'He's only gone to make a film,' Jay reassured William, when she found him still staring at the newspaper story. 'He'll be back.'

'I don't think so, sweetheart,' William answered. 'I'm afraid we're on our own.'

They were waiting for a response from City Television for yet another new series they had proposed to the company. They had already had three ideas and two whole pilot scripts rejected, and now they were waiting for a verdict on their latest. Stuart, their director, had liked it when they had shown it to him in camera, but it was Peregrine ffrench whose support they had to gain in order to get the project to the next stage of development.

He kept the detailed outline for the series for three weeks before he came back to them.

'You clever little people,' he breathed down the telephone at Jay when he finally called. 'How *do* you do it?'

William looked at Jay almost beseechingly and held his thumb first up and then down for Jay to sign which way the wind was blowing. Jay pulled a face. There was no way of yet telling.

'I mean I just love the idea of this streetful of *terrible* people! With their *terrible* problems!' Peregrine continued. 'It's to die for! They are all such purely awful people!'

'Martyn with a y said he wanted – what was it?' Jay paused, trying to remember. 'Yes! Issue-related! Nobody can accuse this idea of being emotional propaganda!'

'I should say,' Peregrine enthused. 'So how about a little lunchie? And a *very* long talkie?'

Jay turned round to William and gave him the thumbs-up.

They ate in the VIP dining room at City Television's offices. Craig Matheson was lunching there with a balding producer known to one and all as The Toad. Peregrine saw William and Jay noticing, and smiled as he shook out his napkin.

'Craig's back in the fold,' he whispered. 'Doing a new drama series for us. About a coal miner who becomes an opera star.'

'Very issue-related,' William said.

'We've actually bought a disused coal mine in Kent,' Peregrine continued, ignoring William. 'It was Craig's idea.'

'It would be,' said Jay. 'Now tell us about *The Neighbourhood*.'

'I can't tell you how much I love it,' Peregrine sighed, breaking his bread roll in an almost religious manner. 'In fact what I'd really like to do is to commission a first script.'

'So OK,' William grinned. 'Let's go.'

Peregrine breathed in very deeply, sighed slowly on the exhalation, and smiled bravely at them.

'It'll only take us a week,' Jay enthused. 'We've half of it done already.'

'It won't even take us a week,' William said. 'We can finish it yesterday.'

'I just wish I'd moved quicker,' Peregrine groaned.

William and Jay stared at him, then at each other.

'Why's that?' William asked him curtly.

'I'm such a silly old windbag,' Peregrine replied. 'I should have had the courage of my convictions. Instead, when it was discussed at the departmental meeting, I just expressed this tiny worry that might it not be more of a ser*ial* than a ser*ies*. But nobody else seemed to think so. Or so it *seemed*, sweeties.'

The writers waited, their hearts sinking rapidly to their shoes. They both knew it was bad news. William had said it would be bad news when he'd asked them to lunch. Peregrine, he had told Jay, never invited them to lunch except to gloat.

'Anyway,' the producer continued, 'the long and the short of it was, this morning at the monthly production meeting, Gareth Williams – you know, God of Plays – he ups and announces *his* new drama series. And guess what? The bitch. It's all about this community and their problems, and they're calling it *The Square*.'

That was the moment the heart went out of William. Jay saw it, and would always remember the look on his face. His mouth was half smiling, but his brow was frowning, and his eyes had gone quite still and dead. Then he simply nodded several times, more to himself than either to Jay or their host, before getting up and walking out of the restaurant.

Jay got up at once and followed, but not before she had leaned across the table and called Peregrine the very worst name she had ever called anyone in her life, and called him it loud enough for everyone else to hear. Then she rushed out after William.

They were soon back at their desk working, but nothing was happening. Jay still felt creative and full of energy, because she was the sort of person who thrived when she was disadvantaged. But William, who before had always enjoyed a battle, now had no appetite for it. Initially Jay was still full of good ideas, but William, having expressed early enthusiasm for them, would then start to pull them to pieces, finding in advance all the faults he reckoned City Television would find. Very soon Jay's own enthusiasm was waning.

It was as if they were both suffering from a debilitating disease. The ideas would still come, but they grew weaker and weaker until finally they were so fragile and under-nourished they no longer even dared submit them for approval. William began to drink, and stay in bed in the mornings, leaving Jay to go for long walks in the Park while he slept.

After six weeks of total non-creativity, Peregrine ffrench called them up.

'It's no longer coming thick and fast, sweeties,' he cajoled. 'In fact it doesn't seem to be coming at all. And Upstairs is getting just a little bit tetchy.'

'The well's dry, old buddy,' William told him, trying to clear a throbbing head with a hair of the dog. 'Nothing's coming to us, and I mean nothing.'

'Well, in that case, my loves,' Peregrine announced, 'let me be your fairy godmother. I have something for you. Our sitcom *Blue Heaven*, yes?'

'Yes,' William replied cautiously.

'A little bit of trouble there,' Peregrine continued. 'Like the writer can't any more. The two bottles a day have finally, alas, caught up on the old grey matter.'

'He's not dead, is he?' William said, suddenly taking fright.

'He might as well be, love,' Peregrine replied. 'He thinks he's Proust.'

'I don't see what it has to do with us, Peregrine,' William reasoned.

446

'Really?' his producer replied. 'Well, let me tell you. I'm putting you and Jay on the show.'

'The hell you are!' snapped William.

'We surely haven't forgotten the little matter of our contract, have we, love?' Peregrine enquired. 'You know as well as I do, William. You still owe us twenty-six whole episodes.'

William and Jay had put up a dartboard at one end of the studio, and they would play a daily match against each other on it in their lunch break. Recently it had been adorned with a large photograph of David Terry, at which they had taken a savage and hysterical delight in throwing their arrows. Now, once they had digested the latest bombshell from City Television, the actor's image had been immediately replaced with a hastily pencilled caricature of Peregrine ffrench.

'He can't do this to us!' Jay seethed, as her first dart landed in the producer's eye. 'The bastard!'

'He's doing it, sweetheart,' William contradicted, taking careful aim at the centre of the drawing.

'They can't *make* us write someone else's show!' Jay replied.

'They reckon they can, honey.'

'Then they can go stuff!'

'Then they can go sue.'

William dropped his aim for a moment and looked at Jay balefully.

'They have us by what you like to call the proverbiballs,' he told her. 'We're under contract.'

'William!' Jay retorted. 'We can't write *Blue Heaven*! You've seen it! It's a terrible show!'

'Then I guess we'll just have to try and make it better, sweetheart,' William answered, before throwing his dart. 'Bullseye.'

Which indeed it was, the dart landing right in the middle of the producer's nose. It was also, alas, the very last score they were to make against Peregrine ffrench for many a long year.

● ● ●

447

In the meantime Meredith hadn't been wasting any time cashing in on the tremendous success of David Terry in *Life With Charlie*. The business was starved of good young light comedians, and most particularly of good and stunningly attractive ones, so everyone was knocking at the door. Meredith let none of them in.

David Terry, however, wasn't at all sure of the game his agent was playing, and kept reminding her of his uncertainty on his daily visits to the office.

'I don't get it, doll,' he drawled, sitting back to front on a chair and gazing at Meredith with his deep blue eyes. 'I thought the idea was to keep the old mush in front of Joe Public.'

'Not in this garbage,' Meredith told him, chucking over some of the scripts she'd been sent on approval.

'You're not going to be offered another *Charlie*, not for a long time. Maybe even never. Those were once in a lifetime, those scripts. What we want now is a different sort of plum. A lead in a Theatre of Today would do nicely.'

The executive producer of BBC's Theatre of Today, Ken Condon, was an ex-child actor like Meredith, although he had never quite achieved Meredith's fame. Even so, as an eight-year-old he too had suffered through two films under the directorship of Basil Landun, and that was enough to forge a life-long bond between the two of them. As soon as Meredith put a call through, he made room in his diary to see her that same week.

He was waiting for her as she got out of the lift on the fourth floor.

'I'd have come all the way down to Reception,' he told her, taking her arm, 'if I could guarantee finding my way back.'

'But you've been here over a year now, Ken!' Meredith laughed. 'It can't be that bad!'

'The people who designed this building,' Ken replied, letting her into his offices, 'based it on Daedalus's labyrinth in Crete. I've only once made it to the canteen and back without having to ask directions.'

They spent the first five or ten minutes in idle reminiscence, now able to laugh at the horrors Basil Landun had inflicted on them. But all the time they laughed and groaned, Meredith noticed that Ken never took his eyes off her.

At the first expedient moment, Meredith brought the conversation around to the purpose of her visit.

'You bet,' Ken nodded, 'I'd love to help you, Merry. I really liked David in that series, you know. It was literate comedy, and he was smashing. But I mean the bloke's light comedy, right? And you know as well as I do, Merry, Theatre of Today doesn't do a whole lot of comedy.'

Meredith was quite expecting this, so she simply side-stepped the implication and enquired what in fact was left on Ken's desk. He told her he had only four remaining plays to produce for that year's strand, and most of them were fully cast up.

'Any exceptions?' Meredith enquired.

'As a matter of fact, yes,' Ken admitted, 'but the delay, or so I'm told, is only technical. We're doing the Pam Shavers play from the Court, *Split*, right?'

Meredith nodded her recollection. She'd seen the play on the first night and, while she hadn't liked it at all, it was a very showy piece for the actors, particularly the leading role of Rick, a biker who moves in with a decaying upper-class family, and having laid them end to end, including the son, ends up as their butler. It was a part tailor-made for David Terry.

'Why's the delay technical, Ken?' she enquired.

'The director wants Tom Kenny,' Ken replied. 'Which would be great, natch. But he's just about to do *Dick Turpin*, and we're trying to work out a way to shoot round him.'

'So in the meantime, why not see David as a long stop?' Meredith suggested. 'If you don't get Tom, David would make a very interesting Rick.'

Ken considered the suggestion, slowly scratching at the

449

slight stubble on his chin, while still appraising the beautiful woman in front of him.

'Isn't he a bit too bloody lardy?' he finally wondered. 'I mean Rick's — well, you saw the play. Rick's bona fide East End.'

Meredith smiled.

'I don't think David would have any trouble with the cockney,' she replied.

David Terry was called to meet the director for the following Monday. Meredith at once rang Polly Stephens, who knew one of the cast of the original production of *Split* at the Court and asked her to get hold of a copy of the script.

Once they had the playscript, Meredith and David worked on the part all of the Thursday night and well into early Friday morning. Meredith finally went to bed at half past three, leaving Terry working his way yet again through the play.

Before the end of trading on Friday, Meredith rang Condon at the BBC, catching him just before he left for home.

'This is very short notice,' she apologized. 'But I don't suppose you'd be free for dinner tomorrow night?'

'As a matter of fact I am,' he told her after a moment's pause. 'I am, that is, but Harriet's not here. She's filming in France.'

'Oh,' Meredith said, her disappointment sounding utterly plausible. 'I didn't realize.'

'I mentioned it when I saw you,' Ken replied. 'She's doing that Colette. With Barbra Stone.'

'Of course,' Meredith sighed. 'For some reason I can't have taken it in.'

She then left a short silence, since she wanted the suggestion, which she was quite sure would come, to come from him.

'I suppose I could always come on my tod,' Ken said, a little cautiously.

'I'd love that,' Meredith agreed, then adding as a rider that there would be other people there.

'OK,' Ken replied with growing enthusiasm. 'Great.'

Meredith made sure there were plenty of other people, and all from the business. One of the perks of being an agent was that when you had an important producer coming to dinner, most actors and writers were only too willing to cancel any previous engagement.

The only person she didn't ask was David Terry.

Who was livid with fury.

'I don't understand you, doll!' he shouted at her down the phone. 'You have all these friggin' plans—'

'Frig*ging*, darling,' Meredith corrected. 'You haven't got the part yet.'

'And I'm not goin' to, not the way you're smartarsing it!' he replied.

'David, darling,' Meredith soothed. 'You come to dinner and he'll be bored of you by Monday.'

'Great,' the actor complained. 'So now I'm boring as well.'

'You just have to trust me on this one, David,' Meredith told him, firming her tone up just enough to make the actor come to heel.

'I've been here before, so believe me. You come here and dine, and you won't get the part for two reasons. One: Ken will have seen you, and we're all very different out of uniform, darling. I may like you as you are, and so may you. But producers don't like to fraternize, particularly *before* making up their minds. And two: you come to dinner and you're funnier than he is, and you make people laugh more – he'll hate you for it.'

'So I won't put on my funny hat,' David interrupted. 'I'll be as boring as all get out.'

'He'll hate you for that just as much,' Meredith replied. 'There's no way you'll win it by coming to dinner. You'll be much better off staying at home and doing your homework.'

Meredith was right on every point. And when he put the phone down, Terry knew it. Which peeved him even more. Which was why the following evening when Meredith was sitting her seven guests down to dinner, David Terry got

451

himself all dressed up and took himself out to The White Elephant.

Where he met Suzanne Altman for the very first time.

Shortly after midnight, when David Terry had settled down to play some serious blackjack, Meredith had said good night to most of her dinner party. One guest lingered, however, exactly as she had hoped he would. As she had been almost sure he would. Certainly by the time he had finished her *Boeuf en Daube Charolaise* the odds on him being able to resist Meredith's charms had shortened dramatically. And once he had sampled her *Corniottes*, and turned to her with a look of utterly blissful astonishment, she knew any attempt he might make to leave with the other guests would be but a social gesture.

'Jesus – I really should go,' he said yet again, looking at his watch at around one o'clock. 'I can't stay here all night.'

'Who asked you?' Meredith smiled.

'I didn't mean that, Merry,' Ken replied, looking for Ken almost embarrassed.

'Neither did I,' said Merry, putting her hand momentarily on his.

They sat and talked for a while longer, and while he kept making leaving sounds every so often, Meredith noticed how more and more half-hearted they were becoming. Slowly but surely she brought the conversation round to the subject of Ken's wife Harriet. Meredith had heard on the grapevine, mostly from Polly, that things were not too good between Ken and Harriet, and that they were spending more and more time apart. And precisely why. Meredith was genuinely sorry when she first heard it; she liked both the partners of the marriage, and their union had seemed one of the more durable ones in a business where five years was a good run.

'So what exactly has been the trouble?' Meredith asked when the subject had been finally broached. 'I'd always looked upon you two as my banker bets in an otherwise impossible race card.'

452

'Why should I bother you with it?' Ken asked, draining his wine glass. 'This is something we all go through in this business, in one form or other. So why the hell should I dump on you?'

'Because I'm very fond of you, Ken,' Meredith told him. 'I always have been. We're comrades in arms. We've been over the top together.'

Ken smiled at her, but then got up and pretended to be interested in her bookcase.

'I know what this is about, Meredith,' he said after a while of silence. 'I get this sort of play a lot.'

'Yes?' Meredith asked him, not at all wrong-footed.

'Trouble is I don't usually get it from somebody so bloody attractive,' he replied.

Ken took off his glasses and, holding them away from him, stared through them up at the ceiling. Then he put them back on and came back over to sit in the armchair opposite where Meredith was sitting on the floor.

'This isn't about anything, Ken,' Meredith said. 'This isn't about anything other than asking you here to dinner this evening. Because I wanted to see you again.'

'It's no good,' Ken replied, looking suddenly and immensely sad. 'It isn't any good.'

Meredith looked at him wonderingly, her brow furrowed, her eyes searching his face. She knew what wasn't any good. She knew because she'd heard it from Polly, who'd heard it from one of Harriet's best friends. But the last thing she wanted Ken to know was that she knew what he meant.

Ken sat in silence, looking at his feet.

'It doesn't matter,' he said finally, shaking his head sadly. 'There's nothing you can do about it. So – you know. Forget it.'

He got up, and smiled at her, but not with his eyes. His eyes showed nothing but despair.

'You really don't want to talk about it?' Meredith asked him once more. 'You'd be surprised how much it helps.'

'You're great, Merry,' he told her. 'And what I said

earlier – about this being . . . you know. This doesn't make any difference, straight up. About David's chances.'

'Oh, forget David,' Meredith sighed. 'You're the one I'm worried about.'

'Well, don't,' Ken said, about to take his leave. 'Because I'm telling you, there's nothing you can do.'

'No,' Meredith agreed, putting herself between him and the door. 'Maybe there's nothing I can do. Or rather maybe there's nothing you think I can do to help. But there is. If it's something physical. Or mental. You know – a block. Or if it's a combination of both, as a matter of fact there is something I can do.'

And there was. She could take him to Annie's, which was precisely what she did. After Ken had sat back down and poured a little of his heart out to her, she put her arm round him, kissed him on the cheek, and then called Annie.

'I have a new friend for you,' she said to Annie, once she and Ken had arrived at the opulent house in Holland Park. 'I was forever hearing from Louis and Baz, and I have to say also from Max, about your famous Lucille. And I really think she can help on this one.'

By now Ken was quite obviously having second thoughts as he stood in the chandeliered hall, his car coat still folded over his arm as if he was waiting for a train. He was staring upwards at nothing in particular, nervously chewing the inside of his lip. By him, waiting to take his coat should he choose to stay, stood an impeccably attired, albeit extremely short-skirted, French maid.

'Céline?' Madame called the maid's attention. 'Be so good as to take Monsieur's coat and show him through to the drawing-room. And then go and fetch Miss Lucille.'

The maid bobbed and moved to take Ken's coat.

'Look,' he started rather uncertainly, then looking to Meredith, 'I'm not absolutely sure about this.'

Meredith smiled back at him reassuringly, but knew better than to take Madame's limelight. This was Annie's show, not her's.

454

'No, no,' said Madame, coming forward and taking Ken's arm. 'You must not concern yourself, my dear young man. We shall take especial care of you. Rest assured, Lucille is the tenderest of creatures. The most understanding and sympathetic young lady.'

Ken hesitated, and then handed his coat to the maid, who smiled blazingly at him, opened the door to another room and stood aside. And before he had time to express any more doubts which might have lingered in his mind, Annie tightened her grip on his arm and swept him away and out of Meredith's sight.

David Terry duly read for the director, Alun Turk, on Monday morning. Turk asked him to wait before disappearing into the next-door office. After a delay of about quarter of an hour, Terry was called through, to meet Ken Condon. He was asked to read once again for both men's benefit, one long speech from the last scene of the play, to which the producer and director paid grave and silent attention. Then they both thanked him formally before releasing him to go home.

'I haven't a bat's,' he informed Meredith as soon as he arrived at the agency.

'Like a bet?' Meredith enquired.

She was arranging a huge bunch of flowers which had just arrived for her. The card lay as yet unopened on her desk.

'You're on,' Terry said, picking the card up. 'Dinner of your choice at the place of your choice at the time of your choice.'

'OK,' Meredith agreed, taking the card back from him. 'I don't know what dish I'll choose, but the Connaught is the venue, and tonight's the night.'

'You're kidding?' Terry asked, his mouth falling open.

'They rang ten minutes before you got here.'

'I got it over Tom Kenny?'

'That's what the man said.'

'Friggin' Ada.'

455

Meredith sighed, but this time didn't bother to correct him. After all, to play Rick the actor was going to have to polish up his cockney. So she just smiled to herself as she put the finishing touches to the arrangement of her flowers.

'Jesus.' David Terry sank into one of Meredith's new deep armchairs, and slowly draped one long leg over an arm. 'I really got it over Tom Kenny?' he asked her once more.

'They didn't even mention Tom, darling,' Meredith replied. 'Ken and the director both think you're something else altogether.'

'Right!' the actor announced suddenly. 'This we most certainly do celebrate, doll! The Connaught, you said! And okey-dokey, the Connaught it shall be!'

He swung himself back up on his feet, and grabbing hold of Meredith hugged her tightly.

'Christ,' he said. 'I don't know how I've kept my hands off you for so long.'

'Maybe it's because you know if you don't, you'll get them smacked,' Meredith answered coolly, while hating what his embrace was doing to her.

'You are just the greatest, Meredith bleedin' Browne!' Terry exclaimed. 'I'll never ever doubt you again never!'

Then he let go of her and frowned. Meredith knew the move. She'd played the scene quite a few times before herself.

'Except I can't do tonight,' the actor said. 'I've suddenly remembered. I got to see my mum.'

'That's all right, darling,' Meredith replied. 'Any evening will do.'

The actor smiled and hugged Meredith again, suggesting the following evening. Meredith agreed and allowed him to kiss her before he rushed away. Then she sat at her desk and opened the card that had arrived with the flowers.

It was from Ken Condon. And it simply thanked her.

456

From the bottom of his heart. And the thanks were not for David Terry. They were for Lucille.

By the time *Split* was screened, to enormous controversy and sensation, William and Jay were on their knees. The day the play was transmitted, their eighth episode of *Blue Heaven* also went out with their names on it and including twenty pages of producer's rewrites. They were now working under a man called Persse West, whose caricatured image had finally even managed to oust that of Peregrine ffrench off the writers' dartboard.

'Why does he spell his name in that fancy fashion?' William had demanded, when the nature of the beast was fast becoming apparent. 'A Percy is a Percy is a Percy.'

'You were fooled,' Jay sighed, throwing a dart at the image before her. 'You believed all that smarm. All that "trust-me" spiel.'

'So did you!' William retorted angrily. 'It was actually you who said "this is the first producer we've been able to trust" for Chrissake!'

'That was because he had a glass eye,' Jay explained. 'I felt sorry for him.'

'I don't think he lost that eye fencing,' William said. 'I think some pissed-off writer poked the goddam thing out with his pen!'

It really seemed to them both that their luck had run out. Even though they had strongly resisted and resented being made to work on somebody else's show, they had finally knuckled down and done their best to do their best. And the results, in their own consideration, weren't bad at all.

Persse West had seemingly agreed with them. True enough, he had made them jump through every hoop of their contract, making them produce three drafts of every episode they wrote, which was allowed for in their contract. And then after they had laboured for days over the final and third draft he would invariably return in preference to their first. But no matter, for he had seemed very

457

keen on their work, and had encouraged them by telling them how much they were improving the standard of what up until then had been a rather shabby and dull little show. In fact both William and Jay had been so impressed by their new producer's apparent diligence, they had been moved to make him a little speech, thanking him for his thoughtfulness and support.

His encouragement had been very necessary, too, because William's confidence was all but gone, and Jay was beginning to suffer from an undue fatigue. In fact, by the time they had finished writing the first batch of thirteen programmes, William had been so worried by Jay's white-washed appearance he had taken her away at once for a fortnight in the south of Italy. The warmth of the Mediterranean and the peace of the little village in which they stayed brought the colour back to Jay's cheeks, and the trials and tribulations they had been through in the previous months faded into a hazy oblivion, helped there by plenty of wine and pasta.

It didn't take long for the good of their holiday to be undone, however, because shortly after their return *Blue Heaven* started its transmission, and William and Jay watched the first episode with a feeling of fast-mounting horror.

'We can't blame Craig Matheson for the changes this time!' William yelled, reaching for the telephone. 'Because the bastard isn't in it!'

'So what's been going on?' Jay asked, deeply upset. 'There's hardly anything we wrote left!'

William looked at her helplessly, waiting for the now ringing telephone to be answered.

'Don't ask me, sweetheart!' he replied. 'All I know is they accepted our final draft—'

'Did they though?' Jay interrupted. 'I mean they may have taken us to three drafts, and gone back to the first. But have we had final payment? Because if we haven't, that means they haven't necessarily accepted it.'

'Of course they've accepted it!' William shouted back at

her after a moment of thought. 'I mean we've written thirteen goddam episodes!'

'That doesn't mean they've actually accepted them,' Jay argued. 'Not unless we're fully paid up.'

William put the unanswered telephone back down, and stared at Jay.

'Of course we're fully paid up,' he said, but without any real conviction.

They rang the producer again in the morning, after they had read some appalling newspaper reviews for what was meant to be their work. By lunchtime he still hadn't returned their call.

William then rang Eric, the young man Max had left in charge of the agency, and instructed him to ring West and find out what had happened.

'Oh and while you're at it,' William added as an afterthought, 'look up to see if we've been paid acceptance, will you, buddy?'

Eric rang them back at teatime to say that West hadn't returned his call either, and no, they hadn't been paid acceptance.

'On any?' William asked. 'Or on all?'

'You haven't been paid acceptance on any of the thirteen, William,' Eric, the most assiduous of young men, informed him.

'What does that mean?' William enquired. 'Besides the fact that we're short?'

'I think that means,' Eric told him, 'they're free to alter and rewrite. For instance I think that would explain last night's freely rewritten first episode.'

William slammed down the phone.

Finally, after three days of waiting for their calls to be answered, William and Jay stormed into City Television and marched straight up to Persse West's office. Naomi, his large and slothful upper-crust secretary, made a half-hearted attempt to stop them going into her boss's office, but William and Jay ignored her remonstrances and burst into the middle of a production meeting.

Persse, in a neat blue blazer and open-necked shirt, was sitting at his desk working on one of William and Jay's scripts with the director. He looked up as the two writers burst in and stared at them coldly with his one good eye. Gone was the warmth, the plausibility, the trust, the friendship. What was now staring at them across a desk was the eye of an assassin.

'Yes?' he asked. 'I'd like an explanation for this, please.'

'Is that so?' William replied. 'Well, we'd like a bit of explaining too.'

'Naomi?' Persse interrupted, calling past William through the open door.

William slammed the door shut and leaned on it.

'We won't be needing Naomi,' William said. 'What we need are some answers. Why haven't you returned our calls?'

'It might not occur to you, William,' Persse answered, 'in fact I'm sure it hasn't occurred to you because you're a writer. And writers seem unable to think of anything or anybody besides themselves.'

'It would have taken five minutes of your time, you bastard!' Jay said through gritted teeth.

Persse stared at her with blank amazement, then turned his attention back to William.

'I was going to ring you back, William,' he continued, 'when I had a moment. I wouldn't have thought it was anything that couldn't wait.'

'Oh, really?' William said, moving ominously towards him.

Jay grabbed William's sleeve, and did her half-hearted best to hold him back.

'Well, I'm very much afraid you're wrong, you son of a bitch,' William continued very quietly. 'You see we want to know what in hell happened to the script we wrote for the opening show, and which you accepted—'

Persse shook his head and held up a hand.

'I never accepted any final script for the first show,' he

replied. 'In fact I never accepted final drafts on any of the episodes.'

'Yes, you did, you bastard,' William told him, still in an ominous monotone. 'You said, fine. Yes, it's great, but I think we'll go back to the first draft after all.'

'Because I wasn't happy with the rewrites, William,' Persse said, frowning at him as if William was a child. 'If I'd been happy with the third draft, I wouldn't have had to go back and start again. Would I?'

William reminded the producer that he had said nothing about 'starting again'. All he had said was that he thought the first draft was better. With which Persse agreed. He had thought the first draft was better than the third, but that didn't mean he accepted it as a finished script. William turned and looked astounded at Jay, who had gone ash-grey. Then he turned back to the producer and leaned his clenched fists on the edge of his desk.

'Are you trying to tell us you haven't accepted any of our episodes "finally"?' he asked.

'Yes,' the producer agreed. 'That's about the size of it.'

'Why didn't you tell us?' Jay enjoined.

'Because I didn't have to,' Persse continued, now with a slightly supercilious smile. 'If you can't deliver the goods—'

'But we did deliver the goods!' It was now Jay's turn to lose her temper. 'We delivered the sodding goods each and every week, and every time you ordered yet another rewrite, we delivered the sodding goods!'

'You weren't available to make any further changes,' Persse informed her coldly. 'And if you're not available —'

'Of course we were available!' Jay yelled. 'We were right there! Sitting at our bloody typewriter! Rewriting every rewrite you bloody ordered!'

'You weren't available for any final rewrites,' Persse insisted. 'And it says quite clearly in your contract—'

'You can take our contract, sunshine,' William cut across. 'And you can stuff it up your ass! We weren't so-called "available" because we were writing the goddam

461

show as it was being recorded! You know that! We hadn't even the time to come into rehearsals!'

'Exactly,' Persse West agreed. 'And I'm afraid if you can't even make time to come into rehearsals, then you really can't be all that surprised if we have to make one or two changes.'

'One or two?' Jay screamed, now practically hysterical. 'You sod – you hardly left one bloody word of what we wrote!'

'That was because, my dear Jay,' Persse said, turning his good eye on her, 'in my opinion there was hardly one word worth keeping.'

William suddenly lunged across the desk and grabbed the producer by his white throat.

'I'd just love to bust you right on your ugly nose,' he hissed at him. 'But the trouble is, knowing you, you'd most likely get off on it.'

William eyeballed the one-eyed and now white-faced producer for a couple of seemingly endless seconds, before dumping him back down in his leather swivel chair. Then he took the trembling Jay by the hand and turned for the door.

Which was opened for them by the director, who hadn't said a word throughout, but who now stood on the threshold of the office, his face glistening with sweat like a boxer after a prize fight.

'I'm really sorry, William,' he whispered. 'You know how much I love both of your work. Really.'

In the following Wednesday's popular newspapers it was reported that one of the latest and hottest tips to play Leslie Unwin's famous spy hero Charles Crown in the first of what was hoped to be a series of spectacular film thrillers was the present toast of the town, David Terry.

12

'I'm a bit worried about you,' William said.

'I'm a bit worried about me, too,' Jay replied.

She was lying in their big bed upstairs in the studio gallery, quite unable to get up and get on with the day, which was totally unlike Jay. She'd been feeling wretched now for some months, but as long as they'd been busy working, she'd pulled herself together and knuckled down. And once she was lost in the mystery of her work, she forgot about her lethargy, and the mysteriously fleeting pains in her muscles and joints, and the loss of all her regular appetites. 'Doctor Writing' was a cure-all, but only as long as Jay actually was writing. As soon as she stopped, once their day's joint stint was over, all Jay wanted to do then was to get into bed and sleep.

'So what did the doc say this time?' William asked, knowing the answer already.

'The same as he did before,' Jay replied. 'That I'm simply over-tired. That I've just been over-doing it.'

'Bullshit,' William said, taking down Jay's much thumbed *Dictionary of Symptoms*.

'You won't find it in there,' Jay sighed. 'Well, at least you will, because the way I feel I seem to have everything from achondroplasia to zoonosis.'

'What are your symptoms exactly?' William enquired.

'Headache, nausea, exhaustion, worry,' Jay grinned. 'The classic writer's complaint.'

'Otherwise known as the Peregrine-ffrench syndrome,' William replied, leafing through the paperback.

'You're really not going to find anything in there,

William,' Jay repeated. 'Only things that will frighten you.'

William closed the book and looked down at Jay. Her eyes were deeply shadowed and she was desperately pale. And William was desperately worried.

'I think you should see a specialist,' he told her, sitting on the bed and taking hold of one of her hands. 'I was reading in one of the medical columns that a lot of these – what shall we say? These somewhat undefined illnesses, they're viral infections. Which they can now identify.'

'And what can they do about them?' Jay asked.

'That I can't answer,' William replied. 'That I guess is for an expert to say.'

The expert's verdict, after running a series of fairly intensive tests, was that indeed Jay was suffering from a virus: most possibly one picked up abroad, commonly known as a harbour virus, usually contracted by eating contaminated seafood. There was no cause for any concern, the specialist told Jay, although she would have to put herself on the easy list while she just sat out the course of the viral infection.

Jay enquired as to whether or not she could continue working, and when in answer to the specialist's questioning she described her workload, he told her most certainly not, at least not at that level of activity. The only cure for what she was suffering from was bed rest, and plenty of it.

William took the news philosophically, telling Jay it would have been a serious setback had they been working on another series of *Charlie*, or a new series of their own. But after the way they had been treated on *Blue Heaven*, there was no problem. He would simply write the series on his own to the worst of his ability, and then let Persse West ruin it even more. His only concession to what had happened on the last run of the show was to insist that his and Jay's names were removed from any forthcoming credits.

So Jay took to her bed, while William worked directly

below on the next series of scripts. Every now and then when Jay was feeling a little brighter, she would tiptoe downstairs and look over William's shoulder, at which William would pretend to be angry. But he never sent her back to her bed immediately. They usually had a cup of tea and a working chat before Jay was despatched back up to the gallery. William knew as well as Jay that were she to be cut off from her work entirely she might never get better.

Even when the work was as dispiriting as the work William was having to do on *Blue Heaven*.

'I don't know why I bother!' William stormed one night when he returned from watching a programme being recorded. 'So OK – they approximate what I've written, but I've gotten used to that! But now the goddam actors are *all* approximating! And as for the so-called star! He's given up approximating altogether and just simply mugs his way through the show!'

William collapsed on the sofa with a full bottle of vodka in one hand and a large glass tumbler in the other. For the next three hours he talked and drank, before finally falling into a deep sleep.

Jay knew better than to try and get him to come up to bed when he was in this state, so she simply removed the empty glass, which was still in his hand, and made him comfortable under a rug. After that she returned to bed, but not to sleep. Because, although she was exhausted and covered in aches and pains, she was too worried about William to settle down for the night.

It wasn't his drinking which concerned her. It was why he was drinking. She now knew William far too well to think that he would ever become a hardened alcoholic. It just wasn't in his character. He was so austere by nature, so self-disciplined, so puritanical. Which was why his heavy drinking was causing Jay so much alarm. William was drinking because he was unhappy, and he was unhappy because of the work he was being forced to do, and Jay knew that no writer as good as William should be working under those conditions.

Besides which, William wasn't the sort of writer who could function on alcohol. Some could. Some could tank up for the morning, work two or three hours, sleep, tank up for the evening and then work into the night without it apparently limiting their output. Or so these writers claimed. Jay knew that some of them were telling no lies. One of such a number, an Irishman who happened to be a great friend of William's, used to spend all his day in the pub, and then come home and work from midnight until six in the morning. And the proof of his particular pudding was that he had two plays on in the West End of London, and another smash-hit on Broadway. It used to boggle William's mind how his friend did it, because one glass of wine at lunch, that was the end of him for the afternoon.

Yet now he was working on half a bottle of vodka before lunch, and half a bottle before six o'clock in the evening, when he would start his serious drinking. Jay was convinced that once he had finished working on *Blue Heaven*, he would come off the juice. What was worrying her more was that William was fast losing his self-confidence. And once that had gone, even if he came off both the bottle and *Blue Heaven*, the experience might have scarred him as a writer for ever.

He might even get the dreaded writer's block.

'Never!' William laughed whenever it was mentioned. 'Jesus, Jay – there's no such thing as writer's block! You either can do it, or you can't! And when these guys say they have writers' block, all it means is that they have nothing to damn well write about any more!'

Watching the process of William's disintegration rapidly accelerate, Jay decided that she had to do something. It was no good nagging William, that she also knew. Being a Piscean, whenever he was given direct advice, he simply swam down into the depths of the pond and stayed there until the storm had blown over. Fishes were difficult. They had to be approached quietly and carefully. One splash and they were gone.

Jay thought she'd found the answer when she unearthed a stage play she and William had started, then had been forced to put to one side once the heat was on with *Charlie*. It was a project they had both been very keen on, and the first act, which was as far as they had got, had worked out very well.

She dropped it in William's lap as he was mixing his first Martini of the evening, suggesting he might like to start working on it again.

'Why?' William wondered, dropping three olives to the bottom of his glass.

'Because I don't think working on just *Blue Heaven* is doing your head any good, Bonzo,' Jay replied. 'This is a bloody good play. You were getting quite steamed up about it.'

William turned the playscript over in his hand but didn't open it up.

'I'd rather leave it until you're better,' he said.

'Rubbish,' Jay retorted. 'You were more or less doing it on your jack anyway, if you remember. While I was working on something else. I read it through this afternoon, and it ain't half good, chum.'

And that was where Jay left it. She knew better than to press William any further. Fish either took the bait or they didn't. Any experienced angler could tell you that.

And sure enough, William finally bit. It took time, but time was all it took. The play lay around for a few days unopened, and then early one morning Jay was awakened from a deep sleep by the sound of furious typing. She crawled to the end of the bed and looked over the gallery rail. Below her she saw William working at the white desk, with just a pot of coffee beside him. There was no sign of the vodka bottle.

Jay smiled to herself and crawled quietly back into bed, where she fell instantly back into a blissful sleep, which lasted well into the afternoon.

She was woken by the sound of something she hadn't heard in months. William was singing. He had a lovely

467

light baritone voice, and he was working his way quietly and happily through George Gershwin's 'Love Is Here To Stay'. Halfway through the second verse he turned and noticed Jay, and sang the rest of it directly up to her, as she knelt on the end of the bed, with her chin on the rail.

'OK, kid?' he asked at the end of the song. 'Fancy a cup of tea?'

'Not as much as I fancy you,' Jay replied.

'How about that!' William laughed, switching on the kettle. 'Guess who must be feeling better!'

They made love while the kettle boiled, and William was quite his old self.

'My God,' he said, rolling over on to his back. 'I'd almost forgotten what it was like.'

'Well, it has been nearly half a century since we last did it,' Jay teased.

William turned his face to her, suddenly very serious.

'Why didn't you say something, Jay?' he asked her. 'Why didn't you stop me from nearly killing myself?'

'Christ, William!' Jay laughed. 'It's bad enough trying to get you to go to the hairdresser!'

'Needing your hair cut,' William replied, 'is a long way from ruining your liver.'

'Not to you, William Kennedy,' Jay said. 'You're a man who makes his own decisions. You're the cat who walks alone.'

For the next two weeks the studio was a different place. Except for Jay's health, life was back to normal, and even Jay's illness seemed to be on the retreat. William had bought her a case of Tokay wine, whose curative powers he had learned from an aunt in New York, and which he now administered to her in carefully measured doses as if it were medicine.

She didn't ask to see the play as it was going along. And William didn't volunteer any information. He just quietly got on with it, working on the scripts of *Blue Heaven* in the morning, which, as he told Jay, he now found as easy as falling off the proverbial log, and then on the play all afternoon and often well into the evening. He had even stopped being angry with Persse West, and now just laughed at him instead, mocking the producer's inept attempts to 'improve' his work, with the result that Persse West, unable to derive the satisfaction he had enjoyed previously from persecuting him, left William alone, and best of all finally started to use episodes of William's almost in their entirety.

The irony was the show improved greatly, and even started to move up in the ratings, but fortunately for Jay's health and William's strength, City Television's executives for once made a right decision and declined to order up yet another series. Most happily of all, William actually got paid completion on all of the final thirteen episodes.

Then one morning Jay woke up very late, and realized that something was different. As always, it took her a while to come to her senses, which was one of the side effects of her viral infection. But once she was fully awake, she realized what it was. The studio was silent.

With an effort she hauled herself out of bed and pulled on her dressing gown. She'd had a very bad night, kept awake for half of it by the terrible pains in her arms. William had mixed her some painkillers, but they had little effect, and Jay had lain awake practically until dawn had broken before drifting back to sleep.

Looking over the balcony she saw the studio was empty. On the white desk below the typewriter stood under its dust cover, a pile of paper neatly stacked by its side. Doing up her robe, Jay made her way downstairs as fast as she could, calling for William as she went. But there was no reply.

The pile of typed sheets on the desk was the play, and, looking to the end sheet, Jay saw it was the play in its entirety. William had finished it. Biting her lip, Jay wondered if she dared, and then, unable to resist the temptation, she removed the title page in order to start reading. But instead of Act One Scene One, she found instead a short typed note from the author. It read:

OK, nosey, if you've got this far, who am I to stop you? Go on, take it back upstairs to bed with your coffee and croissant, and for Chrissake – enjoy! You better, or I won't come home from the dentist! (Bet you forgot!) I love you. W.

Jay didn't go back to bed. She started to read the play standing up, and didn't sit down until she had reached the end of the first act. She didn't even fetch herself a coffee. She simply read it from start to finish in one unbroken session.

And then when she had finished it, she sat back. William was back. William was there. William was himself again.

But most of all what Jay felt was relief. William would in the end be all right. Now she was sure that William would be able to manage without her.

It took William a long time to agree. At first he simply would not hear of it, and came dangerously close to losing his temper with her. But Jay was every bit as stubborn as he, and stuck to her guns. William threatened her, and Jay opened her eyes wide back at him and asked him how he could be so cruel to a sick woman. To which William, tapping his own skull, said that was the only bit of Jay Burrell which was sick. Why was she insisting on such a damn fool thing?

'Because,' Jay coolly informed him, 'I had nothing to do with it.'

'You had everything to do with it, goddammit Jay!' William retorted. 'I'd have never even thought of doing it if it hadn't been for you!'

'Of course you would,' Jay sighed. 'You'd have got there in your own time. You always do.'

'The answer's still no,' William informed her.

'In that case, Mr Kennedy,' Jay replied, 'I shall never work with you again. Now there's a promise.'

Jay finally had to steal the play when William wasn't

470

looking and hide it before he would agree to her demands. Luckily he hadn't yet taken a copy, so she held the nap hand. William held out for the best part of a week, hoping that Jay would be the first to crack. But she wasn't, and it wasn't until William finally promised cross-his-heart-and-hope-to-die that it would be his name as author and his name only that he finally got the play back. His play.

It was accepted by the management of William, Jay and Eric's choice at once, and was in rehearsal within a month. William was more than a little sideswiped by the speed with which everything was happening, but Jay just smiled at him from her bed and reminded him that she had told him the play was brilliant.

'They're not even going to tour it,' William came back with the news one day. 'It's going straight into The Criterion.'

'Where I bet it'll stay for at least a couple of years,' Jay told him. 'Maybe longer. It's funny, and it's sexy, and it's sharp.'

'I still think you should have your name on it,' William said, pouring her a lunchtime measure of Tokay.

'Up yours, Kennedy,' Jay grinned, raising her glass. 'You know I didn't write one word of it.'

'We're a team, kiddo,' William reminded her.

'We're a doubles,' Jay replied. 'And being a tennis freak, you should know that in the majority of cases, the players also compete successfully in singles.'

'OK,' William said, toasting her health in mineral water. 'But the next one's on you.'

'That, as they say in France, Mr Kennedy,' Jay answered, picking up the newspaper, 'is *au choix*. And guess who's finally been chosen to play Charles Crown?'

By now David Terry was almost getting used to the sweet smell of success. It seemed he only needed to be pointed in a new direction and he was off and flying. The notices he had got for *Split* following so closely on his nationally popular performance as Charlie ensured that his was the name on the lips of everyone that mattered. So much so that when Meredith introduced him as a runner in the Who Will Play Charles Crown stakes, the opposition just seemed to melt away. Several of the popular papers ran polls, asking their readers to vote for the Charles Crown of their choice from the shortlist of six nominees, and in all David Terry won by a handsome margin. So by the time it came for the actor to be screentested, it seemed to be all over bar the shouting.

Danny Schwartz and Curly Cale, the film's two producers, were not so easily influenced. They called Terry back for another test, and then went completely to ground. All Meredith's calls were unreturned and, from looking an odds-on certainty, her client's odds started to lengthen ominously. Word was out that Schwartz and Cale wanted the oddball and hell-raising Irishman Jack Duggan to play the part, and that they were already negotiating with his agent.

'That is just plain *ridiculous*!' David Terry ranted down the phone at Meredith. 'Charles Crown is meant to be true blue English! They can't cast some drunken Mick!'

'It's just to bring your price down,' Meredith told him. 'And it's a very old ploy. I used to watch Baz and Louis work this one all the time. It's to make us think you're second-best, so that if and when they do offer you the part – which they will, darling, never fear – it's so that when they finally come to us we'll be grateful and contrite and they'll get you cheap. That's also why they're not returning my calls.'

'So what are you going to do, doll?' Terry asked her, the exasperation barely out of his voice.

'Well, I'm certainly not going to go round and unzip their trousers, if that's what you're hoping, sweetie,' Meredith replied. 'What I'm going to do is stay cool, and I advise you to do the same. Don't talk to the Press, and don't even kvetch to your mates. One word that you're anxious, and you'll halve the price I have in mind, and don't forget, you're taking me to William Kennedy's first night this evening.'

When they arrived at The Criterion, Meredith was careful to let David Terry step out of the limousine first, just as careful as she had been when selecting what to wear for the evening. She had finally chosen a long and sculpted black dress with a single glittering silver sash cut across the bosom, worn under a stunning white mink which she had hired especially. It was an outfit designed to complement her partner, rather than to steal his thunder. Terry, for his part, was in a perfectly tailored midnight-blue silk tuxedo, and a fashionably frilled red evening shirt. Even before he had got out of the limo the screams had started, and the volume of them quite startled Meredith who had only been expecting a handful of hysterical Terry 'fans'. After all, that was all she had paid for.

Yet when she followed the actor out of the car and into the blaze of popping flashlights, Meredith saw that there was quite genuine David Terry hysteria. The police were doing their best to hold the crowd back, but they had obviously been just as surprised by the reaction to Terry's arrival as his agent was. Several girls broke through the cordon to try and grab the actor, and one of them, having managed to reach up and kiss him, ripped his bow tie from his neck and ran off with it. Four policemen quickly grabbed Terry and hustled him into the foyer, nearly knocking Meredith to the ground in the process.

Cale and Schwartz were standing just inside the theatre doors and witnessed the whole thing. Meredith, holding in her hand one of her evening shoes which had been knocked off in the mêlée, smiled to herself as she fitted her shoe back on and thought she couldn't have stage-managed it better. As she straightened up, she saw Shirley Paul, the producers' assistant, heading towards them, so she quickly grabbed David Terry's arm and steered him off in quite the opposite direction to meet somebody from television, a medium which was no longer of the slightest interest to either of them.

473

When the final bell rang to warn the audience the curtain was about to rise, Meredith held Terry back and ordered him to get her another drink.

'If I do that we'll be late,' he complained.

'Exactly, darling,' Meredith replied. 'Now go and get me an orange juice.'

Meredith was a complete expert by now in the field of when to move in, and by the time she swept down the aisle on David Terry's arm to take her carefully chosen third-row seat, she could sense every head turning, and feel the audience almost wanting to applaud. On their progress down the aisle, Meredith stopped and talked briefly to several of the right people, and blew discreet kisses to those sitting too far away to benefit from a more direct greeting. William, who was watching their entrance with Jay from the discreet half-darkness of their stage box, leaned over to his partner and said they were stitched.

'Believe me,' he sighed, 'after that, World War Three would be an anti-climax.'

Jay laughed, kissed William on the cheek, then waved back to Meredith who had blown them her final kiss before taking her seat. This led most of the assembled company to stare up at their box to see whom it contained. William responded by leaning out and bestowing upon the audience a most royal wave.

Two hours later the audience was on its feet applauding William. The play had been a sensation.

At the party afterwards at the Savoy, every pretty woman there it seemed wanted to dance with William. But he declined them all and spent the evening sitting it out with Jay who, although quite well enough to attend the première, was still a little too weak for what she called a knees-up. Jay kept pressing William to accept some of the invitations he was receiving to dance, but he told her he was much happier to sit with her and talk over the excitement of the night. However, he did finally weaken when Meredith came across to their table and asked Jay if she could pinch him for a quick one, and Jay, laughing

474

delightedly, agreed as long as Meredith didn't bring him back pregnant.

William left Jay talking happily to the critic of *Punch*, who she had discovered was an old friend of her erstwhile publisher, and led Meredith out on to the dance floor.

'Brilliant, darling!' she shouted above the music as William led her quite deliberately into an old-fashioned foxtrot while everyone else around them was freaking out. 'It's the best, and the sharpest, and the wittiest comedy I have seen in years!'

Meredith kissed him on the cheek, and William thanked her, steering her effortlessly through the pack of swirling bodies.

'And now you can congratulate me as well!' she continued. 'Curly Cale's just told me David's finally been cast!'

William was delighted and told her so, kissing her in return congratulations.

'So now what?' he asked.

'If you mean what now,' Meredith smiled, reaching up to whisper in William's ear.

'I don't know what you mean,' William replied poker-faced, in answer to her whispered innuendo.

'I'll show you if you like,' Meredith laughed.

'No, thanks,' William replied. 'I'm saving it till I get married.'

They danced some more, and then Meredith steered William to the champagne bar, where it was a little quieter.

'Yes,' she continued, picking up the subject again. 'That's what I'd really like to do. But of course I won't.'

'No, you won't,' William agreed. 'You wouldn't be such a goddam fool.'

The barman handed them their champagne and as he did William caught sight in the corner of his eye of David Terry on the dance floor, smooching with a very tall and very delectable blonde in red.

'Who's that David's dancing with?' he enquired.

'Oh, Christ,' Meredith sighed, 'how should I know? Who's David Terry not been dancing with would be an easier one to answer.'

'Oh, I know who it is, of course,' William nodded. 'Of course, that's Suzanne Altman.'

Early the next morning, when William and Jay were lying in their bed reading the universally good reviews for William's play, Meredith was on the telephone to Polly Stephens, who like most working actresses did not take kindly to being woken so early.

'Can't it keep?' she complained to Meredith, casting one bleary eye to her alarm clock, 'I didn't get to bed until after two.'

'Neither did I,' Meredith replied, 'and no, it can't wait. Meet me outside the front of Harrods at quarter to one.'

Meredith deliberately chose a lunch venue where the ears in the walls did not belong to the business. She had her suspicions, and if Polly went any way to confirming them, she didn't want any spies running backstage and reporting the look on Meredith's face.

'You're right,' Polly admitted, with a face full of chicken pie. 'Walter Ford are wooing him, but it's only what I heard, Merry, you know?'

'There's more truth in rumours than in statistics, darling,' Meredith replied. 'Someone told me he'd been seen with the Altman woman last week at Michael Knight's costume thrash.'

'Who is this bird anyway?' Polly enquired, in between refilling her face.

'Suzanne Altman?' Meredith frowned. 'I thought you knew all the top brass?'

'She's new to me,' Polly admitted.

'Fair enough, because she has only been here a few months,' replied Meredith. 'She's Walter Ford, London.'

Polly stopped eating for a moment, and looked up.

'Ah,' she said. 'Gotcha.'

Meredith pushed her own lunch aside, and lit another

476

cigarette. She had no real appetite; hadn't had one for some days now. Ever since she had first heard the rumours.

'Course the Charles Crown contract's worth a small fortune, I suppose,' Polly continued. 'The agent's whack, I mean. Particularly if they film all the bleeding books. I mean that could be a lot of dosh, right? That could run into real money.'

Meredith nodded. Polly was right. David Terry's film contract was going to be worth a fortune in commission, besides the prestige it would bring Meredith Browne Ltd for being the handling agent.

'Still,' Polly went on, 'you don't have to worry, do you, Merry? 'Cos you got him well tied up, ain't you?'

'Sorry, darling?' Meredith asked, coming out of a momentary reverie. 'What was that you said?'

'I said you don't have to worry, old love,' Polly replied. ''Cos you signed the bugger up.'

'Listen, darling,' Meredith said after a moment, switching tack. 'I want you to put your famous ear to the ground, sweetheart, and find out exactly how hard these rumours are. And I want you to do it now.'

'Yeah?' Polly grinned. 'And what's it going to do for me?'

'It's going to get you that rise in salary for your new telly series, darling,' Meredith answered her, stubbing out her cigarette. 'That's what it's going to do for you.'

'Tell me something, Merry,' Polly asked her as they were descending in the empty lift. 'Is there more to this than meets the eye? Know what I mean? With you and David?'

'David Terry means sweet eff all to me personally, darling,' Meredith replied. 'But he means practically everything to Meredith Browne Ltd.'

Back at the office, Meredith instructed her new assistant Carly Michael to take all her calls for the next hour, while she closeted herself in her inner sanctum, trying to work out a game plan.

She knew if what the rumours were all hinting came true, there was absolutely nothing she could do about it. If her hand-made protégé decided to leave her in order to be represented by one of the most powerful entertainment agencies in the world, she was helpless, because Polly Stephens was wrong. She had not got her client well tied up, because she had made a crucial error, and one that would have had Louis mocking at her from behind the famous lions on his desk. She'd followed the current fashion. If an actor's unhappy, who wants him? That's what all the younger agents said, so why sign him when representing him would be a pain anyway? Meredith hadn't signed David Terry for that reason. Besides, she'd been cocky enough to think that the bastard was so dependent on her he would no more leave her than he'd have bought his mother the much-promised house, poor bitch. And one more thing – Terry had a deep mistrust of putting his cross on the bottom of any contract. It'd taken her long enough to get him to put his money in a bank. Poor habits died hard; he'd have put it all under his bed if he'd had his way. But as Louis always said, there was no such thing as a 'simple man'; now all Meredith had between keeping and losing the most valuable client she was ever likely to represent was a verbal agreement, and that was about as valuable to her as the proverbial good notice in *The Stage*.

No, if David Terry was seduced by the overtures Suzanne Altman was quite obviously being well paid to make to him, then there was only one strike left to her. A strike which would entail another seduction of David Terry, but this time by Meredith. And funnily enough, it was something Polly had said that triggered the idea off in Meredith's mind.

By the time she got the actor on the phone, Meredith had quite conquered the attack of almost hysterical laughter which had overtaken her after she'd formulated her plan.

First she told the actor they should celebrate his casting

in style, to which proposal Terry was only too happy to agree, in principle. Then Meredith reminded him she still hadn't claimed for the wager they had made over his casting in *Split*.

'Right,' Terry answered. 'It was going to be the Connaught, I seem to remember.'

'You agree you still owe me?' Meredith enquired. 'Because as long as we're clear about that, I've changed my mind.'

'You don't want your reward?' the actor asked.

'Oh yes, darling,' Meredith replied, turning her voice to silk. 'You bet your sweet life I want my reward. I've only changed my mind about the venue.'

She then told him she was claiming as her reward an evening at The Bell, a famous hotel restaurant near East Grinstead.

'That's a bit of a hoik, isn't it?' Terry returned, after more than a moment of hesitation.

'Only if we drive back the same night,' Meredith answered, doing her best to sound enigmatic. 'Pick me up at the flat around six.'

Then she put the phone down before the actor tried to persuade her to change her mind, and thought how odd it was that one always knew when the person on the other end of the line was in bed with somebody.

Dinner was superb. Everything was perfection. Meredith had made sure to book a table in an alcove of the restaurant so that her partner would not be bothered either by stares or by autograph hunters during their meal, and her diligence was rewarded. The only people who came near them all evening were the staff.

'You must be very excited,' Meredith asked the actor, as she embarked on her *Poulet aux Ecrevisses* and he cut into his *Filet de Boeuf à la Moutarde*.

'You bet I'm excited,' Terry replied. 'Aren't you?'

'I'm always excited when I'm with you,' Meredith said, startling him into a sudden look.

'I meant about the film,' he explained, staring back down at his plate, unable to hold Meredith's rock-steady gaze.

'Have I said something to embarrass you?' she asked him.

'You embarrass me?' Terry laughed, recovering his poise. 'The boot's usually on the other foot, Meredith darling.'

'Good,' Meredith continued. 'Then as long as you're not embarrassed, I have to tell you, darling, the way you look tonight, I could eat every part of you.'

'I thought I was off-limits,' Terry said with his best boyish grin.

'And so you were.'

'Were? You mean the rules have changed?'

'Rules? Any fool can make a rule, darling. The people to know are the ones who break them.'

Meredith sipped her wine and looked at the rising star. She could see he was worried, at the moment uncertain exactly what Meredith's game was. But she knew once she had convinced him with her sincerity – which she knew she undoubtedly would, since one thing of which the critics had always been unanimously enamoured was Meredith Browne's innate, overwhelming and/or devastating sincerity – once she had David Terry's confidence he would be quite unable to resist her; partly because she knew he could never refuse what he liked to call a bit of free, but more because she had hurt his pride the night she rejected him. And as Meredith well knew, actors did not enjoy having their pride hurt. They lived on it. Pride was of their very essence, and an actor's pride destroyed his objectivity. So when it came to it, David would be only too eager to make love to Meredith, simply just to show her how very wrong she had been ever to have rejected him.

And so she wooed and flattered him, reviewing his successes and wondering at the speed with which he had achieved them. She reminded him how far he had come in such a short space of time, and tantalized him with a vision of the future when he was an international movie star. And all the time Meredith talked, the actor just smiled and ate, listening to her eulogy as if it was a Mozart piano sonata, inclining his head and nodding, or half-closing his eyes and smiling.

'What I love best of all about it,' she told him, at a salient point, 'is that we've done it together. You and I, darling. I found you, showed you the tracks, and put you on them, and you in your turn did everything that was asked of you, and more. You were a brilliant pupil. And now you're going to be a star. Not a television star. Not some major minor-celebrity who goes around opening garages and supermarkets, and whose face the people who pass you in the street keep thinking they really ought to know. But a star in the proper meaning of the word. Everyone everywhere who goes to the movies will know you. They'll know your name and they'll know your face. When people go to see the new Charles Crown picture, it's your face they'll be carrying in their head. It's you the world will see as Crown. Every man in the audience will secretly be wishing he was you, and every woman will secretly be wishing they were yours. When couples make love, women everywhere will fantasize about you, closing their eyes and pretending that it's not John Smith inside them, but you, Charles Crown, David Terry. That's how it's going to be, darling. You're going to have everything you ever, ever wanted.'

By now, the actor had stopped eating, and was looking past Meredith, dreaming in amazement. Meredith guessed that he had never quite seen to what his new-found fame was about to lead. It had just been another job. Albeit a better job, but a job nonetheless. One which he had won over other actors, and one which would make him more famous than other actors. But it wasn't until now that he had realized just how quantum was the leap. And that he wasn't merely going to be a star. He was going to be a god.

'And we did it, darling,' Meredith was continuing, 'you and I together. We're quite a talent, don't you think?'

The actor turned back to her, smiling, and trying to find out exactly where Meredith was.

'You have the personality,' she was telling him. 'The talent, the charisma. And I have the drive. From now on in, I don't see anything to stop us.'

Meredith left a small but deliberate gap as she opened her big eyes on him.

'Do you, darling?' she finally asked.

But by then, the question was purely rhetorical. Because during that momentary pause, Meredith had seen in the actor's eyes and beyond. And in that second she knew the rumour was right, and that the hoped-for lies were truths. David Terry was no longer hers.

They sat and had their coffee and cognac by the fire. Meredith slipped her shoes off and ran a stockinged foot up inside one of the actor's trouser legs.

'What do you want?' he asked her.

'You,' Meredith smiled.

'I haven't brought any things.'

'You don't need any "things". Anyway, it's not your "things" that I want.'

'Sorry, doll?'

'I want you, darling.'

Terry spooned some coloured sugar into his black coffee, then looked up at her with a hooded sort of look which Meredith guessed he was previewing on her before trying it out on the world.

'Yeah,' he drawled. 'OK.'

Just as if he had finally made a decision about walking her home.

Meredith had chosen the best suite, a four-posted bedroom kept for bridal couples and visiting celebrities. Her bags were already in the room, apparently unpacked and tidied away on the case stand. The bed was turned down, and a bottle of bucketed champagne stood awaiting them.

'Nice,' the actor nodded, looking around the suite. 'Very nice.'

'Yes,' Meredith replied, locking the door. 'It's the very best, they have. And I think we deserve it, don't you? After all we've achieved together?'

She came to him and, standing in front of him, took both of his hands. As she did so, Meredith's resolve almost weakened. He was so devastatingly handsome, he was so irresistibly attractive, he was so utterly and remorselessly sexy, that she had to take a very firm hold on her emotions, and call on the spirits that tended mortal thoughts to unsex her there and then.

Which was fine while he just stood before her, holding her hands in his and smiling down at her. That she could manage. But what about when he kissed her? As he most surely was just about to do? What about when he kissed her as he was kissing her now, his tongue inside her mouth, exploring her mouth, and finding the round hardness of her tongue? What was she to do now, as his hands loosened the straps of her dress from her shoulders, and then quickly and expertly unzipped the back? How could she keep her head as he started to kiss her again, his teeth biting into her lips and his tongue rolling under them, and his hands pulling at her dress, pulling the silk of her dress down, taking with it her panties, his hands forcing themselves past the waistband and down the skin of her buttocks until they were under them and lifting her against him, him whose hardness she could now feel pressed against the roundness of her body as her clothes fell to the floor.

She must think of him gone from her. She must think of him as dead. As a dead object. As something finished. He was nothing to her. Yes he was! He was something she hated! That's what he was! And that's what she must remember, now that she was undoing his shirt and running her hand up his back under the material, and then down again, round to the hard flatness of his stomach, undoing the catch on his trousers, as he kicked off his shoes and bent his legs up to himself to remove his black silk socks. And all the time she was opening his trousers and pulling at them, pulling them down as he had unpeeled her from her dress, slipping the trousers from him, and his shorts until it was just him and his pressed so hard and so bare and so huge against the bare of her belly.

I hate you! she thought, how I hate you! You're a bastard! You're a lousy treacherous bastard, and I hate you!

But he was there – his hand was between her legs, urging its way to her, and she knew that once it was there, once he started to arouse her, she would be finished and done; so she struggled and moaned and told him no as if to excite him further, as she tried to ease herself away from his probing fingers, which were pressing and searching around her, to find her, to find the place where he could set her free and make her his. And his mouth was now on her breasts as he bent her backwards, and his teeth were on her nipples which had long ago hardened and become erect.

All the time in between, when he could, he told her how beautiful she was and what he was going to do with her, and Meredith felt herself sinking, and weakening, and losing fast. She was fast losing grip and no longer did she hate him. She just wanted him. She wanted what was so hard against her to be inside her, she wanted it to hurt her, to make her cry out, she wanted the size of it swelling in her, thrusting in her, filling her every corner, being in her everywhere. Oh! she screamed in silence, how much I want you!

Then a moment, a slight pause while he stopped, looking down at her, and Meredith drew breath in time. His eyes were wild for her as she knew hers must be for him, and she could hear her breath inside her head, rushing, gasping, as if they had been running in a heavy sea, their hearts pounding. She could hear their hearts, she could hear and feel hers, and she could hear his thundering like her own, drumming the beat of their desire.

My God, he was saying. My God, my God, he kept saying, but you're beautiful.

And I hate you, she was saying back to herself. I hate you now, and I shall always hate you. Please God, let me just remember how much I hate the bastard.

His arms went around her, one under her back, one under her buttocks, as he lifted her so easily and walked to the bed. He held her for a moment, looking down at her with a look Meredith couldn't distinguish. A look that certainly wasn't love, and which certainly wasn't hate. And then as he laid her on the bed and stood right up, standing over her, she knew what it was. It was a look of conceit.

The look in the mirror clinched it. The look he took at himself in the looking glass put purposefully on the door of the closet opposite gave Meredith the moment she needed to stay resolute, to hold to a course she'd so very nearly lost.

He couldn't resist it. The actor could not help but look to see how he was looking, and how he was doing. Perhaps it was all being logged in those memory banks already, Meredith thought, as she caught the self-admiring glance. Perhaps it was all being locked away for future reference. Something he would be able to reproduce when asked. Yes – I know how that goes! he'd be able to volunteer. And he'd suggest the touch. He'd suggest that just before the man made love to the woman he took a quick look in the mirror, and wouldn't that be brilliant, right? What a character touch!

But in that second of self-regard, he saved Meredith and hanged himself. Between glory and disgrace there's but a step. And with that look in the mirror David Terry took it.

'How do you want it, doll?' he asked, kneeling down beside her. 'Is there any particular way you really like to do it?'

Meredith wanted to laugh inside. She wanted to scream with laughter inside. She couldn't remember when she had last wanted to 'go' as badly as she did now, looking at the actor's so serious face, asking her what she wanted and how, like a doctor visiting a patient. But she didn't 'go'. She just bit the inside of her lip hard and looked back at him, as helplessly as she could.

'I don't know,' she whispered. 'Come here, come and lie here by me for just a moment, and let me make love to you.'

That appealed to Narcissus, who smiled, half-closed his eyes in pleasure, and rolled on to his back.

'OK,' he replied. 'Why not?'

He was making it easier for her now, with his self-love and estimation. He was so busy thinking how grateful Meredith was going to be, he couldn't see the trap he was helping so readily to make.

He did have a magnificent body. Of that there was no doubt, Meredith thought, as he lay there, stretched out across the bed, his arms behind his tousled head. Meredith took a moment to look at him, before she leaned herself across him and kissed him, this time digging deep into his mouth with her curling tongue. Then she slid a hand down his stomach.

'You look magnificent,' she whispered right into his ear. 'Fantastic.'

'Don't,' he urged. 'Please.'

'I've never seen anything quite so incredible, darling. As you just lying there. Just lying there like that. So free. And yet so helpless.'

She still had him hard-held, as he tried to turn himself and take control.

'No!' she ordered. 'You're not to move! Or I shall get *very* angry!'

'Yeah?' he smiled. 'So what?'

Meredith showed him.

The actor laughed. Meredith held him tighter. The victim stopped laughing and looked at her in a barely contained silence.

'What do you want, doll? Just ask.'

'I don't know. Seeing you there like that . . . .'

Meredith allowed the words to drift into the charged atmosphere, all the time keeping both her hands on both his parts, moving them both slowly, squeezing and sliding. She just lay there, slightly to one side of him, looking

486

into his deep blue eyes, knowing she had him in her hands in more ways than one.

'I'd like to make you quite helpless,' she whispered. 'Quite, quite helpless.'

Even though her face was so close to his, that close, Meredith could still see the blue eyes widen. She could also feel his excitement.

'You what? Why?'

'Because you look so magnificent, darling. You look so big. And strong. And beautiful. I want to make you my captive. I want to make you helpless and do things to you. Things that no one will ever have done to you before.'

He breathed in deeply to try and catch his breath. It was the search for breath someone would make after swimming too far under water. It was a fight to find enough oxygen to keep from fainting at a thought. It was the last gasp the captive makes before submitting to the captor.

'Lie there,' Meredith instructed very quietly. 'Just lie there and don't move. You're not to move unless I tell you. Otherwise.'

She smiled down at him from where she was now standing. This time he didn't dare challenge her threat. Because he was already in her thrall. Meredith could see that. She could see from the nervous lick of the lips, the quickening of his breath, from the state of his growing excitement.

'But with what?' he managed to ask in a whisper. 'What are you going to use?'

'I'll think of something,' Meredith replied, moving cat-like round the room and picking up some articles. 'My stockings. Your tie. My scarf.'

She stood at the end of the bed, dangling his bonds before him.

'Not my tie,' he pleaded. 'That's a Hardy Amies.'

'Very well,' Meredith agreed, having espied something much more suitable. 'How about these?'

She undid and offered up the thick silk ropes which held the drapes back on the four-poster.

'OK,' the actor whispered, barely audible.

487

'Not "OK",' Meredith corrected. 'Yes.'

'Yes.'

'Yes, mistress.'

'Yes, mistress.'

It was as easy as that. Meredith could scarcely believe it. One minute he had been the assailant, and it had been her fighting for breath. Now she had him helpless, completely subjugated, before she had even begun to tie a knot.

'My God,' the victim moaned. 'No.'

'Yes,' the mistress replied. 'Now your arms.'

Without resisting, Terry offered her his left arm. Meredith knotted one of her stockings tightly around his wrist, then secured the other end of the nylon to one of the top posts. She did the same with his right arm, spread-eagling him fully across the stretch of the bed. Then she stood back and looked at her captive.

'That,' she finally announced, 'is extremely sexy.'

David Terry smiled back up at her, anxious to please.

'Right,' he said.

'How's it for you, darling?' Meredith enquired.

'Incredible,' Terry replied.

'Good,' said Meredith, pulling up a chair.

As she sat down, her victim turned his head and frowned at her.

'Now what?'

'What indeed?'

Meredith crossed her legs, and sat back in the chair, which she had placed far enough from the bedside to be out of reach. Not out of her victim's reach, because he couldn't move anything. But far enough for him to know she wasn't going to be able to touch him, and thus do anything to or for him.

The frown deepened.

'Question time,' Meredith asked.

'Yeah?'

'No, slave. Not "Yeah". I've just told you. Yes, mistress.'

'Yes, mistress.'

488

'Good.'

'So what do you want to know?'

Meredith waited for full subservience.

'Mistress.'

'Good,' she said. 'You're learning.'

She smiled at him, a clinical smile, the smile of a doctor doing his rounds in the wards, before stretching, yawning and then rising.

'I haven't got many questions,' she told him, going over and opening one of her suitcases. 'Firstly, are you comfortable? I mean, I haven't tied you too tight, have I?'

'No.'

Meredith looked round at her victim, sternly.

'I mean no, mistress.'

'Good.'

She snapped the suitcase open, which was still full of unpacked clothes, and started to search for something. In the mirror she could see her victim straining to see what she was doing, but his utter helplessness denied him any success.

Finding what she was looking for, she turned back and started to pick her clothes up from the floor, shaking them out before laying them on the back of the chair. Panties, slip, bra, dress, and what she had just taken from the suitcase, a new pair of stockings. Then she disappeared into the bathroom.

'Where are you going now?' her victim called after her, with a distinct note of panic, Meredith noted happily.

'Just going to have a quick wash!' she called back.

In fact she wasn't very quick. She was rather slow, taking her time to wash herself quite thoroughly, before dusting herself with Chanel talcum powder and dabbing herself with Joy. Then she wandered back into the bedroom and stood naked for a moment at the end of the bed.

'Come on,' her victim pleaded. 'You can't just leave me like this.'

'I haven't finished asking my questions, darling,' Meredith replied.

She sat back down on the bedside chair and undid the new pack of stockings. She was quite aware she was being well watched, but didn't bother to acknowledge the look.

'Right,' she finally announced. 'Truth, dare or promise?'

'What do you mean?'

'You'll find out very shortly, darling.'

Meredith dropped the stocking packet on the bed and held the new pair of nylons up for examination.

'Answer me truthfully now, sweetheart,' she warned him. 'Because there's no point in lying. Are you, or are you not about to leave me and go with Suzanne Altman to Walter Ford?'

The electrified silence that immediately followed was answer enough. But Meredith wanted it from the horse's mouth.

'Did you hear me, slave?'

'Oh,' the victim finally replied. 'This is all still part of the game, is it?'

Faint hope, Meredith thought, but bothered not to tell him.

'Just answer the question, David. Are you or are you not leaving me and going to Walter Ford, Inc.? The Inc. to include Suzanne Altman.'

'I don't know what you're talking about.'

'Of course you do. It's the talk of the town.'

'Why should I do a stupid thing like that, Meredith?'

'Mistress,' Meredith hissed at him, suddenly bending towards him, pushing her face close to his which was now beginning to sweat.

'Mistress.'

'Yes. I'd be interested to know. Why *would* you do such a stupid thing?'

She kept her face close to his, and then, with a deliberately stagey smile, sat back down on the chair and started to pull on her new stockings.

'Answer please, slave,' she commanded.

All she got was silence.

'Answer me, please.'

The actor saw the look on her face. Meredith could see that from the look on his face.

'I was going to tell you, Merry.'

'Don't call me Merry, please. You never knew me when I was Merry. So please don't you call me that.'

David frowned, bewildered and frightened by the chill in her voice. But more frightened by the knowledge she now had. Even so, he stayed silent.

Meredith stood up, her stockings pulled back on, and attached them to her garter belt. Then she pulled her slip back over her head, followed immediately by her dress.

'What are you doing?' Terry asked.

'What does it look like?' she replied. 'Getting dressed.'

'Why?'

'You haven't answered my question.'

Seeing her slipping her shoes on, and starting to brush out her hair, the victim started really to panic.

'Of course I'm not leaving you!' he shouted. 'I've told you! Why would I do a stupid thing like that!'

Meredith warned him to keep his voice down, while continuing to brush out her hair.

'Is this what all this is about?' Terry hissed. 'Did you set all this up specially?'

'Just answer the question, slave,' Meredith told him. 'Truthfully.'

'I am not leaving you, Meredith.'

'I say you are.'

'Well, you're crazy. Why the fuck should I want to leave you of all people?'

'Why indeed?'

'Why should I leave you and go to Walter Ford? You get forgotten in places like that if you go and have a piss! Of course I'm not leaving you.'

'Promise?'

'Hope to die, Meredith!'

'Then why does Walter Ford, London, tell me otherwise?'

She turned on him, wide-eyed, taking a studied gamble.

491

And the gamble worked, judging from the way her victim turned his head away in anguish.

'I was going to tell you. Really,' he cried. 'It's only a career move!'

For a moment Meredith couldn't quite believe her ears. Then she laughed. She had to. She had to sit on the bed and give in to the utter helplessness of her laughter.

'Seriously,' Terry grinned up at her. 'It's not going to make any difference to you and me, doll.'

'Any difference?' Meredith replied, through her laughter. 'It's not going to make any difference between you and me? The only thing there is between you and me, you bastard, is business!'

Terry frowned at her again, and Meredith as usual was astounded at quite how easily perplexed he became.

'What about this?' he enquired, nodding in the area of his genitals, the main member of which had quite some time ago lost interest. 'I mean we have this. This was all you. You fancy me.'

'No I don't,' Meredith told him. 'I don't fancy slabs of meat. So, just for the record, you're going to Walter Ford.'

'Yeah.'

'After all I've done for you, after all we've been through together. After all I've got you to achieve, you're getting off and going.'

'Look, I told you. It's only a career move.'

'A career move? Eh?'

Meredith bent down to the mirror and reapplied some lipstick, rubbing her lips together and then surveying the result.

'What about Suzanne Altman?' she enquired.

'So what about Suzanne Altman? If you don't fancy me, and I'm just a slab of meat—'

'Which you are. No, you're not. You're also an enormously vain and self-loving mega-shit.'

'So what about Suzanne Altman? What's she to you?'

'I just like to know how the opposition fights. Are you knocking her off?'

The victim took a deep breath and sighed.

'I am not "knocking her off," Meredith. OK?' he replied. 'We happen to be having an affair. All right?'

'Absolutely,' Meredith replied. 'So what are you doing here?'

'I owed you.'

'That's what I thought. Oh – and just before I go—'

'Go?'

There was that note of panic again. Meredith was delighted to hear it.

'As for your affair with Suzanne Altman,' she continued, 'I take it you know all about Billie Swanne?'

'Who's he?' the victim enquired, sounding even less at ease.

'Not he, darling,' Meredith told him. 'She. She's a singer Suzanne Altman's been living with now for about six or seven years. I thought everyone in the business knew. Anyway, have fun. All of you. I'm sure we'll see each other around.'

Meredith snapped her suitcase shut and, picking up both her bags, went to the door.

'You're a mad crazy bitch!' he shouted at her from the bed. 'You can't just leave me here!'

'I don't see why not,' Meredith replied. 'That was the whole idea.'

'The whole idea!' Terry cried. 'You mean you set this whole thing up?'

'Sure!'

'But why for Christ's sake? Why?'

'Don't be silly, darling. You know the answer to that one. What you mean is how? How did I fool you into ending up in this ridiculous fashion? And in case you don't think you do look ridiculous—'

Meredith opened the mirrored closet door and swung it round until she was sure Terry could see himself in it.

'How about that?' she laughed, sharing the image with him. 'How about that?'

Terry started to whimper.

'You bitch, you rotten bitch!'

'You poor darling,' Meredith cooed, 'I'm afraid you forgot one very salient point—'

'Yeah? What?'

For a second David Terry stared at her as eager to learn from her as ever.

'You forgot I was once an actor too!'

She started to laugh helplessly as she headed for the door.

'Please, Merry, please!' Terry pleaded, 'please, let me go!'

'Don't worry,' Meredith called to him as she opened the door. 'Room Service will let you out in the morning. I've ordered you early-morning tea, and a copy of *The Stage*.'

She started to shut the door and then stopped.

'Oh, and you haven't forgotten now, have you? You still owe your dear old mum a brand-new house.'

ACT THREE
SURVIVORS

13

Jay was out at the doctor's when the phone rang early that evening for William. It was a transatlantic call, person to person, from Max Kassov.

William was surprised, because in all the time he had been in America, he had never heard from Max.

'I'm in New York!' he told William. 'I'm going to the première of your play!'

William was so worried about Jay he had all but forgotten that this was the day his play opened on Broadway.

'Why aren't you over here, you crazy bastard?' Max continued.

'I guess because I've seen it, Max,' William replied. 'Several times.'

Max laughed and then got down to business. That was Max. Never one to hang about, thought William, particularly on an expensive phone call.

'Word of mouth is great, Willy boy!' he told him. 'Though of course all depends on the butchers! But if they don't cut it to ribbons, I want first refusal!'

William thoughtfully enquired for what, and Max told him for the film rights, what else? He'd make an offer now, he assured William, but the guy he worked for at Allied Independents was a little on the conservative side, and only liked investing in gilt-edged. So as long as the play got good notices, and consequently good advances, they were in business.

'And if we are,' Max continued, 'I'll want your ass out here and fast! Because I want to sell you to them as the screenwriter!'

Jay came back from the doctor's just as William was concluding the call. Hearing to whom he was talking, she at once wanted to know what was the news, but William was more anxious to learn what the doctor had to say.

'Nothing, William,' she assured him. 'It was just a check-up. So, for God's sake, stop fussing and tell me what Max wanted.'

When William had finished telling her, the colour was back in Jay's cheeks. She was so thrilled for him she threw her arms round his neck, kissed him passionately, and then immediately suggested going out to dinner to celebrate.

'Hold on,' William advised. 'This is all hypothetical, sweetheart. This is Max Kassov abble-dabbling. Firstly the play has got to be a hit—'

'The play is a hit, you lummox!' Jay laughed. 'I tell you it's not a question of winning the race! It's a question of how much by!'

Pessimist that he was, even so William was inclined to think Jay might be right. The play had attracted an extremely starry cast, with two of Hollywood's finest light comedians, Matt Randall and Elsa Craig, in the leading roles.

'So let's go out and celebrate!' Jay urged. 'It's not every day you're the toast of Broadway!'

'You know one of the many things I love about you, Jay Burrell?' William asked as they walked round the block to their favourite local restaurant. 'Your presumption. Most people would wait at least until they knew what the notices were like. But not you. When there's no doubt in your mind, there's exactly that. None.'

And Jay was right. The play was a smash. Max rang them from New York early hours his time and mid-morning theirs to read them the reviews.

'Now go ring the office,' he told William when he had finished, 'and get them to book you on the first available flight over.'

'Book us,' William replied. 'I'll be bringing Jay with me.'

'Sure you bring Jay with you,' Max agreed. 'But she'll be down to you.'

Jay wouldn't hear of it. For a start they were flying William out first class, and they couldn't possibly afford to take her out first class as well just for the hell of it. And then secondly they'd have all her hotel and living to pay for out of their own pockets as well.

'We're about to get rich, kid!' William laughed. 'Think of all those lovely Broadway royalties! Anyway, I'm making enough from the London run practically to hire a private jet!'

But Jay persisted, saying it was just a waste of good money. If William wanted to spend money on her, fine. She needed some new clothes. But she'd only be in the way in America. They wanted William, not her, and the last thing she enjoyed was hanging round hotel rooms waiting for William to return from endless meetings.

'If you get the job as screenwriter,' she promised, 'and they put you up in some sexy little beach house in Malibu, then you try and stop me from being there. But really, in the meantime, William, I'm going to be much more use here. Anyway, who'd look after Gertie?'

William looked at the Yorkshire terrier puppy Jay was holding and stroking in her arms and smiled. Jay was right, as usual. It wouldn't be much of a trip for her, hanging around New York while they dealt, and then hanging around Los Angeles while hopefully they cemented. And besides, William would be worried about her health, and if his mind was elsewhere, he wouldn't be able to give of his best, and as a consequence – fully mindful of what his fellow Americans expected of you when they were paying your way – should he turn in a one degree below performance in front of the studio heads, he was cooked. William was a firm believer in the fact that you only ever got one real good chance. And if and when you did, you had to go for it and for broke.

And so he agreed to leave Jay behind. Jay hugged him, smoothed the frown off his brow, and told him it didn't mean they didn't still love each other just because they were going to be apart for a week or so. Whereas think what it would mean if William landed the job. *Screenplay by William Kennedy, from the original stage play by William Kennedy*. Neil Simon better start looking over his shoulder.

She saw him off from the airport on a bright clear spring day, waving at the silver gleaming jumbo until long after it had disappeared from her view.

Then she fetched her car from the park, and on the drive back to London decided that perhaps the doctor was right after all, and she really ought to admit herself into hospital for the long-time recommended tests.

Around about this time, Meredith also received an unexpected telephone call. It was from Baz, who wasted no time in asking her to meet him for lunch. Meredith, surprised by the totally unanticipated call, discovered only the venue, but not the reason for the meal. That was left until halfway through pudding.

'I heard about David Terry,' Baz said out of the blue, suddenly looking up at Meredith.

'What did you hear, Baz?' Meredith enquired with a smile, knowing it would be nothing untoward. No story had broken about their famous night, nor had there been one breath of scandal, leaving Meredith to assume either that the actor had most probably struggled free before being discovered by Room Service, or failing that, the hotel in question had maintained its famously high level of discretion.

'I heard that he's gone to Walter Ford,' Baz replied.

'These things happen, Baz,' Meredith said. 'Particularly in this business. We all come and go. Is that what you want to have lunch with me for? To commiserate over losing an actor?'

'No,' Baz told her. 'To be perfectly frank, I bring you an olive branch. I want you to come back into business with me.'

500

That was the very last thing Meredith had expected. A business favour, perhaps. An exchange of information, possibly. A sympathetic gloat, most probably. But an invitation to dance? Never.

'Why, Baz?'

'I know we've had our differences, Merry.'

'So why do you want me back?'

The old man sighed and, refusing the cigars on offer from the waiter, took one of his own from an inside pocket.

'Why do I want you back?' he asked. 'Because you remind me of the old days. The times gone by.'

'Long ago and far away?'

'They were good times.'

'Some were, Baz darling. Some weren't quite so hot.'

'I'm an old man, Merry. Now I remember just the good times.'

Meredith picked up her coffee cup and drank from it slowly, buying a little time. Baz didn't want her back for nostalgic reasons. Baz Vogel's strong suit wasn't sentiment. Baz Vogel's bag was acumen.

'What's in it for me, Baz?' she finally asked. 'Because in case you haven't noticed, I've got legs and I'm walking.'

'You're going to miss David Terry, however,' Baz nodded. 'That's going to show at the annual audit.'

'There'll be another one along in a minute,' Meredith smiled, remembering her dear Maxine Gane, who had only recently made a comeback in a phenomenally successful 'soap' and was a star at long last, albeit only a telly star.

Baz regarded the lit end of his cigar, before removing the ash with the tip of his little finger.

'We amalgamate, Merry dear. You come back home—'

'And all is forgiven, darling?'

'You come home, and I make you a partner. Vogel and Browne, Incorporated. As you probably know, I have two young and vital assistants—'

'As you probably don't know, I have one young and vital assistant. Carly Michael. And she's very good.'

501

'So bring her along. She and my two – they run the agency.'

'Yes?' Meredith asked, waiting for the sting. 'And what do I do?'

'You, Meredith dear,' Baz replied. 'You, we send to America.'

She did her best to look nonplussed, but underneath the table Meredith's legs had started to shake uncontrollably. America. If you made it in America, you were made. England was fine for the first part of the game, but the ladders that took you to the top of the board, the ones Meredith was really interested in climbing, they were in America. Besides, the purple patch England had enjoyed in the sixties as far as making movies had gone was over, the bubble burst. It wasn't just the change in the tax laws, it was more to do with incompetence. However much the business in England boasted about their film heritage, the plain fact of the matter was that when it had come to it, when the Americans had arrived loaded with tax-shelter money to make movies in the UK, the film side of the business here just wasn't up to it. She remembered Max publicly going on record time and time again, castigating British film-makers for their sloppiness, their languid attitude to narrative, but above all (Max's favourite hobby horse) for their lack of *definition*.

She remembered his famous but controversial speech at one of the big awards' dinners, when his criticisms so offended some of the more prominent members of British film hierarchy that several parties upped and walked out on him, a moment upon which Max didn't fail to capitalize.

'What you're seeing happening, ladies and gentlemen,' he told the remainder of the gathering, 'is what's happening only in far greater numbers at cinemas all over the country whenever they show British movies! Except the people who are walking out aren't doing so because like our deserters tonight they can't face the truth! No – it's because they're not being shown it! Any version of it! The

British cinema is fey! The British cinema is fast drowning in whimsy! You see an American movie and straight away you know you're in business. Why? Because it has *definition*! It's about something. It's concerned. Or if it's a comedy, it's slick. It's glossy. What do you see when you go to a British movie? Either a vulgar romp, with a cast of actors who would shame a seaside repertory – or an attenuated, navel-examining social anecdote, full of nuance, and implication, but lacking that most basic element of all good movies, *narrative drive*. Hollywood, whatever the intelligentsia might have you believe over here, is far from dead, ladies and gentlemen! Hollywood is up and running! But Elstree isn't! Shepperton isn't! Twickenham isn't! We have no film industry, and we won't have until it gets out of bed with itself. The British film industry is taking itself out, because the British film industry, ladies and gentlemen, the British film industry is incestuous!'

But nobody had heeded the warning. The papers had been full of it for a week or so, and on television the pundits met every now and then on camera to discuss earnestly and caringly about what could be done to save the industry that had made such major contributions to cinematic history such as *The Titchfield Thunderbolt* and *The Blue Lamp*. And then everyone packed their tents and the film-makers went back to making more feeble spy stories and endless *Carry On* capers.

And so Max finally in despair had left and gone to the land in which he believed, and now Meredith had a chance to follow him.

'But as what exactly?' she asked Baz. 'You already have a branch of the agency in New York. Why should you be thinking of sending me out there?'

'I'm not sending you to New York,' Baz told her. 'I want you to go to California. To Hollywood. And not as an agent either. I want you to go out there and work for our company, Diplomat Productions. As a producer.'

Again, Meredith was astounded, but her long experience

as an actress stood her in good stead, the only interest showing on her face was in the raising of one eyebrow.

'I don't know anything about production, darling,' she said. 'You'd be sending out a greenhorn.'

'You don't need to know anything about production, Meredith my dear,' Baz replied, untucking his linen napkin from under his chin. 'To become a producer, all you need to learn is how to read other people's memos upside down.'

Afterwards, Meredith walked Baz back to his office, through St James's Park which was just about to burst into spring and up into Mayfair. She was still curious as to why Baz was inviting her in, as to why he was making her this offer. She knew full well it had nothing to do with wistfulness, but still couldn't guess with complete accuracy at the motivation.

'I was wrong about you and Louis,' Baz finally admitted as they crossed the street. 'I was foolish to blame you for Louis's death. Louis was Louis. Louis did what Louis wanted to do. Louis chose you. You didn't choose Louis. So yes, I want to make amends, of course. But it's more than that, my dear. I'm old now, and I have no children. You were like a daughter to Louis and me. Yes, I know. It's a cliché, but like all those blasted clichés, Merry, it's only a cliché because it's blasted true. So now it's time you came back home. It's time you came back to the family.'

They stopped on the corner of the street, and stood for a moment arm in arm. Then Meredith smiled at him and kissed him.

'You should never kiss old men,' Baz told her, wrinkling his nose in self-disgust. 'Old men smell.'

'This one doesn't,' Meredith replied. 'Except of shaving soap and hair dressing. Which I find quite intoxicating.'

Baz grinned at her, but declined her offer of walking him right back to the office, giving as his reason the fact he had to pay a visit to a sick friend nearby. Meredith kissed his cheek again, and with a wave walked off into her future.

Baz watched her go, a beautiful young woman striding purposefully away from him, with just the right amount of sway to her hips, and the sheen of her long hair catching the spring sunlight. And as he watched her disappear from him, he caught his breath and deeply wished he could learn how to be old.

'We have the results of your tests now,' the doctor announced, 'and you'll be glad to hear they are all completely clear.'

Jay frowned and looked up at him, but didn't feel glad. She knew she should. She knew she should feel overjoyed that nothing had shown up. Particularly since the way she had been feeling these past six months had made her fear the worst. Which was why she had finally overcome her fears and allowed herself to be admitted into hospital, where they had run a very full and comprehensive set of tests.

And they had found nothing wrong. According to the diagnostic specialist who now stood at the end of her bed, she was one hundred per cent in the clear.

'There are still traces of this viral infection you were suffering from, I'll admit that one,' he was saying. 'But then that isn't in any way unusual. Those little blighters can stay in your system for yonks, causing all sorts of mischief. Which could well account for you feeling a bit under the weather now and then.'

Jay smiled ruefully. A bit under the weather now and then. That was how they thought she felt, and that was why she had gone to all the trouble and through all the agony of having herself admitted to hospital, and suffered the indignity and radical discomfort of some very personal tests, simply because she felt a bit under the weather now and then.

'I still feel a bit under the weather, I'm afraid,' she informed the doctor. 'Despite the results of the tests.'

'Yes. Well,' the doctor smiled briefly, tapping his notes with a pencil, 'that's how it goes, isn't it?'

He paused for a moment, drilling her with his rather cold grey eyes, before changing tack.

'You're a writer of course, aren't you?'

'Meaning that explains it?'

'No, no, no, good heavens above, no.'

Meaning yes, yes, yes, Jay thought. Yes, you bet your life it does.

'It's just that some people are more – what shall we say?' A flash of a well-practised medical smile. 'Some people, who do certain jobs, these people are more prone to what you could classify as psychosomatic diseases.'

'Don't tell me, doctor. It's all in the mind.'

'In a manner of speaking, yes.'

The doctor nodded thoughtfully, before putting his notes down on Jay's bed and sinking his hands deep in his pockets, concerned-uncle style.

'I remember you telling me you'd been working very hard, Miss Burrell. Over-hard in fact. On a project in which you took no great enjoyment.'

'That's show business, doc.'

'But really, if we examine your history, that's when the trouble really started. The undue fatigue, the pains in the limbs, the sickness, the headaches, everything seemed to start around this time, and then grow progressively worse. And you admitted you were working under a very great strain.'

Jay considered the points the doctor was making and then nodded.

'Yes. The two things were coincidental. But I haven't been working at all recently. In fact my partner insisted I spend most of my day in bed, so I've not been under any great strain exactly.'

'Not physical, I'll grant you that, Miss Burrell. But you told me you'd still been *worried*. About work. And the prospect of work. And if perhaps you are indeed one of these people I'm trying to describe —'

'Then what I'm feeling, what I'm suffering from, is all in the mind.'

The doctor straightened himself up, and took his hands from his pockets to lean on the bed rail.

'If that's the way you'd like to look at it, then yes – so be it.'

When she was discharged from the hospital later that day, Jay just made it into a taxi before her legs gave way. On the journey home she broke out in a cold sweat of fear, and it was all she could do to stop herself from breaking down and crying. Why couldn't they find anything wrong with her? How couldn't they? She was so weak she could barely open the door to the studio. So exhausted all she wanted to do was go to bed and sleep and never wake up. But she was too tired even to drag herself up the steps to the gallery, so instead she collapsed on the enormous sofa and, curling herself up into a foetal ball, passed quickly and mercifully into unconsciousness.

The telephone ringing woke her. It was transatlantic. It was Hollywood calling. It was William.

William too was lying in bed when he called, but he felt great. In fact he had rarely felt better.

'Guess what, sweetheart?' he asked across the ocean. 'I got the job, goddammit!'

He shifted in his bed and stared out at the early morning sun which was already breaking through the Los Angeles haze.

'I wanted to ring you as soon as I heard,' he went on, 'but knowing the way you sleep nights, I guess you'd never have heard the bell.'

Jay was even more thrilled than he had imagined, and wanted to know all the hows and wherefores. William told her of his endless meetings with the studio chiefs, and how he and Max had thought they were fighting a fast-losing battle, and they were just about agreed to call it a day, when they were recalled at the eleventh hour only for William to be commissioned.

'Max heard afterwards it was Cy Bernstein's wife,' William said. 'Cy's Head of the World, I guess, and he was the one most dead-set against using the originator to do the screenplay. And then suddenly we're having breakfast at The Beverly Hills – where they stick bougainvillaea in your scrambled eggs. Can you believe it? And this guy, Mr Head of the World, he voltes his face and offers me the picture! Because, as Max heard on the vine shortly after, Mrs Bernstein saw me on some damn morning chat show or other and took a fancy! And before you go into one of your contusions of jealousy, sweetheart, Mrs Bernstein is a 160-pound four foot niner with bright purple hair.'

They talked for another five or so minutes about the amazing town that was Hollywood, and William was delighted to hear Jay laughing so brightly and sounding so full of herself. He told her how great she sounded, and Jay answered she was feeling wonderful, and why wouldn't she after such terrific news?

'So all we have to fix up, honey,' William said, 'is how and when to get you out here.'

There was a silence on the line, and for a moment William thought they'd been cut off, before Jay came back to ask exactly what William meant. William realized his error. He'd quite forgotten in all the excitement to tell Jay he wasn't going to have time to return home before starting the first draft.

'They've moved everything forward, you see,' he explained, 'in their typically crazy way. You know, everything has to be now. Then is dead and finished. It's now, now, now. Talk about do you want it good, or do you want it Wednesday, right? The only time they take is to make up their minds. And man, that takes some time. But once they've made 'em up, it's all systems go, go, go! But what's the difference, sweetheart? I'd only really be coming back to collect you. And since I can't do that now, we'll just organize the day between us when you can hop on a plane and get out here.'

On her side of the Atlantic, Jay looked at the telephone she was holding and hesitated. After a moment of silence, the voice in her ear asked her if she still loved him.

'Of course I love you, William,' Jay replied, almost

508

adding that wasn't the point, but instead prefabricating an entirely specious reason. 'The thing is someone's asked me to write something.'

William of course immediately wanted to know what, so Jay quickly had to invent. Fortunately one of her favourite books was lying to hand on the sofa table.

'They've asked me to adapt *The Secret Garden*, William. The BBC. And you know how much I love the book.'

This was something William hadn't expected, of course. They'd worked in harness from the day Max had first suggested it until the day Jay made him continue with his play, so William had all but forgotten Jay had a literary identity of her own.

'Thanks,' Jay said, in response to William's genuine enthusiasm. 'Of course it's not fixed yet. It's nothing definite. But I should know within a week or two.'

Which was how they left it. Besides exchanging more expressions of their love and affection, it was left that Jay would call William the moment she heard anything one way or the other.

Which would buy her just enough time to seek a second medical opinion, which she now knew she urgently needed. Because when she awoke to answer the telephone, there was no feeling whatsoever in her right hand. And now, twenty minutes later when she finally replaced the receiver, there still wasn't any.

Meredith took at once to Los Angeles. It was without doubt one of the ugliest towns she'd ever seen, but it had style. It had energy. Above all, it had *hutzpah*. Agreed, it also had pretensions, and ideas far above its particular station, but that was part of its attraction. It took itself desperately seriously, but while it was doing so it had fun.

At first though, she had found it a little intimidating after the altogether slower pace of London and England, and a totally confusing town to get around. But Trisha from the offices of Diplomat Productions, who was assigned to her as her 'shadow', took a lot of her own time out to show her the town, and before long Meredith, always quick at readapting herself, was driving herself around to meetings as if she was a regular inhabitant.

Often, as she drove along Rodeo Drive, or up to star gaze at the gods' houses in the hills, she thought how far it was from the gloom of her childhood environment. As she motored in her rag-top along the palm-lined avenues, she would think back to the dirty streets of Battersea, to the bombed-out buildings where weeds instead of mortar sprouted in between the rubble. She would admire the California lawns, and immaculate flower beds, and remember how the flowers she had picked from the wastegrounds in her childhood had always been finely coated with dust and soot. And it never seemed to rain. When she had been a little girl, she could only remember the rain and the cold. It seemed the only sunlight she had ever seen had been artificial, a harsh glare that shone down at her from the giant arc lamps in the film studios. But here, in California, the sun was real, and hot, and shining most every day.

Harry was the only drawback. No Harry, and Hollywood could have been heaven. But there was always a price to pay, and Harry was Meredith's. Harry Johannsen was Baz's man in Tinsel Town: Diplomat's number one gun, a slob, a sadist, and a bastard. But a very successful one. The pictures Johannsen made might not win Oscars, but they grossed. His latest, the last one he produced under the Liberty studio banner before joining Diplomat, a thriller called *Blue for Green*, had come in under $4½ million and to date had made back $35 million. That was the kind of return the moguls liked. Yes, they enjoyed a $10 million epic that might well bring in $250 million. Who didn't? But what they were happiest with, at the end of the day, was the neat one. The modest production that came in under cost, and grossed six to ten times its cost. That's what kept them in business, and in women who would do anything.

Harry Johannsen liked women who would do anything.

Particularly to him. Which is why in the main he couldn't stand Meredith. There were other things he didn't enjoy too much about her. Her sang-froid for one. Whatever he threw at her, she took, and took gracefully, without ever recoursing to vulgarities, coarseness, or complaint. She was quick, too. And bright. She was hardly there two days when everyone was telling Harry what a find she was, so witty, so intelligent, and oh boy – so classy! And of course she was British. Harry didn't take to the British. He never had, because he'd been stationed in Oxfordshire during the war as a GI and seen how the British looked down their noses at him, while all the time pretending to be grateful – it made him sick in his shoes. They should be so lucky, he used to tell himself and Meredith regularly. Without guys like Harry the British would still be frog-marching.

But most of all he couldn't stand Meredith because she wouldn't come across. The two girls who had been sent down from New York to be tried in the job prior to Meredith had come across. Harry had enjoyed telling Meredith how good at French they both had been, but he hadn't enjoyed Meredith's reaction because there had been none. In fact Meredith had made some poker-faced remark about how she'd always been brought up not to speak with her mouth full, at which the entire meeting they'd both been attending erupted in laughter, and Harry Johannsen had lost that one hands down.

And she didn't come across. Try as he may, and promise what he would, Meredith Browne was not interested. Harry kept telling her what he could do for her, professionally and sexually, but the lady didn't want to know. He knew why Baz had sent her to him. He'd sent her to torment him. Because as Harry knew that Baz well knew, Harry Johannsen produced all his best work when he was enraged. And Miss Frigidaire Frigging Browne saw to it she kept him just above boiling point.

She had even refused to be impressed by his house. As she drove up to it that first day, Meredith's first inclination

511

had been to laugh, so ridiculous was the building, an absurdity only heightened by the incredible figure who greeted her at the top of a long flight of stone steps.

'Imported all the way from Paris, France,' the figure informed her, as he took hold of Meredith's right elbow. 'The entire flight of steps once graced the entrance of some goddam château outside Paris.'

For their initial meeting, Harry Johannsen was costumed in an outfit he had considered suitable to his abode. And since the house had been roughly fashioned after a typical French château, but in miniature, he had chosen to wear what Harry Johannsen imagined a French vicomte might wear, or more accurately what Hollywood imagined a French vicomte might wear: namely a Douglas Fairbanks-type of loose-fitting silk shirt with enormous collars and puffed sleeves, worn with knee-length embroidered lederhosen tucked into white silk socks, and bottomed off totally inappropriately with a pair of Slazenger tennis shoes. Meredith did what she had always done when the desire to laugh became paramount. She pinched the fleshy part of one thumb as hard as she possibly could with the nails of her other thumb and forefinger and thought of having brain surgery. It never failed. By the time she stepped from her sports car to shake hands with her future employer, she was back in full control.

Harry Johannsen insisted on showing her all around the house. He was proud of it, as he told her. So he should be. It had cost him a goddam arm and leg.

'You want to know whose house this was?' he asked Meredith. 'This was built for Gertrude Malone, at the height of her fame in the twenties.'

'I can just see her in it,' Meredith replied quite truthfully, without adding that she was having some difficulty coming to terms with the sight of Harry Johannsen in it. A house built purposefully for a woman just doesn't look right on a man, particularly a man like Harry Johannsen. Harry needed something modern and brash and vulgar.

The house he had bought was a boudoir of a house, and would always be a boudoir, no matter how he had refurnished it. He looked ridiculous in it, just like Louis Kass had once looked ridiculous in a bowler hat he had gone out and bought himself from Herbert Johnson's in Bond Street.

'It's no good, Meredith dear,' he had sighed, looking at himself wearing the bowler in the hall mirror when he had returned to the apartment. 'I look fine in here. I look great in my Rolls. In this, I look like a winkle.' And then he had thrown it into the back of the closet where it had remained thereafter.

Harry Johannsen's house had the same effect on its new owner. In it, Harry Johannsen looked like a winkle. Worse, he looked like a man who had got out of bed in a hurry and picking up the wrong garment, found himself answering the door in his wife's négligé.

But then, that was Hollywood, as Meredith quickly found out the more she became acclimatized. It was a place full of anomalies and total absurdities, but at which you only dared laugh behind closed doors. Because as Meredith was all too well aware, the most totally absurd people in town were inevitably the most powerful.

William Kennedy also knew this all too well, but being a writer, or rather being 'only a writer' as he took great joy in introducing himself, he didn't have to play by the same set of rules. Writers were mavericks, Hollywood recognized that. Writers, according to Jack Warner, were just schmucks with Underwoods. Writers fitted no known pattern of human behaviour, so the Hollywood establishment patronized them, indulged them, humoured them, but very rarely let them in through their front doors.

This suited William fine. William Kennedy was by nature a loner, as was Jay Burrell, which is why they got along so well together. If they'd been in any way dependent on each other, their relationship would never have lasted. As it was, it was their mutual and fierce love of independence which paradoxically kept them united.

Of course he missed Jay. He missed her every moment he wasn't in his beach house writing. He missed her when he walked the beach each morning and evening, and he missed their long, exploratory and analytical conversations at his solitary mealtimes. Sometimes Max would look in for a couple of drinks, and they would sit and chew the cud as the sun started to disappear below the Pacific horizon, or he would be invited round to Max's where he would eat a poolside barbecue in company with Max's latest girl, and in company with some empty-headed girl Max had laid on for William, and in whom William was not the slightest bit interested.

Max had taken him aside one evening and asked him what in hell was wrong with him?

'This girl I got for you this evening,' he complained. 'Patti. You know how many positions there are?'

'Somewhere around seventy, they tell me,' William replied, throwing the ice from his whisky into a flower bed.

'Patti's invented ten more.'

'Good for Patti.'

'William — it's not as if you're married for Chrissake!'

'That's not the point. Anyway, men are usually more faithful to women they're not married to.'

'It'll help your writing, Willy boy! Look at your shoulders! They're halfway up your head! Take Patti home. Let her help you relax. It'll help the film.'

'I don't need Patti, Max. When I'm writing, that's all I need. I don't need sex. I need a little whisky at sundown, maybe. But sex I don't need. When I'm writing I have neither the time nor the energy for it.'

William wasn't quite so sure of his ground when he bumped into Meredith at one of Harry Johannsen's monthly brunch parties. He didn't even know Meredith was in Hollywood, because Max had certainly never mentioned it, although Max most certainly must have known, because everyone in power knew everything there was to know about everything. William decided Max must

514

have marked and learned the fact and then totally digested it.

He was standing in the queue for food when they met, both waiting to be served yet another helping of utterly tasteless fodder.

'I hope you're enjoying yourself, young man,' Mrs Johannsen enquired as he stood waiting. 'We have eighteen metres of food here, you know.'

'You shouldn't have,' William replied. 'You see I'm slimming. So ten would have been just fine.'

The girl in front of him laughed, and then immediately controlled herself. But not before William had time enough for her laugh to ring bells somewhere in his head.

Even before she turned to him, he knew who it was. And with the recognition came a deep and sudden pang of homesickness, as he flashed back in time to their shared triumphs and despairs.

'William Kennedy!' she gasped. 'For God's sake, I don't believe it!'

And then she put her arms round his neck and kissed him full on the mouth.

They sat some way apart from the rest of the gathering, away from the crowd by the pool, in a sun-shaded part of the garden.

'Doesn't anybody ever swim in their pools in Hollywood?' William enquired. 'In all the weeks I've been here, I don't think I've seen one person in the water.'

'They have people in to swim for them, darling,' Meredith replied. 'Doubles.'

William laughed. In fact they'd done hardly anything but laugh since they'd sat down.

'Who makes this food?' William asked, holding some perfectly tasteless pasta up for inspection on his fork. 'Props?'

'I guess so,' Meredith agreed. 'Except for the really big occasions, when they hand the catering over to Special Effects.'

515

'It's the one thing I miss as an American,' William concluded. 'English food.'

That was enough to open the floodgates of recollection. Putting their tasteless brunch aside, William grabbed a full bottle of Californian champagne from one of the passing waiters, and Meredith and he spent the rest of the midday getting footless and calling up old times. Finally, as people started to drift away to the next social location, William asked Meredith what she was doing out in California?

'Of course you wouldn't read the trades,' she mock-scolded. 'Writers only ever read the sports page.'

'I've even given up the sports page,' William replied, 'now that I've started talking to trees.'

Meredith laughed again, and slipped her arm through William's as they walked towards their cars. On the way she explained how she had been sent out here and why.

'It's my guess Baz wants a piece of the action like Max has,' she said finally.

'I can't see that,' William replied. 'Max is with one of the majors. Your outfit, if you'll pardon me for saying it, is a flea on the dog.'

'It was,' Meredith agreed, 'before I joined it. You see I have a vested interest in pulling at a certain rug.'

'The one Max is standing on?' William asked.

'Keep your eye on the stop press,' Meredith instructed. 'And come to lunch next Sunday.'

They parted with a tentative arrangement for the following weekend. William saw Meredith to her open-topped car, and then as she drove off, her long hair flowing out behind her in the temperate wind, he decided the sudden pang he felt was due either to indigestion, or much more likely, thanks to the time spent in mutual recollection, to *maladie du pays*. He was homesick for England, and it wasn't even his country.

During the week that followed, William finished the first draft of his screenplay and took it in to deliver personally to Max. Max was delighted and told him to leave it on his desk, promising to read it as soon as he had the time. William then told Max that he had no intention of leaving it for Max to bottom-drawer for a couple of weeks while he, William, kicked his heels in his Malibu beach house, which was why he was going to read it to Max right now. Max replied that William had now taken total leave of his senses, because he had a meeting with the studio chiefs in two hours, and before that he had to see his chiropractor.

William flicked on Max's intercom and ordered Max's secretary to cancel the chiropractor.

Then he sat down and started to read his script out loud.

'Wait a minute!' Max yelled. 'What's this?'

'This, Max,' William replied, 'is what a lot of writers do and have always done. Including the great George Kauffman.'

'I don't care if it includes the great Mickey Mouse!' Max objected. 'My sacrum is killing me!'

'By the time I've finished reading,' William assured him, 'the only feeling you'll be having will be one of sheer pleasure.'

He was right. When William got to the last page, Max actually applauded.

'You didn't laugh once,' William complained.

'You'll bet your ass I didn't,' Max said, snatching the script from him. 'I might have missed something. Willy boy, you're good. So let's move it!'

William looked up in surprise.

'Where to, Max?' he asked. 'You said you had a meeting with your chiefs.'

'Too right I do,' Max replied, opening the door. 'And that's where you're going. To give a repeat performance.'

Before she allowed William to return her hospitality, Meredith asked if she could read his screenplay, on the quiet.

'You've seen the play,' William replied. 'Why read the movie?'

'I have my reasons,' Meredith told him. 'And I'd be very grateful.'

There was nothing sexual in her implication of gratitude. But there was a definite other meaning. William's ear was well attuned now to the nuances of Hollywood to recognize the promise of a mutual back-scratch.

'OK,' he agreed. 'But if anyone gets to hear, I'm going to say you broke in.'

The studio chiefs had not been so demonstrably enthusiastic over William's first draft as Max had, but for men who barely seemed alive, they still showed signs of definite approval. However, when the first set of suggested revisions were put to William, he was horrified. He couldn't agree with any of the more major changes requested.

Max marked William's card for him.

'OK – of course there are things you don't like in their suggestions,' he said, 'but that's only your own goddam fault.'

'It's no good you saying goddam, Max,' William sighed. 'Only us Americans can say it and say it right. An Englishman says it and it comes out sounding German. My advice is stick to your own blasphemy.'

'Stop cracking wise and listen, will you?' Max instructed. 'Because I know what I'm saying. Never – and I mean it, Willy boy – never ever again do your best work on the first draft. They're paying you to do two full drafts and a final polish, so take the advice of the guys out here who've been dipping their pens for years. Save best for last.'

'Oh sure, Max. And that way get to lose the job.'

'No way do you get to lose a job like that, believe me. It's like not showing all your best tennis shots during the knock up. You put all your best work into the first draft, and they'll wonder why it's going downhill in the second.'

'It's too late for that now, Max. I've done and delivered draft one.'

'OK. So now do as they say with draft two, and don't argue. Change the order of those scenes, scenes twenty-five to thirty whatever, even though you know it's wrong. Then they'll think they're right, and making them feel they're right, you'll be making them feel creative. And believe me, that's essential. One of the secrets of success in this lunatic town is to make these thick-as-wood philistines feel like Leonardo da Vincis. So you say, thanks, fellahs. Your suggestions – they are something else. How did you get there? I mean I know I wrote it, but I could never have thought of this. And they'll love you. You'll get automatic invitations to every poolside brunch for the whole of the next year. And then when it comes to the final polish they still have to find you something to do, because they're paying you for it. And they don't like the writer to get away with a stage payment unless he's seen to earn it.

'But you stick to your guns here, and say no way. It's perfect as it stands. And they say either you make the changes or we call in another writer. And if they call in another writer, no first-day-of-shoot money for you, and no single credit. So you give in. You bleed a little, you show how much it hurts, but you say: OK, guys. What do you want? I'll do anything, you say, except change the order of scenes twenty-five to thirty whatever. Because nobody makes me change those scenes. They are perfect. So what do you think they'll want you to do? They'll want you to change the order of scenes twenty-five to thirty whatever, the same scenes they ordered you to change on the second draft, they'll want you to change them back to the order they were in before you changed them on their orders, simply because you said no – the scenes stay as they are. That way you get to write the film you wanted to write, and they get the film they think they've creatively helped you to write. It's called How To Write Your Movie Their Way And Still Get To Final Payment.'

William didn't often laugh. William preferred the wry smile, and usually let Jay do the laughing. But Max's lunatic exposé of the mechanics of film-writing really got to him, because more than anything, beneath the barrage of surrealism, Max was speaking the truth. The way to get through the jungle and actually get fully paid up and singly credited, was to write your last draft first and put it away in the closet, and then write your first draft second, or maybe even third, and submit it to the moguls as your first. Max was right. It was pointless putting all your hardest and best work into the first draft, because the producers were bound to trash it, because by the terms of your contract they could make you, and always did make you, write another two drafts. Next time round, William avowed in the letter he wrote to Jay about it, 'His frist droft wud be barley reedible (sic).'

He was writing to Jay because the last time they had spoken she had told him she had to go north to see her mother who was seriously ill, and she wasn't sure when she, Jay, would be back in London. So William wrote to her every day during that spell, sometimes only a postcard or half a sheet, sometimes twenty pages, depending on how much he had to tell her.

Until one night he had a sudden telephone call from Jay to tell him that her mother had died.

'I'll fly over at once,' William said.

'There's no point, William. You didn't know her.'

'That's not the point, sweetheart.'

'It is, really. Anyway, it's only family.'

'And I'm not family?'

'Not in this lot's eyes, William. Not oop 'ere, you're not.'

Jay tried to make a joke, but William knew she was a long way from laughing.

'Will you be all right?' he asked her.

'I'll be fine, William,' she replied. 'Really. I just miss you.'

'I miss you too, honey. Like hell.'

'William?'

'Yes?'

There was a silence before Jay replied. A long silence. William didn't break it, because he knew Jay better.

'William,' she finally said, suddenly sounding as far

520

away as she actually was. 'William, I do love you, you know.'

And then the line went dead.

Meredith had finished reading William's screenplay and knew he was the man she wanted. She had known it anyway, when she saw him at the Johannsens'. But after reading his marvellous script, she knew beyond all doubts.

'If you don't ask me back to lunch soon,' she threatened him on the telephone, 'I really will break in.'

'What in hell's the hurry?' William asked.

'I'll tell you when I see you,' Meredith replied. 'And don't let's ask anyone else.'

She put the phone down and went to work. In ways other than just showing up at Harry Johannsen's house for her daily poolside briefing.

'Hey!' Harry called her from his lounger by the pool as she walked across the lawn. 'There's some dog crap on the lawn! Get the pooper scooper and clear it up, will ya?'

Meredith agreed as pleasantly as she always agreed to do this most disagreeable of tasks, particularly since the dirty dog in question was one of Harry's German Shepherds. Then still holding the full scoop she walked across to where Harry was lounging, talking on one of his four telephones, as if to tip the droppings into a nearby flower bed. But as she went to do so, she suddenly teetered uncertainly on one of her high heels, and, snagging it between the patio stones, stumbled and tipped the entire contents of the scooper into the crystal blue waters of the swimming pool.

Harry put his phone down at once to yell at her.

'What the hell do you think you're doing, you stupid bitch! Look at my pool!'

'I'm sorry, Harry darling, it was an accident,' Meredith replied, examining the heel of her shoe. 'I simply must have slipped.'

'Will you look at my goddam pool, goddammit! It looks like a sewage works!'

521

'I said I'm sorry, Harry. It *was* an accident!'

'I'll have to have the whole thing drained, goddam you! Will you just look what you've done, you asshole!'

'All I can say, Harry sweetie, is, just in case it happens again, next time ask your gardener to remove your dirty fidos. Tony wears much more sensible shoes than I do.'

Harry glared at her, uncertain as to whether or not she had perpetrated her quite deliberate act indeed deliberately, then turned away and stormed into the house.

Before she followed him, Meredith took one quick glance at the pool. Harry was right. It most certainly would need draining.

'We got trouble,' Harry told Meredith when she followed him into the cool of his living room.

'You'll be in trouble, Harry,' she told him back, 'if you don't put some clothes on when you're outside.'

'Don't tell me my natural state embarrasses you?' he asked, feigning surprise.

'Not in the slightest, Harry,' Meredith replied. 'But don't tell me you don't know your libido suffers dramatically if you get sun on your dick.'

'So who says?' Harry retorted, nonetheless casting an anxious eye on his person.

'My old nanny,' Meredith said. 'Who else?'

Having got in the first blow of the day, Meredith pulled a chair up to the desk and started sorting out her papers. She carefully laid out all the documents containing updates on the shooting of Diplomat's latest film, a bank-heist movie called *Silver Sterling* starring Wyn Gates, making sure to put the folder which contained Gates's latest litany of complaints on the very top of the pile.

After Harry had pulled on a pair of faded Bermudas and tossed his baseball cap, the only article of clothing he had been wearing up till that moment, into a corner, he sat his side of the desk and started reading through the documents. He soon came to an abrupt and angry halt.

522

'What the hell is all this?'

'You know what all that is, Harry. That's Wyn Gates still not being very happy, that's what that is.'

'What's the matter with this son of a bitch? We know he doesn't like the director. We know he doesn't like the writers. We know he doesn't like his co-star. Even though she screwed him rotten to get on the movie.'

'You should give him some of your funny stickers, Harry. The ones you put on the ceiling, you know. The ones that say: "*OK. You got the part.*"'

Harry glanced up at her for a moment, with a look of pure hatred, before returning to the list of won't-do's.

'Now he's not happy with the last three days' shoot. He wants us to reshoot. And he wants us to re-cast the bank cashier. What do you think's wrong with the bank cashier, I wonder? Doesn't do a good enough job? And the son of a bitch wants the Marshal re-cast as well. Even though we've got two of the actor's four days in the can! Jesus Christ – who does this guy think he is?'

'Wyn Gates, Harry. That's the name above the title.'

'Wyn God Almighty Gates!'

Harry tossed the report down on the desk and started to roll a fat joint.

'I gave him not one limo, but four. He has four limos at his disposal. He has a private masseuse on call twenty-four hours a day. He has an acupuncturist, and an astrologer. His make-up brushes are special badger hair, he has hot sandalwood towels at the ready, a constant supply of 7-Up, his own personal hairdressers and make-up artists, four chauffeurs, all black – the drivers all had to be black, remember? – and he has a brand-new air-conditioned-six-berthed mobile home, twice the size of his last one. I even have to make sure of his supply of Montezuma Gold.'

Harry paused to lick his joint closed, and then lit it, taking a deep draw.

'But it's still not enough. Every day there's something wrong. Today it's even down to a faucet dripping in his mobile home. What else does the bastard want from me?'

The joint was waved over the desk in Meredith's direction, but she declined. Harry, his temper cooled by the marijuana, grinned stupidly and waved it at her again.

'No, really,' Meredith said. 'Thanks all the same.'

'Come on,' Harry urged. 'It'll help you loosen up.'

'I'm loose enough already, Harry, believe me.'

'You? Loose? You, Meredith baby, this is how loose you are.'

And closing one index finger into as tight a ball as he could along the line of one thumb, held it up to her.

'That's how loose you are.'

Meredith just smiled politely, enduring Harry's insults as always, knowing full well she was going to win this day, and finally every day, because in the brief span of time she had been with Diplomat, she had already discovered that Harry Johannsen, as they said in these parts, no longer knew where it was coming from. And the main reason for this was what he was at present smoking. Harry Johannsen was doing his head, and fast.

'OK,' he finally asked, now well and truly high on his dope, 'so what do you think we should do about this six feet three inches of walking, talking excrement?'

'I think we should listen to what he has to say, Harry,' Meredith answered.

'You think we should fix his dripping faucet?'

'I just think we should listen. Fine, so he complains.'

'He always complains!'

'He's only complaining because he's not happy.'

'Isn't that when people normally complain? Jesus.'

'But we're not really listening, Harry.'

'Fine, sweetheart.'

Harry smiled at nothing in particular then lay back and stared up at the ceiling, before giving Meredith her orders for the day.

'So you go listen.'

One of the many things Meredith was good at was listening. It was something she had learned to do as an actress, something she had learned from Basil Landun. He hadn't told her directly, but one day on the set when he had lost his temper with some unfortunate working actor, out of the ensuing row Meredith had learned one of the secrets of her art.

'Listen, old boy,' Landun had told the wretched mummer. 'If you can't do it, and it's pretty damn obvious you can't, right? the best we can hope to get out of you is to make it look as though you can do it. And you know what the secret of that is, old boy? Just listen. And don't just act listening, like most of you silly twats do. Listen properly. That's all what acting is, you know, old boy. It's listening. Anyone can learn to say lines. Anyone can learn not to bump into the furniture. But the ones we remember as we sit out there in the darkness are the ones who look as though they're listening.'

It had been a turning point not only in that young actor's life, who had gone on to become one of England's more successful film stars, but it had also been a turning point in Meredith's. And once again she could use the technique to her own advantage, as she sat in apparently rapt attention at Wyn Gates's feet.

They were in his mobile home, which was parked that day inside the studios, since they were doing the bank interiors. Gates was eating a fast-food lunch of hamburgers which were being cooked for him by a blonde in a black satin catsuit, while his acupuncturist, a Japanese girl who wore a white medical coat and precious little else, stuck needles in between the actor's toes.

But most importantly, which had won Meredith immediate Brownie points, a plumber was busy fixing the dripping faucet.

'Christ, honey!' Gates drawled in his famous Southern accent to Meredith. 'Why do all goddarn plumbers have to go round smellin' like that?'

The plumber knew better than to argue with Wyn Gates, so he just muttered an apology and went about his business.

'That's OK, man,' Gates waved in the worker's direction. 'Hazard of the profession, I guess. Just must be merry ole hell bein' your poor wife.'

Meredith thought it couldn't have been too much fun being Gates's acupuncturist, judging from the aroma of sweaty feet that even the air conditioning was failing to dispel. But then no doubt the weekly pay packet took care of any such sensibilities.

'You were saying about the scene you have with the cashier,' Meredith reminded the actor, anxious to get him back on the tracks.

'It's not just the scene with the cashier, hon,' Gates drawled. 'It's the whole goddarn script. Fine, the action stuff we've shot, fine. But now we're on to the interiors, and all the talking stuff, man what we're looking at here is just sheet. If you'll pardon the expression.'

Wyn Gates grinned at Meredith, revealing his perfectly capped white teeth. And Meredith just nodded seriously in return, encouraging more from the actor.

She wasn't disappointed. The less she said and the more she listened, the more he talked. And underneath all that laid-back Southern manner, and the 'I am man, you are woman' bit that the actor loved to play, Wyn Gates talked good sense. He knew a bad script when he read one, and he had some pretty good ideas about how to go about improving it.

'But I'm no goddarn writer, hon,' he assured Meredith, who breathed a secret sigh of relief. Because had he been a Craig Matheson, there would have been no way of saving the movie. 'I can barely sign my own name, babe. But what I do know is, come Monday, when they call me for the first of these big talkin' scenes here, I ain't goin' to be available.'

With that he pulled the ring tab on yet another 7-Up and drank half the can in one gulp.

'No, sir,' he finished. 'Wyn Gates just ain't goin' to be around for no one.'

* * *

William returned to his beach house from the studios where he had been to deliver his first set of rewrites as per Max's instructions, and found Meredith awaiting him. She was sitting on his verandah, swinging her bare brown legs through the posts, her linen skirt hitched high above her knees.

William looked up at her and Meredith smiled back down at him.

'Hi, genius,' she said.

'How did you get up there?' he asked.

'I climbed. Come on, open up. I could kill for a beer.'

They drank ice-cold Budweiser on the steps at the front of the house, watching the ocean and talking. Or rather Meredith talked, and William listened, at which he was pretty good as well, but then so he should be. He was a writer.

'You're not asking much,' William said when Meredith was done.

'It's not as if it's the whole movie, William darling,' she replied. 'It's only bits here and there.'

William shook his head although he felt like laughing.

'Did I ever tell you about my English artist friend, Neil?' he enquired. 'He was commissioned to paint a regimental portrait. And when the day came for the unveiling, he was rushed by some high-ranking officer or other into the mess and told they'd left out one very senior member of the regiment. And could he possibly sit down and paint him in. And when Neil refused, they couldn't understand it. They couldn't understand what he was saying about balance and composition. They said look, all he had to do was paint this guy in. Which is what you're asking of me. Don't bother with the whole movie – just paint in a bit here and there.'

William got up and wandered off towards the edge of the ocean. Meredith sighed, and remembered Max's dictum about writers being nothing but old ladies in jeans. How right he had been, she thought as she followed William to the sea. Fuss, fuss, fuss. And always the same old harangue about integrity, and overall artistic control. You ask a writer to drop in a few scenes on a nondescript movie, and you'd think you were asking him to touch up the ceiling of the Sistine Chapel.

'OK, Michelangelo,' she said, catching up with him and taking his hand. 'So you won't bail an old friend out of trouble.'

'You know, I've always believed,' William told her, 'that holding hands is practically as intimate as kissing.'

'So suppose I kiss you?' Meredith asked.

'So suppose you do,' William replied laconically, and then immediately regretted his retort. For Meredith took him at his word and kissed him.

It was the second time she had kissed him like that. Full and soft on his mouth. There was no impertinence to the kiss. There was no sexual challenge. It was just a kiss. A sweet, pure, warm, soft kiss. And in it the ocean's roar was silenced.

'You shouldn't have done that,' William said, taking her by the shoulders and holding her at arms' length.

'I know,' Meredith replied. 'But I'm very glad I did.'

'It won't get me to change my mind.'

'That's not why I did it.'

'Sure it is, Meredith. You said suppose I kiss you?'

'I was changing the subject.'

Meredith was still being held arms' length, but she had William by his eyes. And while he held her by her shoulders, she held him by his eyes.

'It's allowable,' she said, 'if that's what you're worried about.'

'What is?'

'It is. You know the saying. On tour, on location, and in wartime. It's allowable. Because it's understandable, and it's forgivable.'

'Depends who's doing the forgiving, sweetheart.'

'Jay would understand.'

'Sure she would. But you see, it's me. I would never forgive myself.'

528

'You would.'

'I wouldn't. Besides. You want me to patch up this movie of yours this weekend. If I went to bed with you now, I wouldn't want to get out of it for a week.'

Meredith watched him walk back up the beach towards his house, tossing a stone he'd just picked up from one hand to the other. Then she sat down on a rock and gave him an hour to read through the script which she'd carefully left on his desk when they went in for the beers, with the relevant pages marked, before following him in. By the time she had reached the steps leading up to his front door, she could hear him already at work on the typewriter. She paused on the top step before opening the door and tried to think of an applicable term for the technique she had just employed. Reverse seduction, she supposed.

Yes, she smiled to herself, yes, she reckoned that must be it. If she hadn't come on strong for William, she knew he'd have come after her. She knew that from his response to her kiss at that brunch. On tour, on location or away at war, all men were the same. Women too, maybe. But that didn't matter. From where she was standing, Meredith was woman, and William was man. A man away from love. And there was no one more vulnerable anywhere than a man separated from his lover. Yes, William would have come after her, and if he'd succeeded, which he would have done all too easily, since Meredith found him incredibly attractive, then he would have been of no further use to her. The last thing she would have been able to persuade him to do would have been to put the boats out for her drowning movie, had he taken her to bed on his terms that afternoon.

But by her making the move, by her taking the ball and dropping it at his feet, he could then keep his senses and be seen to make a mature and responsible decision. But William, being a sensitive as well as a sensible soul, would need to compensate somehow for refusing her. And of course when you thought about it, there was only one way he could go. Upstairs to his first floor den, his battered old Remington portable, and Meredith's carefully earmarked shooting script.

A well-thought-out piece of campaigning, Meredith thought, reviewing her actions and giving herself a good notice. In fact, judging from the pounding of the typewriter at the window directly above her head, Meredith immediately changed the good review for her successful strategizing into an out and out rave.

The fifteen minutes of rewritten film were with Meredith by late Sunday night. Meredith read through them quickly the first time, to gain the flavour, and then over again but slowly the next twice, just as Max had taught her how.

'It's like buying a house,' he had told her. 'The first look is peremptory. A do-I-like-it-in-general look. Then if you do, you go back, except on your next visits you look for the rising damp and the cracks in the plaster.'

There was no rising damp in William's rewrites, no cracks in the fabric whatsoever. It was seamless.

'Who is this guy, hon?' Gates asked her the next morning after he, too, had cast his eye over the scenes. ''Cause whoever he is, I want him aboard.'

Meredith explained that it was a moonlighting job, and that the author would have to use a *nom de plume* for his additional dialogue credit, since he was contracted elsewhere by one of the majors.

'OK,' the star said. 'I read you. But you just listen here, hon. When this shoot's over, I owe you for this. I owe you and your writer buddy. And I mean it. No shee-it.'

Meredith called William, but got his answering service, so she called round instead. Since the blinds were still down in the bedroom, den and living room, she took it William had crashed out. But since it was now well after midday, Meredith reckoned it would be safe enough to wake him, and started to throw pebbles up at the bedroom window.

After a moment William appeared at the window, naked except for a pair of shorts.

'The chef's off,' he called down to her. 'The restaurant's closed.'

'I only came round to congratulate you,' Meredith called back up, showing him the bottle of champagne she had brought. 'Wyn Gates thinks you're Shakespeare.'

William produced some brandy and some angostura bitters and turned the moderate Californian champagne into delicious champagne cocktails. The two of them sat out in the sun on the balcony drinking the cocktails and dunking thick old-fashioned potato crisps into a couple of dips Meredith had rustled up from the contents of William's refrigerator.

'When you get round to it,' William asked Meredith, 'I want you to credit Jay with the additional dialogue. But don't tell her. I want it to be a joke.'

'No problem,' Meredith agreed. 'And the fee?'

'What is it?'

'If you do the other two or three big scenes – it's not going to be less than eight g's.'

'OK. So we'll give her that as well. We'll send it anonymous. From a fan. A fan of her first book.'

William smiled and looked out across the sea, his thoughts circling the globe.

He still hadn't had any joy getting hold of Jay, despite constant telephone calls. Even the agency wasn't too sure where she was, and thought, like him, that she must still be attending to her mother's affairs. She'd been back in London since the funeral all right, but William had managed to miss her then as well, before she had disappeared again. Strangest of all, though, was the fact that she hadn't replied to one of his letters.

'Not that I expected her to,' William said, pouring the last of the wine. 'The letters weren't like those goddam Latin questions that demand an answer. *Nonne* questions I think they are. Or was it *num*? And what the hell does it matter anyway? Because she didn't write back, and although I didn't expect her to, I'm kinda surprised she didn't.'

531

'Sure,' Meredith replied before lapsing into silence, hoping that William would at last change the subject.

'I just can't help it,' he said finally. 'I just kinda thought she would.'

Meredith rested her last cocktail on the balcony in front of her and took out a small tin from her purse.

'Want to do some grass?' she enquired.

'Sure,' said William. 'I'll try anything that makes the shortest distance between two points even shorter.'

'Christ knows what this'll do to our heads, William Kennedy.'

'How long you been out here, Meredith Browne?'

'Long enough, William Kennedy. Long enough.'

'From the sound of it, any minute now you'll be telling me to have a nice day.'

'Have a nice day.'

'I'm having a nice day.'

'So am I. I'm having a great one.'

She passed the J to William, who took two or three deep draws on it and felt good all over.

'What are you up to, Meredith Browne?'

'I'm going to produce Wyn Gates's next movie, that's what I'm up to.'

'You are?'

'You bet I am.'

'Any minute now.'

'Any minute now what, William Kennedy?'

'Any minute now I tell you – it'll be have a nice day. What makes you so sure you're going to produce Gates's next movie, Meredith Browne?'

'You do, William Kennedy.'

'I do? Why me?'

'Because you're a great writer, that's why.'

Meredith smiled at him, then removed her T-shirt. She wasn't wearing a bra. She smiled again and removed her jeans, before lying back in the hot sun and closing her eyes. William stared down at the perfect girl who now lay at his feet, naked all but for a pair of immaculate white silk panties and a gold chain worn around her waist.

'Whose slave are you?' he asked.

'No one's,' she replied.

'Then why the chain?'

'It was a present.'

'A chain is a chain is a chain. This your regular guy?'

'I don't have a regular, William.'

'Come on.'

'I don't.'

'Why don't you?'

'Because I don't want one.'

William stared at Meredith, still lying smiling with her eyes shut and, seeing the body of a perfect woman, thought how ridiculous that no one was making love to a body like that at every conceivable opportunity. And then, sighing deeply to himself, like a part of the wind that had started blowing off the sea, he leaned his head back and closed his own eyes tightly shut.

'Is anyone making love to you at the moment?' he asked her after an immeasurable silence.

'No,' she answered. 'Not right at this moment.'

'But you have lovers.'

'I have had lovers. Hollywood's hardly a convent.'

'Sure,' William replied. 'And you're no Bernadette.'

After another long, sun-baked silence, William opened his eyes and allowed himself one last sight of Meredith's magnificent body and breasts, before rising and stretching to the full.

'OK,' he announced. 'I'm going to take a swim.'

'Sure that's what you'd rather do?' Meredith asked.

'No,' William replied. 'Which is precisely why I'm going to go take a swim.'

Max and William sat in the viewing theatre long after the president and the vice-presidents of Allied Independents had all filed out. But none of them had left without first individually congratulating both the writer and the producer on what they considered to be a major piece of movie-making.

'You're to be congratulated, Max,' the president had said. 'This is going to prove to be one of the very finest film comedies I personally have viewed in a very long decade.'

William had found himself wondering how much longer a decade could be in Hollywood than anywhere else, when he too was confronted by the president of the studios.

'And Mr Kennedy,' the president had said. 'You can also be proud to have been a major contributor to such a prestigious movie.'

'You're too kind, sir,' William had replied. 'But hell, I only wrote the damn thing.'

'I know,' the president had responded with utter sincerity. 'But that's all the more reason for you to be proud of your participation.'

And now they sat in the silent theatre, Max wondering how much the film would gross, and William how anything in Hollywood ever got to be made.

'What do you reckon, kid?' Max asked him. 'Think we've pulled it off?'

'I couldn't say, Max,' William replied. 'I've never sat through a rough cut before. Let alone a rough cut of my own work.'

'The gods were not angry.'

'Sure. But then there's not a lot of space between their ears.'

'Oh, believe me, Willy boy. They may look stupid. They may act stupid. Most of all, they may be stupid. But when they don't like, you know it.'

'The girl is brilliant.'

'Diane? She's going to be a big star, you watch.'

'But I don't know.'

'Sure you don't, kid. If we did, who'd bother? Can you imagine making movies you knew were going to be hits? I'd prefer to sell meat.'

Max lit a fresh cigar and slipped his feet back into his shoes.

'Go home, Willy boy,' he advised. 'There's nothing left for you to do out here until the film opens. So go home and take a rest. Go home and make love to that girl of yours. You've done great.'

The grin Max bestowed on William was one of his very best and most sincere, guaranteed to melt the toughest of resistances. William slipped his jacket back on and pulled up his tie.

'OK,' he agreed. 'But first, let's go out and get fried.'

Across town, at about the same time, the wrap was being called on *Silver Sterling*. Harry Johannsen had lost close interest in the movie when Gates had been making all the trouble, and had delegated Meredith the job of bringing it in, and hoping the task would prove way beyond her, and that it would break her, since nothing else he had thought up had.

Meredith in turn had done her best to look appalled at the prospect, while secretly testing that the next rung up the ladder was utterly safe. Which of course it already was, now she had the star on her side. The rest of the picture was plain sailing, thanks to William's anonymous rewrites and Meredith's skilful diplomacy.

And she brought the film in two weeks under.

So at the wrap party, the toast proposed by the company president was Wyn Gates coupled with Meredith Browne. Harry Johannsen wasn't mentioned.

At around two in the morning, Meredith decided to go home. But before she could leave, Wyn Gates grabbed hold of her and danced her to his mobile home, where once inside he locked the door, and turned the lighting system down to low.

'OK, hon,' he said. 'Let's party.'

Meredith smiled her best party smile at him, but said she really was done and just had to go home. The star frowned at her, and scratched his chin thoughtfully.

'You wanna go home now?' he asked.

'It's been a long day, Wyn darling,' Meredith replied. 'And I guess I don't have your incredible energy.'

535

'OK, hon. Then let's make it quick,' he said, starting to undo his belt.

'I'm sorry,' Meredith said quickly, to forestall any premature revelations. 'But I don't understand.'

The star stopped his unbuckling and frowned at her, chewing on his gum.

'Now wait up,' he said finally. 'You do give head, right?'

'Wrong, I'm afraid,' Meredith replied. 'It's nothing personal, darling. But it's not part of my act.'

'Your act, hon?' Gates asked, now looking completely baffled. 'You mean you don't want to?'

'Not particularly. No.'

'But hon – after all you done. I told you, babe. I owe you!'

The penny dropped, but Meredith just in time managed to stop herself smiling.

'You really don't want to?' the star asked her again, to make quite sure.

'Really,' Meredith said, kissing him on the cheek. 'Thanks all the same.'

'You're more than welcome, hon,' Gates replied, redoing up his belt. 'Well, I guess I'll just have to come up with somethin' else for you.'

The office got William on the afternoon flight out of LA. He rang Jay from the airport before he embarked, but the number rang unobtainable. He rang from London Heathrow when he arrived, but was still unable to get an answer. Assuming it to be a fault on the line, he finally counted it as a blessing in disguise as he sat in the cab trying to imagine the look on Jay's face when she opened the door to his knock.

It was a fine, warm Saturday morning, and Sloane Street was full of shoppers as the cab swung round Sloane Square and down towards the King's Road. William, clasping the dozen red roses he had bought for Jay at the airport, could barely contain his excitement as the driver pulled the cab up outside the studio. William jumped out, and was too busy paying his fare to notice the sign. He was still too busy lifting his bags out and carrying them to the front door to take proper notice, and even as he stood waiting for his ring to be answered what the sign said had no real significance.

Until he realized the sign was fixed outside the studio, and not, as he had subconsciously assumed, outside the flat next door.

And it was not until he had obtained no answer to his now persistent ringing of the door bell that he stood and stared at the green and white estate agent's poster which now simply read 'Sold'.

14

No one knew where Jay had gone. The house agents were most helpful, but all they could tell William was that the studio flat had been put on the market six weeks ago, and being a very desirable property had sold almost immediately. Miss Burrell had left no forwarding address, simply requesting that any mail should be sent on to her literary representative.

The offices of Max Kassov Ltd incorporating Eric Williams were naturally closed, it being a Saturday, but William telephoned and just caught Eric Williams at home as he was leaving for the Sandown Park races.

'Actually I thought if anyone knew where she'd hived off to,' the acting head of Max Kassov Ltd, London, drawled, 'it'd be you, old thing. She only told us she was taking off to write in the country somewhere, but since she hadn't yet found anywhere definitely, she'd just phone in from time to time. That was the last we heard from her.'

Which had been a month ago. Jay had called into the offices to collect some of the monies she was owed, and promptly disappeared off the face of the map.

Not even any of her relatives whom William tracked down in Danby knew of her whereabouts. She had come up to see her mother in her final illness, and stayed with her until she had died. Then, after one more prolonged visit when she had helped to tidy the family affairs, she had told them all she was going abroad for a sabbatical and left them the agency address should they want to get in touch with her.

'What about any further monies?' William asked their

mutual London agent. 'And what about this work she's meant to be doing? She was meant to be doing an adaptation of *The Secret Garden*.'

'Really?' Mark asked, sounding a little surprised. 'I knew nothing about that, I'm afraid. And as for her monies, she asked for anything that came in to be sent straight to her bank.'

William would have to wait until Monday to make enquiries at the bank, so he checked into a hotel in Basil Street, having sublet his own Hampstead apartment all that time ago when he had finally moved in with Jay. He started the round of telephoning friends. At first he suspected a conspiracy of silence, since no one he talked to could tell him anything more than he already knew.

And what had she meant by telling him she was working on an adaptation of *The Secret Garden* for the BBC when it now transpired she never had been?

By that evening, sick of running up against brick walls, William suddenly remembered Polly Stephens. Jay had developed an unexpectedly warm and close friendship with the bright-eyed and sharp-witted actress, ever since she'd guested on an episode of *Life With Charlie* and endeared herself to everyone. William scanned the theatre columns on the off-chance that Polly might be working in the West End, and as luck would have it, there was her name above the title of a recently opened thriller now packing the audiences into The Garrick.

They dined after the second evening performance in the Savoy Grill, Polly having been all too easily persuaded to drop a previous dinner engagement with one of her stage-door johnnies, as she delighted in her somewhat old-fashioned way to describe her growing army of admirers.

The only thing different about Polly's story, however, was that she had at least seen Jay shortly before she vanished.

'She saw the show then come round after,' Polly told William, 'and we sat and drank the best part of a bottle of wine between us.'

'How was she, Polly?' William asked. 'Did she look OK?'

'You know Jay better than me, William. I mean Jay always looks pale. And she was a bit tired like, because she told me she'd been having to rush about putting her things in store and everything.'

'But she didn't say why? And she didn't say where she was going?'

'She just said she was taking a sabbatical, whatever that is when it's at home. And that she'd be in touch.'

'Did she talk about me?'

'No.'

'She didn't say anything about – about us?'

'Not as far as I can remember, William.'

Polly looked up from her meal and did her best to comfort William with a smile.

'I didn't ask, see,' she continued, 'well – 'cause I didn't know what the score was, like. I mean I didn't know whether or not . . . you know. Whether you and she was still on.'

'That's OK,' William replied, pushing aside his barely touched food. 'I just thought she might have said something.'

'She didn't mention no one else, if that's what you mean,' Polly added.

William pretended to be genuinely comforted by the information, but in reality it brought him little solace. He knew perfectly well that if Jay had found and fallen in love with somebody else, the very last person she would tell in London was her friend Polly Stephens. She would have more chance of keeping such information secret were she to hire an illuminated sign above Piccadilly Circus. She might well have let slip where she was going, but why – never. Jay was a crab, and crabs kept their secrets.

The bank could help no further either. All they were permitted to divulge was that indeed a Miss Jay Burrell held a current account with them, which allowed her encashment facilities at any of their numerous branches throughout the country. But no, regretfully there was no way they could tell Mr Kennedy where, or when, or indeed if at all Miss Burrell was availing herself of their services.

After a further twenty-four hours spent wild-goose chasing, William booked himself back to Los Angeles on the first available flight, which wasn't for three days. To pass the time away, William bought Proust's *Remembrance of Things Past* and three bottles of vodka, before shutting himself away in his hotel room, where he managed to get through the vodka considerably more quickly than he did the Proust.

On the Saturday he flew back out, in the garden of a cottage which overlooked a tranquil stretch of the Thames outside Cookham, a young woman with a braid of long brown hair sat out in the sunshine. Even though the day was balmy and warm, she had a rug over her knees, and a sweater over her dress. On her knee was a jumbo-size notebook, with barely one dozen of its forty dozen pages filled. The notebook was at present closed over, while the writer lay half sleeping in the sunlight. Every now and then she would stir, to open her eyes momentarily as some noise perhaps from the river awoke her, or voices carrying into the garden where she lay from the by-road beyond the wall. Then she would drift back again to slumber some more, lulled by the lapping of the river waters and the hum of the bees in the hollyhocks.

Once, mid-afternoon, without knowing why, she awoke with a start and found herself staring into the clear blue of the summer sky. Above her, after shading her eyes against the sun, she could make out the still plainly discernible shape of a Pan American airliner on its ascent into the stratosphere. The young woman frowned at the disappearing aircraft, without knowing the cause of her perplexity, and stared at it until it was entirely out of her sight, unmindful that the thunder in the air was carrying away from her the one thing she loved more than life itself.

And then, pulling her rug up higher around her, Jay once more fell back into a deep, and for once pain-free sleep.

*Amid growing rumors concerning his future, Max Kassov,
only yesterday Allied Independents' brightest and bluest-
eyed boy, a talent recently tipped as Tab Teffner's immediate
successor, information which came as no small surprise to
Teffner himself who up until that moment had considered his
post as Independents' Chief of Creativity secure for at least
the foreseeable future, flew back into town after a whistle-
stop tour of Europe's financial capitals.*

'I've been doing a little prospecting of my own,' he told me
exclusive as I drove with him back from the airport. 'I have
several sources for investment and capitalization, to which,
if you like, you could say I own sole rights.'

Kassov is looking for more than he has ever looked before.
He would prefer it said that he was looking, assuring me the
necessary finance had been finalised, bar detail. But mindful
of that notorious distance between cup and lip, all Kassov
was prepared to say with any certainty, quoting NASA, was
that he had lift-off.

'If you want me to risk my neck,' he later quipped, 'then I'll
go on record that if The Last Outpost isn't in production by
spring, they won't have to assassinate me. I'll take the
hemlock.'

Kassov is nothing if not a confident man. And he would
need to be. Since the runaway success of Wrong Side of the
Bed, that beautifully scripted (by William Kennedy from his
own Broadway hit) and sublimely played (Diane Felton and
William Payne) movie which was top boxer of 1976, Kassov
has had to sing loud and long for his supper. Though the sequel
to Bed, Warner Hirsh-directed Another Day In The Life Of,
won similar critical acclaim, it failed to sell tickets, due, it
was suspected at the time, to the uncertain casting of Rose
Dimond and Henry LaBara.

'I'll defend that one,' Kassov said. 'Dimond and LaBara
were not second choice. We just didn't want to make another
Felton-Payne movie. What was wrong is that the film went in

too many different directions. It never made up its mind whether it was a comedy or a tragedy.'

So what of the four motion pictures since then, none of which has nudged into the top twenty grossers, let alone the top fifty? Kassov defends his failures with as much passion as he embraces his successes.

'Nobody means to make a bad movie,' he said. 'If they wanted us to make a bad movie, we could make bad movies. That's not the problem. But with Apple Of My Eye *and* Joe and Marsha, *those weren't bad movies. Those were good movies that somehow no one got to see. Wait till you see them again late one nite on TV. You'll grab the lady in the bed with you, or maybe you'll stop grabbing the lady in bed with you – and you'll say "Hey! What in hell is this movie!" I'm not in this business to make bad motion pictures.'*

Nonetheless, this British ex-pat, who arrived in Tinsel Town with such high hopes, admits each day to be like walking the Falls on a tightrope. Not that he'd have it any other way.

'I do it on adrenalin,' he grinned. 'I get off on standing on ledges. Show me a foolproof way of making hit movies and I'll take up door-to-dooring. You look out for The Last Outpost. *If we don't win every Oscar going with this one, that guy ringing your bell about double glazing – that's going to be me.'*

15

Max hadn't had to take the hemlock. Although now, two months into a five-month shoot, and already three weeks over, and with everybody on the unit apparently at each other's throats, he sometimes wished that he had. The trouble had started in the first week on the African locations, when Sally Foote, an idiosyncratic English actress to whom Max had been forced to give yet another last chance, had arrived and at once started causing trouble.

She had been employed for two reasons. Firstly, since her latest marriage, it was the informed opinion that she had dropped her hell-raising ways. Max doubted this, remembering the chaos she had caused on her last come-back movie, *Look To The Rose*, on which she had been replaced after five weeks shooting. Metro Amalgamated, the studio making the film, had been forced back to square one, re-casting Shelley Daytan at enormous expense and with no more success, since Miss Daytan, although unlike her predecessor clean on the drugs and drink front, had just gone into analysis for anal retention, and could not and would not appear in front of the cameras unless her bodily functions were in perfect balance. Consequently the movie went from three weeks to two months over schedule, and cost a fortune which was never recovered.

And secondly Sally Foote had been employed because her utterly brainless and latest husband, Charles Walter-Smith, was one of the movie's financiers. Not the most important of them, but one with sufficient clout to call at least one shot. And that one was the casting of his once famous new wife, who upon arrival on the set had proceeded to set about wrecking the movie as if she was a member of a demolition gang sent in to knock down an apartment block.

'She's drinking,' Victor Nicholson the director told Max on the phone from Africa, 'and she's doing coke. She's so far out of her head, we're going to have to post-synch all her stuff back home. That is if she's still alive. I'll tell you how bad it is. She doesn't know one line of the script. Not one, dammit. So for her scenes, I have to have someone stand out of shot saying her lines out loud so as Sally can pick 'em up. That way at least we've got some lip movement to go on when it comes to the dub. Trouble is her blasted nose runs the whole blasted time.'

'Sack her,' said Max. 'Get rid of the bitch.'

'I'd give my right arm, Max,' Victor sighed. 'But with her goes one million of your precious dollars.'

'I'll turn on another tap.'

'No you won't, dear boy. The word's already out about the trouble we're in. We'll be lucky if all the money doesn't come out within the month, the way things are going.'

'OK, Victor. In that case, I'm on my way.'

Max flew out to the far-distant African location and did his best to negotiate a settlement. But the bad seed had taken root and was spreading its poison throughout the company. In fact only Victor Nicholson's British charm and diplomacy had forestalled a full scale uprising of the natives.

The imported natives that is. The real natives just sat around the set in fascination as the actors and production staff screamed drunkenly and druggedly all night and day at each other.

'She's upset simply everyone,' Victor told Max in confidence the night he arrived. 'She has some extremely distasteful ideas, as well as language. I'm doing my level best to shoot off her and round her, but her part's fairly

545

important to the story, since she's the wife who gets murdered and consequently upon which hangs our tale, so I'm afraid it's over to you, old dear.'

Max tried to reason with the actress, sitting up half the night with her, which didn't faze Sally Foote at all because she was so coked-up she possibly wouldn't sleep for the next week.

'Now you're here, darling,' she promised Max, 'I'll have to behave, won't I? Or I'll be on the next plane home.'

'Or the one before, if you're not careful,' Max warned her, before staggering away to climb into the production's mobile home and a much longed-for bed.

The next morning the actress didn't show at all. They finally found her two days later in a village over twenty miles away in a mud hut with three of the native extras. She couldn't remember how she had got there, but judging from the smiles on the natives' spaced-out faces, it seemed they had all found a satisfactory way to eke out the time.

As predicted, as soon as the troublesome Miss Foote had been sent packing, out came her husband's investment. Max immediately flew to Frankfurt, Geneva and London to try and persuade some of the other backers to up their ante and patch up the loss, but the news of Walter-Smith's defection travelled faster than Max, and he found he was having to spend his time persuading his investors not to put up more money, but to stay in the film at all.

When he was satisfied that he had, and had collected the necessary signed guarantees to finance the next stage of the shoot, only then did Max feel it safe to return to Los Angeles and Hollywood.

But the day after his return he was called into an emergency meeting to discuss the state of the film and its finances. All the concerned studio chiefs were there, in their perfectly ironed short-sleeved white poplin shirts, with their pants hitched up high over their expanding waistlines. Max had always joked when he first arrived in

Hollywood that you could tell the importance of a studio executive by the height he wore his pants. Today he knew he was facing the biggest of the guns, since none of the six men standing awaiting his arrival at the meeting wore their pants lower than their chests.

'There's no trouble,' Max assured them. 'The poison's been rooted out, and Victor is once again at the wheel of a happy ship.'

'There's not a lot of cargo in the holds, we hear, Max,' said Cy Bernstein, sucking at the lemon from his Perrier water.

'There's enough to keep us afloat until the end of the month, Cy,' Max assured him, uncertain of how to handle the running metaphor. 'And when we reach the end of the month—'

'If we reach, Max,' Art Lovinger interrupted. 'If we do.'

'I have written guarantees, Art. We're paid up.'

There was a silence while the studio chiefs stared across at Max, smiling but with hostile eyes.

'Since we consider it to be an if rather than a when, Max,' Lovinger finally announced, 'we'd like to be of help. Which is why we're giving you Sam Russo. Sam's going to help keep an eye on things. Going to help things stay in check. It's all very well for one guy to have his finger in the leaky dyke. But sooner or later he's going to need assistance. You're stopping the flood great, Max. But there could be another leak springing up just down the road.'

Max had been wondering what Russo had been doing there, sitting down the far end of the highly polished table, flicking through the finances. He'd smiled at Max as Max had come in, as much as to say, Max thought, Hi pal. Up yours. Max knew Russo had been after his job since day one, but had discounted him as a serious threat, since the only thing he was known to be good at was playing. Until last month, that was, when he had announced his intention to marry Cy Bernstein's appalling slob of a daughter.

Two weeks later Victor Nicholson walked off the picture, unable and unwilling any longer to cope with the

547

escalating costs and the still feuding company. Max at once recommended they flew Marty Nichols out to bring the movie in, but his advice was ignored and instead the maverick Irving Neufeld was despatched to the battleground, armed with his tame rewrite man, Paul Conti.

They were Sam Russo's suggestions.

Max was furious, even more so when he found permission refused for his own return to Africa.

'Sorry, Max,' Lovinger explained, 'but we need you here.'

'*Last Outpost* is my baby, Art,' Max argued. 'I can get Nicholson back on the shoot, and I can bring the picture in on time.'

'You did your best, Max,' Bernstein assured him, 'and now's the time to step aside. New brooms.'

'And like I said, Max,' Lovinger continued, 'we need you here. We're doing a remake for television of *Little Women*, and you're just the guy to produce it.'

When William arrived at Max's house for the Friday poker game, he found he was the only guest.

'What did I do?' he asked Max, when by nine o'clock no one else had showed. 'Was it something I wrote?'

Max grinned and, loosening his tie, sat down at the card table with a bottle of Old Grouse and two tumblers.

'It was something I did,' he explained. 'Or rather something I didn't do. I didn't look over my shoulder.'

'I heard *Outpost* was in trouble, Max,' William said, accepting a treble whisky. 'But that's the state of the industry right now.'

Max grinned but all William could see were the dark grey lines under Max's eyes.

'Remember what Hitch said to Kim Novak when she was sounding off, Max,' he reminded his friend. 'When she quit bitching, he just looked at her and sighed: "It's only a movie, Kim."'

Max shook his head in reply.

'It's all I've got, pal,' he disagreed. 'And now Sam Russo's in my face.'

William continued to try and cheer his old friend up, but for the first time in a long friendship Max was inconsolable, and for his own part William wasn't exactly feeling like playing the life and soul of the party all evening, since today was the anniversary of the day he'd first met Jay. And although he had spent most of the day trying to forget the fact, memories kept flooding back and by now all William wanted was to be the other side of the Atlantic, dining with Jay at The 31 and holding her in his arms while they danced to 'The Nearness of You'.

Little wonder then that, come midnight, both men were very drunk.

'This is all Seraphina's fault, Willy boy. This is all her doing.'

'Getting fired off the movie?'

'Dying.'

'Like hell it is, buddy. That was her last wish. She said if I can't do anything else, the one thing I'll make sure of doing is getting old Max bumped off *The Last Outpost*.'

'If Seraphina hadn't died, Willy boy. . . .'

Max left a long and pregnant silence, before finishing the remains of his whisky.

'If Seraphina hadn't died, buddy, you'd have divorced her.'

'What did you say!' Max yelled. 'You take that back!'

'I said,' William repeated slowly and just as calmly, 'I said if Seraphina hadn't died, by now you two would have gotten divorced.'

'Jesus Christ, William Kennedy! You'd better get out of here before I kill you!'

By now Max had staggered to his feet and was doing his level best to turn over the heavy table. William, soberer than his friend, simply pursed his lips and pushed the table back down. Then he leaned across and pushed Max back down into his seat.

'Don't go crazy, Max old buddy,' he sighed. 'I'm only telling you something you know full well yourself. Seraphina was something else, sure. She was beautiful. She was perfect. She was an angel. And Christ alone knows how she stuck what you did to her. Burying her away in the depths of that goddam dreadful countryside.'

'I'm warning you, Kennedy!' Max roared, but with slightly less conviction.

'You have no idea of how bored she was, Max.'

'Seraphina wasn't bored, Kennedy! Seraphina lived for me! We were one! She lived for me, I tell you! We had the perfect life!'

'*You* did, you silly bastard. *You* had the perfect life. What you created was a perfect life for yourself. Marrying a beautiful girl, then sticking her away in some draughty old house in the middle of some of the ugliest countryside in England, so no one else could see her, or enjoy her, except you. It's just so much fiction, Max, and you know it. She was bored out of her head. But because she loved you – oh and Christ you've got to believe it, that girl loved you, Max Kassov. And because she did, she stuck out that dreadful life you tailor-made for her, for your precious artefact. But I'm telling you, buddy, as a buddy, as probably the best buddy you'll ever have, old buddy, that if she'd lived, and you'd kept insisting on locking her up in that fusty old house, like some mad old relative, she'd have left you but years ago.'

Max stared at him, rubbing his chin with the nail of one thumb. Then he poured them both some more whisky.

'It was a beautiful house.'

'It was a mausoleum.'

'And as for the countryside—'

'Flat, Max. Very very flat.'

'What do you know, Willy boy?'

'How did you expect a young girl as beautiful as that to live shut away like that, Max? Without anything to do? Without ever seeing anyone? Jeez – talk about selfish.'

'I asked you, what do you know, Kennedy! You're like

all damn Yankees! Jealous of the whole English bit. You never even saw how we lived!'

'Sure we did,' William said quietly, staring down into his glass. 'We saw exactly how you lived.'

That was enough to silence Max. Even through the haze of whisky that was addling his head, he heard something that jolted him back to reality.

'When you were away once, Max,' William continued. 'When you went to the Cannes Film Festival. Seraphina asked us down. In secret.'

'You're lying.'

'It's the truth, Max, so help me God.'

'You're lying, damn you, Kennedy! I tell you, you're lying through your lousy teeth!'

'It was only once, Max. Seraphina was lonely, goddammit. You don't know what lonely is.'

Max was on his feet again, lurching across the table. William shoved him hard and strong straight back into his chair, and then proceeded to describe Max and Seraphina's house in detail, right down to the dishes Mrs Joliffe had prepared them, the fabric of the bed linen, and the colour and scent of the roses in the garden.

'Who else was there?' Max whispered.

'No one,' William replied.

'Oh yes there was!' Max suddenly shouted, caught halfway between tears and rage. 'What about her lovers! What about D! and T! and G! They must have been there, too, yes! All her bloody lovers! Darling D! And wonderful T! And oh so wonderful and fantastic G!'

'There was never anyone else there, Max,' William replied, looking across at Max in astonishment. 'Who's G? And D? And T? I have no idea what you're talking about.'

'Is that so, smartarse!' Max shouted, getting to his feet again and leaning on the table. 'Well, I found her diary!'

Now it was William's turn to be astonished, before he suddenly and thankfully remembered Seraphina's sad little journal.

'Oh Christ,' he groaned. 'I told her to throw the damn thing away.'

'You knew about it?' Max yelled in fury. 'You're telling me she showed it to you?'

'Oh Jesus, Max!' William shouted back. 'Seraphina and Jay wrote it together! For a joke! You know? It was pissing with rain – and it made a change from gin rummy!'

'Jay couldn't have helped write all of it!' Max raged, still on his feet. 'There were pages of it! Pages and pages and pages of it!'

'I guess she just must have kept it up,' William shrugged. 'As a kind of therapy. Sure. In fact I remember her saying something to Jay when they were writing it. About it being positively therapeutic. Do you remember that in *High Society*? Positively therapeutic.'

There was no response from Max. Just silence, and the tapping of one of Max's fingernails on the edge of his whisky glass. Then quite suddenly he covered his eyes with just one hand, leaned back in his chair, and began to weep.

They walked it off on the beach. It had been William's idea. After an hour or so, he'd suggested a walk by the ocean, and had bundled Max in a cab and taken him back out to his rented beach house. They walked until the sun came up faint pink across the still-dark waters of the Pacific, whose tide was turning and building up its strength for its incoming run. They walked mostly in silence, sometimes side by side, sometimes a hundred yards apart, both lost inside their own heads.

When day had broken, they sat out on William's verandah and ate plates of waffles and syrup, washed down with mugs of scalding Blue Mountain coffee.

'Do you know too much coffee can give you cancer?' Max asked.

'There's only one thing that gives you cancer, Max,' William replied. 'Fear.'

'You afraid of anything, Willy boy?'

'You betcha, Max.'

'What?'

'I'm afraid of not being afraid. The day I wake up and start facing things without any anxiety, that's the day I'm cooked.'

They slept all morning on sun chairs out on the balcony, shaded by the overhang of the roof. At midday, William cooked them both some home-made *spaghetti al olio*, which they ate, drinking ice-cold beers. Then they walked the beach again, like the Walrus and the Carpenter, looking for a solution to the many worries that pressed them.

'They're going to fire me, Willy boy, if they haven't done so already.'

'They won't fire you yet. Not unless either they lose the money for the picture, or until Neufeld brings it in.'

'So you got any ideas, writer man?'

'Sure, Mr Producer. One or two. One particularly.'

As they walked, William told Max the rumour was Jules Kahn was leaving Metro Amalgamated to go to HMO.

'So what?' Max shrugged. 'Kahn's barely a vice-president. You want me to step down?'

'Basically yes,' William replied. 'OK, so you were a vice-president at Allied Independents, but then so were fifteen other schmucks, no offence intended.'

Max grinned and chucked a stone into the waves, as William continued to outline his plans. The deal was simple. Max offered himself to Metro Amalgamated in advance of the firing which they all knew was in the offing.

'And what makes you think they'll be falling over themselves to take a drowning man?' Max asked.

'What's in your hand,' William told him. 'Don't think for a moment you're going empty-handed, buddy. You're going with a full house. What's outlined at Allied Independents? I don't mean immediately. We want something under wraps that's being hand-fed for next season.'

Max thought as they walked and tried to remember which projects were hot, and which were just run of the mill. And then he got there.

'You remember *Now You See Her*?' he asked William, who was busy kicking sand. 'That old Ralph Hale classic comedy thriller about the old lady who apparently vanishes during a transatlantic crossing? We're planning a remake for Sue Montgomery and Hatton O'Neill.'

'From now on,' William replied, 'you'd better start calling we them. Have they tied up the rights?'

'I shouldn't think so for a moment,' Max grinned. 'Allied Independents don't like to pay for anything until the last moment.'

'OK,' said William, turning for home. 'Last one to the phone's a betsy.'

By the next morning Max, acting independently but making sure the holding agent knew his name, had taken an option on the rights. By the start of the week after, William and he had drafted a thirty-page step outline of a remake of *Now You See Her* called *Lost At Sea*.

'How about Diane Felton and William Payne as the Loy-Powell-type duo?' William suggested.

'We'll never get 'em together,' Max reckoned. 'They've got awful cautious.'

'They need a movie, Max,' William reminded him. 'Both their last solo vehicles bombed.'

'I don't know, Willy boy. Turkeys make 'em even more chary.'

'So play your trick. The one your father taught you. The she's-doing-it scam to get him, and then the he's-doing-it scam to get her. You said it was foolproof.'

'These guys are more streetwise than that, Willy boy. They'd see that one coming.'

'Run it. Run it at 'em and see. Jeez – what have you got to lose?'

They got into Max's office first thing next morning while the executives were still scattered variously round town at their breakfast meetings. Max got his secretary Barbra to call Diane Felton personally, then sent William out to chat the secretary up and stop her listening in. After

Max had sold the idea of the film to Diane, on the strength of William Payne having professed great interest, Max then did the same run on Payne and sold the idea to him on the promise that Felton was attached.

They then had about a couple of hours, Max reckoned, to pitch the idea to Metro Amalgamated with the two stars' names attached, before anyone started smelling rats.

There was no trouble getting an immediate appointment with Jerry Krugmann, Head of Creative Production, because the major studios were only too anxious to try and poach each other's talent unless the word was out. And while it was rumoured Max was under the axe, at the moment the guy still had his head on his shoulders, and that head was full of bright ideas, one of which he was bringing to Metro Amalgamated.

William was delegated to pitch the idea. William had got even better at pitching than ever. So much so that he had on occasions even been hired to pitch other writers' ideas. And that morning he was brilliant. In an hour and a half he had what had started out to be a stiff and humourless assembly of studio executives totally enthralled.

They were even more enthralled when Max let it be known that Allied Independents were also planning a remake of the same film, but hadn't even bothered to secure the rights.

'So OK!' said Krugmann, stubbing out his Havana. 'So let's get 'em!'

'We already have them, Jerry,' Max said, and went right to the top of the class.

Before they went to lunch, Krugmann had his staff call Diane Felton and William Payne and make them an outline offer subject to script. The message which awaited Krugmann at the restaurant was one of delighted interest from the two stars, and an assurance that if William Kennedy was to be the writer, then they could go straight to talking money.

'At the moment, Max,' Krugmann said as the waiter pulled out his gilt armchair at the table, 'I can only offer you a vice-presidency. Plus of course the production of the movie.'

'I can't think of anything I'd like more, Jerry,' Max grinned in return. 'Except perhaps to top the box again. But this time for you.'

'I'll drink to that,' Krugmann said, and raised his glass to the assembled company.

In the washroom after lunch, as they both took a pee, Max put his arm around William's shoulders and smiled.

'Thanks, pal,' he said. 'I mean it.'

'I did it for both of us, buddy,' William replied, going to wash his hands. 'I'm walking wounded, too.'

Hollywood's a history rather than a town or place. There are the studios, and the lots, and office blocks, and of course there's Beverly Hills, but no one is quite sure where Hollywood either begins or ends. Hollywood is a time being lived out, an industry at work, a business in motion, a parade going by. It's a collection of ever-changing people and ideas, of fashions and modes, of styles and fancies. And it's also a place where, because of its amorphous nature, it is perfectly possible to spend your time seeing only those whom you want to see, and those you don't, not at all.

Meredith was well aware of Max Kassov's presence in Hollywood long before she had even accepted Baz's offer of the Californian posting. In fact Max Kassov's presence in Los Angeles was the spur to Meredith Browne's ambition. However, best-laid plans are notorious for often going astray, and although Meredith had considered all her moves well in advance, nonetheless she had been somewhat disconcerted by the five dozen red roses which awaited her in her office on her arrival at Diplomat Productions.

The attached card had simply read: 'Welcome to Tinsel Town. Best wishes. Max.'

The gesture and the message although spelt correctly had very nearly done it. Max's stunt almost had its required effect. But as Meredith sat at her huge executive desk, she knew if she gave an inch now – by thanking Max for his welcome, showing appreciation of his flowers and his gesture, and gratitude for his concern – she might as well never have bothered. She might as well have never gone after him. She might as well have stayed at home.

So she took a pair of scissors from her desk drawer and cut the head off every single rose. She then replaced the dismembered flowers into their white cardboard coffins and ordered them to be delivered back to Max Kassov at Allied Independents, with no message.

She saw him next at a party, barely a week after her arrival. He was there, in designer jeans, sweat shirt, baseball jacket, with a bigger-than-ever cigar clenched between his teeth. He saw her immediately she entered, and pretended not to. Meredith responded by staring right through him. Not long after, her hostess brought him over to Meredith and introduced them. Meredith smiled at the hostess and said she had already met Mr Kassov, and then enquired the whereabouts of the powder room. Max volunteered to their hostess to show Miss Browne to the comfort station and, without exchanging any further words, led her down a corridor and pointed with his cigar to a room at the end. Meredith thanked him over-politely and walked straight into the room where she interrupted one internationally famous male film star having a pee, and two others doing a line of coke.

It still made her blush when she remembered it, not from embarrassment, but because she hadn't seen Max coming. But rather than go back after him, and try to even the scores on some petty level, Meredith went to ground. This was vendetta, not pass the parcel.

And so they went their separate ways, forever keeping distant eyes on each other, but never disclosing to anyone their former history. William Kennedy was the only man in Hollywood to know the score, but William Kennedy was completely uninterested in the state of other people's relationships. They only ever interested him when he came to sit down and write about them.

'You must have wanted to know how I felt, for God's sake,' Max asked him one night after their weekly poker session.

'You knew she was in town,' William shrugged.

'I didn't know how I'd feel when I saw her again,' Max returned.

'Don't tell me,' William sighed. 'I write much better from ignorance.'

'It was like a slap in the face,' Max confessed. 'I didn't think there was anything left.'

'Nostalgia,' said William. 'And they're not making it like they used to.'

'I'm serious,' Max shouted. 'Don't you ever take anything seriously?'

'Only the lighter side of life,' William replied. 'Listen, buddy. This could be a good thing. The lady could keep you up on your toes.'

'Listen, buddy,' Max concluded. 'As far as I'm concerned, the lady isn't even in town.'

So it wasn't very long after Meredith's arrival in Hollywood that her visible relationship with Max settled down into one of over-polite nods on Max's part, and small hellos from Meredith. In fact since the incident of the gentlemen's washroom, they hadn't exchanged more than the necessary formalities in public, and nothing at all in private.

But they knew, as the saying had it, exactly where each other was coming from.

After Max defected to Metro Amalgamated, clearing his desk at Allied Independents the day before the studio heads convened a special meeting formally to dismiss him, Meredith was offered the now vacant vice-presidency at Allied, with a six-picture deal. It was a good offer, and one which needed careful consideration. So she took a week's vacation in Monterey, packing up her problem to take away with her. After a couple of days, she was still as undecided as ever, so she called Baz up in London to ask for his advice.

If Baz had counselled her against it, Meredith had decided to accept the offer, because if he was reluctant to release her from Diplomat Productions, it could only mean the old man was afraid of the promotion on offer to her, and that if she joined Allied Independents, it would be disadvantageous to Diplomat. If on the other hand he encouraged her to take up their offer, it would mean that Baz considered the job to be toothless, and that Meredith would be just one of many such vice-presidents at Allied, unable to take a swing at anyone.

After an exchange of pleasantries, Meredith put her cards on the table. There was a silence from the other end of the line, and Meredith imagined Baz sitting at his desk, probably stroking one of the famous Lions of Judah which he had purloined after Louis had died, before coming to his decision.

'It's a very big step, Meredith dear,' he came back finally. 'An offer I don't think you should ignore.'

'I'm not ignoring it, Baz,' Meredith replied. 'Why do you think I'm ringing you?'

'Then my advice to you is to take it. My advice to you is to accept.'

'Thank you.'

'It's thank *you*, Meredith dear. I'm very proud of what you've done.'

'Good, darling. Then you can go on being proud, because I ain't going nowhere.'

Events soon proved it was the right decision. Despite being left on the shelf for far too long, *Sterling Silver* eventually opened to good notices, and did very healthy business across the country, without ever breaking any records. But then it was never expected to. It had started out as a bread-and-butter movie which, owing to its casting and the fashion for bank-heist stories, at worst should break even, and at best might go into profit to the tune of about twenty-five per cent of its cost. What happened in fact, due largely to William Kennedy's pseudonymous rewrites, was that the movie went straight up several levels to way above run-of-the-mill, and was in healthy profit within weeks of general release. As indeed were her next three films.

And as a reward for her creativity and in recognition of her loyalty, Diplomat took her out from under Harry Johannsen and promoted her over his head, making her their senior producer. Diplomat also matched Allied's known offer of a six-picture deal, but with one vital difference. Meredith was to be given total creative control.

At once she started looking around for subjects and writers, and one of the first calls she put in was to William Kennedy's agent, from whom she learned William was engaged writing *Lost At Sea* for Max Kassov at Metro Amalgamated. Meredith cursed her luck on this one, because Diplomat had just bought film rights of a bestselling novel called *Lucky In Love* which was tailor-made for William's talents. But two weeks later she had secured the services of another top writer, and after the necessary discussions, put into commission the first draft of the screenplay. Meredith then packed for New York, and took off to see what was new and good on Broadway.

She saw nothing she liked except the première of an off-Broadway production of a new play called *Another Way of Saying It*, the rights for which she bought purely intuitively. While she was waiting for the play to start, idly looking round the attendant audience, she swore she caught sight of Tim Sansom, one of Metro Amalgamated's literary talent scouts. She was pretty sure he'd seen her too, because he immediately hid his face behind his programme. Then the house lights went down, and the play commenced.

Halfway through the first act Meredith smelt a hit. The play was a peach, and told the story of an out-of-town Jewish girl, pretending to have a past in order to give herself status in trend-conscious New York, rooming with a young and dedicated musician, who allows everyone to

560

believe he's homosexual in order to buy himself peace to compose. Naturally they fall in love, the girl convinced she can reform the boy, and the boy equally convinced he can straighten out the girl. The writing was funny, wry and muscular, and by the time the house lights came up in the interval the audience was buzzing.

'Do you happen to know if the author's out front tonight?' Meredith asked one of the theatre staff.

'Sure I do,' the girl grinned in reply. 'That's her standing right there. The lady who looks like she's having twin elephants.'

Meredith spotted an agonized young woman standing by herself at the back of the auditorium, lighting a fresh cigarette from a near finished one while contorting her painfully thin body into paroxysms of anxiety.

'Hi,' Meredith said, when she'd fought her way through the crowd. 'I'm Meredith Browne, of Diplomat Productions.'

'That right?' the girl replied, but from a distance, as if she hadn't heard.

Meredith took a business card from her purse and showed it to the girl, but she barely looked at it. She just nodded, and kept on nodding.

'Can I buy you a drink perhaps?' Meredith offered, and got a surprised and baleful look in return.

'What in hell for?' the girl asked, putting the cigarette to her mouth with a trembling hand. 'I don't know you from nuts.'

'That's right,' Meredith agreed. 'You don't. But perhaps you ought to get to know me. Because I want to buy your play.'

After two double vodkas which the girl consumed straight, one chasing after the other, Meredith reopened negotiations.

'I'm sure you want to get back for Act Two,' she said, 'so I'll be brief. Here's my card, and on the back you'll see I've written a figure. That's just to buy the option. If you agree to sell Diplomat Productions the movie rights—'

561

'The movie rights!' the girl yelped, causing the nearest heads in the bar to turn their way. 'You didn't say anything about you being in the movies!'

Meredith, deciding the girl was bombed out of her head either from nerves, or maybe even from habit, sat her down in a booth away from the bar and talked to her urgently.

'I'm writing down my number at the hotel here in New York, where I'll be till the day after tomorrow, and my other numbers are on the card,' she told her. 'I'm also signing this figure on the back as a good-faith guarantee. We will pay you this amount of money if you grant us sole rights for three months to try and set the movie up. If we fail, you get to keep the money. If we succeed, you get to make a whole lot more. You get to make a lump sum on us buying out rights in the play.'

'Christ,' the girl gasped, half choking on a fresh cigarette. 'How much do I get to make?'

'About half of what you ask,' Meredith grinned.

It was a gamble, but one Meredith felt instinctively worth taking. For all she knew, Act Two might be a turkey, and she might have committed Diplomat for ten thousand unrecoverable bucks, which was twice the rate Meredith should have offered for the first off-Broadway dramatic effort of some freaked-out nutcase.

But by the time the final curtain fell, and the audience was on its feet cheering, Meredith felt her blind faith justified. What remained to be seen was whether the author would keep to her side of the bargain, as Meredith noted not only Tim Sansom dashing round backstage, but also scouts from two of the other major studios. Meredith hung around the perimeter of the ensuing party which was thrown spontaneously in the theatre, in the hope of re-establishing contact with the author, only to see her being hurried out of the building and into a cab by Tim Sansom.

Ah well, she thought to herself, hailing another free Yellow, you win a few, you lose a few.

In the middle of the night, Meredith's telephone rang.

'Hi. This is Myra Munro,' a very wide-awake voice said in Meredith's half-awake ear. 'We met at the theatre. The author of the play, right?'

'Right,' said Meredith, turning the clock towards her and finding it was ten past four. 'How can I help you?'

'You want to meet me for lunch?'

'Is it going to be worth it?'

'You seen the notices?'

'I don't have the papers delivered to my bedroom.'

'Forget lunch. Let's make it breakfast.'

'The notices are that good?'

'They're so good I'm buying.'

'What time do you eat breakfast, Miss Munro?'

'Normally I don't. But today – let's say half seven.'

'Fine. I'll see you downstairs in the lobby at half seven.'

Meredith put the phone down, and lay back on her pillow. It was hardly worth going back to sleep, she thought. So she got out of her bed and pulled back the drapes, so that she could lie watching the dawn break over Manhattan. She found it deeply satisfying. It was like something out of a movie.

'This guy Tim,' Myra Munro told Meredith in between mouthfuls of toast. 'He offered me twice the money you did for an option.'

'Is that why you're buying me breakfast?' Meredith enquired. 'Because if you are, I'd better warn you I don't belong to the no-hard-feelings school.'

'He also said I'd get what I asked.'

'Great. So go for it.'

Meredith glanced across at the girl who had to be busy making up for one hell of a lot of missed breakfasts, the way she was eating.

'You're right,' Myra said, pre-guessing Meredith. 'I haven't eaten since when.'

'Since the play went into rehearsal?'

The girl grinned.

'You got it.'

'I do have quite a full morning,' Meredith said, glancing at her watch.

'Me too. I'm gonna hit the shops.'

'Feel like telling me whose money you're going to spend?'

'Sure,' Myra replied, wiping some maple syrup from her chin. 'Yours.'

After Meredith had lunched with Tony Church, Diplomat's New York Head of Production, and told him of her forthcoming plans – of which he greatly approved – Meredith found herself with a free afternoon. There was nothing she needed from the shops, so she took a look through the movie listings, to look for an undemanding way to pass a couple of hours. She found two foreign movies and one British which she felt she ought to go and see, but in the end she chose none of them, deciding instead to go to the new Charles Crown, starring David Terry.

She'd missed out on the first one, quite deliberately. It had been an instant and smash hit, but somehow Meredith couldn't bring herself round to go see it. It was all still too close to home for comfort, particularly when invited to several notable houses in Hollywood for private screenings. Each invitation she had politely declined, and had stayed home to watch TV instead.

But now in the anonymity of New York, and with the passing of further time, she decided it was time she took a look at the monster she had created. And a monster David Terry now indeed was, monstrously famous according to the box-office returns in *Variety*, and monstrously notorious according to the gossip columns. His name had been romantically linked with practically all the single marquee names, and his bad behaviour had been reported to excess in all of the populist newspapers and magazines. Overnight success had proved, as it usually did with actors, a little too hard to handle.

'Bears of very little brain,' Max had used to laugh, when reading of the loutish behaviour of some overnight sensation. 'Bloody actors.'

And now in the dark of a major New York cinema, Frankenstein sat watching the monster, in company with excited children in company with their excited mothers. On the huge screen in front of the packed audience lay thirty foot of near-naked David Terry, international superstar and sex symbol, and as the women stared up at the projected giant, Meredith glanced at the faces around her while David Terry simulated sex with the girl they all wanted to be, and thought how easily she could have been in real life that fictional girl in David Terry's safe strong arms, that girl made so helpless by his kisses, that girl about to subject herself totally to his will, that girl who was now whispering back that yes, she loved him, of course she loved him, as all these women in the audience imagined they did. Only she, Meredith, so nearly had done so in reality, while all they, the women in the dark, were responding to were the charms and persuasions of a celluloid hero, a man now called irresistible, incomparable, unforgettable, scintillant, luminescent; a glittering, shimmering, glimmering, flickering star flashed on to a silver screen by a silently whirling machine, a man known as David Terry and maybe for ever as Charles Crown, but who had been born as Ted Ernstone, a one-time docker, lorry driver, meat packer and barman. And as she thought of these things, Meredith started to smile. And as the audience around her started to sigh, she started to laugh, because now all she could remember was the thirty-foot man as a six-foot man on a bed, quite helpless, and begging undeservedly to be freed. And with the recollection, her laughter became quite uncontrollable, so much so that in deference to the protests around her, Meredith had to put a handkerchief to her mouth and hurry herself out of the cinema and back into the sanity of real time and space.

*　　*　　*

It was necessary for several of the major sequences of *Lost At Sea* to be shot on location in England. William had sat in on many conferences where the studio executives had tried to find ways to trim what was an already large budget, and while they found several acceptable savings on some of the native locations, the English exteriors were finally accepted, in the words of Jerry Krugmann, as 'wholly needful obligements'.

'The scenes where they find the old lady's nephew,' Max said to William one evening on the beach, during one of their now regular walks together. 'Where in England do you see that happening?'

William shrugged, and stopped to pick an unusual small stone from the sand to add to his burgeoning collection.

'Remote,' William said. 'That's where I see it. Remote.'

'Sure. But remote where? Northumberland? Herefordshire? Somerset? Norfolk even?'

'Too flat, Norfolk, Max. Remember?'

Both the men smiled, the memory of that painful night now a strong link between them.

'OK, Willy boy. So remote where for God's sake?'

'I know where it is, Max. I know it exactly. Even though I've never been there.'

William had stopped walking now, and was standing looking out over the sea.

'I have the picture down to the last detail in my mind's eye,' he continued. 'Christ, what the mind can do never ceases to surprise me. You know if I were an artist, I could paint this place for you. Because for some uncanny reason I know it as if I've lived there. Or as if someone I know lives there. It's that familiar. And by remote, I don't mean that the place is isolated. I mean that it's unspoilt. Quiet. Far from the madding crowd. And so if I say that, it has to be Hardy country, doesn't it? I'd say this place, this little cottage where Guy and Jodie finally stumble upon the old lady's nephew, has to be in Dorset.'

'I like it, William. I like the idea of Dorset. It's very filmic.'

'I believe you, Max. I have to. I've never been there.'

'OK. So it's a small white painted cottage —'

'Thatched. Thatched and white-washed, and it stands outside a small village, looking over fields and if possible up at a church, so when Guy and Jodie are there, trying to get the nephew to talk, we could see the funeral of Fred Eastman going on in the background. So that all the time they're trying to find out the one piece of vital evidence which will help them identify the killer, the only man who could have told them is being buried up on the hill behind them.'

'Perfect,' said Max, staring out across the ocean alongside William. 'We'll send the art department to go find it.'

The cottage was small, thatched and washed light pink rather than white. But otherwise it was exactly as described. It stood outside the village of Wooland, looking up and out at Bulbarrow. In front of it lay farmland, undulating fields where cows grazed, and on the side of one of the hills stood a perfect Norman church, away from the other buildings and separated from the gracious eighteenth-century rectory that had not so long ago still been part of the living.

Jay had lived there now for the best part of three years, alone but content, and that was her view from her study. By her typewriter she kept a pair of field glasses, so that whenever she noticed something of interest just out of range she could reach for the glasses and watch.

She was easily distracted, often preferring to watch the slow progress of some old man walking out of his cottage rather than just sit and stare at the usually blank sheet of paper in her Olivetti.

Sitting there, William had used to remark, staring at a blank sheet of paper until your forehead bleeds.

More often she would watch the birds and, over the time she had spent at her desk, she had become quite an expert bird-watcher, although in order to take her interest the bird did not necessarily have to be rare. Jay could quite happily spend many happy minutes watching a pair of robins fighting over their territory.

But today she was watching a funeral, which was being conducted in the graveyard of the church opposite her window. They were burying Gilbert Sutton, a mysterious old recluse who had gone to his grave, so they said, taking with him the secret to an unsolved mystery, although nobody to whom Jay had spoken seemed to know what that secret was. Jay smiled to herself as she watched the ceremony through her glasses. It was just like something you'd write.

Once the ceremony was over, and there was nothing more to watch, Jay turned her mind back to her work, and within half an hour and two more cups of coffee poured from a Thermos on her desk, she was up and running. In fact she hardly heard Mrs Hunt arrive and start cleaning the cottage. But then Mrs Hunt knew once Jay was working she had to be as quiet as possible. So it wasn't until she started to spray the furniture polish on the pictures hanging by Jay's desk that Jay became fully aware of her.

She smiled at Mrs Hunt and mouthed a greeting but never stopped typing. Jay knew all too well that once she started to talk to Mrs Hunt, despite Mrs Hunt's good intentions not to interrupt what she called the flow, they would be there for the best part of an hour, discussing life in the village in general, and Mr Hunt's varicoses in particular.

Which was all very well when Jay was stuck, or between works, but today nothing must interrupt her. Today she was on a streak. Today at last she was hot.

She hardly heard the telephone ringing beside her, so Mrs Hunt, noticing Jay was making no move to answer it, went and took the call on the kitchen extension.

A couple of hours later, when Jay had come to the end of her streak, she noticed the note Mrs Hunt had left her by the typewriter. It informed her of the whereabouts of the lunch Mrs Hunt had prepared, hidden carefully away from Gertie, Jay's Yorkshire terrier, and that Mrs Randall rang and would Jay call her back as soon as poss?

Jay poured herself a vermouth and stared at the note as if it contained a threat. Which indeed it did, to Jay, the threat being an invitation to dine. Jay hated going out, and rarely saw or spoke to anyone. The village was happy to leave her alone, once they learned her ways, because after all the newcomer was a writer, and, as everyone knew, writers had funny ways.

But Eve Randall was different. Eve was a good and genuine friend, as was her husband Rob. They had met fortuitously at a dinner party Jay found herself attending all because she had said yes when she had really meant no. Her hostess had put her beside Rob, who at once made Jay laugh, as indeed did his wife Eve when Jay got to talk to them both after dinner – which was hardly surprising since, as Jay soon discovered, they were both ex the business: Rob, a retired television producer, and Eve, a retired theatre designer. And so, although Jay was as reluctant as ever to accept to go out, because it had now been nearly two months since she had seen Rob and Eve, and because they were now her only true friends, even Jay in her solitude had to agree that that was too long.

'I haven't the foggiest idea, darling,' Eve said to her halfway through their phone conversation in answer to Jay's query as to who else would be there. 'With a bit of luck it could be just the three of us. But you know Robbie. Once he's got a bee in his old bonnet about having people round, as he still likes to call it, bless him, you never know who he's going to drag up, dead or alive, darling.'

'It's just that I've nearly finished this book,' Jay tried lamely to explain her reluctance, 'and I don't want to get over-tired.'

'I don't know how you do it, poppet,' Eve sympathized. 'I was only saying to Robbie the other night, why don't you take up something simpler, like nuclear physics.' Eve gave a great smoky roar of laughter, and then finalized the time, ringing off quite quickly to prevent any more of Jay's well-known prevarications.

Jay sighed and typed out a note to herself with the date and time of the dinner in capital letters, which she then stuck on a pinboard by her desk. She just hoped if Eve and Robbie did ask anyone else, they'd be what Noël Coward called civilians; that is, nothing to do with the business. Because now that she just wrote books, she felt so differently about her past life. She had weaned herself off the business, and now she was away from it, she saw it for what she thought it was worth: as a world of illusion and make-believe, a sort of alternative Disneyland.

There was a car drawing up on the brow of the hill directly opposite her cottage. Jay at once reached for her field glasses out of automatic curiosity. Through the glasses she saw two men in the car, one of whom got out and shaded his eyes against the sun as he looked down at the village. The other man stayed in the car, pointing his arm first at the church and then it seemed at her cottage. But she couldn't get a clear view of him since the sun was glinting on the windscreen.

She had the other man in her sights perfectly. He was short, and looked plump, and wore jeans and a blouson. He now had a camera in his hands and was taking pictures of the view below. Tourists, Jay thought, dropping her field glasses; most probably Americans.

She returned to her work, and reread what she had done that morning. She became so involved in her reading that she quite failed to notice the car, which had been at the top of the hill a quarter of an hour before, stop briefly in the lane beyond her cottage hedge while the driver took some closer shots of where she lived. She did look up briefly as she heard a car pull away down the lane, but what was in front of her was now of far greater interest, so she gave the visitors no more thought.

Having finished her read-through, Jay then started to make notes for the next chapter of her book, in which she had to deal with the death of her heroine's mother. She shook her head slightly at herself as she wrote, remembering her own mother's death, and wondering how much she should draw from the experience. And then she decided she must of course be as truthful as she could. After all, the only reason she was writing books now was so that her mother could be proud of her, even though her mother was a long time dead.

'How ridiculous,' she suddenly said out loud. 'How silly. How pathetic we all are.'

Then she rolled a fresh piece of paper into her Olivetti and typed out those words exactly, checked them and was well pleased. For they were absolutely perfect for the character about whom she was writing.

Meanwhile the visitors' hired car had stopped in the village and the occupants had got out to seek refreshment in the one and only pub.

Which was how Robbie Randall remet his wife's old acquaintance Paul Luard.

Jay took a great deal of time and care to dress. She always took a long time, but for some reason unknown to herself she rejected three outfits before finally settling on her favourite black velvet jacket, a long-sleeved shirt with a wide collar and lace edgings, and a skirt made of ribbons sewn together. The skirt was long, falling practically to her ankles, which was one of the reasons she had chosen it.

Checking her face in the mirror next, she found that because of the hard work she'd been doing, she was even paler than ever, so she applied sufficient make-up to her skin to disguise the pallor successfully. Then she skilfully pencilled the outlines of her eyes so that people's attention would be drawn there rather than to the thinness of her cheeks. Once she was happy with her appearance, she made her way outside and got into her automatic Mini.

She loved her little car, not only because she had earned it and paid for it herself, but because it was her escape. Without it, and the freedom it allowed her, she had often thought she would be lost. And she loved driving it. On fine evenings, however tired she felt, she would haul herself out into the car and go on long and gentle drives across the Dorset hills, returning home often in the dark, after she had sat and watched the sun go down behind Bulbarrow.

'You've put your hair up,' Robbie remarked as he opened her car door. 'It suits you.'

'It's my Virginia Woolf bit,' Jay grinned back at him. 'I'm trying to look more like a serious novelist.'

'As long as you don't start looking like Lizzie Muddle,' Robbie replied. 'Like one of the great unmade beds.'

As they walked together into the house, Jay wondered why she ever tried to put off seeing Robbie and Eve, since they were both so kind and affectionate, and always made everything so easy for her.

People like me, she thought as she caught sight of Eve waiting in the doorway, don't deserve friends like these.

'Darling,' Eve said, giving her a kiss, 'you're an angel. It would have been perfectly bloody gruesome without you, because dear old Robbie's bumped into some old chum, and there'd have only been little me amongst all these horrid men.'

'Which horrid men, Eve?' Jay asked, trying to keep any anxiety out of her voice.

'I don't know one of them, darling,' Eve replied, 'but the other one's a poppet. He's an old chum of ours. Well, of mine actually. Paul Luard, the designer. Probably a b. before your t., sweetheart, but I promise you he doesn't bite.'

'And the other?'

'The other definitely bites,' Robbie said with his best straight face. 'He's one of us.'

Before Jay could enquire any further there was the sound of a car drawing up outside. Robbie put a glass of wine in Jay's hand and went to greet his guests.

Jay looked out of the window and saw the car which had been on the hill that morning, a shiny new blue Jaguar.

But from what Jay could see, there seemed to be only one occupant.

'Paul and I worked at the Garden together,' Eve was telling her, as the small round man Jay had seen through her glasses got out of the car. 'I suppose you could say I trained him, if you like. He's done a little better than I ever did though. He's now doing frightfully v. well in Tinsel Town. Oh – and here's Richard and Mags. *And* Soozle.'

'I thought you said —' Jay started, only to be interrupted by Eve.

'Darling,' she said, 'blame horrid old Robbie. I had to balance the beastly numbers up, didn't I?'

The rest of the guests were shepherded in by the always even-tempered Robbie, and were all introduced to each other.

'What happened to your chum, Paul darling?' Eve asked him as they kissed.

'If you don't mind,' Paul replied, 'he'll be along later. As soon as he can. Just as we were leaving, a call came through for him from the coast.'

As always, once she was launched and talking, Jay forgot all about her social misgivings and started to enjoy herself enormously. The Randalls' guests were invariably fun as well as nice, and this evening's selection proved no exception. She was laughing so much at one of Paul's tales from Hollywood that she barely noticed the door of the dining room opening and a stranger walking in.

At least he was a stranger to everyone else except Jay.

'Please forgive me,' she heard a familiar voice saying. 'But the front door was open, and I guess you didn't hear the bell.'

Jay knew who it was before she even looked round. She knew even before the new arrival had spoken those first words. She realized she must have known when she was getting dressed, as she was rejecting outfit after outfit, as she had carefully made up her face. Because she had stared into the mirror, she had looked at herself full in the face, and had found herself suddenly, and for the first time in years, saying his name.

William.

'William?'

He had stopped in his tracks, and was looking through the candlelight at someone he had thought never to see again.

'Do you mean to say you two know each other?'

Eve was on her feet, to greet her late guest.

'Yes,' said Jay. 'We know each other.'

'Good heavens above and lordy me,' Eve grinned. 'And where can that have been?'

'It was a long time ago,' said William. 'We worked together once.'

'Isn't it a funny old world?' Eve enquired generally. 'First of all Robbie bumps into my old chum Paul in our local, and now we find our mystery guest is an old friend of our darling Jay's.'

'I'd hardly say friend,' William corrected Eve pleasantly, but with a look to Jay. 'I hardly think it would be fair to call us friends.'

'Well anyway, you know each other,' Eve hurried on, leaving Jay to surmise she must have missed the nuance.

William looked at her and smiled, and his smile chilled Jay to her marrow. She tried to think of something light to say, something bright, something inconsequential and harmless. But nothing came. All she could think of was how much she loved the man who was staring at her with such hatred.

She dropped her eyes and pretended to straighten out the table napkin on her knee while William was introduced all round. Then once he was sat at table, Jay did her best to eat the food which was now choking her, and join in the conversation which soon was in full scandalous flight again.

William found his feet as quickly, as always, and was soon adding that air of urbane detachment that was so much part of William Kennedy. He was sitting by Eve, and out of the corner of her eye Jay watched Eve being enchanted by William's world-weary act. Soozle, a blonde divorcée on William's left, was also obviously bedazzled by him, and took the opportunity whenever Eve had to clear up or fetch the next course to commandeer William's full attention.

Not that William was trying to pay any attention to Jay. He didn't look at her once for the rest of the evening, and between them both they never exchanged another word. Jay learned from Paul that William was over in England helping to choose the English locations for the new movie he was writing. But what astonished her most was when Paul told her about the vision William had carried in his mind about the village, the very village he and William now found themselves in; settings to which he had guided Paul with unerring accuracy, even though he, William, had never before set foot in Dorset.

Jay said nothing of what she felt of this, only to express the usual polite astonishment at such apparent precognition. All the same, she gave a quiet glance at William, wondering whether as he had walked through the door and seen her he had understood the nature of his private vision.

For everyone else the dinner party was an enormous success. It went so well that no one moved from the table when Eve served the coffee, and Robbie poured the liqueurs. It was such a successful evening that no one moved until past two o'clock, when somebody suddenly noticed the time and the usual mock panic to leave set in.

During the ensuing mêlée as the party struggled to leave the tiny dining room in some sort of order and with some sort of dignity, Jay managed to stay in her place – without anyone noticing, it seemed. She sat sipping her dessert wine while Robbie and Eve's guests all said good night, and smiled and blew kisses at Richard and his wife Mags when they looked in and found her at her place.

But Richard and Mags knew Jay, so were unsurprised to see her still sitting at the table. They wished her a fond good night, and then Paul looked round the door and did likewise, telling her she was to look him up in California if she ever made it out there. Jay promised she would, and waved him goodbye.

She heard William thanking Eve and Robbie, but he left without saying farewell to Jay.

'Do you want to stay the night, poppet?' Eve asked Jay, coming back into the dining room and collapsing in a chair beside her. 'I say – that was all rather fun, wasn't it?'

'It was wonderful,' Jay said, finally getting to her feet. 'And no, Eve, I won't stay the night, because I have to let Gertie out.'

'Robbie can do that for you,' Eve suggested.

But Jay, anxious to get herself home as quickly as possible, held firm.

Robbie and Eve took her to her car, and after warm kisses and expressions of eternal affection, Jay drove off down the short drive and into the lane. The night was fine and beautiful, with a moon so bright you could almost drive without headlights. Which was exactly what the driver of the car not far behind Jay's was doing.

She didn't even notice the other car until she got back to her cottage, so deep in her thoughts had she been throughout the short journey. The car behind kept its distance too, driving only on sidelights, but always keeping the Mini just in sight. But once the little car had slowed down to turn into the cottage drive, the following car accelerated and the driver was out of his door and running along on the grass until he was beside Jay.

At first Jay didn't see him for she had turned away from her door to pick up her bag off the passenger seat. But then as she turned back she found her door being wrenched open and a man bending down towards her.

She screamed as loud and as long as she could, but the man put a hand over her mouth.

'Don't be such a fool!' William said. 'It's only me!'

Jay looked at him vengefully over his hand which he had still clamped on her mouth.

'There's no point in screaming,' he continued. 'Anyway – why should you scream? You were the one who disappeared.'

He took his hand away and stared down at her.

'Well?' he enquired.

'Well what?' Jay retorted.

'Christ,' William sighed. 'As belligerent as ever.'

Jay glared at him, and then made a grab to reshut the door, but William beat her to it.

'Get out,' he said.

She shook her head and stared out straight through the windscreen.

'Get out!' William ordered.

'Bugger off!' she shouted back. 'Go on, William Kennedy! Bugger off!'

'I'm staying here until you get out of your goddam car!' he shouted back. 'Even if it takes all bloody night!'

'It will!' Jay promised. 'Don't you worry! I'm staying right where I am! Until you bugger off!'

'Stop behaving like a child!'

'I am not behaving like a child!'

'Of course you're behaving like a child! Now get out of the goddam car!'

Losing patience, William now leaned into the car and started to try and drag Jay out.

'No, William, don't!' Jay pleaded. 'Please don't! No – William! Don't!'

But William was now in a rage, and in a moment he had Jay out of the car and up on her feet.

'If you're going to behave like a child,' he was saying, 'then I'm going to have to treat you like one!'

He had Jay by the shoulders now, and from the look in his eyes Jay thought for a moment he was going to shake her like a rag doll. Instead, after a moment, he suddenly let her go.

As soon as he did, Jay, now quite unsupported, fell straight to the ground.

'What are you doing?' William asked. 'For Chrissake,

what are you doing on the ground, Jay? Get up, will you? For Chrissake get up!'

'I can't,' Jay whispered. 'Sorry.'

'What do you mean?' William asked, bending down to where Jay now lay sobbing. 'What do you mean you can't?'

'I mean I can't get up, William,' Jay replied. 'Not without my sticks.'

He carried her into the cottage. He lifted her tenderly from the ground, and carried her little light frame easily up the path and through the front door.

Then he set her down in a chair, the huge King Lear chair that had once looked so magnificent in the studio but now looked a little out of place in the tiny cottage living room.

Jay just sat there, dwarfed by the chair, no longer crying. Just waiting. Waiting for William to come to. Waiting for him to find the words.

At the moment he was standing at her window, looking out at the night. Every now and then he would heave a deep sigh, and exhale very slowly. Finally he put his hands on the window ledge and, still staring out into the darkness, asked Jay if she had anything to drink?

She told him where the Scotch was and William poured two glasses. He handed Jay hers, and then just stood looking at her.

'What happened to your glasses?' she enquired.

'I wear contact lenses,' William replied.

'I liked you in your glasses,' Jay said, and then sipped her whisky.

William turned away from her and looked round the room.

'I don't believe it,' he said. 'You've still got that terrible hi-fi.'

'Of course I have. It still works terribly well.'

'You need something a bit more state of the art. You can't listen to good music on garbage like this.'

Jay bit her lip and tried to reach her bag which she'd

dropped on the table as William had carried her in. It was almost out of range, but by shifting herself to the other side of the chair, she just managed to reach it. From it, she took her cosmetics, and repaired the ravages of the last few minutes, while William pretended to examine her bookshelf.

'What did you make of *Nearly Never*?' he asked, taking a prize-winning novel down and staring at it. 'I thought it was a crock, personally.'

Jay agreed and put her cosmetics back in her purse.

'OK,' William said, finishing his drink and refilling his glass. 'Right.'

Then he sat down opposite Jay and waited.

'You want me to tell you?' Jay asked. 'You want me to volunteer.'

'Oh Christ, Jay,' William told her, shaking his head. 'I want to know what's happened to you. But I don't know what to say. Why did you just disappear?'

Now that he had found her, Jay knew there was no point in hiding anything from him. So she took another sip from her drink, then put the glass down on the table beside her.

'Well,' she began, following the one word with a deep breath and a raise of her eyebrows. 'You see, they said I was dying.'

'Oh for Chrissake!'

William was on his feet, spilling his drink everywhere. Jay put up a hand. And William grabbed it.

'You can't be dying, Jay! For God's sake you just can't be!'

'Well, as it happens, William, I'm not. They were wrong, and I'm not dying. So there.'

William kept hold of Jay's small cold hand while he pulled a stool round so that he could sit at her feet.

'Go on.'

'The doctor I was going to, remember?'

William nodded.

'He said it was all in my head. But I knew it wasn't. I was just feeling worse and worse each day, and I knew

579

there was nothing wrong with my head. I was too happy with you.'

She reached out and touched William's head. He took her hand and put it to his mouth to kiss her palm.

'Then when you went away that first trip, back to America, I got myself admitted to hospital. Where, to cut a very long story short, they said I had some very rare nervous disorder and would be dead within three years. Up theirs, is all I can say.'

Jay grinned at William and he smiled back.

'That's what I said then as well,' she continued. 'They said it was Alner's Syndrome, for which there was no known cure. And they were very sorry and all that. But that's show business.'

'The three years are well past, sweetheart. And—'

'Yup. And I'm still here. The thing is, William, I haven't got Alner's. I have got some sort of degenerative disease, apparently, although even that's got them worried now. Because you see two years ago I was in the Ironside.'

William frowned at her.

'A wheelchair, William,' Jay joked. 'But now I've progressed to sticks. And this man I've found, this doctor – I'll tell you about him in a minute. He's quite marvellous, and he thinks I could be walking without the stupid things in another six months.'

'So what is it? Do they know what it is?'

'I know what it is. It's the Peregrine ffrench syndrome.'

They both smiled as they remembered Jay's much thumbed medical dictionary, the cover of which showed another medical dictionary with certain pages tagged Headache, Nausea, Sickness, Depression, categories which William had one day connected with his pen to label as The Peregrine ffrench Syndrome.

'Seriously,' he asked.

'In a way I'm perfectly serious, William. That's when it all started. I probably did get a harbour virus or whatever, but I think what they did to us, what I saw them do to you – at least this is what Peter, this doctor, says – we think that tipped some sort of, well, delicate balance. It upset something in me. In my nervous system. Three years ago, all I could move was my head. My feet – just. And my hands.'

'And you had done the Captain Oates,' William guessed, getting up and walking once again to the window. 'You did the noble thing. Trust you. Living out a storyline.'

'Don't mock, William.'

'Oh Christ, I'm not mocking you, sweetheart!'

'I did the only thing. You'd never have stayed in America if you knew I was really ill. You wouldn't be where you are now. I know what you're like. You'd have stayed here, and you'd have tried to look after me. And if I had died, it would have been too much for you.'

There was a long silence, during which William regarded Jay steadily while Jay looked back deep into his eyes. Then he leaned forward and took both of her hands.

'I like your hair up like that,' he said. 'It suits you.'

That was the thing for which Jay had not catered. William being kind to her. William being tender. William being loving. If they were ever to be reconciled, in her mind's eye Jay had seen William angry, William bewildered, William possibly even violent. But she had left no room for William being the gentle and sweet person he was, beneath all that carefully structured urbanity. Which was why she found herself suddenly crying.

William lifted her easily from the great chair and then sat with her on the sofa cradled in his arms, rocking her like a child.

'You should never have come back,' she sobbed.

'That's not your style,' he replied. 'Pure Mills and Boon. That's not Jay Burrell.'

'I'm not Jay Burrell any more,' Jay smiled a little at him through her tears. 'I write books now. Under Nicola Thomas.'

'Christ!' William laughed. 'Nicola Thomas! You never

were any damn good at names or titles, were you, Miss Burrell? Who in hell would buy a book by somebody called Nicola Thomas?'

'Quite a lot, Mr Know-it-all. Four and a half thousand in hardback last time, if you're really interested.'

'If you'd called yourself something like Ophelia Jade, that could have been four and a half thousand times twenty.'

Jay looked round at him for a moment, then lay her head back on his shoulder.

William reached out and picked up a book that was lying nearby on the table. It was one of Jay's novels.

'Nicola Thomas,' he mused. 'It rings a sort of bell.'

'It's what I called myself,' Jay replied, 'when I was working for Max Kassov.'

'Sure. The last time you decanted yourself from my life.'

'Oh yes. That's right, it was, wasn't it?'

William dropped the book back down on the table.

'Know something?' he asked her. 'I don't ever want to hear that goddam name again. Understood?'

'No I don't understand,' Jay said. 'Not quite.'

'If you're going to mess around changing your name, then you might as well change it to mine.'

'That sounds like a proposal.'

'I thought it sounded like common sense.'

Jay sat herself up and put an arm round William's neck.

'I thought you said you'd only get married if you reckoned it was too cold to do anything else,' she said.

'OK – forget marriage,' William shrugged. 'How about a lease?'

'How about if I just change my name back to Jay Burrell?' she asked.

'How come you always have the best ideas?' William sighed.

And then he kissed her.

'You really shouldn't have come back,' Jay whispered as he started to carry her up the narrow staircase. 'You must have been having such fun in Hollywood.'

'You bet I've been having fun in Hollywood,' William replied. 'But you want to know something, lady? Fun's even more fun when there's two of you having it.'

'You don't mean to tell me you haven't been having fun with someone, William?'

William groaned as he lay her down on her bed.

'Trust you to ask a question like that at a time like this.'

'Well?'

'Well nothing. It's none of your goddam business.'

'But you have been having fun,' Jay persisted.

William sat down on the edge of the single bed and turned to look at her.

'I'm a red-blooded heterosexual,' he told her as he started to undo the buttons on her blouse. 'Whose lover ran out on him. And for whom the monastic life has scant appeal.'

'So who's the present lucky lady?'

'There isn't one, Miss Nosey.'

By now William had undone her blouse and was about to loosen the fastening on her skirt.

'You don't have to do this, you know, William.'

'Somebody has to. You look like Elizabeth Barrett Browning.'

'I mean you don't have to make love to me.'

'I know I don't, sweetheart. But I want to.'

William smiled down at her, and then continued undressing her.

'There hasn't been anyone since you,' she told him.

'Good,' he replied as he started to undo his own shirt. 'That's just the way I'd have written it.'

When William had first made love to her, Jay had been surprised that underneath such a debonair and apparently flippant manner had beaten such a passionate heart. And now once again, as William began to make love to her, she was almost as astounded as she had been that very first time in her studio. He was as attentive to her needs as always, and gentle and calming at first. He whispered to her once, anxious lest she be too frail. But Jay assured him

583

as she felt him enter her that there was nothing he need fear, because now that she was in his arms again, now that he was there inside her, now that they were one again, she felt herself growing strong. Strong enough to withstand the increasing power of his love, to bear the weight of his body and the strength of his arms which were now enveloping her. And as her passion grew along with his – until he stopped kissing her and she stopped kissing him and they kissed each other long and deeply as one – Jay felt as if her life blood was being transfused back into her, that she was being brought back to life again, revitalized by William's passion and his love.

And then suddenly there was quiet, and they were lying there together, with just the stillness of the night in their ears; the physicality over, but with the sense of wonder that always followed stronger than it had ever been before.

'My God,' said William. 'Dear God.'

'I know,' said Jay, turning to him and resting her head on his chest.

'Jeez,' William whispered. 'Now that is something you just *can't* write.'

William delayed his return to the States once he and Paul had finished the location recce. He called Max to say that they had found the perfect locales, just as he had described them to him on the beach, and more than that he had found Jay at the end of the rainbow. So he was staying on a while in order finally to persuade Miss Burrell that home was where the heart was, and that while he was so doing he would make the necessary amendments to the script to take into account the detail he had found and was still discovering in the village and its environs.

Jay was refusing to return with William to America because of her dependency on Doctor Mendip. Her version of the game plan was for William to return to California until the film was in production, and then for him to come back to England.

'What then?' he asked.

'Then you can work from here,' Jay argued. 'You're a famous enough screenwriter now for heaven's sake for them either to commission you over there and for you to come back to do your writing, or simply for you to work from here full stop.'

William argued that it wasn't as simple as that, because at the stage his career was he still needed to be where the action was, and that was in Los Angeles.

'If I'd won an Oscar, maybe,' he said. 'Even then, there are plenty of guys who won their Oscar for Best Screenplay, bought themselves a mountain in the South of France under the shadow of which to write, and then nobody remembered to ask them. Either that or the producers were too mean to pay foreign postage. It really does make more sense all round for you to come back out with me. For a start, the climate will suit you better. This is a fine and a very pretty place. But a goddam damp one in which to embrace.'

'I can't leave Doctor Mendip,' Jay countered. 'He's done so much for me.'

'There are some pretty fantastic quacks out on the coast as well, sweetheart,' William assured her.

'This quack reckons he can see this thing off, William,' Jay replied.

It was a painfully difficult decision for them both. Now they had found each other again, neither of them wanted to be apart for a moment longer than was necessary. And while the last thing William wished was to compromise Jay's health, or be the cause of any resultant setback she might suffer, he was convinced he could find her as good if not better medical care in California as she had found in rural Dorset.

Jay was not to be moved, however. Even if it meant a temporary estrangement now, and others during the year, her treatment with Doctor Mendip was not to be interrupted.

'You want me to get well again, don't you?' she would ask William.

'Of course I do,' he would reply.

'Well then,' Jay would conclude, and that would be the end of that particular round.

One day, when Jay had driven herself off to see her doctor, who practised in Dorchester, William read through Jay's latest book without sanction. He was so enthralled by it he didn't even hear her return.

'I don't remember telling you that you could read that.'

William looked round and saw Jay standing behind the King Lear chair.

'This would make a fantastic movie,' he countered, hoping the compliment would help lower the temperature.

'I never sneaked around reading your private work,' Jay continued, unabashed.

'Yes, you did actually, but I'm sorry anyway,' William retorted. 'But I still say it would make a great movie.'

'It's too personal to be made into a great movie,' Jay said heavily, removing the manuscript and putting it back in her desk. 'My face for the world to see.'

'But not too personal to be made into a great novel,' William returned, getting his own back.

'That's my choice,' Jay replied, 'and my choice alone.'

'It was only a suggestion,' William explained. 'It just seemed like a good idea at the time.'

Jay cast him one of her famous looks, and then, picking her walking sticks back up, made her way out to the garden.

William promptly took the manuscript back out of the desk and finished reading it.

As a consequence, they had a fearful argument about it over dinner, Jay maintaining that the writing of the book was a catharsis, and thus not seriously intended for publication, while William tried to persuade her that writers, by the fact of describing their personal experiences, ended up casting light much more generally.

'I don't see it that way,' Jay maintained. 'I don't see why I should necessarily inflict my neuroses on the poor old public.'

'Oh, come on, Jay!' William laughed. 'Writing has always been the result of somebody's neurosis! Think what books would be like if they were written by the level heads! By happy and perfectly adjusted people! My God – there'd be nothing worthwhile to read!'

But while William finally won that round, Jay was still not convinced that she wanted to hand her story over to be made into some 'me-too' *Love Story*.

'Look what it grossed,' William argued. 'Just look what *Love Story* took at the box.'

'And look what they called it,' Jay replied. '*Camille* in nylon tights. That's not how I want to see my story told.'

'A little less of the "my" story bit, if you don't mind, sweetheart. This is a two-hander, remember? Not a solo vehicle.'

'All right, so you come into it, OK—'

'Come into it?' William echoed. 'That's like saying Higgins comes into *My Fair Lady*.'

'The play, you may recall,' Jay answered tartly, 'was originally called *Pygmalion*.'

'It was called *Pygmalion*, knucklehead,' William roared, 'after Pygmalion the King of Cyprus! Who fell in love with a statue! The play wasn't called Eliza!'

'Yes?' Jay replied. 'Well, it should have been.'

To convince her, William wrote a brief treatment of how he would adapt the book to show what sort of film it would make. He did it at times when Jay was off at the doctor's, and at other times when she thought he was working on his screenplay. He even worked on it some nights when Jay was lying fast in a medicated sleep.

Then he showed it to her. It was nothing like *Love Story*.

Jay read it and said nothing, suggesting instead that they go for a drive to the sea. It was a stormy day, so they sat in the car on a headland overlooking part of the famous Chesil Beach and stared at the raging seas far below them. After a while, to improve their visibility, Jay turned on the windscreen wipers, and then sat back to continue their vigil.

'When I first moved down here, I used to drive down here

in the winter,' she said, 'and park the car right on the very edge.'

'Brave girl,' William replied.

'On the contrary,' Jay disagreed. 'It was because I wasn't brave. If I'd been brave I'd have driven it over the side. By parking it right down there on the edge, I was just hoping the wind would make the decision.'

William put his arm round her shoulders and eased her towards him.

'Don't tell me that's still not brave,' he said.

'No,' Jay replied, before turning to smile at him. 'But it'll make a good scene in the picture, won't it?'

16

At the top of the page there are faint traces of text showing through from the reverse side of the paper, which are illegible.

Max Kassov thought it a great scene when he read it for the first time in William's draft screenplay. In fact he thought the whole idea and execution wonderful and was at great pains to tell William so every time they met.

'So why have you still not got it past the bastards?' William asked him yet again during their latest beach walk.

'Jesus, Willy boy! I keep telling you!' Max replied. 'I've told you who's running the shoot now! Christ, you thought the guys running Metro Am before were klutzes! But I can tell you, Ferrachi and Harlan – puh! They make Krugmann and his team of boneheads Nobel Prize material!'

'And all this happened while I was away?'

'You remember what Louis B. Mayer said, don't you?'

'A little before my time at the inkwell, Max.'

'Louis B. said a week is a long time in Hollywood. While you were getting rheumatism in Dorset, sweetheart, it was like the French Revolution here! And we weren't the only ones to get the new brooms through!'

'How come they missed you?'

'I got to stand on top of a closet, Willy boy,' Max grinned. 'As soon as I hear the sound of bristle on wood, I get my feet out of the way.'

'So much as you love my script—'

'Listen, chum. I love your script. I think it's the best thing you've written, you know that. But as I keep telling you. Try selling ice cream in hell, you've got more chance.'

'Or try selling it in space,' William suggested, for once accepting one of Max's cigars.

'Too right, chum. Set it in space. Turn it into a don't-close-your-eyes-or-it'll-get-yer. Make the guy a Thing, and the girl an android, and you'll be writing sequels before they even start shooting. No one wants a decent movie.'

'Except the public.'

'Except the public maybe. And who are they? A lot of pain in the arses who make producers' lives intolerable by refusing to be Mr and Mrs Sub-Average.'

William laughed, but the pain still refused to go away. It had been there ever since he had finished writing the script from Jay's book, and suffered the first rejection from Metro Amalgamated. Max had warned him when he had taken the screenplay to him that in Hollywood unsolicited material was considered suspect, since the moguls had no advance warning of what to expect. If they'd commissioned the screenplay, then they knew roughly what was going to land on their desks. A picture about space, perhaps. Or maybe even another picture about space. But a script of which they knew nothing except what the writer told them — and anyway, whoever believed writers? — no, no. Somebody was obviously trying to pull a fast one on them. Either the script had been paid for and rejected by another company, or else it was the other of the two great untouchables, an unsolicited original, usually known by its shorter but just as worrisome title: an art movie.

'I'm glad,' Jay had told William transatlantically when he had informed her of the continued rejection. 'That must mean it's good.'

'Sure,' said William. 'But I just have this old-fashioned thing about good being seen to be good.'

'Maybe you should stop being so loyal to Max,' Jay suggested, 'and show it around.'

'Yeah,' William agreed. 'Maybe I should.'

But he didn't.

*   *   *

The brooms hadn't just been busy sweeping through Metro Amalgamated. Due to a sudden and inexplicable drop in box-office receipts nationally, and a strongly reported decline in cinema audience attendance across the continent, not only every minor was panicking, but so too and most of all were the majors. Each and every studio spent an unquestionable amount of time in self-examination, some even calling in opportunist psychiatrists who had suddenly developed a specialization in something called creative process analysis.

'Is it a coincidence,' William enquired at his poker school one Friday evening, 'or is it just my dirty writer's mind, or do the first four letters of analysis have a particularly befitting ring to them?'

'Sure,' agreed another writing member of the poker school. 'Though as far as studio heads go, perhaps anusalysis would be even more befitting.'

'As far as most of the studio heads go,' another player said, chucking in his hand, 'by the end of the week there'll be nowhere far enough.'

Most of the rumours were true. Heads rolled. Not one of the major studios escaped without a shuffle, or as the business wisecracked, they all got to be re-cast. Even the Indies, as the small independent companies were known, got affected by the panic, some suffering no worse a fate than being creatively restructured, as a total change of executive staff was being called, while others, the ones whose fortunes were at that moment at a low ebb, were totally liquidated.

Some, the luckier ones, survived by being taken over. Diplomat Productions was one of these.

Meredith had known, like all who kept an ear to the ground, exactly what was going on. But also, like all who thought they lived in secure houses but took heed of the storm warnings, she had put up the shutters and sat back waiting for it all to blow over. After all, her house was in good order. She had brought five pictures already in and under, and the cameras were about to roll on a sixth.

There was a feeling of tremendous confidence within the company, inspired by Meredith's infectious enthusiasm, and her apparently limitless energy. She was also a first-class delegator, leaving her personally appointed delegate, once he was up and running, complete freedom of activity. If anyone was likely to survive the pogrom, the no-risk bet was Diplomat.

'So what happened?' William asked her over sundowners taken on his verandah.

'I guess someone forgot to lock the back door,' Meredith replied.

She had called him as soon as she had heard the news because William was now her best and closest friend in town. And hearing the trouble in her voice, William invited her over at once.

'I still don't understand the reason,' William frowned. 'It's not as if Diplomat is on its knees. Everyone knows the company's strength. Let's face it, everyone envies it.'

'That, darling,' Meredith replied, accepting a second drink, 'I would say is the trouble.'

'But what about Baz? Diplomat is part of Baz Vogel's holdings. And Baz put you over here specially.'

'You're getting warmer, darling.'

'You're saying Baz put you over here specially?'

'Baz is a businessman, William darling. I think they may have made him an offer he couldn't refuse.'

'Do we know who "they" are yet?'

'No one knows any details. Tippi, my PA, she read about it in her paper at breakfast. Can you beat that? She thought it was just a rumour, but when she got to the offices, everyone was walking round like something out of *Day of The Dead*. I was out at a breakfast meeting with two bankers, my costing accountant, and Dan Milner, the Head of Western Pacific Studios, right? who as sure as hell must have known something. But not a word. We all met, and dealt, and went our ways, while all of Hollywood was laughing up its sleeve.'

'You must have talked to Baz?'

'I called him as early as I could. Five-thirty his time, a.m. I got his machine.'

'You've obviously tried the office.'

'He's in a meeting.'

Meredith looked at William ruefully, then raised her glass.

'There's no business like it,' she said.

'Hold on in there,' William said, getting up and going to the verandah windows. 'I know someone who might know something. Just count the pebbles on the beach for a couple of minutes, OK?'

Shutting the sliding door closed after him and leaving a pensive Meredith leaning over the balcony staring out at the ocean, William went and made a call – from his bedroom, to make quite sure of not being overheard.

'What's it to you?' the voice on the other end of the phone asked suspiciously. 'You've not been touting them your wares, I hope?'

'I'm just interested, buddy,' William replied. 'Not interested vested, interested academic.'

'Not that it would harm you if you had been flashing it at them,' the voice continued. 'There were very solid reasons for buying them in. The most solid one is their increasingly good track record.'

'That's what I imagined,' William replied. 'So you'll be keeping the company intact.'

'He that builds on assumptions builds on sand,' came the answer. 'I know the little fish will still be swimming.'

'And surely the big 'uns as well, buddy? What's the point in buying a Mercedes and taking out the engine?'

'None at all, chum. But then that's not what this business is all about, is it?'

William replaced the now dead telephone and stayed sitting on his bed for a moment. Then he got up and walked through to the living room, where he stood looking at the figure of Meredith, who was sitting as she had sat when first she visited his house, with her bare legs swinging through the bars of the balcony. In her unguarded moments, particularly when seen from the back, she looked like a little girl waiting for someone to return.

Then giving a deep and private sigh, William picked up his drink, walked over to the picture window, and, pulling it back open, went out on to the balcony to give Meredith the news that Diplomat had been bought by Metro Amalgamated Pictures Incorporated.

Max had been one hundred per cent against taking over Diplomat, and had made the point as forcefully as was necessary at board level. But the men in suits just sat and stared back at him, as if he was speaking in a totally foreign language.

Finally Joe Ferrachi, the new President of Metro Amalgamated Pictures, a dark rounded man with black slicked-down hair, nodded to Max in indication that he had enjoyed enough airtime, and rose to his feet as Max took the weight off his own.

'Thank you, Max,' he said. 'Yes, I enjoyed listening to that. You spoke most eloquently of the company's needs. Which to your point of view do not include the purchase of Diplomat Productions. You consider the company too small-time for a major like Metro to be concerned with. That their output of one, maybe two movies a year should give us no cause for concern. And that it is better for our prestige, which is a word I appreciate you using so nicely, Max, that it is better for our prestige to take Diplomat out by artistic methods rather than by financial ones. And yes, I understand your argument.'

Ferrachi paused and smiled at Max, revealing a set of gold-filled front teeth. He also produced a comb from his outside top pocket and, during the manufactured silence, ran the comb carefully through his still immaculate hair.

'However,' he then continued, having replaced the comb in his pocket after wiping it off on his fingers, 'however, as we all know, there's more ways than one to skin a cat. And one of the methods I most favour is starvation. You may remember from not so long ago an up-and-coming actress who was working for this very studio. Anne-Marie Hurley. She was going to be a very big number. And what is she now? Now she's a Whatever-Happened-To. I was at Summit Studios at the time, and I tell you, gentlemen, we were extremely concerned at the prognosticated success of Miss Hurley. Particularly when pitted against our own débutante Cindi Heritage, in whom we ourselves had a very major investment. So we bought Anne-Marie Hurley. We bought her contract out, at considerable cost, and then we starved her of movies. We paid her, but we gave her nothing to do. Or if we did give her something to do, it was always the wrong part for her. While of course on the other hand, our own Miss Cindi Heritage . . . well. Last month she won her second Golden Globe. Need I say more?

'So that's my plan with Diplomat, gentlemen. And any other Indies who start getting a little big for their bootstraps. Whoever said competition was healthy wasn't playing with a full deck. I'm right in there with Mr Benjamin Franklin. The guy who wins the race is the guy who runs by himself.'

Ferrachi bowed to his board of directors, and sat slowly back down in his large high-backed leather chair. In a show of appreciation, the members of the board tapped their monogrammed pencils on the table and nodded at their president's sagacity.

All except for Max, who was once more on his feet.

'One last question, Mr President,' he asked, 'if I may. Diplomat's staff, with particular reference to their executives are we to take them on board here after the merger?'

'I would imagine so, Max,' Ferrachi replied with a slow-burning smile. 'As long as they're happy doing it under dustsheets.'

As soon as the meeting ended, Max returned to his office and made a transatlantic call on his private line. It was now midday Pacific time, so with a bit of luck he should just catch Baz before he went out for dinner.

Which he did.

'Don't sell,' Max urged. 'They're going to bury you.'

'I've already sold, Max,' Baz replied. 'They made me such an offer.'

'OK. Fine, that's your business, Baz,' Max said, closing his eyes and sinking into his desk chair. 'But Meredith. Have you thought about Meredith?'

'What are you doing thinking about Meredith?' Baz countered. 'She's my concern, Max. Not yours.'

'I happen to disagree with our President, Baz. I think horses run faster and better when they've got something to race against.'

'Meredith's taken care of, Max. Ferrachi promised me he'd make her a vice-president.'

'Baz—'

'It's a big step, Max. Vice-presidency of one of the majors.'

'Baz, listen to me—'

'I'm an old man, Max. I can't get the trip any more. If you want to talk horses, they're beginning to go away from me. Ferrachi promised me he'd look after Meredith.'

'Ferrachi is going to bury her, Baz. He's going to bore her into resignation.'

'This is nonsense, Max. Meredith is an extremely bright, attractive and capable woman.'

'Ferrachi doesn't employ extremely bright, attractive and capable women, Baz.'

'Yes? And who says?'

'Mrs Ferrachi.'

Meredith was fast asleep on William's sofa when Max called. Between them, after William had broken the news, they'd done two bottles of William's best white Burgundy and, while Meredith had collapsed, William had gone to swim it off. He was just towelling himself down when he saw Max's convertible Mercedes turning off the road.

He got his clothes on and was out on the porch just in time to stop Max from walking straight in.

596

'Hi,' said Max. 'I'm on my way up to Santa Barbara for the weekend, so I thought I'd drop by on the off-chance. Can we talk?'

'Sure. But out here,' William replied. 'I have a guest in there. Female. Crashed out in the living room. Let's walk.'

Max grinned as William locked the house up before setting off down the beach with him.

'What would Miss Burrell have to say, prof?' Max asked.

'It's nothing like that, buddy,' William replied. 'This is an old chum. In a bit of trouble.'

They walked on.

'So what is it you want to talk about, Max?'

'Funnily enough – it's Meredith.'

Max looked round at William, as if anticipating some critical comment.

'So?' was all William had to say.

'Do you know if she's talked to Baz yet?' Max asked. 'I was wondering.'

'She can't reach him,' William replied. 'It's as if he's avoiding her.'

'I should imagine,' Max agreed. 'Judging from my call to him yesterday.'

William stopped and looked round at Max.

'I don't believe this, Max. Meredith thinks Baz set her up out here, and by set her up—'

'It's possible, William. But then in this game, you tell me what isn't. Metro Am have sure as hell paid him more than handsomely for the company.'

'Sure. Well, and so what, Max? It's no skin off your nose.'

'It shouldn't be, Willy boy. No, I should be delighted that probably the best up-and-coming producer in this God-forsaken town is about to have her gun belt confiscated. But I don't know. It must be something to do with the way I was brought up. I have this terribly British sense of fair play.'

William laughed at Max's mock upper-class and then asked him if there was anything Max could do.

'No,' Max replied. 'I don't think there's anything I can do. But I think there's something that I could advise you to do. So why don't we grab something to eat and talk it over?'

Meredith got back into the house just in time as Max and William came back into view. On her hands and knees lest she be seen, she shut the porch door and resnapped the lock shut before she crawled back over to the sofa and back under her rug. By the time William poked his head into the living room to check that she was all right, Meredith was apparently still fast asleep and snoring. William left a note on the table by her head before collecting his jacket and tiptoeing back out.

Max was waiting for him by his Mercedes, a look of consternation on his face. He'd lost his car keys.

'I could have sworn I left the car open,' he told William. 'With the keys in it. Since we were only going for a stroll. But the damn thing's locked and I don't have the keys.'

Agreeing Max must have dropped them on the beach, the two men retraced the steps of their walk, which was no great inconvenience since they had decided to eat at a beachside café less than half a mile from the house and in the same direction they had just been strolling. But there was no sign of the missing keys.

'Don't you have a spare set?' William asked.

'Of course,' said Max. 'But they're at home. And there's no one at home. And home's all locked up.'

'OK,' said William. 'If the worst comes to the worst and we don't find 'em on the way back, you can always borrow my car.'

Max agreed to the proposition, albeit somewhat uneasily, as he was still quite firmly convinced that he had left his car open.

He was right. He had done. And once Meredith was sure he and William were out of sight, she had let herself out of the house, taken the car keys, and locked the car up without exactly knowing why.

She had awoken with a pounding headache as William

was greeting Max on his arrival and, getting up to fetch some water with which to take some painkillers, had overheard Max announcing his weekend plans. Realizing that meant his apartment would be empty for nearly two days, she felt a sudden rush of quite uncontrollable excitement, for which she could find no explicable reason whatsoever. Nonetheless, trusting as always to the strength of her instincts, she knew she had to take his keys because she knew there was something hatching inside her, which given time would make itself known to her.

And when the two men had walked off down the beach, Meredith had sat on the sofa wrapped only in the soft wool of the rug, staring at the ocean in front of her, and wondering what the inspiration was going to be.

Which was when she saw the packets of seeds on William's window sill, and had begun to laugh quite uncontrollably.

While Meredith was driving Max's Mercedes 3.5 convertible back into Bel-Air, William and Max were sitting overlooking the ocean and eating giant Pacific prawns in chilli sauce. William was highly curious as to what Max thought he, William, could do to help bail Meredith out, but was too skilled a games player to come out with it and ask.

Besides, he knew Max better than that. Max liked to eat then talk.

'OK,' said Max, pushing his plate away and draining his Export Carlsberg. 'This movie of yours.'

'I've reset it on Mars,' William replied. 'During the second War of the Worlds.'

'I've an even stronger idea,' Max said. 'Give it to Meredith Browne.'

That was the idea. Take the film away from Metro Am who weren't interested anyway, and even more importantly, who hadn't paid a dime even to read it, and give it to the lady they were trying to kill.

'But they'll take it off her, surely?' William reasoned.

'Not if Meredith goes freelance rather than in the package to Metro Am,' Max grinned.

'But why?' William persisted. 'I thought you two had a kind of Montague-Capulet thing going.'

Max shifted to one side as the waiter brought them their next course.

'You may not believe this, Willy boy,' he said. 'But I believe in your picture. I really think it's your best bit of work. I think it should be made, because I'm like that. When something good comes my way, which it does very rarely, I fight for it. I want to give it life. That's what it's all about. Trying to produce one memorable movie out of the morass of dross. I'd give my right arm to make it, and – this is the bit you may not believe – I seriously contemplated leaving MA and going freelance just to make your movie.'

'But you didn't,' William smiled. 'You came to your senses just in time.'

'You're right, Willy boy, I did. I realized just in time it wasn't my movie. It's a woman's movie. You need a woman to make this movie. The best woman in town. And whether or not it sticks it my teeth to say so, the best gal in town is sweet Meredith Browne.'

She thought perhaps she'd taken Max's keys thinking only to lock his car up and then vengefully hurl the keys into the depths of the ocean. But that was when she had just woken up and was still sitting half-drunk on the sofa, waiting for her head to work itself out. And then when her vision cleared and she had seen the seed packets on the window ledge, the inspiration she had waited for had come to her in a flash, as she realized there was something very much more interesting she could do to exact a revenge on Max Bloody Kassov.

Meredith had never been inside Max's house, but she had passed it often enough. It stood well back from the road but open to view across broad sweeping lawns. There were no gates, and there was no perimeter fence, but

Meredith knew there had to be some sort of security system. Film producers needed safeguards, sometimes even more than the stars they employed, particularly from enraged and vengeful lady film producers whose world they had just helped lay to waste.

So she pulled the car up at the kerb some distance from the house and examined the keys which hung in a bunch under the ignition. One was obviously a front-door key, while several of the others were smaller door keys, and possibly garage keys. But there was one which was very different from the others. A type of tubular key, made of graphite, the sort used to arm and disarm alarm systems, and identical to her own.

Good, thought Meredith, restarting the car and heading it for the entrance to the house. Now all we have to do is find out where the plug is and switch off.

For the benefit of the constant police patrols, to make it look as though Max was at home, she left the Mercedes parked prominently under the mock London street-light outside the front of the house, while she searched discreetly for the security lock. She found it above her head to the side of an overhead light, a place she would never have thought of looking if she hadn't suddenly reckoned that since the key was the same type as her own security key, then the chances were the firm would have fitted the lock in a similar position to hers.

With the seeds safely in her jeans' back pocket, Meredith walked down the white-carpeted hall to where she hoped the second security switch would be, in a box under the stairwell. Sure enough, it was. So now with the whole house safely, she hoped, at her mercy, Meredith went through all the main rooms, hoping and praying her hunch would prove right. And it did. There was thick deep-pile white carpet everywhere.

Of course she had prior knowledge of Max's taste, yet she also knew how tastes changed, particularly out in Hollywood, and particularly if you had an interior designer to plan the furnishings of your house. But

Meredith had banked on Max never losing his love for deep white carpet, with which he had covered all the floors of his old London apartment. Mercifully he had not.

Better still, in the vast drawing-room he had many pieces of matching furniture covered in a deep velour, and best of all, on his king-size bed was a huge fur throwover. Meredith could hardly contain her excitement as she searched around for her next most vital prop.

She found it in the conservatory. She found two of them, to be truthful, and went at once and filled them both with warm water from the gold-tapped circular bath, before returning to the bedroom, where she had decided she would make her start. From her back pocket she took the first of the half-dozen seed packets and carefully opened the top. Then she went all around the room, scattering the seeds deeply and evenly into the deep pile of the white carpet, and into the folds of the fur rug on the king-size bed. Once satisfied with her sowing, she then proceeded to water, taking the cans she had found in the conservatory and carefully sprinkling the warm water through their fine roses all over the wall-to-wall. She then proceeded through the house, sowing and watering the seeds down the landing, the staircase, the hall, into the vast drawing room and all over the velour furniture. She was careful to make the seeds last out, and her diligence was rewarded as she had just sufficient to plant out the eight large items of furniture in the drawing room before her supply of seeds ran out.

Once the drawing-room and hall were well and truly watered, Meredith only had one thing to do, which was find the central heating controls. They were located in a room off the kitchen, and monitored by an idiot-proof master panel. Meredith turned the system from just air-conditioned, to air plus 90°F of heat, and then let herself out, having not forgotten to re-arm the security system.

Then she got back in the Mercedes and drove as fast as she dare back to Malibu, pleased with her evening's work and confident that a temperature of 90°F should be sufficient.

The other gamble was, of course, had she given herself enough time to do the deed and return the car before William and Max got back from the café? She'd allowed herself an hour and a half, which was deliberately on the pessimistic side, because it normally took the best part of two hours to walk to the café, have a two to three course meal with drinks, and to saunter back to the beach house again. But Meredith had also overheard that Max had plans for the weekend, so there was always a chance he would hurry his meal.

As it happened, there was no sign of the two men as Meredith pulled the Mercedes off the main road and coasted down to repark the car back outside the porch. In fact she had plenty of time to leave the keys in the ignition and the car unlocked – a touch with which she was well pleased, because she knew how tremendously it would both irritate and puzzle Max all weekend, if not longer – and she had time enough to collect her things, leave William an affectionate note to make it appear she had just awoken and gone off home five minutes before, and then to drive herself home at a leisurely pace in her own little silver ragtop. All in all, Meredith thought as she tossed her hair free in the light wind, a great end to a really lousy day.

Max returned with William over half an hour later to find his car unlocked and the keys where he thought he had left them. Since there was nothing missing from the car, William and he put it down to some sort of mental aberration. Max drove off for his weekend after extracting a final promise from William that he would have the film script sent round to Meredith. William then let himself into his house only to find his guest already gone.

On Saturday William called Meredith and arranged to drop something in on her that evening. They met at six for drinks, and William told her the story of Jay and her long fight against her illness, and their astonishing reunion, then gave her the script. He told her, as he had promised

Max he would, that he had shown it to Metro Am, who, although they had loved it, were not in the market for this sort of movie at this time. Besides which, William added, it wasn't their sort of movie anyway. This script needed a woman on it, and there was only one girl in town who could handle it. Meredith looked at William, then down at the script in her hands, which she was holding as if it was treasure, which indeed she had already determined to prove that it was. Then she laid it carefully to one side and, kissing William softly and warmly on each cheek, promised him that this day and this moment would mark the beginning of the rest of both their lives.

William laughed and said that Meredith hadn't even read it yet. And Meredith smiled and replied that she had no real need to. She knew this was the moment.

On Sunday morning, two a.m. Pacific time, William called Jay as he did every Sunday to tell her he loved her. This Sunday morning he also told her to whom he had given the script.

'Yes, I know,' Jay's voice said very matter of fact in his ear. 'I dreamed that you did last night.'

On Sunday evening, Max returned from his weekend away to find his home like a hothouse and the carpet in the hall, in the drawing-room, on the stairs, landing, and in the master bedroom and bathroom, and the furniture in the drawing room, and the priceless fur rug on his bed all totally covered in a thick two-inch growth of young and healthy bright green mustard and cress.

'The money,' said Meredith.

'What about it?' asked William.

'The money's the difficulty. It depends what sort you want.'

'The stuff that'll pay the cast and crew'll do just fine, Meredith.'

William and Meredith were sitting in the living room of Meredith's apartment, which was now the production office of Meridian Films, the company they had mutually formed to make *A Story So Far*, as William had titled his film.

'You've been through the costings, right?'

'Six and one-half million, Meredith. Seems right on the line.'

'There's no problem getting that sum, William darling. What I meant by "what sort" of money, is we don't want the sort of money that says no to all our ideas and yes to all theirs.'

'Is there any other sort of money, Miss Browne?'

'I thought we might go for some owe-you money,' Meredith replied. 'I thought we might tap someone's conscience.'

The two of them flew over together to England: William to pick up Jay and Meredith to go and see Baz.

'He's a sick man, William,' Meredith told him on the plane. 'And I hope he may also feel pretty shitty about what he did to me when he sees me face to face.'

'I guess he really thought you were going to be looked after,' William replied.

'Don't you believe it, darling,' Meredith laughed. 'Baz's heart is a crocodile job, and it lives in his inside pocket.'

Jay was waiting for them at the barrier. William could hardly believe his eyes. She looked a different person to the one he had last seen down in Dorset. She had natural colour in her cheeks, her hair was almost fully back to its normal lustre, and she had put on some weight. She also was walking with the help of only one stick.

'I told you we'd lick this thing,' William said, after he'd held her and kissed her.

'I knew you'd negotiate yourself a credit,' Jay sighed, turning to Meredith with a private wink and hugging her warmly. 'Additional recuperative help by William Kennedy.'

'You can't say you haven't started improving dramatically since I walked back into your life,' William argued.

'I don't know about that,' Jay said, taking hold of William's arm. 'What I do know is that you can't say anything to a writer.'

Jay drove them all back into London and dropped Meredith off at Grosvenor House, where she was staying, before driving William down to Knightsbridge.

'I don't get it,' William said, frowning as they passed The Scotch House. 'I thought you said you'd booked me into the Ritz.'

'I was lying,' said Jay.

She turned the car down Beauchamp Place, and then stopped temporarily at the bottom intersection when the traffic lights went against her.

'Ah,' William smiled. 'A trip down memory lane.'

'Do you know something, William Kennedy?' Jay asked him, as the lights changed to green. 'You're corny, even for a writer.'

William smiled at her, and put his arm around her shoulder as Jay turned right and headed for the King's Road. She parked in the first free space she could find. William was about to reason why, but Jay was already out of the car and walking round to William's side.

'Hurry up,' she sighed, opening his door for him. 'Anyone would think you were the one on sticks.'

Then she turned away from him and walked back in the direction of their old studio. William jumped out of the car and hurried after her.

'OK,' he said, catching her up. 'I give in.'

'Really?' she said. 'That's not like you. Happy birthday.'

She put something in William's hand, something in a small box.

'It's not my birthday, Jay,' he corrected her. 'My birthday was two months ago.'

'I know,' Jay replied. 'But I couldn't get your present until now. Aren't you going to open it?'

William opened the present. In the box was a front-door key.

'I bought it back,' Jay said, 'from the sale of one of my books to Hollywood.'

Taking the key from the box, William opened the door and looked inside the studio. Jay had refurnished it exactly as it was, down to the King Lear chair. William stared at it, slowly shaking his head as their past wrapped itself around him and enveloped him. Then he turned and kissed Jay, before lifting her up in his arms and carrying her over the threshold.

'Will you promise me one thing, William?' she asked him as they came in from the street. 'Will you promise me you'll never ask me to marry you?'

'Absolutely right I won't,' William replied. 'As long as you promise me something in return. That if ever I did, you'd turn me down point blank.'

'You betcha,' Jay said, and William kicked the door shut with his heel.

Baz was sitting up in bed reading *Variety* when Meredith arrived, ushered in by a polite but formidable-looking nurse. As the nurse left, closing the door behind her, Baz sighed and shook his head at the retreating figure.

Then he turned his attention to Meredith, and smiled, delighted by her still-as-trim-as-ever figure, shown off to perfection by the rust-coloured leather dress Meredith had bought from Loewe's that very day. She guessed that if the old man was bed-ridden, he'd want to see her looking at her best.

'My,' he said, patting the bed for Meredith to come and sit near him. 'Small wonder Louis lost his senses.'

Meredith kissed his smooth forehead, now mottled with a web of freckled pigmentations, and then arranged herself by him, taking one of his hands.

'Listen,' Baz sighed. 'This is a terrible business, this business of ageing. I tell you, if I'd had any idea I was going to live this long, I'd have taken better care of myself.'

Meredith laughed, and told Baz he looked in great shape.

'Maybe I should have gone to America with you,' he

wondered. 'I hear in America they don't die. They just go to Florida.'

'Maybe you should take a leaf out of George Burns's book,' Meredith replied. 'I saw him In Person last month, and he said he didn't believe in dying. It's been done. Apparently he's working on a new exit. Anyway he said he can't die now. He's been booked.'

That delighted Baz who shook his head and wheezed with laughter. For a while the two of them bantered some more, until finally Baz put his other hand on top of Meredith's and asked her what she'd come for. Meredith put her other hand on top of his and told him. And Baz nodded and asked how much. So Meredith told him, and Baz nodded some more, then asked her to pour them both a glass of champagne from the stoppered bottle which stood in an ice bucket on a table in the window.

'And Metro Am don't want to make the picture?' Baz recapped.

'I'm not going to Metro Am, Baz darling,' Meredith replied. 'I told you. I want to do this independently.'

'Of course you told me. It's my mind. It's too many dry Martinis. But six, six and a half million. With your record, the bank will lend you.'

'The bank won't lend me. Not without strings. And you know the strings they like to put on you. Bankable stars, bankable directors, bankable everything. I want to make this movie unencumbered. And to do that, I need no-string money.'

'OK. OK, I'll lend you. I'll lend you at five and a half over base.'

'Ouch.'

'Take it or leave it.'

'It's not *Gone With The Wind*, Baz. It's not going to be a grosser.'

'Take it or leave it.' Baz shrugged and sipped his champagne. Meredith sighed and did her best to hide her relief.

'Taken,' she said, raising her glass.

The nurse put her head round the door and told Meredith she must leave before she over-tired her patient.

'Her patient indeed,' Baz grumbled, as Meredith tidied him up in his bed. 'Her pay cheque more like. It's never like the movies, is it, Merry dear? Life doesn't send you along a pretty sexy little nurse with perfect legs and a gorgeous little bottom, right? Life sends you nurses like that, with bosoms like bolsters, and backsides like rhinoceroses. And I'm paying.'

'Sack her,' Meredith advised. 'Send out for another.'

'I keep doing that, Merry dear,' Baz replied. 'And every time I get back something worse. I sack this one, they'll send me Joan Crawford.'

Meredith kissed him goodbye, and said she'd put their lawyers together about the finance.

'You do that,' Baz said. 'While I lie here and dream dirty.'

It was only a short walk from Baz's apartment back to Meredith's hotel, but as she strolled along the quiet Mayfair streets, Meredith suddenly thought of something, and, instead of returning to Grosvenor House, hailed a cab and directed it to Holland Park.

When she arrived at her destination she had to ring the door bell of the house three times before receiving an answer. But then knowing what time of day it was, Meredith had anticipated this. Finally an exhausted-looking girl in a towelling dressing-gown opened the door a couple of inches and asked Meredith what the hell she wanted.

'Just tell Madame Pascal Miss Meredith Browne is here, will you?' Meredith requested.

The door was shut in her face and Meredith was left for another few minutes while the message was relayed. She was then admitted by the self-same girl, who apologized for her ignorance, with the sensible excuse that you can't be too careful.

A moment later Annie swept down the stairs, in a superb velvet gown with old-fashioned padded shoulders and enormous medieval sleeves. Considering the hour of the day, and the increase in her age since Meredith had last seen her, Annie still looked magnificent, and every inch the madam.

'My darling,' she said in greeting to Meredith. 'It has been far, far too long.'

In a still-darkened drawing room, not yet quite clear of the evidence of the previous night's activity, the two women sat and talked over new and old times. Finally they came to business.

'And what can I do for you this time, my darling?' Annie asked Meredith.

'I have a friend,' Meredith told her. 'An old friend. Who is badly in need of a loving and gentle nurse.'

Meredith was asleep when the bellhop called. He had a message for her. Meredith took the envelope from him, tipped him, and then retired back to bed to read the contents.

It was from Baz, short and to the point as always, wishing her well with the picture, and informing her that the terms of the loan had been altered from five and a half above base to interest free.

After she had bathed, dressed, and breakfasted, Meredith put a call though to Brown Anderson Ltd, and asked for Marshall Baird's representative. A vacant-sounding telephonist enquired who might be calling, so Meredith told her. The girl said she'd see if she could find someone and put Meredith on hold. After a good three-minute wait, Meredith hung up and redialled. She got the same girl.

'You was on hold,' the girl said.

'I don't go on hold,' Meredith told her. 'Who represents Mr Baird, please?'

'I don't know,' the girl replied truculently. 'I only been here two weeks.'

'Well, find out!' Meredith snapped. 'And get whoever it is to ring Meredith Browne at Grosvenor House at once!'

'I can't,' the girl moaned. 'There's no one in the office.'

'No one in the office! It's nearly ten o'clock!'

'Yeah. Well, no one usually gets in till about eleven.'

At a quarter to twelve, Meredith's phone rang.

'Hello, old girl,' a rather tired voice said. 'I believe you called and bollocked one of my girls.'

'Who is this, please?' Meredith asked crisply.

'This is Bernard Anderson, old love. I look after Marshall Baird.'

'Good. Well, I'm Meredith Browne. I was Head of Production at Diplomat—'

'At where, old girl?'

'Diplomat Productions, Mr Anderson. Hollywood.'

There was a puzzled silence, during which Meredith could hear a cigarette being lit and deeply inhaled.

'Really?' the voice finally came back. 'But you're not American?'

'Mr Anderson,' Meredith said, attempting to cut through the swathe. 'I need to contact Marshall Baird, and pdq.'

'Why would that be, old love? Sorry – someone's come through on the other bloody line.'

Meredith's line went dead. She held the receiver away from her and stared at it, about to slam it down. If it had been anyone else but Marshall Baird she was after, the job would have been lost there and then. But she had promised Baird all those years ago, when he had helped coach David Terry in that vital comedy role, that she would be back to him, and Meredith prided herself on always keeping her word.

'Sorry about that, old girl,' the voice droned back in her ear. 'Where were we?'

'Marshall Baird. I have a film script I want him to read.'

There was another silence, and the sound of another cigarette being lit.

'Marshall Baird?' the voice asked, making no attempt to conceal the surprise. 'A film script?'

'Mr Anderson,' Meredith replied. 'I have to fly back out again tomorrow, and I must make contact with Mr Baird.'

'He really only does commercials, you know. And the odd telly.'

'Just get him to call me, if you'd be so kind. I shall be at this number for the next half-hour, otherwise the desk will take any messages.'

'Marshall Baird,' said the voice, still wondering. 'Well, I'll be damned.'

They met in the hotel bar at six. From his agent's reaction, Meredith had expected to meet a wreck and a has-been. Instead she found waiting for her an extremely trim and well-dressed middle-aged man, little different to the director who had done such great work in such a short space of time on her young protégé.

He greeted her courteously and asked what she'd like to drink. Meredith told him fruit juice, and he ordered himself a tonic water with a dash of angostura.

'I had a problem,' he told her, holding up the non-alcoholic drink. 'Just in case you hadn't heard.'

'I hadn't,' Meredith confessed. 'But as long as you're over it.'

'Oh, I've been dry for four years,' Baird replied.

'But not that busy.'

Baird looked at her with surprise, unused to Meredith's up-front way of dealing.

'Well – no. Not exactly.'

'I'm not surprised. With that agent of yours. What in hell is a talent like yours doing with a klutz like that?'

'I owe him money.'

'Then my advice to you is pay him off.'

'I'm trying.'

Meredith reached into her briefcase, took out the shooting script of William's movie, and put it on the table in front of Baird.

'I'd like you to read this. It's a movie by William Kennedy, based on a book by a girl called Jay Burrell. To me it's quite the best screenplay I've ever read.'

Baird frowned at her, then turned the script round to read the title.

'Why do you want me to read it?' he asked.

'I want you to read it because, if you like it, I want you to direct it.'

Baird sat biting the end of one of his thumbs as he stared down at the script.

'You're sure this isn't some kind of a joke?'

'This is absolutely no sort of joke.'

'If you're offering me a picture to direct, Miss Browne, I really don't have to read it.'

'I want you to read it. I'd value your opinion.'

'Fine. Then I'll sit here and read it right now.'

Meredith took the key of her room from her purse.

'Better still,' she suggested. 'Go up to my suite and read it there. I have to go to a reception, and then on to dinner. I'll call you from the restaurant.'

By the time she called, Baird had read the script twice. Without being asked, he volunteered the opinion that it was a superb piece of work, but that he had some major misgivings. Meredith, her end, was being hurried to table, so she asked the director if he could wait her return so that they could discuss his apprehensions.

'Ring Room Service,' she added. 'Order yourself something to eat. I won't be long.'

When she returned to her suite she found Baird still there, sitting on the sofa with a bottle of brandy in front of him. He looked up as soon as Meredith came in, and saw her stopping in quite visible disappointment by the door.

'It's all right,' he told her. 'The seal's not broken.'

He held the bottle up, and Meredith could see the foil top was still intact.

'So what are the misgivings?' she asked him, sitting herself down opposite him, having hung up her coat.

'Misgiving, Miss Browne. There is only one.'

'I know,' said Meredith. 'What's a girl like me doing offering a guy like you a picture like this.'

She sat back in her chair and stared at the director, who after a moment nodded slowly in agreement.

'For what I did for you,' he said, 'you owe me at the most a half-day shoot on a dog-food commercial.'

'Absolutely,' Meredith agreed. 'I couldn't have put it better myself. And frankly, when that damn fool agent of yours was mucking me about this morning, I really thought that as usual I was misguiding my loyalty. But then I remembered why I asked you to coach David Terry. Because of *My Night with a Star*. I'd just seen your production at The Comedy, and I thought it was the best-directed play I'd seen in years. I wasn't alone. You picked up the *Evening Standard* and the Critics' Circle Awards. So I realized that why I was actually approaching you was because I thought you were quite the best man for the job.'

'Thank you,' Baird said quietly. 'If you mean it, and I now take it you do, I promise you that you won't regret your decision.'

'Good,' said Meredith. 'And I promise you something, darling. If I ever smell drink on your breath, you're fired.'

17

They waited over three weeks. They'd given her two, but more time was asked for, so now it had spread to almost twenty-five days.

'Is this normal?' Jay had asked.

'Out here there is no normalcy,' William had replied. 'If Hollywood was normal, they wouldn't be making motion pictures. They'd be making kitchens.'

While they were waiting, William took Jay to The Cedars of Lebanon Hospital to be examined by a neurologist whom Jay's own Doctor Mendip had recommended her to see. Jay's improvement had continued apace, although she still needed to walk with the aid of a stick.

'Peter Mendip writes me,' the neurologist said, consulting his notes, 'that not so very long ago you were all but paralysed.'

'Yes,' Jay replied. 'They thought I'd had a massive stroke.'

'Yet now you're up and walking on just one stick.'

'But not for long.'

'Pardon me?' The consultant looked up with some surprise.

'Meaning it won't be long,' Jay replied, 'before it's ta-ta sticks altogether. At least it will be if I have anything to do with it.'

'I have a handful of patients like you,' the doctor continued, 'who were all initially diagnosed as sclerotic. But, like you, this group weren't happy with their diagnoses, and came to me for second opinions. And I don't think they are sclerotic. Sure, all their myelin sheaths showed signs of damage, and there was plenty of evidence of impaired conduction. But somehow the cases just didn't patternize into the usual MS syndrome. So like Peter with you, I came at them from another part of the field.'

'Peter was the first man to treat me,' Jay explained, 'rather than the disease.'

'Right,' the doctor agreed.

'Without going anywhere near what you'd call analysis, he opened me right up and took an extremely long look. Then he started to regulate my lifestyle, which was going a bit awry, through pressures and anxieties I didn't even know I had, and put me on a yeast-free diet.'

'Sure.'

'And acupunctured me three times a week. Until I felt like a pin cushion.'

The doctor's expression changed to one of sudden and intense concentration, and he began to nod rapidly.

'Of course,' he said. 'Of course. At which points? The neck, I'll bet. Front and back. The feet. And of course the whole spinal area.'

'Right first time,' Jay grinned, remembering her extraordinary sense of well-being after the initial intensive course of acupuncture.

'Well, of course!'

The doctor was on his feet now, and walking around the room, tapping a pencil in the palm of one hand.

'You had tingling sensations in your limbs to begin with, yes? Which gradually turned to numbness. Your limbs would be quite numb when you woke in the morning. The slightest pressure on a nerve will cause what we all know as pins and needles, and if the pressure continues, then the nerve fibres cease to conduct. Hence the numbness. In normal cases, our cerebrospinal fluid is kept at a constant pressure; but if a part of our nervous system is compressed, that is relayed to our neurones, and there you go. One no-good nervous system. So acupuncture, correctly applied, may well relieve the damaging pressure, and remove the risk of permanent damage.'

'In my case, no may well about it,' Jay replied. 'It did. There's no doubt at all. But am I to gather from your reaction that this is something you haven't tried?'

The doctor smiled and sat back down at his desk.

'No,' he confessed. 'And I have a feeling that this is why you have been sent to see me. Not for me to help you. But rather for you to help me.'

William was pacing the corridors like an expectant father when Jay found him.

'I don't know which is worse,' he said. 'Waiting to hear about you-know-who, or the result of your damn interview.'

On the way back to the beach house, Jay told him of her conversation with the neurologist, and William listened intently, before slapping the steering wheel and shouting that it was just the scene he'd been looking for in the film.

'The patient helps the doctor!' he yelled. 'Christ, it's just great!'

'I'm so glad I fell ill,' Jay said. 'Where would you have been without sick old me?'

William stopped the car at once.

'That's a pig of a thing to say!' he turned on her. 'I'm only trying to make a movie out of something that happened!'

'I spy with my little eye,' said Jay, looking straight out through the windscreen.

'We've been through all this, Jay!' William stormed. 'You wrote the book! And you finally agreed to hand it over! So make up your goddam mind!'

'I'm sorry,' said Jay after a moment, turning to him and putting her hand on his knee. 'I just thought you might have been interested to hear the specialist's prognosis before you started to rewrite history.'

'To hell with writing,' William replied a little sadly. 'It's like a light in your head you can never turn off.'

'I know just what you mean,' Jay comforted him. 'I was trying to see how to incorporate the scene as the doctor was telling me about the proposed operation.'

William stared at her, then killed the car engine.

'Now what in hell are you talking about?' he demanded. 'You told me you were getting better, goddammit!'

'I am, William!' Jay laughed. 'But between them, Peter and this bloke – Doctor Hopper – they've evolved a theory that this compression on my nervous system could be caused by something. An abscess —'

'You'd feel an abscess, for Chrissake!'

'All right – something else then. Anything. A bone misplacement. A cyst.'

'Sure,' said William. 'I see where they're coming from.'

'Not all growths are malignant, William,' Jay sighed. 'If it's a growth at all, which he very much doubts. All he wants to do – and it was on Peter's instigation, because he knows how brilliant Doctor Hopper is – he just wants to have a peek at my plexuses. Whatever they are when they're at home.'

There was no response from William, who just sat staring at his hands which still gripped the steering wheel.

'It's a couple of days in hospital at the very most,' Jay assured him. 'Now drive me home. I'm dying for a swim.'

Swimming was one therapy upon which everyone was agreed. Jay had always been a good and strong swimmer until she fell ill, and when she had recovered sufficient movement in her limbs, the first place Peter Mendip had taken her was a swimming pool.

Now William watched her from the water's edge as she swam against the ocean waves, building up her strength and restoring her confidence. When he thought she'd been in the water long enough, he called her out, then stood and towelled her off as you would a small child. Jay leaned up over the edge of the towel and kissed him.

'Stop looking so serious!' she laughed. 'That was fun!'

'I was thinking of something else,' William said. 'I was thinking about the film.'

But he hadn't been. He'd been thinking about Jay's beautiful legs, and how pitifully weak they still looked.

Then, wrapping the towel around her, he lifted her up and carried her easily back to the house.

The light was flashing on his answerphone. He put Jay down and, having admonished her not to get cold, he ran the machine back to take his messages.

The one he was waiting for was the first one, a call from Meredith. He rang her back at once.

'Hi,' said Meredith when William was put through. 'Guess what? She said yes.'

Once Diane Felton had said yes, they were up and running. Meredith had anticipated the difficulties to start once Felton had accepted, such was her growing reputation for temperament, but besides asking very sweetly if they could employ her usual lighting cameraman, a request to which Meredith was only too delighted to agree, there were no demands made whatsoever. In fact, when it came to the fee negotiations, which is where Meredith really thought they would lose their star, the actress, once she realized the company couldn't pay her money, agreed to do the movie for no fee, just expenses and a percentage of the gross, such was her belief in the script.

She didn't even want approval of her leading man, just so long as she could be consulted. Meredith was happy to oblige, because she had already fought William over some of the suggested actors and they were still in a state of impasse.

'Why not Jon Jones?' the star suggested to Meredith one evening at dinner.

'That was our number one choice,' Meredith replied. 'But Allied have got him signed for *Handshake*.'

'They thought they had,' Felton corrected. 'But he doesn't like the director, Ted Byrne. He doesn't like the leading lady, Felicia Michael. And he doesn't like the script by Herman Prost. I should put in a call. And quick.'

Meredith did, told him the deal, told him Diane Felton

had signed for a percentage, sent him the script round by messenger, and by the next midday Jon Jones was bagged as well.

But the touchstone of the whole enterprise was Jay. Diane Felton followed her round like a little dog, her parasol in one hand and an advance copy of Jay's book in the other. The star had the most delicate pale complexion, upon which she never allowed any direct sun to fall, hence the parasol. But instead of wearing soft blouses and flowing skirts which would have been in perfect keeping with the delicacy of the image, Felton was inclined somewhat incongruously to sport over-large men's trousers, shirts and hats. She was forever out at the beach house, observing Jay, picking her brains, and William used to lean on his balcony and derive enormous pleasure from watching the odd couple strolling arm-in-arm along the sea front: Jay in a simple cotton dress and Felton, as everyone always called her, in baggy pin-striped trousers, collarless shirt, and a floppy white Panama hat. And parasol.

Evenings would be spent around a driftwood fire, which William was instructed to build for them on the beach, where, to the ritualistic passing round of one of Felton's handmaidens, as they got to be called, the script was discussed, bisected, analysed, criticized, disassembled and ultimately put together again. But by that time, William had usually taken himself off for a long walk down the beach to cool off.

'She's a monster,' William said to Jay one night as they cleared up after a particularly analytical session. 'She's just sucking you dry, and when she's finished, and the picture's shot, she'll just spit you out. So watch it.'

'Isn't that just what you do?' Jay asked him back, stacking up the unwashed china. 'Chew on people. Suck them dry and spit 'em out when you've finished with them?'

'The written word's different, Jay, and you damn well know it.'

'The written word's different, I agree. But people are the same.'

'She's never out of your face, dammit!'

'I don't mind, William. So why should you? I love her. Next to you, she's far and away the most interesting person I've ever met. Do you know what she really wants to be? She really wants to be a marine biologist.'

'Sure. So do a heap of people since *Jaws*.'

'Oh God, William!' Jay sighed. 'There are some real people, you know! Not everyone's a let's-pretend!'

'Just as long as you know what she's doing, sweetheart,' William warned. 'Come the dawn, these people pack up their tents and vanish.'

'She wants to get inside my head, William, I agree. But the reason she wants to do that, is one reason and one reason only! She really wants to play your movie to perfection!'

Jay grabbed her stick and hurried as fast as she could upstairs. William sucked his bottom lip, then hurled the tea towel into the sink and walked out to stare at the moonlit sea, to try and rid himself of this quite irrational jealousy.

After a slightly uncertain start, Marshall Baird soon had the cast's full confidence. The near miss was his insistence on having a full read-through of the script before shooting started, as if they were about to rehearse a stage play, not make a movie.

'I don't work like this, Marsh,' Felton informed him as the cast gathered in Meredith's apartment. 'I work organically.'

'Me too,' mumbled Jon Jones. 'I like to work up through a nice tight system of takes.'

'I appreciate that,' Baird replied. 'But I think it would be a help to hear the film as a whole. So that we can carry the picture in our heads.'

'I don't think so, pal,' Jones said, shaking his head slowly. 'It's going to dull my edge.'

'I don't think so either, Marsh,' Felton agreed, taking off her owl-like spectacles. 'It's going to fuck up my id.'

The director nodded as he considered the stars' objections. Then he turned to Meredith as if for a ruling.

'I hear what you're all saying,' Meredith said. 'And I can see there are pros and cons.'

'Fine,' said William, taking his glasses off and staring at the ceiling, which Jay alone knew presaged a loss of temper. 'Then if no one can make up their minds, I'll tell you what we'll do, folks. I'll read it to you. Then you won't get to screw up your ids, or piss on your organics, but the director and me, we'll get to hear how it sounds.'

'Oh come on, like hell you will, man,' groaned Jones. 'That's all my head could take. A writer reading.'

'Sweetheart,' Felton said, reaching out and putting a slender, cool hand to William's cheek. 'It's a great idea but I think no. If it really has to be read, then I think Jon and I should do the reading. Whatever.'

Which they did, mumbling and fumbling a deliberately incoherent way through the first four or five pages. But then, despite their resistance to the idea, the characters and the story overtook them, and they started to perform, particularly when they realized how captivated their audience was. When they finished, over an hour and ten later, the rest of the company — which included the designers and cameraman besides the immediate production crew — burst into spontaneous applause.

What pleased William even more was that all the girls had cried, and even one or two of the men.

'You're a clever old bastard, Marsh,' Felton said, getting up and kissing him on the cheek. 'What time tomorrow?'

Baird squeezed her hand and pointed out who to get her calls from, while Jon Jones came and stood beside him, putting a hand on his shoulder.

'Screw you, man,' he said, nodding very slowly. 'I really mean it. The point is, I was scared shitless.'

And then he and Baird laughed, and agreed to go out and do some beer.

As the meeting broke up, Diane Felton came and sat down between William and Jay.

'You two good people bettin' folks?' she asked, putting on a faultless mid-West accent.

'William bets on anything,' Jay laughed. 'Flies in people's soup. You know.'

'She means flies on the wall,' William said. 'Why, have you got a tip, Felton?'

'Sure thing, Mr Writer man,' the star replied, one hand on each of their knees. 'So choose a number, between one and six.'

'What for?' Jay asked curiously.

'For the number, honey,' Felton laughed, still in her mid-West character, 'of little gold men this here picture of ours is goin' to win.'

When the nominations for the Academy Awards were announced in February, *A Story So Far* was second top of the list, with six: Best Film, Best Screenplay, Best Actress, Best Director, Best Score and Best Art Direction. There was jubilation in the Meridian camp, particularly since in the Best Film category theirs was the only independent movie to get a nomination. Their rivals were all products from the majors.

At best, Meredith had thought they might have an outside chance of winning a nomination for Best Screenplay, and perhaps Best Actress, so to get six exceeded even her wildest bathtime fantasies.

'I reckon there should be an Oscar for best producer,' William said to Meredith at the ensuing celebrations. 'It was like as if the damn thing was on wheels.'

'Garbage,' Meredith replied. 'With a screenplay like that, and a cast like that? Even Mike Victor could have brought this one home.'

'Yes, maybe,' William agreed. 'But instead of that last fine scene in the hills, he'd have had a shoot-out in the subway. And by the by, I have to tell you, before I get completely fried, Marsh did one hell of a job. I had my

623

doubts when you brought him over. I think we all did. But he's a fine director. I mean it. He's a kind of cross between Lubitsch and Cukor.'

'And we haven't made *Love Story*.'

'No, thank Christ you haven't.'

The film had come in a week over, due only to the exceptionally unseasonable weather they encountered on location in England, which William, present for every day of the shoot, skilfully wrote round. It also came in half a million under budget which said it all for Meredith's increasing production skills. She didn't save a dime where it might show. She saved it all from where it never did. From expenses. There was no unnecessary first-class travel, no absurd hotel bills, no lavish partying for the production. In the air, everyone went Club, and on the ground, they all travelled in the production trucks. And when they shot in New York and in England, the cast were invited to stay with friends of Meredith's or Jay's and William's and not just to save waste, but also to keep up the intense bonding that had grown up between the actors, the crew and the production.

'Hey, people,' Felton announced one night in the company bus as they trucked across California. 'This, you know, this isn't a movie. Not as such. No, this is a very real *experience*.'

'What in hell's an experience?' Jon Jones had called back to his co-star, 'compared to a six-foot-square feather bed?'

William, sitting at the back of the bus with a radiantly happy Jay, thought to himself, so what if these people pack their tents and steal away with the dawn? While the caravan was rolling, it was fun, and fun was a commodity in preciously short supply. In fact, William confessed to Jay, as far as work went, he had never had a good time like it.

'Even though they suck you dry?' Jay teased him. 'And spit you out when they're finished?'

'Right,' William grinned. 'So who was party pooper of the year then?'

624

The only aspect of the film none of them could agree upon was the music.

'What we don't want is a Lara's Theme,' Meredith announced.

'*Doctor Zhivago* did for snow what Lawrence did for sand,' William said, quoting one of the criticisms.

'That's funny,' Jay said, 'but not a lot of help. Did anyone here see *L'Affaire*?'

'We don't want a Great Theme,' Meredith continued, unhearing. 'Something which goes to war with what's on the screen. We want something to complement the action, not suffocate it.'

'It was a lovely film,' Jay persisted, 'and it had lovely music.'

'I suppose solo piano's too fey,' William ventured. 'It really shouts here comes the heartbreak.'

'The music in *L'Affaire* was just voices,' Jay said, edgewise.

'I don't really mind piano,' Meredith replied after consideration. 'Just as long as it's not a concerto.'

'It was just voices singing,' Jay prevailed, 'without words.'

'Christ no,' said William. 'A concerto and you're straight into *Brief Encounter*. And *Brief Encounter* our film is not.'

Jay sighed, and then sat back and started humming the theme from *L'Affaire*.

'It needs to be distinctive though,' Baird opined, now entering the fray. 'It needs to have the same feel as the movie. Singularity.'

Jay hummed a little bit louder.

'OK,' said William agreeing. 'But the choice is very limited. Unless you go synthetic, and that's the last sort of sound we want.'

'We don't want a song either,' Meredith concluded. 'Songs over opening and closing credits aren't organic.'

By now Jay was singing, but not too loud, the wordless theme of the French film. William clicked his tongue and flapped a hand in her direction.

'Knock that off for a second will you, Jay?' he asked. 'Because I think I have it. Did any of you guys ever catch a French movie called *L'Affaire*?'

Jean-Paul Clement's score for *A Story* was magical. Using human voice, flute and electric piano, he managed to compose music that was illustrative, sensitive, moving, and quite unforgettable.

'That's just what you want, people,' Diane Felton said when she saw the final dub. 'A terrific drama which the audience goes out humming.'

The reaction at the previews was highly encouraging, with a high percentage of the audiences giving the movie a top rating. Even so, no one was in any way prepared for the notices the movie got on its official opening.

Once or twice a movie comes along that gets called the film of the decade. A Story So Far goes further than that. It's a movie of two, maybe three decades. No, it's more than that. This is a movie of any decade.

(New York Times)

If any of you ever had doubts about Diane Felton's depth, prepare to shed them now. In this deeply-felt movie, Miss Felton shows us that her range doesn't stop, as some suspected, somewhere this side of B, but clearly runs right from A to Z and then some more. She is skillfully supported by Jon Jones, giving his best and thankfully his most comprehensible performance to date, under the consummately delicate direction of Marshall Baird.

(Newsweek)

Baird and his writer William Kennedy have achieved the impossible. They have created a mood rather than a story. And they have kept it alive by their freshness of observation, and their eye for the detail of each small thing around. The pacing is perfect. Comedy is there

626

*when comedy is called for, and real poignancy when
substance is needed. And yet there is not the slightest
trace of effort.*

(New Yorker)

*Not since Capra has so little been made so wonderfully
into so much.*

(Time)

*Felton is wonderful. Jones is wonderful. Baird's direc-
tion is wonderful. Kennedy's screenplay is wonderful.
Clement's music is wonderful. The film looks wonderful.
The film is wonderful. Why are there not enough super-
latives sufficient to describe a movie that revives your
faith in a medium which of late has been dying on its
feet?*

(Hollywood Reporter)

'The *Chicago Examiner* doesn't like it,' Jay said, poring
through William's press cuttings in the beach house. 'It
calls it "an icky bitter-sweetie". And there's a stinker in
The Montgomery Gazette.'

'Jeez,' sighed William, 'just when I was thinking of
moving there.'

'It calls it a "cloying contrivance, directed through a
haze of sentiment by someone on their knees".'

'I think you enjoy reading the bad ones out more than
the good ones, young lady.'

'Well, of course I do, William. It makes a change. You
know how bored I get if I ever have to do the same thing
twice. Let alone a hundred and twice.'

Jay grinned up at him, throwing the mass of rave
reviews they'd collected joyfully into the air.

'Well-who'd-have-thought-it?' she laughed.

William stretched his long legs out a little further on the
sofa and stared at his feet.

'From a girl sliding down a bannister,' he said, 'to this.'

The film had opened the week before in Los Angeles to similar critical acclaim, and was about to go on general release once Meredith had finalized the distribution deal.

'Does this mean you're going to be a very, very rich man, William K?' Jay asked.

'If being rich means not having to work until next month,' William replied, 'then I guess so.'

'Good,' said Jay. 'Then I'll stick around for a while.'

William reached out for the wine and poured two more glasses.

'I thought we might take a vacation,' he said. 'Hawaii maybe. Or the Caribbean.'

'OK,' Jay agreed. 'I'd like that.'

'Really stretch our legs,' William continued. 'Hang out until the film opens in London, spend some time in England, then back for the Awards.'

'You're on,' Jay replied, sipping her wine and then looking at him over her glass. 'Except for London. I'm pencilled in to go into The Cedars that month.'

It was pointless to argue, William knew that. They had been over and over whether or not the proposed operation was necessary, but there was no moving Jay. William had demanded to know why she was so determined upon it, and Jay had said because.

'That's not good enough, Jay! And you know it! Because isn't a goddam reason!'

'All right, William. Because it's my disease, and I can choose to have it treated how I want. I do most other things your way, but on this particular occasion I'm going my way.'

'But there's no reason for them to operate! And if there isn't, I don't want them fooling around with your nervous system! Christ, anything could happen!'

'William,' Jay had said, hoping to put a capper on it. 'I'm having this operation whether you say so or not. I have to have it. I've been waking up numb all down my left side again.'

That at least had temporarily taken the wind out of

William's sails, until he developed a theory that Jay was waking up numb on that side because she was sleeping on it. In fact he became so convinced by his theory he would wake Jay up during the night whenever he awoke and found her lying on her left.

Jay started getting so tired from lack of sleep that she gave up telling William if she was numb.

She also didn't tell him that during one of the tests Dr Hopper had run, he had discovered what appeared to be a small growth on the side of one of her cervical vertebrae.

'I'm not even sure it's a growth,' he told her, looking at the X-ray pictures. 'It could be shadowing. It could be just fibrous tissue. It could be anything. But one thing is certain, it's worth looking at.'

So after an idyllic holiday spent in the end on Antigua, William flew off for the London première and Jay was admitted to hospital.

That was something else Jay had made quite clear. She didn't want William around when she entered The Cedars, and she certainly didn't want him around for the operation.

'You make me nervous, William,' she had told him. 'You get in such a state, you get me in a state. And Dr Hopper says for this to be a success I have to be calm.'

It was a blatant lie as far as what Dr Hopper was meant to have said, but it was the whole truth about William making her nervous. It was bad enough during the week before he left for London. Jay would wake up and find him standing at the end of her bed, staring at her. Or the house would be empty, and she would haul herself out of bed to try and spot the distant figure she knew to be out there on the beach somewhere, throwing pebbles out into the breakers.

And the more she assured him of the simplicity of the operation, the more doubtful he became. At one point he became so depressed and anxious Jay hauled him off to see Dr Hopper in order to have some sense talked into him. Hopper was so strict on William, as well as so convincing, that William cancelled his cancellation and two days later flew out for England.

Nonetheless, he called her at every conceivable opportunity, to make sure of her well-being.

'You can't call me tomorrow, William,' she told him, 'because I'll be in surgery.'

'You're not being operated on until the day after tomorrow!' he argued.

'They've moved me a day forward. No reason, there was just a space, and they want to fill it.'

'The goddam film opens tomorrow, Jay!'

'So do I, William,' Jay cracked, and then, hearing the heartfelt sigh on the line, immediately wished she hadn't.

'William. It's less than having your tonsils out. Now go away and have a lovely première.'

Having established what time he could ring Dr Hopper to find out how it had gone, William finally and very reluctantly rang off.

Twenty-four hours later, Dr Hopper inserted the final stitch in the incision he had made in Jay's neck and, having checked all else was normal, ordered her to be taken down to the recovery room.

'Yes,' he told William on the phone, 'it went just fine. I removed a small growth beside the fourth vertebra, which was undoubtedly causing some undue pressure on the nerves in that immediate area – in fact I imagine on the whole of the brachial plexus. We'll run an immediate biopsy on the growth, the results of which we'll have on your return. Are you still planning to fly back in tomorrow?'

William assured him that he was, and then asked for more information about the growth.

'I really can't say any more, William,' Hopper replied. 'It's not something you know by looking. There was certainly no sign of spread, and without committing myself in any way, if it's any reassurance, on the very few occasions I've come across something like this, they've never proved malignant. OK?'

630

'Thanks,' said William. 'That helps.'

'So how was the movie?' the doctor asked.

'Good,' William replied. 'No, that's not true. It was a smash.'

The plane touched down at Los Angeles airport shortly after six p.m. Pacific time, and from there William drove straight to the hospital. When he got to Reception he asked for Jay's room, but the girl on duty told him to wait while she paged Dr Hopper.

'Is there something wrong?' William asked, his insides suddenly running ice cold.

'Dr Hopper just requested he should be informed of your arrival,' the girl smiled, and then put out her call.

William stood by the desk, unable to sit down, scarcely able to think. If Dr Hopper wanted to see him before he saw Jay, he tried his best to reason, then something must have gone wrong. Otherwise here they were, a day and a half later, and if something hadn't gone wrong William would now be sitting by Jay's bedside.

So what in hell had happened?

'She's in a coma, I'm afraid,' the doctor told him quietly, leading William away from the desk. 'Now before you hit the panic button, let me tell you it's not that unusual.'

'Yes?' William replied. 'I gathered it was something less than having your tonsils out.'

'Nothing is as straightforward as it sounds, William. For an adult, a tonsillectomy can be a major operation.'

'And this? Was this really necessary? Or was it just another piece of surgical experimenting?'

Hopper nodded, and told William he was right to be angry, that his loss of temper was perfectly understandable. Then he steered him into his office and asked him to sit down. William said he would prefer to go and see Jay, but Hopper insisted that he sit down and listen to him before they visited the patient. William obeyed, albeit reluctantly, and Hopper sat at his desk and began to run through the whole series of events.

631

The good news was that the growth which had been removed was not malignant. Nor was there any doubt that it had been the cause of the initial numbness and finally the paralysis in the upper limbs. Why the doctors in London had failed to find it, Hopper imagined, was simply because they hadn't looked for it. There was always an inclination, once any damage was spotted to the myelin sheaths which covered the nerve fibres, immediately to suppose the root cause to be sclerosis, and thus not bother to look any further. That's where Peter Mendip had been so bright. His sort of approach to medicine was to try and think up every possible reason for a symptom, and then gradually eliminate the non-starters.

'But I still can't explain the general paralysis,' Hopper continued. 'Because that would need another growth pressing on the lumbosacral plexus. Or anyway damage in that area. And I can't find the slightest trace of any.'

'It's possible,' William supposed, 'that the total paralysis was auto-suggestive. Or psychosomatic. Apparently Jay lost the feeling in and the use of her upper limbs first, and perhaps if she panicked herself—'

'Good,' Hopper nodded. 'That's good. I really hadn't considered that possibility. That really makes some sense here. Yes.'

But then there was the coma. Hopper established the operation went by the book, and was one hundred per cent correct procedurally, let alone physically. But he had to admit that with neurosurgery, bearing in mind that what was being operated on was a person's central nervous system, even in the most controlled medical environment and with the greatest possible care being taken, any untoward displacement of one nerve fibre, let alone a plexus, could produce a contrary result.

'You mean in a coma.'

'Yes,' Hopper admitted and then under further pressure from William, conceded it could even end in paralysis.

'Then why in God's name did you undertake the operation?' William demanded, getting to his feet. 'When I

632

left Jay she was walking around, and laughing, and talking! What in hell did you think you were doing!'

'William,' Hopper answered, 'we took out a growth the size of a kid's marble. This size.'

He demonstrated.

'Jay was going numb all down her left side again. In another month, maybe less, she could well have been paralysed again.'

'And what about now, doc! She's not exactly leaping around cured, I mean, is she! She's lying there in a goddam coma!'

Hopper took William up to Intensive Care to see Jay, and *en route* expressed the opinion that the coma was only a transient state, that it was just the nervous system expressing a reaction to the surgery.

'Bullshit,' William said quietly. 'You're shooting in the dark.'

For a moment William stood outside the glass-walled room where Jay lay motionless. She seemed smaller and frailer than ever, a little figure in a sea of white linen and a mass of surgical wiring, with the pulse of her life beating a green rhythmic line across a nearby monitor.

Then he went in and stood by her, looking down on the pale beauty of her face and the smallness of her being. He took one of her hands in both of his, and felt it to be cool and dead. And then he sat down beside her, still with her hand held tight, trying to urge some of the life from himself into the pale inertness that was Jay. But she lay quite still and without movement. All the time William sat there, praying to a God he hadn't prayed to in years, promising sacrifices in return for her consciousness, pledging his own life for the return of her own.

Later, as Hopper and he walked down the long corridor away from the comatose Jay, William asked helplessly what was to be done. And Hopper shook his head and told him nothing. All any of them could do now was wait.

William returned to his beach house and unpacked in the company of a bottle of Jack Daniel's. When he had thrown his dirty clothes in the laundry basket and hung up his suits and slacks, he poured himself another shot and sat down on the bed with a large cardboard box on his knees. He remained staring at it for a long time before he opened it. Then he finally undid the ribbon and lifted the lid.

Inside was an exquisite, gossamer-light silver evening dress and matching jacket. There was a purse to match, and a pair of silver evening shoes. Sitting inside the box on his knees was the outfit he'd bought her for the night of the Academy Awards.

William visited her every day. So too, almost every day, did Meredith. Everyone on the film came to see Jay, and Diane Felton would sit for hours at a time in a trance by Jay's bed. Often when William visited he seemed to have to deal with two comatose people, since the actress's trance seemed to be every bit as deep as the patient's coma.

One day, during the second week of Jay's unconsciousness, Diane Felton and William walked for a long time in the grounds of the hospital.

'What causes coma, Bill?' the actress asked him.

'What they call an insult to the brain usually,' William answered.

'Jesus, friend,' Felton smiled. 'Then in this business the likes of you and I should be comatose most of the time. What sort of insult are we talking here?'

'Injury, I guess. A blow. Pressure. Infection. Lack of oxygen. Lack of sugar, as in diabetes. Shock even, in severe cases.'

'Shock even.'

'That's Hopper's banker bet. He says Jay must have a very delicate nervous system, and the operation knocked it off-balance. That her whole nervous machinery is in a state of trauma.'

'Hmmm,' said the actress. 'Right.'

Then she went and fetched her car and drove away.

William's phone rang by his bed at around three a.m. It was Diane.

634

'Hi,' she said. 'Remember the tale of the Sleeping Beauty?'

'Isn't it a little late for bedtime stories?' William asked. 'I heard you read 'em to people before they went to sleep.'

'The Sleeping Beauty was in a coma, right?' the actress persisted. 'And what happened? The guy she loves comes back and what does he do? Awakens her with a kiss.'

'Oh Christ, Felton!' William groaned. 'What have you been doing, dope?'

'I haven't smoked in a month, Bill. And I haven't been near the wine neither. OK – look at it this way. What's the best thing for shock?'

'I don't know, Felton! Warmth, I guess.'

'What sort of warmth?'

'Warm warmth, Diane! What other sort of warmth is there, for Chrissake!'

'Jeez, you damn writers. You're so damn *literal*! Besides just wrapping someone up, in a blanket or thick clothes or whatever, how else can you make a person warm, Bill?'

'Food. Drink. Put him in front of a fire! What the hell are you driving at, Felton?'

'How else can you make a person feel warm, you ape! Not physically! Metaphysically!'

William pulled his knees up under his chin and wrapped one arm around them, resting his head between his knees.

'Are you still there, scribbler?' the voice in his ear asked. 'Because you haven't answered my question. I'll give you a clue. Think of the song Johnny Mathis sang.'

William sat bolt upright. If there was such a thing as Jay and his song, then it was 'Warm'.

'For God's sake, Felton! You got second sight as well?'

'As well as what, Bill?'

'As well as a so-so way with acting. OK – so people make each other warm.'

'Shy, Bill. Not people. Try again.'

'Affection.'

'What's wrong with love?'

'You're not seriously suggesting, are you? That I go kiss Jay awake?'

'Boy – you finally made it.'

'And you're seriously out to lunch.'

'Think about it, scribbler.'

'You are. You're nuts. For a start, the poor kid's tubed up everywhere!'

'I mean it. Think about it.'

'Felton?'

But the line had gone dead.

There was no more sleep to be had, try as William might. So he pulled on a sweater and jeans and went for a walk on the beach. It was a warm still night, and the tide was out there somewhere, just on the turn. For a long time as he walked William just shook his head and laughed to himself, as he considered the absurdity of the actress's proposal.

'Sheer whimsy,' he said out loud. 'Sheer goddam Hollywood schmaltz!'

Medical facts were medical facts, and people in comas did not bust out of them, whatever the fairy stories said. They either gradually recovered consciousness, or else.

Or else.

He knew the phone was ringing before he even heard it. He was fifty yards or so from the house and he started running back before he even heard the bell.

It was Hopper.

'I think you should come over,' he advised. 'There seems to be some regression.'

William didn't even ask what. He just grabbed his keys and was out of there.

He ran from the parking lot into the hospital, and he ran down the corridors and up the stairs, two at a time, three sometimes, running as fast as he could, up to the desk outside Intensive Care. He saw Hopper just coming out of Jay's booth and, brushing aside the medical orderly who was trying to bar his way, grabbed the doctor before Hopper had even seen him.

'How bad?' he gasped. 'What's happened?'

Hopper frowned for a moment, as if he wasn't quite sure who William was, before breathing in deeply and putting an arm round William's shoulders.

'She just started to slip a little,' he said calmly, perfectly calmly. So calmly that William knew he was a worried man. That's how he'd write it, anyway.

'It was about an hour ago.'

When he would have been first out on the beach. When he would have been laughing.

'When I was called, it was because at first they thought she was stirring. There seemed to be some responses.'

That was Diane. That was Felton getting through.

'Then her breathing started to get shallower, and her temperature began to drop.'

Sure. Because she was cold. Because there was no warmth. Of course her temperature would drop. While he'd been shouting schmaltz.

'She's stable now. But I have to tell you, I think there's cause for concern.'

William stopped and disengaged himself from Hopper, turning to look into the glass-walled booth. There was a nurse in there, attending. And another doctor.

'That's why I wanted you here.'

They told him later that he roared. Or screamed. That he made some frightening, primal noise, but William wasn't ever conscious of it. He remembered seeing the nurse's face turn to him in astonishment, and he could just recall pulling the tubes from Jay's mouth and nose as he lifted her featherweight body up from the bed, with the tubes and wires still hanging from her thin pale arms; and he remembered the way her head fell back from him as he held her, and her long mane of brown hair unfurling behind as he put his hand to her head, one hand that was cradling her; and he saw her mouth, and the faint red of her lips, her half-open mouth just before he crushed it with his, as he kissed her and kissed her and held the dying girl to him.

Then he was lying down on a bed somewhere, a dim light above him, shining away from his eyes. There was someone else in the room, a person, a girl, sitting beside him, smiling now at him, putting a cool hand on his arm.

'Jay?'

His voice was a croak, and his lips were bone dry. All his limbs felt heavy, as if they were still asleep even though he was waking. Then the door over there in a wall opened and a man in white came in, to stand by him and bend down close to his face.

'You're crazy,' the very-close face said. 'You could have killed her.'

William remembered the man now. It was that doctor. It was Hopper.

'What happened?' he asked, trying to sit up.

'You went a little wild, William. But it's OK. It's perfectly understandable.'

'Jay?'

'No change.'

Hopper sat on the edge of William's bed and checked his pulse.

'We had to shoot you up, I'm afraid,' he said. 'You were like King Kong.'

'How long have I been out?'

'Nearly two hours.'

'But Jay's no worse?'

'No. Remarkably, under the circumstances – no. But then I'm afraid she's no better.'

The doctor let William's wrist drop, and William lay back on the pillow. Hopper was just in the middle of advising him to go back to sleep until the sedative wore right off when his bleeper went.

'Yes?' he said into the pocket pager. He listened intently, and gave one glance at William. 'I'll be there immediately,' he announced, and started to move. Then he stopped and looked at William.

638

'Your legs working?'

William swung off the bed and tried to stand. He nearly fell, but in a second had regained his balance.

'Kind of,' he replied.

'OK,' Hopper told him. 'Then I think perhaps you better come too.'

The nurse helped William as he stumbled after the half-running doctor in front of him. William cursed his frailty, then swallowed his pride and, putting his arm round the nurse's shoulder, allowed her to help propel him along.

They arrived at Intensive Care to see Hopper standing at the end of Jay's bed, obscuring their view. William grabbed hold of the door frame and pulled himself into the room.

'Hi,' said a small very pale person from the bed.

END PAPERS

They sat surrounded by their peers. By people at whom they had stared out there starry-eyed, out in the darkness, since they were kids. And now there they were all around them, laughing and clapping, living and breathing like other mortals, the gods and goddesses of the screen, magnificent in their finery and jewels, emanating charisma, the stars come down, bringing the heavens to earth for a night.

William had done his best not to rubberneck. After all he was there as a nominee, and although not one of the vast public of fans who had lined the motorcade and massed behind the barriers outside, packed into a gasping sea of adulation, had the slightest idea who he was when he was stopped by the Master of Ceremonies and introduced to the madding crowd, he was still determined to play it mature, and not give the enthralled and starstruck kid inside him one peek out.

Jay, on the other hand, had decided it was May Day, and that she was Queen of it. In her glittering silver dress and jacket she looked like a star, and when she stopped by William's side, and waved and blew kisses at the fans, they roared their worship back at her as if she had been making movies since she was born. They never caught her name, or understood her label. They simply responded to the delight of a beautiful girl who had made it through the night just to be there.

And, once inside the auditorium, Jay did her best to ruin William's composure by nudging him and hissing at him every time she spotted a Fonda, a Bacall, a Stewart or a Hepburn. William finally sighed and warned her if she didn't behave, he was going to ask to swop seats with Charles Bronson, who'd soon keep her in order. Jay grinned and said that suited her fine, and continued to behave like a child at the circus for the first time.

They had dined with Meredith, Felton and Marshall Baird, and none of them had eaten a thing. Marsh admitted that for the first time since he'd been offered the script, he wanted to drink, so Meredith put a bottle of Scotch on the table in front of him, which remained unopened as she knew it would, while Felton bravely lit up a handmaiden, took two draws, and then scampered off to the powder room to be sick. Finally they all sat around waiting for their limos, yawning a lot and making silly jokes, before falling oddly silent, like paratroopers before a drop.

Then Diane got suddenly to her feet.

'Listen, you guys,' she said. 'If we come back empty-handed, so what. Seriously. We all know we made a great movie, and a couple of statues isn't going to alter its value. No. Because anyway, if it's rewards we're talking about, then we've already topped out. Because Jay came back. OK?'

Jay took her friend's hand and Felton just stood there nodding.

'OK?' she asked once more. 'OK.'

Felton and her party were sitting a few rows down from William and Jay, and Meredith and Marshall Baird were a couple of rows back. When William and Jay arrived, Jay saw a sudden but brief look of disappointment cross William's face, as he eased himself and Jay past some of the luminaries already seated in their row.

'What's the matter now?' Jay asked as they sat down. 'Don't you like your seats? They're perfect. Look – we're right in the middle.'

'Exactly,' hissed William. 'They always put the winners on the aisles.'

'Oh, sure,' said Jay. 'I mean this is what? This is about your fiftieth Oscar ceremony, I mean isn't it?'

'I've seen it every year on TV,' William replied.

'So this year,' Jay informed him, 'they changed the rules.'

All the same, Jay's heart sank a little when she saw quite how far down the row they were. William was right. As far as she could recall from watching it on television, the winners were always on the outside seats, or the next ones in.

Felton was on an aisle seat, and Meredith was only two in. And the two favourites for the screenplay award, as William took masochistic delight in pointing out to Jay, were both on outside seats.

'Of course they are,' Jay retorted. 'And if I was organizing this bun fight, that's exactly where I'd put the losers, too.'

William grinned at her, and took her hand.

'Listen, baby,' he said. 'Winning doesn't matter a damn. Felton's right. What matters is you. That you're here. That you're well. And that I love you.'

The ceremony was, as always, immaculately produced and stage-managed. It was hosted by Johnny Carson, who, among many great jokes, told one that had William, who didn't laugh easily, actually in tears.

'You know in 1932?' Carson said, 'Lame-duck President Herbert Hoover was so desperate to remain in the White House that he dressed up as Eleanor Roosevelt. When FDR discovered the hoax in 1936, the two men decided to stay together for the sake of the children.'

The audience roared its approval, and William went into partial hysteria. Jay was about the only person not laughing.

'What's the matter with you?' William gasped during a fortunate lull in the proceedings. 'That's a great gag.'

'Really?' Jay replied. 'I was just thinking what a marvellous plot for a comedy it would make.'

And then the awards ceremony began in earnest, and the atmosphere changed in a second from near-hysteria, to one of barely concealed high anxiety.

Jay could hardly take in the first sets of awards, as the reality of the moment suddenly hit home. But William did, marking them all down neatly in his commemorative programme, as if he was following the tennis finals at Wimbledon.

He barely even looked up as it came to Best Screenplay.

'And here to make the award,' said Carson, 'is Mr James Dexter.'

And on walked James Dexter, fifty years a star, and star of over fifty films. He was slim, tanned and as totally attractive as ever.

'The nominations for Best Screenplay are —' he said in his famous drawl, 'Burt Cummings for *Starwalk*. Miles Enid and Margaret Finesco for *Deep in the Forest*. William Kennedy for *A Story So Far*. Annie Jewison for *Nightwatch*. Mark Hammon for *Two In The Bush*. And Anthony Wright and Frank Cantello for *Catcher's Mitt*.'

'That'll get it,' William whispered as Dexter sliced open the envelope. 'See? They're on the aisle.'

'And the winner is . . .'

And the audience held its collective breath.

'William Kennedy for *A Story So Far*.'

At first William didn't move. Even as the spotlights picked him out, he stayed rooted, as if he had been hammered into place. Then he was aware of someone crying beside him, and he turned and saw Jay, with tears of joy coursing down her face. She had her hands on his arm, and was pushing him.

'Go on, you old fool!' she yelled above the wild applause. 'That's you!'

William eased his way past the others in his row, famous strangers who now clapped him on the back and shook his hands. Then he made the long way down to the stage, doing his best to hurry, but finding his legs barely able to carry him.

James Dexter smiled at him, shook him by the hand, and gave him the golden statue. William nodded, and thanked him, and then turned to the audience.

'Members of the Academy, ladies and gentlemen,' he said. 'I know that writers are meant to be heard and not seen, so I'll be brief. Oscar here ends up in one guy's hands. Sometimes in two. But as you all know, the guy who ends up holding it is just the tip of the iceberg. He's just the representative of a team effort, and I'm no exception. No one, particularly no writer, could have had a greater team. So my team – this is for you.'

William held the statue up to more applause.

'But there's a little bit more to this one. Two bits more. There's the girl who wrote the book. She's sitting out there with you. By the side of my empty seat. To say she was my inspiration would be selling her short. But if I say any more, I won't get supper – so Jay Burrell? This is also yours.'

When the applause died down, William put the Oscar to one side of the desk before continuing.

'It's also for someone who had nothing to do with the picture directly. When I wrote it, I took it to a man who liked it a lot and tried his damnedest to get it made. But it wasn't to be. But this guy didn't set it aside. He said even if he could make it, he shouldn't. A woman should make it. And he pointed me at her. He said there's only one person in town to make this, and that's Meredith Browne. Which is where I went!'

William had to raise his voice over the start of the applause.

'And wasn't he right?' he asked the audience. 'So Meredith, you know this is for you, too! And it's also for the guy who sent me to you! Max Kassov! Because Max – as you know, buddy! If it hadn't been for you – no dice!'

William just held the statue aloft as the applause swelled to full, then, calling his thanks, he left the platform.

At first Meredith just sat stunned as she tried to make sense of the news. Max had recommended her to William. He had told him she was the only person capable of making his picture. Max had sent her gold, and she had repaid the compliment by vandalizing his house.

There was worse to come.

Diane Felton won the Oscar for Best Actress and collected it to wild applause. She was dressed in a man's evening suit and a pair of white tennis shoes.

'Thank you,' she said, staring at the statue as if wondering what to do with it. 'This is great. But let's face it, after all is said and done, a lot more's said than done.'

John Hart was called to make the awards for the Best Picture. As he made his slow way on to the platform, the audience rose and gave the dying man a standing ovation.

'The nominations for Best Picture are,' he read, '*Deep In The Forest*, producer Edward Freimann. *Starwalk*, producer Max Kassov. *A Time and a Place*, producer George Hunter. *Catcher's Mitt*, producer Harry Fine. *A Story So Far*, producer Meredith Browne. And *The Outside Edge*, producer Mike O'Farrell.'

Hart picked up the paperknife and started to lift the back of the envelope.

'The professional money's on *Starwalk*,' William whispered to Jay. 'With six to four on *The Outside Edge*.'

'And I'm changing your name to Jeremiah,' Jay replied.

'And the winner is—' Hart announced, holding the card away from his failing eyes. '*The*—'

Then he stopped and frowned. William's heart was already in his boots. So was Meredith's. Their film began with an *A*.

'I'm sorry, folks,' Hart apologized. 'My mistake. The winner is – *A Story So Far*.'

And now, now that it had come to it, now that the impossible dream she had dreamt had come true, Meredith found herself to be not exultant, but suddenly calm, as if she had just finished crossing a storm-tossed sea and had at last set foot on dry land. She kissed the legendary actor who was making the presentation, then made a short and graceful speech of thanks before returning to her seat.

As she walked back through the tumultuous applause, watched by half the world as she clutched the famous statue to her breast, she thought of her mother and found herself instead of hating her, thanking her, thanking her for having hated her.

As she walked back to her seat, holding the Oscar to her still perfect breasts, slim and radiant in the palest of blue silk gowns, which clung to her figure in places just where it should, Max watched her and thought how even more extraordinarily beautiful Meredith Browne had become.

All in all *A Story So Far* collected four Academy Awards, the last one being for the Best Score. Jean-Paul Clement couldn't make the journey, so Jay, as had been privately agreed between Meredith and William, was deputized by William to collect the Oscar. She was completely astonished when William turned round and told her to go fetch, and at first tried to refuse. But William very kindly, but firmly, guided her from her seat and led her slowly down to the platform, where, having briefly explained Jay's part in choosing the composer, Jay collected Clement's statue.

Best of all, even though she leaned on William's arm, Jay made the journey there and back without sticks.

At the bash afterwards, held as always at the top agent Lefty La Salle's palatial Beverly Hills mansion, the winners all congratulated each other, and the losers commiserated.

For William and Max it was a mixture of both. Max's film *Starwalk* had received five nominations, and failed to get a single award.

'If I can treat the two impostors just the same,' Max grinned.

'You bet,' said William. 'That goes for all of us. Top of the pinnacle now, firewood soon.'

'We've come a long way, Willy boy, you and I. The three of us.'

'Here's to keepin' on trucking.'

William raised his glass, and Max raised his. But William saw little cheer in Max's eyes.

'It's the movie,' Max confessed, as they found a quiet place to talk. 'It's a turkey.'

'*Starwalk*? You have to be kidding. After all those nominations?'

'And after none of those awards. Listen, pal, did I need just one of those statues.'

'OK, buddy. Have mine.'

William offered Max the Oscar he was still holding tight, but the joke was lost.

'I'm serious, Willy boy. The movie's bombing. You know what it cost, don't you?'

'I heard ugly rumours.'

'Well, add a couple of million, and you'll still be nowhere near it. The men in the suits have been waiting for this. Ferrachi's always hated me. I'm a smartarse Brit who wants to make arty-farty movies, as he calls them. And as far as *Starwalk* went, I, not they, notice. Because they weren't the ones who turned down your movie. Hell no. Not that lot of intellectuals. So as far as *Sidewalk* goes, I, me, Max Kassov have lost them the money.'

'Oh-my-God,' said William deliberately slowly. 'So what in hell are you going to do, buddy?'

Max grinned.

'Jump, pal. Before I'm pushed.'

Meredith had heard the rumours, of course. Everyone in Hollywood had. Max Kassov's future was on the line. And, of course, yes he'd table-hopped before, but this time it seemed they were out to bury him, Ferrachi in particular.

'It's just a different ball-game out here,' Ferrachi said to the Press. *'In England, everything's smaller. Including, I have to say, the ability to make movies. Out here, if you want to play with the boys, you got to be up to size. People come out to Hollywood and they shoot a lot off. They say the star system's crap, and everyone goes round taking out what they're not going to put back in.*

And that they're going to clean it up. Clean what up, may I please ask?

'*This place has been going a long time, and we've managed. Hollywood, now and then – and more often it's now, remember, rather than then – we make good movies. Movies that are entirely comprehensible around the world. Not copy-outs from some strange little book that cost about fifty bucks for the rights. Movies. Films that talk to people. That tell them how it is. I regret what is happening here at Metro Am. I think this man has a real ability. But not the sort we need. We're in the business of making movies, not museum pieces. And when I say business, I mean just that. Business.*'

It was a much-quoted interview. But by the time it hit the streets, Max had cleared his desk.

He holed out with William and Jay in the beach house, sleeping most of the week, and playing gin rummy the rest of the time. He planned to fly out and return to England for good at the end of the fortnight.

Before then, however, destiny was busy as always reshaping everyone's ends.

During that week, Metro Am, now radically short of any creative talent, made an extravagant bid for Meredith Browne to join the studio as Joint Head of Production. She refused. They redesigned their offer and she refused again. Finally they offered her sole Head of Creative Production, and still she refused. So in despair they asked her what she wanted. And she said quite simply not to work for them.

Principal Studios then made their bid, which was the one Meredith was waiting for. She knew Sam Harelson's grip of affairs there was practically non-existent; in fact as everyone knew he was an absentee landlord. But so far the board had made no formal move to oust him, simply because they were waiting to bid on Meredith. They came in right at the top, offering her an unencumbered position as Head of Principal Studios, with sole artistic and productive control. They also offered her a salary of $2 million a year, a sizeable holding of company stock, and a percentage of the profits. Meredith's only rider was that she could hand-pick her creative executives. This condition was readily accepted.

By the beginning of the following week, Meredith had a list of proposed appointments. Out of courtesy she informed the board of her recommendations, and the company was at once instructed to go out and hunt the nominated heads. It was noted, however, that the all-important position of Deputy Head of Production had been left without a nominee, and Meredith explained that it was a position she wished to offer personally, as she was none too sure whether or not her candidate was readily available.

Late that Monday afternoon Meredith put a call through and invited the candidate in question in for an interview with her on the following morning.

On Tuesday morning at 10.08 precisely Max Kassov was shown into Sam Harelson's old suite of offices at Principal Studios, which were now of course occupied by Meredith Browne. Meredith had kept Max waiting the regulation five minutes, but Max knew all the moves, so that when Meredith finally called him in, he kept her waiting an extra three minutes while finishing a call he was making on one of her secretary's telephones.

Finally he came through into her office and he stood centre stage.

'Do we kiss?' he asked. 'Or shake each other by the throat?'

Meredith smiled, and simply offered him a chair, the lowest of the chairs available for visitors, before sitting herself down the other side of her desk on an infinitely higher one.

'Excuse me one moment,' she said, signing some documents lying in a folder in front of her, which gave her time to draw breath and regroup.

This wasn't how she had intended to play it. There had been nothing in her scenario to suggest that when Max Kassov actually walked into her office her mouth would go quite dry and her heart would skip a beat. It was preposterous. Nowadays she saw Max round town all the time. Yet now, here on her own stamping ground, at her behest, her heart was pounding in her chest and she hardly dare raise her eyes lest there was the faintest chance she should catch his.

'I notice you have green carpet,' Max said, carefully timed and right out of left field.

'I'm sorry?' Meredith replied, meaning to say something else quite different, but able only to stumble out an unwarranted apology.

'I said,' Max repeated straight faced, 'that I see you have green carpet.'

'This is Sam's old colour scheme,' Meredith blurted out before pretending to sign some more already signed documents. 'I'm having the whole suite refurbished.'

'Refurbished,' Max repeated thoughtfully. 'Well – think about it before you do. Green can grow on you. Or more particularly on your carpet.'

'That was a misunderstanding,' Meredith said, still not looking up, 'for which I'm sorry.'

'Don't be,' Max replied. 'You did me a favour. You took me out of carpet. Now I have Italian floor tiles, which are infinitely preferable. You must come over sometime and slide around.'

'It was a misunderstanding, Max.'

'Sure. And I have a pen just like that. Just like the one you're using.'

Max took his own pen out of his pocket and held it up to show Meredith.

'But,' he continued, 'I find mine writes better with the ballpoint – out.'

He pressed the top of the pen to demonstrate.

'*Comme ça.*'

Keeping her reading glasses on quite deliberately, so

650

that she would not be able to see the puckish grin she was sure would be on Max's face, Meredith looked up slowly and smiled politely, but chose not to reply. The choice was not a hard one, since Meredith could think of absolutely nothing to say in return.

Instead she put her pen down and closed the document folder before rising and walking quite deliberately behind Max's chair, where she stood in equally deliberate silence.

Max craned his head round, to try and get her in his sights, but Meredith had positioned herself most strategically. So Max returned to stare at her empty desk, stretching his legs out in front of him during the silence, and occasionally studying the end of his Havana cigar.

'So,' he said, unable to contain his impetuosity any longer. 'What can I do for you?'

'I think it's probably more a question of what I can do for you, Max,' Meredith replied, turning and putting both her hands on the back of his chair.

'Twentieth are after me,' Max informed his unseen interviewer. 'You do know that?'

'No, I didn't,' said Meredith, now coming round and lowering herself down on to a long low white leather sofa, to sit and stare quizzically at Max still stranded centre stage on his upright chair. 'What I heard was you were going home.'

'Only because I'm not interested in Twentieth's offer,' he replied.

She was sitting upstage of him, just out of his eyeline, making it impossible for Max to see her without turning his head.

'I'm sure you didn't call me in here just to tell me you heard I was going home,' he said, focusing on the toes of his brand-new white Nike tennis shoes.

'You're right,' Meredith replied. 'I called you in to offer you a job.'

Max couldn't help his head whipping round, but Meredith had moved; gone to the door to call out some unimportant instructions to her secretary.

'A job or an olive branch?' was the best reply Max could come up with when Meredith returned, and with that handed Meredith back the initiative.

'A job, Max,' she repeated. 'In my book of rules, a few ruined furnishings merit an apology, or maybe even replacing. But certainly not the offer of an executive position.'

Max stood up and turned to face her, but Meredith walked straight past him to go and sit the far side of her desk.

'Are you saying you want me to come and work with you?' Max asked, turning back to face her across the desk.

'I'm saying that I would like you to come and work for me,' Meredith corrected him, before fanning away some cigar smoke from in front of her face.

For a moment, Max stayed where he was, his knuckles resting on the edge of the huge desk, as he stared at Meredith and into her eyes. Meredith held steady, but had to pinch the fleshy part of one of her thumbs very hard with her nails well out of Max's sight. Max then turned away and, collapsing on to the leather sofa, burst into laughter.

That was something for which Meredith hadn't bargained, and she felt a growing annoyance well up inside her as Max just sat there laughing like a schoolboy. But she would rather be damned than be forced to ask him what he found so funny.

After a while, Max calmed down and shook his head as if he still couldn't believe what he had just heard. Then he drew on his cigar, exhaled the blue smoke and changed the head shake to a nod.

'You're really offering me a job, Meredith Browne,' he stated rather than asked.

'I'm offering you Deputy Head of Production,' Meredith replied. 'And as far as the offer goes, it's a take it or leave it one.'

'I'd like to know why,' Max asked, and in that moment,

the moment Meredith had been doing her level best to avoid, Max caught her eye. And as he caught her eye, so he held it, and Meredith was unable to let go.

Because it was still there. After all that time, after all that had happened, in that eternal split second of initial contact, she knew it and she knew that he knew it. That there it was. *Le rouge regard.*

'Sorry?' she heard her voice asking. 'You were saying?'

'I was saying that I'd give my socks to know why,' Max was replying.

All Meredith knew was that she mustn't drop her eyes first. Not that she could at the moment, because the look between them was like a sealed beam. But when the time came for someone to move, she vowed that it wouldn't be her.

Yet she knew it was going to be. Already her mind was beginning to swim and her bones were quite ceasing to exist.

'I want you to work for me,' she began, and then was about to lapse into a quite enfeebled silence when one of her telephones suddenly rang.

'You're ten minutes in, Miss Browne,' her secretary's voice said in her ear, 'and you asked me to call.'

'Thank you, Betsy,' Meredith replied, smiling to herself as the US cavalry appeared on the hill. 'Put him on, would you?'

She excused herself to Max, finding herself still staring at him. But Max had dropped his eyes the moment the telephone had rung, and now rose to walk around the room, drawing now and then on his cigar as he pretended to look at the pictures on the wall, while in reality he was trying to think up the best way to deal.

Meredith meanwhile kept her mythical telephone call up just long enough to irritate, before replacing the receiver and asking Max politely where they were.

'You were about to tell me why you want me to work with you,' Max reminded her.

'Thank you,' Meredith answered, now totally recovered.

653

'I want you to work for me because I believe in this business two heads are better than one. I want you to work for me because you and I would make a very strong team. I want you to work for me because, if you like, you have the front and I have the backing. I want you to work for me because basically even in this so-called liberated town, they still don't really trust a woman in charge, but a male-female team – that they can't argue with. I want you to work for me because you're damn good, and so am I. And to me two damn goods spell OK – come and get us. I want you to work for me because you're too good to go back to making all that small-time languid, parochial rubbish the rest of them are making back home. You're better than that, and that's the final reason I want you to come and work for me. Because I think it's time you started believing in yourself, Max Kassov.'

She saw that he was staring at her once again, but this time the look was one of utter disbelief.

'I haven't done so bad, you know,' he replied, and somewhat more than edgily. 'I mean you are, as they say, mindful of my achievement out here, Miss Browne?'

'I'm mindful that you haven't seen anything through, Max,' Meredith replied. 'That's what I'm mindful of. You came out here full of it. The wunderkind, the boy marvel, the look-Hollywood-no-hands!-kid. But whenever somebody said boo to you, you cleared your desk. You folded your tent and ran away into the night.'

'That's not fair!' Max protested. 'Jesus Christ!'

'It's fair,' Meredith told him. 'What you mean is you don't like it, because it's true. What you lack, Max, is resolve. You've never been hungry, you see. You've never had to want. You've never had to go to work in the dark of the early morning with your just-in-case money hanging round your neck, not knowing what tomorrow might or much more bloody likely might not bring. Which is why you won't push yourself. Which is why you can maintain an air of such affable arrogance. While finally not really bothering.

'But if you come and work for me, not with me, Max, but for me, I shall see to it personally that you bother. I'll see to it that you stick at it while all those around you are losing theirs. And I'll tell you for why. Because out there – in that crowd of people out there, how many of them have got "It"? Precious few. But you and I have, Max. We've got It. We've got that magic ingredient, the elusive It, which is why I want you on board.'

Max's legs were no longer casually splayed out in front of him and he was staring at Meredith once more, but this time with a totally different regard. He looked at her for a long time, then he got up and walked twice around her office, before standing to stare in silence out of her window.

Meredith waited. She was in no hurry. She'd waited this long, so what was another few minutes?

Finally Max turned to her and took his cigar out of his mouth.

'Got any champagne?' he enquired. 'And by that I mean French.'

'Of course,' Meredith replied, getting up from behind her desk and crossing to the drinks cabinet.

Max watched her, full of admiration as always for the sexy elegance of her figure and her superlative legs. He watched her all the time, as she unstoppered the bottle, and returned across the room to hand him his glass of wine, before sitting on the edge of her desk; but this time on Max's side.

'Are we on, then?' she enquired.

'Oh?' Max answered. 'Listen, we're up and running.'

'Good,' said Meredith, gently shaking out her long auburn hair, cool as ever. 'In that case, here's looking at you, Max.'

'In that case, here's looking at you, kid,' he replied.

They looked at each other and, raising their glasses, they drank. And then they looked at each other some more.

Finally Max removed his cigar from his mouth and gave her his very best cheek-to-cheek grin.

'It's true though, isn't it?' he said. 'There's just no business like it.'

END CREDITS